BOX 8

x 23-04

WHERE THE WILD ROSE BLOOMS

- By -

Carlie G. Butts

2 0 0 1

Carlie G. Butts, Author
101 Eagle Road
North Augusta, SC 29860
(803)279-5988

ISBN 0-7414-0939-9

Published by:

INFINITY
PUBLISHING.COM

Infinity Publishing.com
519 West Lancaster Avenue
Haverford, PA 19041-1413
Info@buybooksontheweb.com
www.buybooksontheweb.com
Toll-free (877) BUY BOOK
Local Phone (610) 520-2500
Fax (610) 519-0261

Printed in the United States of America

Printed on Recycled Paper

Published January, 2002

CONTENTS

CHAPTER: TITLE   PAGE:

PREFACE

This beautiful story with its setting in the Old South during the Civil War era, is the most fascinating story that I've ever read about that time in the history of our country. In an unbiased way, it unveils a forbidden love affair between a white boy and slave girl, as well as other things that took place that so many southern writers somehow tend to overlook. This story, with documented facts supporting it, and being about the Old South, and written by a Southerner, makes it even more intriguing.

By no means, is this one of those so-called "pot-boilers," or "passing-fantasies." This is about real people in real life, and was inspired by stories told by someone who grew up during that time. It's a down-to-earth, and heart-felt accounting of how slaves were treated by their masters, and the way they were treated even after they had been set free.

It tells of many other things that cannot be found recorded in our history books, and brings to light many other things that some southerners had rather overlook. The author carefully takes you step-by-step through that period of time as if you were there yourself, as this beautiful story unfolds. The reader remains in suspense, and awe, until the very end. It is written in such a way so that it can be enjoyed by all races, for it doesn't up hold any particular race, although racist person might think it does.

Best wishes,
Geneva Pelfrey

INTRODUCTION

This fictional novel, is about a forbidden love affair between a slave owner's son and a slave girl, which was inspired by a story that was told to the author in 1947 by an elderly Negro woman. She told a story about the life of her mother who was a slave on a plantation in South Carolina during the 1800's, and she claimed that her father was the son of the farmer who owned her mother as a slave, prior to the Civil War.

Although fictional, it brings to light the many gruesome acts of violence that were imposed on Negro slaves before the war, and freed-slaves after the war ended, when they started working for farmers as sharecroppers. Leaving no stone un-turned, it tells things as they really happened during that era, although they are disgraceful to southern farmers of that time, and brings out many hidden things that no southern writer ever dared mention before.

Certain words that are used in this story were commonly used during that time, although they aren't being used today, and were not intended to degrade black persons, or to express the true way the author feels in his own heart. White persons might feel like it is degrading to their own race, and is primarily intended to be upholding to black persons, which is not true. The author only expresses his version of what he thought happened, based on stories handed down through the years by word-of-mouth by many descendants of slaves, and descendants of those farmers who once owned Negroes as slaves. Although fictional, some of the things mentioned in this story actually took place back then, even though they are deeply regretted by everyone today, including the author.

ACKNOWLEDGEMENT

I will forever be grateful to an elderly Negro woman who sat on her porch during the summer of 1947, and told an interesting story about the life of her mother who was a slave in South Carolina during the 1800's. This is not the actual story that she told about her being the daughter of a slave girl and the son of a slave owner, however after hearing her story I was inspired to write about the way slaves had been treated before the Civil War, and after they had been set free. I thank other older descendants of slaves for their sad and pathetic stories about the life of slaves, for their stories inspired me even more.

I also want to thank Teresa Whitaker and Rhonda Fulmer, employees of the SRP Credit Union of North Augusta, South Carolina, for being helpful in editing and encouraging me with this story. You girls are greatly appreciated.

Most of all, I thank my wife Sara for standing by me during the many times when it seemed like I was perusing an impossible dream. Also, I thank my three sons Ray, Jerrie, and Michael Butts and their wives for their support. A special word of thanks goes to Mike's wife Dawn, for her untiring support in helping to prepare this for publication.

Thank you very much:
Author

CHAPTER ONE

A TINY BUD PUTS FORTH

South Carolina, during the 1800's. Summer was over; the cool days of autumn were here at last, and everyone here on The Simpson Plantation were now enjoying a bit of relief from the scorching days of summer past. Martha, a slave girl, had climbed out of bed before dawn, in anticipation of taking the first trip she'd ever taken in her life. She was to ride into town today with her father on a wagonload of freshly picked cotton, and because it would be the first time she had been to town, or even seen inside a store, she was very excited. She was born on this plantation, and had never been off of it even once for any reason.

The quietness of dawn was disrupted by the noise of mule-drawn wagons, as they rumbled along on the road that led by the rundown shacks where the slaves were housed. This was the time of year when the cotton was being picked and hauled into town and sold, and wagons were lined up for at least a mile along the road. As soon as the cotton had been ginned and baled, it would be taken across town to an auction, where buyers would make their bids to buy the bales of cotton, and then ship them to Europe. The South sold very few products to the North; or the West, for the South did very little to help support the Union.

Negro slaves exclusively operated this plantation, as well as other farms in the South. Not all Southerners agreed when it came to making slaves of other humans, and the majority of Northerners frowned on such practice, however, it was a real way of life for Southern farmers. With the many thousands of acres of farmland, farmers in the South soon learned that the use of Negroes as slaves was the answer to their labor problems. Farmers in the North were not happy because slavery was working so well for the South, but the North didn't have enough large farms to accommodate such vast groups of laborers. All it cost Southern farmers were the few bites of food their slaves ate, the shabby clothes they wore, and the rundown shacks in which they slept at night, following a long hard days work in the fields.

This was to be a very special day indeed for this slave girl, for this trip into town, was something she never dreamed would happen. Although her two older brothers and her father went into town quite often on errands, Martha's mother Liza, had never seen a town since she was a small girl, and was placed on an auction block in Savannah, Georgia, and sold to Nate Simpson's father.

As a rule, a woman slave was not allowed to go off her plantation for any reason, and men slaves must have a written-pass whenever they went to town, or to another plantation. Even then, unless the sheriff really knew to which farm they belonged, they might be mistaken as a slave trying to escape. A crime of this nature was apt to cause a slave to be shot, for if he'd run away from one farmer, he wouldn't be any good to another farmer either. There was a natural hatred for Negroes, not because of what they had done, but simply because they were "black". Although most of them were kind, respectful, and loyal to their master, if they happened to make a mistake, no matter how small it might be, farmers most generally found some reason to punish them just the same. Farmers, felt no mercy for their slaves.

Although the slaves worked all the time, this was the busiest time of the year for Southern farmers, and the workload for the slaves increased significantly. Cotton was the chief money-crop, and it had to be picked and hauled into town and sold, and the slaves were driven from dawn 'til well after the sun went down, seven days a week. Other crops were important, but cotton was given more priority than all the other crops combined.

Martha's father Bill, was the most trustworthy slave on this plantation. He had already hitched a pair of mules to a wagon that had been loaded with cotton late yesterday evening, and was ready to head out toward town. It was quite a long way from this plantation to the cotton gin in town, and it would take almost all day for the mules to make the long trip to town and back. The wagons were loaded each evening, so that the drivers could leave as soon as it was light enough the following morning for them to see how to travel.

Martha's mother Liza, was still here at the shack with her. Although her parents and older brothers had eaten breakfast long before daylight, Martha's mother had a few slices of fatback meat, and a piece of cornbread on the back of the cookstove, keeping it warm for her. She intended for Martha to eat her breakfast, before setting out on the long trip. She had filled a washtub with water last night and had it sitting in the back room, and she intended to see that her daughter took a bath this morning as well. Just as soon as Bill and Martha had left for town, Liza would have to go and help the other slaves pick cotton, and she wanted to make sure that Martha ate her breakfast, and took a bath while she was still here at the house with her.

"Marthie!" said Liza, sternly. "Jus' as soon as you eats yo' break'fus, I's want you to jump in the tub and scrub off rail good." Liza then sat down at the kitchen table, and continued. "I's fetched in a tub of water las' nite fer you, and I's put a cake of lye-soap 'side the tub, and I's want you to use a lot'a soap too. Yo' pappy sez' that you couldn't go wid him less'n you scrubbed off rail good, and he meant that ver'ee thang, too!"

"That don't make no sense!" Martha grumbled, as she started gulping down her food. "I's done washed off in the creek las' Satur'dee, and I's still clean as a pin. The road's gon'a be dusty, and I's gon'a wait 'til I's get back home to take a baf'. Now, ain't that some good thanking."

"It don't matter if you is still clean, you gon'a scrub off 'gain, befo' you's leave the house!" Her mother scolded. "This is a spash'ul day, and yo' pappy don't want you smelling like no mule when you's riding wid him. Less'n you do scrub off rail good like I's say, you ain't going nowhere." Then Liza crossed her arms, and gave Martha that all-too-familiar nod.

"I's wush now, that I wudn't eb'em taking no trip to town," Martha told her, as she shoved her plate back on the table, "fer nobid'ee told me that I would have to do all that, jus' to get to go to a stupid ole town."

Martha knew all too well that her mother was serious about her taking a bath, so she hurried into the back room, climbed into the washtub, and bathed as she'd been told. As soon as she had finished her bath she slipped on her very best dress, and came back into the kitchen to wait on her father, for she knew that he'd soon be there to pick her up. Liza had a pretty red scarf she had been saving for a long time, and she wanted Martha to wear it on her head when she went to town. After all, she wanted her daughter to look nice.

Knowing that Martha would need a place to sit on the wagon, Bill fastened a wide board across the top of the tall sideboards. He pulled the wagon up in front of the shack in which they lived, and sat waiting for her. Martha heard a noise outside, and when she saw the wagon, she became very excited.

"Oh Lord'ee, he done be out there wait'n on me!" Martha screamed, as she scurried toward the door. "Gim'ee that scarf, fer he's gon'a drive on off and leave me! Hurry up, Mammy, and get that thang tied on my head!"

"He ain't gon'a leave you," Liza scolded, as she caught hold of Martha's arm, "but if you's don't be still, I ain't never gon'a get it tied on yo' head."

"Huh, that's what you thank!" Martha replied, as she gradually eased on toward the front door. "He got a big ole whoop in his hand, and when he warps them mules wid it, they gon'a head out running torge town."

"Now, get yo'sef on out of here!" Said her mother, as she playfully shoved Martha toward the door. "And, if you's don't mind yo' pappy, I's gon'a beat the lard out'a you, when you's get back home." Liza chuckled to herself.

"I's know that," Martha called back, as she hurried toward the road, to join her father. "You's aw'ready mad at me as it tis, fer no reason a'tall."

As fast as she could go, Martha went and climbed up the sideboards of the wagon, and seated herself on the board close to her father. Martha had never ridden on a wagonload of cotton before, and she was afraid that she might fall off and get hurt. She figured that if she sat real close to him, she could catch hold of his arm, if she did happen to start to fall.

"There ain't no need fer you to sot all that close to me, fer you ain't left me wid no room to live and brev'," her father fussed, as he tried to push her away with his elbow. "Ain't no use fer you to worry 'bout falling off."

"What is you trying to do?" She asked. "Is you trying to shove me off, and bus' my head on the ground. Is that what you's trying to do to me?"

"Naugh, I's ain't trying to do nothing like that," he told her. "Eb'em if I's tried, I couldn't shove you off. But, if you don't move over a lit'l, I's gon'a make you get off and walk all the way clean to town."

"But, Pappy," she protested. "This is too close up torge Heb'um fer me, and you's better keep yo' arm ready, jus' in case I's do 'cide to fall off and bus' my head. Can't see why you ain't done fell off and kilt yo'sef, a dozen times fo' now."

As soon as the wagon started rolling along, Martha turned to wave goodbye to her mother, who was now standing out in the yard. Martha felt like she was headed for some faraway land, or a place in some dream that she didn't think she would ever visit. As they continued along, she felt compelled to let her father know that she was really enjoying this trip.

"Pappy, I's feel the bes' today, I's ever felt in my lif'," she smiled, and told him. "I's ain't never seed no town - ain't been in no sto' to look 'round at thangs - never is had no new frock befo', neither. The tuther gals is gon'a stick their eyeballs out at me, when they see me walking 'round in a new frock. Yep, that sho' is gon'a be sump'um fer 'em to look at."

For some reason beyond anyone's imagination, Nate Simpson, who owned this plantation, had told Bill to let his daughter ride into town with him today on the wagonload of cotton, and to let her go to the General Store and pick out a piece of cloth, so Liza could make a dress for her and Martha. This sure did seem rather strange to Bill, as well as to everyone else, for farmers seldom ever bought anything new for their slaves. The clothes that slaves wore had been handed down to them by white folks, or were what the slaves had crudely made themselves from pieces of scrap cloth, or feed sacks. They worked in the fields from daylight 'til after the sun went down, and had no need of fancy clothes. Even though Bill didn't understand why Nate was doing something he'd never done before, as a slave, he had no right to question anything that his master did.

Although he was only a Negro slave, he loved his children as any father should, and after having given consideration to what his daughter had just said, he decided to explain something to her.

"Marthie, it sho' be good to have sump'um purdy and nice, but there ain't no new frock, er nothing else that's gon'a change the way we is down inside," he began. "No matter if you's wrop

5

yo'sef up wid' gold, er wear fancy thangs, it ain't gon'a make us be no dif'unt from what we aw'ready is."

"I's ain't sho' what you's meant by that," she replied. "Is there sump'um wrong wid me having a new frock to wear? Ain't you's never been tickled 'cause you had sump'um purdy, and nice?"

"Naugh, there ain't nothing wrong wid that, but we is jus' nigga slaves, and nothing that we's wear, ain't gon'a change what we is," he tried again to explain to her. "You mout strut 'round in a new frock all day, but when nite comes and you's take it off, there you be, jus' a slave, and nothing else."

"Is you saying that all we's fit fer is to be a slave to white folks, and wuk' fer 'em 'til we die?" She asked, seriously. "Ain't we fit to be sump'um else, 'cept fer jus' a slave. Is that what you really mean?"

"We is fit to be sump'um else if we's had a chance, but as long as bref' is in our bid'ee, that's all we ever gon'a be," he sadly explained. "We is black, and dif'unt, and we aw'ways gon'a be looked at like if we wuz trash."

This confused Martha, even more. "I's don't una'stan why you's still got that kin'a notion in yo' head," she replied. "Ain't you got no hope of ever being nothing but a slave? Is that all you thank that we'll ever be, fer the res' of our lif'?"

"Well, it's sort of like this," he continued. "White folks is got a big chain wropped 'round our neck, got our soul in bondage, and our lif' bound up like a fly in a spider's web. They got our head messed up so bad 'til we can't thank fer our'sef, and our mind is been squshed under their foots like squshing a rotten tater. The bes' thang fer us to do, is not to 'spect thangs to get no better, fer they sho' ain't gon'a come our way."

His reply stirred deep within her young heart, and the longer she thought about what he just said, the more she realized that he was right.

As she looked back at her own life she understood why he had made such a statement, for she'd never been able to say or do things the way she felt in her own heart. She had been forced to work from daylight until dark every day of the week for as long as she could remember, with hardly enough food to keep her alive, or sufficient clothes to cover her body. Even when she felt bad a few days each month, she was forced to go on and work as though nothing was wrong. The life of a slave was a difficult one at best.

Nathaniel Simpson, or "Nate" as he was better known, owned a plantation consisting of hundreds of acres of farmland, and he owned several dozen slaves who operated the farm for him. Most of his slaves had been around for several years, and were once owned by his late-father Bill Simpson, while others had been here only a few months. Farmers were always buying new slaves, in order to keep up their young and healthy workforce, and they sold older slaves to farmers who had less strenous work for them to do. Like prisoners, those who had been here only a short time still wore shackles around their ankles, and the shackles would stay there until Simpson was fully convinced that they would not try to escape.

Slavery was all that Martha's family had ever known. Nate Simpson's father at a slave auction in Charleston had purchased her father before he died and his son Nate took over the plantation, and her mother was purchased at a slave auction in Savannah, when she was just a young girl. Martha and her two brothers were born on this plantation, as were most all the other younger slaves whom Nate Simpson owned.

Slavery wasn't only physical punishment for the Negroes, but moral punishment as well, for slaves were forced to obey white men unconditionally, and without question. Though the slaves provided a livelihood for white men they were not considered as being human, and in a manner of speaking, were treated far worse than farm animals. No matter how loyal they were, or how well they worked, they were still hated because they were "black".

Martha's parents had told their own children how they were rounded up in Africa like a herd of cattle, then thrown into the bottom of a musky ship, and brought to America. They were jammed together with no place to sleep, no food or water, no light, no fresh air to breathe, and no bathroom facilities. They told of the many weeks of starvation and thirst, during this long and frustrating voyage, and how they were later lined up like cattle at an auction, then sold to the highest bidder. Liza told Martha how she was snatched from the arms of her mother, and sold to Nate Simpson's father, and how her three brothers and parents were sold to another farmer, and would never be reunited again as a family. She still remembered the pitiful cries of her brothers when they were being separated, and sold to different farmers, and how her mother was slapped and kicked around, simply because she tried to cling to her own children.

Although Bill was just a young boy when he was brought to America, he had not forgotten the dozens of others who had died during this long voyage due to sickness, starvation, and the cruel manner in which their captors treated them. Others, were killed on their way to America, because they were caught trying to steal food to keep from starving, while some jumped into the ocean and drowned, in an effort to escape the cruel, and unbearable punishment being brought upon them. Though he was a young boy, he recalled seeing young Negro girls dragged from the bottom of the ship, sexually molested by shipmates, then thrown overboard and left to drown. He also remembered one girl who died, and was left in the bottom of the ship, where she was trampled under the feet of other fellow-prisoners. Other stories he told bore a pitiful truth of how the dead were sometimes eaten by other slaves, in an effort to avoid starvation.

Nate's father operated this plantation when Martha's parents were brought to America, and they still remembered how cruel, and mean he was to them, even though they were only children, and didn't understand English. It was rather difficult learning how to understand, and communicate with him, since this was the first time that they had come in contact with anyone who spoke the English language. They suffered a whipping many times, simply because of being unable to understand orders given to them, and when they tried, and failed, because they didn't quite understand, they were whipped just the same, because he felt like they had intentionally messed up. They were not considered as human, or capable of becoming anything other than for a slave, and they were not taught how to do anything, except for how to grow cotton. No matter how hard they might work, or how loyal they were, Nate's father never once offered them a word of praise, or thanks for any good deed that they did. As the wagon slowly rolled along, Martha continued to think about what her father said about the new dress, and what he and her mother had told them about how they were treated as young slaves. When she glanced over at her father who now rode along with his head bowed, she realized that he was giving considerable thought to such things as well.

Nate Simpson lived in a beautiful, well-kept mansion that was built on a large knoll overlooking the crude shacks in which the slaves were housed, so he would be able to look out across his plantation, and leave the impression that the slaves must always look up to him. Other than for the slaves whom he allowed to clean the house, and work in the yard, no slave was allowed to come near the mansion unless they had been invited. While the large mansion, and grounds surrounding it were always kept in immaculate condition, the shacks in which the Negro slaves lived were in far worse condition than the barns where the livestock was kept. All such thoughts as these had been cluttering Martha's mind as they quietly rode along, and hoping her father wouldn't get upset at her, she decided to mention them to him.

"I's been thanking over what you and Mammy said 'bout the way youn's wuz treated when youn's wuz fetched over here, and 'bout the way Mos'a Simpson is still treat'n us wuss' than trash," spoke Martha, seriously. "Don't it look like we is being treated awful bad by white folks, and that they don't thank no mo' of us, than they do fer a dog?" "Don't you thank that we's need some credit fer what we's do, eb'em if we's don't get paid?"

Her father didn't reply, instead, he kept his eyes on the line of wagons that were traveling ahead of them, although he did agree with her. He hadn't offered to complain even once about the way that he'd been treated, not even to his own family, or his closest friends, and it bothered him because his own daughter had voiced her opinion, and didn't seem to fear the consequences that might follow. Perhaps, these thoughts would eventually pass from her mind as she grew older - he hoped they would - maybe someday.

"I's know that we is jus' a bunch of slaves, and ain't no good in the eyes of white folks," she continued, "but does you thank that we's ever gon'a own a big ole farm like white folks do, and have them wuk'n fer us?"

Although he had more or less ignored her questions thus far, this really caught his attention, and he decided that he must answer her questions, in one way or another. Unless he did, she was liable to get into serious trouble by asking someone else, and probably end up getting the wrong answer.

"Look'ee here, lit'l gal!" He snapped at her, as he turned, and looked her straight in the eye. "That's what you's call death-talk, and I's don't want'a hear you say nothing like that again. Do you's una'stan?"

"I's didn't mean to get you upsot by axe'n you sump'um, but ever since I wuz jus' a snotty-nosed young'un, you's a'ways told me to use my head," she replied, in a confused voice. "Didn't you say fer me to use my own head, and thank fer my'sef? Ain't that what you's aw'ways told me?"

"Yass'am, that's what I sez, but you ain't gon'a have no head left, if you don't stop thank'n like that," he warned. "Them, is the kin'a words that mout get you kilt, if they happen to get back to Mos'a Simpson."

"Aw'rite then, I's gon'a watch what I sez from now on, and watch who I sez it to, but it sho' ain't gon'a change the way that I's feel deep down in my belly," she replied. "I's mout be kilt a lot'a times fer the way I feel, but I's still gon'a thank that we is mistreated by white folks."

Neither of them said anything else for quite some time, as they continued on their way toward town, while she tried to figure out why he seemed so upset by her questions, and he wondered why she had such thoughts in her mind in the first place. He felt troubled because she had complained about the way slaves were being treated, for a slave didn't dare complain, or find fault with what the white-man did to them. On the other hand he was rather proud of her, even though he feared what was bound to happen, if Mr. Simpson happened to find out how she felt about the way they were being treated. If she had such thoughts as these in her mind at this young age, he wondered how she'd react when she grew older, and if such thoughts might cause her a lot of trouble, should she discuss them with someone else. He had to come up with some way to answer her questions, without letting her know that he thought she was right for feeling the way she did about slavery.

The mules had been pulling the heavy-loaded wagon along for quite awhile now, and Bill decided to let them rest for a few minutes while he took a "trip to the bushes." He guided the wagon over to the side of the road so the other wagons behind him could pass, then he climed down to the ground, and stood with his head bowed for a moment. He remembered what Martha had said earlier, and the questions she had asked, and he felt obligated to do whatever he could to clear things up for his young daughter.

"Well, you's went and axed me some mighty big ques'uns, and I's gon'a try to answer some of 'em, at leas'," he smiled, and looked up at her. "The fus' thang you's need to know, is that ques'uns like that is mighty dangerous, and they liables to stir up a hornet's nest, if they be axed to the wrong feller. Now, that's the thang you's need to be worried 'bout."

"Yass'uh, I's see what you's mean now, and I's got a lot'a learning to do fo' I's grow up," she smiled, and replied. "I's got better sense, than to be axe'n a ques'un like that to jus' anybid'ee. Eb'em if I's don't know what yo' answer wuz, it sho' wuz a good'n, and I's gon'a 'memer it, too."

Bill was pleased that his daughter had confided in him, and hadn't voiced her opinion to someone else. Yet, he wrestled with the fact that he knew that she was right in feeling as she did, and his being able to persuade her not to be so outspoken, without letting her know that he actually felt the same way.

"Well, to tell the truf', I's ain't got no rail good answer to what you's axed me, and the fac' is, nobid'ee ain't got one," he carefully admitted, as he stood shaking his head. "We is jus' slaves, and never will have a lot'a thangs in lif', er have white folks wuk'n fer us. I's want to be free someday, but I sho' don't want'a be kilt, trying to get what I's want. The fac' is, a liv' slave, is better than a dead, free-nigga."

Although Martha was only sixteen years old, she had already suffered more hardships than a white girl her age would suffer in a lifetime, and personally witnessed many cruel, and inhumane things being done to other slaves as well. She had stood and cried, while her mother bathed the backs of her father and two older brothers, after they had been tied to a stake and whipped for making a tiny mistake. Other times, she had seen Mr. Simpson whip a slave until they were hardly able to stand on their feet, then leave them tied to the stake for the rest of the day without a drop of water to drink, as an example to others. Punishment for slaves, had no bounds.

The feelings of a slave seemed to be of little concern to white men, and it seemed to her, that death would be preferred to a life of misery the slaves were suffering. On the other hand, and after having witnessed the way some of the slaves had died, caused her to fear death, even more than a lifetime of slavery. Perhaps death wasn't something to be embraced, as a means of escaping a lifetime of punishment after all, she reasoned.

Following a few more minutes of discussion with his daughter, and a quick "trip to the bushes," they were on their way toward town. Try as he might to dismiss this exchange from his mind, he still wondered if he had given her the right answer. He wasn't sure if he had only confused her more. The longer he pondered her question in his heart, the more he realized that he must come up with a better answer than he'd already given her. He knew her well enough, to know that she wouldn't stop asking until she finally got an answer, and he had rather the answer come from him, than from someone else, or maybe finding the answer the hard-way, by letting Mr. Simpson learn about her thoughts.

"Well, it's like this," said Bill, as they drove past where some slaves were digging up a stump by the side of the road. "When it comes to want'n to be free, there ain't no dif'unce twixt a man and a mule, fer nothing wants to be all bound up, and not be able to live his own lif'. Ever since they jerked me 'way from my mammy, and throwed me in the bottom of that big boat and brung me here, I's wanted to be free. All the tuther slaves feel the same way. As long as I's got bref' in my bid'ee, I's gon'a axe the big Mos'a in the sky to sot me free, and maybe one day He gon'a get tard of me pester'n Him and sot me free, er I's hope He do, anyhow."

"I's glad you said that, fer that's the way I's feel, too, and that's the reason I's axed them ques'uns," she softly smiled, and replied. "Now that you una'stan what I's meant, do you thank we is ever gon'a be free, er is we aw'ways gon'a be a slave fer the res' of our lif'?"

"I's ain't want'n to build up yo' hopes, er make you thank the wrong way, but I do thank we gon'a be sot free one day," he assured her. "Eb'em if we's ain't never sot free, it sho' do make me feel good, jus' thank'n that we mout be free one day. No matter what happens, I's want you to aw'ways keep thank'n that way, fer eb'em if they kill us, they can't take that hope out of our own heart. Thank on that fer a spell, and see if it don't make you feel a lot better."

Indeed, the white-man had succeeded in conquering the life of these poor human beings, and even had their heart and soul in bondage, however, there was no way the white-man could strip them of their yearning to be free. According to white men, all slaves were stupid, illiterate, and void of a heart or soul, yet their desire to be free would never be conquered - never be destroyed.

For a fact, Negroes were born in the thickets and brambles of Africa, and had very little, if any contact with white men until they were brought over to America, yet while roaming around in the wilderness, they were free to live as they pleased. Many did roam around half-naked, without proper food, and many starved to death, and in a manner of speaking, were heathens. Even so, they were free individuals. This is what Bill was trying to point out to his young daughter. Even though he had warned her of the danger in expressing her own opinion of slavery, he certainly didn't want her to abandon the hope of being set free one day, and being able to live her own life, in her own way. Living a life without hope, was more miserable than dying without hope, he thought.

Martha and her father finally arrived at the cotton gin, but it would be quite awhile before his load of cotton would be ginned. Although they started out early this morning, other wagons from nearby farms had already arrived at the gin ahead of them, and they would have to wait their turn. While waiting his turn at the gin, Bill decided to go to the General Store and get the cloth for Martha and her mother, like Mr. Simpson had ordered. Although the wagons ahead of them were from other plantations, slaves always worked together, and Bill asked the driver that was ahead of him if he'd have the cotton ginned for him while he was gone, and of course, the man agreed. Bill smiled, and shook the other slave's hand, and then he and Martha headed for the General Store.

Martha stared in amazement, at the town before her. She could hardly wait to go inside the General Store, and look around. She had never seen inside a store, or ever seen a piece of new cloth, and before she hardly knew what she was doing, she was already far ahead of her father.

"Hold on there, jus'a minute!" Bill called to her. "There ain't no use to be in no big resh to get there, fer the sto' ain't going nowhere. It wuz built back yon'a when the Lord put this ole world together, and it's gon'a be standing rite there, when the Lord comes back to tear it down, too."

"I's know that," she called back, as she kept hurrying along, "but I's want'a take a good look at everthang that's in there. You sez they is got everthang in there, and that's what I's want'a look at fus' - everthang."

She slowed down a bit, and her father caught up with her as she arrived at the rock-walkway, leading up to the front of the General Store.

"Yep, you gon'a see a lot'a thangs in there, but fo' we go inside, I's need to tell you sump'um," said her father. "This is the place whu' all them white womens come to get purdy thangs that you see 'em wearing, and they gon'a get all riled up, if a bunch of niggas comes flocking in on 'em."

"I una'stan what you's mean, but we is got the same rite to be in there, as they got." Martha replied, crossing her arms, in a defiant manner. "Mos'a Simpson sont us here to get some clof', and if they want'a get mad, let 'em get mad at him. Ain't that the way you's feel, too?"

"I's know what you mean, but I's still gon'a take a gander inside, befo' we's sot foot in there," he sternly replied. "If there happens to be a white woman in there, then we's gon'a wait out here, 'til she leaves."

They walked slowly up to the steps leading into the store, and then Bill told Martha to stand quietly, while he peeked inside. Sure enough, he saw a white woman at the counter, and he quickly turned, and went back and joined Martha, who was standing on her tiptoes, trying to see inside the store.

"We gon'a stay rite here fer a spell, fer I's seed a white woman standing at the counter." Bill told her, as he caught hold of her arm, and pulled her over to the side of the walkway. "Jus' as soon as she leaves I's gon'a take a good look, and if there ain't nobid'ee else in there, then we gon'a go in and get the clof', that we's come adder. Be sho' to keep yo' big mouf' shut, and yo' head bowed, when the woman comes out'a the sto'."

A few minutes later the woman walked out the door, and when she saw Bill and Martha standing alongside the walkway with their heads bowed, she frowned at them. Bill sensed that she was upset at the very sight of them, and he decided to speak to her, just to let her know that they did at least respect her.

"Moan'n, Ma'am," spoke Bill, in a very polite, and kind voice. "This sho' is a pow'ful purdy day. Yass'am, it sho' is."

The woman quickly stopped, and shook her finger in Bill's face. "I don't make a habit of speaking to trashy niggers, and I don't appreciate them saying anything to me, either!" Snapped the woman. "When my husband hears about how hateful you spoke to me, and about you spitting on the walkway where we ladies have to walk, you'll be sorry that you opened your filthy mouth!"

"I's sorry if I's upsot you, fer all I wuz doing, wuz trying to show that I's do have some 'spect fer youn's white folks." Bill humbly replied. "Is sump'um wrong wid that?"

"Respect, my foot!" She snorted. "I heard what you said about me when I came outside, and I saw you spit on the sidewalk, too!" Then, she hurried on out to the street, where her driver was waiting for her in a buggy.

14

"What wuz that all 'bout?" Asked Martha. "Is that the way town-folks is 'sposed to talk. I's ain't never seed no town-folks befo', but I thought they would be nice, and fancy-like, and not nasty, like that ole woman wuz."

Bill didn't bother to reply; instead, he walked back up the steps to take another look, to see if another white woman was in the store. When he didn't see anyone except for the manager, he motioned to Martha, and they both slowly walked into the store, as Bill tucked his hat under his arm. Although slaves provided a livelihood for white folks, they were not allowed in a place of business unless they'd been invited. And under no circumstances were they allowed in a place of business, when a white woman was present.

No sooner had they walked about halfway to the counter, Bill glanced over toward where dry goods were kept, and he saw a white woman looking at a piece of cloth. Without saying anything to Martha, he quickly grabbed her arm, and they both hurried back outside. The manager stood behind the counter with his back turned toward the front door, and didn't see them enter, and Bill prayed that the woman hadn't seen them, either. But she had seen them, and she threw the piece of cloth down on the floor, and went storming over to the counter.

"Of all the sorry, low-down things I've ever seen in my life, that beats everthing!" The woman snarled. "It's gotten to a point where a decent lady can't go shopping, without having a bunch of filthy niggers flocking in like a bunch of buzzards! I'm fed up with such things as this, I tell you!"

"What in the world's wrong, Mrs. Wilbanks?" Asked Mr. Wilson. "I didn't see any niggers come into the store, and I don't understand what you mean."

She quickly wheeled around, and headed straight toward the door, with the stunned, Mr. Wilson following close behind her. When she got to the door, she suddenly stopped in her tracks, and pointed her finger toward Bill and Martha, who were now standing next to the steps, with their heads bowed.

"It's high-time, for me to get out of here!" She shrieked. "There's not enough room in this place for a dignified lady like me, and a bunch of filthy, snotty-nosed niggers! You can take this place and go to you-know-where, as far as I'm concerned, for I certainly won't be back again!"

Realizing now, that Mr. Wilson hadn't seen them enter the store, and that he was being blamed for something that he knew nothing about, Bill decided to try to calm the lady down, and get her off Mr. Wilson's back.

"Ma'am, Mos'a Wilson didn't eb'em know that we's walked in the sto', fer he didn't see us," Bill began. "I's didn't see you humped up over there next to the clof', 'til adder we's went inside, and I's rail sorry that we come flogging in on you like that, I sho' is. It wuz all my fault, and I's sorry if it got yo' feathers all fluffed up, like a big ole rooster in a windstorm."

"You ought to know your place, which is out there in the fields with the other trashy slaves!" The woman scolded. "You have no right to be in town in the first place, and unless your master starts whipping you at a stake like he should, pretty soon, you'll start thinking that you're human!"

"Ma'am, I do know my place, and that's the reason why I didn't go into the sto', 'til I thought everbid'ee wuz done gone," replied Bill. "I's sorry, I sho' is, and we won't come flogging in on you like that, no mo'."

She quickly turned around, and shook her finger at Mr. Wilson. "The very idea of you allowing a bunch of niggers to hang around your place of business, burns me up!" She shouted. "The next time I come in here, I'll bet you have one of them running your place. But, there won't be a next-time. When I get through spreading the word about what went on here today, no white lady in her right mind, will even look toward this store!"

"But, Mrs. Wilbanks," the man pleaded, "if you'll give me a moment, I'll explain everything. These slaves belong to Nate Simpson, and if I may say so myself, they are above average. I'm sure they did't mean any harm by walking into the store while you were here, and Bill told you that, himself."

When the woman stepped out on the porch, and saw some men standing across the street from the store, she really tried to "show her butt."

"Those niggers must not belong to anybody who has good sense!" She bellowed in a loud voice. "If they did, he'd have them working in the fields, and not roaming around over town, like a bunch of buzzards! Trash, that's what all of them are! Scum of the earth - scrapings from the bottom of the barrel!"

"Mrs. Wilbanks, you probably know Mr. Simpson," the manager pleaded with her. "He's a respected member of society, a political leader, and has a hand in just about everything that goes on around here. If these two niggers have caused you trouble, or upset you in any way, I'm sure Mr. Simpson will punish them for what they did. Now, please come on back inside, and I swear that you won't be bothered by these niggers again, or by anybody else."

"I don't care who this Simpson fellow is, who, or what he controls, or if he owns the greater portion of South Carolina!" She yelled, more defiant now, than ever before. "His niggers don't have a right to come in here and slobber on everything, and expect refined, dignified ladies like myself to continue doing business with you! There's a limit to what good Christian woman can stand, and I want you to know that I'm fed up with it!"

"I'm sorry, but I didn't even know they came into the store, and I'll do whatever it takes, to get this matter straightened out." Mr. Wilson pleaded. "Come on back, and take all the time you wish to shop, for I really need your business, and the business of your friends too. Will you do that, please?"

"You haven't heard anything, yet!" The woman growled, as she hurried out toward the street. "After we Christian-ladies get together, and discuss how you run a business, you'll be lucky to get another penny from us!"

The woman's hateful words, and demeanor, really took Martha by surprise, for she thought city-folks would be more refined and polite, and not downright hateful, like this woman. Nevertheless, after the woman went out of sight on down the street, Bill and Martha followed Mr. Wilson back into the store. The manager went over and picked up the cloth and put it back on a shelf, and then he came back to the counter.

"All right, Bill, what did you want?" He asked. "I hate what happened a moment ago, but it wasn't your fault, and you don't have to worry one bit, for nothing will be said to Mr. Simpson about it."

"Thank you, Suh'," politely replied Bill. "Mos'a Simpson, he told us to come here and get some clof', but he did't say what kin'a clof' to get. I's 'spose he meant to get sump'um that nobid'ee else wants, fer he wants my woman and my gal here, to make 'em a new frock. Is you got sump'um that ain't good nuf' fer white womens? Sump'um fer slave womens, maybe?"

"I'm not quite sure if I understand what you mean, for nobody ever buys a piece of cloth for their slaves, and especially not Nate

Simpson." Mr. Wilson replied. "Are you sure that Nate told you to get some cloth for your wife and daughter? That's rather hard for me to believe."

Reaching into his pocket, Bill brought out a neatly folded note that Nate gave to him, and handed it to Mr. Wilson. "He scratched sump'um on this here paper, and axed me to fetch it to you," Bill smiled. "I's can't read, 'thout I's got my specs on, and don't know what it sez. It mout tell you the kin'a clof' he wants. Do it say what kin'a clof' we 'sposed to get?"

"Yes, he says for me to give you enough cloth to make two dresses, and for your daughter to pick out the kind she wants," the manager replied, as he placed the note in a drawer. He went over and got the cloth that Mrs. Wilbanks threw on the floor, and placed it on the counter.

"This is the most expensive piece of material I have, and it's enough to make two dresses." Mr. Wilson told him. "I'll let Nate have it at a bargain. It was ordered for Mrs. Wilbanks, but she changed her mind."

"Naw'suh, that's too purdy fer no slave womens," Bill replied, and shook his head. "Mos'a Simpson will skin me liv', if I's fetched that back to him. Ain't you's got sump'um cheaper, sump'um ugly, not so fancy-like?"

"It's all right, and I'll explain everything to him when I see him," the manager said, as he wrapped the cloth in a piece of paper. "He says, that you folks are the best slaves he owns, and I'm sure he won't mind at all."

"Aw'rite then, I's gon'a leave it up to you," smiled Bill, as he handed the package to his daughter. "Be sho' to tell him that it wuzn't sump'um that she picked out, fer you know how he feels 'bout a slave."

"Oh, I know!" Said the manager. "You can't tell me anything about him, that I don't already know, for he's one of a kind."

Martha looked at her father and smiled, as they walked out of the store, and headed back toward the cotton gin. Bill walked at a rather fast pace, for he knew that he had to get back home before the sun went down, for the wagon must be loaded with cotton this evening, so it would be ready for him to head out again, real early tomorrow morning. They'd lost a lot of time back at the store, and he'd have to rush the mules along, otherwise, he'd have to load the wagon after dark, by lantern light.

As soon as he had picked up the receipt for the load of cotton his friend had unloaded for him, Bill and Martha climbed back on the wagon, and headed on toward home. As the wagon neared the edge of town, Bill saw some white women standing on the street, chatting. When he politely tipped his hat to them as he drove by, he saw the same women he had seen at the store, and he felt sure that they were already spreading gossip. This didn't bother Bill, for he'd grown used to having white folks talk about him.

Almost an hour had passed since they left town, and when they came to a place where drivers let their mules drink from a small stream that ran across the road, Bill stopped the wagon to let his mules drink. As soon as the wagon stopped, Martha leaped to the ground, rushed over to the side of the road, and began shaking a bush. At first, her father thought she had dropped the cloth, and had jumped down to pick it up, however, when she started shaking the bush, he had no idea what was taking place.

"What's wrong wid you, no how?" He asked in surprise. "Is you went and los' yo' mind, jus' cause you gon'a have a new frock. Get back up here on the wagen, and stop acting like some kin'a fool. Hurry up, now!"

Martha climbed back upon the wagon, and when the mules finished drinking, they continued on their way toward home. Several minutes passed, as they rode along with Martha holding the bundle of cloth tight against her bosom, and her father still wondering why she had gone over and shook the bush. He hated to make a fool of himself by asking, but he simply had to have an answer.

"I know its gon'a make me look like a fool fer axe'n, but I wush you would tell me why you wuz shaking that bush back yon'a," her father asked, in a confused voice. "If you's got the answer it's fine, but don't mess up yo' head, trying to come up wid sump'um, jus' to make yo'sef look good."

"Pappy, didn't you say, that everthang wanted to be free?" She asked. "Ain't that what you aw'ways told me."

"Yass'am, that's what I's said, but it didn't have nothing to do wid you jumping off the wagon and shaking on a bush, like if you wuz a fool," he replied.

"Well, I's seed a spider wrop'n his ole web 'round a purdy butterfly, and I jumped down and sot it free," she smiled, and replied. "Reck'n if it ever sees me again, it's gon'a 'memer who wuz the one that sot it free?"

"Eb'em if it wuz a good thang that you done, I don't 'magine it's gon'a do that," he replied, as he shook his head. "It ain't gon'a pay no tan'chun to who sot it free, like white folks ain't gon'a pay no tan'chun to us, fer the thangs we's do fer them."

"It mout not, but it sho' do makes me feel better, jus' to know that it's free, like I's hope to be one day," she softly explained.

When they finally arrived at the Simpson Plantation, the sun was sinking low behind the tall pine trees, darkness would soon hover over them, and bring to a close, another long hard day's work in the fields. Women-slaves were allowed to leave the fields an hour earlier than men-slaves, so they could fix supper for their family, and as the shacks came into view, Martha happened to see her mother drawing water from a well near her shack. She could hardly wait to show the pretty cloth to her mother, so she leaped from the wagon, and headed out running toward her mother, holding the cloth out in front of her.

"Hey Mammy!" She squealed, as she ran up to where her mother stood with a smile on her face. "Ain't that the purd'est clof' that you's ever went and seed?" She handed the package to her mother. "Hurry, and say it's purdy!" Realizing that the package wasn't even open, Martha quickly ripped the paper off it. "See there, I's told you it was purdy!"

"Yass'am, it sho' do be some purdy clof'," her mother replied, pressing the cloth against her face, "and it sho' do smells good too. But, it ain't the rite kin'a clof' fer no slave. This is the kin'a clof' that the white womens make their frocks out of. Is you sho' that you's got the rite stuff?"

"It wuz meant fer a hateful ole white woman, and she got mad and throwed it down on the flo', and the man let us have it rail cheap," Martha explained to her. "Yass'am, she got mad'rn a woodpecker wid his pecker broke off, jus' cause me and Pappy went in the sto', while she wuz in there."

"What you jus' said wuzn't nice, eb'em if I's do know what you's meant by it," her mother scolded. "Let's take it inside and spread it out on the bed, so's we can take a good look at it. Yass'am, it sho' gon'a make me and you some purdy frocks, and I's rail happy fer it too."

The Simpson's had a son Mark, and a daughter Susan, and they were quite different in every way. Since early childhood, Mark had played with the slave children, and especially with Martha and her older brothers, but Susan acted as though she was too good to play with the Negro children. Mark slipped food from his house and took it to them, for he knew that their food was rationed, and they hardly got enough to keep them alive. Mark was a kind natured type of person, and even though he was only about seventeen years old, he had always felt sorry for the slaves, and disagreed with the way they were treated. Mark and Martha had grown up together, and they were real close friends.

While Martha was running toward the shack, she glanced up toward the mansion, and saw Mark and his father standing in the yard. She realized that she wasn't allowed to go near the mansion unless she'd been invited, however, Mark was her friend, and she wanted him to see the cloth his father had bought for her and her mother. She felt like she should thank his father as well, and even though she would be breaking a rule, she didn't think his father would mind, under the given circumstances.

"Gim'ee that clof'!" Quickly spoke Martha, as she snatched the cloth out of her mother's hands. "I's gon'a take it up yon'a and show it to Mos'a Mark and his pappy, and thank Mos'a Simpson fer what he done fer us."

Before her mother hardly knew what was happening, Martha started running up the large knoll toward the mansion. Her mother Liza, feared what was apt to happen, for even though Martha might have good intentions, she knew all too well how strict Mr. Simpson was, and he seemed to always look for some reason to punish his slaves, she thought.

"Marthie, you's better get on back down here!" Her mother called out, so that Mr. Simpson could hear her as well. "Get on back down here, fo' I take a stick to yo' black-butt! Do you's hear me, gal?"

Martha acted as though she hadn't heard her mother, as she ran on toward the mansion, holding the cloth out in front of her. Mark knew about the cloth his father had told Bill to get, and he also knew how strict his father was in enforcing his rules, and how quickly he would punish the slaves for making the slightest mistake. Mark cringed, as Martha ran up to where he and his father were standing in the yard.

"Mos'a Mark, look'ee here at what I's got!" Spoke Martha, as she held the cloth up for him to see. "Ain't it purdy, and don't you's thank it's gon'a make me and Mammy a purdy frock. Come on, say it will."

"Yes, it certainly is pretty, and it will make you and your mother some pretty dresses," he smiled, and replied. "Take the cloth and get back home, for I don't have any time to look at it now. My father and I were carrying on a conversation, and you interrupted us. Go on back home, and leave us alone. I heard your mother calling you anyway, so hurry, and get back home!"

"I's tell you what, Mos'a Mark!" She squealed, as tears began to trickle down her cheeks. "I's the happiest gal in the wul'd, and yo' pappy's the one that made me feel this way. There ain't nothing I won't do fer him, to pay him back fer what he done fer me and Mammy."

"I'm sure he appreciates the way you feel, and it came from the bottom of his heart," Mark assured her. "It will be dark soon, and you had better get on back home and help your mother with the chores. Go on back home now, so that we can finish with our conversation."

"Yass'uh, that's what I's gon'a do," she replied. "All I's wanted to do anyhow, wuz to show the clof' to you, and let yo' pappy know that it sho' made me and Mammy happy. Will you tell him that, fer me?"

Mark glanced at his father, who was now looking down toward the shacks in which the slaves were housed, and the strange expression on his father's face, concerned him. He felt like his father resented the fact that Martha had come up there to thank him for what he had done, for his father claimed that slaves didn't have any sense - reasoning ability - or consideration for what anyone did for them. Mark had no way of knowing if it was because the cloth was so pretty, or if it was because one of his father's rules had been broken, but the silent glare on his father's face, caused him to be concerned for this slave girl. As he bowed his head, Mark wondered how he could get this girl to go back home, before any real trouble started.

As though she had read Mark's thoughts, Martha turned, and headed back toward home. However, Mr. Simpson quickly grabbed her by the arm, turned her around, and looked keenly at her. This really shocked Mark, as well as Martha, for up until now his father hadn't said anything. At this point, Mark felt as though everything was about to go wrong.

"Mos'a Simpson, I's ain't sho' what all this means," spoke Martha, with a quiver in her voice. "All I's wanted to do, wuz to show the clof' to Mos'a Mark, and to thank you fer what you's done fer me and my mammy."

"Listen here, gal!" Simpson bellowed. "You know the rules, and you know that no nigger is allowed to set foot in my yard, unless they've been invited. You broke one of my rules, and you'll be punished for that, the same as if you had killed one of my mules, or set fire to my barn."

"But, Mos'a Simpson, I's ain't meant to break none of yo' rules," Martha pleaded. "All I's wanted to do, wuz to thank you fer what you's done. Is it wrong, to thank a feller fer sump'um? Is you mad, cause of that."

"It don't matter what you, or anybody else thinks, I don't listen to any excuses for breaking a rule," he sharply spoke, as he snatched the cloth from her, ripped it to pieces, and threw it on the ground. "I make the rules, and I punish anybody who breaks them, no matter what excuse they might have."

Though this truly hurt Mark, he dared not interfere at all. He knew that his father was a stern individual, and set in his ways, and no one could cause him to change his mind, once it had been made up. The cloth didn't mean all that much, and if this was the only thing that he intended to do, it wasn't all that bad. He certainly was capable, and stubborn enough to do a lot more, therefore, Mark felt somewhat relieved at the moment.

"Now, get that stuff up from there!" He yelled, as he pointed to the strips of cloth on the ground. "Don't set foot back in my yard as long as you live, unless I invite you! Do you understand?"

"Yass'uh, I's do una'stan," replied Martha, as she quickly gathered up the pieces of cloth, "and I's promise not to never do that again."

Mark's mother Julie, had been standing on the front porch while all this was taking place, and when Mark glanced up that way, he saw her shaking her head. She was quite different from her husband, but like Mark, she was limited when it came to involving herself in the ways her husband treated the slaves. She also knew that no one could cause him to change his mind, once it had been made up, and she didn't even try. Nate Simpson had a heart of stone, a mind of steel, and a calloused disregard for the feelings of other persons, including members of his own family. He always demanded respect, even though most times, he didn't deserve any respect at all.

"Hold on there a minute, nigger!" Simpson called out, as Martha started walking toward home. "No need to be in a hurry, for I'm not quite finished with you!"

"Oh Lord'ee, what is it that I's done now?" Cried Martha, as she shook her head, and turned around. "I's ain't nothing but a young'un, and a nigga slave, and I's wush you'd have mu'cy on me. Please, Mos'a Simpson!"

"That's right, you're nothing but a stupid-nigger, but you're plenty old enough to start having babies!" He scolded. "Just for breaking a rule, I'll put the buck with you tomorrow. After he gets through working you over, then maybe you'll see things in a different light, and start obeying my rules."

"Oh no, Mos'a Simpson!" She wailed, as she fell to her knees. "I's jus' sixteen years old, and ain't old nuf' to have no young'un fer you. If you won't do that, I's promise not to never do nothing else wrong."

"No matter what you say, my mind's made up," he told her, as he started to walk away. "After that buck crawls you, like a bull on a young heifer, then maybe you'll calm down a bit. I plan to be right there watching when it all takes place, too."

"But, Mos'a Simpson, I's wush you'd wait 'til I's get older, then I won't say nothing," she proposed. "Please, Mos'a! Will you do that?"

"My mind's made up," he told her, "and you had better stay at home 'til the buck gets there, for I want to watch him work you over real good, before I have to leave for town in the morning."

Since Martha had reached womanhood, a constant fear had gripped her heart and soul, for she, like other slave girls, would have to start having babies for Nate to use as slaves, or to sell to other farmers as slaves. The love that slaves had for their own children meant nothing to white men, for they didn't even consider slaves to be human.

The chance of a slave girl being allowed to select the husband of her own choice was slim to none, and should this occur, the probability of her husband fathering children for her, was highly unlikely. Farmers generally selected a stout, robust Negro man from among his group of slaves for the sole purpose of fathering children for slave women and slave girls. This special chosen man was referred to as a "buck." Farmers thought this would assure them of a healthier offspring, and it was well known that they had no use for a weakling among their work force. If a farmer didn't have a buck of his own, he could rent one from another farmer for a fee. If the child were a boy, the fee for the buck would be much greater than if the child were a girl. When the buck was paired with a young girl, like Martha, white men and boys would watch as though an animal was being bred. They had no respect for the slaves at all.

Mark realized that Martha was a slave with no rights of her own, but he felt that the punishment was far too great, for the "crime" that she had committed. Destroying the cloth was enough to teach her a lesson. Even though she was a slave, she was his friend, and at the risk of having his father turn on him for upholding her, he must do something to help her.

"Dad, I know that it's none of my business how you treat the slaves, but in a way, I think you were just a little too rough on that gal," Mark pointed out, as he watched Martha dragging the strips of cloth along, as she went back toward where she lived. "Putting the buck with her, simply because she wanted to thank you for what you did, does seem like harsh punishment. Like I say, it's none of my business, but I wish you would take a long look at things, before doing something that you might regret later on."

"That's right, it's none of your business!" He scolded. "The sooner you learn to dish out punishment without reservation, or consideration for the way niggers feel, the better off you'll be. If you're tender hearted, when one of them needs to be punished, pay attention to their whimpering, or show concern for their welfare, pretty soon, they'll have you down on your knees begging to them. Nobody tells me how I should spend my money, or how I should treat my slaves. Do you clearly see where I stand?"

"I see your point and understand what you mean, but I still say that what you have planned as punishment, is a bit too harsh for the small mistake that she made," Mark replied, trying to keep a positive tone. "Now, do you see my point, and understand what I mean as well?"

"In a way you're right, and in another way you're wrong," he replied, as he took off his hat, and scratched his head. "Keep in mind that a nigger is like a mule, when it comes to reasoning with them. Unless you work them until they're ready to drop in their tracks, keep them hungry and afraid of you as a rabbit, you'll soon lose control over them."

"I might have gone about it in the wrong way, and left you with the wrong impression, for I was thinking more of their personal feelings," Mark pointed out, more clearly. "She was so thrilled to have the cloth, until she probably forgot all about breaking your rules, until after she had already come up here to thank you. Can you agree with me on that point, at least?"

"But, I accept no excuses, when it comes to breaking a rule!" He angrily replied. "No matter what I might have done for her, and even though she might have wanted to thank me, she had no reason to set foot in my yard, until after she got my permission. If I let her get by, as you seem to think I should, it won't be long until I won't be able to step outside of my own house at night, without stumbling over a bunch of sorry niggers. The way you're talking, it causes me to think that you feel sorry for them."

"No, I'm not trying to defend them for doing wrong, and I don't want you to think that I feel sorry for them, either," he replied. "You own them, and you have a right to do with them as you please. Even so, you'll have to agree that Bill's family is the best family of slaves you have, and they never cause any trouble. She's just a young girl, and she allowed her excitement, to get in the way of her judgement. That's what I meant."

"It's not why she did wrong, it's what she did that concerns me most, and I can't afford to let her get by," his father replied, sternly. "The fact is, I have more respect for my mules, than I have for slaves, no matter how good they are. Like you said, she belongs to me."

At the risk of enraging his father even more, Mark continued. "I realize that you own her, but you should remember one thing," he told him. "It was your idea to get the cloth, which you've never done for a slave before, and I wonder why you did it, anyway. Why did you decide to destroy it, when she only wanted to show her appreciation. Would it be asking too much, to request answer to that question?"

"I do have an answer. It was my idea to do it, and it was for a special reason," he replied. "They worked hard all summer, and this fall as well, and I wanted to do something special for them, that's all. But, it all changed, the moment she set foot in my yard. They belong to me heart, soul, and body, and I can whip, sell, or even kill them if that's what I decide to do. All niggers are nothing but trash, scum of the earth, and scrapings from the bottom of the barrel. Now, does that answer your question?"

"I'm not trying to get you to forget that she did something she shouldn't have done, or that she should go unpunished, but to me, destroying the cloth, was enough punishment within itself," Mark suggested. "She's so young, and I wonder if you've ever thought that she might die, while trying to give birth to a child. If she died, would it bother you?"

"If she was only ten years old, I'd still put the buck with her, for once I make a decision, I stick with it," he replied, very callously. "And if she did happen to die, like we all must do sooner or later, it wouldn't bother me a bit. The buck will be put with her, no matter what you have to say!" Then he turned, and walked up the steps, to go back into the house.

Mark was taken aback by his father's attitude. "Well, I know that she's only a nigger slave, but if she happened to die during childbirth, she'll be gone for a long time," Mark replied, as he opened the door, and followed his father on into the house.

Mark went into the parlor and sat down on the sofa alone, and his father went into the kitchen, to take a sip of whiskey from the bottle he kept hidden in a cupboard. This was a crucial time for Mark, for no matter what he might say, it was likely to create more problems for this slave girl, and for him as well. He liked Martha as a special friend, and though his father was treating her in a very bad way, he must not let it be known how he actually felt about her, or that he had always thought it was wrong to make slaves of other human beings, a fact that neither of his parents knew.

Mr. Simpson came into the parlor a moment later, and seated himself in a chair near the fireplace, for the evenings had already turned a bit cold, and the fireplace was the sole means for heating the parlor.

"Son, I'm not upset at you for voicing your opinion, for we all have that right, but this time your're wrong, dead-wrong," spoke his father, in a stern voice. "Always remember this one thing, when you see me driving the slaves in all kinds of weather, from daylight 'til dark. They aren't human, they don't mean anything to me except for how much work they can do, and when I whip one of them, it's no more than whipping as egg-sucking dog."

Somewhat saddened by the punishment which now lay in store for this young slave girl, and frustrated at his father's stubborn attitude toward all Negro slaves, Mark decided not to pursue the matter any further. He knew that there was no way that he'd ever be able to change him.

Martha's mother had been standing outside, and she had heard everything that took place between her daughter and Nate

27

Simpson, and she saw him rip the cloth to pieces, and throw it on the ground. She dreaded what was to happen to Martha in the morning, and when she saw her coming toward the house with the strips of cloth dragging along behind her, she hurried back inside. She didn't want Martha to know that she'd heard everything that went on earlier.

As for Martha, she hid behind their shack for a few minutes pondering her fate in life, and dreading having to tell her mother what had happened. Then as darkness began to hover over the plantation, Martha walked up the steps to go into the shack. She must talk with someone, for she already felt as though Mark had turned against her, and even God Himself, had forsaken her.

"I's hate that ole fool up yonder!" Martha sobbed, as she finally walked into the shack, dragging the strips of cloth along behind her. "He ain't got no sense, and I's wush he wuz dead and in his grave, er that lightening would strike him 'cross his ole bald-head!"

Liza, had been feeling sad ever since she heard what Mr. Simpson said to her daughter a few minutes earlier, and as she looked at the strips of cloth, she almost burst out crying.

"Say, what happened to the purdy clof'! Who tore it up like that?" Liza asked, as though she didn't already know. "And, who is it, that you's want'a see dead, any how?"

"Ole Mos'a Simpson, that's who!" Martha wailed. "Look what he went and done to the clof'! Cides that, he gon'a put the buck wid me to'mar! I don't want'a have no young'un, and don't want the buck messing wid me."

"Oh Lord'ee, I's sho' hate that fer you," said Liza, her voice choking. "You's need to kalm down a bit and 'lax, fer no matter how much you's cry, it ain't gon'a change nothing." Her heart was breaking for her daughter.

Martha tossed the strips of cloth on her mother's lap, then hurried into the back room, and sprawled out across the bed, crying. "I's wush that sorry goat wuz dead!" She screamed. "He ain't got no rite to do nothing like that to me, fer I's ain't never done nothing to him. That ole fool is crazy!"

It was already pitch-dark, when Bill walked into the shack. He had been busy loading the wagon with cotton, so that he could head out for the gin real early tomorrow morning. He heard cries coming from the back room, and he knew it was Martha. He saw the strips of cloth lying on Liza's lap, and when he looked at Liza, he could tell that she had been crying as well.

"What's wrong wid everbid'ee? Why is Marthie in yon'a squalling like if she been wooped wid a stick, and why is yo' eyes as red as a beet?" He asked Liza, fearing that something bad had happened to them. "And, what happened to that purdy clof', fer it to be tore up like that. Didn't you like it?"

Liza didn't want to discuss the situation so her daughter could hear what she said, so she motioned to Bill to follow her into the kitchen. As soon as they sat down at the kitchen table, Liza told him that Mr. Simpson got mad at Martha, because she walked into the yard without having permission, and about him tearing up the cloth.

"I's hate to hear that, but it wuzn't nuf' to make you scae' me aw'mos to def', like you's done," Bill scolded. "She never is had no new frock befo', and she ain't in no wuss fix now, than she wuz fo' she's got the clof'. She's in yon'a squalling, and yo' face looks like it done wore out two bidee's, and I's thought sump'um awful wuz wrong. I's feel better, and sho' could eat supper. I's hungry nuf' to eat a polecat, fried in kerosene."

"But, that ain't all, fer the wuss part ain't been told," Liza said, as she wiped tears from her eyes. "She ain't never let nobid'ee mess wid her, and Mos'a Simpson is gon'a put the buck wid her to'mar. She's scade aw'mos to def', adder what some of the tuther gals told her what the buck done, when he found out that they had never been busted befo'. That's why she be crying like that, fer she's 'fraid the buck will bus' her wide op'um, fer sho'."

"Oh no!" Sighed Bill. "Is that what Mos'a Simpson sez, er is that what Marthie say is gon'a happen?"

"It's the gospel-truf'," she replied, as tears trickled down her cheeks, "fer I wuz standing in the yard, when he told her. Didn't hear Mos'a Mark say nothing, fer I's don't reck'n he wanted to get 'volved in the mess."

Bill was heartbroken, so he quickly jumped up, and went back outside, for he must be alone for a moment. Although he knew that it was bound to happen to her sooner or later, she was only sixteen, and a virgin, and the buck was a stout, robust man. Like Martha, he hoped that it wouldn't happen until she was at least eighteen years old.

At this time, the Simpsons were having supper, and it seemed whenever there was something to discuss, it always took place while they were seated at the dining room table. No sooner had they started eating. Mrs. Simpson called their attention to the buck being put with Martha tomorrow.

"Nate, I was standing on the front porch when the slave-gal came to show the cloth to Mark, and I heard you threaten to put the buck with her," she began. "You shouldn't have bought the cloth, unless you wanted her to have it, and you don't need to make serious decisions when you're upset at someone. Don't you think you might have acted a little too hastily?"

"You can't deny that Mark's your son, for you two think alike, when things like this come up," he replied, in a stern voice. "The slaves belong to me, and I'll do whatever needs to be done, in order to keep them in line. I never have involved you in other business affairs, and I don't intend to involve you in this matter, either. I do business, in a business way."

"Well, what you did this evening sure wasn't business!" She quickly replied. "It was downright stupid and un-called for, and it certainly didn't create a bit of respect for you in the eyes of that slave girl. In fact, it probably added fuel to the fire of hatred that was already burning in her heart, and in the hearts of other slaves as well. When making serious decisions like that, do you ever take into consideration, the feelings of others?"

"I've already told you that I don't care what happens to any of them, or what they might think of me!" He bellowed. "I did exactly what I should have done at the moment, and I have no regrets! I don't need you, or anybody else to tell me how to handle a bunch of stupid, nigger-slaves!"

"What I really meant," said his wife, "is that she's young, and you are aware of what happened to some of the other young slave girls, when they tried to give birth to a child. You need to think about that for a while, before you put the buck with this girl. It's one thing to rule, but it's something else, when you allow your personal feelings to control your thinking, when making a serious decision like that. Do I make myself clear?"

"You know me!" He blustered, quickly getting up from the table, without finishing his supper. "Whenever I make a decision, I don't care who it hurts, or how many problems it might cause for them. I'm in no mood now to listen to such things, and if you don't mind, Madam, I'm going to sit out on the porch, and hopefully, I'll be able to enjoy some peace of mind. That nigger gal, nor any other nigger, is worth wasting my time on. They aren't fit to discuss."

Mark and his mother didn't discuss the matter further, for they knew for a fact, that Nate Simpson didn't intend to listen to reason. They went on and ate, and tried to cast it from their mind, or at least for the moment.

Down at Bill's house things were quite different, for while Nate boasted of his authority over the slaves, the slaves were worried about what was about to happen to one of their own. They were in a worse situation than were farm animals, for farm animals were properly fed and cared for, got plenty of rest, and were not cursed, and kicked around, just because they make one simple mistake. Although the slaves worked very hard, they were underfed, not properly clothed like human beings, and never had a kind word spoken to them. They were happy this morning, because of the new dresses they would have, but this evening as the sun went down, it seemed like a burial-shroud had fallen around them.

The following morning came too early for Martha, for she had laid awake all night, crying and dreading the dawning of this awful day. She had turned sixteen last week, and what other young girls had told her about what happened to them when they were put with the buck, didn't help her feelings at all. As she lay in bed, and watched the sun shining through the cracks in the walls, she realized that all her fears would soon become a reality.

"Lord'ee, Marthie," sadly said her father, as he stood in the doorway to the back room. "I's dread it fer you, but we is slaves, and we's mout as well get sot fer thangs like this to happen to us, 'til the day we die. Judge'mut, is been sot on you, and it ain't gon'a get no better as long as we got breaf' left in or bid'ee. That's the way thangs is."

"I's hate to have to say this, but I's ruth'u be dead and in my grave, than to have to face the ole buck," she told him, as she noticed tears in his eyes, as well. "Ain't there nothing that youn's can do, to hep' me?"

"Yo' mammy, she gon'a talk wid you fo' she goes to wuk', and I's gon'a say a prayer fer you too," he smiled, and told her. "That's all I can do to hep' you, fer he done passed judg'mut on you, and now you's got'a pay the price."

About an hour had gone by, since Martha's parents and her two brothers Samuel and Elijah, had gone to the fields to pick cotton, and Martha was still here at the shack waiting for the buck to arrive, like Simpson had ordered her to do. Maybe Simpson changed his mind, or maybe Mark had talked him out of it after all, she said to herself. Or maybe, she thought, the old man might have died in his sleep. Martha chuckled at that prospect.

Simpson did not forget, nor had he changed his mind. He had already sent one of his foremen to a nearby farm to rent a buck, and he told the foreman to have him here real early this morning. It was time for breakfast, here at the Simpson mansion, but before Mark seated himself at the table, he went over and peeked out through a window, facing the barn. He saw a robust Negro man down at the barn, and immediately, he recognized him as being the buck who belonged to a neighbor, Ephraim Johnson. For some reason, Mark didn't mention the buck as he sat down at the table. Seeing the buck at the barn, and realizing what was about to happen to Martha, a very strange feeling came over him, one that he couldn't quite understand.

"Say, Dad!" Spoke Mark, as he dipped some food into his plate. "I heard you say that you were planning to go to town this morning, and I know that you planned to put the buck with the gal, but he might not get here until later on in the day. I'm not trying to run your business, but if you would let me take care of the buck for you, you could go on to town earlier. What do you say?"

"That sure surprises me," replied his father, "for I thought all along that you planned to go with us. Have you already changed your mind?"

"Well, I really don't want to go," replied Mark, "for I was in town one day last week. I've started reading the book Mother bought for me, and if you don't mind, I'd like to finish it today. Is that all right with you?"

His father looked at him, and smiled. "I'm glad that you're enjoying the book, for everybody should read more, but I was planning to buy the buggy that we were looking at the other day. Have you changed your mind about the buggy as well," chided his father. "It sure was a pretty thing."

"Oh no, I still want the buggy!" Mark told him. "But it's already up in the morning, and there's no telling when the buck will be here. If you let me take care of the buck, you could head out for town earlier, and it would allow more time for Mother and Susan to shop, for you know how women are. How does that suggestion sound to you?"

"It sounds great to me!" Susan squealed. "Seems like every time we go to town we're in such a rush, until I don't get to do much shopping. Daddy, I think he has a great idea! Thank you, Mark."

"I hadn't given any thought to that," his father replied, looking a bit surprised, "for I planned to take care of her myself. To be perfectly honest with you, I was anxious to see the buck bring her down a notch, or two."

Mark didn't want to play his best hand just yet, for fear of causing his father to become suspicious. "Whatever you decide to do, is fine with me," he replied, as though he wasn't concerned, "but sooner or later I'll have to be handling things myself, and the sooner I start, the better off it will be."

"In a way you're right," said his father, as he leaned back in his chair, and stretched his arms, "for it's no more than breeding an animal."

"You say that niggers are no better than animals, anyway," Mark reminded him, "and she's a nigger, if there ever was one."

"That's exactly right," agreed his father. "There's a mighty few decent niggers left in the world, there's more bad than good, and none worth bragging on."

Nothing else was said for a few moments while they continued eating, but it was obvious to Mark, that his father was giving considerable thought to his suggestion. Nevertheless, he didn't want things to stop while seeming to be going so well, therefore, he decided to see if he might somehow drag his mother into the discussion as well. Susan had voiced her opinion, and it did seem to help quite a bit, and now, if his mother would do the same, perhaps it might help to bring his father around, he thought.

"Mother, what do you really think about our discussion?" Mark asked. "Have you given any thought to me handling the situation for Dad, so that you and Susan can have more time to shop. Susan thinks it's a great idea."

"That's strictly between you and him, for if you remember, he told me to stay out of his business affairs," she sharply replied. "Let your father be the one to make the final decision, for he's going to do that any way, whether we like it or not."

It suddenly dawned on Mark that she was afraid to voice her opinion, and the cold stare of his father as he looked across the table at her, provided a reason for her reluctant attitude. Mark felt as though he had unleashed a wicked monster at their breakfast-table. Perhaps, it would be better to accept his father's philosophy on slavery, and keep peace in the family.

"As you know, Dad claims that slaves aren't human, and to him, they're no better than a plug-mule," Mark said, still trying to get her to voice her own opinion. "This might sound strange coming from me, but I agree with him, when you boil it down to facts. Mother, do you share in the way we feel about the slaves, or do you even care to voice your opinion?"

His mother quickly jumped up from the table, shoved her chair across the room, and stood shaking her finger at him. "It's a shame, and a disgrace what your father is doing!" She yelled as never before. "That slave girl is just as much human, as we are! She's not a heifer, or a hog, and you're not old enough to be witnessing such things!" She picked up the chair and sat back down at the table, then set toying with her food.

Simpson's expression didn't change, and he continued to stare at her, as he had for quite some time, now. "That's where you and I disagree, my dear," he said sarcastically. "Niggers are trash, and even though you disagree with the way I treat them, I don't intend to let up one bit."

"I simply don't agree with what you're doing to that poor girl, for she's human, you know!" She scolded, as her voice choked. "It's bad enough to make slaves of them. Even worse, to treat them like dogs!"

Mark quicly interrupted, trying to take his father's angry focus off his mother, who was now on the verge of tears, all because of him.

"Mother, I disagree with you," Mark lied, "for he owns the slaves, and he has a right to do whatever he wants to do. She's not human, and the fact is, unless we keep the women bred, we soon won't have any slaves to do things for us. It's a way of life in the South. Is that so hard to understand?"

"I'm absolutely ashamed of you, Mark!" She replied, in a tearful voice. "If you were not my own flesh and blood, I'd disown you!"

"Hey, lay off my boy!" Simpson bellowed. "He has a good point, and I'm sure that he knows more about such things than you can imagine. This is about a stupid-nigger gal, not a human being, as you suppose. And, I might decide to let him handle things for me, after all."

"Nate, he's your son, as well as mine, and he's going to learn about such things soon enough, without you rubbing his face in them!" She scolded. "He don't need to mess with the buck, and that gal at all. Have you lost all the sense you were born with, or do you even care what you're doing to him."

"Let me remind you of one thing!" Simpson scolded, as he shook his bony finger at her. "Should I decide to let him do that for me, that's the way it will be! Might do it myself - might let him - haven't fully decided, yet."

Susan hadn't said anything else for quite some time, however, should this discussion continue on much longer, there wouldn't be any time left to do any shopping at all, she thought.

"Mother, don't you think it would be best to drop things where they are?" Susan asked. "After all, she's just a nigger, nothing special, and nothing to get all worked up over, or waste a lot of time on discussing it."

"Keep out of this, little lady!" Her mother scolded, slapping her across the face. "Oh, I'm sorry!" She sighed. "Please forgive me, dear! This has me so upset, until I'm not in my right mind." Tears welled her eyes, and then she reached over, and patted Susan on the arm. "I'm sorry for that, my dear."

"That's quite all right, Mother," Susan softly smiled, as she rubbed her face. "This is getting out of hand, and I wish both of them would stop."

The fear in his mother's eyes caused Mark to cringe, and he decided to go along with whatever decision his father made, and pretend to agree. Mark knew that if his mother had stayed out of this, things would have been different by far, but as it stood now, the chance of his father allowing him to do this job for him, significantly increased by the moment. Without realizing what he'd done, he had brought his father to a crossroad. Now, unless he did allow Mark to go ahead as he suggested, it would appear that he had allowed his wife to control his decisiion, and he certainly wouldn't stand for that.

"Well, I've finally made up my mind," his father calmly said, as he slid his chair back away from the table, then stood up, and stretched his arms.

"What's that?" Asked Mark, like he didn't already know. "Whatever you decide to do, is fine with me. I won't go against your decision."

"Right, or wrong, when John gets here with the buck, I want you to handle this matter for me," said his father, seriously. "Let the buck know that you are in charge, then step back outside, while he does what he's supposed to do. This will probably be the first time for her, and I'm sure she'll put up a fight, but tell the buck to do whatever he has to do."

"Oh, that won't be a problem!" Mark boasted, as he quickly stood up, and stretched his arms. "I'll sock her in the face with my fist, if she causes a problem. The job is as good as done, if the buck ever gets here."

"Do whatever it takes to get the job done, for I want to take Susan into town, and let her get her belly full of shopping," his father smiled.

Mark walked over to a window, and stood looking toward the barn as if he was waiting for the buck to arrive, but the buck was already here.

"Well, I see the buck walking up now," he lied. "And I'd better get on down there, before he decides to leave. I expected him to be here long before now, but he's here, and that's all that matters, I suppose."

The buck's name was Robert, and as soon as Mark arrived at the barn where the buck was waiting Mark motioned to him, and they headed out toward the rundown shack where Martha was supposed to be waiting. Mark had visited the shack as a child, when he went to play with Martha and her brothers, but this would be the first time that he had been there on business. Would he be able to carry out this assignment. He asked himself. He wasn't quite sure, at this point.

"Robert, my name is Mark Simpson, my father put me in charge, and I'll be the one you'll have to answer to, if you don't do your job," Mark bragged, as they walked along. "You have a job to do, and I want you to get it done as soon as possible, for I have other things to do."

"Is she one of them old womens that done had a house full of young'uns, er is she a young whipper-snapper, that ain't never been crawled?" The Buck asked. "I's like them young gals. Hot tails, I's call 'em."

Mark's mission was business, and he didn't have time to listen to foolish talk like this. He had a job to do, and he must do it.

"The feller that brung me here, sez she wuz jus' a young gal, and I's hope he ain't went and lied to me," the Buck blurted. "Did he lie to me?"

The Buck was alrady getting on Mark's nerves. "That's none of your darn business!" Sharply replied Mark. "You have a job to do, and unless you do as you're told, you'll get the devil whipped out of you!"

When they arrived at the shack, Mark shoved the door open without taking time to knock, as if they were entering a barn. When they stepped inside and didn't see Martha anywhere, Mark figured that she was hiding somewhere inside the house. Mark decided to call to her, for she should have known better than to leave the house, after she was told to stay here, he thought.

"Martha, you might as well come on out, now!" Mark called. "We've got a job to do, and the sooner it's over, the better it's going to be for you. Do you hear me, Martha?"

When she didn't answer him, Mark figured that she was probably hiding in the barn, after all. It wasn't like her to not answer him, for they had been friends since childhood, and besides that, a slave must answer a white person, otherwise, they stood a chance of being whipped at a stake. However, when he looked in the back room, he saw her feet sticking from underneath some clothes that were hanging on a nail, on the back of a door.

"Martha, you might as well come on out, for I see your feet!" Mark said, in a stern voice. "Come on out, before I have to drag you out, by the hair of the head!" He yelled again.

Mark waited for a moment longer, and when it seemed like she didn't plan to obey him, he grew very angry. Regardless to their friendship, it was her duty as a slave to obey him without question. After all, he was white, with authority, and she was just a slave, with no rights at all. Then, he thought of the promise he'd made to his father, and he grew very angry.

"All right now, you stupid-nigger, you asked for it!" Mark yelled, as he rushed over and caught hold of her arm, and then jerked her from behind the door. "I don't intend to stand here and beg to you like a darned fool!"

"Please, Mos'a Mark!" She begged. "Don't let that ole sorry man get to me, fer he gon'a beat me half to def'. Ain't we's been friends, ever since we wuz young'uns - ain't we's still friends?" She trembled with fright, at the sight of the buck, and tears trickled down her cheeks.

"Shut up, you sorry hussy!" Shouted Mark, as he slapped her hard across the face, and then shoved her down on the bed. "I don't have time to mess around with you! It's high-time for you to start having babies, and you better let the buck do his job!" Mark saw in an instant, how easy it would be for him to be mean, and cruel to a slave like his father, like everybody else.

Martha was shocked, for she really thought their friendship would have a little bearing, but she knew now, that she had obviously been wrong. The way she was being treated now, she supposed that their friendship didn't make any difference. Mark had been assigned a task, and if he ever intended to become a leader someday, he might as well let this be his starting-place. Why should he allow the pitiful cries of the slave girl to affect his decision, or bother his conscience, he asked himself.

Mark went back into the kitchen, and left Martha and the buck alone, for he was doing exactly what he had been told to do, and he intended to obey his father. He must cast out all his past relationship with her as a friend, for like his father once told him, "You can't be tenderhearted, and be able to handle a bunch of nigger slaves." His father also said- "Hand out the sentence without reservation, or consideration for their welfare." Mark was his father's son, and he wasn't going to let anything keep him from carrying out the order that his father handed down. He sat down at the kitchen table, and bowed his head. He could hear what was going on in the other room.

"Oh, Lord'ee! Cried Martha, when the buck slipped off his britches, and sat down on the edge of the bed. "Get out from here, fer I's ain't want'n you to give me no young'un!"

"There ain't no use fer you to pitch no fit, fer I's got'a get on wid it jus' the same," replied the buck, as he lifted up her skirt. "The sooner I's get to you, the sooner its gon'a be over wid, and all that squalling, sho' ain't gon'a hep' you none."

"Ain't nobid'ee never messed wid me befo', and I's don't want you to mess 'round wid me, neither!" She cried, as he continued fondling with her. "I's shamed fer you to see me naked, so don't take off my clothes."

The buck was anxious now, after she told him that she was a virgin. "Let me get on wid this, er we bof' gon'a be in a lot'a trouble," he told her, as he jerked off her underclothes. "If you's don't let me get to you, then I gon'a have to hit you over the head wid my fist! Do you's una'stan?"

38

From the kitchen, Mark could hear everything they said, and when the buck threatened her, he almost got up to go and protect her. On second thought, he must not interfere. This had to be done. Unless he could take control of his emotions and feelings now, he wouldn't be able to control slaves later, if he inherited this plantation. He must not let this bother him, at all.

"Oh Lord'ee, you's gon'a kill me!" She screamed, when the buck lay down on her. "Please hep' me, Mos'a Mark, fer he's too big fer me!" She twisted, and turned, as she tried to keep him from raping her. But, the robust man was strong, and he began forcing himself on her. "Come in here and hep' me, Mos'a Mark!" She cried out. "I's can't stan', what he's doing to me!"

She was Mark's friend, and this pitiful crying and pleading was starting to tear him apart. But, he had a job to do, and he must convince himself that his duty, should override his personal feelings. She was just another Negro slave, wasn't she? Wasn't he justified, in allowing this to happen? Then, he heard her scream out real loud, for the buck was forcing himself on her, but, when Mark heard him threaten to choke her to death if she didn't lay still, it was more than he could stand. He had to do something to help his friend.

"To heck with this!" Mark cringed, as he grabbed up a butcher knife that was on the kitchen table, and then rushed into the back room. The buck saw the knife in Mark's hands, and thought that Mark was going to threaten Martha with it, if she didn't lay still. He looked up at Mark, and grinned.

"Ain't no use to threaten her wid that knife, fer I's jus' 'bout got her where I's want her," said the buck. "Hold her hands, so she won't scratch my eyeballs out, and I'll wuk' her over, rail good."

In a flash, Mark jabbed the blade of the butcher knife against the buck's side, and the man groaned. "I've heard enough of this!" Mark screamed, as he pressed harder on the knife, "Get off of her, or I'll cut your darn guts out!"

"This don't make no sense," replied the buck, as he still lay on Martha, and looked up at Mark. "I's aw'mos got her, if you'll hold her hands."

Because she was his friend, and the buck didn't seem to want to listen to him, Mark really flew mad. Before he hardly knew what he was doing, he stuck the knife deeper into the buck's side, and then blood gushed forth.

"I told you to get up off her, and that's what I mean!" Mark yelled. "Get up off her, or I'll kill you, you sorry bastard!" Then, Mark jerked the knife back, and held it high above his head, as though he intended to stab the buck in the back, and the buck quickly rolled over off Martha.

"I's gon'a spread the word 'bout what went on here, and you's gon'a be in a lot'a trouble, too," said the buck, as he jumped off the bed, picked up his britches that lay on the floor, and put them back on. "Mos'a Simpson, he sho' is gon'a jump on you, when I's tell him what you's done, he sho' is."

"If you open your mouth to anybody, I'll kill you!" Mark told him, as he placed the butcher knife against his throat. "Shut your darn mouth, and stand over there against the wall, 'til I tell you to move!"

The buck hurried across the room, and leaned up against the wall like he had been told. He knew that Mark was serious, and as he held his hand on the gash that was cut in his side, he could tell that there was something greater than just friendship between Mark, and this slave girl.

"Martha, you've always been my friend, and nothing has changed, no matter what I did or said to you earlier," said Mark, as he spread a quilt over her half-naked body. "I hope you'll forgive me for allowing this to go as far as it did, and I hope you're all right. Are you all right, Martha?"

"Yass'uh, I's jus' fine, now," she sighed, "and I's glad that you's got that buck off me, fer he wuz hurt'n me awful bad." Then she closed her eyes, as though in silent prayer, and Mark gently bowed his head, as he pondered all this in his heart.

Although Martha's mother had gone to the fields to pick cotton, and left Martha alone at the shack to wait for the buck to arrive, Liza kept a watchful eye on the shack while she worked. She had seen Mark take the buck into their house, and even though she tried to convince herself that everything would be all right, she could imagine what her daughter must be going through with at this very moment. Even though she tried, she couldn't hold back the tears as she thought of her daughter, and a woman working close to her, saw her wipe a tear from her eye. The other slave woman's name was Clara Bell. Even though the slaves were constantly watched while they worked, and were not allowed to talk to each other, Clara Bell gradually worked her way over closer to where Liza worked, so she could speak to her.

"I's seed you squalling 'round mite nye all moan'n, and I's know sump'um is wrong wid you," she whispered. "I's like to know what it is, fer it sho' do hurts me, when somebid'ee else ain't happy. Is you sick, er sump'um?"

"But, I's ain't been squalling, and there ain't nothing wrong wid me, in the fus' place!" Liza scolded. "Go on back and stop pester'n me, fer I's a grown womern, and I'll let you know when sump'um is wrong wid me."

"When a feller squalls, sump'um is wrong wid 'em, and you's mout as well go on and belch it out, fo' you's bus' wide op'um," Clara Bell insisted.

Had it been another woman, Liza might have told her, but Clara Bell was a nosey-type of person, and Liza didn't dare tell her the truth. She was ashamed to tell her.

"I's done told you that nothing wuz wrong wid me!" Liza scolded, as she slapped the woman's hand. "Now, do I's make my'sef clear?"

The woman didn't intend to stop prying until she finally got an answer, or until she was able to figure out things for herself.

"Liza, we's knowed each other ever since we wuz lit'l gals," she kept on prying, "and I's know mo' than you's thank I do. I's seed that buck at the barn, and I's ain't seed yo' gal all moan'n, and that tells me all I's need to know. The buck's up there wuk'n her over, and that's the ver'ee reason you's been squalling all moan'n. Now, ain't that the gospel-truf'?"

"Get over yon'a and leave me 'lone!" Liza yelled, loud enough for the others to hear her, and they all looked at her. "Leave me 'lone wid my own trouble, eb'em if I's ain't got none, like I's done sez!"

"I's ain't meant to pester you none, but I's know what's wrong wid you, and I's feel rail sorry fer yo' gal too," said Clara Bell, as she gradually worked her way back across the field. "He's the same buck that wuz put wid my lit'l gal when she wuz thu'teen, and like you's done know, she died, trying to have the young'un. Some of the old womens sez they can't hardly take him, and yo' gal, she ain't gon'a be able to take him, neither."

Although Liza tried to dismiss this from her mind, she knew what happened to Clara Bell's daughter, and she feared for her own daughter. Liza continued to glance up toward the shack while she worked, and she prayed that she would get a chance to slip back, and check on Martha. Maybe the foreman would leave for a few minutes - she hoped so - she prayed that he would.

Back at the shack, and after Mark had promised Martha that he'd come back in a few minutes and talk with her, he took the buck outside. Although he had acted according to his own conscience, his heart was troubled because of what he had done to help the slave girl, and he tried to think of what he should do next. Suddenly, a plan came to his mind. He'd let the buck stay in a shed at the barn, until ample time had passed for the buck's encounters with her, and then he'd send the buck back home, as if he'd done his job. Still, he must let the buck know of his plan, and why all this had happened, in the first place.

"Robert, you might think that I'm crazy, but that gal is my real close friend, and a lot like my own sister, you might say," Mark began. "I won't stand for you, or anybody else to do her harm, and that's why I protected her."

"Then, that makes you be what white folks call a nigga-lover," the buck replied, as they walked toward the barn. "A white feller better not let folks know that he likes a nigga, and spec' to live ver'ee long. Mos'a Johnson went and killed one of his own boys, cause he ketched him wid a nigga gal, then he sez that his boy fell off the barn, and busted his head."

"I heard about the boy falling off the barn, but I didn't know his father killed him," Mark replied. "But I'm not what you might call a "nigger lover" as you might think. I feel sorry for all slaves, even you, for I don't think it's right to make a slave of another human being, be they black or white. We are friends, real close friends, and that's enough said."

"But, what is yo' pappy gon'a do, when he finds out that you wouldn't let me get to her?" Asked the Buck, still angry with Mark. "Is he gon'a kill you, when I's slip up and tell him, fo' I's know what I's doing?"

"If he ever finds out, no matter who tells him, you're as good as dead!" Mark emphatically stated. "And, I'll tell what you told me about Mr. Johnson killing his son. I'll show you where you can stay until I get ready to send you back, but you won't have anything else to do with the girl. And, for your own good, you had better pray that nobody ever finds out about this."

The buck didn't reply, for it was obvious that Mark was serious, and Mark wouldn't have to worry about him saying anything. As soon as Mark showed the buck where he could stay,

Mark headed back up toward the mansion. He planned to enter through the back door, for he wasn't quite ready to face his father. As he started around toward the back of the mansion, his father was getting into the carriage to go into town, when he happened to see Mark.

"Well, how did things go?" Asked Nate, taking Mark aside, so that Susan and her mother couldn't hear their conversation. "Did you have a problem with her, or did she lay there and take him, like she was supposed to do? I'm sure she pitched a fit, for he's a big man, and this being her first time to be put with a buck, wasn't easy for her."

"You know she pitched a fit," Mark smiled, as he balled up his fist, and shook it in the air, "but I took my fist, and calmed her down. I'm sure that I got that from you, for all her crying and begging, didn't bother me one bit. I'll put the buck back with her every day for awhile, or at least until I feel absolutely sure that she's pregnant, then I'll send him back home."

"I had no doubt that you could handle the situation," beamed his father, and then looking at his wife, he added, "this here's my boy, my own flesh and blood, and he knows how to handle slaves. I'm proud of you, Son!"

"Like I said, the buck's in the shed down there at the barn," Mark told him, "and I told the gal to go on to the cotton fields, and that I'd put the buck back with her every day. That's one time, she really got worked over."

"That's fine," Simpson nodded, as he went back to join the others in the carriage, "and from now on, she's in your hands. Set this date down in that ledger that I keep in my desk, so we'll know when to expect the baby."

As soon as the carriage went out of sight, Mark returned to the shack to talk with Martha, before she went on to the fields. He knew that she had probably taken things the wrong way, and might have gotten the wrong impression, and he wanted to clear things up, before they went any further.

"Hey, do you mind if I come in for a moment?" Mark asked, as he knocked on the back door. "I'd like to talk with you, before you go to the fields."

"I's happy fer what you's done to hep' me, and I gon'a axe the Mos'a in the sky to look down and grin at you too," she softly replied, as she motioned for him to come inside.

"Now, let's face facts!" Mark said, seriously. "No matter how much you pray, or whether you want to admit it, sooner or later my father will find out what happened, and we'll both be in trouble. What I hope to do, is to come up with a plan, to prevent us from having any more problems."

"I's hate that I acted like a young'un, but I's ain't never let no boy mess wid me befo', and adder what the tuther gals sez that happened when the buck crawled them, it scade me half to def'," she explained. "He wuz too big fer a mule, much less fer a lit'l gal like me."

"The problem is, my father will soon find out that you're not really pregnant, and I'm not sure how I can explain it to him." Mark replied. "But, I do have a plan, of sorts, and it might just work."

. "What kin'a plan is you got fer me, if you's ain't gon'a let the buck get back wid me?" She asked. "Don't every gal have to let a buck crawl her, fo' she ever can have a young'un? That's what my mammy sez, a buck is fer."

"I know that you like some young boy around here, and if you will let him father a child for you, my father will think it belongs to the buck. How does that sound?" He asked, knowing how foolish it must have sounded to her.

A smile came on her face. "That sounds like a rail good'n, fer you's the only boy that I's like, and you can be the pappy," she replied.

"Hold on a minute! Said Mark, in surprise. "Even if we are real close friends, and I have a special feeling for you, it would be morally wrong, and completely out of the question. Now, do you understand?"

Martha looked as though she was deeply hurt. "I's don't see why not, fer as long as the young'un is got a pappy, that's all that matters," she quickly disagreed. "I's ain't gon'a tell who the pappy is, and if you don't tell 'em yo'sef, nobid'ee won't never know who the pappy is, not eb'em me."

"Either you let one of the Negro boys father a child for you, before word gets back to my father, or I'll have to put the buck back with you," he shook his head, and replied. "I'm in enough trouble as it is, and you'd better get busy, before my father finds out what I've done. Now, do I make myself clear, or had you rather I bring the buck back?"

Mark talked with her for a few more minutes from the bottom of his heart, as he tried to explain why he had helped her. He also told her that he hated slavery, and that he hoped he'd be able to help the slaves gain their freedom one day. Mark tried to point out to this naive girl, the impact that it would have on each of them, and their child, if he should father a child for her.

"That sounds lopsided to me, fer I's thought that all white folks wanted us to be slaves, fer the res' of our lif'," she replied.

"I'm aware of the fact that slaves feel that way, and they have very good reasons to feel as they do, but there's many other folks who think it's wrong to make slaves of other human beings," he pointed out, as he started walking toward the door. "They're afraid to stand up and voice their opinion, or buck against a system that's tearing this young and struggling nation apart. Don't ever tell anyone what I told you, or not just yet, anyway. Give me a few more years to grow up, and get in a position where I'm able to do the way I feel, and you'll see what I mean. Goodbye, Martha."

"Goodbye, Mos'a Mark," said Martha, as he walked out the door. "Me and you is got a secret, and nobid'ee ain't never gon'a know what it tis. I's had a funny feeling in my belly fer you, ever since I wuz twelve years old, and it gets wuss ever day. If you's ever change yo' mind and want'a be the pappy of my young'un, it sho' will make me happy. Why don't you change yo' mind now, and get it over wid?" She boldly offered herself to him.

Mark realized now, that he hadn't even broken through her ignorance by what he had just tried to explain to her, and it really bothered him.

"Martha, that would be wrong," he replied, as he walked across the yard, "and you'll have to put that out of your mind. I'm going back home now, and you need to do some serious thinking about having one of the boys father your child, for this thing is already getting out of hand."

Mark went back home, and Martha started getting ready to go to the fields to pick cotton. They didn't know that Liza had slipped back to the house, and had been listening outside, while their conversation was going on.

"Glory be!" Liza shouted, as she ran inside, and quickly threw her arms around her daughter. "So, the buck didn't get to you adder all, did he? Say he didn't, my lit'l chile."

"That's rite," proudly replied Martha, "fer Mos'a Mark, he wouldn't let him bother me. I's ain't sho', but I's thank Mos'a

Mark is gon'a pappy a baby fer me. Ain't that sump'um! I's gon'a have a baby, and you gon'a have a grand-chile!"

"Don't come at me wid that kin'a stuff, fer I's here'd everthang Mos'a Mark sez to you!" Liza scolded. "I's here'd what he wants to do fer slaves, but he be dreaming - wild dreams, too. Bof' of youn'se is playing wid some rail hot fire coals, and youn's is gon'a get burnt, too. Hurry up now, fer I's got'a get on back to the field, fo' the man misses me."

As they hurried toward the cotton fields, Liza was thinking how lucky her daughter had been. Why had Mark taken a chance, by helping a slave. What if the buck talked, and word got back to Simpson, she thought to herself. Then, her thoughts switched to what other slaves might say. Clara Bell had no doubt already told the others about the buck being put with Martha. She had to come up with some way to help Mark as well, for after all, it was his neck that had been placed on the chopping-block, for trying to help a slave.

"When we's get back to the field, I's want you to act like you is jus' 'bout tuckered out, and can't hardly walk," Liza told her. "If one of 'em do axe you what's wrong, jus' tell 'em that you's ain't feeling no good, and hide yo' face. Then, they gon'a thank that the buck done went and wuk'd you over. Be sho' not to fa'get what I's say, neither."

"That's what I's gon'a do, fer Mos'a Mark, he done put his own'sef on the spot jus' fer me," replied Martha, as she started hobbling along, exactly like her mother had suggested.

"I's 'fraid of what Mos'a Simpson will do to that boy, if he do happen to find out what he's done fer you," Liza worried aloud. "We's need to axe the Mos'a in the sky, to hep' us keep this lie we's 'bout to tell, in the bottom of our belly. I's ain't sho', but I don't thank it hurts nobid'ee to tell a lie, if it's gon'a hep' somebid'ee. Fellers like Mos'a Mark, nohow."

CHAPTER TWO

THE BUD BEGINS TO OPEN

It had been several weeks now, since Mark took the buck down to the shack to father a child for Martha, and though Mark had kept him from doing his job, rumors of her being pregnant, were already spreading around. This did offer a bit of relief for Mark, and his father thought that he had shown other slaves who "ruled the roost," by the way he had treated Martha. Yet, on the other hand, a dark cloud of gloom hovered over Mark, as the truth beat down on him like the sun, on a hot-summer day. What Mark did that day, should have been commendable, but given the time, and circumstances, it might prove to be his undoing, instead.

Nate Simpson knew in his heart that he had acted in haste by putting the buck with the girl, but he'd die before he'd admit that he'd been wrong. And, he was also far from being the type of person to forgive his son for deceiving him. Mark knew all too well that he had placed his life on the line when he helped the slave girl, and he now felt like a man with a divided-soul. He had learned to obey his father without question, out of respect, laced with fear, however, his conscience had been tugging heavily at his heart, over the issue of slavery. He felt that slaves were ignorant through no fault of their own, and he had never accepted the notion, that they were not a part of the human race. His resolve to help these Negro slaves to gain their freedom, seemed like an unattainable goal. Perhaps, it was enough for him just to want to help them, even if there was nothing he could actually do.

The problem at hand plagued Mark's thoughts. Martha was not with child, and time would soon bear out that fact. Each day brought on added anxiety, as he searched for a solution to the problem, and the emotional strain was taking its toll on him. One day while talking with Martha's father, he finally admitted that he had come to a point where he didn't know what to do.

"Bill, I kept the buck from Martha, because I dislike the way you slaves are being treated," Mark began, "and I've often wondered, how you felt about what I did. It's about to get the best of me, which is no doubt very obvious. Do you think that I did the right thing, or is it something that will probably return one day, and slap me in the face? I really would like to know how you feel, that is, if you don't mind discussing it with me."

"Well, that's the kin'a ques'un that's got two answers, and it's pow'ful hard fer me to figure out which one you's need to hear," Bill replied.

"I don't quite understand what you mean," replied Mark, somewhat confused, "for it's not a hard question to answer, or at least, it shouldn't be."

"It's sorter like this," Bill began. "To me, it wuz the rite thang, fer it wuz my chile that you's hep'd. But as fer yo' pappy, he ain't gon'a never trust you wid nothing else. Gon'a call you a sorry nigga-lover, to boot."

"I know how he'd feel if he ever found out what I did, for he's dead-set on not admitting that slaves are human beings," Mark pointed out. "But, what I'd like to know, is if you think what I did was right."

"Well, rite don't sound rite, less'n it's sump'um that we's want'a hear," said Bill. "Eb'em if it do look rite to me and you, it's gon'a look wrong to him, fer he ain't get'n no good out of it. That's why it's got two answers."

"I see what you mean, now," Mark nodded, "but I only acted according to the way I felt in my own heart. Shouldn't I act according to the way I feel in my own heart. Don't I have that right. Shouldn't I have that right, as a human being?"

It suddenly dawned on him, that he was no better off than slaves, for the limitations were somewhat the same. He couldn't go against the rules that his father had laid down, anymore than they could, and he was afraid to voice his opinion, for fear of making his father angry. In a manner of speaking, he was also a slave to his own father, even though he was his father's son.

Sensing Mark's frustration, Bill gently patted him on the shoulder. "The thang that you done wuz rite in yo' eyes, and rite in mine, and all we can do, is whatever that makes us happy," Bill replied. "Nobid'ee never can make yo' pappy feel good, fer he ain't the kin'a feller that's gon'a be happy 'bout nothing, less'n it's sump'um that's coming his way."

All the cotton had been picked and sold, and while Liza was folding up the pick-sacks, and storing them in a shed so they could be used another year, she listened to their conversation. Realizing the predicament Mark now faced because he had helped their daughter, and hoping to lighten the load he had on his shoulder because he had helped her, she decided to let Mark know that they had been thinking of a way to help him.

"Mos'a Mark, me and Bill is been worried mite nye to def' over what you's done fer our chile, and 'bout what will happen to you when yo' pappy finds out what you's done," said Liza, as she walked up, and stood beside Bill. "Like you's done told Marthie to do, me and Bill is gon'a let one'a the nigga boys give her a young'un, and then you won't have to be worried, like you is now."

"Yass'uh, that's what we 'cided to do," agreed Bill. "Fer less'n she do starts looking prag'nut purdy soon, we's all gon'a be in a lot'a trouble."

"I appreciate that, for like I already told Martha, that's about the only way I know to solve the problem," Mark smiled, and replied. "I must go now, and if you folks will do that for me, it sure will be appreciated."

Then, as Mark slowly turned to walk away, he suddenly felt the nagging of his conscience again. Although this would be the solution to his problem, there was something that he didn't quite like about this idea, and he needed to think on it.

"Bill, before you do that, let me try to come up with some other way to get us out of this mess," Mark suggested. "I was thinking of something that might work a lot better, so let me think on it, before you do anything." Mark lied, for he had no other plan, and didn't know which way to turn.

During the following few weeks, Mark constantly thought of what he'd done to help this slave girl, as he searched for a solution to the problem, and the answer to the many questions that cluttered his mind. He spent many sleepless nights wondering why he had gotten himself into this mess, and what he could do to get this heavy load off his shoulder. Most of all, he was at war with himself, for as a child he had innocently played with Martha and her brothers, but now that he was older, the strange feeling he had for her, was far greater than just innocent, childhood friendship. He knew that it must be obvious to her parents, and his parents as well, he thought.

Martha's parents were worried as well, for if Mr. Simpson found out that Martha wasn't pregnant, he'd personally pair the buck with her, until he was absolutely sure that she was with child. He might even kill her, and turn Mark out of his house. They were helpless individuals, Mark as well, and they didn't dare confide in anyone, outside their tiny circle.

One day, while Martha and her mother were down at the creek washing their clothes, Liza reminded her daughter of the problem Mark was now facing, simply because he had tried to help her as a friend.

"This here thang is done got out'a hand," said her mother, "and les' we do sump'um purdy soon, everbid'ee is gon'a be in trouble. We's got'a get busy and get you prag'nut purdy soon, whether you gon'a like it er not, and you mout as well get sot."

"That's the reason I's wanted Mos'a Mark to pappy a young'un fer me, and then we wouldn't be in this mess," replied Martha. "He's the bes' feller I's ever seed, and I'd have the bes' young'un in the wul'd. If youn's could talk him into doing that fer me, eb'em if I's don't want him to, it sho' would make me the happiest gal, you's ever seed."

"Yo' pappy is done talked wid one nigga boy, and he 'greed to give you a young'un," she told her daughter, "so Mark's pappy won't never find out what Mos'a Mark is done fer you. You can pick out a boy, if that's what you want'a do, jus' as long as you's get prag'nut by somebid'ee purdy soon."

"But, I's don't like nobid'ee else, like I's do Mos'a Mark!" She sharply replied. "Ain't nothing wrong wid him being the pappy, neither. Reck'n you could get him to do that, jus' fer me?"

Liza became frustrated with her daughter. "Mos'a Mark, he sez he wuzn't gon'a do nothing like that, and you here'd him say that, too!" Liza scolded her. "It ain't rite fer no white man to mess wid no nigga, eb'em if I's know that it do happen all the time. If Mos'a Mark don't come up wid sump'um else purdy soon, we's gon'a have to put you wid that nigga boy, fer Mos'a Mark, he's the onliest friend that we's got 'round here."

Martha didn't really want to see her mother's point of view. She already had Mark in her sights, and would not be easily swayed.

In addition to this plantation, Mr. Simpson owned a small farm that was a few miles south of here, and he rented it to a man by the name of Powell, who was to keep up the farm for him. He disliked Powell, and he had given thought to selling the small farm to keep from being bothered with this man, for he hardly did anything to keep up the place. Because his father wanted to "own the entire world," Mark felt sure there was no way his father would sell off this small part. Mark also remembered that his father promised him this small farm, when Mark was only twelve years old. At the young age of seventeen, he knew that his father's promise would be well in the offering, if indeed it did come to pass.

One morning while at the breakfast table, following a long and sleepless night, a dim ray of hope began to shine through the dark cloud of gloom, which had been hovering over Mark for several weeks.

"I got a letter from Powell yesterday, and he sent a few dollars for rent on the small farm," Nate told them. "He said he'd like to buy it, too."

"Hey! I was under the impression that the farm would belong to me, when I became of age!" Mark quickly spoke up. "Dad, didn't you promise that farm to me, on my twelfth birthday? Have you already gone back on your word?"

"You never forget anything that I say, do you." Simpson chuckled. "I do remember that, quite well. Don't get upset because he asked me to sell it to him, for that's no sign that I plan to sell. It's just a small farm compaired to this plantation, but if it was handled properly, it could provide a decent living for a fellow just starting out. Powell hasn't spent any time with it since he's been there. Too lazy, I imagine."

"You really had me scared there for a moment, for I've been dreaming about being a farmer like you one day, and that little farm would be ideal for me to start out with," Mark told him. "After all, you did promise it to me."

"The boy is right!" Spoke up Mark's mother. "You promised it to him on his twelfth birthday, the same day you gave him that little pony, which is now the mare, that he thinks so much of."

Well, that extends to threats too, Mark said to himself. His mind began to race. He knew that he must seize this opportunity, in order to help solve the problem now facing him.

"If that be the case, why not turn the farm over to me now?" Mark asked. "Let me get some hands-on experience, and when you retire, I would have enough experience to handle this farm. Now, does that not make good sense?"

He could tell by his father's expression, that this proposal wasn't being taken lightly, and he hoped that his father would accept it. It was his only hope.

"Yes, someday this farm will belong to you, and then you'll find out what it's like to be a farmer, and to handle a bunch of nigger slaves," his father finally said. "Like you said, you need to start off small, and gradually work your way up the ladder, and that speaks well of you, too."

"I really do appreciate that, and the very thought of someday owning this plantation, almost makes me speechless," Mark solemnly replied. "But, you're not about to retire anytime soon, and we both know that. Until then, I'd be a lot better off by trying my hand at running the small farm. I know that I'll be working my fingers to the bone, and I'm going to have setbacks as I work my way up. But, I'll put my heart into it, if you're willing to let me try. What do you say!"

"You sure are an ambitious young man, and I appreciate that, for it speaks well of me," his father chuckled. "This plantation can provide you with all the luxuries of life, but the small farm will only provide you with a living, even if you work hard, seven days a week. That's what I meant."

"I understand that," Mark continued, "but I think that the small farm is all that I need, until I learn a lot more about farming than I already know now."

"Powell is a fairly good farmer, but he only does what's necessary to get by on," his father pointed out. "It's going to take a bunch of niggers about two years of hard-working to get it back in shape, but it will pay off in the long-run, and it certainly would be worth a man's effort, in the end."

Mark was fairly sure that his father would want to wait until he reached his twenty-first birthday before he gave him the farm, but if he could get him to go ahead now, and let him have Bill's family to help tend the land, all his problems would be solved. But, he must be very careful how he went about this scheme so as not to tip his hand, for he was now at a point where he couldn't afford to make another mistake.

"Dad, you really have me excited, now!" Said Mark, as he quickly jumped up from the table. "I'll be eighteen in a few months, and I've often wondered how old you were, when you set out on your own." He already knew, and he sure didn't expect an argument from his father on this score.

"I was younger than you are now, a heck of a lot younger," his father smiled, and reminiced. "I was just a boy, I tell you, too young, in fact."

"Well, unless I do get out on my own pretty soon, I'm going to be an old man, before I know what a stalk of cotton even looks like," Mark teased. "Do you see what I mean."

"You're a lot smarter than that," his father laughed. "I've been giving a lot of thought to letting you take over little by little, like I did, when I let you handle the buck that day. The way you handled that, proved to me that with just a little experience, you could handle almost anything around here."

"I appreciate that," said Mark, trying to remain positive, "but if it's the same with you, I'd rather take over the small farm now, so I can gradually learn as I grow up. And, if you could lend me some slaves to help get it back in shape, I think I could make a go of it. I want you to be proud of me, just like your father was of you, when you first strted out."

"That sounds like a man talking - the same kind of man who took care of the buck, and that gal," his father welled with pride. "But it does require more than just following orders. It takes experience, guts and backbone to run a farm. I'd let you go on down there now, and give you a bunch of slaves to help you, if you were experienced in handling a farm, and a bunch of nigger slaves, but you're not. Now, do you see my point."

"Let me ask you a personal question, if you don't mind," politely replied Mark. "Didn't you have to gradually learn as you went along, and didn't you run into problems, and have to call on your father? It won't be any different with me. With you to rely on, I'll make it, just like you did."

"You sure are real determined, and there's no doubt that you're my son," said his father, "but it takes a tough man, to

53

handle slaves. I sometimes wonder if I'm not too easy on them. Unless you cuss, and kick them around like dogs, they'll lay down on you, and you'll have to beg them to work."

Mark was shocked, to learn that his father thought he was really too easy on the slaves. Although it would be difficult for him to do, he must somehow convince his father that he shared the same belief, if this scheme was ever to work, as he had planned.

"I'm not quite seventeen, and only a child in comparison to a strong and seasoned man like you, but I do have a fair amount of good old common sense, in dealing with Negro slaves," Mark emphasized. "That alone, makes me superior to them, for like you say, they don't have sense enough to come in out of a rain storm. I'm short on experience, like you said, but I'm sure that with your help, I'll be able to handle whatever that comes my way. I'm very fortunate to have you as my teacher - a master at the trade, when it comes to handling slaves."

The last remark was a clincher, for Mark had struck a strong chord in his father's ego. "Yes, I suppose so," his father replied. "I know that you are far from being a fool, and I appreciate your confidence in me, however, and as you just admitted, you lack the experience one needs to be able to run a farm. Maybe it's my fault, for I should have been training you all along, by letting you become more involved in things, while you were growing up."

"No, it's not your fault, for I should have shown more interest, for I'm quite sure you wouldn't have held me back," Mark said, still playing with his father's ego. "Until I get out on my own, make my own mistakes, and find my own weak points, I won't know how to cope with life. And, until I take on a load and try to walk with it, I'll never know how much weight I can carry without stumbling." The weight that Mark had been carrying since he'd helped Martha, had aged him far more than his father would ever know.

"I honestly think that it would be better if you worked for someone else for a year or so, or took an active part in operating this farm, before you went out on your own," his father seriously suggested. "You mean too much to me, for me to toss you into a pack of wolves, with no way to defend yourself, for it's a tough world out there. It's bad enough for someone with experience, and a heck of a lot worse, for someone who is just starting out in life, like you want to do now."

"Dad, I respect your opinion, and appreciate your concern, but asking me to wait until I get experience before I try to do something, is like asking a person to stay away from the water, until he learns how to swim," he replied. "Am I right in feeling that way, or have you forgotten the times you stumbled and fell, before you became strong enough to stand on your own feet."

He had obviously impressed his father, and was surprised that he had been able to hold his ground against such a warrior. Although his father could be rightly termed as a hard-headed, and overbearing person, he was an astute businessman, and when he made up his mind to do something, he most generally stuck with his plan, until he had accomplished his goal. While he didn't want to discourage Mark, or leave the impression that he didn't have any confidence in him, he certainly didn't want to overload him and cause him to fail.

"It's one thing to have lived around a bunch of niggers, but it's a horse of a different color, to be in control of them," Simpson replied. "You don't have to worry about finding your weak points, for the niggers will do that for you, and when they do, they'll use every scheme in the book in order to take advantage of your weakness. They'll have you bowing down to them, like I have them bowing down to me. Does that clear up things for you, or do you think that I.m crazy?"

"I see what you mean, and it does make good sense," Mark lied. "I know that you hate all of them like I do myself, but we must admit that there's one or two, who are better than the others."

"I realize that, yet in a way they're all the same, for it's their nature to cause you to feel sorry for them, like you almost felt sorry for that gal, when I threatened her with the buck," he replied. "The minute you think that a nigger is about dead, he'll jump up and cut your throat." It was clear that he hated all slaves, no matter how loyal and dependable they might be.

"I'm aware of that," Mark returned, "but with you standing by me, and a good bunch of slaves doing the work, I know I can handle the farm. I won't be able to come up to your standards, for nobody can do that, but I'll do my best not to let you down. I'll simply have to learn as I go."

"Don't get testy, boy!" Said his father, sternly. "There's thousands of good honest men in South Carolina, smart men who mean well, but they can't handle slaves. It takes a special breed, men with guts and backbone, and you can bet your life on that.

My policy is very simple. Work them as hard as you can, keep them hungry, almost naked, and even though they never make a mistake, find some reason to punish them just the same."

This game of wits was beginning to wear on Mark's nerves, and he was sure that it showed on his face as well. "I understand what you're saying, and I don't question how you do things at all," Mark replied, hoping to soon wind things down, while he was seemingly ahead. "I know that they have a unique way of getting under your skin, but I think I can handle them."

Nate got up to pour himself another cup of coffee, while Julie sat across the table with her head bowed, where she'd been listening to their discussion. It reminded her of a few weeks back, when they were discussing the slave girl, and she didn't want to get involved. Like then, she somehow felt that her son had an underlying motive that was pushing him to his limits, and she hoped that it would turn out for the best.

"Niggers, are not human," Simpson, protested, as he sat back down at the table, "and unless you keep them under control, they'll start bossing you, as though you belonged to them."

Mark somehow sensed that his father had a strange fear of the table being turned on him one day. Did he actually think that someday, he just might have to serve them. Mark couldn't imagine his father being afraid of anything.

"Maybe someday, I'll be as tough as you." replied Mark, as he continued playing with his father's ego. "All I'm asking of you, is that you let me try my hand at running the small farm, before you give up on me. Never once have I proven myself to you, except for handling the buck, and even then, you gave pacific orders for me to follow. Am I being too demanding, by asking you to at least let me try? We are the same flesh and blood, you know."

Since the outset of this conversation almost an hour ago, his father had succeeded in counteracting everything Mark had to say, or any suggestions he'd made, however, as it seemed now, his father was at a loss for words. Up until now, his mother had managed to stay out of the conversation. However, based on the way his father was looking across the table at her, Mark knew now, that it was only a matter of time, before all this would change.

"Julie," spoke Simpson to his wife, "it looks like the boy is trying to put me on the spot, and I was wondering how you felt about this. Tell me, how do you feel about him taking over the small farm, and a bunch of niggers? I'd really like to know how you feel, if you don't mind getting involved."

Julie was dumfounded, that her husband had even considered asking her about anything, and especially of this nature. "Well, it's like you said a month or so ago, he already knows more than I can imagine," she replied, as she looked over at Mark. "He's young, but if he believes in himself strong enough, he'll be able to achieve any goal he sets for himself. Experience is very important to have, but determination to reach our goal, and confidence in ourself, plays a great part in becoming successful."

"That's just a stock answer, and I want something that's much better than that!" Simpson demanded, arching his eyes. "I want your honest opinion as to how you feel about this! Will I be making an awful mistake, if I let him take over the farm? Don't be afraid to speak up, woman!"

She thought for a moment, for as it appeared, whatever she said, was sure to determine the final outcome. "He's right about not getting any experience, until he tries his hand at something," she finally replied. "You have a very good point yourself, for not wanting him to take on too many burdens at once. He's your son, though, "a chip off the same block," and I suppose he can get the needed experience, as he goes along. The final decision is yours, and I'm sure that you'll do whatever is best for him. Now, that's all I have to say."

Mark beamed, when he heard this, for his mother's statement had obviously made an impression on his father. Mark decided to say nothing more, and leave everything to fate, for he was drained by this exchange as it were. He got up and poured more coffee into his father's cup, then sat back down at the table, and rested his chin in his hands.

Everyone remained silent for a time, as Mr. Simpson sipped on his coffee, and looked across the table at his wife, who wasn't quite sure if she had said the right thing or not. Although deep down inside she dreaded for Mark to try making it on his own, she dared not say as much. She felt like the slave girl was somehow involved in all this, based on what she'd heard. She'd heard two women-slaves talking while they cleaned the mansion one day, and based on what they said, Martha wasn't pregnant. If that were true, it might be best for Mark to get out now, away from everything. If Mark did ask his father to allow Bill and his family to go along with him, it would prove that her theory was right, and explain the reason why Mark was so anxious to leave home. Time would tell, it always does, she thought.

"Well, I don't know if I'm doing the right thing or not, but I've decided to let you go ahead with the farm." Simpson told his son. "It might be the best step you'll ever take in life. Then again, it might be the very first step you take toward your downfall. If it is, you only have yourself to blame."

"I was hoping that you'd say that," Mark smiled, "and should I run into a problem along the way, which I'm sure I will, then I'll call on you."

"And I'll be there, too!" He promised. "You can always count on me, for that's what a father is for." He patted Mark on the shoulder, and smiled.

"I don't intend to set the world on fire," Mark continued, "but I think it will be well worth my efforts, and you'll never regret what you're doing."

"Yes, I think it's the best thing for you," his father replied, "for if you watched me for the rest of your life, you wouldn't get the experience you will get in one day, out there on your own. This means that another farmer is coming up, who knows that niggers are meant to be slaves, and I'm going to be proud to call you my son, when you take a stand to uphold slavery."

"Then, according to what you just said, I can actually go ahead and start making final plans," said Mark, excitedly. "I really feel important - a farmer at the age of seventeen! Can you imagine that, and what all the other boys will think of me."

"Yes, that's right Son, and I promise to back you all the way," replied his father. "No matter what happens, just let me know, and I'll be there."

Mark knew that he wouldn't be able to call on his father if he did fail, for one mistake on his part, and his father would strip him of the farm. He'd have to make it without his father's help and Mark knew that. He'd been able to master one part of his plan, and though the toughest part still lay ahead, he couldn't afford to turn back. He must stand firm, and not lose ground.

"I appreciate your offer of support, and I'll always welcome advice from you," Mark told him. "I'm anxious to get out on my own, and I wondered when you intended to go ahead and finalize the deal," Mark prodded.

Simpson got up from the table, and motioned to him. "Let's go outside so the maid can clean off the table, and we'll sit on the front porch and enjoy the sunshine," said his father, as he walked toward the door. "Spring isn't all that far away, and I'll have things fixed up for you, long before it's time for you to plant your first cotton crop."

As he followed along behind, he tried to mask the disappointed feeling that was caused by his father's last statement, for time was of great importance at this point. Unless Martha started showing signs of being pregnant pretty soon, he'd have the devil to pay. There was no way he could wait until spring, even so, unless he could take Bill's family along with him, it sure wouldn't matter anyway. What if his father wouldn't let them go. Somehow, he must get his father to go along with this part of his plan as well. He sat down on the porch next to his father, and then he glanced down toward the shacks, and noticed several slaves sitting around, and doing nothing. Then suddenly, a thought occurred to him, and he decided to try it on his father, as well.

"Look at those niggers sitting around and doing nothing!" Said Mark, as he pointed toward the shacks. "It's a waste of time to let nice weather like this slip by, with no work going on. If they belonged to me, they wouldn't be sitting around like a bunch of buzzards, for I'd have them cleaning creek banks, shoveling out ditches, or anything else, that needs doing."

"They're caught up with their work, and my foreman said he would let them rest today," his father explained.

"That's where your foreman and I disagree," quickly replied Mark. "Like I said a moment ago, if they belonged to me, I'd find something for them to do."

"But, we have the cleanest farm around," argued his father. "Come next week, you won't see any of them sitting around like that, for he'll have then all at work."

"You misunderstood me," said Mark, as he got up, and went over and stood near the edge of the porch, "for I meant, if they were on my farm. There's a lot of work they could be doing down there. I imagine the farm is covered up with briars and bushes, and it gripes me to see pretty weather like this slip by, when there's plenty of work they could be doing."

Again, Mark had really impressed his father. "You're already sounding like you know how to run a farm, and handle a bunch of slaves," his father replied, as a smile came on his face. "That's the attitude it takes to get the most work out of them, for it really is costly, when they're just sitting around."

59

Mark couldn't make himself stay in one place long at a time even though he tried, and he hoped that his father wouldn't notice his nervousness, and suspect something. He stood near the edge of the porch for a moment longer, while his mind did cartwheels. Then, when he happened to see Martha leaning up against a shack, time seemed to start running at a breakneck pace.

He went back over, and sat down next to his father. He was pleased that his father was giving him the farm next spring, but he might as well wait five years, for it wouldn't help with the problem at hand. He'd been successful in getting his father to go along with him thus far, and he must somehow persuade him to go along with the other part of his plan as well. If he could think of some way to get his father to let him take over the farm now, and if he could take Bill's family along with him as well, all his worries would be over.

"If Mr. Powell is as lazy as you say he is, I'll bet the farm's in one heck of a mess." Mark persisted. "Why don't you let me take some slaves down there now, and start cleaning up the place? If we started right now, we could have it cleaned up by planting time. What do you say?"

"I don't doubt for a minute that the place is in a mess, for Powell acts like he's afraid of work, or afraid somebody will talk about him, if he should happen to do something," agreed his father.

"I can almost see the place now, grown up in weeds and briars, except for a narrow path to the outhouse," Mark chuckled.

"I wouldn't doubt that one bit," his father laughed, "and he might have moved the outhouse upon the porch, to keep from having to walk so far."

"I haven't seen the place in quite awhile," said Mark, "but if I took a bunch of niggers down there tomorrow, it would take them until March to get it ready for planting. Why don't you let me go on down there now and get started, so I won't have to be in such a rush when spring gets here. Doesn't that make good sense. Have you really given any thought to that?"

"You don't give up, do you," spoke his father. "Are you sure that you don't want to wait until after Christmas? It's only a few weeks away."

Mark leaped up from his chair again. He wanted to scream. How could he talk his father into making the decision now, today, even! Too many things were at stake, and too many chances of things going wrong. It had to be now.

"I'm too excited, to wait any longer!" Replied Mark, as he paced back and forth on the porch. "While we're on the subject, I'd like to ask you for just one more favor. Why not let Bill and his whole family go down there with me, and we could get started, while we're having all this pretty weather. I hate them, as much as I hate the other niggers, but they are the best slaves on the place. They won't cause a problem, after what I did to that gal." He really put on an act - he had no choice.

"You're right, they are the best slaves I have, and when you struck that gal with your fist, and made her take the buck, you put the fear of God in the whole bunch," Simpson smiled. "For a fact, you could get a lot of work out of that gal before she gets down with the baby."

Things were looking much better now, Mark thought, and if he kept on like he'd been doing, maybe this part of his scheme would work as well. He didn't say anything for a moment, as he carefully planned the strategy for his next, and most important move. When he glanced toward the front door that he'd left partly open when they went outside, he saw his mother standing there. It was quite obvious, that their discussion did involve Martha, as she suspected, and she shook her head, as she gently closed the door.

"That's the reason, I said that," Mark lied. "Just because she's pregnant, she can't expect me to treat her any different, for it's because she made a stupid mistake, that she's in that shape now. If nothing else, she can burn briars and bushes, and tote water to the others, while they work."

It was obvious that he'd again impressed his father, but the big question now, was if his father would take immediate action. He knew not to be too demanding, but time was running out for him, for Martha as well.

"I see your point about starting while we have nice weather, and I think Bill's family would be the ideal bunch to take with you, and I'll do that for you, too," his father promised. "The big problem now, is what do you plan to do about Powell, for he does deserve some consideration. He has his faults as we all do, but he's human, and he's a white man."

Mark hadn't even thought of including Powell, until his father mentioned him. His mind then started whirling, as he dilligently searched for an answer. He couldn't let his father know that he hadn't even thought about Powell, up until now.

"No, I didn't forget him, although I hadn't gotten around to discussing a plan I had in mind for him." Mark lied again. "I wanted to discuss the plan with you first, for you know more about business, than I'll ever know."

"What kind of deal do you plan to offer him?" His father asked, looking keenly at Mark. "I hope you don't intend to give him part-ownership, for if I thought you were, I'd call off the deal right now!"

"My Lord, no!" Mark quickly replied. "I planned on offering him half of whatever I got from the cotton crop, if he'll help me until I'm able to stand on my own feet. No, I wouldn't attempt to run the farm, unless I had an older person around to help me, for I'm not that stupid."

"I hadn't even thought about that myself, and I think it's a great idea to use him," his father nodded. "That way, we won't worry about you being down there with just a bunch of niggers. He's a white man, and I'm sure that the niggers won't turn on you, with him around." Oh, if his father only knew, how close Mark and these five slaves were.

"Well, I might be young, but I'm not stupid, when it comes to looking out for myself," Mark told him, "and if Powell thinks that he'll continue to do things in a haphazard way, he's got another thought coming!"

"I know that you're smart, and I really think you'll make a go of it, if you'll keep thinking that way," said his father, as he shook Mark's hand, and smiled. "I'm proud of you, and this could be the most important step that you will ever take in life, and maybe it will be."

"Then, it's settled." Said Mark, breathing a sigh of relief. "I promise that you won't be disappointed in me, or regret what you've done."

"It's as good as done." Said his father, seriously. "I'll fix up papers for the niggers today, and they'll belong to you, and I'll go into town early tomorrow morning and sign the farm over to you. It's up to you to decide when to leave. Leave today, tomorrow, or after Christmas."

"I'll go down there and tell the niggers to pack up their rags, and we'll head out real early in the morning," said Mark, as he walked down the steps. "They might pitch a fit when I tell them that they belong to me, but I haven't forgotten how to use my fist."

Mark's first instinct, was to head out running to tell Bill's family what he had planned, but that might give him away, so he slowly walked along, as if it didn't matter to him. Everything had gone his way thus far, and he didn't want his father to question his motive, or have second thoughts.

"Hold on there, just a minute!" His father called. "There's something else that I forgot to tell you a minute ago and it's very important, too!"

Mark quickly stopped, and turned around. What in the world's wrong, he asked himself. Where did I go wrong, this time.

"Tell Bill to grease the wheels on that new wagon I bought last week, for I'm sure that you'll need it," his father told him. "And let him pick out whichever pair of mules he wants, and they'll belong to you as well."

"I sure will, Dad!" Mark happily replied. "I'm sure that we'll find use for them when we get there, and I appreciate that, very much."

"And, tell him to load the wagon with corn and oats, for I'm not sure if Powell has anything for the mules to eat," he added. "Before you leave here in the morning, I'll give you money to start a crop with, and to do repairs on the house and outbuildings, and the niggers will have to be fed."

There were no words to express the relief Mark felt, as he walked on down toward where Bill and the other slaves were enjoying the morning sun. With a great feeling of excitement for the new adventure that lay ahead, Mark thanked God for the turn of events that had taken place this morning, and asked Him to try to hold things together, until they were well on their way.

Simpson went back into the dining room, and found his wife sitting alone at the table, as she thought about the discussion that had taken place between her husband and their son. She had been thinking about what the slave women said about Martha not being pregnant, and how determined Mark had been in his effort to get the small farm. She had overheard Mark ask his father to allow him to take Bill's family with him, and it proved without a shadow of doubt, that Mark was somehow mixed up with the slave girl.

"It looks like the boy finally got what he wanted, and I hope it won't be something that I'll regret later," said Nate, as he walked over, and sat down at the table. "I need a piece of paper and a pen, for I'm going to write him a Bill of Sale for the niggers he wanted to take along with him. He kept right on, until he finally got a farm, and five niggers to tend the land for him."

"When will he be leaving, and which group of slaves does he want?" Asked his wife, as she looked for a piece of paper, and a fountain pen. "How do you feel about him running the farm, and what about that Powell fellow?"

"I'm sure he can handle the farm, for I'm giving him Bill's entire family to take along with him," Nate replied. "As for Powell, I'll send a letter to him by Mark, telling him what I've done, and Mark plans to let him stay there and help him run things, 'til he gets on his feet."

"I sure hope you're doing the right thing," sighed Julie, as she placed a piece of paper, and a fountain pen on the table, "for he's still young, and I wonder if he's not too young. If he happens to fail it might discourage him for life, but I do feel better, knowing that he'll have Bill's family there to help him. Mark and Bill's children have been friends since childhood, but as for Powell, I don't know all that much about him."

"It's what he wanted, and we'll just have to wait and see how things turn out for him," he reasoned, as he prepared the Bill of Sale. "He might change his mind in a month, then again, he might hit it off real well."

By this time, Mark had arrived at the shacks, and he motioned for Bill to come out to the road. Bill knew that something had conspired between Mark and his father, for he had seen them on the porch together. He had no way to know what Mark wanted with him, but as a slave, it caused a strange feeling to come over him, any time a white man asked to speak with him.

"Moan'n, Mos'a Mark!" Spoke Bill, tucking his hat under his arm, when he walked out to the road. "What can I's do fer you, Suh?"

"It's not what you can do for me, it's what I can do for you." Mark smiled. "I'd like for your entire family to step inside the shack for a moment, for I have something very important to tell all of you."

"Aw'rite then, I's gon'a tell 'em what you sez," replied Bill, "and we's gon'a be there in jus' a minute, we's sho' will."

They went into the shack with Mark, and he told them all about what went on between him and his father, and about them now belonging to him. He also told them about the small farm, and about his plan to set them free, if they would help him to get the farm back in shape for planting. This sounded so strange, and farfetched, until they doubted his word.

"Mos'a Mark, why don't you say that you's jus' play-acting wid us 'bout all that you is told us?" Asked Liza. "We's know that you is worried aw'mos to def' over what you's done fer Marthie, and the lie you's went and told yo' pappy. Yo' pappy ain't never gon'a give you no land, not eb'em a shovelful of dirt is he gon'a give you, and no slaves, neither."

Before he had a chance to reply, Bill jumped up. "This ole nigga ain't gon'a run off wid nobid'ee, and get a bullet twixt his eyeballs!" Bill said, as he pointed his finger in Mark's face. "Mos'a Simpson done killed one nigga fer trying to 'scape! I's want'a be free, but a dead free-nigga, ain't worth nothing to nobid'ee."

Mark knew they didn't really understand, and tears filled his eyes, as he thought of how pitiful it was, for one human being, to fear another.

"No, Bill, I'm not running away," Mark assured him. "My father gave all of you to me, you belong to me, and you are now my slaves. He's up there right now writing your names down on a piece of paper, and it says that you folks won't be a slave to him any longer. Now, so you understand?"

"That's dif'unt," Bill grinned. "If our name is scratched on a piece of paper like you sez, then everthang is aw'rite. Now, go on wid yo' tale, befo' you ferget what it wuz."

Mark then explained everything, and told them to be ready to head out by daylight tomorrow morning. He also told them not to say anything to the other slaves. He knew they would be jealous, and with word already spreading around about Martha not being pregnant, they might get word to his father, and things would fall apart. As thrilled as Mark was, he wouldn't breathe a sigh of relief, until he was driving away. He trusted his father's word, but it was a long time 'til morning, and anything could happen.

As Mark walked back toward home, he noticed that his father had come back outside, and was sitting on the porch again. Mark thanked God for everything that had happened, and he knew that it was only because he had included Powell, that caused his father to agree with him. Be it that, or something else, Mark was now the happiest he'd been in weeks.

"What did they say about our deal?" Asked his father, as Mark walked up the steps. "Did you tell them that they belong to you, and that they would have to bow down to you?" He handed Mark a sheet of paper, as he walked upon the porch. "Here's a Bill of Sale, it's legal, and it's been signed by your mother as well, and I'll give you a Deed to the farm, later on in the week."

"I told them about our deal, and how they'd have to bow down to me, and I thought for a minute, that I'd have to take my fist to them," Mark lied, as he folded the paper, and stuck it into his pocket. "If it's all right with you, I think I'll go upstairs and start packing, for I'd like to leave as early in the morning, as possible."

"Go right ahead, for I realize how anxious you must be," his father told him. "After you finish packing, we need to talk, for you'll be dealing with a lot of businessmen, the banker, Mr. Wilson at the General Store, and others as you go along. And, you need to open an account at the General Store, just in case you do need something until harvest time. I'll give him a letter stating that you own your own farm now, and that it's all right to sell things to you on the credit, and to the banker, so he can handle your business affairs, when you start selling your cotton next fall."

After dinner was over, Mark spent most of the afternoon packing things he planned to take with him now, and if things worked out for him, he would come back and get the rest of his belongings later. He did all he could to avoid a conversation with his father, and when he did talk with him, he tried to be as brief as possible, and say only the things that were pleasing to him. It was obvious to his mother that he was doing all he could to keep his father in a happy mood, and while Nate was busy looking over some papers at his desk, she decided to slip upstairs, and talk with her son. Thinking of what she'd heard the slave women say about Martha not being pregnant, and because Mark asked his father to let Bill's family go along with him, gave her reasons to believe that something other than just childhood friendship, lay between her son, and the slave girl.

The door to Mark's room stood open when she got upstairs, and he was busy packing clothes into a suitcase that lay on his bed, so she stood in the hall for a moment, watching. She planned to ask a point-blank question about what was going on, then she decided to wait and see if he would tell her himself.

"Son, do you mind if I come in for a moment?" She politely asked, as she slowly stepped into the room. "Something has been bothering me here lately, and I'd like to discuss it with you. Could I speak with you for a moment?"

"I'm packing up my clothes, but, well, maybe I can spare a few minutes of my time, if you'll be very brief," he replied, fearing what she might have to say to him. "Come on in, for a minute."

"We all make mistakes, but it's better to discuss them with someone, than to keep them bottled up inside," she told him, in a kind voice. "I know that something is bothering you, and it seems to involve your father, that little slave girl, and maybe both. Is there something that you'd like to discuss with me? I'm a good listener, good at keeping secrets, too."

"Mother," he cried, as he threw his arms around her, "my mind is messed up so, until I don't have sense enough to explain it. It does involve the slave girl, but not as you suppose. Could we discuss this later?"

"Yes my son, we surely can," she said, kissing him on the cheek. "I'll always be here for you, and no matter how rough your road might get, God will always walk ahead of you. Keep your faith, and let Him guide your steps."

"Mother, I've lived a miserable life during the past several weeks, which has no doubt been obvious, and even though I did what I thought was right, I'm sure that others will take it the wrong way," he sighed. "Pray that it won't be the cause of my downfall, and no matter what you might hear later, remember that I'm still your son, and that I'll always love you. I'd like to drop this where it is. One day, I'll explain everything to you."

Later that evening as they sat at the supper table, his mother asked him what he planned to take with him. He already knew that she had baked a walnut-cake, and an apple pie for him, and that she planned to fix some ham biscuits in the morning, for him to have to eat along the way.

"I think I've packed just about everything I'll need right now," he told her, as he looked across the table, and smiled. "I'm not taking all that many dress suits, for I don't intend to do any socializing, until I get the farm in shape again. It's going to take a lot of hard work, if I have the place ready by crop-planting time, and I won't have much time left for anything else."

"I'm glad you told the niggers that they belonged to you, and like I said before, you'll have to stay on your toes, to keep them in line," spoke up his father. "I hope that you let them know that you didn't have any more respect for them, than you have for a mule. Did you make that clear?"

"Indeed, I did!" Mark lied again. "I got my point across, and told them that I'd beat them to death, if they stepped out of line. I could tell by the way they acted that they were really afraid of me, and the girl said that she'd make her baby obey me." He gave his father a devilish grin.

"I was kind of worried at first, but I see now, that you've started out on the right foot," his father replied. "Unless you keep them scared, worked to a point of falling in their tracks, and almost starved to death, they'll think you're weak. And, if you show the least concern, or let them think you feel sorry for them, they'll treat you as if you were a slave."

They continued talking for an hour or so, and then Mark excused himself, and went upstairs to bed. He was in need of one good night's sleep, for he hadn't been able to get much sleep lately. Perhaps, now that the burden had finally been lifted from his shoulders, he could rest tonight. As the rays of the moon lit up his room, like the light from the halo of an angel of mercy, he thanked God for what had happened. He resolved to treat the slaves better than they'd ever been treated before, and that they would always be respected as human beings. Then he slept, calm, uninterrupted sleep.

About midnight, Bill slipped down to the barn and hitched a pair of mules to the new wagon, then quietly drove it up and parked it behind his shack. He had already loaded some shelled corn and oats on the wagon, and they planned to load what few things they had on the wagon tonight, and head out before the sun came up, and before the other slaves knew what was happening. As soon as the wagon had been loaded, Martha and her brothers lay down on the bare floor to sleep 'til morning, while Liza and Bill sat on a block of wood in front of the small fireplace, because the shack was now empty.

"Liza, it's hard to b'lev this, fer nothing good is ever happened to us befo'," Bill softly spoke. "We's got'a wuk' rail hard fer Mos'a Mark, and be sho' that he makes it. We's owe him that much, anyhow."

"That's what I's been thank'n too," replied Liza. "I's feel so good in my belly, 'til I's could run clean 'round the wul'd, beller'n like a bull. He be jus' a chile, but there's sump'um 'bout him, that makes me willing to trus' my own lif' in his hands. He be like my chile, my own lit'l boy."

"Well, we's mout as well lye down on the flo', and get some res," yawned Bill, "fer moan'n is gon'a be here purdy quick, and we's want'a be long-gone, fo' the tuther slaves get out'a bed. We gon'a have a new Mos'a, a new shack to live in, and it's gon'a be like we wuz start'n all over again."

The night seemed like an eternity to the slaves, for their excitement had robbed them of their sleep, and when morning finally came, they felt as though they hadn't closed their eyes. Mark, on the other hand, awoke rested and full of excitement for the adventure that lay ahead. Even before the sun came up, Bill hitched Mark's mare to the buggy, and had it parked near the mansion, but the wagon in which the slaves were riding, had already gone down the road when Mark came outside to load his belongings into the buggy. Mark's mother took a box of food she had prepared for him, and followed him outside. She promised to give her mother's old Bible to him when he grew up, so she placed it on the seat of the buggy.

"This is a big step you're taking, and I hope things work out, and I pray that whatever's been bothering you, will soon go away," she said in a kind and loving voice. "Be sure of each step you take, for you won't have anyone to guide you, except for God, and that old worn Bible."

"I love you, Mother, and someday I'll sit down and tell you why I'm doing this" he promised. "It's something that I must do all by myself. I have to prove something to myself, and to others as well. If I didn't have to take this trip, how happy I'd be, but I have no choice, it's my only way out."

Julie seemed to understand. "I know we're living in a strange and mixed up time, for we can't do anything without upsetting somebody, or breaking some kind of rule, if you know what I mean," she told him. "We're in such a hurry to get somewhere, until we don't take time to see the beautiful things of life along the way, and we might not even know when we get there."

Smiling through her tears, she continued. "It's better to set some small goals and achieve them one at a time, than it is to set a large one, and take a chance of falling flat on our face. Like my mother told us children as we grew up, take small bites, and you won't get choked."

"I know, Mother," he replied, hugging her, "but I'm sure I can do this, and I'll never forget the gentle lessons you taught me. I love Dad, and I do appreciate all he's doing for me, but I must prove that it's not necessary for anyone to be as mean, and cruel as he is to the slaves, in order to gain their respect. Mother, I want you to go to your grave with this secret between us, but I intend to prove my theory to the world, before I die."

"Son, I'm sure you can reach whatever goal you set for yourself, that is, if you're willing to accept the suffering and heartaches that are liable to go along with your success," she softly replied. "Just be careful where you set your foot each step you take, for all ground that grows green grass, might not be firm enough to hold up your weight." She waved goodbye, as he climbed into the buggy, and tears welled her eyes.

. Mark gently spoke to the mare as he waved goodbye to her, and he finally set out on his journey. His new home, indeed, his new life lay ahead. His mother stood and cried, while she watched him drive away. His father finally came out on the front porch to see him off, but it was too late, for the buggy was already a long way down the road.

His father felt a lump in his throat, as the buggy sped away. "I have no way to know what's ahead for him, but it's going to be good, I'm sure," spoke his father, as he watched the buggy go out of sight. "He's a good boy, Julie. That's my son, going there, and I'm proud of him too!"

"That he is," she replied, looking up at him, as tears trickled down her cheeks, "but he's so young, too young, I'm afraid. I hope things work out for him, and that he won't run into many obstacles along the way."

"He's going to be a great leader one day, and a strong one too, when it comes to defending our right to own niggers as slaves," Nate boasted. "With more young men like him on our side, the Union will stand up and take notice, for he knows how to keep hammering away, until he gets what he wants."

"If he happens to become a leader, he'll be a good one," Julie told him between sobs, "for his qualities far exceed that of many others I know. He's just a boy, but he has determination, and a kind and decent heart." She said to him, as she walked up the steps, and went back into the house.

Bill and his family had started out in the mule-drawn wagon long before Mark had even finished eating breakfast, however, they still hadn't gotten off Nate Simpson's plantation. Mark's spirited-mare trotted much faster than the mules could walk, and it wasn't very long, until he had caught up with the wagon. Now that they had finally set out on the journey, there was something else that Mark wished to explain to Bill, before they arrived at the farm.

"Hey there!" Mark called out, as he drove up behind Bill's wagon. "I want you to stop for a minute, for I have something else that I want to say to you!"

"What's wrong wid you," asked Bill, after he had stopped the wagon, and walked slowly toward Mark's buggy. "Is you done got homesick, and changed yo' mind?"

"No, you old fool nigger!" Mark teased. "I really do need to discuss something with you, before we get there. Are you too good to talk to me?"

How different the boy is from his pappy, Bill thought, as he walked up to the buggy. However, something about this trip, was still bothering Bill.

"You is got the paper that sez that we's railly do b'long to you, ain't you?" Bill asked, in a serious voice. "They mout come in handy if somebid'ee stops us, and thanks that we's trying to 'scape. Yass'uh, I's sho' hope you's got 'em wid you, and in yo' pocket, I's sho' do."

Mark then took two pieces of paper from his vest pocket, holding them up so Bill could see, even though he knew that Bill couldn't read.

"Yass'uh, that's what it sez, ole Bill and his family b'longs to Mos'a Mark," said Bill, as if he could read. "Now, I's feel a lot better."

"Even though the paper says that you are my slave, you don't belong to me, or to anyone else, for you aren't a slave anymore," he replied. "From now on you folks will be my partners. I'll treat you like human beings, and nobody is going to take a whip to you again. I wanted you to hear that again, to make sure that you understood that my promise to you still stands."

"That sho' do sound good, but you's need to wait 'til you's get thangs up and running, fo' you's stick yo' neck out fer us," Bill told him, as he wiped a tear from his eye. "A feller needs to look at the bottom of a creek fo' he jumps in to wash off, fer he mout bus' his head on a stump."

"I understand, and it does make good sense, but what I told you yesterday will stand until the day I die," Mark assured him. "I'll share what we make, if you folks will help me get started, and I'll set you free, too! Now, let's get going, for I'm anxious to get there, and see how the place looks."

"I's ain't worried none 'bout you," said Bill, as he started back toward the wagon, "but I is worried 'bout that Pow'l feller that's been running that lit'l farm fer yo' pappy. Is yo' pappy and that Pow'l feller cooked up sump'um 'tween 'em?"

"Not that I know of, but I'll handle Powell, when I get there," replied Mark. "I really don't expect any trouble out of him, after I give him this letter from my father. The farm belongs to me, now."

"I's jus' a nigga slave, and ain't 'sposed to know nothing, but I's been wondering what kind'a deal you gon'a wuk' out wid that Pow'l feller, when we's get there," Bill inquired. "And, what is you gon'a do if he sulls up like a big ole bull, and don't go 'long wid you?"

"Well, I plan to offer him half the profit from the cotton-crop, if he'll stay and help us 'til I get on my feet," Mark stated, "and I'll give you folks half of my part of the profit. If he don't accept my offer, then I'll have to do the best I can without him."

"That sounds mighty good to me and you, but you don't know what he gon'a say, 'til you's slap the offer in his face," Bill replied. "We jus gon'a half' to wait and see."

"We had better get going," said Mark, "for we still have several miles to go, and I want to get settled in before dark."

Mark had visited the small farm several times with his father, but as far as he knew Bill hadn't even seen the farm, and he made sure he didn't drive on ahead, and leave him. Mark kept thinking of the Bill of Sale, which was proof that these other humans belonged to him. Should they be stopped along the way, this piece of paper was the only thing to prevent them from being shot for running away. This paper was his "written-pass" as well, and his only proof of what he was doing with these slaves. He must bide his time, and hope that things would change someday for the slaves.

The slaves were happy, as they rode along. "Mos'a Mark is a fine feller, and I's hope thangs wuk' out fer him, too." Liza said, as they followed along in the wagon behind his buggy. "I's done axed the Lord to look down and grin at him, fer what he is done fer us."

"I's hope he don't let his good nature get the bes' of him," Bill softly said. "He acts like he is colorblind, and he don't know the dif'unce 'tween, us and white folks."

"I's knowed ever since he wuz a snotty-nosed young'un, that he wuzn't like the tuther white folks," said Liza.

"He done sot out on his own, and we's got'a stand 'hind him like if he wuz our lit'l boy, and pray fer him, too." Bill added. "We's got'a reach down and pick him up when he falls, hold his han' while he crosses all them big rivers that's 'head of him, and 'courage him, when it looks like everthang is tun'd 'gainst him."

By the time Mark and the slaves arrived at the farm, the sun was already going down, and it would be dark within a few hours. Mark hitched his mare to a hitching post near the edge of the yard, and Bill stopped the wagon down at the barn, like he had been told. The Powells had heard the wagon rumbling up the driveway, and stepped out on the porch to see who it was. Seeing Mark in the buggy didn't bother them, but the Negroes sitting in the wagon, really did concern them. Mr. Powell walked out in the yard, to greet Mark.

"Howdy Mr. Powell...Mrs. Powell." Mark greeted them, as he politely tipped his hat to her, and offered his hand to Mr. Powell. "How have you both been doing? Fine, I hope."

"I can't complain!" Snapped Powell, releasing his hand from Mark's firm grip. "I've seen better times, and I've seen worse too, I suppose."

"This probably comes as a surprise," Mark began, "but I assure you that it's nothing serious, nothing to cause anybody any harm."

"Well, I'm glad to hear that," replied Powell, as he kept his eyes fixed on the Negroes sitting in the wagon. "Your father's well, I take it."

"Yes Sir, quite well, indeed," Mark answered. "In fact, he's been doing exceptionally well here lately, thank you."

"I must say that the niggers in the wagon really does concern me," replied Powell, still keeping his eyes on the wagon. "Are you taking them to the sale at Atkins? I've never known of Nate Simpson selling a slave, unless they were awful sorry. They must be trash. Is that right?"

"You're wrong about them, Mr. Powell." Mark replied, as he took a letter from his vest pocket, and handed it to him. "This letter will explain that my father gave this farm to me, and he gave me those slaves to help tend the land as well. The slaves aren't for sale, neither is this farm."

"Well, I'll be darned, this really is a surprise!" Replied Powell, as he stood reading the letter. "How do I fit into all this mess?"

"That's entirely up to you, seeing that I own the farm, and that I'm here to offer you a deal," Mark told him.

"That's mighty white of him to do something like that, without notifying me ahead of time!" Powell snorted. "Just what kind of a deal do you plan to propose, young man?"

"I'm willing to give you half the profit from the cotton-crop, if you'll stick around until I get my feet placed. The slaves will do most of the work, and I want you to serve as my manager. I expect to get room and board here at your house, which is also a part of my proposal." Mark explained.

Mr. Powell's first instinct was to walk away. He was angry with Simpson for what he'd done, yet on the other hand, his lazy nature caused him to stop and think it over for a moment. The idea of him "managing" the farm, and not having to do any manual labor, struck a responsive chord with him. Still, he must give Mark a hard time, to show his manhood at least.

"The heck you say!" Powell bitterly protested. "I told him in a letter that I wanted to buy this place! Didn't he get my letter, and his part of the money from the cotton I made last year?"

"He did, Sir, but he wasn't interested in selling this farm," Mark told him. "He gave it to me, so that I could get some hands-on experience before I took over the plantation, when he retires. The plantation will belong to me when he retires, you know."

"Do tell!" Powell sneered. "You'll pardon my asking, boy, but just how old are you, eighteen, maybe going on nineteen?"

"Somewhere thereabout," Mark sharply answered. "My age, has nothing to do with my making a deal with you, if that's what bothers you."

"And, how do I know that you're not just making all this up on your own?" The suspicious and disgruntled Powell asked.

"Sir, you have his letter, if you wish to read it again, and you know his script, and signature well," Mark sternly replied. "If you wish, you have my permission to go and ask him for yourself."

Powell knew Nate Simpson all too well, and he didn't want to speak to him about the letter, or anything else.

"That won't be necessary," he grumbled, as he stuck the letter into his pocket. "I'll think on it, and that's all I have to say at the moment. I've always thought things through, before making a decision like this, for it does come as a surprise."

"That's fine," Mark responded, "but if we work together, we both have a chance of bettering ourself."

"He said in his letter, that he promised this farm to you when you were a child, but wouldn't he change his mind, if the offer was right?" Powell asked, still trying to be obstinate. "Money talks, when dealing with him."

Mark was beginning to get upset at him. "What is it going to take to get it through your thick head that he doesn't own the farm, and that I'm not in a notion to sell it?" Mark asked, in anger. "The sun will be down pretty soon, and I wanted to get settled in before dark. Either we work out a deal while I'm standing here, or I'm asking you to get out of my house, and let me handle things as best I can! Do you clearly understand?"

"Very well then, but it seems ridiculous to me for a boy to be in charge of the farm, and a bunch of niggers, but I guess Nate knows what he wants to do, or I hope he does," he grumbled.

Neither of them said anything for a few moments, while Mark looked around at the farm, which looked like it had been deserted, and Powell stood with his head bowed, scuffing the toe of his shoe in the dirt.

The slaves were still sitting in the wagon as they'd been told, and they could only imagine, what was going on between these two.

"I's don't know nothing 'bout that feller, but he sho' run up 'gainst one hard nut to crack, when he run up 'gainst Mos'a Mark," Bill whispered to his wife. "If he wuz able to get us, and this farm from his pappy, he sho' be able to get what he wants out'a that ole feller."

"If ole man Pow'l ain't in co-hoots wid Mos'a Simpson, thangs mout wu'k out fer the boy, but if they is, he gon'a have the devil to pay!" She replied. "I's hope he don't get in a wuss fix, than he jus' got out of."

"Maybe not," Bill sighed. "I's thank the boy is gon'a jump on him, fer I's seed him jerk off his hat, and scratch his head. Let's wait and see."

"Mr. Powell, I hate to ask you to make a hasty decision, but I do need to know, now!" Mark demanded, "Are you ready to give me an answer, or do you expect me to stand here and wait 'til dark?"

"All right, you have a manager for the moment, at least, but I'll ask you not to get uppity with me," Powell finally replied. "I've worked my fingers to the bone trying to keep this place looking good, and now I'll be working as a helper for a boy, who don't know the first thing about farming. It seems as though respect for older persons, is a thing of the past."

"Sir, I've never been intentionally disrespectful to anyone, as far as I know, and certainly not to an elderly person," Mark replied. "I'll be honest and fair with you, the same as I am with everybody else, and I expect the same from you. You can manage the farm in general, and I'll be in charge of seeing that the slaves do what you want done, and you won't even have to bother with them at all."

"I'll thank you to keep the niggers well out of my sight, for I hate them with a passion, and I hate white persons who take up for them," Powell boldly stated. "I'm a true-blooded Southerner, and I'll uphold slavery until the day I die. Niggers were born to be slaves, and that's what they'll always be."

Mark realized now, that he had done the right thing by telling Powell that he'd supervise the slaves, for he'd just rescued them from one person who despised them, and he didn't want them to have to face this again.

They finally reached an agreement, and Mark took the slaves to a house in which they would live, and call their new home. Though the house stood in need of repair, it was far better than the shack in which they once lived, and in a manner of speaking, was a mansion to them. The agreement pleased Mrs. Powell, and she showed Mark to a room where he'd be sleeping. She even invited him to attend church with them, and Mr. Powell promised to introduce him to others in the community as well. Later, when Mark went into his room, he lay across the bed and rested, and thanked God for what He had done to help him get away from the torment he had suffered during the past few weeks.

It was now about three weeks later, Mark and the Negroes had been working real hard, and as it seemed, Mr. Powell was pleased with the amount of work they had done in such a short time. He assured Mark that he would stand by him all the way until he got on his feet, and that he was behind Mark in whatever task he undertook. That's what he said, however, time would tell the truth, as it always does.

Mark and the slaves did the work according to Mr. Powell's orders as the foreman, even though the slaves stayed well away from him, like Mark had told them to do. He hadn't told Powell of his plan to share his part of the profit with the slaves, or his plan to set them free, and he hadn't even mentioned it to the slaves since they'd been here, either. But, he didn't want them to get the impression that he'd forgotten his promise to them. One day when Mark and Bill were sitting on a terrace bank resting, Mark decided to assure Bill that a promise he had made to them, still stood.

"Bill, you folks have worked hard all your lives for a few bites of food, and some handed-down clothes, and it's time for that to end," Mark told him, in a serious voice. "If all goes well, and after I give Mr. Powell his share, I'll divide what's left with you folks, just like I promised. I wanted you to know that I didn't forget, like you might have thought."

"That sho' do sound good, and 'bout the bes' thang that I's ever here'd, but there's one thang you is fer'got," replied Bill.

"What's that?" Mark asked, sincerely. "What did I forget?"

"You's got a paper that sez we is yo' slaves, and you don't owe us not one thang," Bill explained. "What you's done fer Marthie, and the way we is being treated now, is nuf' pay to las' us fer a the res' of our lif'. Yass'uh it sho' is."

"I do have a paper that says you folks belong to me, but it doesn't say how I must treat you." Mark argued. "You folks are friends, and I treat friends as I'd like to be treated myself. And, you will be paid!"

"But, we is slaves, and nobid'ee treats slaves, like they does the white folks," he responded. "That's the way it's aw'ways gon'a be, too."

"I've always had a special feeling for you and your family, and whether folks like it or not, I'm determined to keep my promise," Mark vowed from the bottom of his heart. "I'll go to my grave, before I let you cause me to change my mind."

Bill bowed his head. "I know that you's meant that from the very bottom of yo' belly, but you is still young," he sighed. "You can't let us stand in yo' way, and keep you from being a big man in the South, and being like all the tuther white folks, fer that ain't rite."

"I don't quite understand what you mean," said Mark.

"Well, you's aw'ready done mo' fer us than anybid'ee else is done, and I don't want you to be sump'um that you's don't want'a be," Bill replied. "You got'a be like tuther folks, fer they don't do nothing fer no slave."

"I know what you're trying to say, but I'm not like other persons, and it won't work in my case," Mark rebutted. "I've always hated slavery, and if it takes the rest of my life, I intend to prove that it's wrong. No human should ever become a slave to another person, be they black or white."

"That's like dreaming that you's got a pocketful of money, then wake up, and find out that you's ain't got a penny." Bill explained. "Farmers in the South is aw'ways used niggas as slaves, and it ain't gon'a change."

Obviously, Bill wasn't going to be easily convinced, for he was captured in Africa when he was about four years old, and a life of slavery was all that he'd ever known. Mark wondered if the slaves really wanted to be free, or was this concept, too incomprehensible for them to grasp.

"Bill, you don't have to bow down to me or to anyone else anymore," Mark explained. "I want you to respect me as your employer, and that's all. Maybe if other farmers will learn to respect the slaves, and treat them as human beings, it will create a better working relationship between them."

Bill smiled, sympathetically. "I's know that it comes from the ver'ee bottom of yo' belly, fer we's all have feelings like that sometimes," he replied. "We is here, and we is safe - Marthie too - and that's all that matters wid us. Is you ever told Mos'a Pow'l, 'bout the 'greemut you's made wid us?"

For an instant, Mark grew angry with him, for it seemed like he was trying to block out everything that Mark said to him, however, when he began to look at things from Bill's point of view, he began to understand.

"This here farm belongs to me without any strings attached," Mark began, "and after I settle up with Powell, there's nothing that anybody can say about the way I spend, or divide my share of the money I receive."

Neither of them said anything for a moment. Bill knew that Mark had been serious all along, but he wondered if he'd be able to stand up against Powell, or other farmers in South Carolina. He even wondered what Mark's father would say, when he found out how Mark felt about slavery.

"Mos'a Mark, let me axe you jus' one ques'un," said Bill, as he stood up and brushed the dirt off the seat of his trousers. "Is you ever told ole man Pow'l that you gon'a 'vide yo' money wid us, and do he know how you feel in yo' heart 'bout slavery? Do he know 'bout you gon'a sot us free?"

Mark thought for a moment, as he looked up at Bill, and saw tears in his eyes. "No, I haven't," said Mark. "It's none of his business what I do with my part of the money, and I also have a right to dislike slavery."

"When you's do, that's when everthang is gon'a fall to pieces," Bill warned, "fer he gon'a pitch a big fit."

"My personal feelings shouldn't be of any concern to him, or anybody else," Mark tried to explain, as he also stood up. "Why are you concerned about how others will feel about the way I do things? Leave them out of my affairs, and let me run my own business, in my own way."

"But, I's 'cerned fer you, fer when Pow'l finds out what you gon'a do, the fat's gon'a hit the fire," Bill warned again. "He gon'a spread the word like a pracher spread'n the gospel, and you mout as well look fer that. You's playing wid fire, and you's gon'a get burnt."

"Just let me handle him in my own way, for he don't seem like a bad sort of person." Mark told him. "He's a little lazy, but it seems like he really appreciates what you folks have done, and I don't think he'll mind."

"He be happy now, fer we's doing all the wu'k, and got this place looking like a farm again, but when you pay us, all hell's gon'a tu'n loose," replied Bill, as he chuckled. "I's hope you's rite 'bout him being a good feller, but I's got a feeling that he wants everthang, and a lot mo'."

"What's mine, is mine, and he don't have a right to tell me how to spend my money, or how to treat my workers." Mark clearly pointed out.

"We ain't talking 'bout what's rite, er wrong," said Bill, as he started walking across the field. "If you wuz paying a white man, it would be aw'rite wid him, but he gon'a thank it's wrong, fer you to pay a nigga."

Throughout the winter, the Negroes worked as though their life depended on how much they accomplished, and by springtime the land was ready for planting. The fences had been mended, the outbuildings, and the house in which Bill's family lived had been repaired. Mark had spent the money that his father gave him in a proper manner. Powell had never seen so much work done in such a short span of time. He continuted to compliment Mark on his ability to handle the slaves, and spoke highly of the interest shown by the slaves as well.

Nate Simpson had visited the farm a few times during the past winter, and he seemed pleased with the progress his son was making. He was careful, too, not to stay very long at a time, for he didn't want Mark to get the impression that he didn't trust him. After one such visit, as he was preparing to leave, he felt an urge to openly express his appreciation for what his son had done.

"Well, I'll have to hand it to you this time, Son," Nate smiled proudly, looking into Mark's eyes, "for this place looks the best it's ever looked in a mighty long time. Your neighbors keep asking who I have running this place, but I never tell," his father chuckled. "Somebody has been working hard, and everybody knows that it hasn't been Powell."

"Thank you, Dad, and I appreciate that, coming from you," Mark replied, "but the niggers deserve the credit. They work from daylight until dark every day, except for Sunday, for I let 'em rest that day. I owe you for the things you taught me, for they're paying off now." That compliment, brought a smile to his father's face.

"Powell says that you have the niggers afraid of you, and that you don't have to threaten them, to get them to work." His father beamed, sitting tall in the buggy. "As long as they are afraid of you, they'll turn out a lot of work, but if you let up one bit, they'll sit down, and do nothing."

"Well, I gave them a real good talk before I left home, and again after I got here, and they know exactly where I stand." Mark replied, even though his father's perception was something else, althogether. It was sad to think that the only time he made his father happy, was when he was being mean, and cruel to the poor, helpless slaves.

Then, climbing back down from the buggy, Simpson patted his son on the shoulder. "At first, I thought you were too young to manage a farm and a bunch of niggers, but I see that you're a born slave-driver." Proudly spoke his father, as he pointed at the plowed fields, which looked like a picture. "It's in a child's blood when he's born, for everybody don't have a God-given talent to handle slaves, and you should be proud of that."

"I'm a lot like you when it comes to doing business, or dealing with the other fellow, for when I make a promise, I intend to keep it," Mark replied.

"That's the only way to be!" Said his father. "Keep a tight rein on the niggers every day, and don't ever trust them, for they're unpredictable."

It was obvious, that his father was obsessed with his hatred for the Negroes. He was a good man in many ways, but Mark felt that someday his father's hatred for the slaves would be his undoing. Perhaps he owed it to his father to try to turn things around, as much as he owed it to the slaves.

"These slaves are above average," Mark said, trying not to tip his hand "but I can't tell you anything about slaves, you know them inside and out."

"Speaking of niggers, how's that gal doing?" Nate asked. "She should be as big as a barrel by now. She's young, and Mrs. Powell needs to keep an eye on her. That buck, sure gets some mighty big babies, you know."

"She's fine, and in fact, the way she still gets around, you might think that she wasn't even pregnant," he replied. Then, glancing toward the barn, Mark saw Martha standing in clear view, and he stepped between his father, and the barn. "I don't mean for you to think that I'm rushing you, but I need to get back to the fields. Here, let me hold your coat, while you climb back in the buggy. It's your new coat, the one that I gave you for Christmas, isn't it!"

"It is, and it's the best wearing coat, I've ever had." His father said, as he climbed back into the buggy. "You're not rushing me off, for I need to stop by the General Store, and pick up something for Susan anyway."

Waving goodbye, Mark breathed a sigh of relief. When his father's buggy drove out of sight, he hurried down to the barn, to speak to Martha.

"Martha, have you lost your mind?" Yelled Mark, as he rushed out to the barn. "He just asked about you, and if he had seen you, he would have known that you weren't pregnant! That was stupid of you!"

"I's didn't mean to cause no trouble," she replied. "I's didn't eb'em know that he wuz here, 'til I's come back to get a shovel fer Pappy."

"From now on, whenever he's around, I want you to stay out of sight, for I can't afford to mess up at this point." Mark demanded.

"Yass'uh, I's gon'a do that," she sobbed, "but if ole man Pow'l tells him that I's ain't prag'nut, is you gon'a jump on me 'bout that, too?"

"Powell doesn't even know that you're supposed to be pregnant." Mark told her. "I haven't told him, and I hope he never finds out, either."

Martha mumbled, as she walked away. "Nothing would be bothering us now, if you would'a give me a young'un, like I's axed you to do." Mark shook his head, as he watched her walking away, still mumbling something to herself.

April finally arrived, and farmers always tried to have their cotton crop planted by the first week in April. This way, the spring rain that always arrived during the latter part of April, or the first part of May, would help get the young crop off to a good start, before hot weather set in. Mark was real excited, for this would be the first time he'd tried his hand at farming. Mr. Powell had told Mark only yesterday, how proud he was for the way things were going, and Mark felt like he'd found a real friend, and someone in whom he could confide. Even so, he was waiting until he was absolutely sure about him, before he discussed his plans for the slaves.

Later that afternoon, while they were discussing which field they should plant first, Mark decided to bring up the subject of slavery, just to find out where Powell really stood. Thinking that the man was his friend, Mark didn't stop to think that this might be the biggest mistake he'd ever make. This had been bothering Mark ever since he first arrived, when Mr. Powell pitched a fit, because he had brought the slaves along with him.

"Mr. Powell, I'm not sure how you really feel about slavery, although you said that you hated the ground that Negroes walked on," Mark began. "I have noticed that you never speak to them, and whenever they come around, you walk away. I've wondered if what you said that day was because you didn't get the farm, and that you were upset with my father. Was that the reason?"

"Well, that's a matter of one's opinion, but here in the South, no man in his right mind, has anything good to say about a nigger," he replied. "Maybe it's because they never do anything that's worth bragging on. They don't have any sense, stupid to the core, and don't deserve any credit."

"Like you said, it's a matter of opinion, but Bill and his family really deserves a lot of credit for what they've done," Mark disagreed. "There's no reason to mistreat them, or refuse to recognize their importance, just because they're black. There's no group of white men who would have worked as hard as they worked last winter. They have feelings, just like any other person, and should be treated with respect, like any other human being."

"Even your own father don't have any respect for them, nor does any other true-blooded Southerner, that I know of," he scolded. "As for me, I have too much pride to lower myself to a point of associating with them, for like they say, a person is no better that the one they associate with."

"I'm not saying that it's wrong not to associate with them the same as we do white folks, but it's not right, to mistreat them," Mark rebutted.

"You talk a lot like a darn Northerner, for they claim that we mistreat these poor creatures of God, which is a lie," he returned. "I've never seen any of them mistreated. Whipped at a stake, maybe, kicked in the guts, but they're not mistreated, like you seem to think."

"I'm not as old as you, and might sound stupid at times, but I've seen my father do terrible things to them, unmerciful things, that should not be done to a dog!" Mark scolded. "I agree that a slave, or anybody else should be punished for doing wrong, but not in some inhumane kind of way."

"The niggers you have, belong to you, and you can treat them however you wish, but you have no right to tell others how to treat their slaves." Spoke Powell, in an angry voice. "All I have to say, is that you had better not let them get the upper hand on you, while you're trying to be nice to them."

"I don't intend to allow anyone to get the upper hand on me, even though they might not be a slave!" Mark quickly responded. "I give credit to anyone who deserves it, and it don't take a smart man, to see what's been done around here by the slaves, if I might add. They deserve more than just the food they eat, and the clothes handed down to them, and I plan to see that they get more than that. I'll do that because of how I feel in my heart, not to break customs or traditions, or go against what other farmers do. It might return and slap me in the face, but my mind is made up."

He should have ended this conversation, long before making this comment, but he trusted Powell, and continued.

"Well, exactly what do you plan to do for the sorry bastards?" Powell asked him. "Tell me, what do they deserve! And if you can, tell me what they ever did, to deserve your appreciation."

Mark could sense that he had struck a sour note with Powell. "I want you to know that this doesn't involve you," Mark began, "so you don't need to be worried in the least. But, when we sell the cotton, and after you get what I promised to you, I plan to divide my part with them, because they have worked so hard, since they've been here. They're human beings, no matter what somebody else might say, and I intend to treat them like humans too."

Powell's entire expression, changed. "The devil you say!" He shouted in anger, as he quickly jumped to his feet. "That will be over my dead-body, for I don't intend to work as hard as I've worked all winter, and stand by without saying anything, while you toss our hard earned money to the wind!"

His sudden change, sure caught Mark by surprise. "Hold on a minute!" Replied Mark. "What I do with my money, shouldn't concern you! The slaves belong to me, and I can pay them, set them free too! Do I make myself clear?"

"I don't believe this is coming from Nate Simpson's own child!" Replied Powell. "A nigger doesn't deserve anything for the work he does! If you share your money with them, you'll be branded as a nigger lover! That, my stupid boy, is what I have to say about your idea!"

Mark thought for a moment about what Bill had said earlier, about the way he would probably react, and the only thing he could do now, was to stand firm on his convictions. He had already gone too far, to turn back.

"I might do stupid things, and I'll admit that those Negroes have been my friends since childhood, but that don't make me a Negro lover!" Mark bellowed at him. "I've always hated slavery, and unless I stand up against it, I might as well be a slave myself. Slavery is cruel, any way you look at it, whether it be blacks bound by whites, or whites bound by customs, and traditions, it's all the same thing."

Powell couldn't argue with this logic at all, but because he had very few personal convictions of his own, he scolded Mark.

"You're a fool in my sight, and I know you. You can only imagine what those who don't know you, will have to say about your stupid ideas!" He screamed. "Everybody brags on the way we have improved the looks of this place, and they expect a lot from you, but as soon as they find out what you're doing, it's going to blow up in your face."

"But, Mr. Powell...," Mark began, only to be cut short.

"Don't you Mr. Powell me!" He snorted, as he quickly turned, and started walking away. "From now on, I'll stay out of your way, and I want you to stay out of mine! Now, that's all I have to say!"

This really shocked Mark, for he thought Powell was his friend. Without doubt, he'll tell my father about this discussion - might even add something himself, Mark said to himself, as Powell walked away. Would this be his lot in life, and would he always be afraid to voice his opinion, because it might upset someone. Then, he thought of what Bill once said, "Aw'ways be sho' to tell folks what they want'a hear, so they won't get mad." Bill had been right about Powell.

It was now three days later, and Powell hadn't even spoken to Mark since the day of the discussion. Mark's father had made an unscheduled visit to the farm earlier that morning while Mark was busy in the fields, but Powell made no effort to notify Mark. Mark found out about his father's visit when one of Bill's boys went to draw a bucket of water, and take it back to the fields for Mark and the others.

"Mos'a Mark, when I's went to fetch the water, I's seed yo' pappy talking wid that Pow'l feller, but I's didn't hear nothing that they sez," Elijah told him. "I's thank they wuz saying sump'um 'bout the crop, fer I's seed 'em point'n their fanger out torge the fields."

"I'm glad that you told me, even though he didn't bother to come out here to see me, and Powell didn''t let me know that he was here," replied Mark, as he sipped on a gourd filled with water. "He probably had business here in the area, and stopped by here on his way back home."

The longer Mark thought about this, the more aggravated he became, and by mid-afternoon he'd really become obsessed with wonder, as to what Powell might have said to his father. Finally, he decided to go to the house and ask Mr. Powell about this, and find out why he hadn't been notified.

It had been unusually warm today, and the Negroes had been working real hard since early this morning. Mark told them to go ahead and start doing the chores, while he went up to the house for a moment. But, he didn't tell them exactly why he was going to the house.

Powell was sitting on the porch alone, and Mark stopped at the bottom of the steps, and looked up at him.

"Mr. Powell," Mark addressed him, "I understand that my father stopped by here earlier today, and I wondered why you didn't bother to let me know he was here. I wanted to talk with him about a business matter."

It was obvious, that he was still upset with Mark. "Is that all you come up here for, to meddle in somebody else's affairs?" He asked, in a hateful voice. "I thought that you had come to eat up my hard-earned food, or had you rather eat with the niggers!"

"I've worked all day, and I am hungry," Mark replied, "but first of all I'd like to have an answer to a question, if you don't mind. Can you tell me why you didn't let me know that my father was here this morning?"

"Maybe he didn't come to see you, for if he had, he would have looked you up!" He slyly replied. "Boy, I'll be darned, if you don't beat all I've ever seen! You plan on paying the niggers for working, you claim they are human, and now, you want me to get your permission, before I talk with somebody! I didn't tell him to come and see you, and I'll be darned if I tell you what we talked about, either!"

Mark quickly turned, and walked back down to the barn, for it was obvious that this man didn't intend to listen to reason. He decided to help do the chores, before it got dark. He felt hurt because of what Powell had said, and because he could always talk with Bill, he decided to discuss it with him.

"Bill," spoke Mark seriously, "you told me that all white folks didn't think alike, and that I was different from them all. Now, I want your opinion about something, if you don't mind."

"Well, like yo' pappy sez, we ain't got sense nuf' to get in out of the rain, but I's ready to tell you what I's do know," he replied.

"Well, it's about Mr. Powell, and the way he's reacting to something that I told him the other day," Mark began. "I told him what I planned to do for you folks, and he pitched a fit. He spoke with my father today while I wasn't there, and only God knows what he said. The way he acted a moment ago, really bothers me."

"Like I's done sez, if you wan'a get 'long wid a feller, you's better say what he wants to hear," Bill told him, again. "I's said that the fat would hit fire when you's told him. We's in the South, it's a slave-place, and nobid'ee ain't gon'a change that, neither."

They continued talking until the sun went down, Bill went home, and Mark went up to where the Powells lived, to eat supper. The Powells ate before he came to the house, and when Mark finished eating, he retired to his room to be alone. He somehow felt in his heart that Powell hadn't told his father about their discussion. If he had, and knowing his father as he did, he would have plowed into Mark, before he went home. Was Powell playing games with him, he asked himself. Mark knew now, that he must be on his guard from here on.

Back at the plantation the following morning, Nate was talking about the trip to Mark's farm yesterday.

"Julie, you'll have to ride down there with me one day, and see the place for yourself," Simpson told her. "It don't look like the same place, and I'm glad now, that I let him go ahead. You'll be proud of him too."

"And, how is Mark doing?" Julie asked. "Is he holding up well, and does it look like he's been eating properly? When is he coming to visit us?"

"I really didn't see Mark, for Powell said that he'd gone to visit one of the neighbors, and I couldn't wait until he got back," he replied. "He's all right according to what Powell said, and you have no need to be worried."

"I hope he makes it, and that Powell don't take an unfair advantage of him, because of his good nature," she continued. "What do you know about him? Is he the type of person, who can be trusted?"

"He's not all that bad, maybe a little lazy, but he'll look after our boy, I'm sure," he assured her. "He says that Mark's a born slave-driver, if there's ever been one, and that he keeps his eye on him, every day."

"I've only spoken to him once, and he didn't impress me at all, and I saw nothing in his wife to impress me either," she replied. "I hope you really know this Powell fellow, for I don't trust him at all, and I'm afraid Mark has a rough road ahead of him. You even said that you didn't like him."

"He's not the smartest person in the world, and he lacks a lot in being a good farmer, but I don't think he'd harm anybody."

Nate explained. "He don't want to lock horns with me, and he better not mistreat my boy."

"I've been meaning to ask you, and it always slips my mind, but I wonder how that pregnant girl is doing. Did she have her baby?" Julie asked.

"Powell didn't mention her, and I didn't think to ask," said Nate. "She came from good stock, and I'm not worried about her having a problem."

She knew all too well that he wasn't concerned, and she even wondered if he'd be worried about Susan, if she were in the same condition.

Later that evening back at the farm, Mark was still concerned about what Powell might have told his father. He admitted to Bill, that he'd told Powell all about his plans, even though Bill had warned him against it.

"Mos'a Mark, why did you tell that ole goat what you's planned to do fer us?" Bill asked, seriously. "I's knowed ever since I's socked my eyeballs on him that he wuz no good fer you, and he done told yo' pappy everthang."

"Maybe not, for he's a lot of bluster, and he's afraid of Dad." Replied Mark, hopefully. "I hope he didn't, anyway. Maybe he didn't tell him."

"Well, I's hope he don't get you in no trouble, but mos' of all, you's never shou'da told him nothing!" Bill scolded.

"You're right, for I shouldn't have trusted him," Mark agreed. "He has a good thing going for him, and I don't think he'll let his lip mess him up."

"That's what you's thank, but the older you's get, the mo' you gon'a learn 'bout fellers like him," Bill cautioned.

"I'll have to chalk it up as another lesson learned the hard way," Mark smiled. "But, I didn't count on him going to pieces on me like he did."

Bill, and the others went about doing the chores. Standing there alone, Mark realized now, that Bill had given him some sage advice. In order for him to get along with others, he must only say what they want to hear. Mark then laughed to himself, as he recalled his father saying that Negroes didn't have any sense. Bill had plenty of sense - good common sense. Mark thought that Powell was his friend, when all along, Bill was the only friend he had. Mark then bowed his head, and thanked God again for such a man as Bill.

CHAPTER THREE

THE BUD BECOMES A ROSE

The cotton was now fully grown and the boles would be opening soon, but until the cotton boles opened and the cotton was ready to be picked, everyone could take it easy for several weeks. This was the time when the other crops were being harvested, vegetables canned and stored for winter, and hay cut and stacked to feed the livestock. Nevertheless, knowing that the cotton crop had been properly cared for, and would soon be ready to pick and sell, was within itself a great relief. Other than for occasionally selling a few bushels of corn during the winter months, cotton was the only source of income for most Southern farmers. Some farmers, however, did grow sugar cane and other crops to sell in addition to cotton, but as a general rule farmers relied heavily on cotton for their livelihood.

Since the last encounter between Mark and Mr. Powell last spring, nothing else had been said about Mark's plans for the slaves. There were, however, certain amounts of tension in the air whenever Mark and Mr. Powell were in each other's presence. From the day of their heated discussion until all the work had been done, Powell remained at the house, and didn't offer to lend a hand to help Mark and the slaves. He did, however, continue nagging at Mark every chance he got, and Mark made a habit of staying away from him, other than for having to eat and sleep in the house with him.

It was obvious now that Powell hadn't said anything to Mr. Simpson, for his visits during the past summer were pleasant ones, and Mark did appreciate that at least. Without doubt Powell had told his wife, for her attitude was the same as that of her husband except when Mr. Simpson was around, for then, they treated Mark as if he were their own son. Whatever might be their reason for not telling his father and acting as though they loved him, Mark knew for a fact that they had interest to protect, and he went along with their farce.

Whenever Mark's father wasn't around, the Powells seemed content in causing Mark to live a miserable life, and even though it seemed like they didn't plan to tell anyone of Mark's plans for the slaves, their silence had a price, and they had begun to treat him poorly. They had made a practice of eating alone, and even when attending church they made a point of not sitting close to him. They seemed to delight in causing Mark to wonder if they had said anything to others in the community. Above all, Powell flatly refused to discuss the crop with him, even though he still expected to get his share of the profit.

Even though Mark feared the repercussions, and knew that he was standing alone like a lamb in a den of wolves, he was determined to follow through with his plan. He couldn't afford to break a promise to Bill and his family, for they were like family to him. Regardless to what his father might do when he found out about his plan, he didn't intend to change his mind.

To hate someone because they were "black", made no sense to Mark, but the farners had dominated over the Negroes so long, until setting them free, seemed as incomprehensible to them, as freedom did to the slaves. Mark was aware of that, and even though there were others in the South who felt as he did about slavery, he'd have a hard time in getting them to stand up and voice their opinion. He'd simply have to stand and fight this battle alone, he knew that.

Summer ended, fall was in the air, and Mark knew that it wouldn't be very long until the cotton would be ready to pick. Even though Powell acted like a fool and refused to help make the crop, Mark remembered his agreement to give Powell half of the profit, and he intended to honor his promise. Mark decided to try his hand at some sort of reconciliation with him. He was sure that things would go much smoother, if they could at least be civil.

The following morning, Mark walked out on the porch and sat down with the Powells, who didn't even turn to look at him. This has gone far enough, Mark said to himself, and regardless to what might happen, I intend to bring this to a close, one way or another.

"I'm sorry if I've hurt you folks in any way," Mark began, "but I wish that you'd realize that I have my right to my own opinion, the same as others have to their opinion. This might sound strange coming from someone who was born in the South, but I've hated slavery since childhood. I guess I was born with hatred for slavery, like others were born with hatered for Negroes."

"You had your say, now it's my turn," Powell replied, as he glanced over at his pouting wife. "You want me to go along with you, and it's only fair if you try to see my point of view as well. Nobody..."

"Sir, that's exactly what I've been trying to get you to do, for we each have a right to our own opinion," Mark interrupted.

"Nobody pays the niggers for working," Powell continued. "They get paid by the food they eat and the clothes they wear, and by giving them some place to lay their head at night. That's all they need. Your idea of paying them for something that they're supposed to do for nothing, sounds stupid! And, if you set them free on top of that, it will destroy everything that we've fought so hard to accomplish. What about our Southern traditions and pride. Do you still think that they should be set free?"

"There's a lot of talk about the Union forcing us to set them free, and I wonder if you'll call the Union a Negro lover," Mark replied. "Have you ever thought about that?"

"Then, we will be forced to free them, which is different," he continued to argue. "Even then, the Union can't make us like the black bastards!"

"Sir, let me ask you something, if I may," politely spoke Mark. "During your time as a farmer, have you ever owned, or worked any slaves yourself?"

"I have not!" He quickly replied. "You say you have a right to hate the practice of slavery, and I have the same right to hate the niggers! They are stupid, lazy, and not worth the salt that goes in their bread!"

"But, you must agree that this farm looks good, and we have a cotton crop almost ready to pick, simply because a bunch of lazy, stupid, and ignorant Negro slaves, worked their heart out," Mark rebutted. "Let me also point out, that they worked voluntarily and without any help from you, while you sat here on the porch like a stump in the middle of a field, critacizing, finding fault with them, and not even offering them a drink of cold water. You don't want

91

them to get paid, yet you expect to profit from their work, even though you actually don't deserve anything at all."

"I know, but they worked because you promised to pay them, otherwise, you couldn't have whipped them into working that hard!" Powell scolded.

"That's my point exactly," replied Mark. "I know they have to work for nothing whether they like it or not, but what's wrong with giving them a good reason to work? You stayed on because I promised to pay you for your work as foreman, or you would have left. How can you expect to get paid when you did no work, and not pay them for working? That makes no sense!"

Mark's logic surprised him. "Look, boy," he bellowed, "it's your own money and I agree with that, but this is South Carolina, and we have customs and traditions to live by! You are bucking against something that's been working for the South for almost three hundred years!"

"But, Sir, all I want to do is to obey my own conscience, and the feeling I have in my own heart," Mark replied. "Do I not have that right?"

Powell didn't immediately reply. A moment later his wife jumped up, and hurried into the house. It must have stirred something in his wife's heart as well, Mark thought.

"I'm not arguing with your rights," Powell finally said. "What I really meant, was that anybody who pays a nigger for working, is downright stupid!"

Mark felt tears coming to his eyes. "Even though they are black, and you don't recognize them as being humans, they should get more than a few bites of food, handed-down clothes, and have to live in shacks that aren't fit to house an animal. Deep down in your heart, do you honestly believe that's the way we should treat another human being?" Mark asked, seriously.

"It wouldn't be right if they were human beings, but they're not!" He snapped back. "If you pay them this year they'll expect pay from now on, and so will other niggers on other farms, and we'll have a riot on our hands. They were put on earth to be slaves, and they'll always be slaves."

"Let me tell you something," Mark, retorted. "My father will tell you in a heartbeat that these slaves will work for nothing, the same as if they were expecting to be paid. They've worked their heart out to help me accomplish my goal, and there's nothing wrong with me sharing my own money with them. They will be just as proud to have something to call their own, as you and I."

"I agree, if they knew the value of money," he argued, "but they can't even count their fingers and toes. How can they handle money."

"Sir, my decision is not based on their scholastic ability, or how astute they are in business matters, but solely on principal, and I intend to keep my promise," Mark emphatically stated. "If I failed to keep my promise to you, would you let it slide? No, you certainly would not!"

"There's a big difference in keeping your promise to humans, and keeping your promise to them," he replied, in anger. "Making a promise to them is like promising a mule that you won't make it work, for it don't expect you to keep your promise anyway. The niggers don't expect it, either."

"Come on, now," said Mark. "You know that they do have feelings just like everybody else, and they hurt when stepped on, the same as any other human being. They have good common sense, something that you don't seem to have."

"You should become a lawyer, for you can argue a blue-streak, when you're arguing your point, but I'm still not convinced," said Powell.

"I'm not arguing, just stating facts!" Mark replied. "I plan to keep my promise to you even though you didn't work, and I'll also keep my promise to those who worked. You might as well accept that fact, Sir."

Silence hung in the air, as Powell tried to think of a way that he might get Mark not to pay the Negroes, and Mark tried to come up with stronger words in his effort to convince Powell that he didn't intend to change.

"If a white person worked you would be obligated to pay him, but they're niggers, and you don't owe them anything," Powell finally spoke. "Their sole purpose in life is to be slaves, nothing else, with no questions asked, and no pay at all. They were made black in the beginning, because the Lord wanted the world to know that they were different."

Mark looked keenly at him. "I am aware that you're dead set against the Negroes, but I'd like for you to use common sense for a change," Mark told him. "What kind of crop would we have had, if it wasn't for them? Those five slaves have done more work this year alone, than you've done during the seven years you've lived here! Sir, do you care to argue with that?"

Powell still refused to listen to reason. "You seem to forget that they are slaves, and were put on earth just for that purpose," he disagreed. "You buy and sell them like you do animals, and they should be treated that way as well. Even though they did do a lot of hard work, and improved this place, they don't deserve any thanks, or appreciation for anything."

"Sir, if you agree that they did a lot of work, how can you possibly find fault with my sharing a part of my own money with them?" Mark asked.

Powell didn't reply, for the door opened, and Mrs. Powell walked back out on the porch and sat down. It was obvious by the expression on her face that she had something to say, and Mark was eager to find out what it was.

"I have something that I'd like to say, if my rights haven't been taken away, and given to the niggers, like our money is being done," she finally said.

"Go ahead Madam, and say what you wish," Mark politely replied, "for I voice my opinion, and you have the same right. I have a right to give part of my money to the slaves if that's what I wish to do, and yes, you have a right to disagree, if that's what you choose to do."

"I agree with my husband, that niggers are stupid, and you might as well scream at the moon, for they can't be taught anything," she scolded. "They aren't human beings, and if you talk 'til your face turns blue, they won't understand anything that you've said."

It was clear that neither she nor her husband intended to listen to reason, and Mark decided to be just as rough on them, as they were being on him.

"I don't see that much difference in them and us, except for the color of their skin, and the awesome fact that we haven't tried to teach them very much at all," he rebutted. "They could learn to read and write, and learn how to do other things, if those who think they're so smart would take time to teach them, instead of downgrading them all the time."

"No difference, my foot!" Snapped Mrs. Powell. "They're too stupid, for anyone to teach them anything. Like my husband said, they're not human."

Mark sat and shook his head, for he saw more ignorance in them, than he'd seen in a whole group of slaves. They seemed to have no common sense at all, and were very unreasonable, so he decided to say no more.

Following a few moments of silence, and thinking that Mark was just about ready to give up, Mrs. Powell decided to keep hammering away. She hoped that he'd get discouraged, and go back home. If he did go back, there would be no reason for his father not to sell them the farm, she thought.

"Niggers have been slaves, ever since they were first brought over here," she continued. "They were brought over here to serve white folks, not to be classed as equal citizens, and certainly not to be paid for working for us."

A smile came on Mark's face. "You did say one thing that was right," he told her. "We did, in fact, bring them over here. They didn't jump into the ocean and swim to America, just to become slaves. We've abused them until we finally broke their spirit, stripped them of all their dignity and pride they once had as individuals, and now, almost naked and starving, we're trying to work them to death. At the risk of being called a "nigger lover", I must say that it's no way to treat another human being! It's disgraceful and inhumane, and the way I feel, slavery should be abolished from the face of the earth!"

Mrs Powell softened slightly. "I see your point, in a way, but it's too late to change things now," she replied. "It's like rushing into a house, to rescue someone from the fire. We stand a chance of being burned a lot worse, than the person we're trying to save. It's the same, in trying to help the niggers."

"Our forefathers made a mistake by making slaves of them, and I hope that others will realize that just as I have, and learn from their mistake," Mark told her. "A person ceases to learn when he begins to justify his mistakes, and I hope that I never reach that point. Sometimes, we're forced to walk the road alone, but the only time we're apt to stumble and fall, is when we happen to turn and look back, to see if anyone is following us. I might be the only one to think that way, and it might return to slap me in the face, but I don't intend to stop, or look back to see if anyone else is following me."

"Say what you think. and take whatever stand you wish, but if you decide to pay them, and continue to treat them as though they were human beings, soon you'll find yourself in a worse shape than they're in," she cautioned.

"That's where we disagree," replied Mark, feeling like he had managed to spark her concern, "for I don't see it that way. If shown a little kindness, and concern for their welfare, I'm sure we'd see a great change in the way the Negroes react toward us, as well as toward themselves. Maybe not quite all of them, but at least some, I do believe that, Madam."

Mark sat and waited quite some time for a reply, however, when it seemed as though neither of them had anything else to say, he got up and walked down the steps, for he had work to do down at the barn.

"Give up on that stupid notion of yours, for it's going to mess up things for you," she warned, a second time. "The sooner you admit that they're just as stupid as a mule, and not human, the better off it will be for everybody."

"Madam, I must say good-day to you wonderful folks, for I have work to do at the barn with the 'stupid' Negroes," he said, as he walked away.

Mark realized that Bill had summed these folks up right, and after having talked with them, it caused him to hate slavery even more. He felt like they were not speaking from their heart, but in fear of what someone else might say if they didn't "go along with the crowd." It was much easier just to follow the crowd, Mark thought. Say nothing to upset anybody, do nothing to cause others to dislike them, go with the flow, that's all. Mark knew that he couldn't live that way. There had to be a better way.

Mark made a point of remaining with the slaves all day, and it was after dark when he finally went back to the house. He didn't want to get involved in another fruitless discussion with them; therefore, he went directly to his room without bothering to eat supper. Like Bill once said, "There ain't no way to win when you's argue wid a fool, and you ain't got nothing to brag 'bout, when you whoop a crippled feller."

Sprawled out across the bed, Mark thought back on the discussion he'd had with the Powells this morning, and how difficult they had tried to make things for him. If they had any convictions it didn't show, or they had managed to keep them well hidden. Mark couldn't change them, nor were they able to cause him to change. No sooner had he dozed off he heard a knock on the door, and for a moment it frightened him, for this had never happened before. He jumped up and opened the door, and he saw the Powells standing in the hallway.

"Mark," Powell began, "although we disagree with you, we are concerned for your welfare. This is the South, and we have our customs and traditions that must be upheld, and we're afraid that you're headed for trouble."

"I'm not alone, for if the truth were known there's a lot of other folks in the South who think the same way, but they are simply afraid to speak up," Mark replied. "If I don't take a stand, then I become a slave to the customs and traditions. A slave, is anyone who doesn't have any freedom."

Powell stood for a moment looking straight into Mark's eyes. The boy is a mite too young to make that much sense, he thought. He ought to channel such wit and determination as this, toward other purposes.

"Mark, you won't be anything in the South, except for a small, struggling farmer, unless you decide to change your way of thinking," Powell remarked.

"Becoming great in the eyes of others, don't appeal to me," Mark bluntly replied. "It's that inner peace of mind that keeps my spirit alive. Freedom is very important to me, and I don't intend to become a slave to anyone, or to customs and traditions that you claim are so important to you."

Mrs. Powell decided to speak up, for her husband wasn't getting anywhere, it seemed. "It's all right to hate something, so long as you keep it bottled up inside, while in the presence of others," she almost pleaded. "That's all I ask. Don't be so bold, and don't spill your guts to others."

"I don't see your point," Mark responded, "and I don't quite understand what you're leading up to. I want others to know exactly how I feel."

"It's like when someone comes to visit, and catches you with a dirty pair of britches on," she began, "You can slip on clean britches even though you need a bath, for they will cover up the dirt on your body. Unless folks see the dirt, they won't know anything about it being there. That's what I mean."

Be one person outside, another inside. That's what she actually wanted him to be. His thoughts turned to Bill, "Tell folks what they want'a hear." She would drop dead, if she knew that a "mule stupid" Negro, had given him the same advice. He had one set of standards, and he didn't plan to change.

"I might sound like a fool, and might not see it come to pass, but one of these days Negroes will become equal citizens, and will have the same rights as we have now," Mark predicted. "I must go to bed and get some rest, and we can take this up again at a later time. Good night, to both of you!"

Mark closed the door, and the Powells turned and walked toward the front door. Alone in bed, Mark began to reflect back to when he was a child, and it caused him to grimace as he thought of the way slaves were treated. Everybody makes mistakes, and they should be punished, but they should not be whipped with a leather strap, until their back became a bloody-pulp. Maybe it wasn't slavery that he hated, but the way slaves were treated.

On the front porch, the Powells worried aloud. "That boy is headed for a lot of trouble, if he's not real careful," Mr. Powell observed. "Southerners will not put up with his way of thinking. I hate slavery as much as he does, but I won't admit it to him, or to anyone else. In fact, I really feel sorry for the niggers, but I must keep up my front."

"Since we've been married, I've never known you to be so dead set against niggers, as you've been since he brought them here," she observed. "Can you explain that?"

"I've never owned any slaves, and hadn't given much thought to them, that is, until he said that he planned to pay them," he explained. "But he has a good point, for they are treated worse than dogs. On the other hand, can you imagine what others would say, if they knew I said that?"

"Even if you do feel that way, you're smart enough not to let everyone in the community know how you feel," she upheld him. "The boy has good common sense, but I'll go to my grave, before I agree with him."

"A real smart person can do stupid things sometimes," Powell remarked, "and that's what he's doing now. He's headed for a downfall, along with anybody who is stupid enough to share his ideas, and I don't plan to be one of them."

"You're right," she agreed, "for we're judged according to persons with whom we associate, and I'm afraid that folks might think that we feel the same as he does, as long as he's living here in our home."

"As soon as the cotton is sold and I get my share of the money, I'll let him have this farm and his niggers, all to himself," he replied. "As soon as folks find out that he plans to pay the niggers, we'll be looked upon as trash by everybody, for folks will think we agree with him. Even worse, Nate might think that we put that stuff in his head."

"I understand, but I really hate to move, and have to start all over," she said, sadly. "I wish that we could buy the farm, but I guess that's wishful thinking."

"Yes, I'd like to have it, now that it's been cleaned up, and looks like a farm should, but I don't want to set my hopes too high," he replied. "But if Nate happened to get mad at his son, he might decide to sell it to us."

"We know that Simpson hates niggers with a passion, but we can't overlook how he feels toward his son either," she cautioned him. "That might change, if he knew that his own son really was a nigger lover. I wonder what would happen, if he got word that his son was messing around with that nigger gal?"

"Woman, you really do have an ugly streak running up your backbone, but you do have a good point," he chuckled. "I'll think it over, but it's mighty dangerous to accuse a person of something, unless you have proof."

Morning arrived, and Mark awoke to the smell of coffee brewing, but when he walked into the kitchen, he noticed that the atmosphere was quite differnt than before. Nothing was said about last night's conversation, almost as if it had never taken place. Mark felt strangely uneasy. He found himself faced with regret that he'd confided in Powell.

The cotton was already turning white, and within a few days it would be ready to pick. Bill told Mark yesterday, to ask Powell to take a look at the fields himself, and make the final decision. If he asked Powell to do that, it might "break the ice" this morning, Mark thought.

"Mr. Powell," Mark began, "the way it looks, the cotton might be ready to pick pretty soon, but you need to check it out, and let me know what you think."

"Ain't you and the niggers already looked it over?" Powell snapped. "I thought they knew all about farming, and that they were as smart as white folks."

"I trust your opinion more than I trust my own, for you have a lot more experience," Mark replied. "That's why I asked you to be the manager."

"The devil with the cotton, and your niggers, too!" Powell bellowed, as he struck his fist on the table. "You say they're so smart, so ask them when the stuff will be ready, and leave me out of it from here on."

Mark could feel his face burning with anger. "That makes no sense to me, for you'll get as much money as I will," Mark retorted. "It's your job as foreman, you get paid, and you have more experience."

"Now, see there!" Powell snickered. "You say they're equal with a white man, but when you need to know something, you change your mind. You promised to pay them, so let them earn their money. Let them decide."

"Yes, I'll pay them for making the crop, and I'll have to pay you as well for what you didn't do! How stupid and silly you sound!" Mark scolded.

"When you admit that they're stupid, I'll be glad to help you, but until you do, leave me out of the picture!" He snorted.

It was quite obvious to Mark, that his point of view meant nothing in the eyes of this man, and he was willing to risk everything to prove that Mark was wrong, and Mark felt a chilling sense of dismay coming over him. Hatred was truly a powerful and destructive force, and Mark was about to see it put into action. Although they had different points of view, Mark couldn't see why it should keep them from working together as a team.

"We might disagree on certain matters, but you agreed to manage the farm, and I expect you to do just that, if you want to get paid," Mark clearly told him. "It's your place to make the final decision, not mine."

"That's what I thought too!" Powell snapped. "But, you put the niggers ahead of me, and there's no telling what folks will say, when they learn about me harboring a nigger lover in my own home."

"Sir, I think you're a gentleman, as well as myself, and I don't see why we can't disagree on certain things without you coming apart," Mark replied, seriously. "As long as the work gets done, and we both make money, that's all that should matter. Do you disagree with that, as well?"

"You hurt him real bad, when you said that niggers were as smart as white persons," spoke up his pouting wife, in an obstinate voice. "That makes him look like a fool."

"I agree, that they aren't as intelligent as white persons, but it's not all their fault," Mark countered. "There's quite a bit of difference between being ignorant, and being downright stupid, like you folks seem to be."

"If they're so smart, let them decide when the cotton should be picked," she snarled. "You don't need my husband, with the niggers around."

"She's absolutely right," Powell spoke up. "I'm fed up, with you saying that they're as smart as me! How can you expect me to help you, when you're treating me like trash. I won't lower my standards to please you."

"You just don't understand!" Mark yelled, as he jumped up from the table in anger. "I'm only giving credit where credit is due. Everybody should get credit for what they do, and the Negroes, sure did a lot around here."

"Oh I see now," Powell blurted. "You want me to bow down to them, and kiss their feet, just because they happened to do a little work!"

"Sir, I'm not asking you to bow down to them, and I certainly won't make them bow down to you, like you want them to," Mark scolded. "If that happens to cause a problem, I feel sorry for you, for that's the way it is."

"Look, boy!" Powell yelled. "I hate niggers, and I hate you because you take up for them. I won't have anything else to do with the crop, even if the darn cotton rots in the field. Do I make myself clear?"

"Then, I guess that's it," Mark replied sadly. "I'll do the best I can to handle things, me and my bunch of "stupid" Negroes."

Mark headed for the door, not wishing to argue with him any longer. Mark knew that he was wasting time with them, for they based their theory on what others might say about them, and not on how they felt in their own heart.

"I'm going to laugh, when you mess around with the niggers, and let them cause you to lose the crop!" He said, as Mark went out the door.

"I feel sorry for you, and your lovely wife," Mark countered, "for even a slave wouldn't be that stupid! You're lower down than a slave!"

At that, Powell quickly jumped up from the table, and stormed after Mark. "Listen here, young-sprout!" He yelled. "Nobody is going to ram a bunch of niggers down my throat! The devil with the crop, and you too!"

"Let's just drop the whole thing," said Mark, as he walked away. "If we do lose the crop, it won't be lost because I didn't try. You Sir, don't have any common sense at all, and the worst slave I've ever seen, wouldn't stoop as low as you and your wife have stooped here lately.

As he walked slowly down toward the barn, he realized now more than ever before, that the South was governed by pride, not logic. He was almost sure that within a few days his father would know everything, and he wasn't ready to handle that. He had a cotton crop to harvest, he and a "bunch of stupid niggers," and he didn't intend to allow anything to stop him.

Bill was the most dependable and trustworthy slave that Nate Simpson ever owned, and Mark was fortunate to have him around, especially now, when it seemed as though Powell didn't intend to fulfill his obligation as foreman. When Mark arrived at the barn, Bill and his boys were greasing the wheels on the wagon, for it would be needed to haul the cotton to the gin.

"You're not getting the wagon ready a day too soon," said Mark, slapping Bill on the shoulder, "for the way the cotton is looking now, it won't be too long 'til we'll have to start picking it. You're a good man, and I couldn't have made it this far, without you and the boys."

"Yass'uh, I's told the boys that we'd better get it ready while we had the time, fer adder we get started pick'n the cotton, we ain't gon'a have no time left to do nothing," Bill grinned, and replied.

"When you finish what you're doing, I'd like for you and me to look over the crop, and see if it's ready to pick," Mark told him.

"It's aw'mos as white as my ole head, now," Bill laughed, "and it needs to be picked fo' it dries out too much, fer ever pound counts, like yo' pappy used to tell us. Is Mos'a Pow'l going wid us? He be the man to say when it needs to be picked over, fer he's the main-man, and we sho' don't want him to get upsot wid us."

"I asked him to go with us, but he already had something else planned for today, and he said for us to go ahead and decide," Mark lied, sparing Bill's feelings. "Tell Liza and Martha to come on and go with us, for they worked as hard as anyone else."

"Sounds good to me," said Bill, motioning to Liza and Martha, "fer I's thank they did do some wuk'. Maybe not ver'ee much, jus' a lit'l."

As they walked out across the fields, Mark glanced back toward the house, and he saw the Powells standing on the porch, watching them. Mark didn't beg to Mr. Powell, as his wife no doubt thought he should, and it upset her. Mark might have worked things out with Powell, but his wife was a troublemaker, and she was the cause of all the problems between them.

"That boy has everything, a farm of his own, a father with plenty of money, and he's too stupid to realize what he has," Mrs. Powell said to her husband. "Folks will look down on us, for the way he treats the niggers."

"That's why I keep away from him while we're in church, and don't bother going to town with him, for fear of what others might say," he replied. "If there were some way that we could spread the word about what he's doing so it wouldn't get back to him, we'd have it made. If I wasn't a Christian, and deacon of my church, I'd spread the word, and see what happens."

"God put niggers on earth to be slaves to white folks, and He expects us to keep His plan working," she sneered. "Have you thought about telling his father how he treats the niggers? If you did, he'd probably sell the farm to us, just to teach that boy a good lesson. Have you thought about that?"

"Yes, I have," Powell smiled, and "I know something else that's going on behind Nate's back, that would make him mad."

"My Lord, how could you possibly keep something like that from me, for we never keep things from each other!" She whimpered. "Go ahead and tell me all that you know, for we're in this thing together."

"One day last week while I was in town, I overheard Nate and another man talking about a buck fathering a child for one of Nate's slave girls, and Nate told the man, that he gave the girl to his son," he replied. "Nate said that he'd mention it to Mark, and tell him to pay the fee for the buck. Nate said the girl's name was Martha, and that girl yonder is called Martha, and there's no way she could be pregnant. If that be the case, she should have had a baby long before now, and I think Mark is involved, and he'll have a lot of explaining to do, if his father finds out that she's not even pregnant."

"Yes, I've heard them call her Martha, and she's not expecting a baby, by a long-shot!" She smiled.

"Something's real bad wrong, somewhere," Powell observed. "Whenever Nate happens to be around, that girl is nowhere to be seen. She stays out of sight."

Mrs Powell was enjoying this, for it would give her something to discuss with her Christian-friends. "I can't imagine Simpson saying that she was pregnant, if he didn't have a reason," she frowned. "What do you think?"

"I really don't know," Powell replied, shrugging his shoulders, "but it wouldn't surprise me, if Mark was involved. Maybe that's why he always takes up for them. Maybe he really is her lover, after all."

"If that be the case, it's our Christian-duty to tell his father, for God wants us to keep the devil on the run," she suggested. "Do you agree?"

"I really do," he replied. "It's my duty to tell him, so he can set his son straight, before he wanders off on the wrong path, and away from God."

"Say! Do you happen to know the other man's name?" She asked. "If you told him, then he'd tell Simpson, and it would put you in the clear. We can't let the devil have his way, and deprive us of our rights to use niggers as slaves. God expects us to take a stand for what's right."

"You're right, for I won't be able to sleep, until I find out what's been going on, right under our nose," Powell agreed. "I think the man's name was Johnson, or Johnston, I'm not quite sure."

"Maybe you ought to make another trip to town, and see what you can find out!" His wife prodded. "I won't be able to rest at all, until you do."

"Yes, I need to find out, so I can tell Nate before it's too late to do something about it," he nodded. "I might even tell him about how Mark plans to pay the niggers, set them free, too. Yep! We might just have us a farm, after all. It seems like the Lord is on our side at last."

"Just look going yonder!" She snarled, pointing toward the field. "That gal is strutting along with Mark, like she was a white girl. I'd bet my life, that he's messing around with her. What do you think?"

"I have no doubt!" He replied. "I think I'll go ahead and tell Nate, so he'll know what's going on. If Mark asks where I am, tell him a close friend of mine died, and I went to pay my respect.

Tell him anything, except for the truth. Make up something to tell him. You're good at that."

Mark and his friends looked over the cotton fields, for the earlier they picked it, the more pounds per acre it would yield, and if they happened to be lucky, they might be able to sell it before the market became flooded.

"I'm not an expert at farming, for I've never picked a pound of cotton in my life, but it feels dry," said Mark, as he picked a handful of cotton, and handed it to Bill. "Here, you be the judge!"

"Yass'uh, it sho' do feel dry," replied Bill, as he rubbed the cotton on his face, "but you's need Mos'a Pow'l to say the las' wu'd. He be the feller that 'sposed to runs thangs 'round here, er I's thought he wuz."

"My father trusted your judgement, and now that you're here, I plan to do the same thing," said Mark. "I have no reason in the world, to doubt you at all."

"That sho' do make me feel good, but I's knowed fellers like Mos'a Pow'l all my lif', and I's 'fraid he gon'a get upsot, if we's jump 'head of him, and do sump'um that he wuz 'sposed to do," Bill clearly explained.

Mark didn't reply immediately, for he sure didn't want to tell Bill everything that Powell had said. The slaves had worked hard, and now that they could see the fruits of their labor, Mark didn't want it destroyed by Powell's stubborn attitude. Suddenly, Mark remembered his own words about "giving credit where credit is due." The very thought of Powell saying that Bill was a "stupid nigger," cut deep at Mark's soul. There was nothing stupid about this kind old man.

"I don't know how to say this, except to admit that you were right about Mr. Powell," said Mark, as he glanced up toward the house, where the Powells were still standing on the porch. "He's upset because I plan to pay you folks for working, and he don't care if the cotton rots in the field. I'm sorry to have lied to you, about him having something else to do today."

Bill bowed his head, to keep Mark from seeing the tears trickling down his cheeks. "I's sho' hate to hear that, fer it spells trouble," replied Bill. "You's got a good notion in yo' head, but folks ain't gon'a let it wuk'. It's my fault, fer I's never should'a come down here wid you."

"It's not your fault, I should have kept my mouth shut," Mark admitted to him. "He was mad because he didn't get the farm, and everything else I did that he didn't like, only added fuel to the fire. Even though I hate that it happened, he turned out to be exactly like you said he would."

Bill knew that the burden rested on his own shoulder, and he'd have to be very careful what he said to Mark, so as not to steer him wrong.

"No matter how you's feel 'bout sump'um, sometimes it's better not to say nothing, and not take no chance of get'n hut'," Bill advised. "No matter how rite you is, somebid'ee is aw'ways gon'a say that you is wrong."

"But, he's dead wrong!" Mark argued. "So long as he gets what's coming to him, it shouldn't matter how I feel about other things."

"I's ain't 'sposed to know nothing, 'cept fer how to grow cotton, but I's been 'round long nuf' to know what trouble looks like, when I's see it coming up the road," replied Bill. "This ain't nothing but a slave-country, and you ain't never gon'a change it. Unless you's wake up and realize that mos' folks is slave-haters, you is headed fer a lot'a trouble."

"I know, but unless I stand up against slavery, I might as well become a slave myself,' Mark explained. "I can't help if I feel that way."

"Yass'uh, that's one way to feel, but you's gon'a have trouble fer the res' of yo' lif', cause of us," Bill again pointed out. "You's need to tun' and look the tuther way when they do sump'um to us, fer you can't hep' us."

"I've always hated slavery, and I'll continue to cry out against it, for the rest of my life," Mark swore. "No human, should ever become a slave to someone else."

"I's happy fer the way you's treat us, fer everbid'ee wants to be free as a bird, but it sho' ain't meant fer everbid'ee," replied Bill. "Freedom is good, but the South ain't no place fer no free-nigga, and it never will be."

"Other farmers set their slaves free, and the slaves seem to be doing as well as could be expected, I'm told," Mark offered.

"Freedom ain't what it's cracked up to be," Bill pointed out. "Freedom, is jus' another link in the chain that white folks is aw'ready got 'round our neck, and they gon'a hold on to it 'til the day they die. That way, they can ju'k us back, if it looks like we is get'n 'head in lif'."

Bill's reation, caught Mark by surprise. He didn't think freedom was worth the bother, for slaves would be free in words only, no real freedom at all. Bill looked at freedom, as an impossible dream. He might be right. He was right about Powell, and right about everything else, Mark thought.

Mark had a cotton crop to gather, he couldn't depend on Powell, and these five Negro slaves, were the only true friends he had.

"Bill, if you think the cotton is dry enough, then we'll start picking it tomorrow morning," Mark told him. "Get the pick sacks and baskets ready this evening, and we'll go ahead without Powell, or his lovely wife. I'm depending on you, for I don't know the first thing about picking cotton."

"Mos'a Mark, this is a time when we's got'a do what we's got'a do, to stay 'head of the devil," replied Bill, as they walked back toward the barn. "You ain't got nothing to worry 'bout, fer the Big Mos'a in the sky is on our side, and He gon'a hep' us get out'a this mess too."

Bill and his two boys went back to the barn to finish greasing the wagon wheels, and mending the sideboards, while Martha and her mother made sure the pick-sacks and baskets were in good condition. Mark went back up to the house to where the Powells were still sitting on the porch, looking out across the cotton fields. How lazy he is, Mark thought, as he walked past Powell, on his way toward his room.

"Well, did you and the niggers get the cotton picked?" Asked Powell, in a hateful voice. "You've been out there long enough to pick it, and I'll bet the niggers trampled down half of it."

Mark suddenly stopped, and turned around. "No, we didn't pick any, but we plan to start in the morning," replied Mark. "About half of the boles are open, and Bill suggested that we start picking before it looses any more weight. In my opinion, he's right, even though you might disagree."

"Bill said! Bill said!" Powell mocked. "That's all I hear out of you. That nigger doesn't have any sense, and he doesn't know when to start picking the cotton. But, he's your nigger, and it's your cotton he's wasting!"

"Sir, you'd be surprised how much sense he has, when it comes to growing cotton," Mark said, thinking of Bill's assessment of Powell. "In your honest opinion, and as foreman, would you recommend that we allow the cotton to dry a little longer, and take a chance of the rain damaging it?"

"No matter what that darned, stupid nigger has to say, anybody with good sense, knows that it's not ready to pick!" Powell snapped.

"Sir, I'm not a dog, to be spoken to like that!" Mark scolded. "I'll do whatever I must in order to protect my crop, for I see that you don't care if it's picked, or not. Bill's a slave, but he's honest, and concerned, and he's not afraid of work. You're lazy to the bone, just like my father said, and if I might add, you're disrespectful, contrary, and downright stupid, and unable to listen to reason. Call those slaves stupid, if that's what you like, but I have more confidence and trust in them, than I have in you!"

Mark realized that he shouldn't have repeated what his father said about the man, but he'd grown tired of being criticized, and tired of Powell's lack of common sense and understanding. Even at the risk of Powell telling about what he had planned for the slaves, he didn't want to be walked on.

Powell was taken aback by Mark's words. "Go ahead and depend on a nigger for advice, for I wouldn't help you now, if my life depended on it!" Replied Powell, hatefully. "Keep messing around with that nigger gal, too!"

"Very well, then!" Said Mark. "Just let me handle the crop the best way I can, and stop lower-rating the only friends I have – the five Negro slaves!"

Nothing else was said for a few moments. Mark hated to have to speak to an adult in such a manner, but his patients with Powell, had been spent. Mark slowly turned, to go on to his room.

"Look, boy!" Powell lashed out. "I don't intend for you to live here in my house, and talk to me in such a way! If your father knew how disrespectful you are to me, and my wife, he'd beat the devil out of you!"

"You, Sir, are disrespectful to me!" Mark stood his ground. "We reached an agreement, and I intend to keep my promise. But you, Sir, came apart at the seams, because of my personal view on certain matters. Let me remind you that this is my farm, my house, and my slaves, and I'll still be here after you're long gone! Now Sir, do I make myself perfectly clear?"

"Your problem is, that you don't know a darned thing about how to operate a farm, and you won't listen to me, either!" He snorted.

"But, I've never questioned your ability as a farmer!" Mark replied, in a stern voice. "Your stubborn attitude, and your dislike for the way I treat the slaves, has blinded you from reality. The moment you heard of what I had planned for the slaves you swelled up like a big bullfrog, and acted as though it was coming out of your pocket."

"Then, let me ask you something," said Powell. "If you claim to respect my ability as a farmer, why didn't you ask me to go along with you to look at the cotton, instead of taking that trashy bunch of niggers along? You don't appreciate what I've done around here, and you won't even let me have anything to say, when it comes to making decisions!"

Mark looked at him, and shook his head. "Wy you old fool!" Mark lashed out. "I asked you to look at the cotton, but you wouldn't go with me!"

"I don't remember you asking me," Powell lied. "But, you trust a stupid nigger more than you trust me, and I'm glad that you didn't ask me."

Mark could hardly believe his own ears. Filled with disgust, and totally aggravated, he decided to approach the matter from another angle.

"You might deny what you said, for you obviously put no stock in your own words anyway. But, when I say something, I don't go back on my word," Mark firmly stated. "Sir, do you agree with that philosophy as well?"

Thus far, his wife hadn't attempted to enter the discussion, and because Powell couldn't argue with Mark's last remark, he decided to switch to another subject. Even so, he wouldn't openly admit that Mark was right.

"We're talking about niggers, and if you pay them they'll think that you are weak, and that you need them, and then they'll take advantage of you every time you turn around," Powell snapped. "Other niggers will expect the same thing, and we'll be at war with the black-bastards!"

His tirade was so farfetched, and unimaginable, until Mark decided not to honor it with a reply. He turned, and walked back down the steps, for he knew that it was impossible to reason with the man. Still it was sad, he thought. He decided to go back and help the slaves, instead of going on into his room.

"It's come to the point where I'll have to take the bull by the horns," said Powell, to his wife, as Mark walked away. "I think

I'll head out toward Nate Simpson's place in the morning, and see if I can find out more about the nigger gal. So, Simpson says that I'm lazy!"

"Lazy, who says!" His wife squawked. "Where did you hear that?"

"You must not have been listening, for according to Mark, his father says that I'm a lazy person," he pouted.

"Well, of all the nerve, and after you've worked so hard for all these years, to keep up this place!" She sneered. "I'd tell Simpson all I knew, then add some to it, if I were you! Mark called your hand, and if I were you, I'd lay all my cards on the table."

"You're right, as always," he replied, "and now that he's started this fire, I'll see that it keeps burning. Can you think of anything else?"

"Well, you could say that you caught Mark and that gal in the very act, down at the barn," she coaxed. "Better yet, say that somebody else told you, then you won't be blamed for starting a rumor. I'll back you all the way, and in case you need it, my Christian-friends will help. It's our Christian-duty, you know, and the Lord will bless you."

"I've already told you that we'd have to be awful careful in how we went about this, so leave everything up to me," he sternly replied.

As soon as the dew dried off the cotton the following morning, Mark and the five slaves headed into the fields to start picking cotton, and unless it rained, or they were hindered some other way, they should have it picked over for the first time, in about a week. Mark was happy because they had done so well during his first year as a farmer, and the slaves were looking forward to being paid for working, which would be the first time in their life that they would have something that they could call their own.

Powell slipped down to the barn and saddled his mare, then he headed out for Nate Simpson's plantation in an effort to sow his seeds of deceit, and try to sever the relationship between Mark and his father. Powell and Nate were not close friends, and he was taking an awful chance by trying to create hatred in Nate's heart for his son. However, his heart was set on laying claim to the farm, and he was willing to take that chance. It was almost noon when he finally arrived at Nate's mansion, where he found Nate sitting on the front porch.

" Well, what brings you up this way?" Asked Nate, as Powell dismounted, and tied his mare to a hitching post. "Is something wrong with my boy?"

"Nothing's wrong with him," replied Powell, as he walked up the steps to the porch. "I had some business in this area, and I just stopped by for a brief visit."

Sensing that somethng really was wrong, Nate quickly jumped up, and opened the door. "Come on inside and we'll have a cup of coffee, then you can tell me what's on your mind. I never have thought very much of you anyway, so what you have to say, better be worth me wasting my time on!" Nate said.

Seated at the dining table, as he sipped on a cup of coffee, Powell began to carefully lay out the viscous plan he had for destroying Mark.

"While it's on my mind," said Powell, "I'd like to know if you have a neighbor by the name of Johnson, or Johnston. I'm not sure of his name."

"Yes I do, Ephraim Johnson!" Nate replied. "What business is that of yours? I had no idea that you even knew him."

"And I suppose you've had some business dealings with him, bought slaves from him, sold him some maybe," Powell prodded. "Am I right?"

"I have, a lot of times!" Simpson answered impatiently. "What is that to you, anyway? Has something happened to him?"

"No, it's just that..." Powell purposely stammered. "Oh well, let me ask you something else. Have you rented a buck from him, during the past year or so? I really need to know, before I say anything else."

"Yes, and a couple of times this month," he replied. "In fact, the gal that I gave to Mark was bred by his buck, and she should have had the baby by this time. Has she had the baby yet?"

"Are you talking about Bill's gal, the one they call Martha?" Quickly asked Powell. "Is she supposed to have a baby?"

"Yes, that's her name, Martha!" Simpson growled. "Was it a boy, or girl that she had? I told Mark to ask your wife to watch after her, for that buck gets some mighty big babies, and she is young, you know."

"We must not be talking about the same gal, for the gal that Mark brought with him, is not even pregnant, as far as I know," Powell told him.

"She's what, not pregnant!" Nate bellowed. "Is that the truth, or is that another one of your lies? You've always been a liar, and I'm not sure if you're telling the truth, for that doesn't sound right. I let Mark put the buck with her, and he kept putting him back with her every day, until he was sure that she was pregnant."

"But I'm telling the truth this time, I swear!" Powell said, holding up his hand. "I knew that something was wrong! Now that I know that she should have had a baby, when she's not even pregnant, it explains everything."

"What in the devil do you mean?" Nate asked him. "Are you trying to say that my son is mixed up in this, and that he might be the cause of the gal not being pregnant? Is that what you mean?"

"Yes, I really do!" He replied, acting as if he was about to cry. "This really hurts us, and my wife walked the floors and cried last night, because we think the world of him. We love that boy, as if he were our own child, I tell you!"

Simpson got up from the table, then went over and stood near a window for a moment. He wanted to believe Powell, but he had some doubt. He finally returned to the table, and sat staring at the man for a moment longer. Powell was known to have lied to him before, therefore, Nate wanted to be absolutely sure that he wasn't telling another lie this time, as well.

"According to that, you're saying that my own son lied to me about putting the buck with that gal," he replied. "Is that what you really mean?"

"All I'm saying, is that she's not pregnant," replied Powell. "This has me confused, yet on the other hand, I understand everything now."

"What kind of darned remark is that?" Asked Nate. "You either know, or you don't know! Say what's on your mind, and stop pussy-footing around!"

"I hate to bring you bad news," Powell baited him, "for I know that you love him, and that it's going to hurt you real bad." He bowed his head, as he waited for a reply. He acted as if he was wiping a tear from his eye.

A moment later, Simpson cleared his throat. "And, exactly what has been going on, that you haven't told me about?" He asked. "I'd like to know what it is, good or bad."

"He's your son, but he has some stupid ideas about slavery. He says that he wants to put a stop to it, claims it's not right, displeasing to God, as well," spoke Powell, very cautiously. "He

112

plans to pay the slaves for working, and set them free, too! That's hard for me to imagine, and him being the son of such a great supporter of slavery as you."

Simpson shook his head. "I know my son well, and he's just pulling your leg about paying them, and setting them free," Nate laughed. "He's a genuine Simpson, a slave-driver by birth, and it's in his blood!"

"That's what I thought too, until we both talked it out, and he convinced me that he really was serious," Powell went on. "And like I said, he's going to share his part of the money from the crop with them too."

In an instant, Simpson grabbed Powell by the shirt collar, and shook him real hard. "Don't lie to me, you sorry bastard!" He shouted. "He hates the niggers as much as I do, and he wouldn't stoop that low!"

Shaking himself free from Nate's grip, Powell sneered, as he looked Nate straight in the eye. "You hope so, but you should come around sometime when he's not expecting you, and see for yourself." Powell suggested. "He treats them far better than he treats me, or my poor innocent wife, and that gal, she has real moo-cow eyes for him."

"Can you prove that?" Simpson asked angrily. "Nobody comes into my home and runs my family down, unless he can back it up! I want proof, otherwise, I assure you, that you're a dead-man! Do you understand?"

"My wife will back me up. She won't lie, and she'll place her hand on the Bible, too!" Powell assured him. "She's so hurt, until she can't look at him without crying. The way he treats the niggers, and the disrespect he has shown for us, really has taken it's toll on my poor wife, and me too."

Simpson flew mad. "Get out of my house, you sorry bastard!" He yelled, in a loud voice, as he shook his fist in Powell's face. "I'm tired of hearing all those lies about my son!"

Quickly jumping up from the table, Powell hurried toward the door, for he had clearly angered Simpson. This seemed to have backfired on him, for it now seemed like Simpson was more angered at Powell, than he was at Mark.

"Look, Nate!" He made one last effort. "He got off on the wrong track, for there's talk about him having intercouse with the nigger gal. They say a nigger has a unique way about them, and she's the cause of it."

Simpson got up from the table, and Powell quickly went on outside, for he had always been afraid of Nate.

"Good-day, my lying friend, and make sure that you don't come back around here again!" Nate scolded, as he quickly slammed the door shut.

Julie Simpson and their daughter Susan were away visiting a neighbor at this time, and Nate had no one with whom to discuss this problem, so he paced back and forth through the house, as he tried to sort things out in his mind. Even though he hated Powell, and he knew that he was a liar, yet he seems to know a lot about the situation, Nate thought. Then, he decided to ride over to where Ephriam Johnson lived and talk with the buck himself, for he might be able to shed more light on the subject.

Mr. Johnson was standing near the barn when Nate arrived, and this visit by Nate surprised him, for Nate wasn't a social-type of person. He could tell by the expression on Nate's face, that something was wrong.

"It's nice to see you, Nate!" Said Mr. Johnson, curiously. "Don't tell me that you came to pay the fee for the buck, for it was my understanding that we'd settle up after the cotton was sold. And of course, you sold one gal to Mark, and I expect him to pay me, after the baby is born."

Nate forced a smile, as he climbed down from the buggy. Then, he walked over to where Ephriam Johnson stood with a strange expression on his face.

"No, it's not that," replied Nate. "Something is bothering me about the gal that I gave to Mark, and if it's all right with you, I'd like to speak to the buck about it. Maybe he can set my mind at ease, or I hope so."

Somewhat confused, Ephriam called out to one of the Negroes who were cleaning up the barnyard. "Go down there to the syrup mill where Robert's working, and tell him to get up here, right now!" Then turning to Nate, he said, "If you don't mind, I'd like to know what this is all about."

"Well, according to what someone told me, the gal that I gave to Mark is not even pregnant, and never was pregnant," Nate explained. "Let me first ask the buck something, then I'll explain everything. Might not be anything to it after all, might just be a rumor, could be a lie, too."

A few minutes later, the buck came running up to where they stood near the barn, and fearing that his master was going to punish him for something he had done, he fell to his knees before them. With tears in his eyes, he jerked off his hat and tucked it under his arm, and then he bowed his head.

"Mos'a Johnson, what tis it that you's gon'a whoop me fer this time?" He asked, pitifully. "I's ain't done what you thank I''s done, and I's got proof of that! Now, what wuz it that I's went and done, nohow?"

"Master Simpson wants to ask you a question, and if you don't answer him in the right way, or lie to him, I'll tie you to the stake, and beat the devil out of you!" Mr. Johnson scolded. "Now, go ahead and ask him, Nate!"

"Boy, do you remember being put with a gal over at my place, back before Christmas?" Nate asked. "My son Mark, took you to her."

The man trembled with fright, for even though he hadn't told anybody what had happened, Nate had somehow found out just the same, and he remembered Mark saying that he'd kill him, if this ever happened.

"Mos'a Simpson, I's hate to have to say this 'bout yo' boy, but he jabbed a butcher knife in my ribs, and didn't let me get to her," he replied, as he pulled up his shirt, and showed him a scar. "He say he gon'a kill me if you's ever found out, and now you is, and I's a dead nigga, fer sho'."

Nate's face turned red, with anger, "Let me make sure that I understand you correctly," said Nate. "Do you swear on your life, that he wouldn't let you breed the gal? I'll kill you, if you lie to me! Do you clearly understand?"

"Yass'uh, Mos'a Simpson, it's the gospel truf', it sho' is!" Replied the buck, as his whole body trembled with fright. "Will he kill me anyhow, eb'em if I wudn't the one that told you?"

"Get out of my sight, you stupid, lying bastard!" Nate yelled. "He's my son, and I won't stand here and listen to you telling lies on him!"

"Go on back to work now," Ephriam told the buck, "and I'll handle this with Nate. But, if you lied on that boy, you'll have the devil to pay!"

Simpson stood and shook his head, for it was hard for him to imagine that his own son would do such a thing, and even though he wanted to think the buck had lied, he knew he had not.

"It's hard for me to think that Mark would do such a thing as that, but I know the buck was telling the truth," Nate sighed. "It hurts, to bring up a child in the way you want him to go, and make plans for his future, then learn later that you don't know anything about him at all. I wish now, that he had died when he was just a baby."

"I hate that it happened, if it really did, and I'll beat the devil out of Robert because he didn't tell me when it first happened," Ephriam said, in an effort to make Nate feel better. "Do you want me to do it right now?"

"Do as you wish, for he's your nigger, but he had no other choice than to do what Mark said," Nate countered. "He must be telling the truth, for what he said, backs up what I've already heard. This is one thing, that Mark will regret for the rest of his life, and I'll see to that!"

"I realize how you must feel, but I imagine the girl influenced him," Ephriam told him. "A nigger is good at getting what they want, and I wouldn't be too hard on him, if I were you. He's just a boy, you know."

"I know, but it breaks my heart to know that he'd allow a nigger to cause him to stoop that low," Nate replied. "Keep this between us if you will, for my name is at stake, my reputation, and my southern pride as well."

"Nothing will be said," he promised. "He's still young, and he'll come around one day, you'll see."

Without a reply, Nate Simpson climbed back into his buggy, and sped away toward home. As the mare swiftly trotted along, he regretted that he had been so harsh with Powell, and that he hadn't taken time to hear him out. Without doubt, there was more that Powell could have told him, he thought.

The sun was going down when Nate arrived back at the mansion, and to his surprise, he saw Powell sitting on the porch, smoking his pipe. He hadn't yet told Nate all that he wanted him to hear, and at the risk of angering him even more, he decided to return and complete his mission.

"I know that you're upset at me, but I couldn't afford to leave with bad feelings between us," said Powell, as he got up and walked over to the edge of the porch. "I realize that he's your son, and I shouldn't have said what I did, even though it was true. From now on I'll stay in my place, and tend to my own business too!" He pleaded, trying to get back in good favor with Nate. "Will you forgive me?"

"You made me as mad as the devil, but unfortunately, I owe you an apology for thinking that you lied to me," Simpson replied. "Even though you weren't aware of what it was, you really did stumble on to something. The buck didn't bother the gal, for Mark threatened to kill him, if he did. I'm sorry, but I couldn't make myself believe that you were right about my son."

"I felt bad for having told you, but it was beginning to get the best of me," replied Powell. "I won't say anything about this to anybody else, and I must be on my way, for I've already caused enough damage, as it is."

"You can't cause any more damage than has already been done, and it won't be long 'til dark, so you might as well spend the night," Simpson replied, as he walked upon the porch, and opened the door. "I want to hear everything you have to say about what's been going on down there, but for God's sakes, don't let my wife find out. He's her special child, if you know what I mean."

"I understand, for I had that figured out a long time ago," said Powell. "I hope what he's doing, don't hurt your reputation, for you've done an awful lot to help the South maintain the right to use niggers as slaves."

"I appreciate that, and again, I'm sorry for thinking that you were lying about my son," said Simpson, as he motioned to Powell, to follow him into the house. "I want to know all about my son's dealings with the niggers, and most of all, what you know about him and that nigger gal."

Powell followed him on into the parlor, where he saw Mrs. Simpson reading a book, and she glanced up at him and smiled. She was glad that he had come to visit, for now, she could find out about Mark, she thought.

"Hello, Mr. Powell," she politely spoke. "It's nice of you to visit us. I've wondered how Mark's doing. He hasn't been to visit since last Christmas, and with the cotton now ready to pick, he probably won't have time to get away anytime soon. You should have brought him with you."

He didn't reply, as he followed Nate across the room to a settee, but the coldness of the expression on both their faces, told her that something wasn't exactly right. Realizing that she had no place among such disgruntled persons, as they seemed to be at the moment, she politely excused herself, and left the room. As soon as she closed the door behind her, Powell started telling Nate everything that he knew, and adding other things as well.

"I didn't see this with my own eyes, but according to what one Christian lady told my wife, she caught Mark messing around with that gal," Powell told him. "Claimed that she caught them in the very act, down at the barn."

"Did she actually catch them in the act, or did she just see them in the barn together, and only imagined the rest?" Nate asked, seriouisly. "I know that women sometimes imagine that things happened, when nothing really happened at all. What I want is the truth, and nothing else."

"She actually saw them," Powell affirmed, "and she was almost too upset to talk, when she finally made it up to our house."

"What was she doing at the barn, anyway?" Asked Nate, still trying as he might, to defend his son. "Was she snooping around, when she caught them?"

"She walked past the barn on her way up to the house, for she planned to study the Sunday School lesson with my wife," he lied. "The barn door wasn't closed, and there they were, as plain as day. She stood and watched until it was over. Too shocked to move, I suppose, and all shook up."

"My God, what happened to him?" Nate sighed. "I ought to go down there right now and kill the whole darn bunch, including Mark! I'll do that, too!"

"Don't get yourself in an uproar, for it won't change what's already been done," Powell said, giving him a saintly look. "I thought it was my duty as a Christian to tell you, so that you might correct it, before it went too far. My wife has talked with him many times, and begged him not to become involved with the niggers, but he laughs in her face." Powell laid it on heavy.

They talked into the night, with Powell saying anything he could think of that might hurt Mark, while he tried to embellish certain vital points, that he thought might benefit more. They devised a scheme to strip Mark of everything he had, except for his slaves, and the farm. They claimed it was for his good. They hoped Mark would turn on the slaves, and blame them for everything. The man had spun his web of deceit so tightly around Simpson at that point, until he would have killed his own son, had Powell suggest it.

Early the following morning, Powell saddled up his mare to go back home, for he'd sown his evil seeds. He felt sure that Nate would snuff out the plan Mark had for the slaves, and cause them to hate him because he didn't pay them as he had promised. And, if this happened to Mark he'd throw up his hands and quit, and Nate might sell the farm to him, Powell thought.

"Like I said last night, Brother Powell, keep me posted as to when he'll be collecting for the cotton," said Nate, as Powell climbed into the saddle. "I'll strip him as clean as a hound's tooth! When I'm through with him, he'll wish he'd never lied to me, or looked at that gal's black ass!"

"I'll let you know when he plans to collect for the cotton, for God knows that I need my rightful share," Powell promised. "My wife and I have worked real hard all summer, and now that it's ready to pick, we'll have to pick most of it ourselves. She's picking cotton today, even though she's hardly able to stand on her feet. I must hurry on back, so I can help the poor soul."

"Don't say anything to Mark, or anyone else, except for your lovely wife, of course," Simpson warned. "Keep pushing Mark and the niggers like you've been doing, for the cotton must be picked before the rain sets in."

Powell spoke to his mare, and as she swiftly trotted along, he felt proud that he had accomplished his mission. If things went as scheduled, Mark would be ruined. He proudly rode along, as he dreamed of being a landowner himself.

It was now several weeks later. Even though the Powells hadn't helped Mark and the slaves, the cotton had been picked and sold, and Mark was waiting for the banker to let him know when to pick up his money.

The local banker, Ellis Bland, was in charge of collecting the money for cotton that was sold to Europe, for the South didn't try to support the Union and therefore, it sold hardly anything to the North or the West. If a farmer owed the General Store, or anyone else for supplies, the bill would be turned over to the banker for collection. For a fee, the banker would deduct it from the amount of money the farmer had received for the cotton the banker sold for him, and then the farmer would get what was left. Owners of large plantations, and those who had large sums of money on deposit at the bank, generally controlled what the banker did, as far as helping smaller farmers. It was their way to keep smaller farmers under control.

Mark had just returned from town, where he had gone to pick up some items at the General Store, and while in town, he stopped by the bank to speak with Mr. Bland, who told him that he could pick up his money tomorrow. Mark really was excited, and he could hardly wait to tell Bill.

"Well, tomorrow's the big day!" Mark smiled, as he slapped Bill on the shoulder. "I'll be collecting for the cotton we sold, and unless you plan to do somethng else, I'd like for you to ride into town with me. We need to get there real early, for I imagine that every farmer in the country will be there."

"I's rail happy fer you, fer you sho' wuk'd pow'ful hard all summer, to he'p make the crop," replied Bill, with a grin. "You didn't sot the wul'd on far' as a cotton-picker, but you's done yo' part. Wid a pocketful of money, you can strut 'round like a big farmer now!"

"I wouldn't say that, for one crop, don't make a man a big farmer," Mark replied. "Half of what I get will go to Powell, and of course, I'll divide my part with you folks, like I promised. By the way, if you can come up to the house later on tonight we'll go over the receipts, and make sure that we were credited for each load of cotton that you took to the gin."

"Naw'suh, I's better stay 'way from that Pow'l feller, fer he ain't gon'a like fer no nigga to come flogging in on him adder dark," replied Bill.

"He won't mind, for he says that we made more cotton this year, than he's made during all the time he's been here," Mark told him. "Don't let me down, for I'll be expedting you a little after the sun goes down." They talked, and laughed together for several more minutes, and then Mark walked up to the house to tell Powell the good news.

Though Mark didn't know, Powell spoke with the banker and Mark's father, when he was in town yesterday, and Nate promised Powell that he would stop by later on this evening, for a visit. Mark's mother had overheard them talking when Powell came to visit Nate, and during a heated argument after Powell went back home, Nate promised Mark's mother, that he'd try to work out a deal with Mark. They had planned to stay at an Inn tonight, and following Nate's visit at Powell's house, Nate was to bring Mark back to the Inn, so she could spend some time with him. Although Powell hadn't said anything to Mark about Nate's scheduled visit, they had been busy all day, cleaning up the house.

"Hurry and get finished up!" Snapped Powell. "Simpson said he'd be here a little after sundown. We don't want Mark to barge in, and find us cleaning up the house, for he might become suspicious."

"When you spoke with Nate, did he say why he was coming here?" Asked his wife, as she hurried about.

"No, not exactly," he lied. "All I know, is that he's going to discuss something with Mark, and that he wanted me to meet with him and Ellis Bland, before Bland went to the bank in the morning. We'll meet at Bland's house."

Later that evening, after they had eaten supper, Mark took a box down off a shelf, then went into the kitchen, and sat down at the table. Mark had kept all the receipts from the cotton gin in the box, and he poured them out on the table, so that he could check over them. Even though he hadn't said anything to the Powells about it yet, he wondered why the house was so clean during the middle of the week, and why the Powells were all dressed up.

"Pardon my asking, but why is the house so clean tonight, and why are you all dressed up?" He asked. "Is someone coming to visit, or were you planning to go somewhere?"

"We're not going anywhere, it's already past six o'clock, and nobody is coming, as far as I know," Powell lied. "Because the niggers never take a bath, or sweeps the floor, don't mean that we have to live like them."

"I didn't mean to get your bowels in an uproar!" Mark replied, as he sat and shook his head. "If you were expecting company, I was going to get these papers up off the table, and take them into my room and look at them."

"Why in the devil do you have them scattered out on the table for, anyway?" He asked in a hateful voice. "I hope you don't intend to eat the darn things!"

"Like I told you earlier, I'm to meet with the banker tomorrow, to settle up for the cotton, and I wanted to go over them with Bill, and make sure that we got credit for each load of cotton that he hauled to the gin," Mark explained to him. "I asked Bill to come up here tonight, if it's all right with you."

"Then, you plan to pay them for what work they did!" Powell spoke in anger. "That makes you look like a fool!"

Mark didn't bother to comment. He didn't want to get into another fight with these wonderful folks. He'd heard enough from them already.

A few moments later a knock was heard at the door, and Mark jumped up to go and open the door, for he knew it was Bill. He knew if Powell answered the door he was likely to say somethng hurtful to Bill, and Mark didn't want that to happen.

"Hey, what a pleasant surprise this is!" Said Mark, when he opened the door, and saw his father and his sister Susan, standing on the porch. "Come on in, for it's been almost a year since I've seen you, Susan! Let me give you a big hug." He hugged Susan, then she and their father stepped inside.

After his father shook hands with Powell, and spoke to his wife, he went over and stood near a window, and looked out at the moon, which was shining almost as bright as day. When Susan sat down near the fireplace, Mark saw her glance into the kitchen, and he knew that she was looking at the papers he had scattered out on the kitchen table.

"Don't pay any attention to the mess on the table, for I was looking over the receipts, to see if we got credit for all the cotton we delivered," Mark told her. "We really did well this year, and I plan to go to the bank in the morning and get our money. You folks couldn't have picked a better time to be here, for you can help me celebrate my first year as a farmer."

"This isn't a social call, by any means!" Snapped Simpson, as he quickly turned and looked at Mark. "I'll make this as brief as possible, for it's a family matter, rather personal, you might say."

Mark was frightened. "Is there something wrong back home?" He asked, in great concern. "Is Mother all right? Is there a death in the family?"

His father didn't reply, instead, he went over to where Powell was seated near the fireplace, and shook his hand again.

"I'm sorry for having barged in on you unexpected like this, but I have a business matter to discuss with my son," Nate said, winking at Powell.

"That's quite all right," replied Powell, "for Mark and I were looking at the receipts, to make sure that we got full credit for the cotton we hauled to the gin. It took working together as a team, including the niggers, but we finally accomplished our goal."

Although Mark cringed at the statement Mr. Powell just made about how he had helped make the crop, he decided to let things go as they were, for it was obvious by the expression on his father's face, that somethng was wrong.

"Like Mr. Powell said, we really did have a good cotton crop," Mark told his father. "We stand to make a lot of money, for we managed to get it on the market while the price was right."

"You said that "we" would make a lot of money, and I take that as meaning you and Mr. Powell," replied his father. "Is that what you mean?"

"That's what I meant," Mark replied, feeling a coldness in his father's voice. "Like you already know, each of us will get an equal share of whatever we get for the cotton, and I'm looking forward to having something of my own. This will be the first time in my life, that I've earned any money."

"Making money is one thing, but throwing money away, is somethng that a fool does!" Said his father, in a hateful voice. "We have a few smart men in the world, but more darn fools, than I care to mention!"

"I don't understand what you mean," said Mark, glancing over at Powell. "Go ahead and ask Mr. Powell, and he'll tell you that I haven't wasted a penny of the money that you gave to me! I spent it wisely, like I was taught."

"You might not have wasted any of that money," said his father, "but if what I hear is true, your part of the money from the crop this year, is already being thrown to the wind."

"I'd like to know what you heard, and where you heard it from," replied Mark, as he went back into the kitchen, and sat down at the table. "It's like you say, you can't believe everything that you hear, and I hope you're smart enough not to believe that. It's a lie, no matter who told it!"

Simpson rushed into the kitchen, and jerked Mark up from the table by his shirt collar. "I need to stomp the devil out of you, right now!" Nate yelled at him. "It was stupid of me, to let you talk me into giving you this farm in the first place! You've ruined my name!"

The Powells had turned away, and were now staring into each other's eyes, and Susan sat motionless in the corner of the living room.

"The slaves and I did all the work that was done around here, including making the crop, and picking every bole of cotton with our own hands!" Mark yelled, as he shook loose from his father. "Powell was so darn lazy he wouldn't help tend the crop, and he and his lovely wife, didn't help pick it, either. I don't care what he told you, it's a lie!" Then looking at Powell, he added, "Wy, you sorry, low down bastard! How could you do such a thing?"

"Powell told me that you planned to divide your share with them niggers, and that you planned to set them free!" Simpson

123

snorted, seething with anger. "You've turned out to be a disgrace to South Carolina, and to the name Simpson! I hate you, as much as I hate the niggers you stand up for!"

"I'm sorry, but I don't see it that way," replied Mark. "I'm not doing you, or South Carolina any harm by standing up for the slaves. They're human beings, I'll treat them as such, and I plan to pay them for working, too!"

"Don't ever say such as that to me again!" Simpson yelled, stomping his foot on the floor. "South Carolina is a slave-state, and I intend to see that it stays that way, too! I won't have my friends talking about me, because my son is a nigger lover. I'll see you dead, first!"

"And, my personal convictions don't count any at all," Mark replied. "I am a born citizen, you know, and the Constitution gives me the right to speak out against slavery, if that's how I feel, and I plan to do just that!"

Mark went over and stood in the doorway leading into the living room, and his father stood silently for a moment, with his head bowed. Although Simpson knew that his son was right, he'd never admit it, and now, he must fight this battle on the same grounds, he thought.

"This might be the way things are now," Simpson retorted, "but we're on the verge of having State's Rights, then things will swing our way. Then, I'd like to see you stand up and say something like that!"

"That makes no sense at all," said Mark. "It would be like letting each child do as he pleases, without fear of being punished! You can imagine where that would lead, and how long a family would stay together. I wonder how long this country would hold together, if each state did as it pleased, and passed only the laws that didn't conflict with it's stupid customs, and traditions!"

"That's what's wrong with the South, now!" Simpson yelled, as his anger grew worse by the moment. "We have too many nigger lovers trying to tell us how to run things! I gave you this farm so that you could learn how to handle niggers, but they're handling you! It's a disgrace to my name!"

"You somehow forget that I have my rights as well," Mark retorted. "Those slaves belong to me, and I can't see where I have a right to sell them, but I don't have a right to set them free. Dad, you know better than that."

"When you get to a point where you think as much of a nigger, as you do a white person, you're walking on mighty dangerous ground," sneered his father, avoiding a reply. "You are trying to create a racial problem, and it's liable to get all of the niggers killed, maybe you too, I'm afraid."

Thus far, Powell hadn't said anything, but feeling sure now that Simpson was on his side, he decided to get his two-cents worth in.

"That's what we've been telling him," interrupted Powell. "He acts like we don't know anything, classes us with niggers, and claims that they are as important as white folks. Plans to pay them, set them free, too!"

"Shut up your darn mouth, you sorry bastard!" Quickly replied Mark, shaking his fist at him. "You and your lovely wife are hypocrites, and troublemakers, and bold-faced liars! You're the cause of this, and if you open up your mouth again, I'll beat the devil out of you!"

There was complete silence for a time, for it was obvious that Mark would fight Powell in a heartbeat. Mark walked over to the table to put the papers back in the box, but his father thought he'd turned his back on him.

"Don't turn your back on me, boy!" Simpson screamed, as he kicked a chair across the floor. "I hate niggers, and anybody who stands up for them!" Mark noticed the same kind of hatred in his father's eyes now, as he'd seen in them the day he destroyed the cloth that he bought for Martha and her mother.

"Let me get one thing straight, right now!" Mark spoke in a stern voice. "I resent being called a Negro lover, for that doesn't describe me at all. I still honor you as my father, even though we might disagree, and I wish you'd consider me as your son, and stop referring to me in such a manner. Will you do that? Is it asking too much of you?"

"Then, why do you treat them like you do?" Asked his father. "You know that they have no heart or soul, and no sense to speak of, yet you treat them like white folks, pay them too!" Is that not what you call a nigger lover?"

"You, Sir, taught me to pay my debts, and pay a man when he works for me, as well," Mark replied, in a respectful voice. "The slaves have worked every day since they've been here, and I promised them something if they would help to get the place back in shape, and I plan to do just that too. I'll keep my promise to

Powell as well, even though he didn't help tend the crop, or pick a handful of cotton, for I'm that kind of person. What I pay the slaves will be out of my own pocket, not his, or yours, and you have no room to complain."

His father still wasn't moved. "Go ahead and pay them, but keep in mind, that you'll be dragging the Simpson name through the mud," his father pointed out, quite vividly. "I've worked too hard to let you destroy my name, over a buch of niggers! Honor and power, is associated with the name Simpson, and when you trample on me, I'll use my power to bring you down."

"There's nothing honorable about your name here tonight," Mark reminded him. "You call me a fool and a Negro lover, because I'm doing exactly as you taught me to do - be honest, and pay a man when he works for me."

"A darned fool, that's what you are!" Simpson scolded. "You don't know how to manage a farm, or handle a bunch of niggers, and you need to quit while you can. I'm not sure if you belong to me, and I have my doubts, now."

Mark realized now, more than ever before that he stood alone, except for the slaves who had no right to defend themselves, and were not able to help him. Even his own father disowned him, but he must stand his ground.

"I hate to have to put it this way, but I have no other choice," replied Mark, in a stern voice. "This is my farm, and you don't have a right to tell me how to treat my slaves. I refuse to be a slave to you, or to the customs and traditions of the South, and I won't stand for you to treat me like a slave, or as if I should bow down to you, because of your name."

"I have power, and money," boasted his father, stroking his chest, "and that's what makes the world turn. I have the law in my back pocket, and Ellis Bland at the bank, and just about everybody else around here. Do you say that the name Simpson doesn't mean anything?"

"I'm aware of your importance, for I've grown up with it pounded into my head like the gospel," Mark told him, "but, do any of those whom you spoke of, the law, the banker, or other farmers, care if you should even live or die? I'd rather think not."

"It don't matter who likes me, for I couldn't care less what others think of me!" Replied his father.

"I don't suppose you do, at that," Mark responded sharply, "but all the power and wealth you possess, don't frighten me at all."

"Just for that, I'll strip you as clean as a hound's tooth!" Shouted his father. "You'll be begging to be my stable-boy, when I get through with you! Now, do I make myself clear? Do you really want to see me in action?"

Following this, his father went over and propped his elbow on the mantel, and scuffed his shoe toe on the hearth. Mark's sister went over and whispered something to him, and he patted her on the head. It was obvious, that she had decided to say something in her father's defense.

"Mark, Daddy sized you up right!" She purred. "You've always liked the niggers, as far back as I care to remember, and especially that girl they call Martha. I've noticed the strange way you act when she's around, and the look you give her. Isn't that a sign that you like her, in a special way?"

"No, my dear sister," he replied, "I don't necessarily like the Negroes at all, but I do dislike the way they are treated. There's nothing wrong with being a friend to them, for they are human, whether you think so or not. The only real difference between them and us, is the color of their skin."

"I still remember you slipping food to them, every chance you got," she went on, "and what about the clothes you slipped out of the house, and took down there to them! Have you forgotten about that?"

"There wasn't anything wrong with me playing with them, for I didn't have a brother, and you were too prissy, to play with me," Mark replied. "I took left-over food to them, for it would have been thrown out anyway."

"It wouldn't surprise me, if you've been messing around with the gal, and maybe that's why you didn't let the buck get to her," she teased. "Could it be that you're sweet on her? Is she your black baby-doll?"

"That's quite enough out of you, Susan!" Mark scolded. "But while we're talking about Negroes, why don't you tell them what you and that Negro boy was doing in the barn that day. I'm sure that Dad would like to know what went on that day. Let them hear it from you first-hand, and let them be the one's to decide who's the real Negro lover."

Susan's face went ghostly white. "I, uh, I don't have any idea what you are talking about," she replied, "and Daddy knows that I hate niggers. I've never even been close to one of the nasty things!"

"Well, I'd say you were real close to a Negro that day!" Mark smiled, as he watched her squirm. "What do you have to say, my dear sister?"

"Slap his face, Daddy!" She cried, hugging her father. "He's ruined his own life, and now he's trying to ruin mine! Did you hear what he said?"

"Keep your low-down nigger loving lip off your sister!" His father shouted. "You don't need to drag her down into the hog pen with you!"

"I hate to have to say this," spoke Mark, as he reached over to open the door, "but I'll have to ask you nice folks to leave. I hope, that after you think things over, and realize that I am human, we can get together again for a friendly chat. I really am sorry, Dad."

"Then I'll go," said Simpson, motioning to Susan, "but be sure that you remember what I said." Then turning, and looking at Powell, he added, "Don't forget, tomorrow! Good night Mr. Powel, Mrs. Powell."

With that, Simpson and his daughter walked out the door, climbed into the buggy, and headed for a nearby Inn, to spend the night. Mark gathered up the receipts and put them back in the box, then looked keenly at Powell.

"Mr. Powell, you were too darned sorry and lazy to help us make the crop, and so low down in character, until you couldn't keep from running to him with everything that I told you!" Mark scolded.

"Don't blame me, for something your father said! Powell whined. "I had no more idea that he was coming tonight, than you did!" He lied. "I haven't even seen him, since he was here on his last visit."

"That's a lie, for a friend of mine told me that you spent the night with him, when your lovely wife told me that you had gone to pay your respect to a friend who had died," Mark countered. "You've betrayed my trust, and played the fool, and I'm ordering you out of this house by sundown tomorrow! The furniture belonged to Dad, and now it's mine, so leave it where it is."

Powell quickly jumped up, "That don't give me much time to make plans," he whined, "and that's not fair! You're treating me worse than a dog!"

"Not fair?" Mark snapped. "It wasn't fair for you not to help with the crop, yet you expect an equal share. You haven't shown any respect for me, and I see no need of respecting you. You, Sir, are nothing but trash!"

"Then, you're throwing us out without notice," his wife added, "and God knows that we have nowhere to go. You're tossing us out, like trash."

"Then I suppose that's what it is," Mark replied. "You treated me like trash, and you're being swept out with the same broom."

"And, will you be spending the night here with us?" She asked.

"No, thank you!" He replied, sharply. "I'd rather sleep in the barn, or in the hog pen, than to sleep here another night. I have too much respect for myself."

Mark walked outside and closed the door, then headed toward the barn, for he couldn't stand to be in the presence of these lovely folks any longer. The moon was shining real bright, and as he neared the barn, he saw Bill stånding in the barnyard.

"Howdy, Mos'a Mark." spoke Bill, politely. "The moon sho' is purdy and bright tonite, and that means that we's gon'a have a rail purdy day to'mar."

"I hope so, for tonight hasn't been so great," Mark replied, glancing up at the moon. "Why didn't you come up there, like I asked?"

"Well, I's did, then I's didn't," replied Bill, as he took off his hat, and scratched his head. "When I's seed yo' pappy's buggy, and here'd the racket inside, I's knowed that it wuzn't no place fer me. Then, I's sez to my'sef, Bill, you better keep yo' black-butt down here, and here I is."

"I must say that it wasn't very pleasant, for Powell had told Dad what I told him, and more too, I suppose," Mark told him. "We all said things that we'll regret later, and I'm afraid it's not over with yet. I really feel bad because of what happened, and because I didn't listen to you."

"I's told you that the devil wuz gon'a break loose, but you's didn't take it serious, fer you didn't thank this ole nigga knowed nothing," he replied, as he shook his head. "The devil done stayed quiet as long as he can, and he had to show his butt, one way, er the tuther."

"Well, I won't be bothered with Mr.Powell after tomorrow, for I told him to be out of the house, by tomorrow evening," he informed Bill. "I plan to sleep here in the barn tonight, for I don't trust that man, or his wife. They might melt lead, and pour it in my ear while I'm asleep," he chuckled.

"Sho' can't blame you much, fer being 'fraid of him," Bill agreed. "I's hate that you's got in trouble over us niggas, but I's done seed it coming down the road, and you wuz warned, too. What took place to'nite, is jus' a tiny bit of what's wait'n on down the road fer you."

"Forget about what happened up there tonight," Mark told him, "for it's all over with. Just remember to wake me up real early in the morning, for we need to get started by daylight. Will you wake me up in the morning?"

"Yass'uh, I's be down here rail early-like, wid a big cup'a coffee, and a bite to eats," Bill promised. "Fo' the ole rooster crows, I's be here."

Mark went into the barn where he'd spend the night, and Bill went on back home. Bill acted as though he hadn't even heard anything, but he'd heard what went on between Mark and his father, his sister and Mr. Powell as well, and he was concerned for Mark. He felt partly to blame for what had happend, and vowed to stand by Mark, even if it cost him his own life. Liza knew that Bill went up there tonight, and when he walked back into the house, she began to ask him how everything turned out.

"Well, how did thangs tu'n out up there?" Liza asked, as Bill took off his coat, and hung it on the back of a chair. "How much money is we gon'a get this year? Is we gon'a be rich, like them white folks is?"

"Hold on, jus' a minute!" He scolded. "The truf' is, I's didn't make it to the house adder all. And, I's don't know nothing 'bout no money."

"You's ain't been there!" Spoke Liza, in surprise. "If not, whu' is you been all this time? Does you's eb'em know yo'sef?"

"Well, I's been at the barn looking at the moon, and when Mos'a Mark got there, I's talked wid him fer a spell," he explained. "He gon'a sleep down at the barn to'nite, and he axed me to wake him up, early to'mar moan'n."

"Pray tell! What's he sleep'n in the barn, fer?" She asked. "Ain't he got no bed to sleep in, er is the bed-bugs done took over his bed?"

"Mos'a Simpson wuz up there, and when I's here'd all the cuss'n, yellin', and kicking thangs 'round, I's got out from there," he replied. "The ole man went crazy, and Mos'a Mark had to run him off. He told them Pow'l folks to be out of the house to'mar, too. That boy, he sho' wuz mad, upsot, too!"

"Oh Lord'ee, I's wonder what kin'a trouble that po' boy is gon'a get into next!" She sighed. "I's hate to hear that, fer he sho' be a good boy."

"Yass'am, he sho' is, but he stood his ground," he told her. "Like I's say, his pappy tucked his tail twixt his legs and headed back home, then the boy flew in on that ole Pow'l feller."

"I's glad to hear that, fer them folks wuzn't nothing but trouble," she replied. "Maybe he can get some res', now that they is leaving."

"But, the one I's 'fraid of, is his pappy," Bill pointed out. "He must'a found out what Mos'a Mark done fer Marthie, fer he called Mark a nigga lover. Sez he gon'a take ever'thang 'way from the boy, too."

They sat and talked a little longer, then went on to bed, for Bill was to wake Mark up early in the morning. Simpson classed them as being the "scum of the earth", stupid and ignorant, but they had a heart of gold, and they had as much love for Mark, as they did for their own children.

In the barn, Mark could not sleep. He felt completely alone, and cut off from his family. He wondered how much his mother knew about all this, and why she hadn't accompanied his father and his sister tonight. He felt like crying out, but tears would not come. The Powells, and even worse, his father and his sister had wronged him too.

Suddenly, he remembered the exchange with Susan. His father had somehow not taken up the remark about the buck and Martha. Amid all the uproar, Mark had forgotten all about this. Why had his father let it pass by? And how was it that Susan knew about the situation? Obviously, his father was holding on to this "trump card", to play against him at a later date. His father wasn't apt to forget something so noteworthy as that, for he was the type of person who would use whatever means that were available, in order to accomplish his goal. And, it didn't matter what it might take, or whom it might hurt.

The hour was late when Simpson and his daughter arrived at the Inn, where they would spend the night. Mrs. Simpson had come along with them, but at her husband's request, she stayed at the Inn until they returned. He lied to her, and said he planned to bring Mark back with them, so the whole family could be together for a few days. Julie hadn't seen Mark since he'd visited them last Christmas, and she was looking forward to spending time with him.

Entering the suite, Simpson expected Julie to be sound asleep, but she was wide awake, and waiting. "Where's my boy?" She asked him, beaming with excitement, as they entered the suite. "Why didn't he come back with you?"

"Your boy is the most ignorant person I've even seen, and he has finally lost his mind!" Nate said cruelly. "Your boy's a fool, to say the least!"

Julie was frightened. "Do you realize that he's our own flesh and blood, or do you even care?" She asked. "I didn't hear all that was said when that Powell fellow spent the night with you, but you changed, immediately after he returned home. What did he say to you, that night?"

"He's not a son of mine, and you're to blame for him acting like a fool, and feeling as he does about the niggers!" He scolded. "You always kept him to yourself - away from me - hidden from real life!" It was obvious, that he had turned his anger on her.

Susan ran to her mother, crying. "Daddy, don't do this! Your quarrel is with Mark - not with Mother! She hasn't done anything to you!"

"Go on to bed, Susan, for I'm used to his scathing comments," her mother said, as tears trickled down her face. "Something didn't go his way."

"Do what she said, Missy," Nate said to Susan, "for we might decide to discuss you and that nigger boy! The whole darn family had turned to trash!"

Susan ran into her bedroom, crying as though her heart was broken. Why had she thought herself safe from her father's temper. She felt bad because she took sides against her brother. He's a wild and furious monster, and he's turned against all of us. She lay in bed, and thought to herself.

"What was that all about, anyway?" Julie asked. "It's very obvious that you're upset at Mark for some reason, but where does Susan fit into all this?"

"Nothing to you, Madam!" He sneered, tossing his coat down on the floor, in anger. "My daughter just needs to remember her place, that's all."

"But, would you please tell me what Mark did, to upset you in such a way as this?" She asked. "Did that Powell fellow, start some kind of rumor on my boy? Is that what happened?"

"Your boy's, a darned nigger lover!" He cringed. "He treats the niggers as if they were human beings, and he plans to pay them for working! Nobody in his right mind gives a nigger anything, except for a hard time, and a whipping at a stake! He's ruining my name, I tell you!" He raved on.

"Oh, I see now." she replied. "For a moment there, you had me thinking that he'd done a great wrong. All farmers don't treat the slaves like trash, like some do, and they don't go about hurting their own son, either."

"And, he lied about putting the buck with that gal, for he wouldn't allow the buck to come close to her!" He bellowed, as he paced the floor. "He's a fool, I tell you!"

"I'm not sure that I understand how he lied," Julie observed. "You said she was pregnant, and you said that you told Mark to ask Mrs. Powell to look after her, during childbirth. Didn't you tell me that?"

"She was never pregnant!" He yelled. "He wouldn't let the buck do his job, and he threatened to kill the buck, if anybody ever found out what he did! He took Bill's family with him, so I wouldn't find out about it. He's a darned fool, for he's breaking a southern tradition, and dragging my name through the mud!" He snorted. "I won't stand for that!"

Susan had been listening from the bedroom, and she quickly jumped up and went back and rejoined them. Somehow, she must get back in his good grace. Mark's life as a Simpson was over, and she knew that. She must think of some way to save herself, for she couldn't afford to suffer the same fate.

"This isn't helping matters one bit," Susan interrupted, "for we've let Mark's mistakes put us at each other's throat. No matter what he did to tear this family apart, I still love both of you. Mark's the reason you're fussing like this, and not because you're mad at each other, or at me."

133

"You're right, as always," Simpson smiled, as he motioned to her to come to him. "I'm sorry that I said what I did about you tonight." He placed his arm around her, and hugged her tightly. "Please forgive me, dear."

Julie saw Susan's self-satisfying smirk, and was glad that they had made peace, but her heart ached, for Susan had hurt Mark, in order to accomplish it.

"Mother, you should have heard what Mark said, and right in front of the Powells, too!" Said Susan, as she sat down next to her mother. "He said that I had intercourse with a nigger-boy! How could he say such a thing!"

"None of this makes sense to me! Mark loves you, and I wonder what caused him to attack you like that," she softly replied. "Can you explain why?"

"He's lost his mind, I tell you!" Spoke up Simpson. "The slaves managed to use some kind of weird power to control him, voodoo, I suppose. They brought it with them from Africa! He's not the same boy, I tell you!"

"Other farmers have freed their slaves, and they pay them for tending the land as sharecroppers," Julie countered. "The slaves belong to him, and it's up to him to do as he pleases with them, or I thought so, up until now."

"But, those farmers aren't Simpsons!" Snapped Nate, stroking his chest. "Simpsons, are born slave-drivers - it's in their blood. I won't let him, or anybody else break that chain! I'll kill him, first!"

"According to the Constitution, he has the right to be against something, the same as you have a right to uphold it," she tried to explain to her angry husband. "You've already deprived him of his family, but I wish you wouldn't deprive him of the only friends he has left, his slaves."

"I know, but if I allow him to treat his slaves different from the way I treat mine, what will folks think of me?" He asked. "I won't be able to face others with pride, and pride, is the backbone of the South. I'd rather die as a pauper, and without a friend in the world, than to die without pride."

"Mark must be his own man, like you've been," she told him in a serious voice. "Don't condemn him because he disagrees with you. Your best friends do that every day. Even your own father disagreed with you while you were growing up, but he didn't hate you, or say that you were not his son."

"Let me say this, before I go to bed," Simpson remarked. "I swore that I'd strip him as clean as a hound's tooth, and if I live 'til tomorrow, that's exactly what I'll do! I'll show him how far I'm willing to go to uphold the honorable name of Simpson, a proud generation, born slave-drivers!"

Nate had already said all he intended to say tonight. The three went on to bed, but neither of them were to enjoy very much sleep tonight.

Simpson was so angry with his son. His conscience bombarded his soul, as he lay awake in bed. His son, a nigger lover! Were there any other stand he could take. It didn't dawn on him, that he too, was a slave to customs he was fighting so hard to preserve, which had now separated him from his son.

Susan was almost afraid to breathe, for this evening had really been a terrible strain. Still, she had accomplished quite a lot. She'd been able to get her way with her father, as long as she could recall. She had always taken pains to come between Mark and her father, when she could. Tonight, she had joined with her father against him. So her brother, and his own father wouldn't ever be close again. She wouldn't lose any sleep over it, at least she thought.

Julie lay weeping silently for her son. She knew just how relentless her husband could be. But for him to suddnely turn against his own son, how in the world could he live with himself. She knew all too well that her husband would destroy himself, along with Mark, before he'd forgive, or forget. Julie felt helpless there in the dark. All she could do tonight, was to worry.

CHAPTER FOUR

CARING FOR THE ROSE

Mark awoke early that morning from where he'd slept on a pile of hay in the barn, with some burlap bags spread over him to ward off the cold. He had not slept very well, for his heart was troubled by the horrible events of the evening past. He didn't regret what he had said to Mr. Powell, because he felt all along that Powell might cause trouble, and Bill had warned him of the very same thing. However, being attacked by his own father was somewhat different, and he not only regretted what he had said to his father then, it haunted him this morning as well. He had worked real hard trying to make it on the farm, and the slaves had worked even harder. He couldn't understand why it was so wrong to pay the slaves for doing all the work, yet he was obligated to pay Powell, even though he hadn't done any work at all. How could anyone find justice in such a scenario. Mark knew there was none.

Mark understood how important slavery was to farmers in the South, for the slaves turned out an enormous amount of work, but it upset him to see them mistreated. It made no sense to him. To hate slaves simply because they were "black," was downright stupid. They were created black.

Mark had been awake quite awhile when the barn door opened, and in came Bill with a cup of coffee, a few slices of fried fatback meat, and a piece of cornbread. Mark quickly jumped up, and stretched his arms.

"Moan'n, Mos'a Mark!" Bill greeted him, as he set the cup of coffee and food on a wooden barrel. "I's fetched you some coffee to op'um yo' eyes, and Liza, she went and sont you some vittles, too. The sun is jus' 'bout up now, and when you's eat, and drank the coffee, we can be on our way."

"Thank you very much," replied Mark, as he sipped on the coffee. "While I eat, you can hitch the mare to the buggy, that is, if you don't mind."

"She done hitched to the buggy," replied Bill. "I's couldn't sleep much las' nite, and while the moon wuz shining, I's cured the mare rail good, and her hair shines like she ain't never wore it befo'," Bill chuckled. "She be prancin' 'round out there now, and wait'n on us. She can't hardly wait, to show off her purdy hair to them studs, she gon'a see in town."

"Is Powell out of bed yet, or have you looked up that way?" Asked Mark, as he quickly ate his breakfast. "I heard Dad remind him that they were to do something this morning, but I have no idea what it was. It really doesn't bother me all that much, for after I pay him, he'll be out of my hair."

"Yass'uh, I's peeked 'round the corner, and watched him saddle up his ole mare, then he galloped off like his tail wuz on fire," Bill replied. "Guess he gone to look fer some place to stay, adder you went and run him off las' nite. Yass'uh, he done be long gone, he sho' is."

Mark and Bill climbed into the buggy, and headed out toward town. This was the first time Mark had been in charge of making a crop, and would be the first time he'd ever been to the bank on business. He felt real important as the mare swiftly trotted along, with her blond mane glistening in the morning sun, for he was now an official farmer.

On their way into town they laughed and joked, like father and son were enjoying a trip together. This had been an excellent crop year, and the price of cotton was the highest it had been in quite awhile, and except for what he owed Powell, a fact that galled him more and more, he didn't owe anybody else anything at all. Farmers generally charged things at the General Store, until they gathered their crop in the fall, however, Mark used the money his father gave to him to pay as he went along, which was a part of the deal between him, and his father. After giving Powell half, and sharing his part with Bill and his family like he'd promised, he would have plenty left to tide him over 'til next crop-gathering time. He was grateful to his father for helping him, and it really hurt him, because his father had turned against him. Maybe someday they would be able to settle their differences.

When they arrived in town, wagons and buggies were parked everywhere, and women and childern were going from store to store, shopping. This was a big day for the farmers, and their family as well, and Mark knew for sure that the bank lobby would be filled with farmers, collecting for their crop.

"Park the buggy over there under that oak tree," said Mark, pointing toward a sprawling oak tree, where other horses were hitched, "and maybe my mare can find her a boyfriend in the bunch," Mark laughed. "I'll be back as soon as I can, and don't let me forget to stop by the General Store, on our way back out of town. And, don't doze off to sleep either!" Mark teased.

"I's won't ferget," replied Bill, as he drove the buggy over to the side of the street, and parked it under the tree. "I's gon'a be sot'n here wait'n on you, 'til you's get back wid yo' pocketful of money, I's sho' is."

As soon as Mark entered the lobby of the bank, he suddenly stopped in his tracks, for he'd never seen so many men in one place before. The two long wooden benches along the wall were almost filled to capacity with farmers, some whom he recognized, and others he hadn't seen before. He stood looking around for a moment, then sprinted across the floor to where he saw a vacant spot on one of the benches, and sat down. It was obvious by the way they looked at him, that they wondered what a young man like him was doing at the bank.

"Son, pardon me for asking, and excuse me if I'm wrong, but I wondered if you were somehow related to Nate Simpson," said a man who sat next to Mark. "You sure would pass for being Nate's son, you know."

"You're right, Sir, we are related," Mark smiled, and replied. "He's my father, and my name is Mark. And your name, Sir, if I may ask?"

"George Wilson," the man replied, offering his hand. "I have known your father for a long time, and seeing that you're here representing him, I gather that he's not feeling well. I hope it's not something serious."

"No, he's quite well Sir," Mark replied. "I operate a farm myself, and I came into town to settle up with the banker for the cotton he sold for me."

"I do say!" The man remarked. "You look awful young to be a sharecropper, for most landlords want older men with experience, if you know what I mean. But, I guess that everybody has to start out on his own sometime."

"I'm already eighteen Sir, and I don't work as a sharecropper!" Quickly replied Mark. "I own my own farm, and I'm here to handle my own business with Mr. Bland. This is my first year as a farmer, and I did real well too."

"That's great, and I know that Nate's real proud of you," Mr. Wilson replied. "I must tell my daughter about you, for you're a fine young man," he chuckled.

Smiling, Mark nodded politely, thinking instead, how that his father actually hated the ground he walked on. He would put that out of his mind, though. He had come here on business, and he'd act like a businessperson.

Mark started to reply, however, at that moment the banker opened the door to his office, and looked around at the men who were waiting their turn to see him. A strange quiet suddenly fell over the lobby, for his presence seemed to make the farmers nervous, and they tried to avoid making eye contact with him, and Mark couldn't understand. Mark felt honored, and he looked the banker straight in the eye, and smiled.

"Mark Simpson!" He addressed Mark. "If you'll step into my office, I'll see you now." He then motioned to Mark. "I'd like to get some of you smaller farmers out of the way, if you other gentlemen don't mind."

"But, Sir," Mark protested. "These gentlemen were here long before me, and I'd like to wait my turn, if you don't mind."

"That's all right, for these gentlemen won't mind at all. That will give me plenty of time to carefully go over their accounts with them," replied the banker. The men motioned for Mark to go ahead.

He doesn't act like Nate's son. If that were Nate, he would have trampled over the rest of us to get ahead, Mr. Wilson thought to himself.

Mark followed the banker into his office and closed the door, then he sat down in front of a large mahogany desk. A placard on the desk, bore the name Ellis G. Bland. Mark had been to the bank with his father many times, but he hadn't ever been inside the office before.

"Mr. Simpson, it seems strange to see you here as a farmer, but being the son of Nate Simpson, it doesn't surprise me one bit," said Mr. Bland, looking through a stack of papers on his desk. "If you'll follow in his steps, and be the type of man that he is, you'll go places."

"And, I'm proud of the small farm he gave me, Sir," Mark replied. "This has been a real experience for me, but we did real well this year, and we hope to do much better in the future. Maybe we will."

"You keep saying "we," and I take that to mean you and your father, working together as a team," spoke Bland, bluntly. "Of course, I heard that you had a Powell man working for you, and you could have meant you and him."

Mark thought of how stubborn Powell had acted toward him, and the way his father had spoken to him, only last night.

"Not in the least!" Mark rebutted. "What I meant by we, were the slaves and me. They worked like Trojans, all five of them."

"Like Trojans, or like niggers!" Bland laughed. "Makes no difference to me who it was, they did well. How's your father doing? I'm really not sure, but I don't think he's been in my office, here lately. Maybe so, and it just slipped my mind."

"He's fine, thank you," Mark replied, not wishing to refer to his father any more at this point. "Now, what about the money I have coming to me?"

As if to ignore Mark, he continued on about Nate. "Your father's a real powerful man," he said, as he kept flipping through the papers on his desk. "He's a true-blooded Southerner, and you need to follow his footsteps. The South needs more men like him, to stand up against the Union."

"If you don't mind, Sir, I wish you would get down to business, for I did step out of turn, and I respect the other farmers," Mark told him.

"All right, Mr. Simpson, let me see what we have here," finally spoke up the banker. "Oops, not that one! You have enough liens against you as it is."

"Liens!" shouted Mark, jumping to his feet. "What do you mean? I don't owe anybody one penny, except for Mr. Powell."

"The liens against you are legal, and by law, I'll have to take a certain amount out of what I owe you, to satisfy these liens, plus my fee," replied Mr. Bland. "I must abide by the law, even thoough you might disagree."

"Look, Mr. Bland!" Mark snapped. "I owe Mr. Powell fifty percent of what I got for the cotton, even though he didn't earn it, and your fee for collecting the money from the brokers, and that's all that I owe! That's not what I call a lien, for I intended to pay that anyway!"

"Let me go over them with you one by one, and then you'll have a right to voice your rejection, if you have any," Bland proposed.

"Go ahead and do what you have to do," said Mark. "But I tell you, that I don't owe anybody anything, except for you, and Mr. Powell."

"Very well then," said Bland. "Then, you do owe Mr. Powell half of the money that you got for the cotton, because he acted as your foreman! Is that true?"

"How stupid can you be?" Mark scolded. "I just told you that! Is this some kind of stupid game, that you're playing?"

"Then, let's move along," Bland continued. "Did the Powells furnish you with room and board since back last fall, and did Mrs. Powell do your laundry as well? Scrubbed your clothes, it says here."

"Yes she did, but that was a part of our verbal agreement!" Mark protested. "Is he trying to say something else?"

"But, it's not worded quite like that," said Bland, as he held the paper up for Mark to read. "It says that you were to pay extra for room and board, and for them doing your laundry. It was witnessed by your father, for at the time of the agreement, you were only seventeen, under age, it says."

"Yes, that's my father's signature, but if you'll notice, it has today's date on it, meaning that it was signed today," Mark replied. "You told me earlier, that you hadn't seen Dad this fall, and if that be true, I wonder how his name got on the paper today. The ink isn't even dry yet!"

"I had no intention of getting involved, but Nate and Powell came by my house early this morning, and handed me these papers. Nate demanded that they be filed against you, and I certainly can't buck that man, whether the papers are legal or not, and I hope you understand my position."

"I understand, even though I don't see where you have to uphold somethng that's wrong, and hurt me, just because of him,"

Mark replied. "Go on, and get it over with, for I see now that I'm on the losing side."

"Very well," Bland nodded. "It says that your slaves killed a mule that belonged to Powell. Claims they worked it all week without water, and didn't feed it either. Is that true?"

"That's a lie!" Mark shouted. "All he ever owned, was one old mule, and a mare that's older than I am, which he still has. My father gave me the pair of mules we made a crop with, and a new wagon, when he gave me that farm, but he didn't charge anything for them. He also, gave me some money."

Dead silence hung over the office for a time, as Mark sat quietly, trying to figure out which way he should turn. His father said last night that he'd "strip you as clean as a hound's tooth", and now, he was using Powell to do his dirty work. Mark realized now that it was useless to go up against him.

"Well then, figure up how much he says that I owe him, deduct it from the money you owe me for the cotton, and give me what's left," Mark told him, as he sat and shook his head. "I sure hope they're happy, and that they sleep well tonight, after having done all this to me, and to my slaves."

"Don't get in such a rush, for there's more to come," spoke up Bland, as he looked at another paper, "This one here, makes all the others look sick."

"I don't believe this!" Mark sighed. "If you keep on like this, I'll be in debt to you, for talking to me. Let's hear what it is."

"Well, this one was filed by your father, and I hate to tell you what all it involves," said Bland. "It states that he made you a loan, when you first started out, and he sold you two mules, a new wagon, a mare, a new buggy, and a milk cow. This was dated last fall, and witnessed by Ephriam Johnson, if you care to check the date, and the signatures."

"I recognize both signatures," said Mark, as he glanced at the lien that lay before him, "but I'd say it was written today as well, and backdated."

Mr. Bland looked harshly at Mark. "That's a serious charge you're making against your father, Mr. Johnson, and against me as well," he replied. "If I were you, I wouldn't lock horns with those two, for that would be like locking horns with the devil himself!"

His father's cruelty, had surpassed anything that Mark had ever known him to do before, and Mark's great worry now, was if he'd still have his farm and slaves after today. His father's great wealth, coupled with the influence he had over all the others in the community, rendered Mark almost helpless.

"Mr. Bland, do I have anything left at all?" Mark asked grimly. "After all that, and after you deduct your fee, will I have enough money left to buy a pound of coffee? Or, does the General Store have a lien against me, too."

Bland looked across his desk, and grinned. "Well, you have the tidy sum of thirty dollars, not quite thirty, but I'll round it out to that, anyway."

Mark sat speechless for a moment, as he tried to figure out how a father could do such as this to his own son. He knew he couldn't survive through the winter on such a small amount as that, and he certainly wouldn't be able to plant a crop next spring. This was exactly what his father wanted. He wanted Mark to have to come back and beg to him.

Mark then thought of the slaves. They already felt accountable for what Mark had suffered thus far, and this would prove that they'd been right about his father and Powell, all along. Maybe he could borrow money from the bank, so he'd be able to plant a crop, and give the slaves something for working, as he had promised. He was ashamed for them to find out what happened.

"Sir, I need to borrow some money until I gather my next crop, for this leaves me without any money to operate on," said Mark, almost in tears. "I'm willing to mortgage my farm. It's free and clear. Will you do that?"

"I wish I could, but I have too much on the books, already," replied the banker. "I'm sorry, maybe later. My hands are tied, at the moment."

"But Sir, I must have a loan!" Mark pleaded. "Otherwise, I'm doomed as a farmer. Just a small loan, Sir, enough to get me out of this pinch."

The banker shook his head. "I'm sorry, but your father has control over just about everything that goes on around here. He tells me who I can make loans to, as well," Bland explained. "I can't afford to get on his bad side, for you see what took place here today. Nate Simpson, can bring a man to his knees in a heartbeat. You may go now, for I have others to see."

Mark picked up the money and walked out of Bland's office, and he could tell by the expression on the other farmers' faces, that they had overheard all that was said in Bland's office. He felt as though his world was crumbling in on him, and at this moment, even God had forsaken him. His spirit, pride, and even the faith he once had in himself had been crushed, along with the love he once had for his father, and his fellow man, as well. Bill had forwarned him of what he'd be facing. Mark knew now, that he'd been right. Bill seems to always be right about everything, Mark thought to himself.

Mark stopped on the steps for a moment, as he looked across the street to where his buggy was parked, and he saw Bill sitting with his head bowed. Bill had been so worried about Mark until he couldn't sleep last night, and he had dozed off to sleep, while waiting for Mark to return. He loved this kind old man, and he'd rather take the pistol from his pocket and shoot himself, rather than to break the sad news to him. He even entertained the idea of going back into the bank and demanding Bland to give him back the money he had wrongfully taken from him. On second thought, it would only create more problems for him and for the slaves, who were the only true friends he had left. He thought of what his mother had said on the day he left, and then he walked on across the street, to where Bill was waiting.

"Let's get out from here!" Said Mark, as he quickly jumped in the buggy, and awoke Bill. "I need to get back home, as soon as possible."

"I's ready, if you is," said Bill, as he wheeled the buggy around in the street, and headed back out of town. Then, he happened to remember that Mark planned to stop at the General Store. "The sto', is rite down the street, and I's ain't fergot that you's wanted to stop there, neither."

"I've changed my mind," said Mark, when he saw his father standing with a group of men in front of the store. "Maybe I'll come back tomorrow."

They were not going to stop at the store, so Bill gently tapped the mare with the riding-whip, and she trotted along on their way out of town.

"Hey, don't give those niggers too much money, for it might give them the big-head!" Nate Simpson geered, as Mark and Bill drove by the store. "I guess you see now, what power and money can do. See you later, nigger lover!"

Mark pretended as if he hadn't heard him at all. It was then, that Bill realized that things hadn't gone well for Mark at the bank, but he respected him enough, not to say anything. He didn't want to destroy Mark's pride.

All the way back to the farm Mark didn't speak one word, and Bill hummed a tune as they rode along, for he knew that eventually, Mark would get around to telling him what he wanted him to know. As they drove up and stopped near the barn, Bill noticed that the Powells were loading up a wagon, to leave.

"Mos'a Mark, I's ain't all that smart, but I's got sense 'nuf to know you ain't feeling rite," said Bill, as he slowly climbed down from the buggy. "I's a good lis'ner, and I's got a strong back. If you got sump'um you need to tell somebid'ee, er sump'um too heavy to tote all by yo'sef, jus' tell me what it is, and dump it on my ole back. I'll tote it fer you."

"You're a good man, Bill, and I appreciate that," replied Mark, glancing up toward Powell's house. "I've come through several terrible things before, and I think I can somehow get through this one, as well."

Bill saw instantly, that he needed to change the subject. "I's see that ole man Pow'l is leaving, like you's told him to," said Bill, as a smile came on his face. "They sho' messed up thangs, like when I's busted a rotten egg in the pan wid the good'uns. Now, that sho' wuz a stink'n mess."

"Yes, they sure did mess up things," replied Mark, as he started walking on toward the barn. "I need to be alone to collect my thoughts, and I'll let you know what happened at the bank, and what happened last night, too."

"That's fine wid me," said Bill, as he started unhitching the mare from the buggy. "I's gon'a go up there and see if Liza is got sump'um to eat, fer I's aw'ready hungry 'nuf to eat a polecat, and it fried in kerosene. I gon'a fetch sump'um back down here fer you to eats, too."

"Don't do that, for I'll be on up there in a few minutes," Mark promised him. "I'm in no shape to eat righ now. Maybe I'll be on up there to eat later."

Mark stood in the barnyard for several minutes, while he watched Bill water the mare at a wooden trough that was filled with rainwater, and then he put her in a stall, and fed her. Although he hummed a tune as he worked, Mark knew for a fact that Bill felt a great burden resting on his shoulder, and that his heart ached, because of the love he had for Mark.

As Mark watched Bill walk away, tears welled his eyes. He's a real good person, Mark thought, and he'd gladly take my burdens on his own shoulder, if he could. Wiping the tears from

145

his eyes, Mark went into the barn, and closed the door behind him. His heart was troubled, because he would not be able to keep his promise to Bill, who was the only real friend he had.

"Youn's got back in a hurry, like sump'um got adder youn's," spoke Liza, as Bill walked into the house. "How much money did you's get, anyhow? Let me hold the money in my hand, and see what it feels like."

"Jus' hold yo' taters, womern!" Bill scolded. "I's went and fetched the plate that I's took to the barn this moan'n, and you's need to fix him sump'um else to eat, fer I's promised to take sump'um back to him."

As she followed him on into the kitchen, she could tell by the expression on his face that somethng was wrong. He was excited when he left this morning, but now, he acted like his world had crumbled in on him.

He went and sat down at the kitchen table, and bowed his head. "Sump'um sho' went wrong back yon'a at the bank, and I's don't know what it wuz," he sighed, as tears trickled down his face. "He sez he wanted to stay at the barn 'til he got his head straight, then he gon'a tell me what took place at the bank, and what took place up at the house las' nite, too."

"Oh Lord'ee, I's wonder what it wuz! Said Liza. "He wuz happy as a pig in the sunshine yeserd'ee, er I's thought he wuz."

"Don't know, and guess I's gon'a have to wait and see," he replied, in a concerned voice. "Ain't gon'a mess in his business, by axe'n him."

"Everthang ain't went bad, fer them Pow'l folks is moving out, and it do makes me happy, too," Liza conforted him. "She been busy all day put'n stuff in the wagen, then the ole man come back, and he been hep'n her. I's thank he been looking fer some place fer them to stay at."

"From the way thangs tun'd out in town, I's bet Pow'l, and Mos'a Simpson is been together, trying to mess thangs up thangs fer the boy." Bill observed.

"And, you's say Mos'a Mark is down yon'a at the barn, and he feeling bad, too?" She asked. "Reck'n he jus' got the bellyache, er sump'um."

"He ain't said nothing since we's left town," he replied. "He wuz rail happy 'til he went in the bank, then ever'thang went and fell all to pieces."

"Well, I's glad he run his pappy off las' nite, and maybe that sorry goat won't bother him no mo'," Liza smiled. "Hope he stays 'way from him, too."

"But, he wuz in town today, and he screamed at Mos'a Mark, when we headed back home," he told her. "Mos'a Mark didn't say nothing to him."

"Oh Lord, I's bet it wuz him, and that ole Pow'l feller, that messed thangs up fer Mos'a Mark!" She told him. "Don't you thank it wuz?"

"Go on and fix him sump'um to eats, and maybe he'll tell me what it wuz that happened at the bank," said Bill. "They sez a feller will talk better wid a full gut, and we'll see."

While Liza was warming up the food on the stove, she happened to think of something else, as her imagination began to run wild.

"Say, do you reck'n he done went and got Marthie messed up adder all, and he's 'fraid that we's gon'a find out 'bout it?" Liza's pessimistic nature, was running rampant. "Reck'n that's what he gon'a 'fess up to?"

That flew all over Bill. "Shut up that ole fool talking!" He yelled, and struck his fist on the table. "He ain't gon'a mess wid no nigga, fer he got mo' sense than that. You aw'ways look at the bad side of thangs, and if you's went to buy a mule, you'd raise his tail, and look at his butt fust."

"That ain't it," she tried to explain, "fer I's know what a fool she be 'bout him. She's had a silly grin on her face here lately, and I's bet that's what it is, too. Oh boy, we's gon'a have us a gran'chile!"

At that, Bill quickly jumped up from the table. "I's done sick and tard of yo' ole fool talk!" He scolded. "Gimme them vittles, and let me take 'em on down there to Mos'a Mark, fo' I's railly do get mad at you."

"Take the stuff!" She pouted, as she shoved the platter of food into his hands. "I'll be on down there to see if we gon'a have us a gran'chile!"

He took the food down to the barn to give to Mark, and when he opened the barn door and stepped inside, he didn't see Mark anywhere. Thinking that Mark was taking a nap, Bill called to him, but he didn't reply. He stood for a moment looking around, for the sun was going down, and it was rather hard for him to see inside the barn. He heard a noise at the back of the barn, and when he peeked around a stack of hay, he almost fainted.

"Oh Lord'ee!" screamed Bill, as he threw the food down on the floor, and rushed toward the back of the barn. "What in the wul'd is you fix'n to do to yo'sef?" Bill screamed. "Please don't do that, Son! Please, Mos'a Mark!"

It was obvious, that Mark intended to hang himself. He was standing on a wooden barrel with a hangman's noose around his neck, and he was tying the other end of the rope to a rafter in the roof. Bill rushed over and caught hold of him, as he kicked the barrel out of the way. Mark was now in a crazed state of mind. His eyes looked wild and furious, and he began fighting with Bill, as though he thought Bill intended to hurt him.

Bill finally wrestled Mark to the floor, and removed the noose from around his neck. He sat on the floor holding Mark in his arms, as tears ran from his eyes, while he hummed a sad tune. Bill rocked Mark back and forth, trying to calm him down. Mark trembled with fright. Then, he finally calmed down, and Bill took his coat sleeve, and wiped the tears from Mark's face.

"Mos'a Mark, there ain't no problems big 'nuf to cause you to do nothing like that to yo'sef," Bill sobbed. "Me and you needs to sot down and jaw fer a spell, and you's need to tell me all 'bout what went on in town, today."

Mark was a nervous wreck, as he lay in Bill's arms, and looked up at him. "Bill, I have a serious problem hanging over my head, and I can't seem to cope with it," he sobbed. "I don't know how to begin to solve it, but I know that I can't go on with it hanging over my head."

"I's gon'a be here wid you, through thick and thin," Bill assured him. "You can aw'ways talk wid me, and tell me whatever you's want me to hear, fer I's yo' friend." Bill then stood up, but Mark still sat on the floor, crying like a baby.

"This isn't your problem," he told Bill, "for I brought it on myself by not listening, when you warned me about my father and Mr. Powell. It's not fair to burden you with my problems. You have enough problems as it is, just being black."

"Well, you got'a trus' somebid'ee, and the way it looks now, I's 'bout all you got, eb'em if I ain't 'spose to have no sense," Bill chuckled. "The devil is done jumped on you when you had yo' back tun'd, and now I's got'a pitch in, and hep' you whoop the ole devil off."

"Bill, you're as good as gold, and you're the only real friend that I have except my mother, and I don't know how she feels about me anymore," he told Bill.

Mark finally got up, and they walked over and stood near the door, while Mark told him all about what happened at the bank this morning, and what went on last night as well. Bill didn't know what happened that morning, however, he did know about last night. He'd heard everything that went on last night, which was a secret that he'd keep from Mark, for the rest of his life. Their conversation was suddenly interrupted, when Liza stepped into the barn.

"Is ever'thang aw'rite in here?" She asked, when she saw the food on the floor. "Mos'a Mark, why did you throw the stuff on the flo'? Didn't you's like my cook'n. Did you thank it wuz nasty, er sump'um.

"No, it's not that at all," replied Mark, as he gave her a big hug, and noticed the food on the floor for the first time. "I'm, well, it was just an accident. Bill's been so clumsy here lately, until he'd stumble over his own shadow. I really like your cooking, and I'm sorry that it happened."

Liza suddenly realized that they both had been crying. When she glanced toward the back of the barn, and saw a hangman's noose lying on the floor by the barrel, she became frightened. The first thing that popped into her mind, was that Mark had tried to kill himself, becasue Martha was pregnant.

"Oh Lord, what I's told Bill wuz true!" Liza wailed. "You tried to kill yo'sef, 'cause you's got Marthie prag'nut. We's ain't mad at you, 'cause we gon'a have a gran'chile. Bill, tell him that we ain't mad."

"Have you lost your mind?" Asked Mark, angrily. "What kind of person do you think I am! I respect Martha too much, to do such a thing as that."

"I's knowed that sump'um wuz taking place 'tween youn's," she went on. "And now that we's gon'a have us a gran'chile, me and Bill bof' is rail happy."

Martha had returned from the fields, where she and her brothers had been chopping down some old cotton stalks, for she planned to help her mother cook supper, and do the chores around the house. She had been standing outside the door, and she had heard everything that Mark and her mother had said.

"He be telling the truf'!" Said Martha, as she jerked the door open, and quickly stepped inside. "He ain't never messed wid me! It ain't 'cause I's ain't axed him to, but he keeps on saying that it's wrong."

Then, Bill's two boys Samuel and Elijah, stepped inside the barn to join them, for this was unusual, and they wanted to find out what this meeting was all about. While they were all together, Mark decided to tell them about what happened in town this morning, and why he had tried to hang himself. While he talked, they all stood and cried, for they didn't hold anything against Mark, nor did they intend to allow this to cause them to lose faith in him.

"Money don't mean nothing to us, fer we's ain't never had none," replied Liza, as she threw her arms around him. "You's a rail good boy, and the Lord is gon'a whoop yo' pappy, fer what he went and done to you."

"And Liza, while the Lord's whoop'n him, let Him whoop Pow'l too," Bill told her. "He be a devil, if there ever wuz one, so whoop him too!"

"That's rite, fer he done got yo' money, and I's mad at him too," Liza added. "Money can't buy no clean heart, er no rail friend like you is been to us." Looking at Mark, she smiled, as only a mother could smile.

"She be rite 'bout the money," Bill spoke up. "You don't owe us a penny fer what we's done. We gon'a wu'k this thang out together, and one day we gon'a look in the eyes of yo' pappy, and ole Mos'a Pow'l, and laugh at 'em."

"What you folks just said, has caused me to feel much better," Mark told them, as he slapped Bill on the shoulder. "I had my goal set too high, I suppose, and I feel hurt because I'm not able to keep my promise to you."

"I's know how you feel, but the good thang is, we's all in the same shape, fer none of us ain't got nothing," Bill chuckled. "We's got to 'pend on the Lord to he'p us, fer that's what He 'spects us to do, anyhow."

Then, walking back to where he had tried to hang himself, Mark picked up a note that he'd left laying on the barrel for Bill to find later. He brought it back, and handed it to Bill.

"Bill, here's a signed document which states that all of you are free citizens. You won't be a slave to me, or to anybody else anymore," he told him, in a serious voice. "Each of you are free to leave anytime you wish. You're free to stay, if that's what you want to do. If you folks do decide to stay, we'll work out an agreement where you'll be my employees. You won't be slaves. I promise to pay you a salary, like farmers pay white men who work for them, and you'll be treated with the same respect, as I treat a white person. You're free now, free to leave, free to stay, if you wish to do that."

Neither of them knew what to say. Freedom, was just another word to them, like a lot of other words, they didn't understand. Although Mark made it clear that they had a right to leave, they were not about to leave. But, he had given them a choice at least, something that they had never had before.

"It do make me feel good to be free, eb'em if I's don't know what it tis," Bill smiled, and clutched the paper in his hands. "This is the thang I's been dream'n 'bout, ever since they throwed me in the bottom of that big ole boat, and fetched me over here."

"Like I just said, all of you are free!" Mark told them again. "You are welcome to stay on as my employees, or pack up and leave, if you wish."

Bill looked at the others, then back at Mark. "We wuz here, fo' you got in this mess, and we's gon'a stay on here 'til you's get out'a it, too." Bill clearly stated. "Jus' 'cause the devil throwed sump'um in front of us, to make us stumble and fall, that don't mean that we can't get back up, and try again. We is jus' one lit'l po' family now, wid you rite in the middle."

Mark's eyes welled with tears, as he looked at this kind old Negro slave, who had already been more like a father to him. He still tried to offer Mark hope and courage to go on, when there was none to be seen.

"We already know what can be accomplished by us sticking together, although it was snatched out of our hands," said Mark. "We'll somehow manage to round up enough money to plant another crop, and we'll start all over again."

"Then, its settled fer good," replied Bill, with a grin. "We all gon'a stay rite here, and axe the Lord to look down and grin at us while we wuk', too."

Hearing a noise outside, Mark went over to look out the door. He saw Powell's wagon coming down the road that ran nearby the barn. He grabbed up a pitchfork and headed outside, for he didn't intend to allow him to drive away, as though nothing had really happened.

"Jus' let him go!" Said Bill, as he caught hold of Mark's arm. "There ain't no use fer you to mess up yo' lif', over a sorry pile of trash like that."

"But, this time you're wrong!" Mark shouted, as Powell drove on down the road. "I should kill him, because of what he did to you and me. I'm sure we will meet again one day. When we do, it's going to be a day that he'll never live to regret. He's a dead man, I tell you!"

"Let's go up to the house and get sump'um to eats, fer we got a lot of wuk' to do," Bill said, as he stepped outside. "Now that them folks is gone, we got'a scrub out the house rail good, fer you gon'a be staying there now all by yo'sef. The boys, they can do up the thangs 'round here tonite, so come on up to the house, wid us."

Mark, Bill, Liza and Martha walked back to their house, while Bill's boys started feeding the livestock, and doing other chores for the evening, for the sun was now almost down, and it would soon be dark. Mark and Bill sat by the fireplace and talked, while Martha and her mother prepared supper. While Mark and Bill were talking, something else popped into Mark's mind.

"From here on, I want you folks to refer to me as "Mark", for I'm sick of being called "master", as if I were your Lord, or ruler," he told him. "And I won't call you "slaves", or "niggers", for I have more respect for you, than to address you in such a way. You are human beings; you are free citizens as well. You are my friends. I'll continue to be your boss and your leader, but in the meantime, you have certain rights of your own."

"But, Mos., I's mean, Marr-rk," Bill began. "I's got used to calling white folks that, and it's gon'a be hard fer me to stop saying that."

"I'm sure it will at that," Mark agreed, "but that's exactly how it's going to be. You might as well get used to it."

Bill's boys decided to go possum hunting before they came into the house to eat supper. Mark had eaten supper with them, but before he went on to the house, he sat by the fireplace awhile longer, talking with Bill. As he stared into the fire in the fireplace, he thought of these folks, and how nice they'd been to him, and how thankful he was, because he was still alive. These folks were his friends. He had no need of his father, or Mr. Powell.

When Martha and her mother had finished washing the dishes, they came in and joined Mark and Bill at the fireplace. Mark was reminded of somethng he had almost forgotten, or hadn't thought of for quite awhile. It was the piece of cloth his father had destroyed. Although he had only thirty dollars to call his own for the year's work, he decided to do something special for them, just to let them know that he appreciated what they had done for him.

"Martha, I haven't forgot about the cloth my father destroyed, and if I'm still alive in the morning, I intend to replace it," he told her, leaning back in his chair, and stretching his arms. "Half of the money belongs to you folks, anyway. In fact, we'll all ride into town tomorrow, like one big family. It will mean a lot more to me, than you can ever imagine."

At that moment the front door opened, and Bill's boys walked in. They had been possum hunting. They knew that Mark had set them free, however, neither of them had grasp its meaning. They were not there, when Mark told the others not to be calling him "master", anymore.

"Howdy, Mos'a Mark!" Samuel greeted him. "Me and Lijah went over in the woods possum hunt'n, but the dog treed a polecat, and we left him in the hole. I's didn't 'spect to see you here. Thought you mout'a done went home."

Martha laughed out loud, and Samuel wondered why she had laughed at him.

"What's wrong wid you, Marthie? Sam asked. "Is you done went crazy, er is you los' yo' mind."

"You's the one that's crazy!" She replied. "Mark is done went and sot us free, and we ain't gon'a have to call him Mos'a, like we's been doing."

"Do that be the truf', Marthie?" Asked Elijah. "Is we railly free, and don't have to call him Mos'a, like you sez?"

"We sho' is, fer Pappy's got the freedom papers in his pocket!" Martha squealed. "When the sun gets up to'mar, he gon'a run 'round the wul'd, beller'n like a bull, and telling everbid'ee that we is free at las'!"

"Yes Sam, you're a free man!" Smiled Mark, as he reached to shake Sam's hand. "You too, Elijah, for I have no need of slaves. I only need friends on my side. Call me Mark, from now on. I'm not anybody's master."

Mark and the boys talked and laughed for a while longer, however, Bill sat quietly and listened. As tears welled his eyes, he thought back on how tragic the day could have really turned out. What if he hadn't returned to the barn, and found Mark before he hanged himself. What would he have done, if he had found the boy dangling from the rope. The very thought of this, sent a chill running up his spine. Then, he whispered a prayer, and asked God to "grin at the boy, and look adder him."

Mark's parents and his sister, Susan, had returned to their home on the plantation, however, his mother had hardly spoken a word to his father since their heated discussion at the Inn last night. She tried not to worry herself sick over the problem, and could only wonder what her husband had done to Mark in town this morning, although she'd heard him remark to Susan, about teaching him a lesson that he'd never forget. Mrs. Simpson climbed from the buggy and went on into the mansion. However, Susan waited to go in with her father, for her mother's quietness disturbed her. Susan tried to stay out of her presence as much as possible.

A few moments later when Susan and her father came into the parlor, they found Mrs. Simpson sitting on the settee with her head bowed, crying as if her heart was broken. "What's the matter with you, Julie?" Mr. Simpson asked, as if he didn't already know. "Are you tired from the long trip?"

"Nate, I'd like to know what you and Powell did to Mark today, for I know that it was something awful?" She asked, her voice cracking.

"I did what I had to do to teach him a good lesson," he coldly replied. "He was determined to ruin my name, and he had to be stopped. Was that so wrong?"

"I'm not concerned about your name," she sobbed. "I want to know if you destroyed him, like you have everyone else who has ever dealt with you?"

"No, not completely," he smiled wickedly, "I just let him know that he couldn't buck a man like me, that's all. He'll come crawling back to me like a whipped puppy, and you can have him all to yourself again."

"It was wrong to plot against your own son. It's going to come back, and haunt you one day." She told him, sadly. "You have disgraced your father's name, brought shame to the community, and destroyed your own family,"

"Like I said, I did only what I had to do," he growled.

"What about Powell?" She asked. "Did he take any part in your awful scheme? Did he benefit from your son's hurt, as well?"

"Yes, he was well paid, I'm proud to say," Simpson replied. "Of course, he got half the money, pay for a mule he didn't own, and got paid for Mark's room and board, which Mark didn't owe. Yes, I'd say he did real well."

"You're a monster, Nate! A hell-bound, wicked monster!" Julie shouted, jumping to her feet. "Your pressing urge for money and power, and your hatred for slaves, has conquered your soul!"

"Watch your tongue, woman!" Simpson warned. "You know that I run things around here, and that I always have the last word around here."

"Not this time, Mos'a!" Julie screamed, shaking her finger at him. "I'd like to know how you could sleep, after what you did to your own son!"

"When he took over that farm, he took on the responsibility of a man, and when he challenged me, he locked horns with the devil himself," Simpson told her, in an angry voice. "No my Dear, my sleep won't be interrupted." With a mocking bow, he left the room to go to bed, for it was real late.

Following her father down the hallway, Susan made her way to her bedroom as well, for she didn't want to witness any more of her mother's anger.

Although Julie was frightened and upset, there wasn't anything she could do to help Mark, except to pray for him. Julie sat in the parlor alone during the rest of the night. She knew she couldn't sleep, and she could not bear to be in the same room with her husband tonight.

Early the following morning, Mark and Bill's family boarded a wagon to go into town. He needed some things from the General Store, now that he would be living alone, and he planned to get some cloth for Martha and her mother.

When they arrived in town, Bill drove the wagon up and parked it directly across the street from the General Store. A group of white men were standing near the entrance to the store, and Bill became frightened.

"Them mens over yon'a is got their eyeballs socked on us, and I's hope we ain't in fer no trouble," Bill whispered to Mark.

"Don't worry about them at all," replied Mark, as he quickly leaped from the wagon, "for we have the same right to be here, as anyone else. You are a free citizen, not a slave, and you have nothing to fear. Let's go!"

Although Bill had a paper clearly stating that he was free, he understood how white persons felt about Negroes, be they free, or not.

"It mout be the bes' if we's sot in the wagen 'til you's get back, fer we sho' don't want'a stir up no stink," replied Bill, as he kept an eye on the men. "I's still mem'er when me and Marthie went in there."

"Bill, be rite!" Liza agreed. "We's ain't want'n to get you in no trouble over us, and that sho' looks like trouble, standing rite over there."

"The heck with them!" Mark sharply replied. "Come on and follow me, for I'm not afraid of them, or anybody else. I brought my pistol with me, this time."

When they entered the store, the manager turned his back toward them, and started fiddling around with items on a shelf behind the counter. This really shocked Mark, for he'd been in the store hundreds of times since he was just a child. Just last week Mr. Wilson had complimented him on the way the farm was looking, and the excellent cotton crop he had this year.

After standing at the counter for several moments, it became obvious that Mr. Wilson was either too busy to take his order, or he didn't intend to assist them at all. Mark went over and took a piece of cloth off a shelf, then brought it back and placed it on the counter. Still, Mr. Wilson acted as if he hadn't seen him. Mark gathered up some other items, and placed them on the counter as well. The man still didn't even bother to turn around.

"Mr. Wilson, I'd like to buy this piece of cloth, and these other items I have on the counter, if you don't mind," politely spoke Mark. "I'd like to get back home as soon as possible, for we have a lot of work to do."

"Grab up the darned stuff, and get out of my store!" The man replied, in a hateful voice. "This is a place of business - not a trash dump! There's a group of men standing outside, and you'd better get your niggers out of here, before trouble starts!"

"Hold on a minute, Sir!" Mark snapped. "I have the money to pay for the stuff I want, I'm a citizen and a gentleman! I won't allow you to treat me as if I were a dog. Do you have a problem, in doing business with me?"

"Look, boy!" Wilson shouted, as he quickly turned around. "I know about you treating the niggers like humans, which is wrong! I know that you plan to pay them, too! You're ruining your father's name! I don't like having you in my store, either! Is that so hard for you to understand?"

"So, what you're really saying, is that my father got to you, like he got to everybody else in the community!" Mark replied. "Is that it?"

"If you want to put it that way," Wilson replied. "I don't want to have anything else to do with you, your money, or your niggers! Take what you want and get out, before my store gets burned down." Then, he turned back around, and started fumbling with something on a shelf.

Mark put the money back into his pocket, and then he picked up the cloth and other items off the counter, and they all walked back out of the store.

When they went back outside, Mark noticed that the same group of men who had been standing at the store, had now crossed the street, and joined another group who were standing near where Bill had parked the wagon. As they walked toward the wagon, Bill happened to see something that he thought should be called to Mark's attention, so he nudged Mark with his elbow.

"I's see yo' pappy in 'hind the mens," Bill whispered. "I's wonder what he doing here. Reck'n he done here'd that you went and sot us free, aw'ready?"

"I don't know. He's already taken everything I have, except for my farm. There's nothing else left for him to take," Mark replied. "I hope he's smart enough to keep his lip closed, for at this stage of the game, I'm not for sure if I can hold my temper."

Mark climbed aboard the wagon, and when the others joined him, Bill spoke to the mules, and they headed out of town. No matter how Mark felt about his father for what he'd done to him, this was not the time for him to jeopardize his friends, just to get even with his father. Then, as he glanced back, he saw his father step out into the street behind the wagon.

"I guess that you see who runs this town!" His father yelled. "You had better keep your nigger gal out of town, if you know what's good for her!"

Mark caught hold of the reins and stopped the wagon, and then he stood up in the wagon and looked back at him.

"You might own those men, if you can call them men, but you lack a lot in owning me!" Mark yelled back at him. "I'll bring my friends to town any time they want to come! You, or nobody else, can stop me!"

"The next time you bring that nigger gal to town, you might as well look for trouble!" His father threatened. "Call my hand, and see what happens!"

Arguing with his father in the presence of this "audience" of townspeople seemed ridiculous, to say the least, so Mark decided to say no more. He told Bill to drive on, and forget everything that had been said.

"Can you believe that nigger lover going yonder, used to be my son!" Said Nate, as he went back and joined the others. "The next time he brings the gal to town, I'll pay anybody a tidy reward, if they make sure that she don't go back alive. Are you men interested in making a hundred dollars?"

The men looked at him in amazement. "Surely, you're not expecting a fellow to kill a nigger, right here in town!" Spoke up Edward Baker. "You're asking somebody to murder a nigger gal. You can't be serious, Nate!"

"I'm as serious as a heart attack, Brother Baker!" He replied, in a real serious voice. "I have the law, and the judge in my pocket, so to speak. You don't have to be worried about anything. Do I have a taker?"

Hearing this, the men quickly scattered. "Did you notice the expression on his face?" Whispered Baker. "I think he'd kill his own son, just to prove that he's "king of the roost". He scares the devil out of me!"

"My son and I disagree all the time. He does some things that makes me want to wring his neck, but I'd never make a fool of myself in public, like he did," said another man. "That man's crazy!"

Realizing that he'd been left alone, Nate decided to get in his buggy and go back home. "Weaklings, that's what they are," Nate said to himself, as he climbed into his buggy. "I'll find somebody else. There's other fools, who I can get to do the job for me."

Mark and his friends had been traveling along for about an hour now. As soon as they came to a place where a stream ran across the road, Bill stopped to allow the mules to drink, while the women took a trip to the bushes. Mark walked on down the road several yards, and he stood with his head bowed. Bill remembered the incident in the barn yesterday, and because Mark had hardly spoken at all since they had left town, he decided to strike up a conversation with him.

"There sho' is some strange fellers in this ole wul'd, and the big thang is that we ain't gon'a change 'em," said Bill seriously, as he walked up and stood close to him. "As long as the wul'd stay in one piece, us niggas is gon'a have to put up wid thangs like that. No freedom papers that we got, er nothing else, ain't never gon'a change thangs, from the way they is."

"I disagree with you, Bill," replied Mark, "for if everyone who doesn't believe in slavery, would stand up and cry out against it, we would see things change. I know I'm not the only person in South Carolina who thinks slavery is wrong, but they're afraid to voice their opinion. Although it's liable to cost me everything, even my life, I'll never change my mind."

"That's fine, but look at yo' pappy, tuther fellers, too," Bill tried to prove his point. "They had 'ruther die, than to sot the slaves free, fer that would hu't their pride, and pride, is all that holds fellers like that in one piece. There ain't no way to change 'em. You don't need to try to change 'em, fer it ain't gon'a get done. They won't let you change 'em."

"I'm not trying to change anybody, for everybody has a right to their own opinion," Mark replied. "I don't have a problem with folks using Negroes as slaves, if that's what they want to do, but they shouldn't find fault with me, if I don't want to make slaves of them. Does that not make good sense?"

"Slavery ain't the rail problem," Bill disagreed. "The problem is, that folks ain't gon'a do the way they feel in their heart, 'cause of what folks liable to say 'bout 'em. Pride, and stubbornness, that's what it tis."

"No, Bill, slavery within itself is a real problem for the South, and the root of the conflict between us and the Union," Mark replied. "A law saying it was illegal to bring slaves to America was passed in 1808, but the South continues to go against the law as if it meant nothing at all."

"Slaves, is the bread and butter fer the farmers, and if you's want a fight on yo' hand, jus' try to scrape the butter off their bread," Bill chuckled.

"It's politics, plain and simple!" Said Mark, as they went back to climb into the wagon. "Leaders of the South buck against whatever the Union suggest for the nation, but they tell citizens that their differences is over slavery, which is not true. If the leaders would tell the truth, we wouldn't have any problems with the Union. Wouldn't have any slaves, either."

Mark was right on target, when he gave his assessment as to how Southern leaders covered up the real problem. Though the Union had thus far refrained from taking a real stand against slavery, the South kept pressing the issue in an attempt to get what it wanted. South Carolina had presented a petition for State's Rights; however, it didn't get any support from the North or the West. Because of this, the South denounced what other sections of the country wanted for them. As a result of this, the South was left without any support, other than from its own leaders.

It was early in the afternoon, when Mark and his friends returned to the farm, and they started cleaning up the house, in which the Powells once lived. Mark intended to live there alone. Liza agreed to prepare his meals each day, do his laundry, and clean the house. While the others were cleaning up around the house, Mark found himself alone in the house with Martha. He was coming from another room, they passed in the doorway, and he accidentally brushed up against her breast. Mark smiled at her, but the impressionable young girl, took it to be more than just a friendly smile.

"Mark!" She said, as she caught hold of his arm. "Didn't you's say them freedom papers give me a rite to thank fer my'sef, and say whatever I's wanted to say? Ain't that what you sez."

"Well, uh, yes, they do," Mark, stammered. "And, they give you the right to make your own choices, as well. Now, doesn't that sound good"?

"It sho' do, and now let me tell you what I's thank," she replied, as a smile came on her face. "Ever time I's get close to you, I's get a tickling feeling deep down in my belly, and the older I's get, the wuss it gets. Reck'n it's a loving kin'a feeling I's got fer you? Reck'n it's trying to say that you's like me, and I's ain't got sense 'nuf to una'stan?"

"Please Martha!" Mark spoke softly. "We have already gone over that many times. I've tried to explain the difference between being a close friend with someone, and being in love with them. Your heart is telling you that we are friends, but your mind, is trying to convince you that we're in love."

All the work had been finished inside, and Martha headed toward the front door, with Mark following along close behind. Then, Martha realized that she had left her coat hanging on a chair, and when she quickly turned around, Mark couldn't keep from his body pressing up against her breast, for a second time. This really excited her, and she stood for a moment with her body pressed tight against him, until he politely pushed her away.

"Mark, we's aw'ways been close friend," she began, "but I's ain't had a tickling feeling like that, befo' you kept the buck from me. It gets rail bad when you's bump into me like that. I's hope it ain't sump'um that you mout catch from me, fer that would be awful. Is it sump'um that's slipped up on me, when I wuzn't looking? Is that what it tis?"

"Martha, true love comes from the heart," Mark said kindly. "It starts out by being with someone whom you really like as a friend, and eventually it changes into a stronger feeling, we call love. You begin to feel like they're a part of you, and that you can't live without them. That's what I call love, which is more than just a physical feeling, you might have for someone. I like you as a friend, for we've been around each other since childhood, but I'm not in love with you. Friendship is strong, and friends will die for each other, if need be, but even then, they might not be in love. Now, do you understand how I feel in my heart for you?"

"Yass'uh, I's railly do see what you mean," she replied, not understanding him at all. "When you hep'd me to get 'way from the buck, I's wanted you to pappy a young'un fer me, rite then. Ain't that what you's call love?"

Mark felt his face turn red. "I realize how you must have felt that day, but I also know that you only felt grateful for what I did, and that you were willing to offer your body to me only in appreciation," he explained. "That's the thing that I want you to clearly understand, for we're not in love."

"We growed up together as chil'uns," she persisted, "and now that we's older, don't you ever feel like you's want'a mess wid me? Do you ever feel like that?"

He didn't want to hurt her feelings, and he didn't want to encourage this line of thinking, either. "You and I are different from each other, for you're black, and I'm white, and in the sight of God, it's not right for us to become sexually involved. It does happen today, and probably someday, it might even be acceptable by society, but as for now, it's morally wrong."

"But Mark! She whined, not wanting to give this up. "You's said that I wuz as good as you is, but now, you sez I ain't, and that messes me up."

"Let me put it this way, then we'll call this off," Mark replied, though he doubted that she'd understand. "Birds of all color,

161

Blackbirds and Doves, they all eat together, share the same tree, and bathe in the same water as if they were alike, but when they get ready to have a family, they choose a mate of their own kind. That's the way God intended for my race, and your race to get along. Not to mess up His plan, by bringing a mixed race of people into the world, who are neither black, nor white."

Seeing tears creeping into her eyes, and realizing that it was obviously dificult for her to grasp the reason for him talking this way, he knew he had to steer away from this subject. Shaking his head, he went on outside to join the others, while Martha stood in the doorway, more confused than she had been before. Mark stood and talked with Bill for a few minutes, then they returned home. Mark went back inside, hoping that he hadn't hurt Martha, more than he had helped her.

The Negroes really felt sorry for Mark, for they knew that others in the community would shun him because of his father's vicious attacks, as well as for a strong influence his father had over them. Mark was quite different in many ways from other white persons, and even though he was just a boy in their eyes, he stood head and shoulders above all the other white men they had ever known. Bill loved Mark as though he were his own son, and he pledged to see that Mark regained the same dignity and pride, that he had when he first took over the small farm. While they ate supper, they discussed what went on today in town, and they all agreed to risk their life by standing behind him. Even though they were free, they would never leave, nor forsake him.

While Mark lay in bed that night, his thoughts were plagued by events of the day, starting with what had happened in town this morning, and ending with his conversation with Martha, later. His father's scathing, and somewhat inhumane attack caused him great concern, and he knew that he hadn't seen the last of his father's cruelty. Then too, Mark knew that he did have a sort of strange, and unusual feeling for Martha, despite what he had told her. It haunted him, as much as anything else.

Being a young man of honor, he tried hard to convince Martha that he had no real love for her, however, as he lay here all alone tonight, he seemed to be trying to convince himself as well. No matter how hard he tried to cast it out of his mind, it was ever present, and seemed to increase with the dawning of each day. Perhaps, his father was right to call him a "nigger lover" after all. In addition to all this that was pounding away in his mind like a drum, the responsibility of having to look after the Negroes, now lay heavily on his shoulders as well. He'd brought them here, and he was their keeper, now.

His father had stripped him of everything, including his pride, and will to succeed in life as a farmer, for his hopes of being able to plant a crop in the spring had vanished, along with everything else. Even so, Bill had tried to bolster Mark against such odds, by assuring him that in the end, everything would turn out for the best. They were his only true friends now, however, he feared that their friendship, might eventually become his downfall as well.

Before the Negroes went home, after having helped him clean up the house, Mark told them not to bother with the farm anymore, and let it lay untended. He knew that he couldn't borrow money from the bank, or buy seeds and supplies at the General Store, for his father had seen to that. He also knew that none of his neighors would help him, because of his father's influence over them.

He finally fell off to sleep, only to be awakened at the break of day, by a noise outside. Quickly jumping out of bed, he hurried over to a window, to see what was going on. He saw the Negroes working in a field that lay not far from his house, and it surprised him. He'd told them yesterday that he didn't intend to plant a crop next year. The very thought of them working as if they thought nothing had gone wrong, caused him great concern.

Quickly getting dressed, Mark walked out on the porch, to see if he could tell what was going on. The boys were busy cleaning out the ditches so the rain wouldn't wash the topsoil away, Martha was chopping down the old cotton stalks, and Bill and Liza were on their hands and knees, pulling weeds and briars from along the edge of the field. "Why are they working, when I told them not to?" Mark asked himself, as he shook his head.

"What's going on, out here?" Mark asked Bill, when he walked out to where they were working. "I told you yesterday, that we wouldn't plant a crop!"

"Well, we wuz trying to wuk', fo' you's come out here," Bill replied, as he looked up at Mark, and grinned. "Ain't you's never seed nobid'ee wuk'n befo'."

"I see that you're working, but I told you yesterday that we wouldn't be planting a crop next spring!" Mark replied, somewhat angry with him. "Wasn't that what I said, or did you think that I was only joking?"

"Yass'uh, that's what you sez, but you say that we wuz free, and that we could do as we pleased, too," Bill countered. "Ain't that what you sez, er is you done went and took it back, like yo' pappy took yo' money from you?"

"Yes Bill, you're free, and you do have the right to make decisions of your own," Mark agreed. "But, you need to be working for somebody who will be able to pay you. I don't have any money, and don't have any hopes of having any in the future. Nobody works for me, for nothing. You aren't a slave."

"But, we's ain't wuk'n like slaves, fer we doing what we wan'a do, and a slave can't do that," Bill explained. "The Lord will he'p us, but He 'spects us to he'p our'sef, too. Now, is you gon'a he'p us, er is you gon'a stan' in our way, like a big ole stump, rite in the middle of a field?"

"It seems as though the Lord has forgot all about me," Mark sighed, "but the devil sure hasn't. Every way I turn, there stands the devil. He's always throwing something in front of me, and causing me to stumble."

"Yass'uh, that sounds like the ole devil that I's know, fer he sho' can mess up a feller, in a hurry," Bill agreed. "He sho' is good, at making a feller thank the Lord is fersook him, when all the time, the Lord is peekin' 'round the bushes, ready to jump on the devil, wid bof' feets. The Lord is watching us, and I's bet He sees you standing there feeling sorry fer yo'sef, when you's need to trus' Him, to look adder thangs."

Tears filled Mark's eyes, for he was filled with emotion, as they worked as if their life really depended on how much they accomplished. He felt undeserving of their loyalty, these innocent human beings, who had never known anything in life but slavery. They were the only true friends he had.

"Time is gon'a pass, and we can wuk' it off, er stand 'round and worry it off, like you's doing now," Bill continued. "If the Lord happens to see us wuk'n, He mout send one of His angels to he'p us. When nobid'ee ain't looking that way, He mout slip off and he'p us His sef'. The Lord, He sho' likes to see folks wuk'. Look at the wul'd He built, wid His own hands."

"All right, you ole fool-nigger!" Said Mark, as he playfully jerked off Bill's hat, and slapped him on the back. "Get busy, you sorry slave!" All of a sudden Mark fell to his knees, and started helping them. "Hurry up, for we want this place cleaned up, in time to plant a crop!"

"Now, that's the way to feel 'bout thangs," Bill grinned, as he tossed a handful of grass down Mark's shirt collar. "Get wid it, young sprout!"

All during the rest of the fall and winter, even during times when it wasn't fit to be outside, they continued working as if they really intended to plant a crop, although they knew they would not. Even though Mark felt like it was wasting time he continued helping them, and they didn't even mention what had happened last fall. Everybody worked, nobody complained.

Winter had passed, April was almost here, and had things not fallen apart as they had last fall, they would start planting cotton pretty soon. Farmers always tried to have the cotton planted no later than during the first week of April. The land had been tilled and made ready for planting, ditches had been cleaned to prevent the rain from washing the topsoil away, as they continued praying that they'd be able to plant a crop this spring.

One day while Mark and Bill sat on a terrace bank resting, Mark commented on what they had accomplished, during the past few months.

"Well, we might not see anything growing in those fields this summer except for grass and weeds, but we can boast of having the cleanest farm you'll find anywhere," said Mark, as he looked out across the fields. "If someone didn't know better, they'd swear that we intended to plant a crop."

"Well, you's rite 'bout the place looking good, but you's wrong 'bout not plant'n no crop," replied Bill, as a soft smile came on his face. "We gon'a have a crop, and that's a fac'. It sho' would be bad to let it grow back up, adder we's done wuk'd so hard, and wid fo'ks thanking we gon'a plant a cotton crop, like I know we is. The Lord's gon'a he'p us, but He gon'a do it in His own way, and when He be ready. Yass'uh, that's the kin'a feller He be, gets stubborn sometimes, upsot, when we's don't trus' Him, too."

"That sounds fine," replied Mark, "but short of a miracle, we won't be hauling any cotton out of those fields, this year!"

"But, you's got'a hav' fafe, and keep hoping," Bill told him. "That's the secret, fer the Lord 'spects us to wuk' hard, and be honest. Yass'uh, we got'a do that, er the Lord, He's liable to get upsot wid us."

Mark gently placed his hand on Bill's shoulder. Did Bill know something that he didn't know. Perhaps, Bill's relationship with the Almighty, made him worthy of privileged information, that Mark couldn't comprehend. Whatever be the case, Mark would continue thanking God because this hard-working Negro man was his partner, and his friend.

"Faith can move mountains, they say," Mark nodded, "but it's awful hard to have faith with the devil snapping at your heels, and jabbing you with his pitchfork, every step you take. Do you see what I mean?"

"Well, I's knowed the devil fer a long time, and he ain't the bes' friend a feller is ever had," replied Bill. "But you's got to turn and spit 'backer juice in his eyes, and keep rite on like he wuzn't nowhere 'round. That's the way to treat the devil, fer he sho' hates 'baker juice."

"I understand, and I hate to disagree, or to cause you to distrust God in any way, but I've done all that I can do to get out of this mess, short of stealing or cheating," Mark sighed. "I won't do that at all, I can't."

"We's got some mighty good folks 'round here, and maybe you could axe 'em to he'p us, 'til we's get out'a this mess," Bill suggested. "Is you ever thought 'bout that?"

"I wish I could, but Dad has such a hold on folks around here, until they are almost afraid to breathe, without his permission," replied Mark. "If the truth were known, the devil even dreads the day when he'll have to come face to face with Nate Simpson." They both laughed.

There were a moment of silence, as Bill sat and scratched his head, while Mark gazed out across the fields as if he was dreaming, in a trance, even.

"Speaking of yo' pappy, it give me a good id'ee," Bill finally replied, in a thoughtful voice. "I's got some mighty good friends on his place, and it mout be that I's could get 'em to steal some stuff, to plant a crop wid. We could get the crop planted, and yo' pappy wouldn't never find out."

"That sounds stupid, and I'm ashamed of you for suggesting something like that!" Mark scolded. "I don't know what kind of a God that you worship, but if He allows that, I don't want to know Him! Does Negroes have a special God - one who goes along with such as that?"

Bill slowly stood up, and stretched his arms. "I's been dealing wid the Lord fer a purdy good while now, and I's ain't sho' if He'd thank it wuz a bad thang to do, adder what yo' pappy is done

166

to you," Bill explained. "The Lord made this here ole wul'd, and He 'spects us to keep it planted, no matter what we have to do, to get the seeds. Ain't that what the good book sez?"

Mark laughed out loud. "Don't ask me why, but you do make a little sense after all," said Mark, as he stood up. "An eye for an eye, is that what you mean? In other words, I should steal from him, because he stole from me."

Bill grinned, a wide toothless grin. "Yass'uh, I's guess that's the way I's see thangs -- a toof', fer a toof' -- eye, fer a eyeball," he chuckled.

"No Bill, I couldn't let you do that, no matter what he's done to me, or if I never get a crop planted," Mark firmly stated. "I asked God to work out a way for me to get this farm, and for my father to allow you folks to come along with me as well, and I've asked Him to help me get out of this mess. If I can't get ahead by being honest, and treating my fellow man as I'd like to be treated, then I'll always be poor. Do I make myself clear?"

Bill knew that he was free to do as he pleased, and he could leave if he chose to do so, but his heart was here on this farm with Mark, and he intended to help him. Whatever plan he might eventually come up with, he wouldn't let it involve Mark in any way. He couldn't afford to do that.

Back at the Simpson plantation, Nate had just returned from making a trip to town, for he'd gone to talk with Ellis Bland at the bank, and Mr. Wilson at the General Store, to make sure that neither of them offered credit to Mark, so he'd be able to plant a crop. Still, he was somewhat concerned, for while he was in town, someone told him that Mark already had the land tilled and ready for planting, and he wondered if Mark had outsmarted him.

"I realize that it's stupid of me to even ask," said Julie, as Nate came walking up the steps, to the porch, "but I wondered if you'd been back to see Mark, since that awful night last fall."

"And, why should I do that?" He asked, hatefully. "I have too much pride in myself, to be around a nigger lover! Does that answer your question?"

"I know that you and Powell took all his money last fall, and I wondered if he was going to try to plant a crop this year, or if he had become disgusted, and threw up his hands," she continued.

"According to what I hear, he has the land ready for planting, but he has wasted his time, for I've seen to that," Nate replied, as he reached to open the door, to go inside. "I've made sure that he

167

can't get a loan at the bank, or credit at the General Store, and that stops him cold in his tracks."

"Credit, and money isn't everything!" Julie emphasized, as Nate went on into the house. "There's a higher power than that, if you care to call out to Him for help. Of course, you wouldn't know anything about that."

Simpson's slaves really "hated his guts", but they liked Mrs. Simpson, and she had already set a plan in motion with the slaves to help Mark, should he need her to help him get a crop planted. The slaves were to gather up enough seeds and supplies so Mark would be able to plant a crop, and enough foodstuff so he could survive until next harvest time, and slip it down to him at night. She also had someone in Mark's community watching out for him, and they would keep her informed, as to how things were going for Mark.

Back at Mark's farm, Bill was still concerned about being able to plant a crop, and he decided to explain to Liza, a plan that he had in mind.

"Liza," he slowly began, feeling her out as he went along, "you's know, we got'a have seeds and thangs to plant a crop wid. Mark done tun'd down the plan that I's made to him. Now, I's got another plan in my head. I'd like· to know how you feel 'bout what I's got in my head fer to do."

"Tell me what it is," replied Liza, with a smile. "If it can he'p get a crop planted, it aw'ready sounds good to me, and I's 'gree wid you. What is it?"

"Well, I wuz gon'a sell my'sef back to Mos'a Simpson, so youn's can get a crop planted, and so youn's won't starve to def'," he explained. "Now, that's it."

"You as crazy, as Mark sez you is!" She scolded. "Mos'a Simpson gon'a know that you's doing it to he'p Mark, and he ain't gon'a let you do that."

The boys were outside, but Martha was in the kitchen washing dishes, and she'd overheard what her father said.

"Hey, I's got the bestest plan!" Martha told them, as she came and stood in the doorway. "What if I's went and sold my'sef back to Mos'a Simpson? That would he'p us to get a crop planted, and I's be doing sump'um fer Mark, fer what he done fer me. Now, ain't that a good'un!"

"Good Lord, chile!" Liza wailed. "That ole goat would kill you, jus' as soon as he got his hands on you, fer he done knows all 'bout the buck! He be willing to give up a good seat in Heab'um, and sot in hell on a stump, jus' to get you back there. No, lit'l gal, you's ain't gon'a do that."

"Yo' mammy, she be rite," Bill agreed. "The fus' thang he gon'a do, is sock the buck back wid you, and nobid'ee ain't gon'a be there to he'p you this time. He gon'a kill you, adder the buck wuk's you over."

"He gon'a be so happy to get me back 'til he mout pitch a big party, fer then, I wouldn't be no'whu 'round Mark," she pointed out. "I's done wuk'd it out in my head, and I gon'a head up that way, to'mar moan'n."

Bill and Liza sat speechless. For a fact, her plan was more apt to work, than what he suggested, Bill thought. But, what would Nate do to her. Would he kill her for being a part of Mark's deception. He wondered if he'd stoop so low as to kill her. He'd seen him do some terrible things.

Although her parents knew that she was willing to risk her life in order for Mark to be able to plant a crop, there were underlying motives driving her to a breaking-point, that they knew nothing about. Mark had done all he could to show her that he didn't actually love her, but she was bound and determined to cause it to happen, just the same.

"Let's go on to bed now, and we'll 'scuss it in the moan'n while we eat break'fus, when the boys is here to he'p us make up our mind," Bill said, as he walked toward his bedroom. "No matter what we 'cide to do, we can't never let Mark know nothing 'bout what it wuz that we done."

Neither Bill, nor Liza slept very much at all that night, for they loved their daughter. They loved Mark as well. They knew something must be done in order to get a crop planted. The love these folks had for Mark was unlimited, unimaginable, too. They were willing to do anything, to help him.

It had been two weeks now, since Mark and Bill sat on a terrace bank and discussed the complicated situation they now faced, and because Mark felt that he was mostly to blame, he'd made a point of staying to himself. Mark hadn't spoken to either of them since that day, however what he didn't realize, was that his withdrawal, was actually helping their plan to work.

April arrived, other farmers in the community were already planting their cotton crop, but Mark hadn't planted anything, although the fields were ready. He would stand at his window and look out across the plowed fields, and watch other farmers drive along the main road with loads of cottonseeds, and other supplies, which they had picked up at the General Store. He wondered why this was happening to him. If he hadn't kept the buck away from Martha, and if he hadn't been so eager to prove himself to his father, none of this would have happened, he thought. Should he beg his father to forgive him. Why not sell the farm, and leave the South. All such questions cluttered his mind, and he didn't have the answer to either of them.

Real early one morning, the rumbling of a wagon awakened Mark, and it appeared to be coming up into the yard. Wondering why Bill was driving the wagon around this early, he leaped out of bed, and hurried over to a window to peek outside. To his surprise, he saw one of his father's wagons drive up and stop in front of his house. The wagon was loaded with burlap bags, and wooden boxes, that looked like sacks of cottonseeds, and other supplies. The driver climbed down from the wagon, walked upon the porch, and knocked on the door.

Mark quickly jerked the door open, and stood for a moment looking at the wagonload of supplies, and at the driver, whose name was James.

"Moan'n, Mos'a Mark," spoke James, as he tucked his hat under his arm in respect. "How is you, this purdy fine day?"

"I'm fine, James," replied Mark, as he kept his eyes peeled on the wagonload of supplies, sitting in his yard. "What brings you down here anyway, and where are you headed with that load of stuff, whatever it is?"

"I wuz told to fetch it to you, and I's need to know whu' you wants me to sot it off at," James replied. "Yo' pappy told me to hurry on back, fer you's know how he gets all wuk'd up, when plant'n time come 'round."

"James, are you sure that he sent that to me?" Asked Mark, in a confused voice. "It looks like cotton seeds, and foodstuff, but I didn't order it from him, and I don't know why he told you to bring it to me."

"He loaded it up yeser'dee moan'n, and I's headed out 'bout dinnertime," James told him. "I's got down yon'a at the road las' nite, but I didn't want'a mess up yo' sleep, so I's waited 'til the sun come up, fo' I's come on up here."

Mark could hardly believe that this was happening. "James, are you absolutely sure that he told you to bring the stuff to me?"

Mark asked. "Could you have mistaken what he said, and brought it to the wrong place?"

"Take this stuff down to my boy, that's what he sez," James replied, in a serious voice. "Now, whu' do you's want that stuff sot off at?"

"I'm sure you're telling the truth, even though I don't quite understand, and I suppose he'll send me a bill for it, for he knows that I don't have any money, right now," said Mark. "I hope he don't lay claim against my crop, and take my money, like he did last year."

"I's glad you manchuned money," James smiled, as he took an envelope out of his pocket, and handed it to Mark. "He say to give you this money, and he say he hoped you wuz happy wid the deal you and him made."

"What kind of deal?" Asked Mark, as he quickly opened the envelope, and saw several large bills inside. "I haven't made any kind of deal with him."

"Don't know nothing 'bout that," replied James, "and if you'll tell me whu' to sot it off at, I's gon'a be on my way back torge home."

He told James to unload the supplies under a shed at the barn, while he still wondered why his father had done this in the first place. Did he have a scheme up his sleeve. Was he at last, ashamed of what he'd done.

Regardless to why his father did this, or how much it was liable to cost him later, at least he could plant a crop, Mark reasoned. James placed the boxes of foodstuff on the porch, and unloaded the sacks of cottonseeds, and other seeds under the shed at the barn, and then Mark went in search of Bill, to tell him what happened. Bill saw the wagon arriving, and not wishing to face Mark until he absolutely had to, he made sure that he was as far away from the house as possible. Mark finally found him down near the creek, where he was pretending to be mending a fence.

"Well, your prayers were finally answered!" Mark said, as he ran down to where Bill was working. "I'm not real sure what connection you have with the Lord, but He came through for you once again!"

"What is you talking 'bout?" Asked Bill, acting as though he didn't know what Mark meant. "I's ain't seed you in quite a spell. I's thought you done went and left the coun'ry, er jumped in the well, and drownded yo'sef."

171

"Not yet, even though it has crossed my mind," Mark chuckled. "Although it looked like we wouldn't be able to plant a crop, things finally worked out for us. Yes, we'll be planting a crop, after all!"

"Glory be, and thank the Lord!" Said Bill, as though he was surprised at what Mark said. "How did you's wuk' it out? Did you's find a pot'a gold?"

"I don't expect you to believe me, but Dad sent a wagonload of supplies, and James unloaded them under the shed at the barn," Mark happily replied.

"The Lord, must'a took a big stick to the ole man, and showed him that he done you wrong," Bill chuckled. "Yass'uh, the Lord went and give him a whooping."

"And, there's more!" Mark beamed, as he showed Bill the money that his father had sent to him. "Can you believe this, after what he did to me! It was an act of God, it had to be, for I had nothing to do with it."

"I's thank the Lord fer hearing this old nigga's prayer," said Bill, as he threw his arms around Mark, pretending to cry. "We been saved, 'cause of the prayers that wuz sont up to Him, and 'cause the Lord likes us, too."

"Come on and go with me to the barn," said Mark, as he tugged at Bill's arm, "for I want you to see what all he sent to us. Come on, now!"

Bill realized now, that he did need God's help, as he followed Mark back toward the barn. He had gone with Martha to sell herself to Mr. Simpson, so Mark would have supplies with which to plant a crop, and money to tide him over until next harvest time. He knew that he would have to tell Mark sooner or later, but he had no idea how to go about it, at this point.

"You's rite, 'bout what the Lord can do," said Bill, as they neared the barn, "but we's need to sot down and jaw over what wuz done, fo' we's get too happy over this thang. Can we's do that, fo' we's get to the barn?"

"Oh, we can talk later!" Said Mark, in an excited voice. "Let's be sure of what he sent, then we can tell the others, and especially Martha. I think she worried more about getting a crop planted, than you and I did."

"I 'gree wid you," said Bill, "but we's need to talk this thang over, and we need to do it rite now, too!"

"What's wrong?" Asked Mark, not even bothering to stop. "Do you want to see what he sent? Aren't you glad, that we can plant a crop?"

"Yass'uh, I's glad, and then I's sad too." Bill replied. "You mout not feel so good, when you's hear the truf'. Mout be a lit'l mad at me, too."

When they arrived at the barn, Mark sat down on a sack of seeds and bowed his head. It wasn't quite clear why his father had done this for him, and the unconcern Bill seemed to show, really bothered him. Slowly lifting his head, he looked over at Bill, and noticed tears in his eyes.

"Bill, I'd like to know what's been going on around here, that you're not telling me about!" Spoke Mark, although the strange expression on Bill's face, caused him to dread the reply. "Let me know what you've kept hidden from me!"

"Well, I hate to have to say this, but yo' pappy ain't give you nothing to plant no crop wid," Bill began. "Them thangs you's got, and that money, wuz sump'um that we's done to he'p you, and not nothing that yo' pappy went and done."

"What do you mean?" Asked Mark, almost dreading a reply. "I hope to God, that you didn't steal the stuff from him! Is that what you did?"

"Naw'suh, we's ain't stole nothing" he replied, slowly turning to look away. "Marthie, she got a crazy notion in her head to do sump'um, and none of us could stop her, once she sot her head to do it."

"What was that you said about Martha?" Asked Mark, as he quickly jumped to his feet. "Where is she, anyway? I've looked toward the house every day this week, but I haven't seen her. Can you explain that? Where is she?"

"I's been trying to tell you, that she ain't here rite now," he replied. "But, she gon'a be back, rail soon like. Yass'uh, she sho' will."

Mark felt terrible. "What kind of stupid reply is that?" Mark asked, as he looked straight into Bill's eyes. "I need an answer, and I mean right now!"

"Well, it's sort of like this," Bill began. "Marthie jerked them freedom papers out'a my pocket, then she went and sold her'sef to yo' pappy, so you's could have stuff to plant a crop wid. She gon'a be back purdy soon now, fer I's done jumped on the Lord, and told Him to send her on back here."

"My Lord, Bill, what have you done?" Sighed Mark. "Why didn't you tell me, so that I could have stopped her. Why did you let her do that, anyway?"

"It wuz all her doings, fer we's tried to stop her," Bill sobbed. "That gal made me walk all the way up there wid her, at nite, she sho' did."

Mark cried, as though his heart would break, for he knew that he wouldn't ever see her again, alive, anyway. Then, he grabbed Bill by the shoulders, and shook him real hard.

"Tell me that you're joking!" Mark sobbed, knowing fully well, that Bill was serious. "Please, say that you're kidding me!"

"Naw'suh, I's ain't jok'n wid you," Bill sighed. "You's messed up rail bad when you told her that she wuz free to do what she wanted to do. She went and done zackly what she wanted to do, fer you sez that she had that rite."

"She shouldn't have done that," Mark cried, "for the cotton crop wasn't all that important. She's probably already dead by now, I imagine, but I hope not."

"I's talked wid yo' pappy, to make sho that he treats her rite," Bill replied. "He say he gon'a do that, too. Yass'uh, that's what he sez. Gon'a give her a good deal, he sez."

"I know, but he don't know what a good deal is!" Mark wailed. "Without doubt he'll beat her half to death, might kill her, put the buck with her, I'm sure. She'd be better off dead, than to be back there with him."

"Well, I's trying not to thank 'bout that," Bill replied. "She squalled ever nite, 'cause you wuzn't happy. She wuz hell-bent on get'n thangs so you could plant a crop, 'til it didn't matter what happened to her."

"I know her intentions were good, but she's back in his hands again. She might as well be dead." Mark went on. "No matter what he told you, when he decides to do something, he'll do it regardless to what he promised you, or what anybody has to say. Now, do you unterstand?"

"Yass'uh, I's see what you mean," Bill agreed. "But, that gal is mighty tough to be a womern, and she gon'a come out aw'rite. She gon'a be back here fo' you can say scat, I's know she will."

"But I can't have hope, for thinking of what might have already happened to her," Mark sighed, as tears trickled down his face. "I hate to feel as I do about my father, but after what he did to me last fall, there's no telling what he'll do to her. It hurts, to know that I'll never see her again."

"I's know how you feel, but her mammy done told her what to do if she wuz put wid the buck," Bill tried to encourage him. "Me and the Lord is had us a good talk, and He gon'a slap yo' pappy's face, if he messes wid her."

Mark didn't reply, so Bill turned and walked up toward the house, for he knew there was no way to change things now. He felt that it would be best to leave Mark alone and let him cry it out of his system. Although he didn't dare say anything because he was a Negro, he knew that Mark had been drawn close to Martha by something other than simple friendship.

For more than an hour, Mark sat looking out across the plowed fields, as he thought of the tremendous sacrifice Martha had made, in order for him to be able to plant a crop. He realized that he had a deeper feeling for her, than he dared allow himself imagine. Now that this had happened, he felt as though he might really be in love with her. She was already gone, and he would never be able to tell her how he felt in his heart. Deeply engulfed with sorrow, he suddenly wanted to talk with someone about this feeling he had for her, but he had no friends, except for Bill and Liza.

He walked up to Bill's house, for he must talk with someone. He couldn't go on any longer, with all this guilt resting on his shoulders. When he arrived at the house, he found Liza sitting on the doorstep and Bill standing on the porch, with his head bowed. He could tell that they both had been crying.

"Do you folks mind if I sit with you for a few minutes?" Mark asked, in a polite voice. "I'm in an awful shape, worse than when I tried to, well, you know what I mean. I not only feel hurt because of what Martha did, I feel as though a part of me is missing. I feel like my soul is gone."

"Son, you's don't ever have to axe us if you is welcome here, fer we jus' one mixed up family, wid nobid'ee to 'pend on but the Lord," said Liza, as she caught hold of his arm, and pulled him down on the steps next to her. "Sot here 'side me, and we'll all hurt together, like a family that's los' our chile. Me and Bill is tore up too, so don't be 'shamed to cry yo' heart out, fer you is jus' like our own lit'l boy."

"How in the world can I plant a crop, with me feeling this way?" He asked her, in a soft voice. "Each time I drop a cotton seed, or a grain of corn in the ground, it's going to seem like I'm burying a part of her. This shouldn't have happened. I won't be able to forget this, as long as I live. I'll never forgive myself for not telling her how I felt about her. I can't go on, with this guilt hanging over me."

"I's sorry, too. You ain't never gon'a know how that gal felt 'bout you, deep down in her heart," replied Liza. "She'd walk through a brush pile wid it on fire, er wade 'cross the deepest river fer you. She'd give her lif' fer you, if it come down to that. That gal, is yo' rail friend."

"It's strange how clear things are when you look back at them, after it's too late to do anything about it," Mark went on. "I think she actually loved me, but I acted as though she meant nothing at all to me, and now I realize it was only because of the difference in our color. It's too late to call things back, but I wish now, that I had told her how I actually felt about her."

"Mark, there gon'a be plenty of time to tell her how you's feel," softly replied Liza, as she gently patted him on the arm. "Thangs is gon'a come out aw'rite fer bof' of youn'se, fer she ain't gon'a aw'ways be gone."

"Maybe I can buy her and her baby back next fall, for I know the buck has already been put with her," spoke Mark, as he slowly stood up, then turned to look at Bill. "We'll go ahead with the crop as planned. Even if it takes all the money that I make this year, I'll buy her back. Bill, are you with me?"

"You don't have to axe me nothing like that, Son, fer we's in 'hind you, ever step you take," said Bill, as he walked down the steps. "Now, let's get busy plant'n a crop! We's ain't gon'a get it done, sot'n here squall'n."

To most fine citizens of the South, it was disgraceful for a white person to have special feelings for a Negro, or even regard them as being human, and a true relationship between races, was out of the question. In spite of this, Mark knew that his feelings for this one Negro girl, was quite a bit more than friendship. Though southern white boys were sometimes enamored of the young Negro girls, it was most generally physical, and nothing else. Mark however must admit that his was a deep, heart-felt caring he had for Martha. It was a strange feeling he couldn't explain, one that he couldn't deny, either.

Back at the plantation home, Simpson was bragging at the breakfast table one morning about how he'd brought his insolent son to his knees. So far, he hadn't said anything to his wife about Martha being back on the plantation.

"Just like I said he'd do, your son came crawling to me for help," Nate gloated. "He sold the nigger gal back to me, so that he'd be able to plant a crop this year. I'll eventually bring him down to where he won't have a pair of shoes to wear, a bite to eat, or any place to lay his head."

"That's nothing to brag about, for what you did to him, was low-down and disgraceful!" Replied his wife. "I don't see how you can live with yourself, with food to waste, and money to burn, when he's suffering like that."

"This is a business world!" Simpson sharply replied. "When it comes to making money, or showing my power, I'll do whatever it might take, regardless to who it hurts. If you allow your feelings to stand in your way while doing business, you'll end up like Mark is today. Do I make myself clear?"

"God help you, Nate!" Julie wailed. "You're so pathetic, until I really feel sorry for you. The real fear is that you're afraid if you let up a bit, someone might get the upper hand over you. Isn't that really it?"

"I fear nothing, Madam!" Simpson yelled, striking his fist down hard on the dining table. "I fear nothing, or nobody!"

"Well, you'd better be fearing the mighty wrath of God, and what He can do to you!" She retorted. "You've hurt your own son, until he probably won't have any more confidence in you, or in himself either."

"I should hope not!" Simpson snapped. "He's a liar, and a nigger lover! How can you uphold him, when he lied about putting the buck with that gal? He schemed and lied until he cheated me out of a farm, and five slaves!"

"But, the girl was a virgin and so young!" Julie said tearfully. "When she cried out, he responded in the only way he knew how. That, my stupid, and inconsiderate husband, is what you call humanity, which is something you don't know the first thing about, or have any knowledge of, whatsoever."

Her husband was an unmovable force. "I'm not concerned whether she was a virgin or not!" He blustered. "Mark betrayed me, his own father!"

She was still afraid of her husband, but she grew more and more weary of his cruelty for their son. She wondered if he'd ever let up on Mark.

"Nate, you know absolutely nothing about humanity! Those children grew up together, if I need remind you," she told him. "They're real close friends, but your dirty mind keeps telling you something else. Is that not the real problem; the fact that he gets along with Negroes, and you don't?"

"Regardless to what you might say, there's something more than just friendship between them too!" He sneered. "I honestly believe, that Mark's in love with the black-hussy. It's a disgrace to the South, the world, even! That's the reason I feel as I do. Now, do you understand?"

"I understand what you mean, for I'm also against interracial involvement when it comes to romantic relationship, but I'm afraid that you're driving them into a situation they might not have gotten into otherwise," she cautioned. "Mark needed a friend, so he turned to anyone who could afford him with friendship. Can't you see that's exactly what you've done to him?"

"You're wrong about that!" He sharply replied. "Anyway, I have that gal here with me now. I can hardly wait, to put the buck back with her. I intend to show her who's boss, even if the buck has to beat her to death. That's the kind of person I am. I'll always be that way, I guess."

After hearing this, Julie decided to try another approach. "You somehow forget what your father did for you, for he stood by you until you finally got on your feet," she reminded him. "You seem to forget all the mistakes you've made, or that you gave your father a reason to disown you. I recall a similar mistake you once made that brought shame to your family, so, you have no right to treat Mark, as though you have lived a perfect life. Like my mother used to say, "The stew-pot, can't call the skillet black". The greatest mistake that anyone can make, is when he tries to justify his own mistakes."

"I know what you're referring to, but that was a long time ago. We need to talk about the present time," he scolded. "I gave my son a chance to make it in this world, but instead, he's trying to ruin my name. I made a mistake, when I gave him the farm. He's a nigger lover, born and reared here in my own house, right under my own nose, if you please!"

"I might be wrong, but I think Mr. Powell is the cause of the problem that's come between you and Mark," she replied. "He was mad at you, so he told lies on Mark, just to get back at you. Am I right, Nate?"

"No, he wouldn't lie to me, for I've known him a long time," he replied. "His wife's a good Christian woman. He claims that her and another woman from the church, caught Mark and the gal in the very act. I'm a churchman myself, so it's hard for me to think that she'd actually tell a lie, just to hurt him. Church workers, don't do things like that."

"A church-worker, is she!" Julie chuckled. "Well, you're a deacon, and look at all the God-awful things you do. Look at how you've cheated and lied your way to success. You take advantage of poor farmers, every day. You joined with others, in stripping your son of what he rightly earned."

"You've already said too much as it is, woman!" He snapped. "Keep your lip off my friends, off me, too!"

"No, I haven't said enough!" She quickly replied. "My father once said that a lie could get up and be around the world, before the truth got its shoes on, to get started. You, my dear husband, have been taken in by a lot of cheap, vicious gossip about your own son."

A chilling silence fell over the room. Julie went quietly into the cook room for more coffee. It was very obvious, that she wasn't able to win in the battle to defend her son. There must be something else that she could do.

Although Susan hadn't said anything, she had been listening to every word that was spoken. Susan had sided with her father last fall. She knew that she had to do whatever she could in order to stir up this family "stew pot".

"Mother, have you forgotten the awful things that Mark said about me last fall," she pouted, when her mother returned to the room. "If I were guilty of the things he said about me, you would disown me as your daughter."

"Well you claim that Mark lied about you and that Negro boy," said her mother, "yet you believe what Powell said about Mark having an affair with the Negro girl. Isn't that a little lopsided?"

Susan's true color suddenly showed through. "The difference is, I'm not a nigger lover, like my brother!" She replied, in anger.

"Both of you are my flesh and blood. I love each of you, like any good mother should love her child. I'm not accusing either of you of being guilty of doing wrong," she replied. "I haven't seen either of you do such a thing. Until I do, I have no right to pit one of you, against the other."

"But Mother!" Susan whined. "I'm a fine southern lady! You taught me not to get involved with a nigger, in such a way. But as for Mark, he's always liked that nigger gal. Could it be, that he's your pick in this family?"

"You claim that you hate Negroes, but you really have no way to prove how you feel, deep down in your heart!" Her mother scolded. "You claim that you are innocent, and without proof, it would be wrong for me to doubt your word. He also claims to be innocent. I'll treat him with the same respect that you ask for yourself. We should be friends, with persons of all races."

"The devil with friendship!" Nate shouted, as he quickly jumped up from the table. "He's been messing around with that nigger gal. I'll do whatever I have to do, in order to bring him to his knees. That sorry, nigger lover!"

"Haven't you done enough to him already, without trying to do something else even worse?" Julie asked. "Have you completely lost your mind?"

"He can go ahead and plant a crop, for I have the gal now. We're even as far as I'm concerned," he bellowed, as he left the room. "I'll make her work 'til she drops in her tracks, then as soon as the sun goes down, I'll put the buck back with her until I'm satisfied that she's pregnant."

Though not all farmers hated Negroes as Nate pretended, they must keep up this facade, if for no other reason than to keep others from branding them as a "nigger lover". It was no secret that some white men had sex with the slave women, and white women had sex with slave men, but it was rarely discussed in public. White persons denied it - slaves certainly wouldn't tell.

THE ROSE IS TRIED BY FIRE

It had been three weeks since Nate Simpson had sent a load of cottonseeds and other supplies to Mark, because of a deal that Martha and her father had worked out with Nate without Mark's knowledge. Although Mark used the seeds to plant his crop, he regretted how it all had come about. Even so, Mark's enthusiasm while he planted the crop, was duly overshadowed by his deep concern for Martha, and her present well being. Nevertheless, he worked just as diligently with Bill and the other Negroes, almost in a robotic way at times, for the money he hoped to get for the cotton, would be his only means of being able to buy her back from his father. Perhaps, the only way he'd be able to save her life, as well.

The ominous reality was ever present with him, whether he was working, or resting. Was Martha still alive? On the other hand, he felt sure that if she had been killed, his father would have no doubt delighted in "rubbing his face in the fact", which gave Mark some hope. The thought that Martha was probably still alive was indeed the only thing that kept Mark going. The hope that he might be able to buy her back this fall, gave him some courage, at least.

Martha's parents were beginning to fear for her life, as well. If their plan had worked as they hoped it would, she should have been back home by now. Had they overlooked some vital detail in their plan? They wondered.

"I's don't know what happened to her," said Bill one evening as he and Liza sat by the fireplace, "fer if thangs wuk'd like we's had 'em planned out fo' she left, she ought'a done been on back home. Reck'n her nerves failed?"

"Bill, I's wush you hadn't said that, fer I's been worried all day 'bout the same thang," replied Liza. "Knowing ole Mos'a Simpson, he mout'a tied her up hand and foots, and crawled her fo' he went and put the buck wid her."

"Lord'ee Jesus!" Sighed Bill. "That ole goat ain't got no sense. Yass'am, he mout'a had his eyes sot on her, adder all. I's 'memer when he put a buck wid a gal that wuz nine years old, 'cause she chopped down a few stalks of cotton. Marthie is older, and she mout not have no problem wid him, like that lit'l chile did. I's gon'a try not to worry too much."

"Maybe the buck won't eb'em get to her, a'tall," said Liza. "I's sewed a big butcher-knife in her frock to sca' him wid, 'til she can slip off and come back home. Maybe her nerves won't fall to pieces, er I's hope not."

"I know it's been aw'mos three weeks, but it's a long way from there to this place, and we's got'a make oursef' thank that she's aw'ready on her way back home," Bill suggested."

"I's aw'ready done that," replied Liza, as she went and turned down the quilt on their bed. "Mark's worried too, fer I's here'd him squall'n down at the barn the tuther day, and axe'n the Lord to he'p her. Twixt me and you, I thank he loves Marthie. What do you thank?

"I have to 'gree wid you," replied Bill, "but that's got'a stay twixt me and you. I's ready to go to bed, fer I's got a lot'a wuk' to do to'mar."

Bill and Liza slept, physically exhausted from the long day in the field. They were emotionally drained, by the many days they'd worried about Mark and Martha as well. Mark and Martha were still just children, as far as Bill and Liza were concerned. Their well-being, as well as their future rested heavily on Bill and Liza's shoulders at this point.

Mark had worked extra hard today, as well. Thoroughly exhausted, he went in and sprawled out across the bed, to take a nap before he ate supper. Sheer fatigue finally caught up with him, and he slept on until the wee hours of the morning. Then, he was awakened by the sound of someone knocking on the front door. Still not quite awake, and wondering why he had allowed himself to take such a long nap, he got up and felt his way over to the door. Realizing that it must be very late, for it was dark inside the house, he wondered who could be knocking at his door at such a late hour. Maybe something's wrong down at Bill's house, he thought.

"Who is it?" Asked Mark, still half asleep. "What are you doing here, at this late hour?"

"It's me!" A soft voice whispered. "Op'um the doe', and let me in. Did you's hear me?" Still, Mark couldn't recognize the voice.

"Who did you say you were?" He asked again. "You're whispering, so talk up, so I can tell who you are!" Mark called out, in a louder voice.

"It's Marthie!" She yelled, as she shook the doorknob. "I's back home, so let me in the house!"

At that point, Mark almost jerked the door off its hinges, for he finally recognized Martha's voice. To his happy surprise, there stood Martha on the porch, very much alive. The moon wasn't shining very bright, but Mark could see well enough to know that it was her. Though he was looking straight into her eyes, he still thought he might be asleep, and dreaming.

"Lord have mu'cy!" Squealed Martha, as she lunged forward and threw her arms around him. "Is you glad that I's come back home? Is you, Mark?"

"Co..., come, uh, come on in, Martha," Mark stammered, as he pulled away from her, and stepped back inside. "Let me turn the lamp up, so I can take a good look at you."

Closing the door, Mark went over to a table where he kept a kerosene lamp burning low, and turned up the wick. Martha had followed him into the living room, and when he turned around, he saw that she was muddy and dirty, and her clothes all tattered and torn.

"I's know that I look like a mess," said Martha, as she held the front of her shirt together, for a button was missing. "We's had a hard time get'n here, fer we's come through the woods and swamps all the way, to be sho' that nobid'ee didn't seed us. But, I's here at las'!"

"Did you say that somebody came with you?" Asked Mark, looking keenly at her. "Where are they now? Who came with you?"

"That's rite, they sho' did," she replied. "James come wid me, but he done gone back home now. Yo' pappy locked me and the buck in a building down next to the barn, but adder yo' pappy went somewhu', yo' mammy come down there and let me out. She says she railly hated what he done to you, and felt sor'ee fer my fo'ks, and she let me out'a the building. Adder she kicked some boards off the side of the building, she told James to fetch me back home."

"Wait just a minute!" Said Mark, in a confused voice. "Did you say that my mother helped you escape? Are you really telling the truth?"

"Yass'uh, she sho did," she assured him. "She sez she wuz praying fer you. She sez she wanted to see you rail bad, too. Yass'uh, that's rite."

"God bless her!" He tearfully replied. "I really thought that she might hate me just like my father, but I'm glad she don't. I still love her."

"Naugh, she ain't mad at you," replied Martha, as she went over and sat down on a settee. "She eb'em went and axed 'bout my fo'ks, too. She sez fer you not to feel bad at her, fer what yo' pappy went and done."

"I started to ask if you stopped by to see your family before you came up here, but I'm sure you did," said Mark. "What did they have to say about you being back home? Were they as surprised to see you, as I am?"

"Naugh, they don't eb'em know that I's back," she informed him. "I been worried so much 'bout you, 'til this is the fus' place I's come to. I's thank mo' of you, than I's do my own fo'ks. Now, aint that sump'um!"

"Sit right there, while I go and tell them that you're back," said Mark, as he hurried toward the door. "They love you, as much as anyone else."

Mark ran down to where her family lived, and pounded on the door with his fist. "Hey! Get out of there, for Martha's back!" He yelled. "Did you hear what I said? Martha's up at the house!"

"Yass'uh, I's hear you!" Bill called back, as he began shaking Liza, to awaken her. "I's be on up there, jus' as soon as I's jerk on my britches!"

Not even taking time to awaken the boys, as soon as Bill and Liza got dressed, they headed up toward Mark's house. They didn't know what to expect, or what they should say to Martha, if the buck had been put with her.

"If the buck got to her, you's mout need to talk wid her, so she won't come all to pieces over what happened," Bill suggested.

"I's hope nothing happened, but if she be liv', that's all that matters," she replied, as they hurried along. "We'll jus' have to wait and see. Maybe he didn't eb'em bother her. Maybe she be aw'rite, er I's hope she is. If she still be liv' when we's get up there, that's all that I's 'cerned 'bout now."

Mark had already returned to the house, and was tossing wood on the fire to ward off the chill of the early morning, when Bill and Liza rushed in.

"My baby, my lit'l baby gal!" Liza wailed, as she ran over and threw her arms around Martha. "Lord'ee chile, we thought you wuz dead, never gon'a see you again! Thank you Lord! You's ain't dead neither, is you, chile?"

"Naugh, I's ain't dead, and I's glad to be home, too," Martha sobbed, as she hugged her mother. "Sot down here 'side me, fer I's still too scade to be thank'n rite. Ain't got it through my head that I's back, yet."

Mark knew nothing about the plan for Martha's escape, so he kept quiet as he listened to them crying, and rejoicing over Martha's return. How could his father say these folks had no heart, or any love for their own, Mark thought to himself, as he stood and shook his head. Then, Bill walked over and stood near the settee, as tears trickled down his face. He gently patted Martha on the head, as he stood quietly for a moment, looking down at her dirty clothes.

"Marthie, we's all glad that you's back, eb'em the boys too, fer we 'bout went crazy while you wuz gone," Bill said, tearfully. "The Lord must'a got a lit'l tard of us pester'n Him, and 'cided to send you on back home."

"I'm glad, too," Mark spoke up. "Bill kept on saying that you'd be back one day, but I had my doubts. If you feel like talking, I'd like to know what happened up there, and how my mother became involved. Do you mind?"

"Nothing happened, 'cept that he made me wuk' by myse'f, and wouldn't let none of the tuther slaves come 'round me," she began. "Ever'thang went 'long jus' fine 'til 'bout two days ago, then it all started."

"I'm not quite sure if I understand what you mean," replied Mark, with a puzzled expression on his face." Explain that to me, if you don't mind."

"Well, yo' pappy brung that same ole buck and locked him in that building wid me, and told him to beat me to def' if I's didn't let him crawl me," she continued. "Then, yo' pappy stood outside listening, fer awhile."

"Oh Lord, I figured that he'd do that!" Mark grimaced, as he walked the floor. "He's that sorry, and low down, even if he is my father!"

"Cal'm down, so I's can finish telling my tale," said Martha, a bit more calm now, than before. "It's gon'a get a lot wuss'a, fo' I's get through telling what happened."

"Go ahead then," said Mark, as he stood looking at her. "I'm sick and tired of being left in the dark, like I've been ever since you've been gone."

"Adder yo' pappy locked the doe', he stood outside listening, fer I seed him through a crack in the wall," she went on. "Then, the buck started in to messing wid me, and I's knowed that nobid'ee could he'p me. I didn't have no way to do nothing to help my'sef, wid yo 'pappy standing outside.

"Oh Lord, he wuk'd you over, didn't he, chile!" Liza cried. "I hope the Lord will fergive me and Bill, fer what we's went and hep'd you do!"

"Let me go on wid' my tale!" Martha scolded. "When the buck jerked up my skirt and sprawled out on me, it wuz over, fo' you could say scat."

"My God, he finally got to you, like I thought!" Mark spoke up, gritting his teeth in anger. "That makes me sick at my stomach, for it all came about, because of me. I'm sorry Martha, for it was my fault, and I feel awful."

"Naw'suh, that ain't what happened," she told him, trembling. "When he started poking at me, I's slipped the butcher knife out'a my skirt, and socked it to the handle in his guts. He didn't eb'em scream. He jus' blared his big eyes, and he went limber as a dishrag. He acted like he wuz dead, too."

"Martha, did you really kill him, did you?" Asked Mark, in great concern. "Is he really dead, or were you just kidding us. Where did you get the knife?"

"Mammy fixed it in my skirt," she replied. "He ain't gon'a be bothering no young gals, 'less the devil is got slaves, and needs him. Don't know whu' the devil wuz barned, but if he's from the South, I's know he got slaves."

Mark went over and turned the lamp down low, then hurried to the door, and locked it. He knew that if this happened two days ago, his father already had some men out looking for her.

"Martha, are you sure that you killed him?" Mark asked, seriously. "You might have thought that you killed him, and you didn't kill him at all."

"Naw'suh, he be good'n dead," she replied. "While yo' pappy wuz standing out there, I's screamed like he wuz killing me, and I could see a big grin on yo' pappy's face. When another slave come up and said sump'um to him, he left in a hurry, and I's ain't seed him since then."

"Well, how did you manage to get out, if he locked the door, with you two inside?" asked Mark. "Oh yes, you said Mother helped you!"

"Yass'uh, I's laid there wid him on top of me 'til I's knowed yo' pappy wuz gone, then I's rolled him over 'hind the bed. I's left the knife in his guts, fer I don't thank Mammy wanted me to brang it back," she explained.

"How did my mother get involved?" Mark asked. "Did she accidentally see you in the building, or did she happen to hear you pretending to cry?"

"Later that day I's hear'd a racket outside, and I's knowed fer sho' that Mos'a Simpson had come back," replied Martha. "I's knowed that he wuz gon'a kill me, 'cause I's kilt the buck, and it scade me mite nye to deaf'. When the doe' opened, it wuz yo' mammy. She told me to hurry and get out, and that James would see that I's got back home."

"My God, I'll bet my father's furious!" Said Mark, as he paced the floor in the darkness. "We need to keep our voices down, for I'm sure that he'll be here looking for you, sooner or later. He might be here now!"

"James and me didn't see nobid'ee when we's got here, and didn't run into nobid'ee 'long the road, neither," she told him. "Yo' mammy sez that she wuz gon'a make it look like I's broke out, so she kicked some boards off the side of the building. Say she gon'a make sho' that nobid'ee knowed that James come back wid me, neither. Yo' mammy, she be a rail fine feller."

Mark was proud that she was alive, but he feared what his father was sure to do later. "Martha, do you think James might tell

187

about bringing you here?" Mark asked. "I don't know him all that well."

"Naw'suh, he won't say nothing fer he done all too mixed up 'bout ever'thang," she assured him. "I's told him that the buck wuz taking a nap, and yo' mammy told him that yo' pappy wanted him to fetch me back home."

"I hope you're right," replied Mark, still worried. "Did my mother know that you had killed the buck, or did you even mention it to her?"

"Eb'em if she didn't see him in 'hind the bed, I's thank she knowed that sump'um happened, when she didn't see him nowhu'," she replied. "She told me to get back home and hide rail good, while she tried to figure out some way to he'p me out'a the mess I's got into."

Although Bill had hardly said anything up to this point, he was thinking of what Simpson was liable to do, when he found out what happened. He knew for a fact, that this would be the first place he'd come looking for her.

"Marthie, we's gon'a have to keep you out'a sight 'til we's find out what Mos'a Simpson is gon'a do," Bill warned her.

"That's right, for he's not likely to let this pass so easily," spoke up Mark. "He already paid me for you, with the supplies and money he sent to me, and now he'll have to pay for the buck. He'll come looking for you."

"But, what is we gon'a do?" Sighed Liza, as she hugged Martha. "He'p us thank of sump'um to do, Mark!"

"You'll just have to do the best you can, until I'm able to come up with something," Mark replied. "I'm sorry Martha, for it was all my fault."

"Don't blame yo'sef fer nothing," said Martha, as she and her mother got up off the settee. "Jus' look at all the thangs that you's done fer us."

The Negroes slipped back down to their house, leaving Mark standing alone in the dimly lit room, while he tried to sort through what took place. He was thrilled to have Martha back, but what bothered him now, was how long this was apt to last. His father would come here looking for her, and when he found her, he'd kill her for sure.

Simpson returned home the following morning, after he'd been away for two days looking at some more land he wanted to buy. Julie was sitting out on the front porch when he returned, and as he walked up the steps, he began to brag about how he'd taken advantage of another farmer who had a streak of bad luck, and was forced to sell his farm. Julie hardly paid any attention to him while he continued to rave, as he sat in the porch swing, for she was more concerned about how he'd react when he learned that Martha had escaped, and the buck was dead. He finally stopped talking, took off his coat and threw it over the back of the swing, then walked back down the steps.

"I think I'll look in on the buck and that gal, for he's been locked up in there with her for two days, and I'm sure he's worked her over by now," said Nate. "I finally taught her a lesson, about breaking my rules."

"You don't have a heart, and I wonder sometimes if you even realize there's an Almighty God watching you!" Julie scolded. "She came back to this God-awful place just to help your own son, but you even hate her for that. Could it be that she wouldn't let you mess with her, like you've messed with some of those other slave girls, or is it bacause you're jealous of her and Mark. Could it be, that an old man is jealous of his son and a slave girl?"

"The devil you say!" He bellowed, as he kicked over a pot of flowers that were sitting on the doorstep. "I've never messed with a darned nigger, so don't come at me with that."

"I imagine that the girl's dead by now, for you told the buck to do whatever he had to do, in order to make her submit to him," Julie said, dramatically.

"I don't care if she's dead or not!" He smiled wickedly. "I should have taken care of it before, instead of depending on your nigger loving son to do it for me!"

"Well, I don't want to hear about it!" She said, flouncing her skirt, as she quickly hurried back into the house. "Nate, you're downright stupid!"

Simpson laughed to himself. "That woman sure has a weak stomach, for anything that happens to the niggers," he mumbled to himself. "How could I have ever married such a bleeding-heart type of woman, anyway? All women are the same way." He felt proud of himself, as he walked toward the barn.

Inside the mansion, Julie stood near a window in the parlor, so she could see her husband, when he arrived at the barn. She knew that Mark would be blamed for this, like he'd been blamed for everything else that had gone on around here. She also wondered, if what she had done to help Mark and Martha, might in turn, create more problems for them as well. She hoped not.

When Nate arrived at the building, he quickly unlocked the door, stepped inside, and looked around. "Time to get up, you lovebirds!" He chanted, in a mocking way. He didn't see anyone inside, but the stench that hung in the air almost made him sick. "What's that awful smell?" He yelled, as he placed his hand over his nose. "Did you have to kill the sorry hussy?"

When he walked over and looked behind the makeshift bed, he saw the buck laying on the floor, with the butcher knife sticking in his stomach. Holding his nose, he noticed that some boards had been kicked off the building, and he knew then that Martha had escaped. Furious, he quickly stormed back outside, and then went back up to the mansion to tell his wife what had happened.

When Julie saw him rushing toward the house, she sat down and picked up a book, as though she had been reading. She wondered if she had locked the door back, after she had let Martha out. She hoped she had, anyway.

"That darned sorry hussy, killed the buck!" Nate yelled, as he stormed upon the porch, flung open the door, and rushed inside. "I should have killed her when she first arrived, for now, I'll have to pay for the buck!"

"What happened Nate?" She asked. "Did I hear you say that somebody was dead? Is that poor girl dead? Please, tell me that he didn't kill her!"

The angry Simpson, struck the wall with his fist. "That 'poor girl', as you call her, stuck a butcher knife in his guts! She probably killed him right after I left, for he's already rotten. Your favorite son is to blame!" He fumed.

"Mark?" She asked, now crying for real. "How could he have killed him? He hasn't even been around here, since God knows when! How can you blame him?"

"He had a hand in it, for no stupid nigger is smart enough to plan such a thing as that!" He snorted. "She didn't have a knife when I searched her the day she arrived, and somebody had to give it to her, after she got here."

"If you say she didn't have a knife, then somebody else might have killed him. Don't blame her, or Mark for something they didn't do," she protested.

"Say what you like, for I know that you're on his side, but I'll eventually find out, and I'll see that he reaps what he sowed!" He told her. "An eye for an eye!"

"My God Nate!" She cried. "You hate him so, until you're willing to do anything to destroy him, aren't you. You call him a Negro lover, because some of his friends are Negroes, and now you accuse him of murder, just because you think that one of his friends killed the buck. That's stupid!"

"I'll have everybody in South Carolina searching for her, and when I get my hands on her, she'll have the devil to pay!" He boasted. "I'll chop her into pieces, and tie a piece of her around each nigger's neck, as an example of what will happen to them, if they try a stupid thing like that."

Hearing this declaration, Julie left her husband standing alone with his anger, for she couldn't bear to look at him any longer. Julie knew that Mark and Martha were in more danger, than ever before. She hoped they would decide to run away - to the North perhaps - never to be seen by Nate again.

Still angry, Nate had one of his foremen search his entire plantation, including the shacks, barns, outbuildings, and the woods as well. He sent word to other farmers, telling them that if they shot her, he'd pay them a reward. He sent a man over to tell Ephriam Johnson what had happened, and then he told some of the slaves to throw the buck's body into a gully where they threw dead animals, so the buzzards could devour him. Even so, he figured that she had slipped back to Mark's farm, therefore, he had a man camp out close by where Mark lived, so he could watch for her, and report back to him.

Since she returned to Mark's farm that night, Martha hadn't been allowed to go outside during the daytime. When it became necessary for her to go out at night, her mother went along with her. It had been three weeks since she'd returned, and Mark figured that if his father planned to do anything, he would have already made his move. Still, he wanted to make sure, before letting his guard down, for Mark's mother had sent word to him by a neighbor, warning him what his father had planned. Thus far, he hadn't seen anyone snooping around.

One afternoon when Mark and the others returned to draw a fresh bucket of water from the well in the yard, Martha stepped outside and joined them. This really upset Mark, however, it didn't seem to bother Martha.

"What are you doing out here? Asked Mark. "I've already told you, that Mother said somebody was watching the house! You'll have to stay out of sight for a few days longer, or until it's safe for you to come outside."

"That ain't fair!" Martha complained. "I's want'a be outside wuk'n, like everbid'ee else, and not stay all cooped up inside, like a chicken."

"I understand, but you see what he did when you came up to the house that day to show me the cloth," Mark replied. "He'll kill you, because you killed the buck. He has somebody watching this place, day and night. I wouldn't be surprised, if they were looking at you, right now."

"He ain't got nobid'ee watching the place," she protested. "If he's got somebid'ee watching, I's ain't seed 'em looking in the windows at me, er when I wuz outside the tuther day."

"Hold on a minute!" Said Mark, in shock. "Have you been outside during the day, since I told you not to come outside? Have you?"

"Yass'uh, I's come outside the tuther day, but I didn't see nobid'ee down at the road, 'cept fer a tramp," she told him. "When I's yelled out at him, he jumped on his horse, and run off in a hurry."

Mark suddenly felt faint. "Oh my God, Martha!" He sighed. "That was a man my father had posted at the road, and he saw you for sure! Get back inside as quick as you can, even though it might already be too late!"

No sooner had she turned to go back inside, a noise was heard coming from down the road. They saw Simpson's buggy speeding toward the house, with three other buggies, following along close behind.

"Hurry and get back inside! Mark yelled. "It's my father, and he has a large group of armed men with him! Run for your life, Martha, and pray that he didn't see you!"

Martha ran into the house and slammed the door, but Mark knew that it was already too late. He saw his father stand up in the buggy as he drove up and stopped in the yard, and point his finger toward the house.

Mark quickly turned to Bill, with panic in his eyes. "What will we do now?" Asked Mark. "He saw her run into the house, and he'll kill her, as sure as the world!"

Before Bill had a chance to reply, Nate leaped from his buggy, and rushed up to where they stood near the well. The expression on his father's face was frightening, for Mark had seen this same expression, many times before.

"Hello Dad!" spoke Mark, his voice cracking. "What brings a busy person like you, down here on a weekday? Is Mother sick? Is Susan all right?"

"I'm looking for that darned murdering nigger gal, and from what I saw a minute ago, I've come to the right place!" Simpson bellowed, as he jabbed the barrel of his rifle up against Mark's chest. "Now, where is the hussy?"

"I'm not sure what you mean, for the only woman around here is Liza, and she's standing right over there!" Replied Mark, as he slapped the rifle away from his chest. "Who are you looking for? Did one of your slave women escape?"

"Don't act like a darned fool, for you know who I'm looking for!" Nate yelled. "I saw her go in the house, so you'd better call her back out here!"

"You're not making sense, for no one around here has killed anybody, that I know of," replied Mark, turning to Bill's family. "Bill, did you kill someone without telling me. What about you, Liza. What about you boys."

Before either of them could reply, Nate fired a shot into the air, which caused them to flinch. "I've had a man watching this place, and according to him, he saw the sorry hussy standing in the yard the other day," said Nate.

"You know that you can't believe everything you hear, and he probably saw Liza standing in the yard, and mistook her for Martha," Mark argued. "That's who he saw."

"The devil you say!" Nate snorted. "I personally saw her run back into the house as I drove up, and so did my men! I know she's hiding in there."

Although very frightened, Mark continued acting as though he didn't know what his father was talking about, for there was a slight chance that he didn't see her run into the house after all. If he had, he would have gone storming into the house without asking questions, Mark thought.

"Have you looked around your place for her?" Mark asked. "I understand that she sold herself back to you, she belongs to you, and she knows she'll be killed, if she tries to leave your farm.

Furthermore, I haven't even heard anybody say anything about someone being killed. Who got killed, anyway?"

"You're a darned liar!" Nate yelled. "You know all about the buck being stabbed to death with a butcher knife, and about her escaping, too!"

"Say what you wish, but the last time I saw Martha, was a few days before she came back to your place," Mark lied, in order to protect her.

Simpson then turned to Bill and Liza. "I don't suppose either of you two black bastards have seen her, either!" He jeered.

"Naw'suh, I's ain't seed her since I's come wid her up to yo' place, and yo' boy, he sho' didn't know nothing 'bout that neither," Bill told him.

"You darned lying nigger!" Shouted Simpson, as he struck Bill across the face with the rifle butt, knocking him to the ground. "She's hiding in the house, and you'd better call her out here, before I kill all of you!"

Suddenly, Samuel spoke up. "Mos'a Simpson, that wudn't Marthie that you seed run into the house. That wuz another gal, and she come up here to see me this moan'n. Her fo'ks wouldn't like it if you's kilt her, thanking that it wuz Marthie. They mout get mad at you, too."

"All of you are darned liars!" Simpson shouted in anger, as he fired another shot into the air. "I'll kill the whole darn bunch, if you force me to go in there and drag her out! Do you want to challenge me?"

"Look Dad, we haven't seen Martha," said Mark. "Anyway, you know that a little girl like her, couldn't have killed a big man like him. Did anyone see her kill him? Did you see her kill him, with your own eyes?"

"No, I didn't actually see her kill him," he replied in anger, "but according to the way it looks, she stuck the butcher knife in his guts, shortly after I had locked them in the building. I don't know where she got the knife."

"Then, why come here, looking for her?" Asked Mark. "You just said that she killed him, so look around up there for her, and stop bothering us."

"Hold on there, boy!" He shouted. "All this started because you lied to me about her being pregnant, like you're lying about her not being here! I'm here to find the murdering hussy, and I won't leave until I do!"

Mark realized that his back was up against the wall, so he decided to try some legal tactics, for after all, he had nothing to lose at this point.

"This is my property, and you have no legal right to be here, without my permission!" Mark replied, in a stern voice. "You don't have a right to accuse me, or my workers of a crime like that, so leave us alone!"

"I always keep the law on my side," Nate chuckled. "I have power, authority, and enough money to back up anything that I decide to do. Must I show you, that I'm willing to back up my words with action?"

"But where is the law now?" Asked Mark, as he looked around as if he was looking for someone. "Where are the legal papers, that give you a right to be trespassing on my property, without having my permission?"

Simpson's face was now red with anger, as he cocked the rifle, and aimed it at Mark's chest. "I came here to do a job, and I'm willing to kill you in an instant, if you try to stop me! Must I prove my point?"

"Dad, you've always boasted of being a reasonable type of person, and if you don't mind, I'd like to make you an offer," Mark suggested. "Neither of us will lose anything, or have to back down. What do you say?"

"Hey! Don't make me laugh in front of my friends out there," his father sneered. "What kind of offer do you propose, pray tell?"

Mark thought he might have brought his father to a bargaining table. "Drop things right where they are, and when I gather my crop, I'll pay Ephraim Johnson for the buck, and reimburse you twice the amount that you paid me for Martha," Mark proposed. "What do you say?"

Slapping Mark's hand away, Simpson shouted. "I don't shake the hand of a nigger lover, and I don't need your money! I'm here to get revenge, even if I have to wipe out the whole darn bunch in the meantime! Do I make myself clear?"

"Well, I made you an offer and you refused to accept it, and that's all I can do," replied Mark. "Now, I must ask you to get off my land."

"I don't make deals with a liar, or a nigger lover!" Nate scolded, as he motioned to the men, who had come along with him. "Come on fellows! Tie the men to that clothesline post, then kick the darned woman in the guts, for we have a job to do!"

Immediately, the men hurried over to where Nate stood. "What about your son, Nate?" One of the men asked. "Should we tie him to the post, as well?"

"Of course, for he's lower down, than the niggers he upholds!" Nate told them. "Treat him like he is, a trashy nigger lover!"

The men tied Mark and the Negroes to a clothesline post, while Liza stood and watched, as she dreaded what was sure to happen to her young daughter, who had gone into the house to hide. Then, Nate took his foot and kicked Liza in the stomach, and she fell to the ground, groaning with pain.

Looking around at the men who were helping his father carry out this act of violence, Mark saw his old Sunday School teacher, and a longtime neighbor. He felt pity for them, for he realized that they had become entangled in his father's web of deceit, like all the others with whom his father had dealt.

"All right fellows some of you can go inside and drag her out, while the rest of us watch the windows and doors," Nate told the men. "Be careful, for she's hnady with a knife, but bring her out, dead or alive!"

Four of the men stormed into the house to search for Martha, while Nate and the others remained outside, with their weapons pointed toward the windows and doors. Mark could hear the men inside, kicking and tossing the furniture around as they searched for her. A few minutes later they stepped back out on the porch, but Martha wasn't with them, which did give Mark some hope. Maybe they couldn't find her, or maybe, they had a change of heart, and decided not to go along with this act of violence after all. He hoped they had, anyway.

"Sorry Nate, but nobody's in there!" Said one of the men. "What do you want us to do now?"

"Tear the whole darned house apart!" Simpson demanded. "I saw her go in the house with my own eyes, and she hasn't come back out. She's in there, I tell you!"

"Elmer's right, for she's not in there," said another man. "We searched the houes room by room, and couldn't find her. Unless she crawled up into the chimney and hid, I don't know where she could be. You might have been wrong, I mean, about seeing her run into the house."

Mark could hardly believe his ears. Like he first thought, the men might have changed their mind, and decided not to go along with his father. Because the men were unable to find her, even though Mark knew that she was inside, perhaps his father would go on and leave them alone, Mark thought.

"I told you that she wasn't in there, but you wouldn't believe me," said Mark. "She's probably hiding on your place, right under your nose!"

Nothing was said for a few moments, while Nate stood with his head bowed, and the men awaited further instructions. It seemed as though Nate was now at a crossroad, and Liza decided to add something to what Mark had said, in hopes of convincing him that Martha was not here.

"Yo' boy didn't know nothing 'bout her coming back to yo' place," softly spoke Liza, as she held her hand on her stomach. "As fer as I's know, she is still up there at yo' place. Go up there, and look fer her."

"It makes no difference what any of you say, I saw her run into the house, and close the door behind her, and she's still in there!" Nate assured them.

"Unless she happened to climb up inside the chimney, like Elmer said, I have no idea where she could be." One of the men again pointed out.

"You're probably right," Nate agreed. "Let's set fire to the house, and we'll try to smoke her out, then we'll shoot her like a rabbit on the run!"

The men gathered up some dry grass, and piled it up at each corner of the house, then set fire to it. In an instant, the dry boards on the wall started to burn, then the fire quickly spread to the wooden shingles on the roof, and within minutes, the entire house was engulfed with flames. Mark knew that she was inside, with no way to escape. If she didn't come out she would be burned alive, and if she did come out, she would be shot. Mark knew there wasn't any hope for her, and he blamed himself for what was happening to her now.

"Fire some shots into the house, and maybe she'll run out so we can shoot her, before she burns to death!" Simpson shouted. "I'll get more good out of shooting her while she's running, than I will, if she burns to death inside the house."

"There's no reason for all that!" Mark screamed. "Why don't you act like a human, and listen to reason, for the men already said that she wasn't inside?"

"Shut your mouth, you lying nigger lover!" Simpson snorted. Then turning to the men, he said, "Go ahead fellows, and let the rifles bark out, real loud!"

As the fire roared and the shots rang out, Mark's heart ached, for Martha could not escape death at the hands of his father. How in the world could one human, be so cruel to another. Mark asked himself. His father always said to "pass out judgement without reservation, or consideration." He was doing exactly what he'd always told Mark to do.

"Oh Lord'ee, I's hope our plan wuk's, and that she comes out'a the fire liv'," Bill prayed out loud. "Please Lord, he'p that po' lit'l gal get out'a that far."

"What was that you said Bill?" Whispered Mark. "Do you know something, that I don't know? Please tell me, if you do!"

"Naw'suh, I's guess not, jus' praying out loud, I's guess," he replied, in a soft voice. "Trying to keep legs under my prayers, that's all."

Simpson stood with his hands on his hips until the roof caved in, then a smile came on his face, for he knew Martha was dead. He walked over to where Mark was tied to a post, and waved Martha's freedom paper in his face.

"Here's the darned so-called freedom paper that you gave her, which isn't worth the paper it's written on!" He jeered, as he tossed the paper down at Mark's feet. "I'll go back home now, and you don't owe me anything, for that fire paid your account in full." Then Nate and the other men quickly climbed back into their buggy to leave.

Just as quickly as they arrived, Simpson and his friends left, leaving Martha burning to death in the fire, and Mark and the others tied to a post near the edge of the yard. Mark bowed his head in shame for having such a man as this for a father, and for the hurt he had brought on Bill's family, because of his firm stand against slavery.

Quickly jumping up, Liza went over and untied Bill and the boys, and they hurried toward the house, that was nothing but a pile of burning timbers. The heat was almost unbearable, but they had to search through the burning timbers for Martha, or enough of her for a proper burial, at least. This really upset Mark, for they worked as though they really expected to find her still alive.

"Poor Martha!" Mark sighed, as he looked at the heap of burning timbers. "I hate that she had to die like that, but I guess she's at peace, something I will never be able to enjoy. Liza, I'm not ashamed to tell you that I really did love her, but it's too late now, for she's gone forever.

"They sez, true love never dies," Liza told him, as tears trickled down her cheeks, "and that there ain't no fire that is able to burn it up, neither. Marthie sho' wanted to hear you to say that, and she will, maybe someday."

"I hate myself for not telling her before, but here I sit, watching while she burns up in the fire, wishing that I had," he wailed. "I couldn't search through those ashes for her, and I don't see how they can either. I wish now, that I had died in the barn that day."

"Mark, there ain't no use fer you to fall to pieces," said Liza, as she untied his hands, "fer the Lord can spit on the fire and put it out, fo' that po' chile burns to deaf'. Bill sez, for us to put legs on our prayers."

Mark sat with his face in his hands, as he listened to the cracking fire. It seemed to grow hotter each moment, as Liza looked out toward where Bill and the boys were pulling and tugging at the burning timbers, as they searched for Martha's body. Oh, if Mark only knew what kept them going.

"Liza, this is awful," sighed Mark, as he stood to his feet, and started walking toward his house. "There's so much hatred in the South, until I can't afford to call this my homeland anymore. As soon as I pack my clothes I'm leaving this God-awful place. There's nothing left for me to live for."

She really felt sorry for Mark. Liza and Bill had begun to think of Mark as their child, and were more concerned for him, than his own father was. Now that he had openly confessed to his special feelings for Martha, which she and Bill already knew, it caused her to feel much closer to him. Her heart almost broke, as she stood and watched him walking away.

"Oh Mark!" She cried. "Please don't go off and leave us in this mess, fer we's got'a have faif' in the Lord! Come on back and he'p us look fer the po' chile. Please he'p us, jus' this one mo' time!"

"How do you expect me to have faith, when God has turned His back on me?" He asked, not even bothering to look back. "Find some quiet place to bury her where her grave won't be trampled on, like she has always been trampled on. I hope God will forgive me, but I'm going to kill my father for what he did

199

here today. I'm going to leave the South, and all this hatred, for there's nothing left here for me but memories of sorrow, and unending pain and misery."

This was the most pathetic sight Mark had ever seen, for even though the house had burned to the ground, Bill and the boys worked feverishly while they called Martha's name, as though they expected her to answer them. The crying, praying, and begging God to spare Martha's life, was tearing Mark apart. Even though their face and hands were blistered and bleeding, and their clothes all scorched and burned, they kept on working and humming a mournful tune. He was not able to take any more of this, so he started to run toward home.

Then, he suddenly stopped and looked out across the fields of cotton that were growing well, and he was reminded of the awful price it had cost him, the life of a very dear friend. He also remembered promising the slaves that he'd take care of them, but look at all the heartaches and sorrow he had caused them to bear. He asked God to forgive him for what he had caused these poor slaves to endure, because of his stand against slavery. Then, he remembered Bill saying to him one day: "It's gon'a be like this fer us, 'til the day we's die."

"Lord, have mu'cy!" cried Liza. "There's my lit'l baby gal, and she sho' do look bad, too! My po' baby, let me get my hands on you!"

Mark almost fainted, for they had obviously found Martha's body. "Oh my Lord, the poor thing is dead," Mark sighed, as he continued on up toward his house. He wanted to stop and look at her for one last time, but he couldn't.

"Mark! Come back down here and see what we's found!" Liza called to him. "Get on back here, fer this is sump'um that you's got'a see fer yo'sef!"

"I can't, for I'm already sick at my stomach, so go ahead and bury her," he cried. "It's my fault that she's dead, and I can't bear to look at her."

"But, you's got'a take a look!" Liza pleaded. "You can't leave us in a mess like this, wid no house to live in, and nothing to live fer, when you is gone. Come on back, Son, and look at her fer the las' time, fo' you leave!"

Mark stopped just short of the house. Liza was right; he couldn't afford to let them down. He had to help them bury Martha, for he owed them at least that much, for what they had done for him. However, when he looked back, what he saw was more than his eyes could believe. There stood Martha in the road, and even though she was covered with dirt and ashes from head to toe, she was alive. This can't be! I saw the house burn, with her inside! He thought.

Mark stood for a moment dumbfounded, thinking that he was looking at her ghost. Then it dawned on him, that it really was Martha. "Oh my God!" Cried Mark, as he ran toward Martha, with outstretched arms. "Thank the Lord, you're still alive!"

Mark stood for a moment with his arms around Martha, and cried as though his heart would break. He didn't think that he'd ever see her alive again.

"Martha, how did you hide from those men, and how did you endure all that heat, without being burned to death?" Mark asked. "I saw the house burn, and even the devil couldn't have withstood all that heat. Do you mind telling me how you managed to escape, for it's tearing my mind apart."

Then up walked Bill, with his clothes scorched and burned, his hands and face blistered and bleeding, and his eyebrows singed. Mark then looked at the boys, who actually looked worse than Martha, even though she had just come out of the burning house. Mark placed his hand on Bill's shoulder, and smiled.

"We all saw her run into the house and she didn't come back out, but here she stands, very much alive!" Mark reminded him. "Tell me if you can, how Martha managed to come through all that heat without a hair on her head being singed. Now, old man, let me hear you explain that, if you can!"

"Well, she be liv', and I's thank the Lord fer that, eb'em if she do look like she been in a hog pen," Bill chuckled. "God is a purdy good feller, but He 'spects us to put legs on our prayers, too. Yass'uh, that's what we done, we's put legs on our prayers, when we axed Him to he'p Marthie."

"Hold on a minute, you old fool nigger!" Mark teased. "That wasn't an answer to my question at all. I want to know how it really happened."

"Ever nite while you wuz worrying 'bout yo' pappy coming here to look fer Marthie, me and the boys wuz busy digging a hole in the ground under the back porch," he began. "Then, we's throwed some ole quilts in the hole, and poe'd water in the hole to keep the quilts wet. I's thought sump'um like this mout happen, and if it did, she could wrop up in them ole wet quilts, and she wouldn't be bunt up. That's how we's put legs on our prayers."

"That's hard for me to believe," said Mark, "for I haven't seen a spoonful of fresh dirt anywhere around your house. Can you explain that?"

Bill smiled, and winked at Liza. "You see, we's went and dumped the dirt in that ole dry well down b'low the barn, so you wouldn't see it," Bill explained.

"I'm glad, for it saved her life, but why didn't you folks tell me ahead of time, so that I wouldn't have worried myself almost to death?" Asked Mark.

"The Lord be a purdy good feller, but He gets mad, when somebid'ee gives His secrets 'way," Bill smiled. "Now, that's the reason why we didn't tell you."

"Let's draw a fresh bucket of water from the well, then you folks need to go down to the creek and wash off," Mark told them. "I'll have to gather up some clothes for you to wear, and you'll have to live with me until we can build you another house. Put legs on our prayers!" Mark chuckled.

It was almost sundown, when Simpson returned home. He had told his wife that he was going to Mark's place to look for Martha, and for the past hour or so she had been sitting on the front porch, waiting for him to return. As he walked up on the porch and sat down, she saw a satisfying smirk on his face, and it bothered her quite a lot. She knew that there were no limits to how far he'd go to get revenge, and she worried about what he was apt to do to Mark, when he found Martha on Mark's farm.

"Well, that put an end to one sorry hussy!" Nate boasted. "I watched as the house burned to the ground, with her inside. Yep! She burned to a crisp, right before my eyes! I made your son stand there and watch, too!"

Julie quickly jumped to her feet. "What do you mean by the house burning with her inside?" She asked, as her face turned ghostly white. "Did you set fire to the house, with that poor girl inside? That's horrible!"

"There's nothing horrible about killing a nigger, who's caused me as much trouble as that sorry hussy has caused!" He smiled. "I saw her run into the house so I burned it down, with her inside."

"Where was Mark at the time?" She quickly asked. "Did you hurt him? I hope you didn't kill him, too! My God Nate, did you kill your own son?"

"No, your precious son wasn't hurt, but like I said, we tied him to a post, so that he would have to watch, while she burned to a crisp," he replied.

"Are you sure that she's actually dead?" Julie asked, hoping that he only thought that she was dead. "Did you actually see her charred body?"

"No, but I saw her run into the house right before we set fire to it, and I watched the roof burn and fall in, and she didn't come back out," he firmly stated. "A rat couldn't have escaped all that heat, and I'm pretty sure that I heard her scream out real loud, when the roof fell in. She's dead, all right."

"That's awful, Nate!" She sighed. "I don't see how you can claim to be a Christian, and do such things. How in the name of God, can you sit there with a smile on your face, with such as that hanging over your head."

"Listen woman!" He scolded. "I did what I should have done, a long time ago. She's dead now, out of my hair for good, and away from Mark, too!"

Julie hurried back into the house, for she couldn't bear to listen to her husband bragging any longer. She was heartbroken, and ashamed of him.

Word soon spread like wildfire about Martha's death, and when the slaves on Simpson's plantation heard about it, they grew very angry. They loved Bill and his family very much, and they didn't intend to allow Simpson to go unpunished. The men slaves got together one afternoon, to discuss their plan for revenge.

"Fellers, we done got mos' of the cotton, and corn planted," said one of the slaves, named Luke, "and we's need to learn that ole goat a good lesson, fer what he done to Marthie. He got'a pay, fer what he done to her!"

"What is you got in yo' head, fer to do?" Asked another slave. "Tell us what you gon'a do, so's we can he'p you wid yo' plan, whatever it be."

"Well, we's need to soak the res' of the seeds in kerosene, so they won't sprout, when we's plant 'em," Luke explained. "Then at nite, we's gon'a pull up mos' of the plants that's aw'ready growing, so he won't hardly have no crop left growing in the fields. Is all you fellers in this wid me?"

"We sho' is," one of them replied. "I'll get all the kerosene out'a the lamps in our shacks, and we'll start to'nite."

CHAPTER SIX

THE ROSE BLOOMS ON

It was now several weeks later, and the news of Martha's death had spread as rapidly as did the flames that had supposedly taken her life. Mark planned to let everyone continue thinking that Martha was dead, for he figured that it would be best for her own personal safety. He knew that if his father thought that she was still alive, he'd return and kill her for sure, for he wasn't the type of person to allow himself to be outsmarted by anyone, and especially not by a Negro. Her family had lost everything in the fire, however, knowing that Martha was still alive, outweighed their loss.

A neighbor had an old house on his farm, and he gave it to Mark if he and Bill's boys would tear it down and haul it to his place. Other farmers in the community helped Bill and his boys rebuild the house, local churches furnished their house with odd pieces of furniture, and donated clothes for Bill and his family as well. During this time, Martha stayed out of sight, for Mark planned to keep this secret from everyone for a while longer. Amid all the heartaches, and setbacks they'd recently suffered, Mark and the Negroes continued working together as a team, if for no other reason than to prove to Mark's father that they really could survive on their own.

Mark's cotton crop was growing just fine, for which he was very thankful, for it was sure to be his saving grace. The price of cotton was on the rise, he had no liens against him, and if he were favored with good weather, his crop would be even better than the one he had last year. Maybe God hadn't forsaken him after all, he thought.

Though Mark's house was adequate and comfortable, he had already dreamed of building a new house for himself one day. He felt that if his father would go on about his own business and leave him alone, he could most likely become a successful farmer in time. He vowed not to allow greed, and thirst for power to overcome him. He could never become the type of person his father was, no matter how rich and powerful he might become.

Mark did have a lot of pride, southern pride, and he realized that. Wealthy farmers in the South enjoyed a high social status, and they didn't hesitate in flaunting their prosperity at every opportunity they had. Mark was aware of how that a bigger and nicer home would be an advantage to him in gaining a higher social standing in the community. He was more concerned with winning respect and admiration of others by his high moral standards, and the way he respected and treated his freed-slaves, than he was in gaining great wealth and power.

The great concern and respect Mark had for the freed-slaves, coupled with the love and admiration they had for him, made them an unbeatable team. Mark could depend on Bill's guidance in operating the farm, his family was loyal to him in seeing that all the work was carried out right, and they knew that Mark was their genuine friend, although he was a white person. For the first time in his life, Bill felt like his knowledge and ability was appreciated, and the fact that Mark treated each of them like human beings, caused Bill to realize that Negroes were worth something after all. One day while Bill and Mark were looking over the cotton crop, Mark decided to tell him about a plan he had in mind for the future.

"If we have the kind of crop this year as I expect, and unless something else happens to set me back, I'd like to start making plans to build myself a new house," Mark told him. "When, or if that happens at all, you folks can move into my house, and I'll let some of the other Negroes I plan to hire, move into the house you now live in. How does that sound?"

"I's glad that you want a new house, but the one that you's stay in now, is too fancy fer a bunch of niggas," Bill replied. "What do you's want wid a big ole house, wid nobid'ee living in it but you. You's gon'a look like a black-eyed pea, rolling 'round in a big ole hamper basket."

"I have a reason, and a very good one, too," Mark replied. "If I become successful, then I need to look successful, right down to the house in which I live. When the other farmers see that I'm prospering by treating my freed-slaves fair, and respecting them as I do white folks, they might follow my lead, and treat their slaves the same way. What do you say?"

Bill thought for a moment, as his mind flashed back to Mark's father, and the way he had always treated his slaves. He also remembered what had happened to Mark not so long ago, because he took up for Bill's family.

"Well, it's aw'rite fer you to have a fine house, but you sho' don't need to 'spect other fellers to start treat'n their slaves no better," Bill replied. "They ain't gon'a say that we is human, and they sho' ain't gon'a pay us fer wuk'n neither. That's a fac', that you's got'a learn to live wid."

"I'm not so sure about that," Mark replied, "for Southerners are pretty impressionable, if I may say so myself. If some of the fine citizens see that I'm prospering by the way I treat my workers, they might come over to my side in spite of what my father might have to say against them."

"I's still say you is wrong 'bout 'em paying a nigga fer wuk'n, but you's rite 'bout want'n a fancy house," Bill smiled. "Then, you's need a lit'l gal of yo' color, to live wid you. Yass'uh, a big house, and a purdy woman, sho' is what you need. Is you ever thought 'bout get'n a purdy white gal to live wid you, er is you ever been sweet on a gal in yo' lif'?"

"Well, I've chatted with the banker's daughter at church, but it's always been rather friendly chats, and nothing serious, or romantic," Mark replied.

"That's fine, but is you talked 'nuf to her, to find out her name?" Bill asked. "Is you thought 'bout axin' her name, fo' you axe her to marry her?"

"Her name is Carolyn, Carolyn Bland, and she's the prettiest girl, I've ever seen!" Mark bragged. "But, I'm sure her father would never permit me to call on her, for he and I aren't the very best of friends."

"But, if you's had a purdy new house, and a pocketful of money, it would make him change his mind in a hurry," Bill laughed. "Money, sho' can change thangs in a hurry, yass'uh, it sho' can."

"Well, a new house and a wife is a long way off, and they might never come my way," said Mark, as he started walking across the field. "I'll have to be making a lot more money than I'm making now, to afford a new house, and as for a wife, that's something that I haven't even thought much about."

Though Mark had admitted to Liza that he loved Martha, he'd never gotten around to telling Martha in person, and he wondered now, if he ever would tell her how he felt about her. This was during the time she had sold herself back to his father, and again when he thought that she was dead, however, now that she was alive and with him every day, he hadn't said anything else. Mark knew that he had a special feeling for her, but he also knew that a true, romantic relationship with her was impossible. Even Martha felt that her deep caring for Mark must be kept under wraps. After all, she was officially dead. She continued to remain out of sight to the public, and Mark hoped that they could keep this secret for a while longer, at least. He had a plan in mind, but he didn't dare discuss it with anyone, not even with his closest friends.

It was now several months later, the cotton was almost ready to pick, and Mark's anxiety grew stronger with each passing day. From all indications he'd have a bumper crop this year, therefore, he made arrangements with other freed-slaves in the area to help Bill's family, and he promised them a fair share of the crop as well. Though their former masters had set them free, and they had a right to work with whomever they chose, their former masters frowned on Mark because he agreed to pay them, just like other farmers paid white persons.

As harvest time drew near, Julie Simpson wondered if her husband planned to sabotage Mark's crop this year, like he did last year. One morning at the breakfast table, she dared to broach the subject with her obstinate husband.

"Well, I wonder what will happen to Mark this fall," said Julie, as she sipped her coffee. "What do you plan to do to him this time?"

"Nothing should happen, if he stops messing around with those trashy niggers, and treating them like human beings!" Nate snorted. "What did you mean by that?"

"Well, the last Negro you accused him of messing with, died when you set fire to their house," Julie snipped. "Who do you suppose he's messing around with now, her mother! I wouldn't doubt that's what you're thinking."

"That sounds stupid!" He replied, curtly. "He can't expect to prosper, and fool around with a bunch of niggers, for it's already been tried before."

"That really doesn't answer my question!" She scolded. "You cheated him out of everything he had last fall, this past spring you killed one of his slaves, and I wonder what you have in store for him this fall."

"Things like that don't bother me, for he stepped out of line, and he got exactly what he deserved!" He snorted. "I uphold the laws of the land, and I take a firm stand against injustice. I'll do whatever I must, to bring a fool like him to his knees. Now, do I make myself clear?"

"Someday, you'll pay dearly for what you did to him," she scoffed at him. "Vengeance belongs to the Lord, and He'll do the repaying. God won't let you go unpunished, and you might as well get set for His wrath."

"Well, if it comes, let it come." Simpson smiled smugly. "I'll defend what I believe in, and I'll kill if need be in order to protect my name, and social standing in the community. God has nothing to do with what a man does to protect his interest, even though it might mean destroying someone in his own family, in order to accomplish his goal."

Julie bit her lip, as she looked across the table at him. "You might not think so, but if you'll compare your crop with other crops in the area, you'll see that something went wrong," she protested. "Something happened to cause your crop to fail, while the other farmers have an excellent crop. You don't suppose that God might have had a hand in causing the failure, do you."

"So, you're an expert farmer, now!" Simpson shouted. "I had a bad crop, like we all have at times, no big deal. I don't want to hear anything about my crop. That's none of your concern. None of God's, either."

"Very well then," she replied. "Let me finish, then I'll leave you with your hatred for your son, and your disrespect for God. If every white man who has messed with a Negro woman suddenly died, the cemeteries would be filled to the brim. According to what I've heard some of the women slaves say, you'd be first in line to be buried. You're trying to show up Mark's faults, while you're trying to keep folks from looking at your own faults."

Without even offering to defend himself, he jumped up from the table, and stormed out of the room, wondering how much she really knew about him.

Within a few weeks, the farmers had picked and sold their cotton, and they celebrated an excellent crop-year, that is, except for Nate Simpson. He had a miserable crop, to say the least. What his slaves had done to revenge the death of Martha, had surely taken its toll. Regardless of how he might feel deep down inside, he wasn't the type of person who would admit that this might have been an act of God, or something that was brought upon him by other persons, even the slaves, because of what he had done to them.

Early one morning, Bill and Mark boarded the buggy to go into town to get the money for the cotton the banker had sold for him. They were happy for the excellent cotton crop, with which they had been blessed. The Negroes had not been paid for working before, or even offered a word of thanks or appreciation for the hard work they had done, therefore, Bill looked forward to being paid for the first time in his life. Most of all, Mark was thankful that he would be able to show his appreciation by paying Bill and his family, as well as the other freed-slaves, who had helped them pick the cotton.

"Well, I've always heard that Negroes didn't know anythng at all, but I must admit that you've taught me more about life than anyone else I've known," Mark said to Bill, as they rode along. "Above all, you have taught me how to put legs on my prayers," Mark chuckled. "You helped to mold my life, and you showed me the importance of holding on, when all my hopes had vanished.

"Well, lif' is the portion of time that we's 'joy while we live," replied Bill, seriously. "You mout live to be a hun'dud years old, but if you's ain't never 'joyd yo'sef, then you ain't never lived. Yo' pappy is got money, and a lot'a land, but he ain't never lived nar'ee day in his lif'. He is a dead man, walking 'round like a ghost, scarin' other fo'ks to deaf'."

"I thank God every day for you folks, and how He has kept me from doing a lot of things that I would have regretted later," Mark told him. "We all had to suffer a lot, but it has drawn us closer together as a team."

"You's thought the Lord fergot us, but look at what He done fer us," Bill reminded him. "We's had a hard time, but none of us ain't starved to deaf', er if we is, I's ain't missed nobid'ee."

"Back last spring when everything looked awful bad, you kept on humming as though you didn't have a care in the world," Mark told him. "I would like to know how you acted so happy, when all our hopes were gone."

"When I wuz jus' a lit'l boy, and felt bad 'cause they jerked me out'a my mammy's arms, and brought me over here, I's seed sump'um one day that caused me to see thangs in a dif'unt way," Bill began. "I's seed a bird in a bush, and it wuz sang'n like nothing wuz wrong, then I's noticed that it didn't have but one foots. When I's looked in a nest close to her, I's seed three tiny birds. Then, I's knowed that she wudn't sang'n cause she had one foots, but 'cause of the babies she had in the nest. No matter what happens to us, if we take time to look 'round, we can aw'ways find sump'um good in lif', and sump'um to sang 'bout."

They talked, and laughed together all the way to town, for Mark loved the old Negro man, and Bill thought as much of Mark, as he did his own children.

As soon as they arrived, Bill parked the buggy across the street from the bank, and Mark quickly leaped down and walked briskly inside. He sat down on a bench with other farmers, who were waiting their turn to go in and speak with the banker, Ellis Bland. Memories of what had happened to him last year came flashing through his mind, when the banker finally opened the door, and stood in the doorway for a moment, looking straight at him. "I wonder what I'll be facing this year," Mark said to himself.

"Gentlemen, as I've done before, I'm going to get the smaller farmers out of my hair first, so that I'll have more time to spend with you fellows," the banker explained. "So, you'll be first, Mark Simpson!"

"But Sir, that's not fair to these gentlemen!" Mark protested. "If you don't mind, Sir, I wish you would let these gentlemen go ahead of me."

"Son, this is my bank, and I set the rules!" Sharply replied the banker. "Either you do exactly as I say, or you can come back sometime later!"

A sinking feeling came over Mark, as he went into Bland's office and sat down. Had his father been here earlier, to spread his poison. Was he in for another fight with Bland, like he faced last year. He certainly hoped not.

"Well, it looks like you did real well this year, and most of all, or at least according to my records, you have no liens against you," Bland said, as he looked at some papers on his desk. "Everybody is talking about your cotton crop, and the new ground you cleared and planted this year, which speaks well of you, as a young man just starting out."

"Thank you, Sir!" Politely replied Mark. "To be honest, I was hoping that we wouldn't have another fight, like we had the last time I was in here."

"I realize how you must have felt, and I'm sorry that I was caught in the middle of things," spoke Mr. Bland, seriously. "I couldn't afford to take a chance of having my bank closed, by not going along with Nate."

"And this year, Sir!" Spoke Mark, cautiously. "What did he order you to do to me, this time around?"

"Nothing at all," Bland smiled. "He's upset because of the poor crop he had, which quieted him down a bit, I'm sure. He was in here a few days ago to withdraw money, so he could buy corn and feed for his livestock. No, he didn't say anything about you, for a change."

"Yes, I heard that he had a bad crop, but I can't make myself feel sorry for him, not after what he and Powell did to me last year," Mark replied.

"If you don't mind, I'd like to know how you managed to have such a good cotton crop, when so many larger farmers fell short," inquired Bland.

Mark chuckled, as he leaned back in his chair. "I'll tell you, just like a Negro friend told me," said Mark. "You have to ask for God's help, but you have to put legs on your prayers, as well."

"Legs on your prayers, you say!" Bland mused. "That's a real good idea you have there! I'll have to remember that one, for sure."

"Thank you, I thought so myself," Mark smiled. "I've had a lot of help from my Negro partners, otherwise, I couldn't have done so well."

"I don't know who's your foreman, since Powell left, but whoever they are, they sure know how to grow cotton," Bland remarked. "Who's your foreman?"

"This might sound strange, but I have a freed Negro slave handling everything for me," Mark proudly told him. "He's the best there is."

"Seems like I heard somebody else say that, too," he replied. "You need to be very careful about bragging on a nigger, for it might upset other folks. Your father said that one of your niggers died in a fire back during the spring, when lightening struck their house. Is that right?"

"Lightening!" Snapped Mark. "My father, and a group of fine citizens set fire to the house, with the poor girl inside! A free slave was killed, and in my book, that was murder in the first degree, if I might add."

Bland sat shaking his head. "I'll tell you now, freeing the slaves could get a person in a lot of trouble," he warned. "If you'll look around and ask questions, you'll find that folks in this area, are touchy about freeing them."

"There's nothing touchy about treating other folks with respect, regardless of the color of their skin," Mark countered. "The Negroes work for me, and I'll pay them, just like I'd pay a white person. Anybody will work harder, if he knows that he'll get paid. It's the same with freed-slaves."

"You might justify what you're doing from a monetary standpoint, however, socially, and politically it's unacceptable," Bland rebutted. "Soon it will smother you completely out of society, and cause other farmers to dislike you."

"Sir, how am I hurting other farmers, by paying my workers?" Mark asked. "It's not coming out of their pocket, or out of yours, either!"

Bland leaned back in his chair, clasp his hands behind his head, then he looked keenly at Mark. "In determining what's right or wrong, you should look at who's doing it, for that makes a world of difference."

"That makes no sense at all." Mark firmly stated. "Wrong, is wrong, no matter who it might involve! Even a Negro slave has enough common sense to know that!"

"Well then, let me give you an example," Bland replied. "I've seen you talking with my daughter at church, and folks tend to look down on me, because I allow it to happen. Even the pastor of our church, wonders why I allow her to associate with someone who treats niggers like human beings. Now, can you see where you're doing wrong, and how it causes other persons to look down on you?"

"My father, Mr. Powell, and even you yourself cheated me out of what was rightly mine, yet all of you maintain a high social standing!" Mark scolded. "I find it difficult, to become excited about becoming a member of a so-called social group that steals, lies, and plays the hypocrite in church! How in the name of God can you folks profess to be Christians, yet stoop so low?"

"Let me put it another way," Bland persisted. "If you don't do what you promise to do then you have lied, but should a politician, or a menber in good social standing do the same thing, they're not considered as liars. If you do something it might be considered as being wrong, yet another person can do the same thing, and it might not be considered wrong. It's not what's done that matters so much, it's who did it, that counts the most."

"Oh, I see now!" Said Mark. "It's wrong for me to free the slaves, then pay them a salary for working, but it's not wrong for other farmers to set their slaves free, then cheat them out of everything they earn. Mr. Bland, is that the kind of philosophy that you wish to get across to me?"

Bland shook his head, as he placed Mark's money on the desk. "I see that I'm making no headway, so I'll drop the subject," said Bland. "Remember what I said about treating the niggers like human beings, for it won't work."

Without a reply, Mark picked up the money, stuck it into his vest pocket, and then headed back outside. As he crossed the street, he saw one of his father's slaves talking with Bill, and he thought that trouble might be brewing. When he heard Bill laugh, he realized that they were only having a friendly talk.

"Howdy, Mos'a Mark!" Spoke the slave, whose name was Lester. "I's ain't seed you in a coon's age, and everbid'ee is been axin' 'bout you."

"I'm fine, Lester," Mark replied. "If you and Bill want to chat about something, I'll go on and leave you fellows alone."

"I's come wid yo' pappy to town to pick up some stuff, and when I seed Bill sot'n here, I's 'cided to jaw wid him fer a spell," he replied. "Don't let me hinder youn's, fer we wudn't saying nothing that made no sense."

"Talk as long as you wish, if you can make any sense out of what that old stupid-nigger has to say," Mark chuckled. "I was only kidding, for Bill's my very best friend. He's free now, and so are all the others in his family."

"Me and the tuther niggas on you pappy's place is been talking 'bout what happened to Marthie, and how sorry it wuz of

Mos'a Simpson, to bun' her up like that," said Lester. "She wuzn't a bad gal, eb'em if she did kill that ole buck."

Mark glanced at Bill, who had a grin on his face. "Yes, we miss Martha a lot, for as you know, she and I grew up together," said Mark. "While we're talking, I'd like to know what kind of a crop my father had this year. We had a real good crop this year, and I hope he did, too."

Lester turned to see if anybody was watching them. "He ain't had much of a crop this year, and he come to town today to buy some corn and stuff to feed the mules this winter," Lester told them. "He sho' be mad, too."

"I can't imagine what happened, for he always has the best crop of anyone in the community," Mark pried. "Bad things do happen, no matter how hard we try to prevent them, I suppose."

"Like the preacher sez, the Lord is a funny kind'a feller," Lester told them. "He ain't gon'a look down and grin at no ugly feller, and yo' pappy is been pow'ful ugly. I's thank the Lord went and got mad at yo' pappy fer what he done to Marthie, and He give yo' pappy a good whoop'n."

"Your preacher is a wise person," replied Mark, "but he'll never get my father to believe him. He thinks that he can get along, without having to ask anybody to help him. He doesn't even think he needs God's help, either."

Bidding Lester goodbye, Mark climbed into the buggy, then he and Bill set out on their way back home. Simpson drove his buggy to town, and Lester drove a wagon to haul back the supplies Nate came to purchase. When Lester returned to the wagon Nate was waiting for him, and from the expression on his face, it was obvious that he had seen Lester talking with Bill and Mark.

"I saw you talking to that sorry nigger lover, and it makes me as mad as the devil, too!" Simpson snorted. "I'm warning you now, to stay away from him!"

"I's sorry, fer I wuz jawing wid Bill, 'cause I's ain't seed him in a pow'ful long time," Lester cowered. "Naw'suh, I's ain't said nar'ee word to yo' boy, I's sho' ain't. Didn't let him say nothing to me, neither."

"That's a darned lie, for I saw him shake your hand!" Simpson replied in an angry voice. "Did he ask about me, or about the kind of crop that I had?"

"Naw'suh, he didn't axe nothing 'bout you er yo' crop," he lied, "and I sho' didn't tell him nothing. Didn't tell him that you wuz mad 'cause you had a bad crop, neither. Didn't say nothing 'bout you running out'a feed."

"Did he say anything about lightening striking a house, and killing that sorry hussy, they call Martha?" Nate inquired.

"Naw'suh, he sho' didn't," he lied again, "and I's didn't tell him that you's sot fire to the house, wid Marthie still inside the thang, neither."

"Get in the wagon and follow me," said Nate, "for I want you to take a load of corn and feed back to my place. You're a dead nigger, if I ever hear tell of you talking with Mark or Bill again. Let's go!"

Mark and Bill had been riding alone for quite awhile, and when they came to a crossroad, Mark told Bill to turn up a side-road. Mark planned to speak with a carpenter about building a new house, and realizing that it would take at least two years to complete it, he wanted to know when the carpenter would be ready to start. When they arrived at the man's driveway, instead of going on up to the house, Bill drove the wagon to the side of the road, and stopped. Bill sat silent for a moment, with his head bowed.

"Why did you stop here?" Asked Mark, somewhat confused. "I told you that I wanted to speak with the man about building me a house. Would you mind telling me what's wrong? Don't you want me to have a new house?"

"No matter if you's ain't said nothing 'bout yo' pappy not having no good crop this year, I's know that you is been wonder'n what happened," Bill told him. "Now, ain't that the truf'? Ain't you's wonder'n what happened?"

"Well, yes, it's been on my mind," Mark admitted. "There must be a very good logical reason, for he has plenty of help, and the weather's been perfect for growing cotton. Bill, do you know something, that I don't?"

"Yo' pappy sez that no nigga ain't got no sense, but the slaves wuz upsot fer what he done to Marthie, and they 'cided to learn him a less'n," replied Bill. "That's why he ain't had no good crop. They went and messed him up."

"It seems like you're trying to tell me something, and I wish you'd go on and get it off your chest!" Mark scolded.

Bill told him what Lester and the others had done to prevent the corn, and cottonseeds from sprouting, and about pulling up the other plants at night.

"Now, is you mad at me 'cause I's let him tell me what they went and done to yo' pappy's crop?" Bill asked him. "I's didn't axe him to tell me."

"No, I'm not mad at you, or them either, however, no matter what they did to hurt him, it wouldn't have brought Martha back, had she really been dead," Mark explained. "Do you really think it would have helped?"

"Naw'suh, I's reck'n not, but I's bet it made him thank back on what wuz done to Marthie, and to you too," Bill reasoned.

"I agree," said Mark, "but in reality, persons like my father refuse to consider what they do to others as being wrong. He's told me many times, that he thought God had blessed him with a special ability to take advantage of the less fortunate persons, and scheme his way to success."

"I's ain't rail sho' what you's mean by all that," said Bill. "Is that sump'um bad?"

"He claims that it doesn't bother him one bit to take advantage of other persons, or to strip them of what they own, "Mark replied. "He certainly won't let this one bad crop keep him from doing what he does best, being cruel, mean and overbearing, and cheating his way through life."

"My Lord!" Bill sighed. "He's got'a be one unhappy feller, wid nothing left to sang 'bout. He ain't like that lit'l bird that I's told you 'bout."

"Happy or not, if he ever finds out what his slaves did, they'll have the devil to pay!" Mark cautioned. "I hope and pray that he never finds out."

When they arrived at the carpenter's home, Mark found him to be friendly and nice, even to Bill, and because he didn't have anything else scheduled for the moment, he told Mark that he'd be able to start his house immediately. He promised to meet with Mark the following morning to discuss his plans, and lay out the location where the house was to be built.

The house Mark planned to build was indeed a mansion. A big twelve-room house, with a large front porch, a balcony, with four large columns out front. He also agreed to remodel the house in which Mark now lived, for Mark told Bill that he could occupy it, after he moved into the new house.

As they drove back home, Bill was excited because Mark was going to build a new house for himself, and Mark was glad that he was able to pay the workers for what they had done to help him.

Another man who owned a larger farm that adjoined Mark's farm had his property for sale, and Mark planned to buy it as well. He wasn't able to build a new house and buy the land all at the same time, therefore, he agreed to pay the carpenter as he went along, and pay for the land when he sold his cotton next fall. This would add a hundred acres of land to what Mark already owned. The farmer agreed to sell his slaves to Mark as well, and help Bill manage things for Mark. Although he wasn't happy with the idea of Mark freeing the slaves, then paying them, he finally agreed to go along with Mark, and pledged his support for Mark's plan to help the slaves.

At the break of dawn the following morning, the carpenter whose name was Alton, arrived at Mark's house with his workers. Feeling a bit proud because of his success this year, Mark went with Alton to the top of a large knoll, and showed Alton where the house was to be built. Several sprawling oaks already stood on the knoll, and Alton agreed to locate the house so that the oak trees would remain as a part of the natural landscape. He planned to set out other oak trees alongside the driveway that was to lead from the main road, to the new house when it was completed.

"Mr. Simpson," said Alton, respectfully. "I've heard quite a lot about the stand you take against slavery, and I want you to know that there are many others who feel the same way, but they're afraid to voice their opinion. I'm here for the sole purpose of building your house, not to criticize, or to find fault with you. I tell everybody how I feel before I start working for them, and so far, I haven't had any problems with the issue of slavery."

"That'a fine with me, for I appreciate a person who's willing to come out and state how he feels, whether I agree with him or not," Mark replied. "I'm also glad to know that there are others who agree with me, for I sometimes get the feeling that I'm standing all alone like a lamb in a den of lions."

Alton looked at Mark and smiled. "You'd be surprised at how many of your neighbors agree with you, but they're afraid to speak out, for fear of causing others to look down on them," he added. "Fear, is a destructive force, in my way of thinking. As long as southern leaders can keep the citizens afraid to speak out against slavery, they have them under control."

"As for me, I'm not afraid to speak out against whatever I think is wrong and unjust, for I have that right as a citizen," Mark told him. "I know that some folks hate me for treating Negroes with respect as human beings, however, I'm upset at them, because they treat Negroes like dogs! I've learned that we all have feelings, regardless of the color of our skin, and we hurt when other folks trample us under their feet. That's the reason I treat others the way I would like to be teated, be they black or white."

"I admire you for standing up for what you believe, but in my business, I more or less keep my opinion to myself, otherwise, folks wouldn't be asking me to work for them," Alton explained. "That's why I wanted to get all this cleared up, before I started working for you. Is that a problem for you?"

"Of course not!" Replied Mark. "I don't force my personal opinion on my neighbors, and I wish they would respect me in the same way. I see that you have a Negro on your crew, and they seem to get along well together."

. Alton looked around, as if to see if anyone was listening. "I bought him when I first started out in business, I set him free, and he's still with me," Alton told him. "Regardless of what folks say about me working him, or about paying him like I pay the white men, I'll keep on doing what I think is proper and right as long as I'm in business, or until he decides to quit. As long as he works like a white man, he'll be paid like one, too."

"I'm glad that you feel that way," said Mark, "for it gives me strength to go on, knowing that I'm not alone in the way I feel."

They shook hands, and then Alton walked away. "I'm really enjoying this, but I'm not getting any work done," said Alton. "Maybe we can get together later and finish this discussion, for we do have a lot in common."

Time seemed to fly at a breakneck speed, for it was now a year and a half later. News of the beautiful mansion Mark was building had spread throughout the area, and needless to say that many of his neighbors were jealous because of Mark's rapid success. Others actually feared his success, for they thought that Mark might become as powerful, and influential as his father. His mother was pleased with his success, and the mansion she'd heard he was building, for she knew that he had finally triumphed over the many obstacles his father had thrown in his pathway. She wasted no time in telling friends and neighors of her son's success, and she asked them to pray for God to watch over him.

In anticipation of another excellent crop-year, Mark bought a second farm adjoining his property to the north, and like before, he bought the slaves and set them free, then hired the freed-slaves to work for him. He also hired the farmer to help another white man and Bill manage his farm. Mark was now well on his way to success. With about forty former-slaves to tend the hundreds of acres of farmland he now owned, Mark was destined to become one of the largest farmers in South Carolina. Other farmers envied his success, yet they refused to admit that his practice of freeing the slaves, then hiring them to work for him, was a good business policy. Even his father did everything that he could to downgrade Mark, by making sure that his friends understood that Mark's view on slavery, and his respect for the Negroes as human beings, were far from the way that he felt himself.

One day while Mark's parents were riding into town, his mother decided to mention Mark's success to her husband, and see how he reacted.

"Nate, while we're this close, we ought to ride on down and visit Mark," said Julie. "I've heard so much about the beautiful mansion he's having built for himself, and I'd like to see it, if you don't mind."

"You know that I hate him because he freed the slaves, then turned around and started paying them for working, and I don't intend to associate with him, in any way!" He snipped. "He's ruining my name, disgracing other farmers in the community, and bringing shame to South Carolina as well."

"Say what you wish, but you should at least give him some credit!" Julie scolded. "I know that you've heard about the beautiful mansion he's building, the other farms he's bought, and the dozens of slaves that he bought and set free. That shows that he's becoming successful."

"I've heard about that, and I give him credit, credit for being a darned fool," he laughed. "He's spending everthing, and saving nothing. If he has one bad crop-year he'll be wiped out. A fool and money will soon part, and I'll be right there to wipe him out, when he stumbles!"

"Have it your way, Nate, but I plan to attend the open-house party he'll have when his house is completed, whether you like it or not," Julie replied. "Someday you'll regret the way you've treated him, and treated me as well."

Another year quickly passed, during which time everything seemed to work in Mark's favor. He had purchased another adjoining farm and the slaves that the farmer owned, which enlarged his plantation to well over four hundred acres of choice farmland, and he had about seventy freed-slaves working for him. Alton was making some final touches on his mansion, and within a few weeks it would be ready for Mark to occupy. Mark and Carolyn Bland, the daughter of the local banker, had been seeing each other every weekend here lately, and Mark planned to ask her to marry him within the near future. His father could only wonder how Mark had accumulated so much in such a short time, and it made him angry when others reminded him of his son's success.

Mark had ordered the furniture for his house from abroad, and other than for a few pieces that were soon to arrive at Charleston, the house was completely furnished. Each evening after Alton and his workers went home, Mark let some of the slaves clean up around the house, while he and Bill's family went about arranging the furniture, and hanging drapes over the windows. In keeping with southern customs, Mark must appoint a Negro man as butler and a Negro woman as maid, and every Negro on his plantation hoped to be chosen. One evening while he and Bill's family were dusting and polishing the furniture, Mark decided to let them know how he planned to fill these positions.

"Well, I've decided to let Martha be my maid, and you, Liza, will do the cooking, and help Martha clean the house," Mark told them. "Unless I change my mind, I'm going to let Sam serve as butler. Of course, each of you will be paid the same as if you were working in the fields."

Immediately, Bill stepped out in front of Mark. "You's ain't got thangs wuk'd out rite, and everthang is gon'a be messed up." Spoke up Bill, while he playfully strutted across the floor. "Let me put on that suit, and everbid'ee is gon'a thank that you's fetched in a feller from Savan'ee, er Charl'sun, to be that butler thang! Yass'uh, I's the ver'ee feller fer that job!"

"You old fool." laughed Mark. "You're too old to even help yourself, and I'm sure you couldn't help anyone else. I'll lay you out there on the front porch for folks to wipe their feet on, before entering the house."

"That's rite!" Liza chimed in, playfully kicking Bill on the butt, as he continued strutting around. "You 'mind me of a big crippled billygoat, jumping up and down in hot fire coals. Stop that, you ole fool nigga!"

A few days later the house was completed. Mark had the Negro women clean the house from top to bottom, the Negro men smoothed the driveway and painted a fresh coat of whitewash on the trunks of the trees that lined the driveway, while Mark moved his personal belongings into the mansion. Reluctantly, Ellis Bland allowed his daughter Carolyn, to help the women arrange the furniture, however, he demanded that his driver bring her back home before sundown. Mark teased her about marrying him, and moving into the mansion with him. She was ready to do just that, but Mark had a few things he wanted to clear up between he and his father, before he officially asked her to marry him.

Eager to show off his beautiful house, Mark decided to have a gala party, and invite not only his family and personal friends, but prominent persons in the area as well. Though he wasn't actively involved in politics, he thought about inviting the governor of South Carolina, to make a particular impression on his fellow farmers. And of course, he planned to invite larger farmers to the party, just to prove to them how profitable it had been for him to set his slaves free, and then hire them back as employees. He knew there were others who were anxious to see his house, if only out of curiosity, and he being a proud southern gentleman, wanted to give them an evening they'd never forget. Most of all, he wanted to make an impression on the local banker, for he hoped to marry his daughter in the very near future.

Since the day of the house fire, nobody had seen Martha except for Mark, her family, and a few real close friends. Even then, their friends were not told that her real name was Martha. At Mark's request, they called her Clara Bell, even though they didn't know why. It was only after Mark had planned a party to show off his new house, that he devilishly came up with the idea to bring her back to life. He could hardly wait to see the expression on his father's face, when he found out that Martha was still alive.

The day of the party finally arrived, and while seated at the dining room table this morning, Mark's family discussed the invitation they had received by special carrier. His mother was excited, for this would give her a chance to visit with him, for she hadn't seen Mark for quite awhile.

"Like I said earlier, if his house is half as pretty as I've heard folks say it is, it's going to be a sight to behold," said Mrs. Simpson, with a big smile on her face. "Nate, aren't you excited about his new house, the success he's made, and the name he's made for himself? Aren't you proud because such a successful young man is our own son?"

"No, not in the least!" Nate scolded. "I don't care about attending the party, for I'm afraid that my presence might tend to ruin my good name. If he hadn't invited the governor, I wouldn't even think about going."

"The governor of South Carolina!" Susan squealed. "Will he really be at Mark's party?" She asked, in disbelief. "Daddy, you must be kidding!"

"From what I hear, he'll be there," he reluctantly replied. "This is an election year, and I imagine other politicians will be there too. But, they won't be back, after I tell them how Mark treats the niggers. They'll probably run him clear out of the country after tonight."

"You just won't give up!" Julie lashed back. "Even though he's finally proven to you, and to others that he can make it on his own, you're still deadset on destroying him. You might have to call on him for help one day."

"That my dear, I seriously doubt!" He snapped. "I'll attend that party and put on an act, but I hope it falls apart right before his eyes, so that I can personally witness his downfall. I pray to God, that it will."

"I wouldn't count on that if I were you, for after all you've done to him he's still going strong," said Julie, as she got up from the table, to go into her room. "Susan, you need to pick out the prettiest dress you have to wear to the party. I want you to look real nice, in the presence of the governor."

"I will Mother," replied Susan. "Even though Mark probably paid him to be there, I still want to meet him."

As the sun began to set this evening, the grounds around Mark's new house were bustling with people from nearby farms. Special guest were arriving in fancy buggies and carriages, and it was evident by their attire, that they all considered this a very special occasion. Just like a professional butler, Sam announced each guest who entered, and after a brief tour of the mansion, they all gathered in the parlor for a friendly chat, and a social drink before they were called to dinner. Thus far Mark's parents and his sister hadn't arrived, and realizing that the time for the party was fastly approaching, Mark began to think that they might not attend at all. He hoped they would, for if they didn't attend, what he had in mind, would have to be called off.

On the beautiful front porch, Mark greeted the banker and his wife, and their lovely daughter Carolyn Bland. Then seeing the governor in the parlor with members of his staff, Ellis Bland hurried inside. When he entered the parlor, he realized that the governor and two other men were discussing Mark, and how he had achieved so much, in such a short span of time.

Wishing to be included in the conversation, Bland chimed in. "Yes, it's amazing how far he's come in about five or six years," Blamd spoke up. "The thing that bothers me most, is his radical idea about Negroes. He has a crew of freed-slaves running this farm, and he pays them a salary, the same as if they were white men. Can you imagine that! Paying a Negro for working!"

The governor quickly looked at Bland. "All I know about him, is what my advisors told me, but I'm sure that they didn't tell me everything," the governor replied. "He does seem to me like a fine person though."

"I believe that you have already met his father, haven't you?" Mr. Bland asked. "They are as different, as night and day."

"I've heard of his father, Nate Simpson I believe, but I've never had the pleasure of meeting him," the governor replied. "I have heard that he's quite a businessman. He upholds our southern traditions I'm told, and we need more men like him in the South."

"I was under the impression that you two actually knew each other, for he speaks highly of you," Bland replied. "Nate has a lot of influence over the folks in this area, and they generally do what he tells them to do."

"To be perfectly honest with you Sir, I'm only here to meet some of my constituents from this area," the governor explained. "The young Simpson is very impressive though. I'd like to get to know him better."

"He certainly is that!" Replied Bland, as other men began gathering around. "But, he's against using Negroes as slaves, and he treats them as though they were human. He even opened up accounts for them at my bank. Can you imagine a Negro, with money in the bank? He does some stupid things, I tell you."

"In all fairness, I must say that it's his money," stated the governor. "He can squander it on a beautiful mansion like this, gamble it away, or pay the Negroes for working. I can't control how he spends his own money."

Well aware that a good-sized crowd had encircled them, Bland felt like he had been backed into a corner. "I'm afraid that it's going to stir up trouble with other farmers," Bland replied. "I've discussed it with other farmers in the community, and they all seem to be highly upset with him."

"Maybe so, but I see that those farmers have gathered here tonight to eat his food and drink his liquor," replied the governor, not wishing to tip his hand. "Sometimes a dog's bark, is worse than its bite."

"I see what you mean, your honor," Bland chuckled. "I guess we all are a bit curious, at that."

"Indeed, curiosity did kill the cat, so they say," laughed the governor. Then the governor excused himself, but not before telling Bland that he'd like to speak with him in private.

After a brief period of perfunctory conversation with some others in the group, Bland also excused himself, then sought out the governor for a private chat. The governor was waiting in Mark's study, while he stood looking at the handsome collection of bound volumes in the massive bookcase.

Entering the study, and quickly closing the door behind him, Bland approached the governor. "This study sure is quite nice!" Bland observed.

"It certainly is, and I'm impressed by young Simpson, for this collection of volumes is somethng to be proud of," the governor replied. "The longer I stay here, and the more I hear about this fellow, the more I'd like to really get to know him, learn what makes him so unique, and how he operates."

"You wanted to talk with me, didn't you Sir?" Mr. Bland interrupted, as if to jog his memory. "Was it pertaining to Mark Simpson?"

"It was indeed, for I'd like to learn more about him, if you don't mind my asking," he replied. "You mentioned his ideas on slavery, and the way he treats the Negroes. Is there something else I should know about him? I must admit that something is working awfully well for him."

Bland scratched his head. "I know first-hand, that he opposes the use of Negroes as slaves," Bland stated. "He bought up all the land that surrounded the small farm that he started out with, and the slaves that belonged to those farmers as well. He freed the slaves, then started paying them a salary."

"It's his money, and whatever he wishes to do with it is his business, I suppose," the governor again reminded him.

"Well, it's fine if he wants to free the slaves, but paying them a salary like if they were white, sure cuts against the grain!" Bland replied.

"Even though we might disagree, it's working for him, or so it seems," the governor carefully replied. "But, if we should go to war over slavery, having young men like him in our ranks, sure would play havoc with our chances of winning. You good citizens should point out to him, where he's going wrong."

"It won't work in his case!" Bland clearly stated. "He has already come through hell to get where he is today, and it only made him stronger. His own father took every penny he made the first year he started farming, and look at him now! I don't expect his father to even be here tonight."

"So, they don't get along real well?" The governor asked. "Maybe they have decided to settle their differences, now that the son is prospering so well."

"Not to my knowledge!" Bland answered. "His father has done everything imaginable to destroy him, even down to killing his favorite slave girl. I really think it galls his father, because his son disagrees with him on slavery."

"I've never met his father, but I'm inclined to think that there's quite a bit more than slavery, involved in this case," said the governor. "Could be a matter of jealousy in his heart, that causes him to hate his own son."

"For a fact, there could be at that," Bland agreed. "He owns about six hundred acres of land, and has about seventy freed-slaves working for him, and on a salary, if I might add. Unless somethng happens to slow him down, give him ten more years, and he'll probably have you looking up to him. I tell you now; he gives me the jitters when he walks into my office. I act as though it don't bother me, but I'm afraid of what he's capable of doing."

"Mr. Bland, success and power are two difficult things to argue with, any way you look at them," said the governor. "I agree that he'd be mighty hard to handle, if he's challenged, without a lot of forethought."

Bland looked at him, and shook his head. "That's why I'm so careful what I say too him," he replied. "My daughter is smitten by him, and I don't dare say too much to her even, for fear of driving her into his arms."

The governor walked over and sat down at Mark's desk, then bowed his head in deep thought. Bland went over to the door, and peeked out to check on his daughter. Suddenly, the governor raised his head, and looked up at Bland.

"I've been giving thought to something, and if it were handled properly and diplomatically, your problems might be solved," said the governor.

"I'm listening," Bland replied, "but let me tell you now, Mark Simpson is not what you call an ordinary young man. Nobody threatens or bluffs him into doing what he doesn't want to do. Exactly what did you have in mind, Sir?"

"I didn't intend to go against his wishes, or suggest anything that might cause him any harm," the governor explained. "I'm his servant, and I didn't come here to persecute him, or create any kind of problem for him."

"Sir!" Bland interrupted. "Just what do you have in mind for him, that might cause him to change his way of thinking? It better be something real good!"

"Well, if you folks would appoint him as leader in community afairs, and social activities as well, he'd change in a heartbeat in order to maintain his social position," the governor proposed. "Once a person achieves a position of power, and authority, it's rather hard for him to give it up, even for what he might consider a noble cause. Better yet, I could offer him a position in my office, if you folks will support me on Election Day."

It was obvious to Bland, that he was only playing politics. "Sir, you'll have a hard time in luring him into something like that," Bland replied. "He isn't the type of person who can be led around by the nose, and I'm quite sure you won't change his mind about slavery. I've even tried to..."

Their conversation was interruped by the sound of Sam's deep gruff voice coming from the hallway, "Ladies and Gentlemens, din'a is suv'd!"

"We'll try to continue our discussion later," said the governor. "Mark did ask me to speak at dinner, and I'll somehow work all of this into my speech."

"Good luck!" Said Bland, as they headed toward the dining room. "Let me tell you now, this young man is going to be a hard nut to crack!"

Guest were now milling around everywhere. Some were still touring the house, while others were outside enjoying the fresh air. Mark helped Sam gather them into the large dining room, where eight tables were beautifully set with fine china and crystal. A large buffet table held a sumptuous feast. Mark made a point of positioning himself at the far end of the room, facing the guest.

Mark was pleased that almost everyone who had been invited were present and seemed to be enjoying themselves, yet his heart was sad. Although he sent a special invitation to his family, thus far, they hadn't arrived. He took a quick glance toward the door, and when he didn't see them anywhere, he decided to go on with the party without them.

"Ladies, Gentlemen, and our Honorable Governor of South Carolina, it's a real pleasure to welcome each of you to my home this evening," Mark politely said. "I hope you're enjoying yourselves, and will continue to do so." He then saw his parents and his sister Susan entering the room, then he added: "I would like to extend a special welcome to my parents and to my sister Susan. I will feel honored to have you three sit at the head of the table with me as my special guest." He smiled, as he motioned to the three chairs sitting nearest him. "Help yourselves to the food, for I have a surprise for each of you when we finish dinner."

Julie hugged her son so tightly, until he could hardly catch his breath. His father managed a superficial smile and a handshake, and Susan gave him a mocking curtsy. His mother was thrilled to be here, but it was obvious to him that his father and sister, were only here out of curiosity. They were here, and that's all that mattered, for he'd be able to go on with the plan he had for everyone after dinner. Mark smiled, as he turned to look at Carolyn, who was seated next to he and his parents.

They began eating the delicious food that Liza and the other Negro women had prepared for this special occasion, and they chatted with each other as if no ill will had ever been between them. Mark had asked the governor to make a speech after dinner, for after all, he must not only be a gracious host here this evening, he must show at least some support for the governor as well.

Immediately after dinner, the governor stood up and made a few comments, which in Mark's opinion, were only in an effort to entice him to give up his idea about slavery. He hesitated for a moment, and sipped some water from a glass sitting by his plate, then continued:

"Futhermore, I wish to commend our host on his tremendous success as a farmer and landowner," said the governor, as he continued to patronize Mark, shamelessly. "If I had a man like him on my staff, there's no limit to what we could do for this great state." He then leaned over and whispered, so that only Mark could hear. "I'd like to have a word with you in private, if I may, for I have an offer that might interest you."

Everyone applauded the governor, as he sat back down in his chair. Ellis Bland felt somewhat relieved, for he felt sure that the governor had impressed Mark. But he was wrong, as was the governor himself, to think that Mark would humble down for a promise of political gain. This gathering was intended to prove to everyone that he hadn't changed, and that society and politics didn't play a part in what he had planned. Although he really loved Carolyn, and hoped to marry her someday, no one except for Bill's family, knew what he had scheduled to do after dinner.

"Thank you, Honorable Governor, for your timely comments," Mark said, as he looked at the others and smiled. "I'm sure that you'll get the votes you need from these good citizens here this evening." He then quickly changed the subject. "I had some special wine imported for this occasion this evening, and it will now be served." Mark clapped his hand lightly.

This was Martha's cue to enter the dining room, and in she came, proudly carrying the carafe of wine. As planned, she stoppeed beside Mark's father's chair, though at first he didn't pay any attention to her. Mark nodded, then she moved up a little closer to his father.

"Mos'a Simpson, would you's like to try this spash'l wine?" Martha asked politely. "They sez that it's the ver'ee bes' wine, that ever wuz made."

Glancing up at her, Simpson was about to lift his glass, when he suddenly dropped it, breaking it into dozens of pieces. "I, uh, I'm sorry, the glass, it slipped," said Simpson, as his face turned ghostly pale. "My hand it was wet. The glass, it slipped."

"What's wrong with you?" His wife whispered. "Your face is as white as cotton, and you're shaking like a leaf. What's wrong? Are you sick?"

"Look at that Nigger gal, and you'll see what's wrong!" He whispered, as he pointed to Martha. "She's the same gal who was burned to death. It's the dead-gal, and she came back alive. She's a ghost!" He was terrified.

"Be quiet Nate, for you're mistaken," she whispered, as a shiver ran up her spine. "Calm down a bit, and get hold of yourself."

"I saw her run into the house, and she didn't come back out, and I watched the house burn, and fall in on her," he mumbled. "She's dead, I tell you!"

"Perhaps it's your conscience bothering you," she whispered, and patted him on the arm. "She just looks like Martha, that's all, so calm down."

"But, she called me by my own name!" He countered, still trembling. "How could she have known my name, if it wasn't her?" He asked, his voice quivering.

Julie looked keenly at her, as she served wine to the other guest. For a fact, she does look a lot like Martha, she thought, but that girl died in the fire. Still, Julie took pleasure in watching Nate squirm, as he kept his eyes on the girl. This really is good for him, she thought, and good for his conscience.

Almost everyone in the room were staring intently at Martha now, as they wondered why she had made such an adverse affect on Simpson. Even those who knew about the incident hadn't personally seen her before, and they didn't associate her with the girl they heard was killed, when lightening supposedly struck the house in which she lived.

"What in the world's wrong with you, Dad?" Mark asked. "Don't you like the wine, or do you resent a Negro serving you?" Mark knew that he recognized Martha, and that he was stunned to see that she was still alive.

"Nothing's wrong, nothing at all," he stammered, as he kept his eyes on Martha. "I was just reminding your mother, that she forgot to bring your gift with her. Oh well, she can send it to you later."

Everybody knew that something was amiss, for Simpson's face was as white as cotton, and he trembled so, the wine sloshed about in the glass he held.

"My father looks as though he's seen a ghost," Mark explained. "He's no doubt thinking of the girl who died in the house fire. Word has it, that the house was struck by lightening, but my father ordered some prominent citizens to set fire to it, with that same girl inside. Yes, the girl who just served the wine, is the very same one who was in the house that day. He'll be all right in just a moment, so go ahead and enjoy yourselves."

The guests complemented Mark for the dinner and the wine he had imported for this special occasion, and without exception, all extended their thanks to him for a lovely evening. Some of the guest returned to the parlor to talk, while others gathered in small groups outside to chat. Mark had been called aside by the governor for a private conversation, and Mark took him into his study, and closed the door.

"I was in here earlier with Mr. Bland, admiring your beautiful volumes," the governor told him. "Where did you happen to find these, anyway? This has to be the finest collection of books I've ever seen. They are nice."

"Thank you Sir," replied Mark, with a smile. "They once belonged to my grandfather, they are as old as the hills, but they have a lot of sentimental value." Then cutting through the small talk, Mark asked the governor a direct question. "Your Honor, what do you wish to speak with me about?"

"I really could use a young man of your caliber at the State House," the governor responded. "I need somebody who's willing to stand up and fight for what he thinks is right, like I've heard you are."

"Sir, you don't know anything about me, and you hardly know my name," replied Mark. "Shouldn't you get to know me a lot better, before making such an offer?"

"If we had some younger men in office, with new ideas, we would see a lot of changes," the governor continued. "As it stands now, the Union wants the South to abolish its customs and traditions, and stop using slave-labor."

"Please, Governor!" Mark said, disapprovingly. "I'm sure you're aware of my stand against slavery, my respect for Negroes as human beings, and about my policy of paying them for working. Did you think that you could change my mind?"

"You're as stubborn, and hard-nosed as Bland said you were, and unwilling to see the other person's point of view," he replied angrily. "We're part of the South, you know, and unless we take a stand for our rights, we should move up north. That's the kind of person I need in my office. Do you accept?"

"Not interested, Sir!" Mark smiled. "A slave, is a slave, whether he is bound by chains, customs, traditions, or anything else that deprives him of a right to function freely as an individual. Sir, if I'm against using Negroes as slaves, why would I want to give that up to become a slave to the state, or to you, if I might add? I won't be bound, and I won't bind others."

"You're going to find yourself in a lot of trouble, unless you change the way that you feel about slavery!" He cautioned. "Be realistic, Son!"

"Perhaps it's you, Sir, who needs to be realistic!" Mark countered. "If you have nothing better to discuss, Sir, I wish to be excused."

"I thank you for a delicious meal, and an eye-opening evening, for it was one that I won't forget," said the governor. "Now, I bid you good night."

"And a pleasant one to you, Sir," Mark replied. "You can be sure that your presence here has meant a lot, and you're welcome to visit me anytime you wish, Sir."

The governor left the study to seek out Ellis Bland. When he found Bland in the parlor, he and Nate Simpson were in deep discussion. When Nate saw the governor in the hallway with a disgusted expression on his face, he cut Bland short, and went to where the governor stood alone.

Extending his hand, Simpson smiled. "What a great honor it is to finally meet you! I was afraid that you had already left," Nate said.

"No, Mr. Simpson, I've been chatting with your son," the governor smiled, and replied. "Intriguing young man, your son. One of a kind, too."

"Intriguing?" Simpson laughed, winking at Bland. "I'd hardly say he is that! He has some strange ideas, Sir, and he didn't learn them from me!"

"If you gentlemen will excuse me, I'll be on my way, for I have a million things to do next week," the governor told them. Turning to Bland, he added, "You're right, he's not an ordinary man!" Simpson looked perplexed, but Bland knew what the governor meant.

Simpson stood and shook his head, for he thought the governor was talking about him. "What did he mean, by me not being an ordinary man, Ellis?" Asked Simpson, curiously. "What gave him that impression of me?"

"No, he wasn't talking about you," replied Bland. "Let's just say that he was duly impressed by your son, as are most folks here tonight. We'll have to admit that he's done well, considering the obstacles he had to overcome."

Without a reply, Simpson left the room, as he continued searching for the phantom-maid. His heart was filled with regret for what he'd done to Mark in the past, and he couldn't imagine how Martha escaped the burning inferno.

In the parlor, Julie Simpson and Carolyn Bland were sitting side by side on the settee talking, when Mark decided to join them.

"Son, I'm really enjoying this evening," said his mother, as he sat down beside her. "This beautiful house, and the expensive furniture, really speaks well of your accomplishments." Then turning to Carolyn, she added, "I had no idea that you and this lovely lady had been courting for almost three years. Planning to get married soon, I suppose?"

Mark smiled, as he looked at Carolyn. "I'm not so sure about that at the moment, but yes, we've been seeing each other for quite awhile," he replied. "She's the daughter of the banker, Ellis Bland. I'm sure you know him."

"I think we've met," Julie nodded. "Now let me ask you about something that's been bothering me, if I may. It's about your maid, who looked an awful lot like the girl who was, well, you know. She upset your father more than he has ever been upset before, and for a moment, I really thought it was her."

Mark and Carolyn looked at each other, and snickered. "You have a right to feel that way, for it really was Martha," Mark replied, seriously.

"Oh, I see now," smiled his mother, "her name is also Martha. I didn't think she was Bill's girl, for she is dead. How silly of me."

Mark sat and shook his head for a moment. "No Mother, that girl whom you saw tonight really was Martha, Bill's girl. She didn't die in the fire, like you thought she did. I'll tell you all about it one day."

Julie's eyes filled with tears. "But why didn't you let me know that she wasn't dead, and spare me a lot of grief, and heartache?"

"I was afraid he'd find out, and really have her killed," he explained. "Mother, I've been through hell since I first came here, and without Bill and his family, I couldn't have survived. They stood by me through everything that my father brought upon me, picked me up when I fell, and they encouraged me even when it seemed as though God had forsaken me. They are my only true friends."

"I understand, but he'll be furious when he finds out that she didn't die in the house-fire," Julie reasoned. "I wish he could have found out about it before tonight, for he'll likely think that I had something to do with it."

Then Carolyn spoke up. "I tried to talk him out of it, but he refused to listen to me. I knew that his father would probably get upset, but you know how he is at times, bullheaded, and stubborn to the core," she teased.

"Then, you knew about this all along, didn't you?" Asked Julie, thinking that she and Mark must be very close, for him to confide in her so.

"No Mother, she didn't know anything about this, until after she arrived this evening," Mark replied. "I didn't want anybody else involved with what I had planned. This seemed like a good time to bring Martha back to life."

"Well, you certainly did get your father's goat, and I hope it doesn't return to haunt you one day. Maybe it won't," she smiled.

"I hope not," Mark agreed, "but the look on his face at the table, sure was worth waiting for. I didn't think that he'd ever accept the fact that she was still alive. Made him feel like he'd failed, once in his life."

They talked for a little while longer, and then Mr. Bland came to the doorway and spoke to his daughter. "Carolyn dear, we must be going," spoke Bland, in a polite voice. "Mark, you have a beautiful home, and I've enjoyed the party. My wife's sister is ill, and we planned to visit her on our way back home."

"I'm very sorry to hear that," Mark responded sincerely, as he quickly stood up, and shook Bland's hand. "Please give her my regards."

"I hope your sister-in-law will recover real soon, and Carolyn, it's been a pleasure meeting you," Julie added. "I hope we'll meet again, real soon."

"Thank you both, very much," Bland smiled. "Come on Carolyn, for we must say good night to the others, and your mother is waiting for us."

After seeing the Blands off, Mark returned to the parlor to continue the conversation with his mother. He invited his family to spend the night in his new home, and his mother accepted, contingent of course, on her husband making the final decision. She knew that he hadn't changed his feelings toward Mark, and what happened here earlier this evening, might have magnified the tension between them.

After the guest had departed, Nate came into the parlor and sat down in a chair near the fireplace, and bowed his head. Mark didn't think that he would go to bed, without lashing out at him about what happened earlier.

"That was a stupid trick you pulled on me, and it made me look like I was a fool, in the sight of the others!" Nate snapped. "She resembled Bill's gal there for a moment, then I realized that she was dead. It would take a stupid person, to think that she could still be alive. I saw her burn to death."

"But, that really was her!" Replied Mark. "She walked right out of the fire, I tell you. She's as much alive, as you and I."

"The devil you say!" Nate yelled, jumping to his feet. "I saw the house burn to the ground with her inside! Where can I find a place to sleep in this trash dump? I'm not a fool, for I saw her burn to death, with my own eyes!"

Susan was just entering the parlor, and was standing near the stairs when he made that statement. The maid had already shown her where she could sleep, and she also thought the maid looked like Martha. "Come with me, Daddy, and I will show you to your room," said Susan, as she caught hold of his arm. "If you folks don't mind, I think I'll go on to bed myself, for we'll probably be leaving real early in the morning, anyway." Then, they both went upstairs to go to bed.

Julie could hardly believe that her obstinate husband had agreed to spend the night in Mark's home. He must really be exhausted, she thought.

Before joining her husband upstairs, Julie hugged Mark, and patted him on the back. "You've given me something to smile about," she told him. "I was beginning to think that I'd never see you again. He wouldn't have brought me this time, if he hadn't heard that the governor would be here."

"I've missed you too, Mother!" He softly replied, "You've known all along that I hated slavery, haven't you? I've always hated slavery, and I always will."

"Son, I thank God that you're not like your father," she replied. "What you did this evening, really floored him. If he admits that Martha is alive, he'll be admitting defeat, and he won't ever do that. Good night my son, and I'll continue to ask God to watch over you."

"Thank you, Mother," Mark smiled, "and I'll ask the Lord to watch over you as well, for at this point, we both are in desperate need of His help."

Over the ensuing years many things happened, both good and bad. Southern states were gradually growing farther away from the Union, which caused great concern. For one thing, the Union imposed a higher tariff on goods that were shipped to southern ports, than goods that were shipped to northern ports. In fact, the South was paying 75% of all taxes received by the Union.

The Union opposed slave labor, but because of all the other problems that it faced, it certainly didn't want to risk creating more problems, by rebelling against slavery. The country was actually falling apart, and even though some claimed to have a solution to the problem, they were not willing to compromise one bit, in order to bring about a solution. The North was jealous because the South was prospering by using slave-labor, and the South was determined not to abolish slavery, even at the risk of an all-out war. The South wanted to have it's own way, like a spoiled child, so it stood against whatever the North or the West proposed for the good of the country. It soon became a stalemate of grand proportion, and the results were, nothing was done.

Mark continued to prosper amid the jeers of neighbors and other farmers in South Carolina, while he continued freeing slaves, then paying them like he paid white employees. Not only were other farmers upset with him, other freed slaves were upset as well, for they were not afforded the same opportunity in life, as were Mark's freed-slaves. Though free, they continued working for almost nothing at all, and were fortunate to have a few bites to eat, and some place to lay their head at night. This angered other farmers who also worked free-slaves, and hardly paid them anything; therefore, these angry farmers began to spread rumors about Mark, in an attempt to ruin his reputation.

Mark took all this in stride, however, for he was doing what worked best for him, and for the freed-slaves as well. He hoped that other farmers would see the light, free their slaves, and start paying them a salary, the same as they did white workers.

Mark and Carolyn Bland had grown real fond of each other. Although Mark hadn't said anything to her about it, he planned to ask Carolyn to marry him, the next time he went calling on her, which would be next Saturday evening.

Saturday finally arrived, and as he drove his buggy up into the yard, he saw Carolyn and her mother sitting in a swing on the porch. As soon as he had hitched his mare to a post, and started up the walkway, he saw her mother get up and go back into the house, which really concerned him. Other times he had called on Carolyn, her mother would sit and chat with him for a moment, before she went inside, and he wondered why she hadn't spoken to him this evening, as well. Nevertheless, he walked upon the porch, and sat down beside Carolyn in the porch swing.

"I don't think your mother likes me anymore, for I saw her jump up and go inside, the moment I arrived," Mark observed. "She used to sit and talk with me for a moment, before leaving us alone. I think your father has turned your mother against me, becasue we disagree on the way I treat Negroes. He'll have you turned against me, if you aren't careful."

"Daddy might not like you, but Mother does," she assured him. "She knew that we'd rather be alone, and that's why she went inside. You do want us to be alone, don't you? Do you want me to call Mother back out here?"

"Why would a man want to be alone with such a pretty girl as you, in the first place?" He teased back. "You're only the sweetest, and most beautiful girl in the world. What an unpleasant combination!" They both laughed.

"Well, look at you, Sir!" she mocked. "You're only handsome, kind, rich and successful. Nothing to brag about!"

Then a sober expression came on his face. "Carolyn, we have known each other for a long time now, and I wonder if we could make it, if we decided to get married someday," he said softly. "Have you given any thought to that?"

She looked a bit surprised. She knew that Mark was a shy type of person as it were, and she realized that it must have been difficult for him to say. "Did you mean that as a proposal?" She softly whispered. "Do you really want me to be your wife, or were you just teasing?"

"Uh, well, I'm not sure," he nervously replied. "I mostly wanted to see how you felt, I guess. You don't have to be in a hurry, and you can wait 'til next Saturday to decide, if you wish, longer, if need be."

Caroly smiled, and gently kissed him on the cheek. "Mark, I don't have to wait a week, not even 'til tomorrow, for I already know what I want to do," she murmured sweetly. "I'd be proud to be your wife, and the mother of your children. The answer to your question, is yes!"

"I appreciate that, but marriage involves more persons than just the two who are getting married," he pointed out. "We need to consider them, and how it will affect their lives, before we make a final decision."

"Well, I'll say!" She said, somewhat confused. "Just who, and how many persons do you wish to marry? Is it me, Carolyn Bland, who you want to marry, or do you want to marry my friends, my parents, even?"

Mark laughed, realizing how dramatic he must have sounded to her. "No, I don't want to marry everybody," he replied. "I really love you, Carolyn, and if we should get married, I want us to be able to enjoy a happy life together, that's all. I'm aware of how your father feels about me, and I'm sure some of your friends don't like me either, and without their blessings, it would cause you misery, and heartaches for the rest of your life. I love you, but I don't want your parents or your friends to look down on you, just because of me."

"It doesn't matter how others feel about us, so long as we are happy with each other," she softly replied. "I realize that some folks look down on you because of your stand against slavery, but I agree with you, and I'll stand by you as long as I live. I love you, and no matter what my parents or anybody in the community has to say, it won't change the way I feel about you."

"I don't doubt that your love for me is true, and I love you, but we will be much happier together with your parent's blessings," he persisted. "At least, we'll have two persons on our side. Now, do you understand?"

"Look, Mr. Simpson, do you want to marry me, or not?" She teased. "You ask me to marry you, then you turn around and try to talk me out of it."

"I guess I'm just a crazy man, madly in love with the most beautiful girl in the world, that's all," he smiled. "You are beautiful, you know!"

"In that case, you're forgiven," she said, as she gently leaned her head over against his shoulder. "My father will be coming around, and so will all the others, you'll see. So, don't worry about what they might have to say."

Inside the house, her father's curiosity was beginning to get the best of him. Somehow, he sensed that Mark's visit this evening, was more than just an ordinary date with his daughter. As he paced the floor, he began to worry out loud, when he saw his wife sitting on the settee, with a smile on her face.

"I wonder what they're talking about our there," he said, as he went and peeked out through a window. "They sure are sitting mighty close for some reason, and they're whispering back and forth about something. Do you have any idea what they are talking about, or do you know anything about their plans?"

"It wouldn't surprise me at all if they were making plans to get married, or I hope so, anyway," his wife replied. "They've been courting for four or five years, and it's about time that they were getting married."

"You have to be joking!" He snapped. "I can't imagine my daughter being married to a nigger lover! Have you ever thought what folks would say about us, if they got married? It would ruin all of our lives forever!"

"But, he's one of the richest "nigger lovers" in the country, and one of your largest depositors, you know!" She scolded. "He's not a child, or poor, like he was when you and Nate stripped him of everything. Try that on him now if you will, get Nate to help you, and see how far you get!"

"No matter how rich he might be, he's nothing but trash in my sight!" He continued. "No matter what it takes, I don't intend to let my daughter marry him. If you know what's good for her, you'll talk her out of it."

"Have you ever thought that she wouldn't be deprived of anything in life, if she married him? She asked. "They love each other, and if they want to get married, nothing that you say, will stop them. She is of age!"

Bland's face was now red with anger. "He's nothing but a troublemaker in my book." He said, almost whispering. "My daughter deserves better."

"Ellis, why don't you go out there right now, and tell him exactly how you feel, and stop talking trash behind his back?" She asked. "Shut up and leave them alone, and let them get on with their lives together, in peace!"

"If his money didn't mean so much to my bank, I'd go out there right now and kick him off the porch!" He snorted, still pacing the floor. "Let me get back to reading this book, before I really get mad." He sat back down, picked up the book, and continued to read.

His wife knew that he didn't want to discuss the matter any longer. Even though he tried to present a gruff exterior, he was somewhat ambivalent about everything in life. He claimed to uphold slavery, but he had never owned any slaves, and he claimed to be an honest, Christian-businessman, yet he involved himself in crooked deals with Nate Simpson, and other low-class citizens. She could only hope that he didn't interfere, if they really did decide to get married.

Mark and Carolyn stepped off the porch, went out the walkway to the gate, and then stood holding each other for a moment, while they looked at the crescent moon. "Carolyn, you've made me very happy tonight, the happiest I've been in all my life," said Mark, "but..."

"But?" she asked.

"But what?" He responded.

"It sounds to me, as though you have some reservations about marrying me after all," she explained. "Am I right? Is something bothering you?"

"Not really,' he replied. "I just think it's only fair to talk it over with your parents first, and not let them think we're trying to slip something over on them, that,'s all. There's no way that we could expect to be happy together as husband and wife, if it caused hard feelings with your friends and family."

"It's none of my father's business who I marry, and as for what others in the community might say, I couldn't care less!" She protested, as tears came to her eyes. "It won't be the first time a couple got married, without having their parent's permission! Everything will fall into place, you'll see."

"I had no intention of upsetting you," Mark sadly told her, as he wiped a tear from her cheek, with his hand. "It will mean so much to me, if you discuss it with your parents, then give me an answer. Will you do that?"

"All right then, I promise," she sniffed, "but I don't see any point in it, for I am of age, you know."

"That's my girl!" Mark smiled, knowing that she was upset. "It's rather late now, and while the moon's shining bright, I'd better get going. I'll be seeing you at church tomorrow, I hope. Please don't forget the party we plan to attend next Saturday night. If you still want to marry me, then I'll officially announce our engagement at the party. I do love you, Carolyn."

"And I love you," she said tearfully. "Good night, and I'll be looking forward to attending the party, and hearing you announce our engagement."

Carolyn stood for a moment looking at the moon, and then she went back inside to where her parents were sitting in the parlor. Her first instinct was to go on to her room and say nothing, but she had promised Mark. Honesty meant very much to her. Mark was depending on her to keep her word, and she knew that.

"Is Mark already gone?" Asked her mother, when Carolyn sat down in a chair at the far side of the room. "I didn't think it was all that late."

"Yes, he's gone, and I'd like to discuss something with both of you, then I'm going to bed," she replied sheepishly, as she looked over at her father. "I have something to discuss with you both. And Daddy, I want you to hear me out, before you make a comment, either way. Will you do that for me?"

"I am civilized," he replied, not taking his eyes off the book, "which is more than I can say about some folks! I hope it don't involve Mark, or the conversation that you two had out there on the porch tonight."

"It does, for he asked me to marry him, and of course, I said that I'd be happy to become his wife," she smiled, and replied. "I'm very happy because he asked me to marry him, and I wanted to share my joy with you."

Suddenly, her father let the book slip from his hands, and fall on his lap. "What was that you just said? Would you let me hear that again!" He shouted, in angry.

"Mark asked me to marry him, but he wanted me to discuss it with you, and give him an answer next Saturday," she proudly announced. "We're planning to attend a party, and he wanted to anounce our engagement there. But first, he wanted to get your approval. Wasn't that nice of him, to want your approval first."

Quickly jumping up, Bland threw the book against the wall. "That will be over my dead body!" He yelled. "I'd rather see you dead, than to marry him!"

Carolyn bowed her head, and began to cry. Then, her mother went over and kneeled down by the side of her chair, and hugged her tightly. "Everything is going to work out just fine, I'm sure," her mother comforted her.

"But, he's already asked me to marry him, and I said I would," she began to cry even worse. "Would you mind if I married him? I do love him, Mother."

"He's a wonderful person, and he'll make you a fine husband," she smiled and replied. "It's in all parents to want their child to be happy, whether it be in marriage, or anything else. If you're happy, then I'll feel happy too!"

"Thank you, Mother," smiled Carolyn. "You make me feel good, and maybe someday, I'll be able to say the same thing to my own daughter, when she plans to get married. I'll never stand in the way of her happiness."

"If you two love each other, then it don't matter what anyone else has to say, not even your own parents," her mother winked, and told her. "Go ahead and marry him, if that's what you really want, and I'll stand by you as long as I'm alive, even though I might have to stand alone."

"Woman, you're crazy!" Bland shouted at her, in anger. "And Carolyn, if you go against my wishes and marry him, you won't be welcomed back in my house! He's no good for you, and no good for the community, either!"

"No, Daddy, not everybody is against him," she murmured. "It's only those narrow-minded hypocrites in the community, and those who are jealous of things that he's accomplished, by being honest and fair to all human beings."

"Obviously, you don't even care what I think, either!" He scolded. "You're willing to marry him, even though it ruins my good name, aren't you?"

"That's not fair, Ellis!" His wife countered. "She's a fine girl, and I don't see where your so-called "good name" is in jeopardy. I would like to see the expression on the faces of your friends, if your book could be opened for them to read. Mark is open in what he stands for, but you, my dear husband, sneak around like an egg-sucking dog and do your dirty work, or like a cat covering up its mess. That's what I think of your good name!"

"Daddy, I really do love Mark, and that alone should count for something," Carolyn spoke up. "He's kind, understanding and above all, he's a gentleman. I plan to marry him, whether I have your blessings, or not."

"He's nothing but trash, scum of the earth, and a nigger lover!" Her father bellowed. "You deseve better than someone like him, and I don't intend to stand by, and see you throw your life away. Now, that's all I have to say!"

He quickly stormed out of the room, and left Carolyn crying her heart out over what he'd just said. What a shame, her mother thought. He's willing to allow prejudice, and politics to rob his daughter of her happiness.

"Mother, I don't intend to let him stop me, even if I have to leave home to accomplish my dream," Carolyn sighed. "I let him do that to one nice boy a few years back, but not again, not to Mark Simpson. Do you blame me?"

"You're old enough, and smart enough to know what you want to do, and you don't need anyone else to make up your mind for you," her mother told her, as tears welled her eyes. "He's afraid that if you marry Mark, he won't be able to boss you around, like he does now. Deep down inside he wants you to have a happy life, I'm sure. Just give him time, and he'll come around."

"You'll forgive me, if I have a hard time believing that," said Carolyn. "I can't believe that he said I'd ruin his good name. How could he say such a thing as that, and especially about such a nice person as Mark Simpson!"

"That was cruel, but he was angry," said her mother. "I don't think he really meant it to sound that way. We'll just have to wait and see and hope that things work out."

"Whether he meant it or not, it really hurt me, and I'm sure that he will cause trouble for us, before it's over," she sighed.

Her mother got up and walked over to a window, and stood looking up toward the beautiful crescent moon, while she thought about Carolyn, and the problems now facing her. She knew that if things didn't work out for her daughter this time around, she'd probably never let herself fall in love with anyone else.

"Go ahead and marry him, and leave your father out of the picture," said her mother, as she wiped tears from her eyes on the window drapes. "He'll get tired of being left outside, and he'll come around, you'll see."

"I certainly hope so," replied Carolyn, as she got up and walked toward her room. "Thank you, Mother, and good night."

Her father didn't get very much sleep that night, and he didn't even take his family to church the following morning, for he intended to do all he could to prevent Carolyn and Mark from seeing each other. Should he take Carolyn to church and she told

Mark what happened after he left, they just might run away and get married for sure, he thought.

Monday morning found Bland in a foul mood, and it showed on his face when folks came into his office.

"Ellis, you look like you've lost your very best friend," said Simpson, as he walked into Bland's office. "What's wrong? Did your sister-in-law die?"

"I'm afraid it's too late to do anything about what's bothering me at the moment," Bland replied. "It's something Mark did to Carolyn, which is going to disgrace her name in the community forever, and mine, too."

"I tried to tell you about him, but you wouldn't listen, and he finally ended up getting her pregnant!" Nate grinned. "Maybe you'll listen, the next time."

"Heck no, she's not pregnant!" He scolded. "They plan to get married in a few days, and there's nothing I can do. Do you have a suggestion?"

"Not right off, for with everything going for him like it is, he's going to be hard to handle," Nate explained. "The only possible way for us to destroy him now, is to get an insider to do it for us, and it must be somebody that he's apt to trust."

"That's the problem, for he don't trust anybody, except for the niggers he set free, and there's no way one of them would turn on him," Bland shook his head, and replied. "He's already ruined your name, and if he marries her, my name will be ruined as well. Nate, you've got to help me!"

"I'll do what I can," Nate promised, "but like I said, it's going to be hard for us to bring him to his knees, and even harder to get somebody else to do it for us. At this point we're both helpless, for he has the upper hand."

Throughout the week that followed, Carolyn kept to herself, pondering the situation, and praying that things would work out for her. Her father hardly spoke to her all week, and when he did, it was in a hateful voice, that caused her to cry. In spite of this, her mother insisted that she follow her heart, and do whatever she thought was best for her, and Mark.

For Mark, the week crept by, and it seemed like Saturday would never come at all. He could tell by the sad expression on Bland's face when he went into the bank one day, that Carolyn had already told him of their plan to get married. Mark could only imagine what her parents were saying about their marriage, but he had a feeling that it wasn't something positive.

Today was Thursday, and Mark had just returned from town, where he'd gone to pick up the engagement ring he'd ordered earlier. He decided to show it to Martha, and ask her how she felt about him getting married. Martha was in the kitchen helping her mother prepare dinner, and Mark called her aside.

"Martha, I"d like to know how you really feel about me getting married to Carolyn Bland?" He asked, seriously. "I remember what you said earlier about how you liked her, but are you real happy about me marrying her, and starting a family of my own? Just tell the truth, no matter how you feel."

"Yass'uh, I sho' is!" She cheerfully replied. "It sho' is gon'a be nice to have a purdy woman sashaying 'round the house, and smellin' good. And a bunch of snotty-nosed young'uns running 'round, sho' will top thangs off."

Mark wasn't exactly pleased with her reply, for he sensed that she hadn't fully expressed her feelings. "Are you sure that it won't bother you, to have another woman in the house with you?" He teased. "I've heard that there's no house big enough to accomodate two women, and I don't want to create any more problems for myself, than I already have," he chuckled.

"Like I sez, it's gon'a be jus' fine," she assured him. "Me and Mammy is been fuss'n over who wuz gon'a take care of her. Mark, will you let me be looking adder her? If you would, it sho' would make me happy."

"Of course I will, if that's what you want," Mark promised. "I know you two will hit it off together, like two peas in a pod. She already likes you, and I'm sure that you'll learn to like her as well. I'm proud of you, Martha, and nobody will ever take your place as my dearest, and best friend."

"The thang me and Mammy wuz wonder'n 'bout, wuz when is you gon'a make up yo' mind to fetch her in here, fer us to look adder," she replied.

"I plan to ask her next Saturday, and if she says yes, I imagine we'll be getting married pretty soon," he told her. He took a velvet-covered box from his vest pocket, and showed her an exquisite diamond ring he'd purchased that day. "What do you think she'll say, when I give her this ring." He handed the ring to Martha, and smiled. "Do you think she'll like it?"

"She be a fool, not to like it!" Martha gasps. "I's ain't never seed one befo', but it's the purd'est rang I's ever seed! Yass'uh, it sho' is purdy."

"Well, I hope her father won't get upset about us getting married, for I haven't even mentioned it to him," Mark frowned. "Maybe I should have waited until after I spoke with him, before I even bought the ring for her."

"Jus' who is it, that you gon'a mar'ee?" She asked. "Is you gon'a mar'ee the ole man? I's hope you don't fetch him in here fer me to have to take care of, and stumble over him, ever step I's take. Why do you have to axe him, if you's gon'a mar'ee her! That don't make no sense, do it!"

Mark stood there looking at Martha, almost as if seeing her for the first time. She truly was a beautiful black woman with small, defined features, and the darkest eyes he'd ever seen. It occurred to him that she was not all that different from Carolyn, except for the color of her skin. Carolyn had already made the same observation, about their marriage not being any of her father's business. Under different circumstances, Mark thought, he could probably give his heart to Martha, but she was black, and he was not. It wouldn't work out here in the South, not in a million years, he reasoned.

Mark had heard the nasty little inuendos made by some of the fine folks around town, about the Negro maid who lived in his house. Why do people think the worst of things, all the time. Mark simply couldn't understand. Men and women could be friends with each other, without sleeping together, as some had accused him and Martha of doing. Why was that so difficult for some folks to understand.

At long last, Saturday evening finally arrived, and Mark had asked Elijah to take him to Carolyn's house in his new two-seated buggy (surrey), and then take him and Carolyn to the party. Mark had told one of his lifelong friends about his plan to ask Carolyn to marry him, and his friend had scheduled a special party for the occasion, and invited several of Mark's and Carolyn's friends. Mark being a rich Southerner, he planned to arrive at the party in style. Tucking the small box containing the ring into his vest pocket, he went and climbed in the buggy, and they headed out toward where Ellis Bland lived. Carolyn didn't know anything about the ring, and Mark planned to slip it on her finger at the party later that evening, when he announced their engagement.

When they arrived at Bland's house, Mark walked upon the front porch and knocked on the door, and to his surprise, a Negro man came to the door. For a moment, Mark stood looking at him, for he was surprised to see him here.

"I'm Mark Simpson, and I'm here to take Carolyn to a party," Mark told him. "Sir, would you please tell Carolyn that I have arrived.."

"Yass'uh, Mos'a Simpson, she say you wuz coming," the Negro man replied, astonished at how polite Mark had spoken to him. "Miss Carolyn, she be aw'mos ready now. Come wid me to the parlor, whu' you's can wait fer her."

Mark seated himself in the parlor, and waited for her. He had brought a beautiful bouquet for Carolyn, and he placed it on a table next to his chair. A moment later the hallway door opened, and he stood up to greet her. Instead of it being Carolyn, her father walked in, and closed the door.

"Good evening, Mr. Bland!" Mark cordially greeted him. "How did things go for you this past week? Fine, I hope."

"Thanks to you, it didn't!" He snapped. "You have been calling on Carolyn for a long time, and up until now I've tolerated it for her sake, but the time has come for me to put my foot down, and bring things to a halt."

Mark looked at him in surprise. "I don't quite understand what you meant," Mark replied. "We've been seeing each other for years, and so far, you haven't said anything about it. Why are you acting like this now?"

"Courting is one thing, but marriage is something else!" He snarled. "She told me about you proposing, and it made me as mad as the devil too!"

"But, Mr. Bland, we love each other very much, and I told her to ask you about it, before we even set a date," Mark explained. "It's not like as if we were trying to hide something from you, or get married without your permission."

"Let's get one thing straight!" He bellowed. "I allowed her to be your friend, but I won't allow her to be your wife! Do you clearly understand?"

"But Sir, I'm not a pauper, and she'll never go lacking for anything that she wants in life," Mark pointed out. "More than that, we love each other an awful lot, and that's what makes a marriage work, not money, and certainly not our social or political standing in the community."

"You have plenty of money, but no common sense!" Bland scolded. "You're a troublemaker, to say the least, and the stupid ideas you have about slavery, and the way you treat the niggers, will be your downfall."

"Have you really been thinking that way all along, while you complemented me on being successful?" Mark asked, in an upset voice. "In other words, you have been lying to me, so long as I made deposits at your bank!"

"I told you what I wanted you to hear at the time!" He sharply replied. "To be perfectly honest, I've told my friends that Carolyn was ashamed of you, and that she only talked with you at church, because you didn't have any white friends at all. Now, does that tell you anything?"

His comment really cut deep into Mark's heart. "I have quite a number of friends, both black and white," Mark told him. "They are true-friends, not lousy hypocrites, or two-faced liars, like some persons I know!"

"Well, I'll say!" Bland snapped. "Then tell me, if you can, how many agree with you, that slavery is wrong! Name one white man, who agrees with you!"

"Sir, the Constitution which gives you a right to voice your approval of something, gives me the very same right to disapprove," Mark rebutted. "If you buy a mule, it's yours to keep, or turn loose in the woods. The same goes with buying slaves, for I can keep them, or turn them loose. No human, black or white, was put on earth to become a slave to another person."

"Darn the luck!" He shouted. "Niggers were brought over to this country to become slaves to white persons! But no, you set the bastards free!"

"Sir, about seventy-five years ago our forefathers fought and died to get away from an unjust, slave-like system that the British was imposing on them," Mark reminded him. "Now we, their descendants, are doing the very same things with Negroes. Tell me, where can you find justice in that?"

Bland didn't reply, for Mark's question had left him without a meaningful response. Mark's success alone, attested to the validity of his methods, even though it caused Bland and others great distress. Then Carolyn stepped into the room, a vision of pink, all dressed for the party. Bland saw her from the corner of his eye, as she stood smiling at Mark, for Mark had sat back down in his chair, while waiting for her.

"Get back into your room, this moment!" Bland shouted. "I'm not finished talking with this nigger lover, and you have no place in here!"

Mark quickly jumped to his feet. "Sir, I resent that remark!" Mark told him. "Carolyn and I have a party to attend, and I don't have any more time to argue with you. Are you ready, Carolyn?"

"Sit back down, Mr. Simpson!" Bland yelled. "And Carolyn, you might as well return to your room and take off that fancy dress, for you're not going anywhere tonight! Not with him, anyway."

Carolyn ran back into her room in tears, and sprawled out across the bed. She had no idea what was taking place until she came into the parlor, but with her bedroom door now open, she could hear them screaming and fussing.

Mark quickly jumped up, and shook his fist in Bland's face. "You inconsiderate hypocrite!" Mark lashed out at him. "You claim that you're afraid that I'll hurt her, but you don't mind hurting her yourself. You don't deserve to be her father!"

"My daughter is none of your darned concern!" Bland scolded. "I'm doing what I think is best for her, and one day she'll thank me. I don't agree with the way you treat niggers, and I don't intend to stand by and let you drag her down with you. I'd rather see her dead!"

"You and a lot of others try to force me into accepting your theory, but you refuse to even listen to my point of view," Mark frowned. "That makes me a slave to you, Sir, with no rights, or any way to defend myself."

"Then, why don't you leave the South, go up north, and suckle up to all the other nigger lovers?" Bland sneered. "I'll even pay the train fare!"

Mark was becoming annoyed with him. "Other farmers have set their slaves free, yet you say nothing to them," Mark protested. "Tell me if you can, why can't I do the same thing? They realized that it was wrong to be making slaves of other human beings, but I'm not allowed to think that way."

"They freed the slaves, because they didn't need them, but they certainly didn't hire them back to work for them," Bland argued. "There's not anything wrong with freeing them, but it's wrong to pay them for working, when there's plenty of poor white men who need the money."

"If God ever made a mistake, it was when He didn't make everybody colorblind," Mark replied. "No matter if it's wrong to pay them, or regardless of what my fellow-farmers have to say, it works well for me. They're jealous because I'm prospering, and afraid to follow my lead, for fear of what others might say."

With that, Ellis became enraged. "I won't allow my daughter to be out of my sight with you!" He snorted. "Go home and get in bed with that nigger gal that you call your maid, and let her ease your pain as usual."

"My maid and butler are brother and sister, and yes, they have a separate room in my house," Mark countered. "If I may ask, where does your own butler live? In your house, with your wife and daughter while you're away. Is that where he lives?"

"That's none of your business!" He snapped. "My friends call me a fool for allowing you to call on my daughter on weekends, then lay up with a nigger gal during the week. It's a disgrace to the Simpson name!"

"There's no way to get through your dirty mind," replied Mark. "I don't suppose it would help if I placed my hand on the Bible, and swore that I have never slept with that Negro girl, or any other girl, black or white."

"You'll never get me to believe that, for you're too fond of her, not to be sleeping with her." Bland growled. "Even your own father, knows that."

That did it, for Mark stood right up in his face, and began storming in a loud voice. "Listen, you bigoted old fool! That girl and her family are the only true friends I have in the world! They stood by me when you helped strip me of everything, and stuck with me through all kinds of hell. There's no way you can measure up to them, and you're not fit to walk on the same ground they walk on! That, my stupid, incondiderate friend, is my honest opinion of you!"

Bland's face was red, and the veins in his neck looked like they'd burst open. "I'm ordering you out of my house right now!" He shouted, pointing to the door. "And, I'm ordering you to stay away from my daughter!"

"Very well then, I'll stay away from your house and your daughter, but as sure as Monday morning comes, I'll be at your office to withdraw all my money from your bank!" Mark told him, as he slapped Bland across the face, knocking him back down in his chair. "If you as much as bat an eye, or move a muscle, I'll beat the devil out of you, in your own house!"

Mark stormed out of the house, then went and joined Elijah in the buggy, to head back home. "Drive me back home, Elijah!" Said Mark, as tears filled his eyes. "That man's as crazy as a bat, and downright stupid!"

Before Elijah could turn the buggy around, Carolyn came running out into the yard crying, and headed toward the buggy. "Wait just a minute, Mark! I'd like to talk to you, before you leave! Daddy doesn't run my life!" She cried.

This really broke Mark's heart, and he quickly jumped down from the buggy and ran to meet her, and held her tightly. "I love you Carolyn, but he is so consumed with hatred, until he'll never give in," he cried. "It won't work, he's dead set against me, and we could never be happy together."

Her face was soaked with tears as he held her close to him. "But Mark, I have my own life to live, and my future's at stake, not his," she cried. "It doesn't matter if he never speaks to me again, just as long as I'm happy."

"I know, but marriage is risky as it is, and problems like we are having here tonight, will only lead to more serious one's later," he softly replied. "I can't bring that on you, I love you too much."

"But, mother likes you, and her blessings is all we need," she continued to plead. "She told me to follow my heart, and I really do love you."

"I appreciate that, and I like her too, but your father will never allow me to become a part of the family," he told her. "That's not the way for two persons to start out in life, it won't ever work."

It was obvious, that Mark wasn't going ahead with his plans to marry her. "Then you don't love me, like you said that you did, do you?" She cried, and asked him. "Isn't that it, you don't really love me?"

"No, it's because I love you, that I'm dropping things where they are at the moment," he replied. "I'd rather die loving you, than to go against his wishes and marry you, and cause you trouble for the rest of your life."

"I'll always love you, Mark," she vowed, "and one day we will be living together. Please don't take that hope away from me."

"I'll never fall in love with another girl," he told her. "I must go on home now, for I've had enough for tonight. Good night, Carolyn. I love you."

Brokenhearted and sad, Mark climbed back into the buggy, and told Elijah to drive him back home. It was obvious that Mark was in no condition to talk with him, so Elijah sat quietly, as they went on their way.

As they rode along, Mark wondered why all this was happening to him, and instead of it changing his view on slavery, he vowed to be more against it now, than ever before. It was love that had brought them together, and because of his love for her, and not wanting her to have to live the life he was already living, he was now leaving her.

CHAPTER SEVEN

THE EVIL GARDNER

It had been quite awhile now since Mark had even spoken to Carolyn Bland, for she had stopped attending church, and taking part in social events of the community. Even when others visited Bland's home, she made a point of staying well out of sight, and her mother would cover for her by telling their friends that she was visiting someone else at the time. Other than for occasionally at church, Mark hadn't even seen her father, for since Mark had withdrawn his money from Bland's bank, he had no reason to associate with him. Since the night he and Bland had a fight, Mark had taken a greater stand against slavery, and had begun to more openly express his point of view, and lash out at others because they still used other human beings as slaves. His life had become nothing but a living-nightmare, with no real purpose at all.

He continued to buy other farms, and mostly because these farmers would sell him the slaves as well, so he could set them free. Word had spread around as to what he really had in mind, and most slave-runners refused to sell him any slaves at all, because they knew that he would set them free. He now had well over a hundred freed-slaves on his payroll, and because of his increased stand against slavery, he bore the horrible brand- "nigger lover." Even though some proclaimed that they shared his viewpoints, Mark realized that they were doing this only while in his presence. When they were away from him, like most other persons in the South, they were afraid to say anything against slavery.

Contrary to popular belief, slavery didn't originate in the South as Mark soon learned. Slave labor was not practical for smaller farmers in the North, therefore, it was introduced to the South. In the South, with the vast amount of farmland, where cotton was the chief money-crop, it required a considerable amount of labor. Slavery seemed to be the solution to the labor problem, and using Negroes as slaves, soon became concentrated here in the South. A great many foreign countries profited by selling slaves to America, and by the year 1860, there were about 4 million Negro slaves in America, one third of the total population of all the slave states.

The longer Mark studied the history of slavery, the more he found it to be evil and distasteful. From his own experience as a farmer, he knew that using Negroes as slaves was not necessary for survival, or for success. He refused to support the theory, that slavery really was necessary in civilizing the allegedly barbarous Negroes. Mark knew for a fact that the overall purpose for the Negroes being brought to this country, was to work as slaves for the white persons, and nothing else.

Mark's father had bragged about how almost thirty years ago, during 1830, South Carolina had threatened to withdraw from the Union, unless it got it's way. It claimed that the Union didn't want the South to use slave labor, which was not the whole truth. The Union didn't want any human being to become a slave, however, there were many other differences that were threatening to tear this young and struggling nation apart. Because the South didn't get it's way, and like an obstinate stepchild, it started rejecting whatever rules the Union handed down. However, the average citizen was led to believe that the problems were being caused by slavery alone. Soon the rebellion against the Union became an ominous fact that more serious problems could result, if it wasn't handled in a proper way. Mark could see "the hand writing on the wall." The North wasn't without fault, and Mark knew that. It was evident, that an unmistakable element of jealousy did exist between small Northern farmers, and large plantation owners in the South, Mark Simpson included. After all, using unpaid slaves as laborers soon proved to be profitable for southern farmers.

Although Mark Simpson was considerably younger than most farmers, he had great insight into the many problems that plagued the entire country. Unless the South and the North could settle their differences, all previous threats were sure to become a reality. Unless they reached an agreement, he could not see a way out, short of an all-out war. He loved the South, but he disagreed with the way the leaders were misleading the people. He didn't expect a proud Southerner to accept a Negro as their equal, but if they would only set the slaves free, perhaps the Union might look more favorably on his homeland, he thought.

A few years ago, Mark's father had helped a young man by the name of Joe Wilson to buy a small farm, and just recently, Mark bought the farm from him. This young man knew quite a lot about farming, therefore, Mark decided to hire him to help Bill manage his plantation. This pleased Bill, for he needed help in supervising more than a hundred workers. Joe Wilson and Bill seemed to get along real well together, and Mark thought they would make a good team.

Since having come to work for Mark, Joe and his wife Elizabeth, visited in Mark's home many times, and Mark and Joe became great friends. They had a small child, and Martha began to look forward to their visits, for she enjoyed playing with the baby. Joe soon won Mark's trust, and Mark felt comfortable discussing things with him, even his somewhat controversial theory of slavery. Joe left the impression with Mark that he was repulsed by the way Negroes were being treated by white men, which caused Mark to like him even more. Although Mark got along well with other white men who worked for him as foremen, he had a special liking for Joe Wilson.

With his great wealth, one might think Mark would be the happiest person on earth, but nothing could be further from the truth. He was unaccepted by social groups in the comunity, and considered unworthy to become a member of the political arena, because of his stand against slavery. Some claimed that it was because Martha lived in his house as maid, which wasn't true, for every wealthy farmer had a maid living in their home. The truth was, he'd shown the other farmers that he could prosper by freeing the slaves, and paying them to work for him. Some farmers freed their slaves, but they didn't dare give them anything for their labor, except for a few bites to eat, worn out clothes, and a rundown shack in which to live. This is why other farmers didn't like Mark, and not necessarily because Martha lived in his house.

Needless to say, Mark had given considerable thought to selling his farm and going to Ohio to live with relatives, and if it were not for the true love and respect he had for Bill's family, he would probably elect to do just that. Mark could not abandon these wonderful folks to escape his own heartaches, for all he owned today, was a result of their standing by him through all the many years. The only way he'd even think about going away, was if he could find a person to look after them while he was gone. Although they were free, he knew that they could not survive without someone to watch over them, and keep white persons from taking advantage of them.

One Sunday afternoon, while Mark and Joe Wilson were riding their horses around over the plantation, Joe sensed by the tone of Mark's voice, that he was bothered about something. Mark had been acting a bit strange since he went to town a few days ago, and it caused Joe great concern. Mark didn't deny that he still loved Carolyn Bland, and even though the chances of them getting back together were slim, he still hoped they would get married someday. Joe thought that Mark might have tried to patch things up between him and Carolyn, and she turned him down, or that he might have had another run-in with her father, for Mark had already told him all about what happened that night.

"Mark, you haven't acted just right here lately, and I must say that it's beginning to bother me," Joe told him. "I hope it's not something that I've done, but if it is, I wish you'd come right out and get it off your chest."

"Strange that you asked, for I didn't realize that my frustration showed all that much," Mark replied. "I should be the happiest person on earth, but I'm as miserable as a pauper, and as sad as a person without a friend. I know it's hard for you to understand, and it's just as hard for me to explain."

"I might not have a solution to your problem, but I'm a good listener, if you care to discuss it with me," Joe responded, kindly. "I find that it does help sometimes, if we discuss our problems with others."

Mark stopped his mare, turned around in the saddle, and then looked keenly at him. "Joe, is your father still living?"

"No, he died when I was fifteen years old," Joe sadly replied. "Not one day goes by that I don't think of him, and how kind, and loving he was to each of us. I still have fond memories of him, for which I'm thankful."

"I envy you, for I can't say that about my father," Mark told him. "The only memories that I have of my father, are his acts of cruelty, and I hate that."

"I'm sorry, but I haven't heard of his death," replied Joe. "Of course, I haven't seen him in quite awhile, and I suppose that's the reason."

"No, he's still alive!" Mark nodded. "He's done some awful things to me down through the years, and the problem is, I don't know when he might decide to strike again. That's why I can't let my guard down, and enjoy my life like other folks, for I sleep with one eye open, and have no peace of mind."

"That's awful!" Joe remarked. "He should be proud because you followed in his footsteps, and became one of the largest farmers in South Carolina."

"But I haven't, and that's the point!" Mark explained. "I have become just as successful, but I refuse to treat Negroes like trash, and I don't try to cheat my way through life. That's why he has nothing to do with me."

Joe shook his head. He'd only dealt with Nate Simpson once, and he would never forget it. Nate once held a lien on his farm, and he'd never forget how demanding and hateful Nate acted toward him. He understood what Mark meant, by his father being mean and cruel. A burned child dreads fire, he thought.

"That's a shame, and I can see why you're so bothered," Joe replied. "Like I said, my father's dead, but I'm sure that I would have been much better off now, if he were still alive. He never gave me one reason to question his love for me."

"That means more than all the money in the world," sighed Mark, as tears filled his eyes. "That feeling of love will always remain in your heart, like the hatred I have for my father, will always remain in mine."

"That's sad," Joe agreed, "but you'll have to shake if off, and rely on your friends for comfort. Forget about it, and keep moving right on forward."

"Now, that brings me to the second phase of my problems," Mark frowned. "My real friends consist of five Negroes, Bill and his family. Other than for them, everybody else looks down on me because of my stand against slavery. My father stripped me of everything I earned the first year I started out, and he lurks in the shadows waiting for me to stumble, so he can wipe me out again. I stand alone, like a lamb in a den of wolves."

Tears came to Joe's eyes as well. "I'm sorry to hear that, for I know it must be something that's hard to deal with," he said kindly. "As for the way other farmers feel about you, I think it's pure jealousy. They see how that you've prospered by treating Negroes right, and it galls them an awful lot, simply because you have outsmarted them, that's all."

"I understand," said Mark, "but I also know that they had rather simply get by on the skin of their teeth, than to prosper in life, by following my lead."

"Let's not forget politics, for it plays an important role in this, too," Joe pointed out. "If the slaves were free they'd be able to vote, and present leaders who uphold slavery, might be voted out of office. Negroes aren't all that stupid, although some folks think they are. Am I right?"

"Joe, you've made some valid points, and I appreciate that," Mark smiled, and told him. "I already feel better, knowing that I have at least one person who sees things my way. I really do appreciate that, Joe."

"Any time." Joe smiled. "I'm a good listener, even though I might fall short, when it comes to solving your problems. I do understand how difficult it is for folks to admit that they've been wrong for all these years, and whether or not you agree with me, it does take a lot of giving and taking to accept a former slave as an equal citizen. I just learned to do that myself, only after I came to work for you, and really got to know Bill."

"Listen, Joe!" Mark said seriously. "I've been thinking very seriously about leaving this part of the country, and getting away from this mess for a while. I feel more like it now, than ever before, thanks to you."

"That's fine, but wherever you go here in the South, you're going to face the same problems you face now," Joe warned. "Where are you going, or do you have your mind made up yet?"

"Some of my mother's folks live in Columbus, Ohio, and I thought I might go and live with them for awhile," Mark replied. "The only drawback, is that I don't have anybody to take care of things while I'm gone, however long that might be. Then again, I might never come back."

"That's a long way from here, and besides that, I'm not sure who would be able to handle things for you," Joe replied. "This is a mighty big farm, and you have over a hundred Negroes to look after, and finding somebody who's able to handle this monster of a farm, certainly won't be easy."

"I feel sort of like I've been caught between two evils at this point in my life, and if I could get away for a few months, even a few weeks, it would help me quite a lot," he replied.

Maybe it's because of his broken engagement with Carolyn. He might have changed his mind a bit about slavery. Maybe he realizes, that it wasn't worth the hassle after all. He has plenty of money, and could travel the world, so why don't he take a vacation. Maybe he's too bold in the way he takes a stand against slavery, and voicing his opinion, Joe thought.

"Have you thought about easing up a bit, and not being quite so bold in voicing your dislike for slavery?" Joe asked, seriously. "If you did, I'm sure that folks would ease up on you, and make life a little less diffucilt for you."

"Not in the least!" Mark quickly replied. "Even if I were a pauper I'd feel the same way, for slavery is wrong, and it should be abolished. The only thing I ask, is that I be allowed to think as I please about slavery, the same as I respect their right to uphold it, and let me waste my money on Negroes by paying them, if that's what I wish to do. That's all I'm asking."

Although Joe thought that Mark was assuming an awesome task in attempting to change the South's view on slavery, he'd been fair and honest with him, and he couldn't complain, Joe reasoned. Maybe Mark should get away for a while.

"Maybe it would be best if you did get away for awhile, then you would be able to look at things from a distance, for sometimes it's hard to see things, when they're right under your nose," said Joe. "The Negroes like you, and I'm sure they'd keep on working as though you were still here, which would make it easier for the person whom you left in charge. Although they are Negroes, you won't find a better white family, than Bill's family, and they'd make sure the others kept things going while you were away. I didn't think that I'd live to see the day when it happen, but even your white foremen respect Bill."

"But the big question is, who will I get to supervise them, and to make sure that things are run right while I'm gone." Mark replied. "Say! Why couldn't you and Elizabeth move into my house, and look after things for me! I'm sure you could handle things just fine. What do you say?"

"Hold on a minute!" Joe protested. "I've run my own farm, which is like nothing compared to this plantation, but I'm not sure if I could handle a big place like this, even if I tried. You need to find somebody else."

"Sure you could!" Mark argued, as they rode back toward the barn. "You know a lot about farming, and you strike me as being honest, and trustworthy as well. If you'd treat the Negroes as I have, I'd turn this farm over to you in a heartbeat. Bill will help you, for his qualifications exceeds that of most white persons I know, and most of all, he's honest."

"I agree that he's a fine person, and like I said before, even your white foremen respect him, and ask him for advice," Joe replied.

"I know, and it means something for a white man to admit that a Negro has some sense after all, but you still haven't answered my question," said Mark, as they arrived back at the barn. "Will you handle things for me?"

"I don't claim to know it all, but I think I could handle the supervision part, if Bill will promise to oversee the workers," Joe replied. "But, only if you promise to come on back, if I happen to run into a problem."

"I certainly will, and I thank you for taking a heavy load off my shoulder, for it was getting awful hard to carry," smiled Mark, as he offered his hand.

"And, I thank you for trusting me," said Joe, as they shook hands. "All I promise, is that I'll try to do my best, and that I'll never let you down."

"Then, I'll go into town tomorrow and speak to my attorney, and tell him that you'll be in charge," Mark told him. "It won't be long until the cotton will be ready to pick, and I want one-half of the money divided equally among all my workers, black and white alike. And of course, you'll be paid an extra amount for your service, in addition to your present salary."

"I hardly know what to say, for this is the best offer I've ever had come my way," Joe smiled. "I understand how you want the farm run, but before you leave, explain any other particular thing that I need to know."

"I intended to explain certain things to you and Elizabeth together, but I might as well tell you now," Mark began. "Leave your furniture where it is now, and use my furniture as if it were yours. Let Sam continue on as butler, and Martha as maid and cook. She's a real good cook, and she'll be a great help to Elizabeth, in helping tend to your child."

"Fine with me!" Joe agreed. "Is there anything else that you can think of, that I should know about? Something that you might have forgotten."

"Of course, I want all my workers to be well fed, properly clothed, and I don't want them working on Sunday, or when it's unfit to be outside," clearly stated Mark. "Don't ever call them 'niggers' or slaves, and regardless to the color of their skin, they must be treated equally, and they must be paid equally too. Have I made myself clear?

"Consider it done!" Joe promised him. "I'll need to be off tomorrow to pick up our clothes and personal items, and Elizabeth needs to go into town and get some things for herself and the baby. Will that be all right?"

"That's fine, for I need to talk with Bland at the bank, and let him know that you will be in charge," Mark explained. "I'll have him handle the sale of the cotton for you, and handle money matters for me as well. I'll call all the workers together tomorrow evening, and explain everything to them, so they will know what's going on. I'll see you tomorrow evening."

Although it was hard for him to do, Mark went to the house and explained his plan to Martha and Sam. He hated to leave, but he had to have some rest, and beyond that, some peace of mind. He felt sure that he had made the proper decision, but as the case had been so many times before, events to come, would probably prove him wrong. Time would tell - it always does.

Sadness filled the hearts of Martha and her brother, and Mark would spend an almost sleepless night while pondering over his decision. His heart ached, as he thought about Carolyn, and how wonderful it would be if she were here with him now. Someone to lean on, someone who really cares.

Early the following morning, Mark went into town to take care of business matters, before turning the farm over to Joe Wilson. Though he hadn't spoken to Bland since he closed out his account at the bank, Mark knew that he had to leave some money on deposit for Joe to use, and let him know that Joe would be in charge while he was away. He also wanted Bland to keep half the money from the crop on deposit, to use to pay taxes on his property, and for whatever Joe might need in order to keep things going smoothly. He spent the least amount of time with Bland as possible, for Mark still hated the very sight of him.

"Mr Bland, I'm placing a lot of confidence in you, which I know is wrong in the first place, but I have no other choice at this point," said Mark, as he started to leave Bland's office. "For once in your life, I hope you can be honest enough to handle my business while I'm gone, and not let my father get the upper hand on me, or let my farm go to the dogs. Will you do that?"

"You don't have to worry one bit," Bland replied, "for what you've told me, will remain a secret between us. "Nate won't know anything about what you plan to do, unless you tell him yourself. I don't trust that man."

"You'll forgive me Sir, for doubting your word, but time will tell," he lashed out at Bland, as he left the office. "Time heals wounds, it also causes scars. I still bear some of the scars, that you placed on me."

Joe and Elizabeth had also gone to town, and when Elizabeth finished with her shopping, they headed back toward home to pick up their clothes and other personal items they planned to take back to Mark's house. Before they got out of town, Nate Simpson walked out of the bank, stepped out into the street, and flagged them down. They'd been laughing and joking up to this point, however the very sight of Simpson put a stop to that. Joe quickly glanced over at his wife and shook his head, as he drove the buggy up to where Nate was standing in the street, smiling.

"Good morning, Joe, Mrs. Wilson," spoke Simpson politely. "When I was in the bank a minute ago, Bland told me that Mark planned on being out of the country for awhile. Going to Ohio, I understand. I'm aware that you sold him your farm, and that you work for him, and I was wondering if you knew why he was leaving, and when he planned to return."

Joe was somewhat intimidated by Simpson, so he answered him softly, as he winked at Elizabeth. "Yes, he's going up north, but I don't know how long he plans to be away," Joe replied. "Word sure gets around, for he told me only yesterday, and you already know all about his plans. That's strange."

"From what I hear, you'll be running the place while he's gone," Simpson said slyly. "That's a mighty big place, and unless you're a nigger lover like him, it's going to be a mighty tough job. You and him must see eye-to-eye on everything, for him to trust you. Two peas in a pod, they say!"

261

Joe knew that Simpson had his wicked heart set on something, and he was weary of telling him anything. He remembered when Nate held a lien on his farm, how overbearing he was, and he didn't want this to happen again.

"Yes, he asked me to look after things while he was away," Joe carefully replied, in a diplomatic voice, "but we don't see eye-to-eye on everything as you suppose. We are business partners with no time to argue, unless it has to do with matters that might affect the operation of the plantation."

"By that, I take it that you'll continue paying the niggers for working, just like he's been doing," Nate probed. "Is that what he told you do?"

"Sir, you have nothing to do in the matter," sharply replied Joe, "and if you'll excuse me, I still have a lot of things to do today."

"I didn't mean to upset you," Simpson replied, changing his tone, "but Mark and I sure have had somewhat of a strained relationship, and it probably still shows. If you have no objections, I'd like to visit the plantation sometimes, that is, after he's gone."

Seeing another buggy approaching, Simpson quickly bid them good-bye, and hurried into a store. It was Mark, and he had seen his father.

Mark drove up and stopped alongside Joe's buggy. "That was my father that I saw run across the street, wasn't it?" Mark asked, somewhat confused. "I can see him now, peeking from a door over yonder." Mark then pointed that way.

"It was," Joe replied, still somewhat shaken. "He ran out in the street and stopped me, but when he saw your buggy, he took off in a hurry."

"What did he have to say?" Mark asked. "He must have said something you didn't like, for you're a little pale, and frazzled looking."

"He didn't have time to say very much, and if I look frazzled, it's only because I still remember my past dealings with him," he replied.

"I'd rather he didn't know anything about my plans, for he's liable to cause trouble while I'm gone," Mark stated. "I'm sure that he'll eventually find out though."

"Then, perhaps you shouldn't go," spoke up Elizabeth. "We don't want to have any trouble with him, or with anybody else."

"Don't worry, for he won't cause you any kind of trouble," Mark smiled. "He'll no doubt be so proud that I'm gone, until he'll pitch a party. I told Bland not to say anything to him, and he promised that he wouldn't."

Joe heaved a sigh of relief. Should he tell Mark that Bland had already told his father. He decided to say nothing, for he didn't want to tangle with Simpson, yet he didn't want to deceive Mark. Still he feared that Nate might try something after Mark was gone, but he hoped not.

Joe and Elizabeth went on home to pack up their belongings, and Mark went back to his plantation.

As soon as Mark arrived, he called Bill's family aside and explained his plan to them. Though they were heartbroken, they seemed to understand why, or so it seemed. Bill assured Mark that he and Joe would get along just fine, and this caused Mark to feel somewhat better. Then Mark assured them that nothing would change, and that Joe would continue treating them as they'd been treated before, and he asked them to respect Joe as well.

Later that afternoon, Mark called all his workers together and explained his plan to them, and he told them that Joe would be watching over them while he was away. He assured them that everything would remain the same, and he asked Joe to say a few words to them.

Joe also assured them that things would remain the same, and he promised to treat each of them equal, regardless to the color of their skin. He looked at Bill and smiled, then told them that Bill would be in charge of the workers as before, and that Sam and Martha were to stay on in Mark's house as maid and butler, just like Mark requested. Although they hated for Mark to go, they felt sure that Joe would treat them like he'd promised, then they all returned home as they each waved good-bye to Mark, and wished him well.

Friday came, and following a private conversation with Bill's family, and after having given Martha and her mother a big hug, Mark went and climbed into his buggy where he sat for a moment. He looked up toward the mansion, then at Bill's family, who stood there in the yard crying.

"I'll be writing to Joe, and he promised to keep me informed as to how things were going," he told them. "Good-bye, and I'll pray for you!"

"Yass'uh, we's know that," Bill sobbed. "And put rail long legs on yo' prayers, too! Good-bye, and we's hope to see you rail soon."

Elijah drove the buggy, so that he could bring it back after Mark boarded a train to Ohio, and as they rode along, Mark had a weary feeling that things might not go as he expected. More than once, he almost made up his mind to go back and call off the trip, but he had Joe's word that everything would remain the same, and he tried to cast it out of his mind. Mark needed some rest, to say the least. Joe swore in the presence of everybody that he'd treat all the workers with respect and dignity. Would he do that? Mark still wondered.

Three weeks had passed, and thus far things were going along as smooth as could be expected under the new management. Joe and Bill seemed to get along real well together as a team, and Elizabeth was thrilled to have Martha taking care of the house, and helping her tend to her child. Elizabeth wasn't accustomed to all this help, and soon began to enjoy this kind of life-style.

Mark had built a church for the Negroes, and except for tending to chores and taking care of the livestock, they didn't do any work on Sunday. He even allowed them to stop working at noon on Saturday, so they could go to a creek and take their weekend bath. Joe honored this practice as well, for he swore to Mark that he wouldn't change anything.

Then one day things began to change, as though a dark cloud of gloom had hovered over the plantation, for at last Nate Simpson had come to call. While Martha served tea to him and the Wilsons in the parlor, she could feel the icy chill of Nate's stare. He's thinking of the party here earlier, she thought.

"Well, I see that Mark's nigger maid is still with you," Simpson said to them, as Martha left the room.

"Yes, and I don't know how we could ever do without her," Elizabeth spoke up. "Martha's a wonderful person, a real good housekeeper, and an excellent cook."

Simpson almost strangled on his tea. "Is her name Martha?" He asked, as a strange expression came on his face. "Is she really Bill's gal, the one that was...?"

"That's right, and her name is Martha," Elizabeth told him. "Her entire family are wonderful folks, and they don't come any better than Martha."

"So, she really is Bill and Liza's gal, is she?" He asked again.

"She is, and why do you keep asking?" Elizabeth inquired. "I sure would like to know why you're so concerned about her, for it really does bother me."

"Oh, I was thinking that something happened to her, that's all," replied Simpson, as he turned to Joe. "Let's step outside. What I have to discuss is strictly business, and it might be boring to your lovely wife."

"Very well Mr. Simpson," said Joe, in an uneasy voice, "but I must get back to work shortly. I hope this discussion won't take up a lot of my time."

"It won't," Simpson told him, "and Mrs. Wilson, I enjoyed the tea, and your gracious hospitality. You're a wonderful hostess." Nate led the way, as he and Joe walked out into the yard.

Elizabeth watched from the parlor door as Joe stood talking with Simpson, and wondered why she wasn't allowed to listen. Joe's gestures, and his facial expressions told her that Joe was upset, and more than a few times, Joe tried to walk away. At one point, Nate shook his finger in Joe's face. For several minutes, they stood and exchanged words she could not hear. Then Nate jumped in his buggy, and quickly sped away.

Quickly going out to join her husband, Elizabeth found him trembling with fear, or anger, or perhaps a combination of both.

"What did that old fool say to you?" She asked, almost in tears. "I saw him shaking his finger in your face, and I started to come out here and thrash him over the head with the broom! I've never seen you so frightened. Tell me what he said, to upset you so. Did he threaten you in some way?"

"Lizzie, we need to talk, real bad," he said, his voice cracking. "Tell Martha to look after the baby for a few minutes, while we go down to the creek where we can be alone. I don't know what to do, for he controls everything, and everybody around him. He's a demon from the pits of hell."

Martha watched the baby while they were gone for almost an hour, and when they returned; Elizabeth had a strange expression on her face. Being bothered somewhat by the sudden change, Martha decided to see if Elizabeth would talk to her.

"Miss Liz'buth," said Martha softly, "I's glad you's let me look adder the baby, fer it takes my mind off Mark not being here. Is youn's ever hear'd from Mark since he been gone? Is he scratched youn's a letter yet?"

Elizabeth didn't reply, instead, she sat quietly with her hands folded on her lap, staring into space as though she hadn't heard Martha. It was obvious that she was upset about something, and as Martha left the room, she felt sure that it must have been somethng that Simpson had said to Joe.

Later that afternoon, while Martha was in Mark's room folding up some of his clothes, and putting them in a cedar chest, she began to cry. Somehow she hadn't seen Elizabeth enter the room, however, when she turned to walk out of the room, Elizabeth was standing right next to her, with her hands propped on her hips. Martha looked at her and smiled, and wiped tears from her eyes.

"Shut up that crying, you stupid nigger!" Elizabeth scolded. "Finish up your work, before I slap your face!"

"I's sorry 'bout that," Martha sobbed, "but when I's see thangs that he wore, it brangs back memories. We been friends since we wuz younguns, and I sho' do miss not having him 'round here to talk wid."

"Well, he's not here now!" Elizabeth snapped. "He's gone, and as far as I'm concerned, you're nothing but a sorry nigger slave!"

"But I's a free-nigga now!" Martha told her. "Mark give us a paper that sez we is free, and it's over there in his trunk, rite now!"

"Yes, I've seen those precious papers you're talking about, which aren't worth anything unless you have them with you," she snarled. "They're in that trunk, where they'll stay, too!"

"Yass'am, Mark sez he'd keep 'em there fer us, 'til we's need 'em," she replied. "We don't never need 'em, 'cept fer to show folks, that we is free."

"As long as the papers are in that trunk, you're my slave, and so are the other niggers around here!" Elizabeth yelled. "Mark's not around anymore for you niggers to suckle up to, and you need to keep that in mind."

Martha noticed that she was shaking like a leaf, and it was obvious that Nate's visit earlier today, was the cause of it. At the risk of upsetting her even more, Martha decided to see if she could find out what had happened.

"Miss Liz'buth, is sump'um went wrong when you and Mos'a Joe went down to the creek, to cause you to be upsot wid me?" Martha asked. "If I done sump'um wrong, I's wush you'd belch it out, and tell me what it wuz."

Elizabeth wouldn't look Martha in the eye. "You don't have any business in Mark's room, so get busy doing what needs to be done around here," sharply replied Elizabeth. "What's in there, is none of your business."

"But, me and Mark wuz brung up like kinfolks," said Martha. "Yass'am, that's 'zackly what me and him is, kinfolks, sort of like one big family."

"I'm not a fool, and I wasn't born yesterday!" Elizabeth screamed. "If the truth was known, you two have secrets that would shock the world. The reason Mark didn't get married, is because he had you to sleep with."

"It ain't rite fer you to say that!" Martha protested. "We is jus' rail good friends. Nothing ain't 'tween me and Mark, 'cept fer good ole friendship, and that's the gospel-truf'."

"I'll bet the girl refused to marry Mark, when she heard that he had been wallowing around with you!" She sneered, as she quickly left the room.

Martha sat down on the trunk and cried, and prayed that Mark would return home soon. She really did love Mark, and it was obvious that he cared for her as well, but thus far, he had managed not to become romantically involved with her. She had offered herself to Mark many times, but he being a man with high morals, and respect for both races, had somehow managed to keep things under complete control.

A short time later, Martha slipped quietly into the kitchen, for it would soon be time for her to start cooking supper. Even though Simpson's visit earlier was still bothering her, she decided to say no more, and see what happened, for it was obvious that his visit had something to do with what was happening now.

After Martha kindled a fire in the cookstove, she moved quietly while she went about doing her work. However, a noise from the doorway startled her.

"Martha, you called me a liar, and I don't appreciate that at all," said Elizabeth. "That's something a nigger don't get away with, in my house!"

Martha turned to look at her. "But, I's ain't called you no liar, fer my folks learnt me better'n that." Martha quickly replied.

"There, you just did it again!" yelled Elizabeth, as she ran across the kitchen, and slapped Martha's face. "Maybe you'll learn someday!"

"You's gon'a be sorry fer that when Mark gets back, fer he sez he wuzn't gon'a let nobid'ee mistreat us," Martha warned, as she rubbed her face.

"I want you to get this one thing straight!" Elizabeth yelled. "We're in charge now, and we don't care about Mark. Less about you niggers, and your so-called freedom papers! This is our place, now!"

What she just said, cut deep into Martha's heart. "Mos'a Joe, he sez he wuz gon'a look adder us while Mark wuz gone," Martha argued. "Promised to take care of Mark's place, too. Now, ain't that what he sez?"

"How stupid you are!" Elizabeth scolded. "He went to Ohio to live with his folks, has no plans of ever coming back, for there's nothing left here for him, anyway. We'll run this place, the way we want it run from now on."

It was very obvious that Nate's visit had somehow altered the plan. Martha's heart was filled with fear, and hopelessness. Nothing would be the same as it was before Mark left. It was hard for her to imagine that a person could make such a drastic change within a few short hours, and she didn't think this was coming from the bottom of Elizabeth's heart. There had to be somethng behind this. Maybe Nate had demanded that she change. Maybe Nate was holding something over their head, Martha said to herself.

Throughout the remainder of the evening, Elizabeth continued nagging and fussing at Martha, and finding fault with her work. Martha decided that she'd heard enough, and at the risk of being thrown out of the mansion, she made up her mind to defend her rights as a human being.

"Miss Liz'buth," Martha said politely, "you's been talking to me like if I wuz a dog, and you know that I's ain't done nothing. Sump'um happened rite adder old man Simpson left, and that's why you been talking like you is to me. That ole goat messed up everthang, messed up yo' head too, didn't he."

Elizabeth quickly left the room unable to respond, and Martha knew that she had struck a chord of truth in the young woman. Heartbroken and sad, Martha walked down to where her parents lived, for she had to talk with someone. She had never felt so hurt in all her life.

Martha told them about everything that had gone on up at the mansion, and how Elizabeth suddenly changed, after Simpson came to call. They really were surprised, for everything had been going along real well. Just today, Joe told Bill that he planned a barbecue for the workers, in appreciation for the way they had continued to work, since Mark went away.

"I's seed his buggy go up that way this moan'n," said Bill, "and rite off, I's knowed that he wuz up to sump'um bad. Did you's happen to hear what he sez to them folks?"

"Naugh, but it sho' did cause Miss Liz'buth to change," Martha told him. "I's ain't seed Mos'a Joe since him and her went down to the creek, but if it done him like it done her, we gon'a have the devil to pay."

"I's can't 'magin what happened, fer he wuz pow'ful nice to me when we's talked this moan'n," replied Bill. "He ain't never talked ugly to me, and if he did, I didn't hear him. Don't know what took place, but you can't tell when the ole devil is gon'a swat you wid his ole tail."

"Jus' wait and see how he acts to'mar," Martha suggested, "fer I's got a feeling that he gon'a be jus' like Miss Liz'buth, changed all 'round."

A noise was heard outside, and Bill rushed over to a window to peek outside. The sun had gone down quite some time ago, but the moon was shining bright, and he saw Nate's buggy headed up toward Mark's mansion. This is the second time today the ole goat is been up there, Bill said to himself.

"Oh Lord'ee, it's that ole goat again!" Bill grimaced. "That makes two times he been here aw'ready, and somebid'ee sho' is headed fer a lot'a trouble."

"Lord he'p us!" Liza sighed. "I know he's out to hurt Mark someway, and I's wush that we could find out what he gon'a do this time."

Bill stood watching until Simpson drove up and stopped in front of Mark's house, got out of his buggy, and walked up on the porch. Bill put on his coat and hat, after he watched Simpson enter the house.

"I's thank I'll slip up there and see if I's can find out what he got in his head fer to do this time, fer it can't be nothing good," Bill told them.

"Be ca'ful," Martha cautioned, "fer the way Miss Liz'buth jumped on me, they mout kill you. That ole goat done got 'em all messed up in the head as it tis, and there ain't no telling what they mout do."

Bill slipped quietly up to the back of the mansion, then got down on his hands and knees, and crawled around to where he'd be under the dining room window. Slowly raising his head and peeking inside, he saw Nate and the Wilson's sitting at the table talking, and he listened to them.

"Where is that nigger maid?" Nate asked, in a grumpy voice. "And the butler, where is he?"

"Martha went to visit her folks, and she hasn't come back yet," replied Elizabeth, a look of disgust on her face. "I've come to the conclusion, that she's Mark's lover, or so it seems."

"And Sam, he and some of the other niggers went fishing," Joe spoke up, "and there's nobody here but us and the baby, and he's asleep."

"That's fine, but just to be on the safe side, Mrs. Wilson, I want you to go to the window and keep an eye on the yard," Simpson suggested. "I don't want anybody to slip up and hear what we're talking about."

Almost mechanically, Elizabeth hurried over to the window, and looked out across the yard. Then Nate started talking to Joe.

"Like I said this morning, I went out of my way to get your tail out of a crack one time, and it's time for you to return the favor," Nate began. "You sold your farm to Mark, but I would have paid you twice that much for it. I'm sure that you remember me lending you some money, don't you?"

Joe sat shaking his head for a moment, and right off, it appeared to Bill that Nate was holding something over Joe's head. Maybe they're not real close friends after all, Bill thought.

"Yes Nate, I remember," Joe finally replied. "But I almost had to kiss your butt to get the money, then you hounded me every day until I paid it back plus outrageous interest, if I must say. One of the happiest days of my life, was the day Ellis Bland marked the note paid in full."

"Is that a fact!" Replied Simpson coldly, as he took a folded paper from his vest pocket. "Well, I say that you're wrong, for this copy tells me that the note never was paid, as you claim." He then handed the paper to Joe.

Joe thought this morning, that Nate might try to do something in order for him to get the upper hand, and it had now come to pass. Although the official transaction between them had taken place a few years ago, the ink on the paper was as fresh as the tea in the cup Simpson was holding. The lien had not been marked paid, as Joe thought.

"This is illegal, and you know that!" Joe protested, quickly jumping to his feet. "This is not the same paper that I signed, and it won't stand up in any court of law! The paper's new, and the ink's still fresh."

"Wy Joe," Simpson whined, as he pretended to be offended. "You're insulting my integrity. I would never do anything illegal, and you know that."

"What you're saying then, is that unless I help you destroy Mark like you suggested, you'll use this against me!" Joe snapped. "That's what you had in mind this morning, wasn't it?" Joe sat back down at the table.

"I'd say that's a fair estimation of things, as they stand now," replied Nate, smiling wickedly. "And, as for what you've heard about the way I manage to get the upper hand on folks, you need to believe that, and a lot more."

Joe remained silent for a moment, as he thought about what Nate had said this morning about treating the Negroes like slaves again, and not paying them for their work. He realized now what Mark meant, when he spoke of his father's cruelty. There's no wonder why Mark hated him.

"Just how do you intend to make me pay again, when the note has been paid already?" Joe asked, realizing that he'd been caught up in Nate's web of deceit, like others had been. "I left the original copy with Bland at the bank, and it's marked paid. Now, where do you stand, if I may ask?

"Well, I stand to collect!" Replied Simpson, as he put the paper back in his pocket. "This is the copy Ellis had in his files, and he let me borrow it to show to you. If you noticed, it hasn't been marked paid."

Elizabeth was now in tears as she stood listening to them, and then realizing how cruel she had been to Martha, it broke her heart. It wasn't her nature to be cruel to anyone, and she hoped that God would forgive her. She wiped tears from her eyes on the window drapes, then turned and looked back at Simpson.

"Mr. Simpson, why don't you get somebody else to do this for you?" She asked. "We aren't thieves, as you suppose. We're just a couple of young folks, with a baby to rise, and I wish you'd go on and leave us alone. Mark trusted us, and it's not right for us to let him down."

271

"You had better coach your wife in the fine art of doing business, and in treating niggers as they should be treated," Nate told Joe. "She sounds like my wife, a bleeding heart all the way."

"Leave my wife out of this!" Joe scolded. "She's already hurt Martha by following your instructions! Bill and his folks are my best friends, and they are as honest and trustworthy, as any white person I know."

Nothing was said for a moment as Bill listened, and he realized that what Elizabeth had said to Martha, hadn't come from her heart. He wondered if they would be strong enough to stand up against Simpson, in his plan to destroy his own son. He realized that there was no limit to what Simpson might do.

"You still remember what I said this morning about that maid, don't you?" Nate snarled. "She's probably into that African voodoo, because I personally saw her burn in that fire, but she's still walking around. She's some kind of spirit, a ghost, I tell you!" His face was ghostly pale.

After realizing that he didn't stand a chance in court against such a man as Nate Simpson, Joe thought it best to go along with his scheme. Oh, how he wished that he'd never accepted Mark's offer, and paid more attention to what Mark said about his father, but it was now too late.

"What else do you have in mind, in addition to what you suggested earlier this morning?" Joe asked. "It's wrong, and I know that it's going to return to haunt me later, but I'll follow your orders, as best I can."

"Now, that's more like it," Simpson grinned smugly. "But first, I would like to know if you've heard from Mark since he's been gone."

"Yes, I got a letter from him the other day, and he said that he made the trip to Columbus, Ohio just fine," Joe answered. "He told me to keep him up to date on how things were going, and he also asked if I had seen you lately."

"That's fine, and you need to reply as soon as possible," Nate told him. "Tell him that everything is fine, and that you haven't seen me. Tell him to let you know when he plans to return, for you want to pitch him a party."

"Then, I'll get a letter off to him tomorrow," Joe promised. "I hate to lie to him like that, but I'll tell him exactly what you told me to say."

"Good enough, Wilson," Nate smiled smugly. "I won't be back around, so long as things go my way, and you keep playing my game, like I explained to you earlier this morning. Don't look so glum, and out of sorts, for you'll benefit in the long run. If you'll do exactly as I say, we'll gradually take this plantation away from him. Good-night, to both of you."

Joe and Elizabeth stood and watched, as this monster of a man left their house. A sickening, eery silence hung over the room, as neither of them could bear to speak to the other for a time. They hadn't been brought up this way, and they felt that it was morally and spiritually wrong as well. There was no doubt, that it would haunt them for the rest of their life.

"We have no choice now, but to do as he says," Joe finally said, looking pitifully at her. "He has us over a barrel - nobody to talk to - nowhere to turn for help. I'd rather be shot, than to betray Mark in such a way."

After Simpson drove away, Bill slipped quietly back home. His heart was heavy because of what he'd overheard tonight, but not knowing exactly what to expect, caused him to feel even worse. He'd like to warn the others, so they would know what to expect, but he had no idea what Nate had told Joe earlier.

As soon as he stepped inside his house, the others could tell by the sad expression on his face, that he was deeply toubled. He went over and sat down in a chair near the fireplace, and bowed his head. A few moments later, Bill lifted his head and looked up at Liza, as tears trickled down his cheeks.

"Well, we mout as well get sot fer trouble, but there ain't no way fer us to know what it's gon'a be," he sighed. "I's hear'd some mighty nasty thangs said up there tonite, and I's wush now that I's stayed at home."

"What kind'a thangs did you hear?" Asked Liza. "Wuz they saying awful bad thangs 'bout Mark, 'bout his farm, and maybe 'bout us, too?"

"They sho' wuz!" He quickly replied. "Eb'em if I's didn't hear everthang that they sez, I's hear'd 'nuf to know that they gon'a take this farm 'way from Mark."

"That's awful, adder he done wuk'd hard to get it started, and got a rail purdy house built, too," Liza sighed. "I's wush that we knowed what to look fer, befo' it comes flogging in on us. Can't you find out what it tis?"

"Like I's sez, I don't know what it is, er when it's gon'a come, but it's done on its way," Bill replied. "They is good clean folks, the kind ole man Simpson likes to mess up, like he done Mark. He gon'a make 'em do thangs that's 'gainst their own good jug'mut. Thangs that they don't wanta do in the fus' place. He's sot out to mess 'em up, and us too."

"That's 'zackly why Miss Liz'buth talked to me like that," Martha spoke up, "fer the Lord don't make us so we can change that quick. He sho' mus' be holding sump'um over them Wilson folks, to make 'em change like that."

"He do, fer I's hear'd him say that Joe owed him some money on some land, er sump'um," Bill explained. "All we can do now, is to axe the Lord to pitch in and hep' us, and hope that Mark comes on back home."

From that night on, things became more and more difficult for Martha and her brother Sam, while they worked in the mansion. As it seemed, the Wilsons didn't have a kind word to say to either of them, and it was obvious that this was a part of the scheme Nate was forcing them to help him execute. The other workers noticed a change in the way Joe treated them, for he hardly ever spoke to them anymore. When he did speak to them, it was in short, curt sentences. They also noticed, that Joe didn't meet with Bill each morning, to lay out the day's work as he had done before. Thus far he hadn't acted like that to white workers, but Bill knew that they could tell that things were not the same with Joe, for he had seen them gathering in small groups, and heard them whispering to each other. He figured that they were talking about Joe.

Martha tried to listen at every opportunity, to hear anything being said between the Wilsons that might give her a clue as to what Simpson was holding over them, or what he had ordered them to do. One night she crept quietly to their bedroom door and, laying her head on the floor next to the open space at the bottom of the door, she listened to them talking in bed.

"Mr. Simpson talked with me in town today, and he said for me to get the cotton picked as soon as possible," Joe whispered to his wife. "He also told me to tighten up on the Negroes, and start treating them like they were slaves again. He wants them stripped of their freedom, and make them bow down to me, and beg for something to eat. He don't want me to pay them anything for working, like Mark did either."

"What about the white workers?" Asked Elizabeth? "Does he have anything special in mind for them? Will they be treated the same as the Negroes?"

"He wants me to pay them when I sell the cotton, and tell them to leave, without the Negroes finding out anything about what happened," Joe explained.

"I know, but the Negroes will expect to get paid, for you told them in the presence of Mark, that nothing would change," she reminded him.

"I'm not supposed to say anything to them until after the cotton is sold, then I'll tell them that they won't get a penny," he whispered. "He wants me to cut down on their food supply, and sell any of them, who causes me trouble. He also wants them to have to bow down, and beg for food, for he claims that's the only way to handle a Negro. He wants me to call them "niggers" and slaves, for he claims that the word Negro, is too good for them."

"And, what's in it for Simpson, for engineering this mess he's managed to get us mixed up in?" She asked, obviously annoyed. "We'll probably end up in a worse mess now, than we were in before Mark bought our farm."

"No, he claims that he don't want one penny for himself. Can you believe that he'd say somethng like that." Joe chuckled. "According to what he said, the only thing he wants out of this is the property, and nothing else."

"But, where does that leave us, when he does take over this plantation?" She asked. "Once he gets his claws on something, he never lets go, and then we'll be left out in the cold. Have you ever thought about that?"

"According to what he said, as soon as he lays claim to the farm, it will be divided equally between us." Joe enthustiastically pointed out to her. "I think he's on the up-and-up this time, for he said that in the presence of Mr. Bland. I really do think that the man has changed."

"My Lord, Joe! What if Mark happens to find out about the awful scheme that's being worked behind his back?" She asked. "There's a lot of folks on this place, and what if one of them finds out, and gets word to Mark!"

This was getting very interestng, so Martha pressed her ear hard against the bottom of the door, for she didn't want to miss a single word they said.

"Who's going to tell him?" Joe asked her. "I'm not going to write him a letter and tell him, Nate certainly won't say anything, and Mr. Bland has sworn not to say anything either. Those stupid niggers aren't smart enough to figure out what's going on, and we're as safe as can be. Let's go to sleep now, and we'll talk more about this tomorrow."

Martha almost laughed out loud, at what Joe just said about the Negroes. Here she was, a so-called "stupid nigger", listening under the door during the middle of the night. Stupid, or not, she came up with this idea without help from anyone else, she thought. In the morning, she vowed, they had to come up with a plan whereby they could protect Mark from this den of wolves, that were set out to destroy him.

Early the following morning, Joe boarded Mark's buggy, and headed toward Nate Simpson's plantation, for it was time for him to set another part of this scheme into motion. He would replace Martha and her brother with some Negroes Nate had selected to serve as Joe's butler and maid. Nate had a similar plan for Bill as well, and Joe intended to stay in Nate's good favor. In the very beginning, Joe was bitterly against Nate's scheme, however, he'd been deluded into thinking that Nate was honest. Joe even thought now, that Mark deseved what was happening to him, because he'd walked away from his plantation. Now that he was destined to becomeing a rich and powerful farmer, Joe's friendship with Mark, had at last taken a back seat to a heart filled with greed.

Martha also got up real early this morning, for she was anxious to go and tell her folks what she had heard last night. Yet, she couldn't help feeling sorry for the Wilsons, for they too, had been caught up in this web of deceit, Simpson had placed in their path. Her parents sat and cried, as they listened to the sad story Martha told them.

"I's ain't a bit 'sprized at nothing you sez, fer I's done seed all that coming down the road torge us," said Bill, "fer Joe ain't tough 'nuf to hold his ground wid that ole goat. We is been sot free, and Joe is Mos'a Simpson's slave now."

"Well, I's better get on back, fo' Miss Liz'buth wakes up, fer she's done mad at me," said Martha, as she walked out the door.

"And watch yo' tongue, fer you's done in nuf' trouble wid them fo'ks, as it tis," her mother cautioned. "No matter what they say, jus' go on and be stupid-like, sort of dumb, fer that's the way they thank we is, anyhow."

276

Later that afternoon as the sun was going down, Joe still hadn't returned to the plantation, and Martha decided to cook supper, for she knew how hateful he acted, when supper was late. Martha hadn't heard their conversation before Joe left this morning, and she had no idea where he had gone, or what they had in mind to do next. She hardly got started cooking supper when Elizabeth came into the kitchen, but she could tell by the way that Elizabeth acted all day that something was wrong, and the expression on her face now, caused Martha to be on the alert for anything to take place.

"Martha, Joe and I were talking, and we've decided that we don't need you any longer, and I'm telling you now, to leave." She said, coldly.

"Yass'am, I's done seed that coming, but befo' I's go, I wush you would tell me what I's went and done to you folks," replied Martha, sadly.

She wouldn't face Martha, as she stared out the window. "My husband don't like your cooking, or the way you clean house, and quite frankly, I don't either," Elizabeth replied. "You're needed out there in the fields, anyway."

"But, when Mark left, he told youn's that me and Sam wuz to stay here in the house, and bof' youn's 'greed on it, too," Martha protested.

"Maybe then, but things have changed," Elizabeth said sternly. "Pack up your things right now, for I want you and your brother to be out of the house before my husband gets back. Do you understand?"

"I's know youn's is running thangs now, but what you gon'a say when Mark gets back, and finds somebid'ee else humped up in here?" Martha asked.

"The heck with Mark, and what he says!" She scolded. "He's gone, and he won't be back again, and you might as well get used to that."

"Oh Lord'ee, sump'um done happened to him!" Martha cried. "Tell me what happened. Who kilt him? Where is he gon'a be bur'ed? Oh Lord, I's hate that he done left this ole wul'd! Po' Mark, he be dead," she sighed.

"No, you stupid idiot, he's not dead!" she curtly replied. "He realized that his stupid ideas wouldn't work here in the South, so he went to live with the other nigger lovers. This is our place, we'll run things as we see best for us, and you niggers will be our slaves from now on."

"You's wrong 'bout him," cried Martha. "He ain't never gon'a let us down, fer he ain't that kind'a feller. Mark, he done got us out'a one mess wid ole man Simpson, and he ain't gon'a let us get in no mess wid youn's folks, neither."

"Listen, you stupid nigger!" Said Elizabeth, as she shook her finger in Martha's face. "I'm telling you now, to get out of this house for good!"

"Befo' I's go, do you wants me to cook supper fer you, and Mos'a Joe?" she asked. "I's be glad to do that fer you."

"Indeed not!" Elizabeth scolded. "Joe's bringing two good niggers to be looking after things around here, and the sooner you leave, the better!"

Martha ran to her room, for it would be pointless to argue with the woman any longer, she thought. She would take a few of her personal belongings with her this evening, and then come back tomorrow to get her clothes. She wished there were some way she could get in contact with Mark, and let him know how things had changed since he'd been away. But, there was no way.

A few minutes after Martha arrived back at her parent's house, which was the house in which Mark lived after the Powells moved out, Joe returned home in the surrey that belonged to Mark. Martha saw a Negro woman and man sitting in the back seat. In a wagon that followed close behind were a white man and woman, and by the many boxes and trunks they brought with them, it was obvious that they planned to stay for quite awhile.

She watched the Negro man and woman follow Joe into the mansion. The white man got out of the wagon, and left his wife sitting there alone, then he walked up on the front porch. Joe came back out on the porch and joined him a moment later.

On his way back home, Joe had stopped by the fields to talk with Bill, and he told Bill to come on up to the house, for he had something to discuss with him. When Bill arrived, he saw a strange white man on the porch with Joe, so he politely stopped, tucked his hat under his arm, and stood there with his head bowed.

"Bill, I want you to round up all the niggers, and have them up here before dark," Joe told him. "It will be dark soon, so you'd better hurry, for I want everyone of them to come up here. We're going to have a meeting."

Bill sensed that trouble had already begun, so he decided to pretend that he didn't have any idea what was taking place.

"I's glad that you's gon'a have a meet'n, and I's see that you done got a preacher-man humped up there on the porch wid you," Bill replied. "When we get through shout'n 'round in yo' yard, you ain't gon'a have a blade of grass left in yo' yard. Thank the Lord, we's gon'a have us a meet'n at las'!"

"Not a darn church meeting, you stupid nigger!" Joe scolded. "Hurry, and get them on up here, and make them stay off the grass in my yard." Then, Bill headed toward the barn.

Bill had already told the other Negroes what Martha had heard the Wilsons saying, and what he had heard while listening near the window, and they agreed that some kind of trouble was brewing. He had also told them about Joe asking him to come up to the house, and they had already gathered behind the barn, to find out why Joe wanted to speak with Bill.

"Mos'a Joe, he sez fer everbid'ee to get on up to the big house, fer he gon'a have a meet'n," Bill told them. "He's got another ugly feller up there wid him, and thangs sho' don't look good."

An elderly man named George spoke up. "Bill, is you got any way to know what kind'a meet'n he gon'a have?" He asked. "Do he wants all the womens and younguns up there, too?"

"He sez fer everbid'ee to be there, but the way thangs is been going on lately, it ain't gon'a be nothing good," Bill replied. "They is done run Sam and Marthie out'a the house, and they brung in two other niggas to take their place. I thank the man up there now, is gon'a take my place, but he aint said nothing."

"But, that ain't what Mark sez, when he left!" Said George. "Mos'a Joe must'a los' his mind, fer this ain't his farm, and we ain't his slaves."

"That's rite," Bill agreed, "but Mark, he ain't here, and Mos'a Joe is went and got messed up wid ole man Simpson, and we's got the devil to pay!"

Bill turned and started walking back up toward the mansion, with all the others following along close behind. They gathered near the edge of the yard, and stood with their heads bowed as they trembled inside with fear, while they tried to figure out what this meeting was all about.

Then Joe stepped out to the edge of the porch. "I want you to pay real close attention to what I'm fixing to say, for I don't intend to repeat it," Joe yelled. "Mark is gone, and probably won't ever be back again, and I wanted you to know that things will be run different, from now on."

Joe then motioned to an unfamiliar man who was standing on the porch, and he walked up and stood by Joe's side.

"This here is Mr. Henry Graham, and you'll call him Master Henry, for I'm putting him in charge over all of you slaves," Joe told them. "I demand that you do as he says, no questions asked! Master Henry and his lovely wife will spend the night here with me, but tomorrow, after Bill's house is cleaned out, they'll be moving into it. Now, is that clear?"

"But, Mos'a Joe!" Replied Bill, his voice cracking. "Mark told me to be over the tuther workers, and fer me and Liza to stay in that house, adder this big house wuz' built. And, you's told him that you wouldn't change thangs."

"That was then, and this is now, and things have changed!" Replied Joe, in a hateful voice. Then turning to Henry, he added. "His name is Bill, and he's the one I told you about earlier, but you'll know how to handle him."

"Mos'a Joe, you promised Mark that you wuz gon'a look adder us while he wuz gone, and that you would treat us good," spoke up Martha. "He sez fer me and Sam to stay in the big house, and fer Pappy to run thangs like Mark let him do, when he wuz here. You's 'greed wid that too, you sho' did."

"Shut your darned mouth!" Joe growled. "Henry, she's going to be a troublemaker, if she's not handled right. In fact, she was supposed to have been burned to death in a house fire. Nate says that she's a walking-ghost. She's the one who's been shacking up with Mark, his lover, mind you!"

"They must have been real close, for her to call him by his given name," Henry replied. "Don't worry, for I'll handle her, and the old man Bill, too."

Nothing else was said for a moment, as the Negroes stood with tear filled eyes, and they wondered how Joe could be so cruel and mean to them, after Mark had placed so much confidence in him. Then Bill shook his head, as he stepped up closer to the porch.

"We is been sot free," he told them. "We ain't slaves no mo', and you promised Mark that you would treat us like humans. Why is you went back on what you promised Mark fo' he left? Why is you treat'n us like slaves?"

"I don't know anything about that, for Mark has never told me that any of you were free," Joe flatly lied. "If that's true, let's see your freedom papers!"

"Mark sez he gon'a keep 'em in his trunk fer us, fer he looked adder us sort of like a pappy, I's guess," Bill replied.

"Hold it, right there!" Henry spoke up. "Without proof, you are nothing but slaves, and you'll be treated like slaves! I've already told the sheriff to shoot any of you on sight, if you tried to escape."

"That's right," Joe agreed. "In fact, I told Mr. Graham to shoot any of you who tried to escape, refused to work, or talked back to him or me."

"Mos'a Joe, we ain't gon'a leave, fer this is our home," Bill sobbed, as he looked up at them. "All we axe from you is a lit'l 'spect, and that all of us be treated like human-folks, that's all."

"That makes me laugh!" Henry hissed. "From here on, you'll have to work from sunup 'til sundown, seven days a week. Mess up one time, complain about something, or refuse to work, and you'll be shot! Do I make myself clear?"

"And, your food supply will be cut back," Joe added. "I won't have any more fancy eating, like while Mark was here. All you'll get, is barely enough cornmeal and fatback meat to keep you alive. You're slaves, now!"

"But Mos'a Joe, we got'a eat, if you 'spect us to wuk'!" Bill pitifully replied. "That ain't no way to treat a dog, and you done know that."

"Starting tomorrow, you'll work like slaves are supposed to work, and you might as well get used to it," Henry scolded. "Now, get on back to where you stay, and come daylight, sick or well, I want you in the fields."

This was a grievous turn of events for the Negroes, to say the least, and they turned and slowly walked away, knowing that in a span of just a few weeks their lives had been turned upside down. Prayers of these lonely Negroes tonight, and prayers for Mark and his return, no doubt bombarded Heaven.

The weeks were abominable. The Negroes were driven from daylight, until well after the sun went down, with hardly enough food to keep them alive. God help them, if they even tried to slip bread to the fields for the children to eat during the long day's work, or drink water, without Henry's permission.

One day, a woman killed a rabbit with a rock, and hoping to cook it later that night for her children, she hid it in her bosom. Henry saw her stick the rabbit inside her blouse. He took the rabbit away from her and cut it up into small pieces, then threw it away. Then he whipped her with a leather strap, until she was hardly able to stand on her feet, while she cried and begged him for mercy. One of her small children ran up to help her, and Henry slapped it so hard on the head, until blood came from the child's ears.

Not even before Mark bought them and set them free, had they been treated in such a dastardly manner. Even though Nate Simpson never came around, these poor Negreos knew that he was a key player in this viscous game, but his role, seemed to be aimed more at striking whatever blow he could to Mark, as well as his security. These free-slaves, were merely pawns of these three treacherous conspirators.

The meager allotment of food that was given to these workers was cut even more, and sufficient food was only a memory. Henry Graham seemed to take some sadistic pleasure in eating large quantities of food in the presence of these hungry workers, even the children. Once after Joe had given a party for some of his friends, Henry made the Negroes bury the abundant leftover food in the ground, daring them to eat even a morsel. Then, to make sure the Negroes didn't return at night and dig it up, and eat it, Henry soaked the ground with kerosene. His penchant cruelty for them, seemed to have no bounds.

Though the cotton had already been picked and sold, by no means were the Negroes allowed to slow down one bit, for Henry always had something scheduled for them to do. It was never too wet or cold for them to work, it seemed, and even on Sunday they worked just the same. The small church Mark had built for them was stacked full of hay, even though the barns were not quite filled, and Henry made them plow up the graveyard where many of their friends were buried, and tear down the rock headstones. He watched their houses every night, listening for the slightest complaint, and they didn't dare go outside, for fear that he might think that they planned to escape.

In Ellis Bland's office one rainy morning, he and Joe were discussing the crop on Mark's farm. "You had a good crop this year," said Bland, "but I'm sure you had your hands full, for that's a mighty big place, Mark has."

"Don't give me all the credit, for it was Mr. Simpson who set everything in motion," Joe stated. "Give him the credit, for I only follow his orders."

"Well, how are things going?" Bland asked. "Does Nate come to check on you? Knowing him, I'd say he's there every day, snooping around."

"No, he rarely comes around at all," replied Joe. "I guess he trusts me to take care of things for him. He does his part, and I do mine."

Ellis Bland snickered aloud, and was about to respond to the remark, when he suddenly stopped short.

"What were you about to say?" Joe asked, seriously.

"Oh, it was nothing, nothing at all," replied Bland, smugly.

"Oh yes you were!" Joe insisted. "It was something about Nate, and him trusting me, wasn't it? Go ahead and say what's on your mind."

"Joe, I've known you for a long time now, but I've never known of you getting involved in something like this before," said Bland. "Be careful, for Simpson didn't get where he is today, by trusting folks. Watch out for the trap that he might have set for you, and don't get caught up in it."

"You're wrong about him!" Joe protested. "Mark's gone, and he probably needed somebody to take Mark's place as his son, and he turned to me. I don't believe what folks say about him, not what Mark said, or you, even."

"So be it, but I know how he treated his son," Bland warned. "Nate is a man to be reckoned with, and I even tremble, when he steps into my office."

Joe had obviously forgotten how Simpson had coerced him into going along with his scheme. Simpson had a very unique way of entangling a person in a web of deceit, and causing them to lose sight of reality, and common sense.

Bland sat for a moment, and thought back on how he had helped Nate strip his own son of almost everything, and here sat another young man Nate would no doubt treat the same way, and maybe even worse, with Bland's help.

"Well, what do you think about Henry Graham?" Bland asked. "I hear that he works for you now. I hear that he's a hard-nosed type of person."

"He's that, and even more!" Joe smiled. "When he speaks to the niggers, they jump like they had been shot. They're scared to death of that man, and to be honest, I am too."

"I don't have any proof, but I heard that he killed one nigger because he talked back to him," Bland gossiped. "That, I believe, was somewhere in Georgia, around Augusta, maybe. I think the law is looking for him."

"Yes, I've heard that too," replied Joe. "Now if you'll give me what money that's coming to me, I'll be on my way. It don't look like the rain is going to let up, and I need to get on back home."

"Very well then, let me explain how the money was divided," said Bland. "Half of the money will be divided between Nate and me, and you get the other half. Nate said that you were to divide your half with Henry. Am I right?"

"But, what about Mark?" Joe asked. "Simpson said you would deposit half of it into Mark's account, to be used to pay taxes, and other expenses related to the upkeep of the farm. What about the taxes you were supposed to pay, for even Mark told me that you agreed to handle that for him."

"Joe, do you really think Mark deserves anything?" Bland asked. "Did he help you and Henry harvest the crop, or help drive the slaves, and make them work?"

"I see what you mean," said Joe, as he signed a receipt, not even taking time to read it. "If he didn't work, then he shouldn't get paid, I suppose."

"I'm not going to pay his taxes like I promised, or the General Store for things that you charged to his account, either," Bland chuckled. "If he does come back, he'll find that he has nothing left. His farm will be sold to the highest bidder, and you know who that will be, Nate Simpson."

Just about the time Joe was ready to leave Bland's office, in walked Nate Simpson, as wet as a dog.

"Well, what do you know," smiled Nate, "just the very two gentlemen I wanted to see, and in the same place! Joe, I take it that you're here to collect for the cotton crop. I hear that you and Graham had a good crop this year."

"We did, and as you know, we got it to the market while the price was the highest it's been in years," Joe boasted. "Yes, we made a lot of money." Joe showed him the recipet.

Though Joe hadn't noticed, he had signed a receipt stating that Bland had given him all the money, instead of just half, as Joe thought. It didn't show where any money had been deducted for Nate Simpson, or Ellis Bland.

"So I see!" Said Nate, as he looked at the receipt. "I suggest that you hold on to that receipt, too. Do you already have your part of the money from the crop?"

"Indeed I do," smiled Joe, patting his coat pocket. "Mr. Bland took out half for you and him, and I'll share my half with Henry."

"And you say Ellis has my share!" Simpson asked, shaking his head. "My share of what, may I ask?"

"Your fourth of the money that we got for the cotton." Joe explained. "Bland gave me half of the money, and he kept half to divide between you and him, like we agreed."

"Hey, I don't even know what you're talking about!" Nate responded. "I have nothing to do with the money you make out there, for it belongs to you."

"But Mr. Bland already deducted half of the money, and like he said, you and him will divide it between the two of you. Am I right, Mr. Bland?" Joe asked, in surprise.

"Wait a minue! Said Nate. "If you'll notice, that receipt shows where you got all the money. According to the law, you will be responsible for what you charged at the General Store, and the taxes that are due on the property."

Joe looked completely bewildered. He stood up slowly, as he looked over at Bland, who was now busy looking at some papers, probably Nate's.

"Well, uh," Joe stammered. "Mark told me that Mr. Bland promised to pay the taxes, and for what I got from the General Store, from Mark's half of what money we got for the cotton. Mark also said that Mr. Bland was to deposit the balance of his half of the money into his account, to save for him. I thought I was supposed to give you fellows half of my part, and not half of everything that we got, as Mr. Bland claimed. I don't understand what's going on here at all."

"You sure don't!" Simpson said sharply. "Good-day, Joe! Hold on to the receipt, for you just might have to present it as evidence one day."

Joe walked out of Bland's office with a sickening feeling in his stomach. Was that what Bland meant, when he told me to be careful. Joe asked himself as he walked toward his buggy. Nate had made a deal with him - he remembered it well, but now, he acted as though he knew nothing about it. Perhaps Simpson doesn't trust Bland, and didn't want to discuss it in his presence, that's all it was. Joe decided to dismiss it from his mind, and he headed home, with his ill-gotten money in his pocket.

Back at Bland's office, Nate laughed as he took a pot off the heater, and poured himself a cup of coffee. "We finally found ourselves a fool, and we've got him by the seat of his britches," Nate chuckled. "The poor fool is mixed up so, until he don't know if he's coming or going!"

"I know, but he might back out on us before we complete what we've set out to do," Bland cautioned. "He doesn't seem to have very much backbone at all."

"He's not going anywhere," Simpson said smugly. "He knows that all this will fall back in his lap if he tries to weasel out, for he has no proof that we had anything to do with it. I know about Henry killing that nigger, and he'll keep Joe in line, in return for me keeping my mouth shut. I won't deal with anybody, unless I can get the upper hand. It's my way of surviving."

"I sure hope you're right, but I still have my doubts," Bland told him. "Let me give you what you have coming from Joe's crop, or Mark's crop, I should have said."

"See there, Bland!" Nate smiled. "Here we are with half of the money, and he has all the obligations resting on his shoulders, with no proof that we got one penny. That my friend, is exactly how I do business."

As Joe rode back toward Mark's plantation, he thought about the money he had made, and how good it felt to be successful. He decided that the best way to impress Simpson, was for him to become just as ruthless as Henry, and be a better farmer than Mark thought he was. Mark, there was that name, popping into his memory, and creeping into his thoughts as he rode along. Well, what about Mark, he thought. He left his farm for me to look after, and if he thought anything of it, or the niggers, he never would have left.

Later on that evening, Bland and Simpson sat in the hotel restaurant and ate dinner together, while still gloating over the wicked plan they had engineered to eventually put Mark out of business, and take the plantation away from him.

"This scheme, is working out a lot better than I ever thought it would," Simpson laughed. "All I have to do is wait 'til the taxes get behind, then I'll pay them, and take over. I hold something over the Tax Collector's head, and he promised to fake a sale, and then declare me the highest bidder. I told my wife that I'd ruin Mark, and I'm well on my way."

"I know, but what about Joe Wilson?" Bland asked. "He somehow gives me the jitters."

"What about him, and his jitters?" Nate asked. "What causes you to be so worried about him. Do you know something about him, that I don't know?"

"Nate, do you really intend to divide up Mark's plantation with him, like he said you promised to do?" asked Bland. "I remember you telling him that, in my office one day. He actually thinks that you'll keep your word."

"Wy Ellis, you insult my intelligence!" Simpson teased. "Do you really think I'm that stupid. I thought that you knew me a lot better than that."

Bland had always thought that Nate was only using Joe, and as soon as he had done Nate's dirty work, Nate would drop him. For a moment, Bland felt as though he was doing wrong by helping Nate, for Nate couldn't be trusted, and he didn't trust anybody else, either. He also knew that he couldn't back out now, any more than Joe could. Nate also had him in his pocket, so to speak, he reasoned.

It had been raining all day, and seemed to get worse as the sun began to set. In front of Mark's mansion in the soggy road, quietly stood the workers who had been called up there by Joe. He told Bill that he wanted to discuss the money he'd received for the cotton, and in turn, Bill passed the word to the others. There stood Bill, not a dry thread on his body, wondering why he had bothered to come up here in the first place. Some thought that they would be paid, but Bill didn't have the slightest idea that either of them would get anything.

"I'll tell you now, George, we ain't gon'a get nothing," Bill whispered. "I's know, by the way he been treat'n us here lately. Jus' wait and see."

"Then why is he axed us to come up here in the rain, if he wuzn't gon'a give us nothing?" asked George. "That don't make no sense, do it?"

"But pappy!" spoke up Martha, as she peeked from under a burlap bag, she held over her head. "Maybe he done got scade, and 'cided to give us sump'um adder all. Maybe Mark sent him a letter, and told him that he be coming home. Hey, that's it! Mark, he is coming back home!" She squealed.

"I's sho' wush that wuz the truf'," replied George. "If Mark wuz here, he sho' would pitch a fit, fer the way Mos'a Joe, and Mos'a Henry is been treat'n us."

Then, the front door to the mansion swung open, and out stepped Joe with dry clothes on, and eating a piece of cake. Then close behind him came Henry Graham, with a shotgun in his hand. They walked out to the edge of the porch, and stood looking out over the wet, anxious group of workers. Mixed emotion filled their hearts, for some thought they'd be paid, and some didn't. They would soon find out, for Joe tossed the piece of cake across the yard, cleared his throat, and held up a handful of money.

"All right, you wet bunch of slaves, I have something I'd like to say to you," Joe began. "We had a good crop, and we made a lot of money, and I want to pay those who were responsible for turning out such good work."

The poor Negroes grinned and chanted with joy, for they were almost sure they would be paid after all. Joe and Henry looked at each other, and smiled wickedly. They knew what the Negroes were thinking, just like they knew that they were wrong, dead wrong.

"Be quiet, and listen to me!" Joe yelled. "I just came from the bank a moment ago, and I have the money we got for the cotton. I know you are only slaves, and don't have anything to say about how I run things, but I wanted you to see me divide up the money. Half of it goes to Henry because he worked so hard, and the rest of it belongs to me, for this farm belongs to me."

Joe gave Henry some money, and then they both went back inside, and closed the door behind them. Inside the house, they laughed and shook hands.

"I couldn't have done better myself," said Henry, as he shook Joe's hand, and smiled. "You learn fast boy, and we're going to make a good team."

"Thank you, and you're a good teacher," replied Joe. "I made more money this year alone, than I've made during all the years that I've been farming."

Outside, there was dead-silence, except for the pounding thud of the rain as it beat down on the poor helpless slaves. They continued standing there in the downpour, silently looking up toward the closed door, with tears of sorrow, intermingling with the rain on their faces.

The front door to the mansion opened, and Henry emerged with the shotgun still in his hand, to go back home. He suddenly stopped, and looked at them.

"What are you darned fools still hanging around here for?" Henry yelled. "Don't you have sense enough to go on home? Go on back home, for we have work to do tomorrow, rain or shine."

Hearing the shouting, Joe came out to see what was going on. "What seems to be the problem, Henry?" Joe asked. "Why are they still here?"

"I think these darned slaves are hard of hearing!" Henry replied. "If I shot into the crowd and took out one or two, maybe they'd see who's in charge around here." He cocked the shotgun, and aimed it directly at Bill.

"Hold on there!" Yelled Joe, as he caught hold of the shotgun. "Be calm for a minute longer, and give them another chance to make up their mind to leave."

"That's the trouble now, they've been treated like humans!" Henry said, in an angry voice. "Kill the one called Bill, for he's the ringleader of the bunch! His gal is just as bad. I say, kill all the sorry bastards!"

"Mos'a Joe, if you ain't gon'a give us no money, will you please give us a few mo' bites to eat?" Bill begged. "We all is 'bout starved to def'."

Though his pitiful begging was getting to Joe, because Henry was present, he couldn't allow his conscience to be his guide. And Nate Simpson lurked in the shadows, a man he feared more than he feared Henry. He had to keep up a front, even though it meant trampling on his conscience.

"Shut up, Bill, and tell the others to go on back home!" Joe yelled, trying to impress Henry. "You're nothing but nigger slaves, so don't think that I'm going to treat you like humans. I won't give you any more food."

Hungry, soaking wet, and feeling like they didn't have a friend on earth, the lonely Negroes slowly turned, and headed back home. They had been cheated out of their share of the crop, denied extra food they desperately needed, and had no access to the papers that showed they were free. What real purpose did it serve to be free, alive even, Bill thought, as he plodded along in the mud?

"Po' Mark," sighed Bill, as they walked along. "He don't know one thang 'bout what's going on, and we ain't got no way to let him know."

"You know that none of us can't read er write, and the only way we gon'a let him know, is to scratch out a letter, and send it to him," Liza replied.

"Well, Pappy sez that the Lord 'spects us to use our head, and I's gon'a do that ver'ee thang, too," Martha told her. "I's gon'a axe the Lord to he'p me thank up sump'um, fer if He don't, we's all gon'a be dead purdy soon."

Later that evening back at their house, Bill's family sat huddled around the small fireplace, as they quietly prayed and asked God to help them. Then, all of a sudden, Martha quickly jumped up, and shouted in a loud voice.

"Glory be! Thank the Lord!" Martha shouted. "The Lord done went and whispered in my ear, and He told me how we could get out'a this mess. He sho' did."

"He done what?" Bill asked. "Is the Lord done told you sump'um all that quick? Is you sho'? He ain't had time to hear you yet."

"Pappy, you sez fer us to axe the Lord fer he'p, and then we's got'a put legs on our prayers," Martha reminded him. "Well, the Lord, He done told me whu' to find some legs, to put on mine!"

"Yass'am, that's rite," replied Bill, "but I sho' didn't thank the Lord would hear you that quick. What did He say fer you to do, nohow?"

"He say fer me to slip up yon'a and get them papers out'a Mark's trunk, then all this trouble would stop," she smiled, and replied.

"Lord'ee chile, you's gon'a get ketched, and kilt, too!" Liza warned her young daughter. "I's knowed the Lord fer a purdy good while, and He be a rail good feller, but He ain't gon'a tell you sump'um that's gon'a get you kilt. You's need to come up wid sump'um bet'rn that, fer that ain't gon'a wuk'."

"Naugh, I's ain't gon'a get ketched, and I's ain't gon'a be kilt, fer the Lord told me what to do," Martha protested.

She even had her brother's excited. "What kind'a plan did the Lord put in yo' head?" Asked Sam. "If the Lord told you to do sump'um, then He 'spects you to tell us what it tis. Do you's still happen to 'memer what it wuz?"

"Well, I's gon'a get them freedom papers out'a the trunk, and head out to whu' Mark is," she explained. "When I's tell him what's going on back here, he gon'a come running back home."

"Marthie, you can't get to whu' he be," spoke up Elijah. "It's a mighty fer piece from here to Oh'hie, wherever that be."

"Then, I's gon'a get the letters that Mark sont to Joe, fer they gon'a tell me whu' he stays," she replied. "We'll scratch out a letter and send it up there to him, fer the letter will know how to find him."

"That sounds good, but how is you gon'a get back in the house to get them papers?" Bill asked. "They done run you out'a the house, and said fer you to stay 'way from up there, too."

"Pappy, you's rite mos' of the time, and you mout be rite now, but if we don't try sump'um, we all gon'a starve to def'," she explained. "All we can do is to axe the Lord to he'p us, fer if He don't, we's all gon'a wake up dead one moan'n, and won't never know what happened."

CHAPTER EIGHT

WEEDING OUT THE BRIARS

Word of Mark now being in Ohio, and having someone else managing his plantation while he was gone, had finally reached his mother, and because her husband had not mentioned this to her, she wondered if he had anything to do with it. She had recently received a letter from her cousin in Columbus, Ohio, and was told that Mark was visiting with them for a while. His mother was pleased to learn that he was happy in Ohio, for he'd faced some difficult times back home.

One cold afternoon, when Nate came into the parlor and sat down near the fireplace to get warm, Julie decided to mention this to him. Nate seldom ever spoke Mark's name, and she didn't know if he'd even discuss the matter.

"I got a letter the other day from my Cousin Helen in Ohio, and she said that Mark was visiting with them," Julie began. "I was wondering if you knew anything about it, and if so, why hadn't you told me."

"I heard that he was gallivanting around over the country, but nobody has ever told me where he is," Nate lied. "As far as I'm concerned, he can stay with the nigger lovers. He was nothing but a troublemaker while he was here, anyway."

"Do you know who's looking after things while he's away?" She asked him. "Whoever he is, I hope he treats the Negroes like Mark treated them."

"How should I know?" He sharply replied. "Knowing him, he probably has a nigger managing it for him. What he does is his business. I don't care if it grows up in weeds and briars, while he's gone."

"To be so young when he first started out, and having to face all the difficult times along the way, I think he's done well for himself," Julie told him, in a caring voice. "They say he's one of the richest men in South Carolina, with hundreds of acres of land, and only God knows how many slaves he's bought and set free. Our son has come a long way, and I'm proud of him."

"Like I said, what he does, is his business," Nate stated again. "Would you mind changing the subject, before I really get wound up?"

"I'm sorry, if I upset you by showing concern for our own son," she told him. "If you were half the man he is, the world would be a lot better off."

For weeks after that rainy night, Martha thought of nothing but some way to get the freedom papers, and a letter with Mark's address, so they could get word to him. Even so, unless she could find someone trustworthy to write the letter, they would get into worse trouble. Still, she kept the faith, and she asked God to help her. As the long days and sleepless nights dragged on, she found herself daydreaming of the day when Mark would ride up in his buggy, and order these two horrible taskmasters away from the plantation.

One day while Bill was cleaning up around the barn, Nate Simpson came by for an unscheduled visit with Joe. Simpson had more plans for Mark's demise, and he wanted to lay them out for Joe and Henry. Joe and Simpson sat on the front porch talking, and Bill decided to see if he could find out what Simpson had in store this time around. He slipped up to the mansion, and sat down on the ground at the end of the porch, and listened intently.

"Mark would probably kill both of us, if he knew what was happening while he's away," said Joe. "He really likes Bill's family, and in every letter he writes, he asks about them, and tells me what to say to them."

"I sure hope you don't tell them what he says," replied Simpson. "We're taking a chance as it is, out here in the open where they can see us."

"As far as I know, they don't even know that I've heard from him since he left," Joe assured him. "They can't read anyway, you know."

"Good man, Joe!" Simpson nodded. "Keep up the good work, and you'll be a rich man pretty soon, a property owner, too! You're going places now, Joe."

Joe happened to recall that one day in Bland's office. "Why did you deny any knowledge of the scheme, when we were in the bank that rainy day?" Asked Joe, seriously. "Were you afraid to discuss it in front of Mr. Bland?"

"Uh, well, how clever of you to notice that," Simpson lied. "I have to word what I say very carefully when he's around. Bland's a two-faced person, and I hate that kind, for you never know when they might turn on you."

"Well, I've done everything that you've told me to do," Joe told him. "When Mark comes back he won't have anything left, for I've seen to that of course, with Henry's help. Henry is my kind of a man."

"That's good to know," Simpson smiled. "I went ahead and paid the white men you still have as foremen, and those who left as well, for word might get back to Mark that you didn't pay them, and he might come back home. Your foremen are the only one's who know about our plan, but they won't talk."

"I haven't told anybody, for you've been too good to me," Joe smiled, as he looked over at Nate. "Like you say, we both will benefit from this, and I give you all the credit for being honest and straight with me."

"And, I thank you from the bottom of my heart for what you're doing, and I'll continue praying for you," Nate replied. "It's nice to lay down at night with a clear conscience and sleep like a baby, knowing that you've done right."

"So far, everything is going along as planned, for I let them know that I'm the boss, and they're scared to death of Henry," Joe boasted. "We make up a good team, you know."

"I know, for Henry knows how to handle niggers," Nate told him. "Do you have any troublemakers, that you're aware of? If so, we need to weed them out as soon as possible, for we can't afford to have any trouble, not at this point."

"No, not except for Bill," Joe answered. "He does talk back to me, and he has a lot of influence over the others. We probably should get rid of him and his girl too, for other than those two, none of them have sense enough to get in out of a rainstorm. I'm actually afraid of those two."

"Then, get rid of them." Simpson agreed. "Of course, they could have an accident, for accidents do happen, you know. Keep telling Mark that you have things under control, but don't ever mention my name in your letters."

"Don't worry, for I haven't even mentioned Henry's name to him," replied Joe. "By the way! When are you planing to take over, and divide the farm between us? I hope my part includes this house, for it sure is nice."

"Don't get in a rush, for we still have a lot of things to do, before that happens," Nate told him. "I don't like to rush into anything."

"Oh no, I'm not rushing you at all, for I ralize that you know what step to take next, and when to take it," Joe cowered.

"I must go now, for I have a lot of things to take care of before the sun goes down this evening," said Nate, as he walked down the steps. "I'll watch after the business end of things, and you can handle the niggers."

Bill's heart ached, as he slipped back down to the barn, but this threat on his life was secondary to the pain he felt for Mark. I'll have to get word to Mark. My life depends on it, and so does the lives of all the others, he thought.

The following morning, while Martha was hanging out clothes at her house, Elizabeth stepped out on the porch at the mansion, and called to her.

"Martha, I want you to come up here!" Elizabeth summoned. "I'd like to talk with you, about something."

"Yass'am, Miss Liz'buth, I's coming!" Replied Martha, as she hurried up to the mansion. "What is it, that you gon'a jump on me fer, this time?"

"Don't get the wrong impression, gal," Elizabeth replied, trying to seem stern, "but I'm asking for your help, this time."

"I's here, and ready to do what you's want me to do," spoke Martha, in a polite voice. "Does you still mem'er what you wanted me to do, er is it went and slipped out'a yo' head? It does happen like that, sometimes."

"My nigger maid Bertha, is a real good cook, and a fine housekeeper, but she's no good at tending to the baby," Elizabeth explained. "Little Joseph screams his head off when she comes around him, and I need to get some rest."

"Yass'am, you's do look tuckered out, and frazzled, too," replied Martha, "but what do you's want me to do 'bout it? Sang to you, maybe."

"Well, when it comes to tending to him, you're the best," Elizabeth told her, as a soft smile came on her face. "He seems to like you, too."

"Is you trying to say you's want me to come up here and sot wid him one day?" Martha asked. "I's be glad to do that, fer he sho' be a fine boy."

"Yes, a few hours every day, so that I can get some rest," she politely replied. "But, I don't want Joe to know that you're here. Do you understand?"

"Yass'am I una'stan, but he ought'a know that you's got'a get some res' sometimes," Martha smiled. "When does you want me to come up here?"

"Joe generally takes a nap right after lunch, and after that, he's out there in the fields, 'til dark," Elizabeth explained. "Watch when he leaves tomorrow, then slip up here and tend to the baby, so I can take a nap."

"I's be rite here, soon as he leaves," Martha replied. "I's been missing lit'l Jos'f. Ain't hugged him in a long time, neither."

Martha nodded, then scurried back to the clothesline. She'd get to be in the house again, even if only a short time each day, and she had hopes of getting the freedom papers, and Mark's address. She felt like this was a way the Lord was answering her prayers, and she looked up, and gave thanks.

Martha seemed to glide through her chores during the next few days. Each morning, she did her yardwork, and helped her mother around the house, and then after Joe finished his nap, she tended to the baby for Elizabeth.

Elizabeth was delighted, since she could take a nap, or read a book, and not be disturbed. Bertha was more than glad to have Martha in the house, for she couldn't tolerate any child. Martha was happiest of all, because she not only adored the baby, but because she was in the house, and learning about the routine of the day. Soon she'd come up with a way to get the papers from the trunk, and no one would be the wiser, she thought.

Martha certainly did have a way with little Joseph. It was almost as if the child knew instinctively when it was time for Martha to arrive. He'd pull up in his crib and look out the window, and how he would giggle, when he saw her approaching.

Once Martha was inside, he would reach for her, and then hug her real tight, while tugging at the braids in her coarse hair.

Though Elizabeth pretended not to be impressed, Martha could see that she was touched by Joseph's affectin for her. How sad it must be to have to put up this act, Martha thought. Elizabeth was such a beautiful young woman, with long raven hair, and cream-white skin, and Martha knew that somewhere deep beneath this contrived exterior, was a kind-hearted, possibly even a sad, and broken-hearted young lady.

One afternoon while Martha played with the baby, Joe happened to return a bit earlier than they expected. Martha saw him ride up on his mare and hitch her to a post at the barn, then she hurried downstairs and told Bertha, and in turn, Bertha hurried out to the porch where Elizabeth was reading a book, to tell her. Elizabeth became frightened, for she certainly didn't want Joe to know what she'd been doing behind his back.

"Tell Martha to slip out the back door!" Elizabeth told her, as she laid the book down on the porch. "Bring the baby to me, and I'll keep Joe out here long enough for Martha to get back home. I don't want Joe to find her here."

"Yass'am, I'll fetch the youngun," said Bertha, crossly, as she hurried back inside, to where Martha stood holding the baby. "Gim'ee that young'un!" She snapped at Martha, as she jerked Joseph from Martha's arms. "His mammy is want'n him out yon'a wid her."

Elizabeth quickly took the baby from Bertha, and hurried down the walkway to meet Joe, and detain him long enough for Martha to get back home.

"Look Joseph, it's Daddy, and he came home early!" Elizabeth said to the baby, as she handed him to Joe. "Give Daddy a big kiss."

Joe took the baby, and held him high in the air. "He's daddy's big boy, that's what he is!" Joe teased. The baby cooed, and smiled. "Have you had a good nap today?" Joe asked, lovingly.

"Tell daddy that you just woke up," said Elizabeth. "Come on up and sit down on the porch with us, Joe," she said, demurely.

"That's fine with me," Joe smiled, "for I have something that I want to talk over with you, anyway."

They walked upon the porch and sat down in the swing, and Joe started in telling her what he had on his mind.

"I heard about a sale, where a farmer is selling all of his equipment, along with his livestock, and I wanted to look at a pair of mules he has for sale," Joe told her. "He lives at Beckville, not all that far from where you're family lives, and you can visit with them, while I attend the sale. What do you say?"

"Oh could we, really!" She squealed. "I have't seen them since a week after the baby was born, and Mother wasn't feeling too well. I'd love to see them, and I'm sure they'd like to see the baby. I'm ready to go, right now!"

"I was thinking about taking Bertha with us to tend to the baby, and help around the house while we're there," Joe told her. "That will give you more time to visit with your folks."

"Bertha?" She asked, frowning. "Well, yes, that's fine, but what about her husband, Chappie. Is he going with us, too?"

"No, I think he'd better stay here," Joe replied. "I'm afraid that the niggers might break into the house, if everybody is gone. I've noticed quite a bit of whispering going on between them here lately, and I'm afraid they are up to something of no good. No, I don't think we'll take him with us."

"That's fine, but I'm afraid that she won't like to go off and leave him here alone," replied Elizabeth. "I don't think that she can trust him."

"Well, that's too bad!" Joe frowned. "We won't be gone all that long as it is, and she'll do what I tell her to do, for she's our slave."

"When do you plan to go?" She asked. "I need to know ahead of time, so I can pack our clothes, and I want to take that new quilt, and give it to Mother."

"The sale is this coming Friday, and I thought we'd leave fairly early on Thursday morning, and spend Thursday night with your folks," he replied. "Henry will take care of things while I'm gone, but I need to let him know ahead of time, so he can keep his eye on the house. I'll be back by dark."

Bertha had been standing near a window watching them, and as soon as Joe left, she went back outside to talk with Elizabeth.

"Miss Liz'buth, did Mos'a Joe 'spect sump'um wuz wrong, when you went and told him that Marthie is been slipping up here and playing wid that youngun? Was he mad 'cause you ain't been telling him 'bout it?" She asked.

"No, I didn't tell him," replied Elizabeth. "By the way, I need to tell you something, so sit down in the swing for a minute."

"What is it that you's want'a jump on me 'bout?" She asked. "I's ain't done what you's thank I's done, and I can prove it by Chappie. Now, what is I done, that you's don't like?"

"We're going on a trip this coming Thursday morning, and we're taking you along with us, to tend to the baby," Elizabeth began. "You can take an extra change of clothes with you, for we'll be spending the night."

"My Chappie, is he gon'a drive fer us?" She asked, in a tone that really annoyed Elizabeth. "He be a rail good driver, and he done aw'ready knows whu' youn's is head'n out to. Whu' is youn's going to, nohow?"

"No, he'll stay here and look after the house while we're gone, for we're afraid somebody might break in and steal something while we're away," Elizabeth replied.

"Oh my Lord!" Bertha gasp. "I's better stay here, fer they mout hurt my hus'bun, when they break in the house. Yass'am, I's gon'a stay wid him."

"That won't work, for my husband has already made plans for you to go, so you might as well get ready," Elizabeth told her. "My mother is sick, and we want you to help around the house while we're there, too."

"What's wrong wid yo' mammy?" Bertha nagged. "Is she done got old and wor' out, er did her young'uns run her crazy. Young'uns will do that. That's why I's ain't never went and had none. Don't want'a be run crazy, like she be."

"No, she's not crazy!" Elizabeth scolded. "Mother's suffering with some kind of paralysis, and she's unable to get around on her own, anymore. Bertha, you can go on back to work now."

She could tell by the way Bertha mumbled to herself as she slowly got up to go back inside, that she wasn't happy because her husband wasn't going with them. Chappie was somewhat of a rounder, and she feared what might happen, if he was left alone. As she slowly walked toward her room she met Chappie, and she slapped his face, as they passed in the hallway.

"My God, womern, is you los' yo' mind?" Asked Chappie, as he stopped, and turned around. "What wuz that fer? What is I done to you?"

"That, wuz fer sump'um that you's ain't never done, that I's know you gon'a do, jus' as soon as I's get gone," she said, as she went on into her room.

Elizabeth carried Joseph out toward the barn, hoping to find Martha. She needed to start packing for the trip, and she wanted Martha to tend to Joseph, while Joe was gone to talk with Henry.

"Martha, are you in there?" Elizabeth called, when she saw that the barn door was open. "If you are, I'd like to talk to you."

"Yass'am, I's in here!" Martha called back, with a sound of fear in her voice. "I's sorry that Mos'a Joe went and ketched me up there, and I's hope he didn't whoop you, er nothing." Then, she stepped outside.

"No, thank the Lord, he didn't see you," Elizabeth smiled, as she handed the wiggling child to Martha. "Take him, for he's having a duck fit to get to you," she laughed. "Joe's working, and he won't be back 'til dark."

"Come here, you lit'l punk'n bug," Martha grinned, as she took the baby from his mother. "We's good buddies anyhow, ain't we, lit'l feller."

"Let's go back up to the house, and you can tend to him, while I pack up my clothes," Elizabeth told her.

"Is you gon'a leave Mos'a Joe?" She asked, in a puzzled voice. "And, if you go off and leave him, is you gon'a take him wid you, er will he stay here?"

"No, I'm not leaving him," she smiled. "We plan to visit my mother this coming Thursday, and we'll be away for a day or so. I sure wish you could go along with us to tend to the baby, but I'm afraid to mention that to him."

Martha was disappointed, for even though the Wilsons would be away, with Bertha and Chappie still in the house, she wouldn't be able to get the papers from Mark's trunk. Bertha and her husband occupied Mark's room, which complicated things.

"We're taking Bertha with us, to help around the house, but we're leaving Chappie here, in case some of the nig..." Her voice trailed off.

Martha went on up to the mansion, and tended to the baby while Elizabeth started preparing for the trip ahead. Martha was thrilled because Chappie was staying. He's so simple minded, she thought, until anybody could walk on past him, and take whatever they wanted. Everything was going to work out for her after all, she hoped, and she could hardly wait to tell her folks.

"Glory be, and thank the Lord!" Martha yelled, as she went running into her parent's home, later that evening. "The Lord is done ready to answer my prayer!"

"What's wrong wid you, chile?" Her mother scolded. "You know better than to come in here screaming like that!"

"Miss Liz'buth and Mos'a Joe is gon'a take a trip, they gon'a take grumpy ole Berthie wid 'em, and leave ole Chappie in the house," she excitedly told her. "Now, ain't that sump'um fer me to be happy 'bout?"

"Well, I's 'spose he ain't 'fraid to stay by his sef', fer he's growed up now, and he ain't no chile," Liza replied. "The way you's acted, I's thought that you done got them papers."

"Don't you see!" Martha smiled. "Chappie is done messed up in the head, and I's can get the stuff, rite out from under his nose."

"You's better be ca'ful, fer he mout not be as stupid as you thank he is," her mother warned. "He be what they call one of them skirt-chaser, too!"

"Don't worry 'bout me," she winked, 'fer I's done took care of a bigger man than him. Jus' sew another big ole butcher knife in my frock," she chuckled.

Liza slapped Martha's face, before she hardly realized what she had done. "I's sorry, but you ain't 'sposed to laugh 'bout nobid'ee get'n kilt," Liza scolded.

"I wuz teasin'," cried Martha, "but you aw'mos knocked my teef' out!"

"But, that sho' wuzn't funny!" Liza sobbed. "When you get to whu' somebid'ee being dead sounds funny, you's done standing at the ver'ee gates of hell."

Later, when Bill came into the house, Martha told him what she'd already told her mother. Like her mother, he was a little skeptical of her plan.

"It sounds good in a way, but ole Chappie is standing in the way, like a big stump in the middle of a field," he observed. "What pesters me, is how is you gon'a handle him. Is you got that figured out, too?"

I's gon'a sashay up there and act like I's want a man, then I gon'a axe him to go down to the barn and wait fer me," she explained. "When he heads torge the barn, I's gon'a slip in and get them papers, and run back home."

"But, what if he don't go to the barn?" Bill asked. "What if he grabs hold of you, and drags you in the house. Is you ever thought 'bout that?"

"Oh, he gon'a do what I sez," she assured him, "fer he done socked his froggie eyes on me, when Berthie wuzn't looking."

"Marthie, we done is aw'mos los' you twice befo', and this time mout turn out to be a clincher," her mother frowned. "I's wush you'd thank up sump'um else to do, fer that plan don't sound too good."

"If we's don't get them letters that sez whu' Mark is, and scratch him a letter, none of us is gon'a be left liv'," she explained. "If they do kill me, it ain't gon'a be no wuss than to starv' to def', like we is doing now."

Martha finally convinced them that her plan might work. Later that night, Bill slipped around and discussed it with his special friends, and they agreed to help him. They had nothing to lose, they thought.

Wednesday evening, before they were to set out on the trip early the next morning, Joe and Elizabeth discussed the trip.

"I'm so excited, I doubt if I sleep a wink tonight!" Elizabeth told him. "Mother and Daddy will be shocked, when we come riding up in Mark's beautiful surrey. It really would knock their eyes out, if we had a Negro man driving for us!" Her face was all aglow.

"But, I'm taking a wagon," he told her. "I might need it, if I buy some pieces of farm equipment, and I don't want your father anymore mad at me, than he already is. I'll have two seats fixed on the wagon, and we'll be fine."

Early on Thursday morning, they set out on the trip. Her parents, Arthur and Betsy Garrison, lived on a small farm near the edge of town. For several years, her mother had been suffering from paralysis, she was unable to stand on her feet, and hardly had any use of her arms. Arthur and his sister Agnes took excellent care of Betsy, and though helpless, and often in a great amount of pain, she never complained, or became disagreeable.

Elizabeth could hardly wait to see her parents. Little Joseph was almost two years old now, and she knew what a delight it would be to her parents, and her Aunt Agnes, to see him.

Joe was anxious to boast to his father-in-law of his position as manager of a large plantation, and newfound wealth. Even so, Mr. Garrison wasn't all that pleased with his daughter's choice of a husband, but he tried to keep his personal feelings all to himself, for the sake of his daughter's happiness. He'd always thought of

Joe as being a bit spineless, and feared that he'd sooner or later dissappoint or desert Elizabeth, when she needed him most.

Aunt Agnes was busy sweeping off the front porch, and Mr. Garrison was sitting on a bench in the yard, when they heard a noise from down the road. As far as Aunt Agnes knew, they were not expecting any visitors, and the very sight of a new wagon coming toward the house, surprised her.

"Arthur!" called out Aunt Agnes, to her brother. "I see a wagon coming toward the house. It looks like three people in it, as near as I can tell from here. Were you expecting company?"

"Not as I know of," he replied, as he quickly stood up, and looked down the driveway. "Look Agnes! It's Liz, as sure as the world!" He yelled, as he stood looking at the wagon. "Agnes, its Liz, coming to see us!"

"Surprise, Daddy!" Elizabeth shouted, as the wagon finally pulled up and stopped in the yard. "Hey, Aunt Agnes!"

Arthur helped his daughter down from the wagon, and hugged her for a long time. Then it was Aunt Agnes' turn.

"Liz, you are the spitting image of your mother, when she was about your age," smiled her aunt. Elizabeth then handed the baby to her. "My, you're a heavy little fellow," Agnes said, as she hugged Joseph. "You're a fine boy."

Joseph was passed around and admired, and he seemed to love every minute of it. Joe sat in the wagon for a moment watching them, and then he climbed down, and went over and offered his hand to his father-in-law.

"I hope we're not intruding on you in any way, by barging in on you folks like this," Joe politely said. "I was going to a sale over near Eldridge in the morning, and while I was already coming this way, I decided to let Liz and the baby visit with you folks for a day or so. Is that all right with you?"

"A week, would be better!" Garrison laughed. "Come on into the house, and see Mother." With his arm around Elizabeth, they headed inside.

"Is she any better, Daddy?" Asked Elizabeth, softly.

"I'm afraid not, she has a good day now and then, never will be well, it don't seem," he replied. "She's in the parlor, and I'm anxious to see how she acts, when she sees you and the baby."

Mrs. Garrison was sitting in a rocking chair near the fireplace, with a beautiful crocheted shawl draped over her legs. She began to smile, and cry at the same time, when she saw Elizabeth.

"My baby, you finally came to see me," she sobbed. "Come and let me get a good look at you." She tried to reach up for Elizabeth, but her hand fell limp on her lap. "It's been such a long time, and I've missed you so much here lately."

Elizabeth was heartbroken, for in a short span of a few months her mother had lost a lot of weight, and she looked frail and weak. Her skin had almost lost all its natural color, but her eyes were still strong and blue, truly the only thing that looked the same about her.

"Oh Mother," Elizabeth cried, as she hugged her, "it's so wonderful to see you again. I brought your favorite grandson to see you, if I can get him away from Aunt Agnes."

Agnes handed the baby to Elizabeth, and slid a chair over close to where Betsy was sitting. "Sit down there, Liz, so your mother can place her hand on the baby. She's been asking about you and the baby, every day."

Elizabeth sat down near her mother, and then Joseph grasp her mother's finger, and babbled. Betsy smiled, and then a faint tint returned to her cheeks.

"Hello there, big fellow," Betsy said to Joseph. "Are you enjoying your visit with Grandpa and me. We've been wanting to see you for a long time."

Joseph grinned and babbled as if trying to answer her, as he held on to her finger. Thank God the baby isn't afraid of her, Elizabeth thought.

"Mother, I brought my maid along to help with the cooking and cleaning, while we're here," Elizabeth told her. "She's still outside, for I wanted to get your permission, before asking her in."

"Tell her to come on in," said her mother, "for we certainly don't want to leave the impression that we have no manners around here."

"But she's, well, she's a Negro woman, Mother," Elizabeth added.

"That doesn't matter!" Her aunt spoke up. "She's human, and she needs to feel welcome in our home. Have you forgotten how you were raised?"

Elizabeth felt small and ashamed, as she turned and looked at Joe, who stood with his head bowed. She ran to the front door and looked outside, with Aunt Agnes close behind, then she saw Bertha sitting on the bench in the yard.

"I'm sorry to have abandoned you," said Elizabeth, "but I was eager to see my mother, and I guess I forgot all about everything else, and you too."

"Including her manners!" Agnes laughed, as she walked out and placed her hand on Bertha's shoulder. "I'm Agnes, this silly girl's old-maid aunt. Can I show you to your room, Madam? And let me welcome you, to our humble home."

Bertha looked befuddled, as she stood up, then turned to face Agnes. She had never been spoken to so politely, in all her life. She was shocked.

"Yass'am, I's sho' would like that," Bertha drawled, "fer I's do need a lit'l res', adder the long ride in that ole bumpy wagen."

"We have a small room off the kitchen, but I'm sure you'll find it to be comfortable, and I'll put some clean sheets on the bed," Agnes smiled, as she motioned to Bertha to follow her. "I'll have dinner ready, in a little bit."

Elizabeth went back and rejoined her parents in the parlor. She sat and held her mother's hand, while they talked about everything that came to their mind, while Joe was outside unloading things from the wagon. This is strange, Elizabeth thought, for it seems like Mother is trying to relive her life.

"Mother, you'll have to come and see our new house. It's a mansion, and we're enjoying it," Elizabeth told her. "It's really not ours yet, but maybe it will be someday, for we hope to buy it pretty soon. We're taking care of a large plantation, while the owner is visiting relatives in Ohio." She was not about to tell her mother the whole truth.

Her father went outside to help Joe unload the wagon, and to show Joe where he could put the mules, and feed them. Joe was anxious to brag about his great fortune, and Garrison knew that, so he decided to lead Joe along.

"Well, how's that little farm of yours doing?" asked Garrison. "We had a good crop-year this time around, and I wondered how you made out."

"Well, we don't own that little farm anymore, and you might even say that we outgrew it," Joe began to boast. "We live in a beautiful mansion, and take care of one of the largest plantations in South Carolina. I'm recognized now, as being one of the largest farmers in the state."

"Sure you are," Garrison joked, "and I was appointed governor of South Carolina, just this past week. We're really going places now!"

"Seriously, I'm managing Mark Simpson's plantation, while he's up in Ohio, visiting relatives," Joe explained. "I got involved with Mark's father, Nate Simpson, and by this time next year, I'll own half of the plantation."

"Nate Simpson, you say," Garrison replied. "I hear that he's screwed, and controls everything, and everybody he has any dealings with. Am I right?"

"You're right, Sir," Joe smiled. "He and his son don't get along like a father and son should, and he turned his attention toward me. Seems as though he's searching for a lost son, you might say."

"The way I hear it, you'd be better off not to get involved with that man at all," Garrison replied. "I hear that Nate, and that crooked banker, Ellis Bland, almost destroyed his son a few years back. He's like a snake hiding in the grass, and he knows when to strike, and who to strike at, too."

"He's always gone out of his way to help me," Joe lied, trying to defend Nate. "He's been a lot like a father to me, here lately."

"Just remember what he did to his son," Garrison cautioned. "He's using you 'til he gets what he wants, then he'll drop you like a rotten apple."

"I don't believe all that folks say about him," Joe protested. "We have confidence in each other, and we trust each other. It's as simple as that."

Garrison suddenly remembered all that he didn't like about Joe. He was the type of person who looked for an easy road, a pie in the sky, something he could get for nothing. Garrison feared for his daughter, and he'd have to speak with her about this. Maybe she'd listen to reason, for Joe would not, he thought.

Early the following morning, Joe headed out for the sale where he planned to look at a pair of mules he hoped to buy. Elizabeth had brewed some coffee before her husband left, and she was still sitting at the kitchen table, when her father got out of bed, and came into the room.

"Do you have an extra cup of coffee, my dear?" Her father asked, when he sat down at the table. "Make mine black, or do you still remember?"

"Of course I do!" she said, as she poured the coffee. "A girl still remembers her parents, even after she's married, you know," she teased.

"I didn't have a chance to talk with Joe all that much yesterday, but he left the impression that things were going well," he said. "Is that right?"

"Yes, we live in a beautiful mansion, and Joe's managing a plantation for a friend while he's away," she replied, "and it's just . . . "She could not stoop so low, as to lie to her father. "Daddy, it's awful!" She cried.

"Shhh, don't wake up everybody," he whispered. "Let's go to my room, so we can talk." They walked down the hallway to a small room, where her father did his bookwork. He sat down at the small desk, and closed the Bible he had been reading last night, then put it on a shelf, and she sat down on the small cot, where he usually took a nap during the afternoon. As she glanced around the room she saw one of her pictures on the wall above his desk, and a picture of her mother, on a shelf next to his Bible.

"I want to know what's really going on between Joe and Nate Simpson, if you don't mind," he said. "I'm your friend, as well as your father, so talk to me like you'd talk to a friend. Now my friend, how have you been doing?"

"Daddy, it's just awful! She sobbed. "Nate Simpson has turned Joe into a monster, like he is himself. He's talked Joe into helping him work a scheme to take everything from Mark while he's away. Nate's a horrible man!"

"Why didn't Joe refuse to go along with him?" He asked. "I realize that Joe borrowed some money from him, but he paid Nate back, plus an ungodly rate of interest."

"But Nate came up with a false lien, that he's holding over Joe's head," she explained. "Nate's so rich and powerful, until the law is even afraid of him, and with Mark gone, he'll take the farm, with Joe's help. Henry and Joe are abusing the poor Negroes, starving them to death, and treating them worse than when they were slaves. It's awful, what's going on down there!"

"I've heard that about Simpson," he said, "but I never thought he would bother my own family. I've never had any dealings with him, though."

"I wish now, that we hadn't either," Elizabeth whinned. "He demands that we mistreat the Negroes, but they're freed-slaves now, and Mark trusted Joe to look after them while he's away.

Joe don't pay them like Mark did, he refuses to give them enough food to eat, and Henry even locked up the church Mark had built for them, and plowed up their graveyard. Joe even threatened to run me off, unless I treated the Negroes cruel and mean, like he and Henry is doing. That's the kind of hell I'm going through!" She cried, as she jumped up, and went over and threw her arms around him.

Tears came to his eyes, as he bowed his head, and she went back over and sat down on the cot. "Joe didn't mention that to me, at all," he sobbed.

"I know, for he's somehow forgotten his promise to Mark, as well as what he promised the Negroes," she added.

"I try to live right, but part of living right, is not to stand idly by, and let the devil run over us," he replied. "I'll beat the devil out of him when he gets back here, for he has no right to make you do such things! You have a place here, you and the baby, but not Joe. I've never liked him."

"I can't seem to get Joe to understand, but he's allowing Nate Simpson to come between us, and causing me to hate him," she continued. "You've always taught me to respect everybody, both black and white, and it hurts me to have to treat Negroes like trash, just to please my husband. I'm at a point where I hardly know what to do anymore, or where to turn for help."

"You're right, for they are human," he agreed. "We must never let Agnes or your mother know anything about this, for it would worry them absolutely to death. It's awful hard for me to handle, and I'm a tough ole dude."

"I wish I didn't have to go back, and could stay here until Joe realizes where he's going wrong," she said, in a pitiful voice. "I feel as though I'm spitting in God's face, when I say hurtful things to the Negroes. I slip away and cry to myself, later. I can't go on like this, very much longer."

Neither of them said anything for a few moments, as he sat with his head bowed, wondering why Joe had allowed himself to become entangled with Simpson in the first place. And of course, he was thinking of his daughter's welfare and happiness, as well as that of his only grandchild. Maybe it would be best if his daughter and grandchild did stay with him for a while, he thought. He'd have to think of something, so Joe wouldn't become suspicious.

"It might be best, if you stayed here with us for a while," he told her. "When the doctor was here last, he said she didn't..." He stopped all of a sudden, and tears trickled down his cheeks.

"Oh no, tell me that it's not true, Daddy!" She wailed. "Has she gotten all that bad, since I've been away?"

"She's gradually slipping away," he told her, "and that's why I'm glad you and the baby came to visit, for it seems like a dose of medicine to her, you might say. I wish you would ask Joe to let you and the baby stay on with us a few weeks. If you like, I'll ask him for you."

"That's fine with me," she agreed. "Maybe he'll think things over while I'm not there with him, and come to his senses. If I had Mark's address with me, I'd write a letter to him, and let him know what's going on back here. He doesn't let me read the letters he gets from Mark, and he certainly won't let me know what he writes and tells Mark. He keeps the letters from Mark in a trunk that Mark left in his room, and he dares me to even go near the trunk."

"You need to stay away from there," he advised. "Maybe one day he might see where his family is more important, than Nate Simpson."

"God, I hope he comes to his senses," she sighed, "for he's changed so much here lately, I hardly know him. I'm afraid it's going to be hard to get Simpson's influence out of him, and he's afraid of what Henry might do, if he doesn't obey Simpson. Henry Graham, is the man who's behind what Nate wants Joe to do against Mark, for Nate holds somethng over Henry's head, as well."

"I don't know Mark, but from what you say, he's a fine person," said her father. "I'd write to him myself, if I had his mailing address."

"Mark's a wonderful person, and he thinks everything is going along fine, for nobody has told him any different," she pointed out. "There's no telling what he might do, if he found out what Nate and Joe were doing behind his back, while he's gone. He'd probably kill both of them, for he thinks the world of those poor innocent Negroes, especially Bill, and his family."

"He's bound to find out sooner or later, and I don't want you and my only grandchild to be caught in the middle, when he does," he emphatically stated. "When Joe gets back, he and I will have a little discussion, for somebody has to knock some sense into his head, before it's too late."

"Daddy, please don't do that!" She pleaded. "I'd rather he'd never know that I told you anything about what's going on. Will you promise?"

"Very well then," he promised. "I'll never let him know the real reason I want you to stay with us. I'll word it in a way, where he'll never know."

When they heard someone in the kitchen, they ended their discussion, and returned to the kitchen and joined the others for another cup of coffee.

Back at Bill's house this morning, Martha was busy planning her strategy for tonight. She was to go to Mark's mansion as soon as it got dark, and persuade Chappie to go to the barn and wait for her, then slip into Mark's room and get the freedom papers from the trunk. If she were lucky, she'd be able to get one of the letters from mark in Ohio. She couldn't read, and it would be dark inside the room, so she'd have to quickly grab up whatever papers she could find, and get back out in a hurry. However, there were no assurances that Chappie would even fall for this scheme, but she hoped he would.

Bill, and some of the other men were preparing for the role they'd be playing in this scheme, for if they didn't play their part well, Martha couldn't carry out her part either. Their life now depended heavily on her plan working. Though some doubted that it would work, it was their only hope. They realized as well, if they were caught in the act, they'd be killed. Death, was death, regardless to how it came about, they reasoned.

As a part of their plan, as the sun went down, Bill and some of the other men brought a load of firewood up to where Henry lived, and began stacking it on the front porch. When they saw Martha slipping along behind Henry's house, on her way up to the mansion, they were to make as much noise as possible, and hopefully, cause Henry to come out on the porch. If this worked, Henry would not see Martha, as she slipped past his house. When Bill saw Martha slipping along in the moonlight, he nodded his head, which was their cue, and the other men began to slam the wood down hard on the porch.

"What in the devil's going on out here?" asked Henry, as he came and stood in the front doorway. "Why are you fools making all that noise?"

"I's sorry 'bout that," said Bill, as he turned to the others. "Youn's fellers better stop making all that loud racket! Do youn's hear me?"

They mumbled something to themselves, and after they quieted down a bit, Henry turned to go back inside. Not quite sure if Martha had arrived at the mansion, and wanting to keep Henry out front, they slammed some more wood down on the porch. It worked, but this time when Henry came out, he had a shotgun in his hand.

"There you go again!" Henry bellowed. "It looks like I'll have to stand right here, and watch you fools! Stop making all that darned noise!"

"Yass'uh, it sho' do looks like you gon'a have to stay rite there to keep us from tearing the po'ch down," calmly spoke Bill. "I's sorry 'bout that."

"You darned niggers are so stupid, I don't see how you manage to find the way back home at night!" Henry laughed, wickedly.

"Yass'uh, we is stupid, and that's a fac'," said Bill. "I's don't know how we ever found yo' house, so we's could make all that racket. You better keep yo' eyeballs on us, fer we mout mess up rail bad, the next time."

Bill knew that Martha already had plenty of time to reach the mansion by now, and they quickly finished unloading the wood, and returned home. Henry went back into the house, and quickly slammed the door behind him.

"I didn't realize that a nigger was so darned stupid!" Henry said to his wife, as he sat back down at the fireplace. "They didn't even know that they were making as much noise as they were, until I mentioned it to them."

"Then, some people think they're human!" said his wife. "Like you said, they do things, and don't even know why they're doing them." Oh, if he only knew how smart they really were!

Martha had arrived at the back of the mansion. Tapping on the back door, Martha stood looking very disheveled. She had mussed up her clothes while she walked along, and unbuttoned the top of her dress, partly exposing one breast. She had gotten some hay from the barn, and stuck it in her hair.

Chappie was surprised when he opened the door, and found Martha standing there, looking this way. "What is you up to now?" He asked, as he gasps at her for a moment. "You's done know that nobid'ee ain't here, but me."

"I's know that," she purred, "and that's the ver'ee reason I's come up here. I's hope you ain't messed wid one of the tuther young gals aw'ready, and don't want'a give me what I's want."

"What wuz that!" he quickly asked, looking at Martha's breast. "Come on in the house, and let me see if I's got what you's want, you sweet dar'lin."

"I's been down at the barn wid a rail young boy, and adder he got me to want'n him, he wouldn't do nothing," she whinned, pulling some pieces of hay from her hair. "I's feel awful, fer I ain't never had no man mess wid me, and I's wondered if you would he'p me get rid of the jitters."

"I's be glad to hep' you, if you'll come inside wid me," he replied, as he gently rubbed her cheek. "Marthie, I's thank I's got zackly what you need."

"You know my name, don't you, Chappie!" She whimpered, as she took his hand, and rubbed it on her breast. "Oh Lord, that sots me on fire!"

"I's sho' do know yo' name, Marthie," he drooled, "and I's had my eyes sot on you, fer a long time. Come on in, and I'll get rid of them jitters."

Martha had everything going her way, and she knew that she must keep them moving along, before Chappie became suspicious.

"I's 'fraid to go in there, but if you'll come on to the barn, I'll let you doctor me," she replied, gently squeezing his hand. "It started down at the barn, and it's gon'a finish up down there too."

"Ain't nobid'ee gon'a see you in the house," he insisted, pulling her up close to him. "Gim'me a lit'l kiss, Marthie."

"I's can't do nothing here," she said, twisting out of his grasp. "Come on to the barn where I's done got a bed made in the hay, fer I's gon'a wait on you. Please Chappie, don't do me like that young boy done!"

Chappie was so excited he could hardly hold his breath, for he knew that a real adventure lay ahead for him. He went inside and quickly splashed some smelly cologne all over his face, and then headed out toward the barn, to where he was sure the desirable Martha was waiting. Instead of going to the barn, Martha hid behind some bushes, and as soon as Chappie passed on his way to the barn, she slipped into the house.

Although the moon was shining, it was dark inside the house. Other than for a lamp that was burning in the hallway, and one in the parlor, the entire house was dark. Nevertheless, Martha knew her way around, and she rushed into Mark's room, opened the trunk, and grabbed a handful of papers and envelopes, and stuffed them in her bosom. As she ran back outside she happened to drop one of the letters on the back porch, but she was afraid to take time to pick it up. Thank God, my mission was completed, she thought, as she ran real fast back toward home, with the papers stuffed in her bosom.

Down at the barn, Chappie opened the creaking door, and stepped inside to join Martha. "Oh Marthie, yo' honeysuckle is here," he called softly. "Tell me whu' you is, dar'lin, fer I's got what you's been wait'n fer."

As another part of the plan, three Negro boys were hiding in the barn, in case Martha happened to need them. Realizing now that Martha's plan was obviously working, they tried to detain Chappie as long as they could.

"Marthie is back here wid me, and I's done what she wanted you to do fer her," one of the boys called back. "She's too young fer you, and she wuz on fire fer a man, and she couldn't wait fer you to get here."

Chappie was angry and embarrassed. His ego was deflated, for he knew now that Martha had played a trick on him, though he didn't know why.

"Tell that sorry hussy that she'll pay fer this!" He barked, as he stormed out of the barn.

By this time, Martha was back at home, spreading the papers she had taken from the trunk, on the kitchen table. The documents might as well be written in German, or French, for the Negroes couldn't read anyway.

Bill picked up one of the papers, and held it close to a lamp that sat on the kitchen table, and grinned. "That rite there sez Bill," he told them. "That's my freedom paper, fer Mark say when I's seed that scratched on a piece of paper, it wuz mine. That say, ole Bill is free, it sho' do."

"Then, the tuthers mus' b'long to us," Liza smiled. "I's bet that stack of letters is from Mark. Marthie, you sho' done good."

Martha quickly bundled up the papers and letters, and wrapped them up in a scarf she had tied on her head. Indeed, she had accomplished the first part of her mission, however, a greater part still lay ahead, for she must now find someone to write a letter to Mark. The problem with that, she didn't know who to trust, not even another farmer in the area, for they were absolutely afraid of Nate Simpson. At this point she didn't know what to do, for without doubt, Joe and Henry would eventually find out what she had done, and in addition to that, the chance of her being able to get off the plantation to find somebody to help them, was almost impossible.

Then, a knock was heard at the front door. When Bill opened the door, he saw his friend George, with a frightened expression on his face.

Without even saying anything to Bill, Geroge hurried into the kitchen to where he saw Martha and her mother standing at the table. "Marthie, we's got'a get you out'a here, as quick as we can!" George told her. "Hurry, and get out'a here!"

"What's wrong, George?" Asked Martha. "You's look like you is scade to def'. What do you mean, by get'n me out'a here?"

"Henry's womern seed you running back from the big house, and he done out there looking fer you!" He replied frantically. "You's done got Chappie mad at you, if you's done what you say you wuz gon'a do to him, and if Henry axe him, he gon'a spill the beans 'bout what happened."

"George is rite," said Bill. "Take them papers and get out'a here, and don't stop, 'til you's get word to Mark! Hurry and get going chile!"

Frightened, and not knowing what to do, she quickly grabbed up the papers she had bundled in her scarf, tucked them under her arm, and headed toward the back door. "I's ain't sho' whu' she stays, but if I's can find Miss Carolyn, she gon'a be glad to scratch out a letter to Mark."

"Hold on jus' a minute!" Said George, as he caught hold of Martha's arm, when she reached to open the door. "I's used to stay wid Mos'a Robert Harper, and he's a fine feller. I's gon'a take you to whu' he stays, fer I's purdy sho' that he'll scratch out a letter fer us. Let's get going!"

"But Mos'a Henry told the shef' to shoot us if we's 'scaped, er run 'way," Martha warned. "I's better go by my'sef, and that way, I's be the only one that gets kilt."

"Well, we's aw'mos dead as it tis," said George. "Get'n kilt fer trying to hep' our'sef, ain't no wuss than starving to def', while we sot here and do nothing."

"Aw'rite then," Martha smiled, and hugged her mother. "Don't 'spect me back 'til I's get word to Mark, er when you see the buzzards tote'n me off, in tiny pieces." Then, Martha and George went out the door.

Up at the mansion, Henry Graham pounded on the back door. "Chappie, this is Henry, and I want you to get out here!" Henry called. "Get out here, you sorry black-bastard, for I need to talk to you about something!"

"What's the matter, Mos'a Henry?" Asked Chappie, as he opened the door, and saw Henry standing there on the porch with a shotgun in his hand. "Is somebid'ee sick, er did you's die in yo' sleep, er sump'um?"

"My wife saw a nigger gal running away from this house, and I wondered if you knew anything about it," Henry replied. "Did you have a gal up here in the house with you tonight? Don't lie to me, nigger!"

"Naw'suh, nobid'ee ain't been here wid me," he whinned. Then, deciding to shift the blame to Martha, he added. "That hussy that b'longs to Bill wuz up here to'nite, but I's didn't let her in the house."

"You'd better not lie to me!" Henry snapped, as he glanced down, and saw something lying on the back porch. "What's this?" He asked, as he picked up the letter Martha had dropped earlier. "Where did this come from?"

The light from the hallway shone through the door, and Henry saw that it was a letter, so he held it up and took a closer look.

"It's a letter to Joe, from Mark, and I wonder how it happened to get out here," said Henry, in amazement. "Somebody had to drop it here after Joe and his wife left, for Joe keeps such stuff as this in a trunk. Let me go inside and look in the trunk, and see if anybody has messed with Joe's papers."

Shoving Chappie aside, Henry grabbed the lamp that was sitting on a table in the hallway, and hurried into Mark's room. When he opened the trunk, it was obvious that someone had bothered it, for everything was cluttered up, and not one letter could be found. Then, he noticed that the freedom papers that Mark was keeping for the Negroes, were also missing.

"Darn the luck!" He swore. "The trunk has been cleaned out, which makes you a liar! Is there any chance that Bill's gal got into the house and did this?"

So that's it, Chappie thought to himself. She tricked me into going down to the barn, while she took the things from the trunk.

"I's hear'd a racket down at the barn, and I's bet she snuked in here, when I's went to see what it wuz," he lied. "Yass'uh, that's what she done."

Henry was furious, as he rushed back outside. "She's not going to get by with this!" He vowed. "I'll find the letters and papers before the sun comes up tomorrow, or I'll kill every darned nigger on the place!"

His first thought, was that she was hiding in the barn, for she knew that he'd look for her at her house first, he figured. When he didn't find her at the barn, he headed for her house. Without even taking time to knock, he took his foot and kicked the door open, then rushed inside.

"Where is that darned black-hussy hiding?" Henry bellowed, pointing the shotgun at Bill's chest. "Are you going to tell me where she is?"

"Mos'a Henry, is you axe'n me 'bout Marthie?" Asked Bill, frightened by the expression on Henry's face. "Is that who you is come here looking fer?"

"Yes, and I plan to kill the hussy!" Henry screamed. "Are you going to tell me where she is, or will I have to kill all of you?"

"We ain't seed her in quite a spell, and don't know 'zackly whu' she be at now," Sam spoke up. "She sez that she wuz gon'a leave this place one of these days, and I's bet that's whu' she be now, gone and left."

"Don't lie to me!" Henry yelled, as he jabbed the shotgun barrel against Sam's chest. "I've been known to kill niggers, for lying to me!"

"Naw'suh, I's ain't lying," Samuel cried. "Marthie, she be a headstrong kind's feller, sort of crazy like, and she mout do jus' 'bout anythang."

"Yes, she's a darned fool for sure!" Henry said, as he moved the shotgun away. "I knew that she was a murderer, and now shes a darned thief."

"Why is you calling her a thief?" Asked Liza, pretending that she didn't know what he meant. "What did she take out'a yo pocket, yo' chaw'n backer?"

"The sorry hussy can't read, and I don't see what she wanted with the old letters from Mark, and the freedom papers for you niggers!" He snorted.

Bill heaved a sign of relief, for he knew now that she had managed to get what they needed, Mark's return address. This satisfying moment, however, was suddenly overshadowed by fear for Martha's life. Henry was determined to find her, and he was not about to give up the search.

"Simpson will be as mad as the devil, when he finds out about this!" Henry told them, as he rushed back outside. "I'll find her tonight, before Nate finds out, and before Joe gets back. I'll have to find her."

Although Martha and George had been gone quite some time now, they still hadn't gotten off Mark's plantation, for it consisted of hundreds of acres of farmland, in addition to several acres of timberland. Although the moonlight did help some, they had to wade through swamps, cross-creeks, and stumble over rotten logs in the woods, in addition to clusters of vines and briars, as they avoided the roads to keep from being seen. They waded across a wide creek, and then they decided to sit down on a log, and rest for a few minutes.

"George, we's done been walking a hun'dud miles, and you's ain't said one word since we's left the house," Martha told him. "What if that man stubs up and won't hep' us adder we's get there, and sots the law on us too."

"Oh, he gon'a hep' us aw'rite, fer he be the same kind'a feller that Mark is," he assured her. "He bought me when I wuz jus' a youngun, then he tun'd me lose when he started hate'n slavery, like Mark do now."

"I's hope he do hep' us, fer we can't go back now, adder what I's went and done," Martha sighed. "We be dead if he don't hep' us, and jus' as dead if we's didn't get 'way from Mos'a Henry."

"Well, we's ain't get'n nowhu' sot'n here," said George, as he stood and looked at the moon. "We's got two er three mo' farms to cross for we's get to Mos'a Robert's place, and we's better get going, fo' the moon goes down."

Back at the plantation, Bill and Liza sat and prayed, and asked the Lord to look after Martha and George.

"That gal is got a spash'l way 'bout her, and I's ain't sho' if it's the Lord, er the devil that makes her do some thangs she do," said Liza. "She be bound, and 'termined to get word to Mark, eb'em if she do gets kilt."

"You's rite 'bout her, but we's need to go on to bed and get some res', and leave her in the hands of the Lord," Bill replied.

"Eb'em if Mos'a Henry is still looking fer her, sump'um tells me that she gon'a be jus' fine."

Even though it was now past midnight, Henry was still out there searching for Martha, but he had no clue as to where she might be. Even though Negroes were considered to be stupid in the eyes of most white persons, they had managed to come up with this scheme all by themselves, and so far, it was working. They also knew that they must continue to keep Henry distracted, until Martha had plenty of time to get away. Two boys faked a fight, and Henry fired a shot into the air, as he ran down the road to see what was going on.

"What in the devil's going on here?" Asked Henry. "What are you stupid fools fighting about, anyway?"

"I's got mad at James fer what he went and said 'bout Marthie, fer she be my gal," replied Leroy. "She ain't done what he say she went and done."

"Well, what about Martha?" Henry asked, hoping that they just might know where she was hiding. "Where is the sorry hussy hiding at, anyway?"

"James sez she run off wid another boy, and they headed out 'cross that bunch of bushes," replied Leroy, as he pointed in the opposite direction, from the way George and Martha had gone. "She wuz my gal, fo' she run off."

"She's anybody's gal, you fool!" Henry replied. "She won't get very far before daylight, then I'll have everybody around here out looking for her."

Deciding to call off the search, Henry went back home to go to bed, even though he wasn't likely to get much sleep tonight. He wasn't worried too much about Joe, but Nate Simpson was something quite different. He knew for sure that he couldn't afford to let Nate know that she had escaped.

Martha and George kept plodding along through the night, and up into the following day, as they carefully slipped across other plantations on their way to where Robert Harper lived. It was late in the afternoon when they finally arrived at his farm, and when they crossed over a rail fence that surrounded Robert's farm, George fell to his knees, and thanked God for watching over them on their journey. Muddy, dirty and wet, and their clothes torn to shreds, due to crawling through vines and briars, they made their way toward Robert's big house that sat on a knoll overlooking his farm. When George saw Robert standing in the yard, he took off his hat, and humbly fell to his knees.

"Mos'a Robert, this here is ole George!" He called out. "Do you still mem'er me. Ole George, that's who I is."

"What brings you back here?" Robert asked. Then seeing him more clearly he added. "What's wrong with you, for it looks like you're bleeding awful bad?"

"Naugh, there ain't nothing wrong wid me, 'cept fer a few scratches, but the gal here, she mout need a lit'l tending to," replied George, as he got up and put his hat back on, then walked toward him.

"I'll have her looked at," replied Robert. "I was on my way down to the barn, and if you'll follow me, you can sit down and rest, while you explain to me, what you're doing here. And, young lady, what's your name?"

"They calls me Marthie, and George hep'd me get 'way from somebid'ee that is nasty and mean to us niggas," she replied. "He fetched me here to see if you would he'p us out'a the mess that we's done went and got in."

When they arrived at the barn, Robert pointed to a stack of lumber he was using to repair the barn. "Sit there on that stack of lumber, and tell me all about it," he said.

They took turns telling him about the problems they were having since Joe had been placed in charge of Mark's farm, about him being in cahoots with Nate Simpson, and their plan to strip Mark of everything. They also told him about having to go hungry, and how brutal and mean Joe and Henry were to them, while Mark was away. Tears came to Robert's eyes as he listened, for what they had told him today, was far worse than anything he could have ever imagined.

"That's awful, and these men must be real stupid, to get involved with a man like Nate Simpson," Robert sighed. "He's the last person on earth, that you would want to have anything to do with. Dealing with Nate Simpson, is like dealing with the devil himself, or so I've heard."

"Then, you mus' is done had sump'um to do wid him befo'," Martha said to him. "Yass'uh, he sho' be awful bad, jus' like you say he is."

"Not really, but I've heard of his reputation, which is enough for me," replied Robert. "What is it, that you folks would like for me to do for you?"

"We want you to scratch out a letter, and send it to Mark, and tell him how thangs is been going on, while he been gone," Martha told him.

"I've heard that he was up north somewhere, but I don't have his address, and I can't help you, even if I wanted to," said Robert.

Then Martha pulled a bundle of papers and envelopes from her bosom, and handed them to him. "This is what I's took out'a Mark's trunk, but none of us can't read, and they mout not be no good to you, adder all."

Looking at one of the envelopes, Robert saw a return address. "Yes, this is what I need! He's living with John Harkins, in Columbus, Ohio."

"Yass'uh, that's whu he sez he wuz going," Martha smiled. "Will you scratch out a letter to him, and tell him everthang that we's told you?"

"Yes, I'll do it in the morning," Robert replied, as he started walking back toward the house. "Sit right there, while I go up to the house and round up something for you folks to eat. You can stay here on my place until I get a reply from Mark, or until he gets back to South Carolina."

"Thank you, Suh," said George, "and I's gon'a axe the Lord to look down and grin at you, fer what you is done fer us."

In Ohio, Mark had just told his great aunt how lucky he'd been, to find a trustworthy person to look after things while he was away, as he sat and wrote Joe another letter. He also planned to write to his mother, and have his aunt put her name on the envelope so his father wouldn't destroy it, and claim that he hadn't written to her.

In Beckville at the Garrison farm, Arthur stood in the yard and talked to his son-in-law, Joe Wilson. Joe had just returned from the sale, and was very angry because his deal on some mules he hoped to buy, hadn't worked out.

"That was a waste of time!" Joe snapped. "I'll have to find another man who has some mules for sale, for I needed them for next year's crop."

"Joe, I have to tell you something," Arthur spoke softly. "It's a very serious matter, and it concerns all of us."

"What's wrong?" Joe asked, trying to be calm. "Does it have anything to do with me, with Liz, maybe?"

"It's my wife, for she's dying," he tearfully replied. "I hate to have to say it, but she won't be around very much longer. The doctor said there's nothing else that he can do for her, and it's only a matter of time."

"I'm awful sorry to hear that," Joe replied. "Have you told Liz, or had you rather that she not know just yet?"

"Yes, I told her the day you went to the sale," he replied. "I wish that you would encourage Liz to stay on here with the baby for a while. It would mean a lot to her mother, to me too, to have them here during the last days."

"If that's what she wants, she can stay as long as she likes, for I won't stand in her way," Joe replied. "Is there anything else we can do?"

"Having Liz and the baby around, is the best medicine you could give her mother," Arthur told him. "Thank you, Joe, for being so kind."

"Will you need Bertha too?" Joe asked. "If you do, she can stay as long as you need her."

"No, we won't need her, but I appreciate the offer," Arthur replied, as he turned to walk away. "My sister Agnes, loves her like a sister, and with the housework to do, it keeps her mind off Betsy, for a time at least."

"I need to be heading back home real early tomorrow, and unless you have something that you'd like for me to help you with, I'd like to spend the rest of the day with my wife and child," Joe told him. "When I get back home I'll have one of my drivers bring Liz and the baby some more clothes, for we didn't know that things would turn out this way. It's no problem, though."

Early the following morning, Joe and Bertha headed back home, with Bertha sitting in the back of the wagon, so he wouldn't have to talk to her, on their long journey back home. Bertha smiled and waved goodbye, when the wagon began easing away from the house.

"Bye, Miss Liz'buth! Bye, Miss Ag'nus! Bertha called back. She'd never been treated so kind by white folks. She almost didn't want to go home, and then she happened to think of Chappie. If that rascal is been fool'n 'round while I's been gone, I's gon'a box his jaws, she said to herself.

Back at Mark's plantation, Henry had gotten up earlier than usual, and he called all the white foremen together to form a search party. He had searched alone for Martha all day yesterday, for he hoped that he'd be able to find her before they found out that she was gone, for he feared that word might somehow get

321

back to Nate Simpson. He expected Joe to return home today, and he wanted to find her before he arrived.

"What's this all about, Henry?" One of the foremen asked, when they met Henry at the barn. "Why did you want us to bring our shotgun? Is there a mad-dog roaming around somewhere?"

"That darned sorry gal of Bill's, broke into Joe's house the other night and took all his money, and some important papers from his trunk," Henry told them. "I want you men to comb every inch of this place for her, and shoot her on the spot, no questions asked. Get the papers back and I'll give you twenty dollars apiece, and all the liquor you can drink. Let's go, fellows!"

The sun was almost down when Joe returned to the plantation, and he was a bit surprised, when he saw Henry and the foremen sneaking through the bushes, as if they were out looking for something. He stopped the wagon in the road, and then called out to one of the men.

"What's all this about? Joe asked. "Did somebody spot a mad-dog in the area? Is that what you fellows are looking for?"

"We're looking for Bill's gal, for Henry said that she slipped away from the place the other night," the man called back. "Henry's walking toward the wagon now, so ask him, for he can tell you more about what happened."

Henry walked out to the wagon to talk with Joe. "We had a little trouble the other night," Henry began. "Bill's gal went into your house and took the freedom papers, all the letters that you received from Mark, and the money you had in the trunk as well. I can see why she took their freedom papers and the money, but I don't see why she wanted the letters. None of them can read."

My money! Joe thought. How did he know that I had some money hidden in the trunk. He probably took it, and blamed it on her, he reasoned.

"Darn the luck!" Joe snapped, kicking his foot against the front of the wagon. "When did all this take place? Where were you, when all this happened?"

"Night before last," Henry answered. "She went up there after dark, and tricked Chappie into going to the barn, while she went in and got the stuff."

"The moon was shining real bright, and it looks like you would have seen her when she went by your house, if you had looked outside," said Joe.

Then Henry happened to remember the noise that the Negroes made that night, and he knew now, what it was being done for. A stupid nigger outsmarted me, he thought.

"Well, uh, I was sick that night, and went to bed right after supper, and my wife was busy reading a book," Henry lied. "Anyway, it was about midnight when she did it, according to what Chappie said. Woke him up, he said."

"Have you already talked to her folks, and searched the house from top to bottom?" Joe asked. "She once escaped from a burning house, you know."

"That's the first place I looked, but they don't know anything," replied Henry, resentfully. "But she's a dead-nigger, when I lay my eyes on her!"

"But she's a live-nigger now!" Joe replied. "Remember, she has letters from Mark to me, and the freedom papers, which could spell trouble for us."

"She can't read, none of them can, and what do you suppose that she wanted the letters for?" Henry asked. "That's just like a stupid nigger, though."

"Well, I'd say that she planned to use her freedom papers for traveling, but I can't understand what she wanted with the letters from Mark," Joe told him.

"For traveling, you say! Henry questioned. "The letters do have Mark's return address on them. She might be able to reach Mark after all."

Joe laughed. "Do you have any idea how long it would take her to get all the way to Ohio?" He asked. "Even if she made it, we'll have things wrapped up before Mark gets back here. We have nothing to worry about, my friend."

"Guess so," Henry nodded, "but it still bothers me. She's a cocky type of nigger, and she might try anything. She was smart enough to work a scheme to get into the house that night, with help from some nigger men, and so far, she's managed to hide from us."

"I'm going on to the house, and you might as well call off the search for today," Joe told him. "I'll question her folks myself, for I'd bet my life that she's still here. Might be hiding right in my house, in yours, even."

"Where's your wife?" Henry asked, just then realizing that she wasn't in the wagon with him. "Did she leave you?"

"Her mother's dying," Joe replied. "Her father wanted her to stay there with him, until it was over. Her father and I are great friends, and I simply couldn't turn him down, after he begged so pitifully for her to stay."

"Humm, too bad," Henry said superficially. "I'm sorry to hear that, but we all have to die sooner or later, no big deal, it happens every day."

Joe drove on to the mansion, and while Bertha unloaded the wagon, he went down to talk with Bill and Liza about Martha. He found them standing outside.

"Henry told me, that Martha took some things out of Mark's trunk while we were gone, and I'm here to find out where she is," Joe barked. "If you know where she is, you'd better tell me. If Henry gets mad, he's liable to go wild and kill every nigger on the place. Why did she take the stuff, anyway?"

"Mos'a Joe, I's didn't see Marthie take nothing out'a no trunk, and ain't seed her since she went and left here the tuther nite," Bill carefully worded his reply. "I's swear, I's don't know whu' she be at, rite now."

"I don't believe a darn word that you're saying!" Said Joe. "You're nothing but a troublemaker, and I'll bet you put her up to it, didn't you?"

"Naw'suh, Mos'a Joe, I's ain't put her up to nothing," he replied. "She be my chile, but sometimes she uses her own head, 'bout thangs."

Stomping his foot on the ground, Joe quickly turned, then hurried back up toward the mansion. Henry was waiting in the yard, when Joe arrived.

"They didn't know anything, did they?" Asked Henry. "I told you, but you wouldn't listen to me. She's a smart hussy, and she'll cause us a lot of trouble before it's all over."

"Tomorrow morning I'll make them tell me, or I'll take a whip and beat it out of them." Joe tried to impress Henry, with his gruff exterior.

"Why not shoot them, and get it over with?" Asked Henry. "Unless you do it now, they'll wind up killing you. That's the way of a nigger."

Joe cringed, when he saw the terror in Henry's eyes. "We'll both go down there and talk with them tomorrow, for I want to give them another opportunity to tell me where she is, before I decide what to do. I'm tired, and I'm going on to bed early. I'll see you tomorrow. Good evening, Henry."

Henry mumbled something to himself, as he quickly turned and walked back toward his house.

Nate knew that Joe wasn't likely to do bodily harm to the Negroes, as Nate wanted done to them, so he had Henry Graham brought in to do the dirty work for him. He knew that Henry would do what he'd been told, for Nate held something over his head, like he did everyone else he dealt with. He planned to drop Joe, as soon as he'd taken over Mark's plantation.

The following morning came far too soon for Joe, for no sooner had the sun come up, Henry came knocking at his door. Joe would give anythng now, if he could call back the threat that he'd made in Henry's presence.

"You're out awful early, Henry," said Joe, when he saw Henry standing on the front porch, with a shotgun leaning against the wall. "I haven't even had a cup of coffee yet, so why don't we put this off, until another time."

"If you intend to beat the truth out of them like you said, you can't sit around and wait 'til they go to work," replied Henry, as he held up two short pieces of chain. "I came prepared, as you can see."

"I see you did," yawned Joe, looking at the chains. "Let me get dressed, and drink a cup of coffee, and I'll be right out."

Henry went with Joe inside, and joined him with a cup of coffee. Joe sat sipping on his coffee, as he looked across the table at Henry, and he realized that Henry knew he was taking as much time as he possibly could. He gave some thought to telling Henry that he'd changed his mind, for Henry was only one of his employees, but he was actually more afraid of Henry, than he was of Nate. He had to go ahead now.

Joe finally finished drinking his coffee, then reluctantly, he slipped on his coat, and then he and Henry went down to where Bill's family lived. They were already outside and ready to go to work, and when they saw the pieces of chain in Henry's hand, they almost fainted.

"Mos'a Joe, I's told you that I's don't know whu' Marthie be, and I's hope you b'leave me," spoke Bill, pitifully.

"I didn't believe you then, and I don't believe you now!" Joe yelled, in an effort to impress Henry. "Go ahead and tie Bill and the boys to one of the clothesline post, and we'll take the chain to them!" Joe winked at Henry, for he really didn't mean it at all.

Henry quickly grabbed hold of Bill, then led him over and tied him to the post, with a piece of rope he already had in his pocket. He told Joe that he needed more rope with which to tie the boys, and then he headed toward the barn.

Joe walked over and stood next to Bill. "Bill, you'd better go ahead and tell where she is, before he gets back," Joe said, half begging. "Henry don't have a heart, and he's liable to kill you. Now, where is she?"

"You's mout whoop me to def' fer not telling whu' she be, but none of us ain't seed her, since she left here," he solemnly replied.

"Have it your way, but when Henry gets back, there's no telling what he might do," Joe warned, as he went over, and picked up Henry's shotgun.

Soon Henry returned with more rope, and he tied Bill's boys to the other post. He picked up the pieces of chain he'd thrown on the ground, and then walked over to where Joe stood, with the shotgun aimed at Bill.

"Here Joe, I brought two chains with me." Henry grinned. "One for you, and one for me."

"Well, uh, maybe I ought to hold the shotgun on them, for they just might try to break loose, while you're whipping them," Joe stammered, as he looked at the chains. "You let one get away, and we can't afford that to happen again."

"They ain't going nowhere, Joe!" Henry insisted. "You're the one who threatened them, and not me. All I'm doing is following your orders."

"What about Bill's wife?" Joe asked, obviously stalling for time. "She might go and tell the others, and then we might have a war on our hands."

Immediately, Henry went over and caught Liza by the hair of her head, and dragged her across the yard. Then, he kicked her in the stomach, and she fell to the ground, groaning with pain.

"Let her be!" Bill pleaded. "She be jus' a po' ole innocent womern, and she ain't done nothing to you! Beat me to def', if that's what you want'a do, but keep yo' filthy hands off her!" Bill was clearly angry with them.

"Come on Joe, and let's get this over with," said Henry, as he gave Joe one of the chains. "Or, don't you have the guts, to back up your threats."

Joe went over and stood behind Bill for a moment. He hadn't ever been in a fight before, and he certainly hadn't ever beaten an innocent man with a chain.

"Go ahead, Joe!" Henry prodded. "You're the big boss, so go ahead and carry out your threats, like a boss should!"

Then, Joe struck Bill across the back with the chain, and Bill cried out in pain, as blood gushed from where the chain cut deep into his flesh. Again, and again Joe struck him, and the more Joe saw blood the more he hardened his heart against the voice of his conscience. Between the two of them, they soon had the poor slaves beaten almost to death. As it seemed, the more they cried for mercy, the more Joe enjoyed beating them. Henry stopped beating them, when he realized that they had rather die than to tell where Martha was, but Joe continued as though he'd lost all sense of reason.

"That's enough!" Henry told Joe, as he jerked the chain out of his hand. "Let them think it over, and they might remember where she is. I didn't mean for you to kill him."

Throwing the bloody chains down at the Negro's feet, Joe and Henry headed back toward the mansion. When they came to a row of hedge bushes, that flanked the walkway between the smokehouse and the kitchen, Joe suddenly stopped. He held his head in his hands, and threw up violently.

Henry laughed to himself as he went on home. I gave him a good lesson in how to handle slaves, he thought to himself. Maybe he won't be playing the big shot, any time soon.

Still in pain, Liza went over and untied Bill's and the boy's hands, and gently tore the blood-soaked shirts from their backs, then she hung them over the clothesline, for all the other workers to see. Her heart ached for them.

"They went and whooped us free-slaves, didn't they, Liza," Bill said, as he took his hand and wiped the blood from his face. "Oh Lord, he'p Marthie to get a letter scratched out to Mark, and send him on back, fo' they kill the res' of us." Then, he collapsed in Liza's arms.

Liza finally managed to get Bill and the boys back inside, and she gently bathed their backs with warm water, and applied salve to their wounds. It was obvious that they wouldn't be able to work for some time now, yet on the other hand, it wouldn't surprise her, if they were forced to go on to the fields and work today. Joe and Henry's cruelty, had no bounds.

Joe stayed to himself for the rest of the day, and nausea engulfed him, as he thought about the chain as it cut into the Negroes' back. He hardly closed his eyes all night. The following morning, Henry came and knocked on Joe's door, wide awake, and smiling.

"We need to have a little talk," Henry told him. "I've sent the foremen out to search again, but we need to decide what we'll do, if they don't happen to find her. We need to decide what to tell Nate Simpson too."

"Excellent idea, Henry!" Replied Joe. "Come on inside and let's have a cup of coffee, while we plan our strategy."

"Joe, are you feeling all right this morning?" Asked Henry, as they went into the dining room, and sat down at the table. "It couldn't be, that you're upset over what happened yesterday. To the niggers, I mean."

"It's Bertha's cooking, that's what it is," Joe lied. "I get this way after each meal, or when she brews coffee, for her cooking gives me the bellyache. A man can't think straight, with his belly aching. I need to look for another cook, otherwise, I might as well hang it up."

They discussed the situation, and finally decided to tell Nate that she'd run away, but nothing about the freedom papers, or Mark's letters. They knew she couldn't use them anyway. Oh, if they only knew what she had done.

"We'll tell him only what we want him to know, and nothing else," Henry said, as he got up from the table. "But, we must keep our stories straight."

"Agreed!" Said Joe. "Now, you'd better get out there and look after the niggers, for with the foremen out looking for Martha, they'll have a party."

"That they will," Henry laughed. "By the way, do you plan to talk with Bill again today?" Henry asked, just to see Joe squirm.

"Well, uh, I think it's a waste of time," Joe said, as his face suddenly turned pale, "for I don't think they know where she is. If they had known, they would not have taken a beating, without breaking down and telling us. I think she acted on her own, and nobody else knew about her plan."

The days slowly dragged on, while Bill and his boys tried to recover from their wounds, as they wondered if Martha had been able to get word to Mark, or if her and George had been shot along the way, for trying to escape. If they had been killed, it would have been kept a secret anyway, they reasoned.

As for Martha, she didn't know what was happening back home, and she had no way of finding out, or letting them know that she was still alive. She had helped to pass off the time by helping Mrs. Harper around the house, while she patiently awaited a reply from Mark, or his return. At this point, she didn't know if Mark had even received Mr. Harper's letter, or if he ever intended to return home at all. Did he think that much of them after all? She wondered.

It had been two weeks since Mr. Harper mailed the letter. He had written a five-page letter, telling Mark everything that Martha and George had told him.

One morning while Martha was drawing a bucket of water from the well near the edge of the yard she glanced down the road and she saw someone coming toward the house on horseback. Frightened at first, thinking that it might be Henry, or Joe, or maybe the sheriff looking for her, her first instinct was to run into the house and hide. However, when she took a closer look at the way the rider sat tall in the saddle, it suddenly dawned on her, that it was Mark.

"Whooppe, Whooppe, its Mark!" She yelled, as she threw the water bucket down, and ran toward him. "It's me Mark, it's Marthie!" She screamed so loud, until George and Robert came outside, to see what had happened.

Mark galloped toward her, then leaping from his saddle, he ran to her and hugged her real tight, while George and Robert stood watching.

"Wy, that's Mos'a Mark coming there, it sho' is!" Said George, as tears of joy came to his eyes. "Yass'uh, Mos'a Robert, he done went and got yo' letter."

"So it seems," smiled Robert, as Mark and Martha came walking on toward them, hand-in-hand. "Of course, I've never personally met Mark Simpson as far as I recall, but he sure looks like a real fine gentleman."

"He sho' be a fine feller," said George, "and I's thank we mout be some kind'a kinfolks, cousins maybe, fer he sho' is been good to me."

"I'm Mark Simpson, Sir," politely spoke Mark, as he reached out to shake Robert's hand. "I appreciate the letter, even though it was sad news."

"Robert Harper, Sir, and it's my pleasure," Robert smiled pleasantly, as he shook Mark's hand. "I only wish that I had known of this earlier, but I didn't, and I hope the letter wasn't too late, to be of some good."

"I shouldn't have left them in the first place, shouldn't have trusted Joe, and shouldn't have second-guessed my father," Mark replied. "Trying to escape my own hardships, it looks like I've created problems for others who were willing to give their life for me. It's my own fault that it happened, and I pray that God will give me a chance to correct my mistakes."

"Don't blame yo'sef," Martha said softly, "fer adder the way everbid'ee treated you, you sho' needed some res'. We done been through a lot, but nothing like you is been through fer us."

"Mr. Harper, I'd like to rent a horse and buggy, so I can take these folks back home, and find out what's going on," said Mark. "I rented the mare from the livery stable in town, and I'll pay for someone to take her back, that is, if you don't mind."

"No problem," smiled Mr. Harper. "In fact, I just bought a new surrey a few weeks back, and you're welcome to use it, free of charge. And yes, I'll have my foreman return the mare for you."

"I'll return it tomorrow, along with rent for using it, and of course, I want to pay you for housing my friends for all this time," Mark smiled, as he patted George on the back. "I should have known that my father would probably do something like that when he found out that I was gone, but I can't imagine how I misjudged Joe Wilson, so badly."

Mr. Harper shook his head, as he walked toward the barn to tell a worker to hitch a horse to the two-seated buggy, and allow Mark and his friends to be alone for a few moments.

"Mos'a Joe is scade to def' of yo' pappy, fer he changed rail fast, the fus' time that he come to see 'em," Martha explained. "He mus' is be holding sump'um over their head, fer to make 'em change so quick, like they done."

"That adds up, but what I'd like to know, is how this Henry fellow became involved," said Mark. "Where did he come from, and who is he?"

"He come from the pits of hell, if you's axe me," spoke up George. "He be a devil-man, and ten times wuss than yo' pappy is ever been!"

They stood and talked while Mr. Harper was getting the buggy ready, then after spending a few minutes talking with Mr. Harper, Mark and his two friends climbed in the buggy and headed out toward his plantation. As the mare gently trotted along, Mark wondered just how things would be when he arrived, and if they were as bad as Mr. Harper had explained in his letter. He reached into a bag and took out his pistol and stuck it in his belt, for he had no idea what, or whom he might be facing when they arrived.

The sun was setting when they finally arrived at the plantation, and then he began to realize how strange things seemed, for he didn't see anyone in the fields working, or even at their houses. Nevertheless, while George unhitched the horse from the buggy, and put her in a stall, Mark and Martha went on into the mansion. Bertha was cooking supper when Mark walked into the kitchen, and stood behind her for a moment. When she turned, and saw Mark standing there in the kitchen, she was shocked, for she had never seen him before.

"What is you doing in here?" Asked Bertha, in surprise. "If you come to see Mos'a Joe, he ain't here rite now."

"Where is Joe, anyway?" Mark asked. "Is he somewhere around here, in town, or maybe out visiting a neighbor?"

"Him and Mos'a Henry is out looking fer . . ." She suddenly stopped, when Martha stepped into the kitchen. "They be out there looking fer her!"

"It appears to me, that they're looking in the wrong place," Mark smiled, and said. "Martha's right here, alive and well, as you can see."

Bertha grabbed up a butcher knife, and held it up as if she intended to stab Mark with it. "Chappie!" She yelled. "Come in here quick, and hep' me!"

However, her husband didn't come into the kitchen, as she had asked.

"Put that knife down, for nobody is going to hurt you." spoke Mark, in a demanding voice. "All I ask, is that you to tell me where Joe is. Now, where is he?"

"Miss Berthie, you's better do what Mark sez, fer he be the owner of the place!" spoke up Martha. "He be the one, I's told you 'bout."

"Oh Lord, Mos'a Mark!" She howled, dropping the knife to the floor. "Is you raily Mos'a Simpson's boy? Is that who you raily is?"

"At your service, Madam," Mark mockingly bowed. "Now, if you'll gather up your clothes, I'd like for you and your husband to get out of my house."

"Yass'uh, Mos'a Mark," she cried, as she left the room. "We gon'a be on our way soon as I's find my hus'bun, and we's get our rags packed up."

When Joe returned and saw a strange buggy parked in the yard it upset him very much, for he figured that Nate had come to call, and he dreaded having to tell him what had happened. Then, he hurried inside.

"Who's here, Bertha?" Joe asked excitedly, as he rushed into the parlor, and looked around. "Whose buggy is that out there? Do you have guest?"

Then, Mark stepped from the kitchen, to where Joe could see him. "By no means, am I a guest, or I don't think I am!" Spoke Mark, sarcastically.

"Mark!" Joe gasps. "How ni-ice to see you again! Wha, what a nice surprise!" Joe stammered, wondering just how much Mark really knew about what had happened.

"I can imagine how surprised you must be," said Mark, as he stared into Joe's eyes. "You didn't expect to find me here, did you, Joe?"

"Oh, I'm glad you're home!" He blabbered, instantly deciding to lie his way out of everything. "I planned on writing to you tonight, and asking you to come back home, for I can't handle things anymore. Everything fell all to pieces around here, after Elizabeth left me. What hurt so bad, was that she just grabbed up the baby one day, and took off with another man!"

"I don't blame her one bit," replied Mark, unmoved by Joe's phony act of emotion. "Nice try, Joe," he added.

Then, Joe realized that Mark must already know something about what had been going on, and knowing that Mark disliked his father, Joe decided to shift the blame to Nate Simpson. Maybe that will work better, he thought.

"This is something that your father cooked up," Joe babbled on, as tears really filled his eyes. "You know how he hates you, and how he controls just about everybody in the country. I tell you, it's all his fault, not mine!"

"What did he promise you, great riches and power beyond your wildest dreams?" Mark asked, as he shook his head. "Is that what he did?"

"Mark, I'm real sorry for allowing your father to talk me into doing what I did, and I'll help you to get back at him," Joe whimpered. "He brought a man in by the name of Henry Graham, and I was afraid to challenge that man."

"You're such a liar, Joe, until it makes me sick as a dog, just to look at you!" Mark scolded. "I'm sorry now, that I ever met you, you sorry-bastard!"

"I tried to do what you said, but they wouldn't let me," Joe whined. "It was your father, Ellis Bland, and Henry Graham who set out to destroy you, and they forced me to go along with them. Please believe me!"

"Is that the truth, Martha?" Asked Mark, glancing behind him. "Is Joe really telling the truth about what happened, or is that just another one of his lies?"

There were a moment of silence, then Martha stepped into the hallway, and Joe's face turned ghostly pale.

"Naw'suh, he ain't telling the truf'," she replied. "He had a hand wid what wuz done, 'long wid yo' pappy and Mos'a Henry. They all had a hand in what went on, and Mos'a Joe be the main one, and he made Miss Liz'buth be mean to me, when she didn't want'a be. That's the gospel truf', too!"

"She's a lying nigger!" Joe cried, as he fell to his knees. "I'll swear on the Bible, if that will help you to believe me!"

"Wy, you sorry, low-down bastard!" Yelled Mark, as he took his foot, and kicked Joe in the face, bursting his nose. "See how fast you can get your butt out of my house! And, don't ever let me lay my eyes on you again!"

As Joe turned to leave, Henry Graham knocked on the door, and Joe almost fainted, when he heard Henry call out to him.

"Joe!" Henry called out. "Are you in there?"

"Yes, he's in here. Come on in!" Mark called back.

Upon entering the room Henry noticed a strange expression on Joe's face, and then he knew that something was wrong when he saw Joe's nose bleeding, and a stranger standing there with a pistol in his belt. Henry had never met Mark before, however, when he saw Martha standing behind him, he then realized that this must be Mark Simpson. But, how did she manage to get word to him, Henry wondered, as he stood speechless.

"So you must be Henry Graham, I gather," said Mark, not even bothering to introduce himself. "Is that your name?"

"Yep, Henry Graham's my name," he coldly replied. "And, who are you, if I may ask? Would you happen to be Mark Simpson?"

"Joe was telling me, how that you and my father conspired to cheat me out of everything that I owned," said Mark. "He claims that he's innocent of any wrong doings, and he claimes that it's all your fault. Is that right, Henry?"

"Wy, you sorry bastard!" Henry yelled, lunging at Joe, and knocking him to the floor. "I'll kill you, for that!" Then, they began fighting.

Then, picking up a chair, Mark quickly smashed it to pieces across their heads. "Get out of my house, both of you!" Mark bellowed.

With blood coming from a deep gash in Henry's head, they both quickly ran outside. Mark knew that they had mistreated the Negroes, but had he known the truth, as he'd learn later, he would have shot both of them there on the spot.

Martha had gone into the kitchen to make sure that supper didn't burn on the stove, now that Bertha was leaving, and a moment later Mark went into the kitchen and joined her. Then, Bertha came into the kitchen, dragging a large bag of clothes along behind her.

"Whu' is my hus'bun?" She wailed. "If he wuz here, he'd tell you that me and him didn't have nothing to do wid what went on 'round here. Yo' pappy sont us here to wuk' in the house, and that's all we's know."

"I understand, and I know you're telling the truth, but I don't want you around here anymore," Mark said kindly. "Now, do you understand?"

"Yass'uh, I's sho' do una'stan," she replied. "Me and Chappie ain't got no place to stay at, fer yo' pappy knows that we's seed what went on here while you wuz gone, and he gon'a kill us. Will you not let him kill us?"

"Don't worry, Bertha," Mark smiled. "I promise not to let anybody hurt you, or your husband, for Martha has already told me about you folks."

"Then, I's 'spose what the tuther niggas sez is the truf'," she smiled, and replied. "Then, you's do treat niggas, like they wuz human-folks."

"That's what I've been trying to tell you ever since you's been here, but you wouldn't listen to me," Martha spoke up.

The fear in Bertha's eyes tore Mark apart. "Bertha, stay here and fix us some supper," Mark told her sincerely. "When Chappie comes home, I'll try to work out something. Forget what I said to you earlier, and I'm sorry,"

"Thank you, Mos'a Mark," Bertha smiled. "And Marthie, I's sorry fer the way Mos'a Joe, and Mos'a Henry went and treated yo' brother Sam, I's sho' is."

Martha quickly turned, and looked at her. "What wuz that you's said 'bout Sam?" Martha asked. "Would you tell me what they went and done to him?"

Realizing that Mark and Martha knew nothing about what had happened, she began to cry uncontrollably. "That sorry bunch went and hung'd yo' brother in that walnut tree, down next to the barn," she told them, as she pointed toward the barn. "They sez that he wuz messing wid Henry's ole ugly wif'."

Mark held Martha as she cried, but for Mark, tears would not come. He'd become so consumed with grief, until all he could do at the moment, was simply stand there and hold Martha, while she cried.

The sun was now almost down, and Mark wondered why the workers hadn't started doing the chores for the evening. It's strange he thought, for I didn't even see any of them when we first arrived.

"Bertha, where are all the workers?" He asked, seriously. "They need to get the chores done before it gets dark. Do they always work this late?"

She hadn't seen any of them for several days, and she hesitated for a few moments, trying to think of an easier way to tell him. Then slowly turning, she looked at Mark, as tears trickled down her face.

"I's raily don't know whu' they be at," she began, "and I's don't know if they is dead, er 'liv. They aw'mos beat Bill and his boys to def', fer not telling them whu' Marthie wuz. I's ain't seed none of 'em fer three, er foe' days, and Mos'a Joe, he been out looking fer 'em all day."

"I's got'a find Mammy and Pappy, and see if they is still liv'," Martha cried, as she headed toward the front door. "Mark, will you hep' me find 'em?"

"Of course I will, for this is awful," he told her. "I had no idea that all this had happened, or I would have killed Joe and Henry, while they were in the house. They're gone now, but their day will come!"

They left Bertha sobbing, as they headed toward where the Negroes lived. The door to the house in which Bill's family lived was standing wide open, and they didn't see anyone in the other houses either. And, they hadn't seen George since he went to put the horse in a stall, for he was searching for the other workers as well. He had an idea where they might be hiding, that is, if they were still alive, but even then, they wouldn't dare return until they had been told that the coast was clear, and George knew that.

"Reck'n whu' they all is?" Asked Martha. "Does you thank that they wuz all kilt, like Berthie sez my brother wuz?"

"I hope not," replied Mark. "All we can do now, is to hope they managed to escape, and that we can find them, before any real harm comes to them."

"That's it!" Martha said, forcing a smile. "They is all looking fer me. And, I's bet Li'jah is rite in the middle of the bunch, too!"

Then, they heard someone talking, in a low voice. "Marthie, this here is me, Li'jah, and I's hiding rite over here. Is you sho' that's you, Marthie?"

Martha and Mark saw Elijah hiding behind some bushes, then Martha ran and threw her arms around him, and they both stood and wept pitifully.

"Li'jah, is Sam dead, like Berthie sez?" She asked, as they stood there holding each other tight. "Is it the truf'? Please say that he ain't dead!"

"He sho' be dead," Elijah sighed. "They hunged him in that walnut tree, then they shot him full'a holes, wid him crying and bag'n fer mu'cy."

"Why in God's name did they kill him?" Mark asked, although he had already heard it from Bertha. "He was the type of man, who didn't bother anybody."

"They sez he wuz fiddling 'round wid Mos'a Henry's wif', but it wudn't the truf'," he replied. "Berthie give him a piece of cornbread fer killing a chicken fer her to cook, and they ketched him eat'n the bread. We all 'bout starved to def', fer they won't give us nothing to eats."

"My God!" Mark sighed, and asked. "What got into them, to cause them to do such things? Have they lost their minds?"

"I's hate to say this, but yo' pappy made 'em treat us like that, and it wuz him, that shot Sam," Elijah replied. "I's hate that I's had to say that."

"I might have known that he had a hand in it," Mark grimaced. "Elijah, do you know where your parents are hiding, or if they are still alive?"

"I's fix'n to axe you the same thang," he replied. "Pappy sez fer me to run and hide, adder they kilt Sam, and aw'mos beat him and Mammy to def', wid a piece of chain. The reason that I's come back, wuz to see if they wuz still 'liv, but so fer, I's ain't seed 'em, nowhu'."

"Elijah, did they ever whip you and Sam with a piece of chain, like they did your parents?" Mark asked, dreading his reply.

"Yass'uh, they sho' did," he replied. "Rite adder Marthie left, Joe and Henry beat all of us rail bad, and kicked Mammy in the guts too."

"The devil you say!" Shouted Mark. "Was Joe really all that cruel, even though he promised to look after you folks?"

"Yass'uh, they took tun's whoop'n us," Elijah sighed. "They whooped po' ole Pappy, 'til the bones wuz sticking out'a his back, but he didn't tell 'em whu' Marthie wuz gone to. He couldn't walk fer a week."

Neither of them said anything for a moment, as they watched Henry's wagon speeding down the road, with Henry and his wife sitting in the wagon, and Joe running along behind. Maybe its best this way, Mark thought, for they would have been killed here tonight, had they not left.

Though it was almost dark, when Elijah turned around, Martha saw the deep gashes in his back that were made by the pieces of chain, when he was being whipped.

"Lord'ee Mark, look at Li'jah's back!" Martha wailed. "Look at what them ole fools went and done to him!"

"That ain't nye as bad as Pappy's back is," said Elijah. "When you see him, you's gon'a see bones sticking out'a his back, ribs sticking out'a his side, and his arms 'bout beat off. He sho' do look awful, Mammy too."

"I simply can't take any more of this," Mark sighed, feeling sick at his stomach. "Let's find your parents, for I'm sure that they're hiding around here somewhere."

Martha started walking down a road that led across the fields toward the creek, and as soon as Elijah stepped out into the road, he and Mark followed her down the road. Martha was several yards ahead of them, and then she let out a loud, pitiful scream.

"Lord'ee Mark! Lord'ee Li'jah!" She screamed. "Oh Lord, come here rail fas', fer I's done found 'em!"

Running to her, Mark could see that she was just about ready to pass out. She was clammy, and reeling on her feet, as she stood pointing toward what had to be the most gruesome sight he had ever seen. In the twilight, Mark saw two bodies hanging upside down from a tree, and there was no doubt, that these were the bodies of Bill and Liza.

Martha collapsed in Mark's arms, and Elijah ran across the field to where the two bodies were hanging from a tree, near the edge of the road.

"Oh Lord, have mu'cy on us!" Elijah screamed. "It's Mammy and Pappy, and they been hung'd, and shot full'a holes! Oh, Jesus God, hep' us!"

Mark eased Martha down on the ground, and ran to Elijah's side. Then, he saw the bullet-riddled bodies of Bill and Liza, hanging there in grim display. The gashes in Bill's back, were gruesome evidence, even there in the twilight, of the horrendous beatings he'd suffered, and Liza's head had been smashed.

"Whoever did this to them, is not human!" Mark choked. "And, whoever did this, will pay dearly for what they did, with their own life," he vowed.

"Lord'ee Mark! Marthie and me is the only one's that's left in our family, wid Mammy and Pappy dead," Elijah sighed. "Is Marthie gon'a be aw'rite?"

"She'll be all right in a few minutes," Mark assured him. But he knew that she would never be all right. Nothing would be all right again, not even himself, for a part of him now dangled from that tree, and he felt like his soul had vanished.

While Elijah went to hitch a pair of mules to a wagon to haul the bodies away for burial, Mark took Martha back to the house to be with Bertha, in this time of sorrow. He took some quilts from a closet, in which to wrap Bill and Liza's body. His first thought, was to bury them near the small church that he'd built for the Negroes, but they were like family to me, he thought, and I want them to rest eternally near where I live. Even though Mark didn't know, Henry had made the Negroes plow up the graveyard, and tear down the rocks that once stood as headstones, and fill the church with hay.

Mark went back and sat down on the ground, near where his closest friends still hung from a tree near the edge of the road, and wept bitterly. Although his father had stripped him of everything, and branded him as a nigger lover, and his hopes and dreams of marrying Carolyn Bland were crushed under the heel of her father, nothing hurt him more than what had happened here. Then, after he and Elijah cut the bodies down, and wrapped them in quilts, they gently put them into the back of the wagon, then Mark led the mules slowly back up toward his mansion. It was already dark now, so Mark went to the well house and got a kerosene lantern, lit it, then went back to the wagon.

"Elijah, where did they bury Sam? Mark asked. "Were you there, when he was buried?"

"Naw'suh, I's don't know whu' he wuz bur'ed at," he replied. "I's done went and hid, and don't know nothing 'bout what they done wid his bid'ee."

"If it's all right with you and Martha, we'll bury your parents behind my house, and when we find where Sam was buried, we'll move his body there, to be near them," Mark told him. "And, if we don't ever find his grave, then we'll put up a marker near them, anyway."

"Mark, you sho' is a pow'ful good feller, clean to the core, and you's thank as much fer us, as you's do fer yo' own folks," Elijah reasoned. "Yass'uh, you is like kinfolks."

"No, I'm really to blame for all this," Mark wept aloud. "Two precious persons are gone, and I wasn't even around to let them know that I really did care for them, or to tell them how much they really meant to me. They were as black as the darkest night, but their love shined along my pathway as bright as the noonday sun, and their heart was as clean as snowflakes, falling on the face of a newborn baby. I'll go to my grave, regretting that I wasn't here in their time of need, and I won't have a minute's peace of mind, until I personally witness the deaths of all those who were involved in their deaths."

"But, you's did show 'em that you's loved 'em while they wuz still 'liv, and when they died they took that feeling wid 'em, fer Pappy aw'ways sez he gon'a love you like his own boy," Elijah comforted him. "They is sot'n up in Heb'um now, wid their feets dangling in that big river, looking down at you. Yass'uh, they be up there grinning at us, rite now."

Mark and Elijah worked by lantern light, digging two graves only a short distance from the back of his house. Martha and Bertha joined them later for the burial, but before lowering them into their graves, Elijah asked Mark if he would say a few last words over them. Martha had given Mark the letters, and freedon papers when he returned, and he still had them in his pocket.

"You are free at last, Bill and Liza," Mark cried, as he gently placed their freedom papers on their chest. "Rest in peace, my friends, and enjoy an eternity of freedom, which is somethng that you didn't enjoy while on earth."

Martha and Bertha went back inside, while Mark and Elijah heaped a mound of dirt over the graves. When the mules were put back in their stalls, Mark and Elijah went back inside the house, and joined them.

"I's worried 'bout Chappie," Bertha sighed, "fer I's ain't seed him all day. Will somebid'ee hep' me look fer my hus'bun?" She pleaded.

"Elijah and me are going to look for the others, and we'll look for your husband too," Mark told her. "Get the latern Elijah, and we'll go and look for the others, that is, if they're still alive."

They went to the barn and looked around, but they didn't see or hear any of them. "Where do you suppose they went, anyway?" Asked Mark. "Surely, Joe and Henry didn't kill all of them, when they killed your parents."

"Wait jus' a minute!" Elijah smiled, and told him. "Hep' me climb up on top of the barn, fer I's jus' thunk'd of sump'um."

Although it was now well past midnight, Mark gave Elijah a boost, and he took the lantern and climbed up to the very peak of the barn roof. He began to slowly swing the lantern from side to side, as if giving a signal, while he called out in a loud voice, as though he expected someone to hear him.

"Come on back, fer the Mos'a is here!" He called. "Come on home, fer we is saf' now!" Mark's heart broke, as he thought of the love these Negroes had for each other. Even white persons, don't have that kind of love for their own, he thought.

Mark slowly turned to go back to the house, for it was obvious that they were gone for good, or were dead, and this pitiful calling was getting on his nerves. How in the name of God, could anyone be so cruel and mean, to such a humble group of folks as these, he asked himself.

Suddenly, there seemed to be a faint, mournful sound breaking the silence of the night like a chant, or a very sad song. The sound became more audible every minute, and Mark then realized, that Elijah had been giving a signal to the other Negroes that the coast was clear. They had heard Elijah calling and saw the light from the lantern, and climbing from their places of hiding, they began their long march back home.

Mark then let out a joyful cry, and ran down the road to meet the Negroes, who were finally returning home. Although he couldn't understand a word these folks were saying, he threw his arms around two of the men's shoulders, and he proudly walked along with them. Far in the back of this group of sick, weary, and heartbroken slaves, he heard the voice of George saying, "We's coming home, Mos'a Mark! Yass'uh, Mos'a Mark, we's coming home at las'!"

THE ROSE HAS MANY THORNS

Mark's unscheduled return from Ohio, had been a bittersweet turning point in his life. The horror he'd encountered had left him seriously disheartened, and his sincere vow to see that his friends had not died in vain, was all that sustained him now.

Martha and Elijah worked just as hard as ever at the mansion, which they shared with Mark, but much of their spirit was gone, buried with their parents and brother no doubt. Although they never found Samuel's grave, they placed a third marker by their parent's graves as a visual aid for them, and for others who loved their brother.

The plantation was in disrepair when Mark returned, but the freed-slaves seemed to welcome the tedious work restoring it as therapy for their broken hearts, and diminished spirits. Without exception, the Negroes respected and adored Mark, and would have gladly worked without pay, had it been necessary.

The memory of the beatings and starvation, were beginning to fade in light of Mark's kindness and generosity. There was now plenty of food, and another successful harvest would ensure them of more of the same.

Although Mark had not come in contact with Joe or Henry since he ran them off, he had kept up with their whereabouts. Joe had gone back a few times and tried to make up with Elizabeth, but it hadn't worked out. Already mad at him for allowing Nate Simpson to lead him around, when she heard about the deaths of Bill and Liza, her hatred for Joe increased. As for Henry, he was still on the run as he was when Nate first found him, and despised by those in the area who knew how cruel and mean he had been to Mark's workers. Thus far, Mark hadn't done anything to Henry or Joe. or even to his father for what they did while he was away, but the loss of his dear friends still lay heavy on his conscience, and the thought of revenge, was deeply embedded in his heart.

Mark tried to rise above the hatred that he felt for them for what they'd done to his friends, but he could not. Had it not been for the deaths of these real close friends, he might have found a vestige of forgiveness in his heart. But as he looked at the three grave markers, he knew that he would likely burn in hell, for he could not forgive them for their role in this tragedy.

Though Mark's plantation and the residents were beginning to recover, the same could not be said for the South. It was obvious, that its conflict with the Union was growing worse, which was indeed a trying time for this young and struggling nation. Southern states were bound and determined to have their way, and any hope of compromise seemed unlikely, if not impossible.

Rumors of war continued to echo throughout South Carolina, and it sparked mixed emotions among her native sons and daughters. For many, it created fear that their customs and traditions would be destroyed, and would disrupt their present lifestyle. Others welcomed a war, as a means of proving to the Union that it could control individual State's Rights. As for Mark, he stood in the middle, so to speak, for he'd fight to protect his homeland if need be, though he disagreed with what the majority stood for, the right to own slaves.

Abraham Lincoln described the country as "a house divided, half slaves and half free." Much attention was forcused on the North-South situation, but in reality, the nation was divided into three major parts, Northeast, South, and West. They each suffered internal problems, but they each looked at the other parts of the country, as being the reason for their sufferings.

The Northeast and the West saw eye-to-eye on many things, and therefore, they had a natural trade relationship. But the conservative, aristocratic South had little to do with the support and well-being of the Union. Although other sections were somewhat demanding, the South was more vocal in its demands, and left the impression that the South was better than other parts. In short, the South wanted to handle its own affairs, and not comply with Union regulations.

Another year had now passed, and Mark and the Negroes celebrated a kind of life-after-death, as another bountiful harvest was gathered. At last, prosperity was again within their reach, and the many sorrows of the past became stepping-stones to the future. All of his white foremen went to work for someone else right after Mark went to Ohio, and many of the free-slaves left shortly after Nate Simpson came into the picture, for they couldn't work for Joe and Henry. Mark contacted each of them after he returned home, and assured them that they would be paid for working, during the time that he was away.

The day came for Mark to settle up with the banker for the cotton he had sold for Mark, and he asked Martha and her brother to go into town with him to pick up his money, for they were closer now, than ever before. Following the death of Bill, George was placed in charge of supervising Mark's workers, and soon Mark learned to trust him, as he once trusted Bill. Mark planned to have a barbeque to show them how much he appreciated them, and hopefully, get their mind off the past.

"George, I want you to go and tell everybody that they'll be paid for the work they did this year, just as soon as I get back from town," said Mark, as he climbed into the surrey. "And, tell them that we have a barbeque planned for this evening. How does that sound?"

"Sho' sounds good to me!" George smiled. "Does you want me to kill that big ole red hog that we's been feeding all that corn to, the one that's so fat, 'til you can't see his eyeballs?"

"Kill two hogs, if you think we can eat them," replied Mark, winking at Elijah, who was sitting in the back seat, "for we might still be celebrating, when the sun comes up tomorrow. And George, I don't want to make you mad, but if you'll look on a shelf in the well-house, you might find some spirits in a bottle, to help your ole bones work better." They both laughed.

"Mark, can we's have some baked sweet taters, to go 'long wid all that barbeque?" Asked Elijah. "Make him bake a bushel of sweet taters."

"Baked potatoes, for Mr. Elijah too!" Mark chuckled. "Will you eat them all, Sir?" He joked.

"Naw'suh, jus' a belly full, that's all," laughed Elijah. "I's sho' the tuthers will want some too, that is, adder I's get all I can eat."

"Well, I's better get crack'n, fer the way youn's is talking, you's mout starve to def', fo' I's eb'em get that ole hog kilt," said George.

On their way toward town, Mark and Elijah laughed and joked as usual, but Martha seemed quieter than she'd ever been before. This bothered Mark, for she acted like she wasn't feeling well, or was worried about something.

"Martha, are you feeling all right this morning?" Mark asked, as the mare swiftly trotted along. "You act to me, like if something is bothering you."

"Don't know what it tis," she muttered, as tears filled her eyes. "Ever since I's had that dream las' nite, it makes me feel like sump'um bad is 'bout to happen to me, er to somebid'ee else. It makes me feel awful bad."

"Don't worry about that," said Mark, "for bad dreams cause us to feel bad, but remember, dreams aren't real. So try to forget all about it."

"It's hard fer me to 'splain," she replied, "but I's feel like I's felt rite befo' we's found Mammy and Pappy, hung'd in that tree."

"Don't say thangs like that," Elijah scolded, "fer it's li'ble to cause us not to 'joy the party when we's get back. Pappy would say, not to drag the past 'long wid you, and aw'ways look fer sump'um to sang 'bout."

"Yes, he probably would, at that," Mark told her. "He'd probably say for you to pray for better times. Put legs on your prayers, too."

She looked at Mark, and smiled. "Yass'uh, that's 'bout what he'd say," Martha sobbed. "You is rite, bof' of youn's is rite 'bout him."

They had been traveling along for almost an hour, when suddenly a man on horseback came galloping up the road behind them, and Mark glanced back to see whom it might be. Mark didn't know him, however, when he rode up alongside the buggy he called Mark by name, and Mark quickly stopped.

As Mark climbed from the buggy, he intentionally opened the front of his coat, to expose the handgun in his belt. Seeing the handgun, the man quickly dismounted, and identified himself.

"I'm Willie Hendricks, Robert Harper's foreman," quickly spoke the man, as he keenly eyed the handgun. "Mr Harper sent me to give you a message, but George said that you were already on your way to town, so I followed you."

"How are you, Willie, I'm Mark Simpson, and I'm glad to meet you," Mark smiled, and offered his hand. "What kind of message do you have for me?"

"Mr. Harper is concerned for your welfare," Willie began, "and he asked me to warn you of a possible conflict that might lay ahead. He's not positive that anything will really happen at all, and his warning, Sir, is based on the conversations he's overheard between other persons."

"A conflict, you say!" Replied Mark, in a rather confused voice. "What kind of conflict, if I may ask? That seems to be just about all that I've ever had, anyway."

"Well, I hate to have to say this, but according to a rumor that's been spreading around, your father plans to have someone kill that Negro girl, the next time you bring her into town," Willie explained in a low voice, so the others couldn't hear. "Your father claims that you're ruining his name, or something like that."

"I appreciate you warning me," said Mark, "and tell Mr. Harper to come by my place and visit with me sometimes. You are quite welcome too, Willie."

"I'm sorry, but Robert can't walk, for someone took a pot-shot at him, and injured his spine," Willie sadly replied.

"Oh Lord, who would have done a thing like that, for he's one of the most respected farmers in the area," asked Mark, tearfully.

"Nobody has any idea," Willie told him. "He was walking around the edge of the field one morning, and someone must have been hiding in the bushes, and shot him with a rifle. We didn't find him until later that evening, and he's mighty lucky to even be alive. He did hire a Negro man named Ike, just a few days before it happened. Then Ike left the next day, but I really don't think Ike did it. I think Ike left, because he thought he might be accused of doing it, because he's a Negro. Can't be sure of anything, these days, though."

"Well, give him my regards, and tell him that I'll drop by for a visit in the near future," Mark replied.

"I'll tell him, Sir," Said Willie, as they shook hands. "Keep your eyes open while you're in town, and watch your back."

Mark stood and watched Willie ride away, as he searched for an answer to the many serious questions that now cluttered his mind. There was no doubt that his father had made such threats, and if he had talked Joe into doing what he already did, he'd get someone to do this as well, he thought.

Climbing back into the buggy, Mark was a little hesitant about going into town, but he had to collect for his cotton crop. He planned to get some items from the General Store on his way back home but, after what Willie said, he changed his mind. I'll just have to be careful, he reasoned.

"What did that man want wid you?" Asked Elijah, as they rode on toward town. "You's look like you's did, the nite I's took you to see that purdy gal, that you wuz gon'a mar'ee. Do you still 'memer that nite?"

"I remember, and I'll never forget, but this is not like that by a long shot," Mark replied. "He was telling me about Mr. Harper getting hurt."

Realizing that Mark didn't want to discuss the matter, Elijah decided to change the subject. "Is that them taters, I's smell cooking," he asked, in a cheerful voice. "I's bet that's what it tis, and I's can't wait to get back and eat 'em."

"Wy, you ole fool!" Martha laughed. "George ain't eb'em got the hog put on the fire yet, and you know that he ain't never went and baked no taters."

They finally arrived at town, and Mark noticed that everyone began to act in a strange way, all of a sudden. Some of the men climbed on their horses and galloped out of town. Others walked behind the buildings as if they were hiding from someone, and the women and children, hurried inside the stores. Suddenly, what Willie had said, came flashing back across his mind.

A small group of men were standing across the street near the hotel, but as Mark parked the buggy near the bank, they didn't act like it bothered them, because he had the Negroes in the buggy with him. Maybe I'm allowing all this to mess up my mind for no reason at all, he said to himself, as he climbed out of the buggy.

"You two sit right here, while I go into the bank, and don't say anything to anybody, no matter what they might say to you," Mark instructed. "It does seem strange, that so few persons are on the street, but you don't need to worry, for I'll be back in a minute. Elijah, you can sit up front with Martha, just in case that something happens, to spook the mare."

Elijah climbed into the front seat of the buggy with Martha like Mark had told him, and Mark sprinted across the street, to the bank. When he opened the door and walked in the bank, he was surprised not to see a single farmer waiting their turn, and the door to Bland's office stood open. When Bland saw Mark in the lobby, he motioned for him, to come on into his office.

"Well, we meet again, Simpson," Bland said curtly, not even bothering to stand up and offer his hand, as usual. "Have a seat, and I'll be with you shortly."

Mark was rather stunned at Bland's appearance. He had aged so much since their last meeting, and his hands shook as he riffled through some papers that were stacked on his desk. Bland seemed to be a bundle of nerves which caused Mark to almost feel sorry for him, but there was no pity left in his heart for this unreasonable and stubborn man.

"Well, it looks like your farm paid off real well again," finally spoke Bland, as he looked across the desk at Mark. "It hasn't been the best year to grow cotton, and a lot of the farmers didn't do quite so well."

"We all worked very hard," Mark sternly replied. "My workers really do know how to grow cotton, and they certainly deserve all the credit."

"And, you still have a bunch of niggers working for you," Bland asked, in an accusing voice. "I might have known before even asking, for you've always relied on trashy workers, the scum of the earth, if I might add."

"Ellis, you're walking on mighty thin ice with me as it is, and I've made up my mind to do whatever it takes, even physical strength if need be, to make sure that you, nor anyone else walks over me," Mark replied, sternly. "I do have the same workers as I had before, except for those whom the good citizens killed off. If anybody is scum, it's you, Sir, for you lied to me, cheated me out of what I earned, and one day you'll dearly pay for it. Again, you and my beloved father failed to bring me to my knees while I was away, and now that I'm back, I've taken a firmer stand against slavery, than ever before."

Bland's face turned pasty white. "I wish that you'd lean more toward the ways of your father, and his way of thinking," Bland rambled on. "We need a lot of strong men in the South now, more than ever before."

"How could you suggest such a thing, after what my father and that group of henchmen have done to me," asked Mark, very annoyed. "Do you expect me to forget how you and him set out to destroy me, and forget about my friends that were killed. Do you have any idea, what you're asking of me?"

"What I'm saying, is that we need young men like you with guts, to stand up against the Union's demands," Bland nervously explained.

"To be a leader, you must first figure out where you're going, before you ask someone to follow you," Mark pointed out. "If a man don't know where he plans to go, he won't know when he gets there. You must be sure that you are on the right path, before saying that it's right for others."

"But our demands," Bland said weakly. "We need somebody who has enough guts to stand up to the Union, and let it know that we mean business."

"Then you need my father!" replied Mark. "I'm sure that if he, and his henchmen would take a chain to the Union, like they do to the slaves, then the Union would leave us alone. A leather whip, or a piece of chain, is all they think of when a slave steps out of line, so why not treat the Union the same way."

Bland quickly changed the subject. "Carolyn still loves you as much as ever before," he mumbled. "She hasn't spoken to another boy since you left that night. I couldn't allow her to become your wife, and take a chance of having my name completely ruined," he rambled on, his lips quivering.

Mark had not allowed himself to think of Carolyn for many years now, but her father's reference brought everything back in a flood of emotion.

"Wy, you old stupid fool!" Mark snarled. "Her future happiness didn't mean one darned thing to you that night! You might as well have killed both of us, for you ruined both our lives, for the sake of saving your so-called good name."

"But, she's my daughter, and my only child, and I had to look out for her, and protect her as I saw best," he whined.

"Yes, she does need protection from you, not from me!" Mark shouted at him, as he jumped to his feet. "Give me my money, for I can't stand to be around a man like you any longer. You make me sick at my stomach, Mr. Bland!"

Mark picked up his money, and headed back outside, for the very sight of this man, disgusted him. Then, he happened to remember what Willie had warned him of earlier, and he realized that it might not be a good idea to leave the Negroes sitting out there alone any longer.

Just as Mark reached to open the door and go back outside, he heard what sounded like someone screaming. When he stepped outside and looked across the street, he almost fainted. He saw Martha kneeling on the ground, and holding her brother's bloody head on her lap, and he ran as fast as he could to where they were.

"My God, Martha, what happened?" Mark wailed, as he went and kneeled down beside her.

"They went and kilt the las' brother I's had!" She screamed. "They busted his head wid a stick! Oh Lord, the las' one of my family is dead!"

There was no doubt, that the brutal blow to his head had instantly killed him, and for this, Mark was thankful. He gently eased Elijah's head from her arms, let it lay on the ground, and then covered it with his coat. Then he helped Martha back into the buggy, as he thought about what Willie had told him earlier.

"Who did this, Martha?" He asked, as he jerked the pistol from his belt, and looked around. "Would you recognize him, if you ever saw him again?"

"Naw'suh, I's didn't get a look at who done it," she told him. "We wuz sot'n there talking 'bout the barbeque, and he shoved me over in the seat foe' I's knowed what wuz happening, then I's here'd the stick hit him. He fell to the ground wid his head bleeding, and when I's raised up, I's seed a man wid a stick, running 'way. It wuz somebid'ee that looked like Mos'a Joe, but I's ain't rail sho' who it wuz."

"I understand, but did you hear anybody say anything?" He asked. "Could you recognize his voice, if you ever heard it again?"

"Naw'suh, nobid'ee ain't said nothing, and like I sez, all I seed, wuz a man wid a stick, running 'way," she sobbed.

Some men stepped out of the hotel across the street, and stood looking in that direction. A moment later, one of them stepped out into the street.

"What happened to your nigger?" The man yelled. "Did he go to sleep and fall out of the buggy, and bust his head?" Then, they all began to laugh.

"Stop laughing at him, you sorry- bastards!" Yelled Mark, as he fired his pistol into the air. "Which one of you sorry bastards killed him?"

The shot quieted them down, and they stood looking at each other, like as if they were afraid to move. Maybe they're not guilty, and I do need somebody to help lift his body up into the buggy, Mark thought.

"Then, if you fellows aren't guilty of killing him, maybe you'll help me put him in the buggy," Mark said, as tears trickled down his cheeks. "Would one of you fellows give me a hand."

Immediately, the men scattered like a covey of birds. Realizing the men were not going to help him, he decided to try to do it himself. Then, a Negro man walked up to where Mark was trying to lift Elijah's body.

"Mos'a, Suh," spoke the Negro man, as he took off his hat, and tucked it under his arm. "I's been over yon'a wait'n on a feller, and I's be rail glad to he'p you put the boy's bid'ee in the buggy."

"You're very kind Sir," spoke Mark politely, "and I thank you for being kind enough to help me. Did you see it happen, or better yet, did you see who did it?"

"I's ain't want'n to stir up no trouble," replied the man, "but the man that done this, sho' mus' be as mean as he looked."

"Then, you did see who did this, didn't you," replied Mark, as they placed Elijah's body on the back seat.

"Yass'uh, I's seed a man slip up 'hind the buggy wid a stick," replied the man. "The way it looked to me, he wuz gon'a hit the gal, but this feller shoved her out'a the way, and the man hit him."

"Did you know the man who did this, the farm he owns, or which farm he might work on?" Asked Mark.

"I's ain't from 'round here, and don't know nobid'ee," the man explained to him. "Ain't never seed the man foe' today, and ain't seed him adder he run in 'hind that building 'cross the street. Don't know nobid'ee, yet."

"Well, you know me." Mark smiled. "I'm Mark Simpson, and this man was a very dear friend of mine. The girl up there is his younger sister Martha, and they live on my farm." Mark shook the man's hand. "And your name, sir, if I may ask!"

"They calls me Ike," the man replied. "And, Miss Marthie, I sho' is sorry fer what happened to yo' brother."

"Thank you for hep'n Mark put his bid'ee in the buggy," Martha told him. "You's a rail good feller, Ike, and I's hope we meet 'gain one day."

Although he had no doubt that his father was somehow involved, Mark wouldn't be satisfied until he found out who killed his friend. Ike saw what happened, and who did it, and I must learn more, he thought.

"Ike, I hate to keep bothering you with questions, but is there anything else you know about the man who did this?" Mark asked. "Did you hear anybody call his name, or did you happened to hear him say anything at all?"

"Well, him and another feller is been standing over there talking fer a long time fo' you come to town, and I's did hear the man call him Joe," replied Ike.

"Joe!" Mark snapped. "Ike, was he a real tall man with dark brown hair, and a rough-looking face?"

"Yass'uh, that 'scribes him purdy good," he replied. "He wuz rail tall and skinny, like a beanpole, and his face looked mighty rough, too."

"Joe Wilson, that's exactly who it was!" Mark said sharply. "That sorry weasel is still around, and the other man was probably his no-good friend, Henry Graham."

"Mos'a Mark, you's done got me scade now, and I's wush you'd take me wid you to yo' place," Ike said pitifully. "The man done knows that I's seed him kill the boy, and he libel to kill me too. He eyeballed me rail good, fo' he run in 'hind that building. Will you please take me wid you?"

"But who do you belong to?" Asked Mark, as he saw the same kind of fear on his face, as he'd seen on many slaves' faces before. "Who's your master?"

"I's a free-slave wid papers to prove it, and I's come to wuk' fer Mos'a Harper, fer everbid'ee sez he wuz a fine feller," Ike explained. "I's wuk'd fer him 'bout a week fo' he got shot, and 'cause I wuz a new nigga, and wuzn't knowed by nobid'ee, I's thought they mout blame me. Then, I's left."

"Well, who were you waiting to go to work for today?" Mark asked. "You did say that you were waiting for somebody, when you saw this happen."

"I's met Mos'a Johnson this moan'n and he say he'd let me wuk' fer him," he replied. "He say he treats his wuk'urs good, and pays 'em good too, and he wanted me to join his happy bunch. Yass'uh, that's what he say."

"Ephriam Johnson, is that his name?" Mark asked. "Is that his new buggy parked over there across the street?"

"Yass'uh, that be his name," Ike replied. "He sez that he done sot his slaves free, and wanted me to be part of his happy family of wuk'ers."

"Ike, that man told you a lie!" Said Mark, sharply. "He's awful mean to his slaves, and none of them are free. Get in the buggy, and go with me."

Hearing this, Ike climbed into the back of the surrey, sat down next to the body of Elijah, and then Mark sped out of town. Mark knew that if Ike went to work with Ephriam Johnson, he'd never be free again. Why did I bring these folks to town with me in the first place, he asked himself as they rode along, and why didn't I listen to what Willie told me, and take them back home.

Nate Simpson had been hiding in the hotel, watching his son from a window on the third floor. His foreman Bill Walker, who had assisted Joe in killing Elijah, walked in and set a mug of ale on a table in front of Nate.

"I know that you have been looking for Joe, after he did what I paid him to do, and I wonder if you ever found him," said Nate, sipping on the ale, as he stared out the window. "I hate that he killed the wrong nigger, but we'll just have to get that gal later, I suppose. There will be another time."

"Yes, I found him hiding behind that vacant building down the street, and he was trembling like a leaf," Bill replied. "He's standing out there in the hallway now, and still shaking like a scared rabbit."

"Well, bring him in here!" Simpson growled. "I want him to explain to me why he killed the boy, instead of the gal. I paid him to kill her, not him!"

Then his foreman opened the door, and motioned to Joe. When Joe stepped into the room, he was still trembling uncontrollably.

"Mr. Simpson, did, uh, well, did Mark happen to see you?" Joe asked, as his whole body trembled. "Reckon he knew it was us, who killed the nigger?"

"Hey, what did you mean by us?" asked Nate, angrily. "I had nothing to do with killing anybody, for I have proof that I was sitting right here in my room."

"No matter what you say, you're in this as deep as I am, for it was your idea to kill that gal," Joe whined. "You did promise me a hundred dollars if I'd kill her for you, and that makes you just as guilty as I am."

"Hold on a minute!" Said Simpson. "Yes, I told you to kill the gal, but I watched her ride out of town, very much alive." Quickly jumping up, Simpson caught hold of Joe's coat collar.

"You killed an innocent man, and you can't say that I told you to do that. You could hang for what you did."

"Why are you so concerned about which nigger I killed?" Joe asked, as he jerked free of Nate's mighty grip. "When I was out there at Mark's place, you didn't care which nigger I punished, or killed. You're the one who told me to kill that gal, and if I happened to kill the wrong one, you're just as guilty in the sight of the law, as I am."

My fault!" Said Simpson. "I had nothing against that boy, and it looks like you've killed an innocent person. Yep, I'll have to see that our sheriff hears about what you've done here today, for I'm a law-abiding man, you know."

"You're as crazy as a bat!" Joe screamed, as he quickly lunged forward, and caught Nate by the neck. "Like Mark said, you are nothing but a darned fool!"

The foreman intervened then and held Joe's arms behind him. He knew that Joe was angry enough at this point, to kill Nate.

"Joe, you messed up the plan that Bland and me had for taking over Mark's farm, like you've messed up everything in your life, even to your marriage!" Nate snorted. "One more mess up, and you're a dead-man."

A crazed expression suddenly came over Joe's face - one that frightened Nate Simpson - a man who wasn't afraid of anything.

"I'm a real dead-man all right," Joe said, glossy eyed, and trembling, "but you won't get the pleasure of killing me!"

With that, Joe broke away from the foreman, and then hurled himself through a third-story window, to his death on the rock sidewalk below. Nate rushed over to the broken window, and looked down at the street below.

Not wishing to appear shaken by Joe's death, Simpson turned and looked at his foreman, and brushed his hands together, as if brushing off dirt. "That's another worry off my shoulder," he said stolidly, "for sooner or later, that man would have caused me a lot of trouble. I'm glad he's out of my hair."

"I know that his wife left him, but should we notify her, so that she can give him a decent burial?" asked the foreman. "He was human, you know."

"Absolutely not!" snapped Simpson. "And, don't let anybody know that we knew about him killing that nigger. Mark thought a lot of that nigger, and to be perfectly honest, I'm afraid that he'd kill me if he knew that I had a part in what happened. Joe's dead now, let him carry the blame on his conscience to his grave, on with him to hell, even. By the way, let me pay you for the wonderful job you helped Joe to do." He then handed the foreman some money.

When Mark's surrey arrived back at the plantation, George was cooking the hog over an open-pit, while the others did whatever they could do to help him prepare for the feast that lay ahead for this evening. When Mark stopped near the barbeque pit, instead of driving on up to the mansion as he most generally did, and motioned to him, George walked out to see what was wrong.

"I's been sort of worried 'bout youn's," said George, seriously, 'fer a man come by axe'n 'bout you. When I's told him that youn's wuz done aw'ready gone to town, he headed out that way in a rail big hurry."

"I spoke with Willie, and I appreciate your telling him that I was headed into town," replied Mark. "You did the right thing, George, and I appreciate that."

Then, George saw an unfamiliar Negro man sitting in the back seat, and on the seat beside him, was the lifeless body of Elijah.

"Oh, Jesus God!" George screamed. "Is that Li'hah, looking like he done been kilt? Is he railly dead? Is that why he looks like he do?"

The others heard what George said about Elijah, and they quickly gathered around to see what had happened. Then Martha climbed down from the buggy, and went around to the other side, and stood by George.

"Yes, my brother is there wid his head busted op'um, and he be kilt dead too," she told them, pitifully. "It wuz Mos'a Joe, that done it. He tried to kill me, but Li'jah shoved me out'a the way, and the man kilt him."

"Yes, I'm fairly sure it was Joe, and of course, he was acting according to my father's instructions," said Mark, as he climbed out of the buggy, then went over and joined them. "I feel like it's my fault for taking them with me in the first place, after what Willie told me." He then burst out crying.

George placed his hand on Mark's shoulder, "It wuzn't nothing that you went and done, so don't blame yo'sef," he comforted him. "The ole devil done sot out to kill all of Bill's family, and he ain't gon'a tuck his tail 'tween his legs and leave, 'til he kills the las' one of 'em, neither."

"I have to find some way to stop all of this," Mark cried, as the others lifted Elijah from the buggy, and placed him on some burlap bags that they had spread on the ground. "He was my friend, like all of you are, and I'll always feel like it was my fault."

Ike had been sitting quietly in the buggy until now, and then slowly climbing down, he went over to offer his comments.

"I's mout not have no rite to say nothing, but all the way from town you ain't done nothing but blame yo'sef fer what happened," Ike began. "If you's treated him all his lif', like you's done treated me today, that boy sho' is lived a happy lif'."

"That's rite," quickly replied George. "Now, we's got'a dig a grave and bur'e him, and say some purdy words over him, and let the Lord know that he is on his way to be wid his folks again. He wuz a fun-lover, and I's thank he wants us to go on and have a party. Do youn's fellers 'gree wid me?"

"George is rite," Martha spoke up, "fer like he sez', Li'jah would want us to go on and 'joy the party, and that's zackly what we gon'a do."

Mark then reached over and placed his hand on Ike's shoulder. "This here is Ike, and I talked him into coming to live with us," said Mark, "and he is an eye-witness to what happened in town today. I want you folks to treat him well, like I'm sure you will, for he almost didn't get to be here with us."

"That's rite," said Ike, "fer I wuz wait'n to go and start wuk'n fer Mos'a Johnson, when all this happened. Mos'a Mark sez the man wuzn't 'zackly what he say he is, then I's 'cided to come here and live wid you folks."

"Oh Lord, he be nothing but a slave-hater, and slave-killer, and you'd be better off in hell, than to live wid him," said George. "You's better thank the Lord that Mos'a Mark come 'long, and fetched you here."

Mark told the men to carry Elijah's body to where his parents and brother were buried behind the mansion, and Martha went inside to get a new quilt that she had just finished, in which to wrap his body for burial. When she stepped inside, she could tell that Bertha had been crying, however, Martha knew that she had no way of knowing that Elijah had been killed.

"Miss Berthie, I's the only one left in my family now, fer Mos'a Joe went and kilt Li'jah, while we wuz in town," Martha cried, and told her.

"Oh Lord, not the las' one you's had lef!" Bertha wailed, and threw her arms around Martha, and they both wept together. "You the only one left now, and I's bet they gon'a be adder you next."

"Come on wid me, Miss Berthie," Martha said softly. "Come and stand by me, while we's bur'e my brother. Then, we's gon'a 'joy the party, jus' like I know that Li'jah wants us to do."

Elijah was buried next to a grave in which his brother Samuel's clothes and personal belongings had been buried in his memory. Thus far Sam's grave had not been found, and nobody really knew what happened to his body.

Though heavyhearted at Elijah's untimely death, the Negroes ate George's delicious barbecue, and dedicated the sweet potatoes to Elijah's memory. When everyone had finished eating the barbeque, and Bertha had placed some pies on the table, Mark told them that it was time for everyone to be paid.

Mark took half the money he had gotten for the cotton, and divided it among the workers, in equal shares. He included Ike as well, even though he hadn't done any work at all, for Mark wanted him to feel welcome.

"Mark, I's sho' do thank you fer the money," said George, as he grabbed hold of Mark's hand, and shook it. "You's the only white feller that I's know that pays a nigga fer wuk'n, and I's sho' proud of you too."

"No, it's I, who should thank you folks," Mark told them. "If it hadn't been for you good folks, we wouldn't have a reason to celebrate. I won't ever be able to thank you folks enough, for what you've done for me."

Bertha turned to Martha, and whispered in her ear. "He be the bestest man I's ever seed, and I's wush sump'um would come 'long to make him happy. Maybe a purdy womern fer a wif' and a house full of snotty-nosed chil'uns, too."

Mark's personal life however, was a non-issue at this point, compared to the many events that were beginning to unfold around him. As it had threatened to do since back in 1830, South Carolina withdrew from the Union in December of 1860, and by March 1861, Mississippi, Florida, Louisiana, Alabama, Texas and Georgia had also withdrawn from the Union. These states were soon known as The Confederate States of America, and they immediately elected Jefferson Davis as President, with its temporary headquarters being set up in Montgomery, Alabama. Although Mark was not involved in politics, he automatically became a citizen of this newly formed government, and his primary concern, was for those slaves he had set free. He feared that this new government might not recognize their freedom papers as being legal. Mark was no longer a citizen of the Union, and he now stood at the mercy of a group of leaders whom he knew for a fact, would be upholding the use of Negroes as slaves.

The average citizen knew very little about the politics which had kindled this fire between the North and the South, and many went about their business uninformed, or under-informed about the real issues. Each part of the country had its own theory as to what was causing the conflict, and seemed to have the solution to the problems at hand, however, neither side was willing to give in, for fear of appearing weak in the sight of others. The way it seemed to Mark, neither side intended to budge, and war would probably be the only solution.

The General Store, which was owned my Mr. Wilson, was a place where folks not only bought supplies, but learned about things that were going on all over the community, and the entire country as well. Although most of the products he sold were guaranteed to be genuine, the same couldn't be said for the information one might gather at this public meeting place. Nevertheless, no matter what a person might have to say, good or bad, they were most likely to find someone who was willing to listen to them, and just as likely to find someone who took what they said as being true.

Mark had gone to the store to pick up some supplies, and as usual, while he was there, Mr. Wilson began filling him in on the latest gossip. It became obvious to Mark, that Mr. Wilson had been brainwashed by politicians, just like most everyone else in the South had been.

"Well, we finally pulled out of the Union, like we threatened to do about thirty years ago, and now we can do as we please," said Wilson, as Mark came into the store. "How do you feel about our new government, and the fact that we won't have to bow down to the Union, and kiss it's butt, every time that we want to do something?"

"Sir, it depends on one's personal point of view, I suppose," Mark spoke in a stern voice. "As they say, a picture always looks good to the person who painted it, but the buyer always looks for flaws, before he invests his money. Withdrawing from the Union might look good to the politicians who caused it to come about, but that doesn't mean it's best for our country, or that everyone should agree with their decision, simply because they say that it's best for us."

"I understand what you're saying, but the primary reason for electing men as leaders, is so that they can make decisions that we're unable to make, and take a stand for what they think is best for everybody," he rebutted. "And, as citizens, we must stand by their decisions, regardless to the outcome. Do you agree with that? Isn't that what leaders are for, anyway."

"In a way, yes," Mark replied. "But there comes a time when we citizens should be notified ahead of time of pending decisions, how they will help our country, and yes, how they might hurt us in the long run as well. I honestly think that it should have been put to a vote, and let the citizens decide for themselves, for all of us will be affected by their decision in some way."

"I disagree with you, for I trust our leaders to make decisions that are best for us and our country, and you should too," Wilson told him.

"The decision to withdraw from the Union, was made by greedy politicians who didn't even stop and consider the end results, or how that the average citizens felt about it," Mark pointed out. "Seems to me, they should have informed us citizens ahead of time. Many of those living up there in the mountains of the Pickens and Greenville Districts of South Carolina, probably don't even know that we even withdrew from the Union. And they probably won't know, until they are called up to fight for somethng that they don't even understand. That's the point I wish to make."

By this time, others had come into the store, and were listening to their discussion. When it seemed as though Mr. Wilson didn't have a reply at the moment, one of them spoke up.

"Excuse me, Mr. Simpson," said one of the men. "If you don't mind, I'd like to ask you a question."

"Go right ahead, Sir," Mark replied, very politely. "I might not answer your question in the way you'd like, but I'll answer honestly, and according to how I feel in my heart, and of course, you have a right to disagree."

"Now that we're no longer a part of the Union, what will happen to those niggers, that you bought and set free?" The man asked. "You know the South is known for upholding slavery, and I wonder if they will become slaves again."

"Let me clear up something for you, then I'll answer your question," he replied. "I don't have any "niggers" working for me, but I do have Negroes on my payroll. Since so many of them have suffered and died at the hands of the upstanding citizens of this community, I consider it disrespectful to address them as being 'niggers'." And Sir, I wish you wouldn't either."

"This was once a slave-state, and now it's a slave-country, because we no longer belong to the Union, and the main reason we left the Union, was so that we would be allowed to use niggers for slaves," the man pointed out. "Do you plan to buck against The Confederate States of America, like you have those of us who upheld slavery? Do you think that you are big, and powerful enough now, to take on all the southern states?"

"Sir, I'm not bucking against anybody, or anything," Mark rebutted. "In my opinion I still have rights of my own as a citizen, even though we might be going under a different name. I don't know all that went on between leaders of the North and the South to bring this about, but I'm sure there was more than just a disagreement over a bunch of Negroes. I set my slaves free, and they'll remain free as long as they're on my farm, and I'm alive."

"We'll see!" snipped the stubborn man. "You might as well get ready to burn those so-called freedom papers, for they're no good to the niggers now."

This heated discussion continued on for quite awhile, and the longer Mark and this man talked, the more Mark realized that this man had been brainwashed by politicians, like most other citizens of the South. He decided that it was useless to try to explain something to a person, unless he was willing to look at both sides, and be at least reasonable. So, Mark paid for the supplies he came to get, went and climbed into his buggy, and headed back toward home.

Later, while on his way back home, Mark admitted to himself that this new form of government would indeed, have an impact on the way he felt about using Negroes as slaves, and his reason for freeing them as well. The South wouldn't listen to the Union, and now that it had withdrawn from the Union, he knew for a fact, that it wouldn't listen to him, he reasoned.

Even after he arrived at his plantation, what the man said at the General Store still bothered him very much, and he wondered how many other persons in South Carolina shared this man's views. Mark liked George, almost as much as he once liked Bill, and that evening when George returned from the fields, he decided to discuss the matter with him.

"George, things are looking mighty bad since South Carolina withdrew from the Union, and I must admit that it has begun to disturb me an awful lot," he told George. "Unless the South and the Union are able to iron out their great differences, I'm afraid it's going to lead to war. It seems like everybody is eager to fight, but nobody seems willing to sit down like men and discuss the problem, or listen to the other person's point of view."

"I's see what you mean, but they been fussing fer a long time, and so fer, nothing ain't happened," George replied. "It reminds me of two tomcats wid their tails tied together, and hanging over a clothesline. They scream, and yell at the other'n, but neither one can't figure how they got in a mess like that, and they can't thank of no way to get loose."

"Like I told you, when South Carolina withdrew from the Union, I was awful afraid we'd be in trouble, and now that the other states have joined, it does bother me quite a bit," Mark explained. "If this thing does lead to a war, I wanted you and the others to be on the lookout for almost anything to happen, for at this point, I have no idea how it might affect you folks."

"Well, if a war do come, it sho' will be hard on us niggas, fer we gon'a feel the blunt of thangs," George replied. "I's hear that the giver'mut told the South to run the slaves off, put 'em on a boat, and send 'em back to whu' they comes from. Yass'uh, the slave is gon'a feel the wuss part of whatever do happen, if a war comes."

"How do you figure that?" Mark asked. "It's the white folks who are mad at each other, so how do you figure that it's going to hurt you folks?"

"The fus' thang, its gon'a be a lot like digging our own grave," George slowly replied. "If we's hep' the South win this war, then we gon'a be put in chains and shackles, and if we's don't fight, then the South is gon'a kill us fer sho'. They sez that being dead, ain't sump'um that nobid'ee never learns to like, no matter how it comes, and I's 'gree wid 'em, too."

"Well, the way things look now almost anything might happen, and it sure wouldn't surprise me, if we were in war before we even get another cotton crop planted," Mark worried. "According to what I hear, South Carolina is willing to go to war, even though the other states don't join us."

They continued discussing the situation for quite some time, then George went home, but Mark sat alone until late that night, trying to figure out what part he'd have to play, if a war really started. Each time he and George met, it seemed like they always ended up discussing the possibility of war, and how it might affect the free-slaves, and Mark as well.

Mark had no way of knowing just how close he'd been in predicting the war, for on April 12, 1861 Confederate troops from South Carolina fired on Union troops that were stationed at Fort Sumter, which lay in the harbor of Charleston. On the very next day, the garrison was forced to surrender to confederate troops, and on April 15, Lincoln ordered that all the nations laws be enforced. This order by Lincoln, was taken by the South to be a declaration of war.

Shortly thereafter, four additonal states joined The Confederate States of America. Arkansas, Virginia, North Carolina and Tennessee. Up until this point, the Union chose to sit back and see what the South would do next. When these other four states joined the Confederacy, the Union realized that it now faced a serious situation. For the past several years the South had shipped a greater portion of its products to Europe, and it thought that these countries were their friends, and would offer support during a war. Lincoln had reasons to predict the same thing, therefore, on April 19; he ordered the blockade of all southern ports. With very few factories in the South, this really posed a problem for the Confederacy, and even before the war really got started, there were some doubts about the South winning in an all-out war. And, their friends from Europe didn't offer to help the South, for they wanted to wait and see if the South showed a possibility of winning in this war, before they offered any support. They didn't want to end up supporting a loser.

Then on May 21, 1861, Richmond, Virginia was chosen by the Confederacy to become its new Capitol, which greatly bothered the North. There was no doubt that a greater concentration of southern troops would be situated dangerously close to the North. The war was really raging on, however, until spring of 1862, volunteers had done the fighting, and many lives had already been lost in this bloody conflict between two neighbors.

The spring of 1862 brought a new surge from both sides. Fort Donaldson fell to the North, taking a grim total of 4,500 lives. Both sides suffered a greater loss at Shiloh. On April 16, the

Confederacy began drafting young men for service. This really concerned Mark Simpson, since every able bodied man between the age of 18 and 35, were ordered to sign up for at least three years of active duty. Though he had no desire to go to war, there was no way short of his deserting to avoid it, and he had no intention of doing that.

Mark's chief concern was for the Negroes, and he wondered what would happen to them, if he were called into battle. He knew they could survive as farmers without his help, but were not able to defend themselves, should trouble arise between them and white men. Though he disagreed with the reason for the war, if drafted, he'd fight to defend his homeland. He appreciated the Negroes for the concern they had for him, and to show his concern for them, he decided to call them all together one day, and explain everything to them.

Early one morning, Mark stood on the front porch and looked out across a sea of grim faces, as the Negroes stood quietly in front of his mansion. Many things crossed his mind, and he felt tears coming to his eyes, as he thought of how loyal they had been to him over the years.

"Well, the war is getting out of hand," Mark began, "and if things keep going as they are now, everybody is going to suffer. Although I disagree with the reason we're fighting, I hate not to fight for my homeland. Now that they have started a draft, it looks like I'll have to fight, after all."

"But, ain't the North our enemy?" Asked George, very seriously. "Ain't we's 'sposed to kill off the enemy, befo' they come down here and kill us?"

"I don't like the word "enemy", George," Mark replied. "This is sort of like two brothers, or two neighbors fighting over something they disagreed on, instead of sitting down and trying to settle their differences like men. This is a war that should have never gotten started in the first place, and I think it's going to bring pain and sorrow that will continue to hurt us down through many generations to come."

"The way you's talk, you don't want'a fight," said George, "but the big quess'un in my head, is you gona'a jine in and fight wid the tuther fellers?"

"Well, if they draft me I'll have no other choice but to fight," replied Mark sadly. "No matter which side wins, both sides will lose something that they will never be able to regain. Let me put it this way. Our leaders claim we are fighting for State's Rights, but the majority of those who are fighting and dying out there on the battlefields, don't even know what that means."

Martha was standing in the doorway behind Mark, and she began to cry when Mark indicated that he might have to go war. She still remembered what happened to her family when he went to Ohio a few years ago, and she felt that the same thing would happen, if he happened to leave again.

"But none of us wants you to jine the war, jus' so that you can get shot and kilt," she wailed. "It ain't yo' war in the fus' place, and you gon'a be fight'n fer sump'um that you ain't had nothing to do wid. Can't you tell 'em that you don't like the war, and that you ain't gon'a fight?"

"Like it or not, if I have to go, I will," he responded. "On the other hand, the North hasn't started drafting men yet, and I suppose that I could go back to Ohio and stay until the war is over. I wouldn't be fighting for something that I don't believe in, which is, to make slaves of other human beings. That's what most folks claim this war is about, but in my opinion it's a political struggle. A rich man's war, and a poor man's fight."

They continued talking for quite awhile, then the Negroes went on to work as they normally did, but they were obviously heartbroken because Mark finally said that he would go and fight, even though it meant leaving them alone. The war was just as confusing to them as it was to Mark, and after he explained to them how serious the war had already become, and the probability of his being killed in the war as well, it caused them even more sorrow and grief.

Several of Mark's friends had already volunteered for duty, and now that the draft had started, other farmers in the community wondered why he had not reported for duty as well. The sad part about this war is that it wasn't an all-out battle between everyone in the South, and everyone in the North, as one might suppose. There were just as many in the South who opposed this war as there were who supported it. Father's disagreed with their sons, brothers disagreed with each other, and sometimes more conflicts could be found in the home, than was being experienced on the battlefields. Though Southerners were reluctant to admit to such facts, there were probably more average citizens in the South who opposed the war, than were those who agreed with it. Hardly anyone knew anything about the war, or how it got started, other than what leaders, and greedy politicians had told them.

The war raged on, and Mark realized that he must either sign up for duty, or stand a chance of being put in jail, or even killed for not obeying orders to join the Confederate Army. He spent several sleepless nights, and many weary days, pondering the decision in his heart. Then one morning while eating breakfast, he decided to tell Martha what he had finally decided to do.

"Well, I've finally made up my mind about the war," he began, "and I've decided not to leave the South, no matter what happens during this war."

"Whoopee! Thank the Lord!" Martha yelled, as she went over and gave him a hug, as he sat at the table. "That's the bestest news that I's ever hear'd!"

"I hate to have to say this, but I really don't think the South has any chance of winning this war, for the North has too many advantages over us at this point," Mark admitted. "Yet on the other hand, the draft has given a new twist to the war, and now we'll have more men fighting on our side. I'm sure I'll be killed if I don't report for active duty, and I'll be taking a great chance of being killed if I go to war, so I've decided to fix up a place here on my farm, and hide out until it's over."

"That sho' do sound good to us," spoke up Bertha, as she poured him some more coffee. "Me and Marthie is done 'scussed that, and we's bof' been hoping that you wouldn't go off to war, jus' to get yo'sef kilt."

Mark now stood at a crossroad, for he no longer had the Union on which to rely for support in his crusade against slavery. It was unlikely that he'd be able to buy his way out of the war like some were doing, because of the way he had rebelled against the South prior to the beginning of the war. He would have to go ahead and enlist, to avoid getting into trouble, even if he decided later on to change his mind, and hide out until the war was over. To complicate matters even worse, his brother-in-law, Susan's husband, was in charge of the District Recruiting Office, and if nothing else, Susan and her father would be watching very careful to make sure that Mark enlisted.

Although Nate Simpson hadn't spoken to Mark since Mark returned from Ohio a few years ago, because of Mark's stand against slavery, Nate didn't imagine that his son would allow himself to be drafted. Nate was really shocked when Susan and her husband John Phillips, came to visit one day, and John told him about Mark enlisting.

"Nate, I suppose that you've already heard about Mark signing up for duty with the Confederate Army," John stated. "He sure has guts to go to war and fight for our rights to own niggers as slaves, after he fought so long to set his slaves free. To me, that means that he's changed his mind since we pulled out of the Union, and now we have him on our side at last."

"John, you've got to be joking!" Simpson jeered. "He wouldn't join with us under any circumstances! That bleeding heart ain't about to fight in order for us to keep slavery in tact, no way at all."

"Say what you like, but I personally swore him in the other day, and told him that he'd be notified when to report for duty," John replied. "Could be more to him, than you know. If he'll fight as hard for us to keep the slaves, as he's fought to free them, he'll be an asset to our ranks."

"Well, I'll be darned!" Simpson smiled. "I can't imagine him going to war to defend our rights to own slaves. That's not like him at all."

"It surprised me too, but a man has the right to change his mind, and I'm glad he did," replied John. "When the war is over, and we have a legal right to use niggers as slaves, he'll become one of the largest slave owners in the State of South Carolina, with all those niggers he has on his farm."

Later on that evening after Susan and her husband went back to their home near town, Mrs. Simpson decided to ask Nate to take her to visit Mark before he reported for duty. Although he hadn't told her that Mark had signed up with the Confederate Army, she had overheard John telling him about it, and now, maybe he'd look at Mark in a different light, she hoped.

"Nate," she begged, "will you take me to visit my son this weekend? I'm growing worse each year, and I might not live until this war is over, and I'd like to see him again before he has to report for duty. The way our young men have been killed here lately, his chance of coming back alive, is slim."

"Julie, how did you know about that?" Asked her husband. "I didn't tell you about him enlisting. Where did you hear about that?"

"Well, while I was talking with Susan, I overheard John telling you about it, and that's how I know," she replied. "He is our son, and I am concerned very much for his well-being, even though you might not be."

"How dare you eavesdrop on our conversation!" He bellowed, as he quickly stormed out of the room, avoiding her plea to take her to see her son again.

In the meantime, while Mark was waiting for his notice to report for duty with the Confederate Army, he had been taking care of business. He discussed a plan with George and Ike in private, on how he planned to avoid going to the war. Other than for these two men, along with Martha and Bertha, no one else knew anything about what he had planned. He had talked with Robert Harper and had Ike's name cleared, and Ike was no longer accused of shooting Robert.

Robert's attacker had been none other than Chappie, who had been paid by Simpson to kill Harper for helping to bring Mark back home. Needless to say, that Chappie's unsuccessful attempt on Robert's life had cost him his own life as well, a fact that his wife Bertha, would never know. According to what Mark had heard, Nate had Henry to kill Chappie, to keep him quiet.

Following Mark's orders, George and Ike had been working every night for about two weeks now, digging out a small room underneath the kitchen of Mark's mansion. They worked during the night, to prevent the others from finding out about what they were doing, and they dumped the dirt into an abandoned well to hide the evidence. When others asked why Ike and George slept every day, Mark told them that he had them standing guard at night, in case Union troops tried to attack them. The only access to the room was by way of a trap door in the kitchen floor, and the door was hidden with a rug Martha kept spread over it. Unless Mark changed his mind, and went on to war anyway, he planned to stay in the room until the war was over, and spread the word that he'd slipped back to Ohio, to live with relatives. This way, none of the Negroes would be punished, for folks wouldn't think that the Negroes were helping him to hide out here on his own farm. He had Ike and George to make a small table for the room, and a makeshift bed, and he would keep a kerosene lamp in the room. He hadn't fully explained just how he planned to use this room, and one day while Martha swept off the rug that lay over the trap door, she decided to ask Mark about it.

"Mark, you ain't told nobid'ee why you's had that big hole dug under the kitchen, and I's got sump'um to axe you," said

Martha. "Is you gon'a stay in the room 'til the war is over? Is that what you went and had it fixed fer? If you's do, you gon'a be as blind as a bat, when you come back out. We done got 'nuf to do as it tis, 'thout having to lead you 'round by the hand, blind."

"I plan to go down there whenever somebody comes around, otherwise, I'll stay up here, and out of sight," he explained. "Don't let anybody know about that room, and be sure to spread the word that I went back to Ohio, that is, if and when I decide not to enter the war. I haven't made up my mind yet, so be sure not to say anything, until I tell you. No matter if your life is threatened, don't let anybody other than for you and Bertha know about the room, for my life will depend on it. Will you keep it a secret?"

"You don't have to worry 'bout that, fer nobid'ee ain't never gon'a learn nothing 'bout that room," she assured him. "No matter if they say they gon'a kill me, and eb'em adder I's done been kilt, I's still ain't gon'a say nothing."

"That's the way it's got to be," said Mark, as he got up from the table, "and tell Bertha to do the same. I might even change my mind and go on to the war after all, for I haven't really decided, one way or another."

Every day brought on more new and horrible tales about the war, for Union troops had already captured New Orleans and Yorktown, and were now on the move toward Richmond, Virginia where the Capitol of the Confederacy was now located. By now, the outlook for southern troops was very bleak, for each battle seemed to chalk up another victory for the strong, and well equipped North. Although the South hadn't given up hope of eventually winning the war, at this point at least, it didn't seem to Mark like this hope was well founded. He had kept up with news about the war, and he knew about all the factories that were located in the North, with so few being located in the South, and the possibility that the South could keep its troops supplied looked grim. Even so, and with ports being blockaded to prevent help coming from foreign countries, leaders of the South kept claiming that they would eventually win.

In late May, Union troops captured Corinth, Mississippi, and the fall of Memphis, Tennessee at the hands of Union troops was another serious blow to an already battered South. As the battles raged on, seemingly out of control, the draft soon began to systematically strip the South of all its able-bodied young men in its desperate effort to eventually win. Mark suddenly began to shift gears in his resolve to stay out of the senseless war. His heart ached for families of those young men who had already given their life, and those who were still suffering and dying on the lonely battlefields far away from home, and a new sense of patriotism overcame him. He knew that he could not go ahead with his plan to hide in the secret room, while so many of his fellow Southerners fought and died for their country. He would fight with his brothers - he must fight to defend his homeland - he had no other choice.

His decision to go into battle for his homeland was the right choice, he assured himself, for even his enlisting had already begun to cause many of his neighbors to regard him differently. His greatest worry now, was what would happen to the slaves he had freed, if the South won. One afternoon while sitting out on the front porch and talking with Martha, he made up his mind to obey his own conscience and report for duty, regardless to what he thought about the war.

"Martha, I've come to the conclusion, that it will be best for me to join the Confederate Army after all," he told her. "I have to help other southern men defend our homeland, even though I disagree with our leaders, and the real reason for the war. My friends have their rights as well as I, and I'll fight for my rights for freedom of the slaves, alongside those who are fighting for a right to own slaves, while we fight for our homeland. South Carolina is my home, and no matter how I disagree with its leaders, that don't relieve me of my obligation as a citizen to defend it. Whether we win or not, I'll live the rest of my life here, and I don't want to go to my grave regretting that I let my fellow-Southerners down when they needed me most."

"And, if you does go to war, that means that we's ain't gon'a never see you again," replied Martha, tearfully. "The war wuz meant to kill ever good man in the country, and let the trashy mens stay on here to take over, and run thangs the way they want 'em to go. Ain't that what a war is fer?"

"No, that's not what the war is all about," he replied, in a soft voice. "I'm a native of the South, and I can't allow my brothers to be slaughtered on the battlefields without offering to help them. I'm not gong to desert them, any more than I'm going to desert you folks. It's that simple. I must stand by them for what they're doing for me now, the same as I'll stand by you folks because of what you have already done for me."

"I can see now, that you's aw'ready done went and made up yo' mind to get kilt in the war, and I's wonder how long it's gon'a be, fo' you head out torge the war, wherever that be," she replied.

"I plan to leave early tomorrow morning, and I want you to tell the other workers that I'd like to speak with them before I leave," he told her. "Tell them to be up here at the break of dawn, tomorrow. Although I won't be using the secret room after all, it might come in handy one day, so don't let anyone know that it's there under the kitchen."

Mark spent the rest of the day, sitting outside on a bench underneath a big oak tree, near the graves of Bill, Liza, and their two sons. He thought about the first year he spent on this farm, which was only a few acres then, and how they stood behind him then, and all during the following years. He loved his mother, but his real love seemed to be buried in the four graves there before him. Then, there was Carolyn, a name he hadn't even thought of in quite some time now, yet his love for her was as strong as ever. Then, as he thought of his father, memory of his cruelty came flashing across his mind, as it blotted out every childhood memory he once had for him. Then his mind suddenly turned to Joe Wilson, and how cruel and overbearing he'd been to Bill's family. The four graves at the edge of the yard, would always remind him of how easy it is to misjudge someone, like he had misjudged Joe.

The following morning, all the Negroes gathered in the yard below the mansion to hear what Mark had to say, and stood silently as Mark talked to them about his decision to join the army, and how he'd made preparation for them while he was away. He had spoken to Willie Hendricks, Robert Harper's foreman, and he promised to look after the Negroes for Mark when he went to the army, and to handle business matters.

"I'll be back in no time at all," Mark told them, "and you folks don't have to worry about anything. You have plenty of food stored away, and enough feed for the livestock 'til harvest time, and I've asked Willie Hendricks to look after you folks, and to sell the cotton for you. No matter what happens, I want you folks to stay on the farm 'til I return, whenever that might be."

"But, this war mout las' fer a long time," George sighed. "What if you is in the war fer the res' of yo' lif'. What if you's like the war, and 'cide to stay and fight 'til everbid'ee 'cept fer you is been kilt?"

"I don't expect that to happen, and with all the extra men signing up for duty, I hope to be back in time to help plant a crop next spring," he smiled, and told them. "Just look for me, when you see me again."

This was a sad day indeed, for these lonely Negroes, for Mark had finally left them to go and fight for his homeland, something they couldn't understand at all. They loved Mark, and would have gladly taken his place, for they were afraid that they would never see him again.

One of the Negroes drove him into town in a buggy, and after he talked to several others in town about the war, he went to the Recruiting Office, where he talked with his brother-in-law John Phillips, for a few minutes. Although this made only twice that Mark had spoken to John, it soon became obvious that his father had handpicked him for Susan.

"Mark, this is an honorable thing you're doing for the South, and when we come out of this war as winner, we'll be living in a new world," John smiled, and told him. "I've heard about your previous stand against slavery, and now that you've changed your mind, I hope we'll be able to see more of each other, when the war is over. Your father is even proud of you now."

"John, there's a lot that you don't know about me, and I'm learning other things about myself as I go along, but sometimes we have to do things that we don't want to do, in order to eventually get what we want," Mark replied, in a stern voice. "I'll fight for my homeland, but that doesn't mean that I'm in full accord with the way its being run, for its leaders are blinded to reality, and unwilling for anyone to show them the way to go. It's been a pleasure meeting you, and we'll meet again one day, even though I'm not quite sure under what circumstances it might be." Then, Mark went back outside, to wait for the train that would soon be taking him north.

Later, as he waited in town for the train that would take him north where he'd soon meet his enemy, who not long ago was his neighbor, a dashing figure in a makeshift uniform, Mark heard someone call his name. Turning to respoind, thinking that his brother-in-law had called to him, he saw his father proudly walking toward him, with an outreached hand.

"Well, if I wasn't seeing this with my own eyes, I wouldn't believe that it was happening," said Nate, as he offered his hand. "Let me have the honor of shaking your hand, and thank you for finally seeing the light. Now that you've decided to fight for our rights to own slaves, it makes me feel like we never had any differences of opinion at all. I'm proud of you, Son."

"Sir, I disagree with what this war stands for," said Mark, in a serious voice, "and I'm not all that anxious to risk my life, but the love I have for my homeland overshadows all that, I suppose. I took a stand against those who used Negroes as slaves becasue I love the South, and that same love is what's making me go to war to defend the South. Like a family, children disagree with their parents, and parents disagree with their children, but it doesn't mean that they shouldn't fight to maintain their family ties."

"Give them northern fools the devil, Son!" His father smiled. "Don't be worried about your farm while you're gone, or your niggers, for I'll see that nothing happens to them, and that's a promise. Those words come from a father to his son, not as a businessman, and not a man who is any longer one of your enemies. That's enough said, and I wish you luck."

"Thank you, Sir," Mark said, dramatically saluting his father. "I'll do the very best I can to win this war, if only for you, Sir."

As his father walked away, Mark heaved a sigh of relief. He had finally rallied some support at least from his greatest adversary, and felt sure that the Negroes would be safe while he was away, no matter how long that might be. Mark thought back over the years, and summed up his father well. My father is proud of me, only when I go against my own convictions. In this one instance, however, Mark knew that the lives of his friends would depend primarily on his father's word of support while he was gone. Although his father had been mean and cruel to him down through the years, Mark still had faith in his father's promise, and even though he and his father might clash again when the war was over, while he was away he had no need to fear. His father's word was enough.

Sad to say, but many had underestimated the gravity of the war effort, for the fighting would not subside for quite a while. As the horrors of this war loomed heavily on the horizon, neither the North nor the South could claim an overall victory, though both sides had very high hopes of eventually being the winner. It might be said, that the North with its unlimited supplies and manpower, had finally clashed with the South's mighty unbeatable pride, determination, and willingness to die to defend what seemed right.

As Mark heard the train whistle blowing, he choked with pride as he began to think back on some of the things that had kept the South fighting, although all odds were against it winning. Then, he thought back on how the pride that one man had for his homeland, had given great hope to the Confederacy. Maybe by joining the army himself, it might be the beginning of a new, and different relationship between my father and me, he thought.

Robert E. Lee was in the Union Army when Virginia joined The Confederate States of America, and because Virginia was his homeland, he refused to remain in the Union Army, saying, "I can't take up a sword against my own homeland." He then joined the Confederate Army, and because of Lee's abilities as a soldier, and the fact that he knew quite a lot about the Union Army, he was immediately placed in charge of the Confederate Army, and given the rank of General. This brought him to a crossroad, because he was from Virginia, and in an effort to keep him in the Union Army he was offered a ranking position. He refused this offer, and now being in command of the Confederate Army, he was feared by many of those with whom he once served, yet highly respected for his character as a true gentleman. The fact that they now had a man of Lee's character in charge of the Confederate Army became a shot in the arm for the leaders of the newly formed Confederacy, and the hope of winning, significantly increased.

The second battle of Bull Run, proved to be an undeniable feather in the hat of General Lee, and did much to boost the flagging morale of the Southern troops as well. This dubious accomplishment, however, soon lost most of its glamor in light of the bloody Confederate retreat in a battle at Sharpsburg. To make a bad matter worse, Abraham Lincoln issued a temporary Emancipation Proclamation on September 22, 1862. This struck a more serious blow to the South than many of the battles it had already lost, Mark reasoned, as the troop train chugged on northward, loaded with many young men who no doubt would never return.

Each time Mark Simpson went up against the enemy, it caused him to wonder why he had become involved, and why Southern leaders didn't call this war off, for it was becoming obvious to him that the South couldn't possibly win, with the way things were going now. From the winter of 1862, through the spring of 1863 the war raged on, as both sides continued to strike heavy blows against the other, time and again, in an all-out effort to win.

Although Union forces now held many strongholds in the South, still neither side could honestly say that they were winning. Mark fought on; the war seesawed back and forth, while each side was sure of victory one day, and admitting defeat the next. Each time his Company had to retreat, and regroup for another seemingly lost-in-advance battle, he wondered why the Southern leaders kept on sacrificing young men's lives, for what seemed to him like a worthless cause.

On October 18, Confederate forces invaded Kentucky, only to be halted by Union forces, which were dealt a crushing blow, with total casualties reaching 12,000 at Fredricksburg alone. The Confederacy would have little cause to stand on their laurels, however, since it would soon be forced to retreat in the Battle of Murfreesboro, and some 9,000 casualties on each side, bore testimony of the repercussions of a bloody war.

Until January 1863, the sole motivation of the North was to try to bring the South back into the Union. However, on January 1, 1863, Lincoln freed the slaves, and the purpose of the North in this war became two-fold. Starting as of this day, not only would it fight to preserve the Union, but would fight to abolish slavery as well. In March 1863, the North also began drafting men between the ages of 20 and 45, and the war raged on.

Early in the spring of 1863, Northern troops were defeated in the Battle of Chancelorville, while General Grant's army defeated Confederate troops during this same time frame in Mississippi, as they began to beseige Vicksburg. It seemed a never-ending trade-off in Mark's opinion, as more lives were lost.

The summer of 1863, however, would prove a turning point in the war, with the overwhelming defeat of Southern troops during The Battle of Gettysburg. Up until now, Mark had not been presented with an opportunity to surrender, short of deserting the South, and though enemy forces were gradually marching deeper and deeper into southern territory, Southern leaders still had hopes of winning the war.

To Mark, it seemed that each battle was worse than the one before, as the casualties mounted higher and higher on both sides of the conflict. During a battle at Chickamauga, a few miles south of Chattanooga, an enormous number of lives were lost in only two days of fighting that claimed 28,500 casualties.

Victorious at Chickamauga, Southern troops then forced enemy troops to retreat into Chattanooga. However, Southern troops didn't follow Northern troops into Chattanooga, instead, they occupied Lookout Mountain that stood just south of town, and Missionary Ridge that stood southeast. Northern troops were now suffering starvation, for Southern artillery stationed above the city controlled the roads into it, as well as the Tennessee River, making it impossible to receive food supplies, and ammunition.

Hearing of this situation, General Grant quickly moved part of his troops into Chattanooga as reinforcement, and later on in November, dealt a heavy blow to the southern strongholds above the city. Then, in an attempt to retaliate for the great defeat at Chickamauga, troops from the North stormed up Missionary Ridge without being given orders to do so, and within an hour, defeated the Southern troops on their own ground.

The determination of Northern troops grew stronger with every victory it tallied, and Southern troops waned as supplies dwindled, and manpower rapidly decreased with each battle they lost.

The war became a living-nightmare to Mark Simpson, for in reality he did not want to fight in this war at all. Not because he was a coward, or that he didn't love his homeland, but because he knew that it could have been avoided in the first place. His southern pride, however, coupled with his deep desire to save the South from complete destruction, gave him a good reason to continue to hold on, and do whatever he could to help win this awful war.

To fight with hope of winning was one thing, he thought, as he witnessed many men perishing on the battlefields. To fight with no hope of winning, was a travesty of bravado that became increasingly difficult to witness.

CHAPTER TEN

THROUGH A BATTLE OF TIME

By the winter of 1864, Mark felt as though he'd already spent a lifetime in this awful war, and the certainty of defeat, now haunted him at every turn. His plantation seemed very far away now, but the memory of his friends somehow provided a dim ray of light, in this otherwise dark and hellish existence. He had no real friends here, only a few comrades like him, fighting, and dying for a cause they didn't understand, and hoping for victory, that never came. One day he'd learn a man's name, only to forget it the next day, after seeing him killed in battle. He tried to rest at night, and forget about the battle he had gone through that day, but the pitiful groaning and crying of the wounded men that lay around, haunted him until the dawning of another weary day.

The opportunity for him to surrender had not presented itself, and he was not about to desert his friends, no matter what he thought of the war, for his pride would keep him there, even if it cost him his own life. Even though all odds were against him now, his Southern pride, love for his homeland, and true respect for his leaders, kept him there. Like his other Southern comrades, he would continue to fight until the South won, or until he was hauled off dead, after having given his life for the cause.

The Confederate troops were in a sad state indeed, for even though their pride was strong, their supplies had exhausted. The small Southern factories were unable to supply its troops with sufficient ammunition. Many times, they were forced to go into battle with only sticks and clubs with which to defend themselves, and even after death, they proudly held these crude weapons tight in their still, and lifeless hand. Northern troops admired their courage, and many times they would spread their jacket over the face of a dead Confederate soldier, to show their respect for the dead man's courage. At the very outset of this bloody war, Northern troops felt almost sure that they would come out as winner, but they underestimated the pride and courage of Confederate troops that would keep them fighting to the bitter end.

Early this morning Mark was awakened from a short and restless sleep, by the sound of cannon balls as they whistled overhead, aimed at a small group of Southern troops that were coming to relieve them. The sun rose at last on a pathetic scene, as dead and wounded men lay scattered about, further attesting to what was sure to be the South's impending defeat. Mark's Commander warned them yesterday, that thousands of Northern troops were camped in the area, and unless help came soon, they faced complete disaster.

A group of Southern troops finally arrived at where Mark and his men had been pined down on top of a wooded knoll for several days, and were shocked to find so few South Carolina soldiers still alive. They were told that hundreds of Southern troops were holding their gound against the North, and they were sent to help wipe them out. Mark Simpson was happy to be among those survivors, although only a few were still left, and he welcomed the arrival of troops from Alabama, who had come to help them.

"I'm glad that you fellows were able to make it," Mark said to a soldier when the group arrived. "We've caught the devil during the past several days, and we haven't advanced a hundred yards. How many men came with you?"

"Well, we started out yesterday with about six hundred men," the soldier told him, "but as you can see, there's less than a hundred of us left. Most of the men are sick, and unable to fight. Every soldier the North has, must be camped right around here, from the way they bombarded us all night."

"It seems that way," replied Mark. "The cannon balls whistling over us last night, didn't let us get very much sleep. They've had us pined down for three days, we're about out of ammunition, and we haven't had anything to eat, or any water to drink for three or four days."

"What's your plan?" Asked the soldier. "Do you think we should bunch up and hit them head on, or try to sneak around, and hit them from the rear? If we spread out, it might look like there are more of us, than just a few. By the way, who is in command of your men?"

"Our Commander was killed late yesterday evening, and it's up to us to do what we think is best, I suppose," Mark replied. "If we could manage to slip across that clearing up ahead, then we could hide out in the bushes until more reinforcement arrives, for we're sitting-ducks where we are. Anything will be better than sitting around here. What do you think?"

"Sounds good to me, for we don't have a Commander either, and I'll signal for the others to follow me," said the soldier, as he motioned to his friends who had come along with him.

The small group of South Carolina and Alabama soldiers got down on their hands and knees, and started crawling through the thick clusters of briars, as they made their way toward a cluster of trees beyond a small clearing. As it seemed, they might be able to make this move without harm, for they didn't see any Union soldiers, and for a brief moment, their hopes were high. As soon as they were about halfway across the clearing, Mark stood up and started to run, and the others followed after him. In an instant, Union soldiers began firing from both sides, and from ahead of them as well. For hours, it seemed, Mark's men and their friends from Alabama took a pounding, and by noon, only a few of them were able to slip back to where they had been for several days. Although they started out with about a hundred men, less than a dozen made it back, and most of them were seriously wounded. Mark somehow wondered how, or why he had been one of the survivors.

Hidden from the enemy behind a thick cluster of bushes, and surrounded by many dead and wounded soldiers from the battle yesterday, Mark began talking to the young man from Alabama about the situation they now faced. Although Mark was in his thirties, the young man from Alabama didn't look as though he was more than sixteen years old.

"I don't know about you," said Mark, "but I was wondering just how many of us really know what we're fighting for. It's obvious, that we're losing."

"I don't guess we're supposed to ask why, but I've wondered about it ever since I first joined up," replied the young man. "Everybody else in the community had been called to fight, so I decided to join them. I don't think I had what you might call a good reason, except that I heard they needed more men to help win the war. So here I am, for whatever reason it might be."

"Although you don't have a uniform, or a cap with a symbol on it, because you are with the group from Alabama, I take it that you're also from Alabama," said Mark, as he eyed the young man keenly. "Am I right?"

"Yes, my name is Jim Ables, and I'm from a small community just south of the Tennessee border, called Bridgeport, Alabama," the young man replied, as a soft smile came on his face. "I'm proud of Alabama, and if I had any reason for being here at all, I guess it would be pride, and nothing else."

"I'm Mark Simpson, and I'm from South Carolina," Mark responded. "I'm glad to meet you, Sir." The two then shook hands. "There's so many differences of opinion about this war, and I wondered how you really felt in your heart about it, if you don't mind my asking."

"Seems like a waste of time and lives, if you don't mind me being so blunt about it," Jim replied. "If folks keep getting killed like they have since I signed up, there won't be anybody left to fight pretty soon, then the war will have to stop on its own. That's exactly how I feel about it."

"You're awful young, what, about seventeen?" Asked Mark seriously, as he shook his head. "You don't look quite old enough to be drafted."

"Right, I turned seventeen last month!" He beamed. "Some folks say that I look a lot older, but I'm not. In fact, I'm the baby of the family."

"So, you say you don't know what this war is about," Mark inquired. "You're not alone, for I feel the same way at times. Our leaders would like for us to believe that it's all about slavery, but I know better."

"I'm not really sure, but I've heard that it was because the Union didn't want us to use niggers as slaves, but that don't make sense," replied Jim, in a confused voice. "If anything, it makes us slaves to the niggers, for we are out here fighting to save them, and they wouldn't do that for us. Looks to me like our leaders think more of the niggers, than they do of us."

"I see your point, and I agree that this war isn't worth what it's going to cost us in the end," Mark told him. "Does your folks think it's worth the lives that have already been lost, just to be able to own Negroes as slaves? Is that what the leaders in Alabama tell the citizens?"

"I'm sorry Mark, but I don't have any family left, that is, except for my mother, and she might be dead by now," replied Jim, tearfully. "My daddy was killed at Chickamauga, a long time ago, and last week, my only brother died in my arms. I guess that's why I'm still here, for I don't have anything left to go back home to, or anything to live for anymore."

A lump came in Mark's throat. "I'm sorry to hear about what happened to your father and brother, and my heart goes out to your mother," Mark replied, as he wiped a tear from his eye. "This war can't last too much longer, and my prayer is, that we'll both be back home pretty soon. I joined in an effort to help the South, but it turned out that I'm only helping to destroy it."

For hours it seemed, they sat and talked about many things back home such as the economy, the way they felt about the war, anything else that happened to come to their mind. Mark felt that he'd found a kindred spirit in Jim, for he was just as ambivalent about the war as he. How sad to fight for something that you don't believe in, Mark thought, and much sadder still, to die under those same circumstances. For many generations to come, both sides were bound to feel the blunt of the hatred that had been created between these once close neighbors, who were now bitter enemies, all because of a war that should have never been fought anyway, Mark thought.

Then suddenly, Mark and Jim realized that they hadn't heard a single shot in quite some time now, and they decided to climb to the top of a large knoll to see what might be in the valley below. They had sat there and talked for a long time, for the sun would be down in a few hours, and they didn't think the Union soldiers would have packed up and left all this quick.

They cautiously made their way through the thick underbrush, until they'd reached the top of a large ridge, and from this vantage point, they hoped that they could gain some insight as to what they were up against. Easing along on his stomach, Mark came to where he could see clearly down to the valley below, and he was absolutely stunned at what he saw.

"My God, Jim!" Mark whispered. "I'll bet there's 10,000 Union soldiers sitting around like buzzards, waiting for us to make a move! I wish you would look at that wagonload of rifles, and ammunition, and that other big wagonload of foodstuff sitting there, and going to waste."

"I see, and especially the food, with us up here starving to death," Jim replied. "It looks like every soldier they have, is sitting around down there eating, and enjoying life, like nothing was happening."

"They look like they're not afraid that we'll bother them," Mark replied in a low voice, "but I'll bet they have their beady eyes on us, right now."

"That's right, Reb! I do have my 'beady' eyes on you, and my rifle aimed at the back of your head!" Came a voice from behind. "Raise your hands real slow, and you won't be shot, for there's no way for you to escape."

A cold chill came over Mark, like as if the hand of death had been placed on him. "Sir, do you mind if we turn around and face you?" Asked Mark, as he lay motionless, with his hands on the back of his head.

"Turn around real slow, and sit up on the ground," the voice replied, in a stern tone. "Don't try anything, and I promise not to shoot you."

Mark and Jim slowly turned, and sat up on the ground, as they faced their captor. They looked up at the Union soldier, a young man in his mid-twenties, well dressed, and with a sparkling new rifle pointed at them. Though Mark had often embraced the idea of being captured, now as he looked down the barrel of the rifle, he had second thoughts of becoming a prisoner of war after all.

"Sir, do you intend to shoot us here on the spot?" Asked Jim, his young voice cracking. "All my folks have been killed in the war, I'm the only one left except my mother, who is down at Bridgeport, Alabama. Would you not kill us, like we were a couple of wild dogs? Please, Sir," he begged.

"Are you fellows scouting out the area?" Asked the Union soldier. "Word has it, that about ten thousand Southern troops are headed this way, and we're here to stop them, before they cross over the river into town."

"You have to be joking, Sir," smiled Mark. "We're the only one's in the area, except for about a dozen wounded, and several hundred dead, who are back down there a ways. I hope you believe me, for that's the truth."

"Is that a fact," asked the soldier. "We were really expecting a lot of resistance, and that's why there's so many of us camped around here now."

"Sir, we've already lost just about all the men the South can afford, and we're losing the war as well," Mark pleaded. "I'm disgusted with this war, and I hope you don't kill us, for we're no threat to you any longer."

"Now, that wouldn't be sporting at all, would it, Reb," the soldier then chuckled, causing Mark and Jim to feel much better. "I know we're winning the war, and we already have too many prisoners." The soldier then hesitated for a moment, as he looked keenly into Mark's eyes, as if trying to figure him out, or trying to decide what he should do next.

"This might sound stupid," interrupted Mark, "and don't laugh at me for saying this, but it seems like you and I have . . ."

"Tell you what, Rebs!" The soldier broke in. "I'm willing to offer you a deal, seeing that you fellows look like you've just about had it."

"Go ahead and speak whatever's on your mind, for we're listening with both ears," Mark replied. "Anything you might have to offer, will be better than what we have now, for at this point, you hold our life in your hands."

"First, I'm going back to camp and get you fellows some food to eat, for it looks like you're just about starved to death," he began. "Then, when you fellows finish eating, I want you to head back south, and don't stop until you get back home. You aren't alone in being disgusted with this war, for my only brother, well, he's not with me anymore." A tear trickled down his cheek, and he turned and looked away. "Just sit there where you are, and I'll be back in a few minutes with some food for you fellows."

"But Sir, aren't you afraid that we might jump up and leave, or shoot you in the back when you walk away? Asked Mark. "Have you thought about that at all. We are your enemy, you know."

"Let's just say that we're some neighbors who happen to disagree on something, and our leaders were unable to settle the argument," the soldier smiled, and replied. "I'm not afraid, for with ten rifles pointed at you from the bushes over there, you won't try anything. Let me have those beat up rifles. I hate to say this, but those rifles look worse than you fellows do. I'll be back in a few minutes, and you have my word on that."

Mark and Jim looked dumbfounded, as the soldier made his way back toward the camp below. Since being in the war which now seemed like a lifetime, Mark hadn't spoken to a Union soldier before. For some reason, that soldier looks familiar to me, he thought, as the soldier walked away. Oh well, it's because he's being so nice to us, that makes me feel that way, he reasoned.

"Mark, do you really think he'll bring us some food like he said, and let us go back home?" Jim asked. "He acted like he felt sorry for us, but that's not the way the enemy should act toward a prisoner. He probably plans to feed us, then kill us with a full stomach, to ease his conscience."

"Can't rightly say," Mark answered, still being bothered by the thoughts that cluttered his mind about the kind Union soldier. "He acted sincere, and maybe he'll do exactly what he said, or I hope he does, anyway."

"We can't forget that he's our enemy, and what if he goes back down there, and has the men turn the cannons loose on us," Jim nervously replied. "What do you think."

"Then, it's been a pleasure knowing you, I guess," Mark replied. "Maybe he won't turn on us after all, but with ten rifles pointed at us, I don't see where we have any choice, other than to believe him. He was a young man, and when he tells the older men about us, there's no telling what might happen."

For what seemed like an eternity, they sat watching and waiting like they had been instructed to do, still not sure what might happen next. Then, just as the young soldier had promised, up he walked unarmed, with a large sack on his shoulder, and a bucket of water in his hand.

"Mark Simpson, here's some food for you fellows, and I brought a couple of blankets for you to use, until you get back to your plantation in South Carolina," said the soldier, as he set the sack on the ground. "I brought you some water too, for you will probably needed it."

"Sir, how did you happen to know my name?" Asked Mark, as he quickly stood up, to take a closer look at him. "I don't recall mentioning my name earlier."

The soldier smiled, as he reached to shake Mark's hand. "Your name, Sir, is Mark Simpson, from South Carolina, a plantation owner. I met you at my father's store, when you and him sat and talked about the way things were going on in the South. Yes, I'm Henry Watkins, from Columbus, Ohio."

"I remember you now, you little squirt!" Mark said, as he gave him a big hug, and patted him on the shoulder. "Boy, am I glad to see you! Never in a million years, did I think that I'd ever meet somebody I knew out here."

"Same here Mark," replied Henry. "But, I wish it could have been under different circumstances. Now go ahead and eat, for the sun's going down, and you'll have to be on your way pretty soon."

"Maybe we'll meet again someday, or I hope so, if you ever happen to come down to South Carolina," Mark told him.

Henry and Mark talked, while Mark and Jim ate the food, but something was still bothering Mark about the situation.

"I know that you have men hiding in the bushes around us, and hundreds of other armed men in the valley, and what's to keep them from killing us when we head out toward home?" Mark asked. "I'm sure you're not going along with us. They won't know that you told us to leave, and they'll kill us."

"There never were any men hiding in the bushes, and you could have taken off without anyone seeing you, but you didn't," the soldier replied. "Like I said earlier, we know that the war is just about over, and we already have too many prisoners to take care of as it is. You won't be harmed, or at least not by Union soldiers, for we have orders not to shoot any Southern soldier who is headed south, and unarmed."

"I appreciate that, but what about other soldiers that we might run up on, after we get out of this area?" Asked Mark. "How are they going to know that you gave us permission to leave the war, and go back home."

"Although it's not a written-command, General Grant asked us not to take any more prisoners, or kill any more Southern soldiers unless they threatened to kill us," he explained. "We were told to give food to those who willingly gave up the fight, denounced the Southern cause, and admitted defeat. We have hundreds of Southern soldiers walking into our camp and surrendering, in order to get food to eat. Even though we don't take them as prisoners, they keep on hanging around our camp, just to be fed."

After Henry and Mark talked for a few minutes longer, Mark and Jim packed up the leftover food to have to eat later, picked up the wool blankets Henry had brought along, then headed toward the valley below. In the valley below, they walked directly into a group of Union soldiers. No matter what Henry had said a few minutes ago, the sight of these armed men frightened them, so they quickly raised their hands in surrender.

"That's all right Rebs," said the Union soldier, when he saw the fear in their eyes. "Just keep on going south, and you won't be harmed. Tell all the other Rebs along the way to do the same thing, to avoid being slaughtered, for we have them outnumbered. Will you do that, for the sake of saving lives?"

"We will Sir, and that's a promise," replied Mark. "We have no idea how this war got started, or why we've been fighting, unless it's Southern pride, and the love we have for our homeland. I hope you understand."

"I'll admit that you Rebs do have pride, and guts too, for you keep right on fighting with sticks and clubs, knowing fully well that you'll be killed," replied the soldier, unpretentiously. "Not more than a month ago, we captured a whole company of you Southern soldiers, and not a single one of them had a rifle or a pocketknife. Go on back home fellows, for you've done your part in trying to win this war."

"We're on our way," said Mark, as he walked on, "and I'll pray that the Lord blesses you for your kindness, Sir."

Tears then came to the soldier's eyes, when he saw that Jim and Mark were barefooted, and they had a piece of scrap carpet draped over their shoulders, because they had no coat to wear.

"Stop by that wagon down there ahead of you, and tell the man to fit you fellows up with a pair of shoes," the soldier called out. "Tell him to give you one of our jackets too, if you're not too proud to wear our color."

Day after day, Mark Simpson and Jim Ables continued on southward as they had been instructed, passing fully equipped Union camps at every turn, passing on by all but unnoticed. Those few Confederate encampments they came upon along the way however, provided a much different prospective, for many starving, crippled and dying soldiers lay about, with their pride being the only thing seeming to keep them there. It was these sad and bitter experiences, that caused Mark's conscience to breathe down his back, still he and Jim trudged on, spreading the word of warning they'd been asked to do. They were scoffed at for going back home, and accused of deserting by some Confederate soldiers, but because their life had been spared once, this didn't seem to bother them. The awful war was over, as far as Mark and Jim were concerned.

All along this desertion route southward, they heard many stories of how prisoners were treated on both sides, which offered them some measure of logic for their release. In southwest Geogia, 30,000 Union prisoners were crowded into a log stockade, which covered an area of only 16 acres, and about 12,000 graves where Northern prisoners were buried, bore pathetic witness to the poor conditions that existed. Likewise, the North had a problem in trying to house its prisoners, since the Confederate forces were in need of food and shelter, until whole companies would march into their camps, and surrender in masses.

The South in general, was suffering tremendously, for the war had finally driven the economy to a breaking point, and dwindling resources had evaporated to nothing. The people were unable to support themselves, much less support an army, and living conditions were deplorable. Were it not for their great Southern pride, the war might have ended long before now.

Mark and Jim continued plodding along, exhausted and hungry, for the food given to them by the Union soldier, had already exhausted. After what seemed like a month of plodding along toward home, they finally made their way across the mountains of North Carolina, and had crossed over into South Carolina near a small town that was called Pickens. This small town was nestled deep in the foothills of the Blue Ridge Mountains, and was the headquarters of the Pickens District of South Carolina. Here, they would part company, for Jim would head on southwest, on his way toward Alabama, and Mark would head directly south, toward his plantation that lay farther down in South Carolina.

"Well, we made it this far without running into any serious problems, and I must say that it's been a pleasure having you with me," said Mark, while he and Jim sat on a rock, resting. "This is where we part company, maybe forever as far as I know, and I hope you find your mother well when you get home. You have a long way to go before you get to Alabama, but you'll make it."

"I've enjoyed your company as well, and I hope that you'll find your fine mansion still standing, and your workers still alive," replied Jim. "I heard about Sherman destroying Atlanta on his march to the sea, and how he destroyed everything in sight, as he plundered across the coastal section of your state, but maybe he missed your place."

"I hope so too, not for my sake, but for the sake of the loyal Negroes on my farm, that I've already told you about," Mark said, as tears came into his eyes. "My mother was ill when I left over two years ago, and she might have died, while I was gone. But, I know that your mother really will be proud to see you when you get back, though."

"Yep, she's all that I have left, except for my dog, that is, if they are still alive," Jim forced a smile. "If they haven't sent my brother back home yet, I sure hate to tell her what happened, for he was her favorite among the two of us, if you know what I mean."

"Yes, I know how it feels to be the black-sheep of a family," Mark told him, thinking of his own family. "My sister, was my father's favorite, and it does give a fellow the feeling that he's not a part of the family."

"Take care of yourself Mark," said Jim, as he shook Mark's hand, "and I hope you find everything all right when you get home. I know that folks in my community will shame me for leaving the war, but a live coward, is better than a dead hero, when we had no chance of winning in the first place."

"Goodbye Jim," Mark replied, "and I pray that the Lord watches over you all the way back to Alabama. Like you said, folks will call us a fool for not staying in the war, but I'm thankful that I'm able to go back home, and wasn't left laying back there on some lonely battlefield."

Mark traveled on alone, carefully slipping by villages and towns, to keep from being seen, and he stayed off the main roads, for fear that someone might recognize him. As he made his way on past Anderson, Abbeville, and Edgefield on his way back to his plantation, he wondered if he'd find his mansion still standing, or if any of his workers would still be there. A great many former slaves had fled to the North for fear of being killed by their former masters, and The Confederacy had promised 200,000 of them freedom, if they would fight for the South. He had no way of knowing what his workers had done.

He'd also heard of the raid Sherman made through the South, but he didn't know just how destructive this raid had been. In December, Sherman and about 60,000 troops from the North had occupied Savannah, after having marched from Atlanta in a 60 mile wide path, destroying everything in sight. On their long march to the sea, they burned crops, homes, and entire towns, as they killed livestock, and polluted wells. Railroads were torn apart as well, and the crossties were used for firewood. The rails were heated in the fire, and twisted around big trees, and were called "Sherman's hairpins", or "Sherman's neckties". They had no mercy on the poor defenseless Southerners, or respect for the women and young girls, for they molested, and raped them while members of their family stood helplessly by. As if that wasn't enough humiliation for these poor folks, their houses would be burned, and dogs and cats were killed, and used to pollute the water in their wells.

Following the long march to the sea, Sherman and his troops turned eastward, and crossed the lower part of South Carolina, plundering, and destroying their way into North Carolina, then on into Virginia, where they joined with Grant's forces. However, as luck would have it, they bypassed Mark's plantation, and didn't do any damage at all, as he'd learn later.

The closer he came to his home, the more frightened he became, for he was more likely to be recognized. Many other Southerners had deserted the war as he was doing now, but in his case, it would be looked upon quite differently. If caught, he would probably be shot for deserting, simply because he disliked slavery before the war started. Even though he had risk his life many times for the South, simply because he'd returned before the war was over, or before he was killed, folks in his community would hate him as much as ever before. If he could somehow make it back home, and if his plantation had not been destroyed, and if his workers were still there, he planned to hide out in the secret room under the kitchen floor, until the war was over.

It was about ten o'clock at night, when Mark finally arrived back at his plantation, and instead of going up to the mansion, he stopped at the barn to rest, and savor the feeling of being back home. He saw no light burning up at the mansion, or in either of the worker's houses, and it caused him to wonder what might have happened while he'd been gone. His father swore that he would look after the Negroes, Mark remembered that, and he trusted his father to do that, but something else could have happened beyond his father's control. He might have died, even, my mother too, he thought.

He finally slipped up to the mansion, walked up on the back porch, and stood for a moment listening to see if he could hear any voices inside. Then he tried the back door and found it locked, like he'd told Martha to do every time she left the house. He was afraid to break a window and go in, for there was no telling who might be inside. Then, he decided to go back down to the barn and wait there until daylight, then he'd decide what he should do next. After all, he was in need of rest, and a good night's sleep."

It was obvious that someone had been here not very long ago, for as soon as Mark opened the barn door and stepped into the hallway, he heard the mules eating corn. By no means did this mean that his workers were still around, as he first thought, for he had asked Willie Hendricks to look after things while he was gone, and his father had promised to help him as well. He was "dead on his feet" so to speak, so he decided to make a bed in the hay and sleep there tonight, and worry about tomorrow when it came. Although the moon was bright, it was rather dark inside the barn, so he felt around until he found a pile of hay to use as a bed, then he layed down to rest.

Completely exhausted from the long journey back home, he soon fell off to sleep. This would be one of the few night's sleep he'd get, without having to listen to the groans of wounded and dying men as they lay on the ground around him. However, he'd been used to sleeping very lightly, and even the slightest noise would awaken him. This night would not be different, for no sooner had he dozed off, he was awakened by the sound of someone coughing, and it sounded as though they were inside the barn with him. Quickly sitting up, he realized that he wasn't the only one inside the barn tonight. With his eyes trying to pierce the darkness, and even afraid to draw a deep breath for fear that they might hear him, his imagination began to play tricks on him.

A moment later, he heard someone moving in the hay not very far away from him, and then he really became frightened. He had no weapon, not even a stick, or club, and it was too dark inside the barn to find a pitchfork, so he decided to try and bluff his way out of this situation.

"All right now, you had better come out with your hands up, before I open fire on you!" He snapped.

There was dead silence, and he knew now that he must press the point, for whoever was in the barn, knew that he was there as well.

"This is your last chance, before I start shooting!" He called out, in a loud voice. "I have my rifle cocked, and aimed right at you!"

"Mark, is that you," a soft Negro voice asked. "Is it railly you, er is you somebod'ee else, 'sides who you is?"

"Yes Martha, it's me," cried Mark, as they both jumped up. "I can't see you, but I'm glad to hear your voice."

Then, they stood holding each other for a few moments, as they both cried as though their heart would break. How good it feels to be home at last, Mark thought to himself, back with someone who really cares.

A moment later, Mark went over and peeked out through a crack in the barn door. "Has anybody been around here asking about me?" He asked her. "I mean, within the past month, or so."

"Yass'uh, they sho' is," she replied, as she went over and stood next to him at the door. "Some Fed'rate soldiers, and a feller that sez he wuz yo' brother-in-law, er sump'um. When I's told him that you wuz still in the war, they say that you done run off and left, er 'scaped, one."

"I wonder how they found out, for nobody who actually knew me, knew about what I did," he assured her. "So many men were blown all to pieces, and that could have happened to me as well, as far as anybody knows."

"They sez, that a feller from Alabam'ee wuz ketched over in Geogia jus' a few days ago, and befo' they went and kilt him, he told 'em that you and him went and 'scaped the war at the same time," she explained.

"Yes, I did escape, if that's what they want to call it, and with a young man from Alabama," Mark grimaced. "He probably told them about it to save his own life, but he was killed anyway. That figures."

"That's why I's been sleeping in the barn, fer I's thought they mout burn the house down, thanking that you wuz hiding in it," she told him. "I don't guess you want'a hear this, but ever few weeks since you's been gone yo' pappy is been here, axing if we's had sump'um to eats, and if thangs wuz aw'rite. Mos'a Willie, he been like a pappy to us, fer he comes 'round ever week and hep's us, and to make sho' that nobid'ee ain't bothered us."

"I appreciate what Willie has done, and of course, I'm glad that Dad kept his promise to me as well, but I imagine all that will change, now that he has found out about me leaving the war," replied Mark. "Where are all the other workers? Did they leave and go up north, like I heard a lot of the slaves have done? Are you the only one that's left?"

"Yass'uh, some did left, like you sez, but the mos' of 'em is still rite here on the farm," she smiled, and replied. "They been hiding over yon'a in a big gully that's kivered over wid vines, 'cept ever day when the sun comes up, they head out to the fields to wuk'. They call it their vine-shack, they sleep there ever nite, and eb'em a buzzard flying over, can't see 'em hiding in that place. Ike and George sez they is yo' boss-mens, and they sho' do make a good team, too. Ike, he found him a galfriend adder you's left, and he sho' is happy 'bout that. Sez they gon'a get hitched purdy soon."

They stood in the barn and talked for quite awhile, about almost anything that came to their mind, the war, his father looking after them as he'd promised, and how they had managed during this awful conflict. They finally slipped up to the mansion, and Mark climbed down into the secret room, for he was in desperate need of rest, and a good night's sleep. Martha went to where the others were hiding in the vine-covered gully to tell them that Mark was home, and to warn them not to say anything about it. Like Mark had told her, she told Ike and George to slip up to the mansion after dark every night, so Mark could discuss the day's work with them, and advise them as to what they should do the following day. He planned to stay hidden in the secret room, until he received word that the war was over.

Although Nate had kept his word to Mark about looking after his farm and workers while he was gone, as soon as he got word of Mark's desertion, everything suddenly changed. He ranted and raved, as he told his sickly wife about what Mark had done, although Susan and her husband had already made a point to tell her what an awful thing Mark had done.

"That darned sorry son of yours has walked away from the war, which goes to show that he's a yellow-bellied coward!" He spat. "I wish now, that I had not looked after his niggers while he was gone, for that goes to show that he don't appreciate a darned thing I did for him. Look at the shame and disgrace he brought on me, his family, and to others in the community."

"But, the war is all but over," Julie said weakly, not telling him that she already knew, "and there's nothing much left to fight for. Our spirit is broken, our pride is gone, and if he did give up the fight, I'm happy to know that he's still alive. So many of the men won't be coming back."

"But, he's a darned deserter in the eyes of everybody, and they look down on me for what he did!" He continued to rave. "Are you saying that I should be proud that he deserted. Is that what you really mean."

"Well, what about all the other men who deserted, the sons of your great friends, if I might add," she asked. "The Wilson boy, two Smith boys, and a host of others right around here left the war, but I haven't heard you branding them as deserters. He only did what hundreds of others have done, yet I don't hear folks in the community down grading them, like you do Mark."

"That's quite different, a heck of a lot different!" He snarled. "They upheld our Southern customs and traditions before the war started, then they went off to war to defend our right to maintain our proud Southern heritage."

. "Slavery, is what you really mean, isn't it?" She asked. "They defended their right to be mean and cruel to other humans, that's what you really mean, isn't it."

"But, he has always hated me for the way I felt about niggers, and now he has turned against his country as well," he bellowed. "Pride in our homeland is what has held the South together this long, and pride is what's helping win the war, not cowards, or deserters. The biggest mistake I ever made, was when I didn't let Henry Graham kill every nigger he had on his place when he went to Ohio, for I had a man, who would have done it for me."

Julie didn't even bother to reply, instead, she lay in bed crying because of what her husband had said about their son, as she wiped tears from her eyes on the pillowcase, for she was almost too weak to talk any longer. Julie was aware of the fact that he had watched after Mark's farm while Mark was at war, simply because he had made Mark a promise, but now that Mark was back home, it caused her to realize that this loyalty had turned to revenge. The fire of hatred had been rekindled.

"I see that you're not going to listen to reason, when I'm discussing something that your beloved son did, so I might as well stop where I am," he scolded, as he left the room. "I'm going to ask some men to keep their eye on his place from now on, for sooner or later, he'll come sneaking back home like an egg-sucking dog, and then he'll have the devil to pay."

In Mark's case, Union forces were not the enemy to be reckoned with, not at this point, however. His father would prove more of a threat to him than a whole garrison of Union soldiers.

He had been hiding in the secret room under the kitchen ever since he returned home, only slipping out at night to advise the Negroes what they should do the following day. He had no way to know just how much longer the war would last, what lay ahead for him and his workers, or what his neighbors thought about him. Willie Hendricks still kept making his weekly trips to see after Mark's workers, and to help them manage things until Mark returned, and Mark had asked Ike and George to ask Willie about the war, and then pass the word on to him that night.

"Like Mos'a Willie sez, mite nye all the mens in the South is done went and got kilt in the war, and the soldiers that ain't kilt, ain't got nothing to fight wid," George told Mark, one night. "He say there ain't no flour to make no bread wid, and if a feller is lucky to find some, a sack of flour, is gon'a cos' three hun'dud dollars. He sez he went to buy a pair of shoes from the sto', and they cos' him two hun'dud dollars. Sez the South is jus' 'bout as po' as us niggas is, and everbid'ee is starving to def', too."

"I appreciate that information, although I wish it could have been better than you described it," said Mark. "Keep asking him every time he comes around, for he'll tell the truth, and make sure he tells you when the war comes to an end, so I can get out of that room. Although the others know that I'm back home, please don't say anything to them about the secret room, for they might become frightened, and tell somebody."

"I's gon'a do that, fer I's done sick and tard of the war, and I's can't wait 'til you can get back out there in the fields wid us," said George, as he walked back toward the door to leave. "There ain't nuf' of us left to tend all the land, but we gon'a do the bes' we can to make nuf' stuff to eat, eb'em if we ain't gon'a get nothing fer the cotton crop."

This was a disasterious, and pathetic time for the South. It was obviously losing a war that it thought it could win. The war had completely destroyed it's economy, stripped it of almost all its able-bodied men, and those who had been left, were barely able to support their own self. Neighbors were being forced to steal from other neighbors, in order to survive. The Negroes were leaving to go up north, or joining the Union army to have food to eat, still leaders of the South refused to admit that it had lost the war. Upset because they were losing the war, they were taking their spite out on the Negroes who were still here in the South, and sometimes they would fly mad, and kill the poor Negroes, for no reason at all. Had it not been for Mark's father keeping his word, the same fate might have come upon the Negroes who worked for Mark as well.

Late one night after George and Ike had returned home after having talked to Mark, and Mark had returned to the secret room, he heard a loud noise just above him in the kitchen, mingled with the sound of men's angry voices. Mark suddenly realized that the voices were those of white men, shouting at some of the Negroes they had obviously rounded up, and brought into the mansion. These men were questioning them about Mark's whereabouts, for they had heard that he had deserted the war, and they figured that he was hiding out somewhere on the farm. As Mark would learn later, one of his father's men had seen him talking with George in the kitchen one night, while a lamp burned in the hallway.

"All right now, you sorry black-bastards, you might as well tell us where he's hiding, if you know what's good for you!" Yelled a voice, that Mark knew was the voice of his brother-in-law John Phillips. "We know for a fact that he's hiding around here, and unless you niggers tell where he is, we're going to kill every one of you trashy bastards!"

"Is that what you's brung us up here fer, jus' to axe us whu' Mos'a Mark is," asked George, in a calm voice. "You's need to be looking fer him in the war, wherever that mout be, fer that's whu' he wuz head'n, when he left here 'bout two years ago. Yass'uh, he went to the war to get kilt, like the tuther mens done, but I's ain't sho' if they got 'round to killing him yet."

"That's a darned lie, for we know that you are one of his favorites, and that you know where he's hiding!" Yelled another man, as he struck George on the head with the butt of his rifle. "Unless one of you tell us where he's been hiding since he returned home, the whole bunch will be in trouble. We're here to kill a darned sorry war-deserter, and if we don't find him, then we'll kill us some niggers, instead."

"George be telling the truf', fer none of us ain't seed him since he left to go to the war," spoke up Martha. "He mout be done kilt, er got his head blowed off wid one of them cannon balls, as fer as we know. Like George jus' sez, go and look in the war, fer that's whu' you gon'a find him."

"Shut up, you sorry hussy!" Barked another man. "You're the hussy who's been shacking up with him, and I know that you'd

394

lie for him. We need to kill all you sorry bastards, and that's exactly what we're going to do, before this night is over."

"Oh no, Mos's, please don't kill us," Martha begged, "fer ain't none of us never seed Mos'a Mark, since he left fer the war." She referred to him as "Mos'a Mark", while in their presence.

"We'll soon see about that," said John, as he motioned to the others who were inside the house with him. "Get all these sorry bastards outside, where the other men are waiting, and unless they tell us where he's hiding out, then we'll kill every one of the sorry bastards! Shove 'em outside, before I start shooting them right here in the house."

Mark could hear the shuffling of the Negro's feet, as the men shoved them toward the back door. Frightened at what was about to happen to them now, and feeling sorry for the Negroes for risking their own lives to protect his, Mark decided to climb out of the secret room, and go face them. No sooner had he climbed up the small ladder and lifted the trap door, he heard shots ring out, and then he eased the door back down. Surely, they won't kill those innocent folks, he thought. Then a number of other shots rang out, and as the pitiful cries and screams from the Negroes filled the moonlit night, he realized that the men had really killed the poor innocent Negroes after all. He heard the sound of horses, as they quickly galloped away.

Mark stood up in the room, then let out a pitiful scream as though he had been shot himself, for he knew now that the men had been serious about killing the Negroes unless they told where he was hiding. They had rather die than to tell where I was hiding, he cried, as he thought to himself how loyal and true they had been to him. And, my father claims that they have no heart, or soul, no sense or concern for anyone, and are lower than the scum of the earth. If he could call back just ten minutes of his time, he'd gladly face the men, and take whatever punishment that lay in store, but it was already too late.

Mark sat on the edge of the cot for a few moments and cried, as he rested his head in his hands, and wondered how these men could have stooped so low as to do such a thing. In a way, he was glad that the South was losing the war, for if they treated Negroes like this now, he could only imagine how far they would go in mistreating them if the South was allowed to maintain slavery. He felt guilty, ashamed, and dirty because he had allowed this to happen to them, but he had no idea that the men would go this far.

Mark trembled with fright, mingled with anger, as he slowly climbed from the secret room to go and see about his friends, knowing fully well that their chances of being alive were slim. As he stepped out on the back porch, laying there in the moonlight was a dismal sight indeed. He could hardly even bear looking at the bullet-riddled bodies of his friends laying there on the ground before him. Ike, George, Bertha, and several others whose faces he could not see, and God help, Martha herself. There she lay in the yard along with all the other victims of the heartless assassins. This was far worse than any of the battle scenes he had ever encountered during the war. They were not just nameless, faceless men lying there; these were his true and loyal friends. He knew he must get away from this God-awful place, for there wasn't anything left now for him to live for, and he had lost all hope of the South ever changing its attitude toward the Negroes, or at least not while he was still alive. He regretted now that he had returned home, regretted that he'd been spared during the war, and wished that he'd been killed while on his way back home, like Jim Ables.

He walked slowly, and reverently across the yard, as he headed toward the barn to saddle his mare, and slowly glancing down at Martha and the others who lay sprawled out on the ground, he became sick at his stomach. Mark loved the South, and he had risk his life to save it, although he disagreed with making slaves of other human beings, and disagreed with slaughtering them without any reason at all. All the threats that he had heard in the past had come to pass here tonight, and at long last, he realized just how far some persons would go, in order to uphold their stupid, and inhumane ideas. If I ever make it out of the South alive this time, I'll never return, he thought, as he slowly made his way toward the barn in the moonlight, hoping not to be seen by anyone.

After spending some time at the barn, thinking about what had happened to his friends, he started riding off with no plan of ever returning. Suddenly, he decided to ride by the house and take another quick glimpse at his friends, before leaving the South for good. He held his hat in his hand, and rode very quietly past these martyrs, and prayed that their killers would someday suffer the same fate. He put his hat on and started to ride away, when he thought he heard a noise, and then turning in his saddle, he sat for a moment listening.

"Hep' me," a faint voice groaned. "Please Lord, hep' me." Then nothing else was heard for a few moments, as Mark sat quietly in his saddle.

"Who was that?" Mark called out, thinking he might have imagined hearing someone. "Come on and answer me!" Nobody answered him.

Then quickly leaping from his saddle, he began to check the bodies one by one, in hopes of being able to find at least one person still alive. Although he was heartbroken and sad because of what had happened here tonight, still he was thankful because some of his workers had been spared. As it seemed, they only wanted to kill Martha, and others who were real close friends to Mark.

"Oh Lord, have mu'cy on us," the weak voice came again. "Oh Lord, won't you please hep' us?"

Realizing now that it was Martha, Mark went quickly to where she lay, and checked her pulse. Though weak, she was still alive, and he hoped that others in the group were alive as well.

"Please don't die on me, Martha!" He cried, as he lifted her head that was covered with blood, hoping to make her more comfortable. "Hang on as long as you can, for you can't leave me here alone like this!"

Mark lifted her up into his arms, and then carried her back inside, and layed her down on a settee in the parlor. After washing her face and head with cold water, he could see that one bullet had creased her skull, which had obviously knocked her unconscious, and another had cut an artery in her neck. Mark felt sure that the men thought she was dead; otherwise, they wouldn't have left her there for dead. Mark put a tight cloth around her head, and held a cloth firmly against her neck, in an effort to stop the bleeding.

"Please speak to me," Mark pleaded, as he looked into her horrified eyes, and cried. "Please say something to me, Martha."

Then she slowly lifted her hand, and placed it on her head. "My head is 'bout to kill me," she cried. "Them mens went and shot us, fer no reason in the wul'd. Jus' started shoot'n, like they wuz crazy, er sump'um."

"I'm sorry Martha, for I thought they were only bluffing in order to find out where I was, and I didn't expect them to go this far," Mark sighed. "I'm to blame for trying to save my own life, while I put your life at stake, along with the lives of all the others."

"It wuzn't yo' fault, fer they wuz drunk as a skunk, and they come here tonite to kill us, eb'em if they found you," she softly whispered. "There wuz some mo' mens wait'n in the yard, they all had guns, and they all wuz drunk, too."

"Martha, you might not feel quite up to talking now, but I sure wish that I knew the names of those who did this," he said to her. "I know that my own brother-in-law was involved, for I heard his voice, but I couldn't figure out who the others were. Did you recognize any of the others?"

"I wuz too scade' to know nothing, when they drugged us outside, but I's did see yo' pappy, fer he wuz the one that shot me," she replied. "Did they kill the tuthers, er is I the only one that got shot? I wuz the ver'ee first one to get shot, and don't 'memer nothing else adder that."

"Yes, George, Ike, and Bertha are dead, along with several others I haven't taken a close look at yet," he sadly replied. "Martha, I hate to ask you so many questions until you get to feeling better, but are you absolutely sure that my father shot you? Could you be mistaken at what you saw."

"Yass'uh, he sho' did shoot me," she assured him. "And I's seed that ole Pow'll feller, the feller that runs the General Sto', and one of the mens that used to wuk' fer you, fo' you's went and run him off fer talking hateful to us."

"Powell, he's still in cahoots with my father, is he?" Mark asked, even though he didn't expect a reply. "Herbert Smith, the man that I run off from here for talking hateful to you folks, and Mr. Wilson, who operates the General Store. That figures."

Eleven of Mark's closest friends had been slaughtered tonight, but he was thankful that the rest of them had been spared, and though sad as it were that they had been killed, they were willing to give up their own life, rather than to tell where Mark was hiding. The others had heard the gunshots, and came to see what had happened, and when Mark peeked out through a window, he saw them standing in the yard.

Just as soon as Martha was able to sit up, Mark took some quilts from a shelf in the hallway, and went outside. Mark wanted all his friends to have a decent burial. He helped the others load the bodies into a wagon, then they took them down to the small church Mark had built, to bury them. Even though Henry Graham had made the Negroes plow up the graveyard and remove the rock headstones, when Mark returned from Ohio, he asked the Negroes to mound up graves where they thought someone was buried, and had them to place the rocks back at the mounds of dirt, as markers.

Mark realized now, that everyone knew that he was hiding out somewhere on his plantation, and that someone would be watching his house day and night, or at least until the war was over. And if they found out that Martha was alive, they would not only return to kill her, but all the others as well. He could not allow this to happen, so he told all the others to spread the word around that Martha was dead, and keep on saying that they hadn't seen him since he'd left to report for duty with the Confederate Army.

During the next few weeks Martha remained in the mansion, for Mark had a reason to believe that his father knew about every move the Negroes made, and Mark knew what his father would do, if he found out that he had failed to kill her a second time. Mark prayed that this awful war would end, so he'd be able to get away from this God-awful place. He was so disgusted over the way the Negroes were being treated, and as the war slowly wound down, it seemed as though the hatred for them increased with each passing day.

A few weeks later, on Sunday, April 9, 1865, General Robert E. Lee agreed to meet with General Ulysses S. Grant of the Union Army, for Lee realized that the South could not win the war, and to avoid further bloodshed, he decided to surrender, and bring this bloody conflict to an end. The two Generals agreed on liberal terms of surrender, and officially the war was over, even though a number of small Southern troops fought on, not willing to admit defeat.

Though the war was over, it would take many years for the South to regain even a part of it's ability to survive on it's own, for it had lost just about everything it once proudly boasted of, including all its young men. The slaves were set free, and farmers who were forced to free them under orders of President Lincoln were angry. They ran the former slaves off the plantations, and they were forced to survive as best they could. As for Mark, he kept his workers, and though he was unable to pay them, due to the economy in the South after the war, they worked on together as before, and they all gladly shared in whatever they were fortunate to achieve together as a team.

CHAPTER ELEVEN

AS THE LAST PETAL FALLS

"The war is over! The war is over!" This happy cry was being echoed all across the land, and especially throughout the South, for it had suffered much greater loss in property damage, and the economy had also completely exhausted, even before the war was over. The cost in human lives, and property damage to both sides was devastating, but the past four years had left the South in an awful dire condition, to say the least. Farms now lay in charred ruins, and all the hopes and dreams of the Southern farmers were possibly destroyed forever. The spirit and pride of Southerners had been crushed underneath the heel of their enemy to the north. Though they would never be able to engage in another war against the North, and were now no more than footstools, for many generations yet to come, parents would instill in the hearts and minds of their children, distrust and hatred for their Nothern neighbors.

While the ending of this bloody war did bring a halt to the fighting and dying on the battlefields, it did little to relieve the suffering of those who were trying to survive in the South. Even though the post-war reconstruction program did offer a promise of help for the South, in many ways, it took away what the war had not already destroyed. For a fact, the North still hated the South because it withdrew from the Union in the first place, and officials of the government didn't take immediate action in offering relief to the South, now that the war was finally over. The Freedom Act was initially intended to assist all the freed-slaves, but those in government who opposed it, began to accuse its agents of fraud, and party politics. Though Southern citizens hated Lincoln, and accused him of starting the war in the first place, Lincoln, actually felt pity for the South, and wanted to help it to get back on its feet.

Years crept by, and the South was slow to heal. Although the South swore to support the Union, in reality it had not. The slaves had been set free and were given a right to vote, but in the South there were some restrictions, for Negroes were still considered to be inferior to white persons.

Negroes continued to work for white people in the South, not as slaves as before, but as sharecroppers, and though they were cheated of what they earned each year, they dared not complain. Though free, they still feared what might happen if they rebelled. Hooded vigilantes had begun harassing the Negroes by raiding their homes, beating, and sometimes killing them. Local members of law enforcement seemed to look the other way when such as this happened, and were believed to be a member of the hooded-mob as well. Negroes could not turn to anyone for help, the Law, or sworn leaders, either.

Fortunately, Mark Simpson somehow managed to keep his plantation. He used the freed slaves as before, and paid them a fair salary. Negroes from other farms were aware of how Mark treated his workers before The Civil War, and now that they were free to work for whomever they chose, they came to Mark's plantation seeking work. Although Mark had nothing to do with them coming to his farm in the first place, and was unable to give all of them work to do, other farmers in the area blamed him just the same, and called him a "nigger lover". Though it seemed that they had somehow forgotten all about him leaving the war, they certainly hadn't forgot about the firm stand he took against slavery before the war started. During his first post-war visit with the local banker, Ellis Bland, he was reminded that the hatred others once had for him, was still very much alive.

"Well, Mr. Simpson," said an old and broken Ellis Bland, "I see you're still in the cotton business, although many other farmers threw up their hands and quit, after what happened to them during the war. You were among the very few farmers in the area who escaped total destruction when Sherman's men swept through the South, and even today, some folks wonder why he bypassed your farm, in the first place."

"So, what you say, is that I had something to do with him bypassing my place!" Mark scolded. "And, I suppose they claim that my leaving the war before it was over, caused the South to lose. Is that it!"

"No, I didn't mean it that way, but because your farm wasn't bothered at all, you had a better chance of restarting, than some of the others had," he explained.

"That's right, Mr. Bland." Mark replied, as he sat watching the hands of the aged banker shaking, as he sat behind his desk. "I'm working hard, trying to recover from what the war cost me. I don't imagine that we'll ever really recover, not in my lifetime, for we lost more than we'll ever regain. Firing the first shot of the war, was the biggest mistake South Carolina ever made as far as I'm concerned, except for using Negroes as slaves, for it cost several thousands of lives, and millions of dollars in damage, all because our leaders were too proud to compromise. What made it so bad for those men who suffered and died on the battlefields, was that they really didn't know why they were there, or what they hoped to accomplish by fighting."

"I'm glad it's over, even though we're in worse shape now, than before it started," Bland rambled. "As it seems now, just being able to survive is a luxury, not to mention the hardship we face at the hand of the Union, as we wait for it to let us get back into the Union again."

A smile came on Mark's face, for this gave him an opportunity to lash out at the old man, and refresh his memory.

"Sir, if you remember, long before the war started, I cautioned you about what would happen," Mark reminded him. "If farmers had let up on the way they treated the Negroes, the Union would have backed off. But you and a lot of others, including my father, called me a 'nigger lover'. Do you remember that, and how you said that I was bringing shame to your family, and the community, for treating my workers fair, and paying them."

"Yes, I vaguely remember you saying something like that, but at the time, it sounded rather foolish," Bland admitted. "No use to cry over spilled milk, as they say, but I agree that you became successful by paying the niggers, and other farmers didn't want to admit that you were right. I operate a business, and in order for me to survive, I have to agree with whatever the majority of my depositors think is best. And you didn't seem to care what others thought about you, which I couldn't understand."

"Mr. Bland, if you don't mind my asking, how is Carolyn? Is she as kind and sweet as ever," Mark inquired. "I still think of her quite often, and if things had worked out for us, we would have been happily married today. Might have even had a family of our own, someone to leave my farm to, and someone to carry on after I'm gone."

"But, I do mind!" Bland snapped. "She's changed so very much, don't speak to me anymore, and don't even attend church. Thanks to you for that, for you stepped between her and me, and severed our family ties."

"But you deserve blame for that!" Mark scolded, remembering that one night at Bland's house. "You treated her worse than a dog, or worse than some folks did their slaves, so don't come to me complaining about a problem that you created for yourself."

"Look here!" Growled Bland. "She's my daughter, and she's of no concern of yours, and I don't want you to mention her name in my presence again."

"That's fine with me, but the money you owe me is my concern, and if you will count it out to me, I'll be on my way," snapped Mark, as he stood up and tapped his finger on the desk. "I thought that by losing the war, it might stir up the minds of such persons as you, and cause you to look at what such an attitude has cost us, but I was wrong, I suppose."

"I know that you still like the niggers as before, but you had better be careful how you suckle up to them from now on," Bland warned. "There's a new Christian group called White Supremacy getting started in the South, and it's gaining a lot of support, and they'll handle the niggers the way they should be handled. We might have lost the war, but we certainly didn't lose our will to always keep the niggers in line."

Mark was in no mood to talk with this man any longer, so he put the money into his pocket, shook his head, and walked out of Bland's office. On his way back home, he couldn't keep from feeling a bit sorry for Mr. Bland, for it was men like him who had caused the war, and it would be men like him who wouldn't ever accept the fact that all humans were equal, regardless to their race, or the color of their skin.

Mark had heard many horror stories about the group of so-called Christian men who now roamed the countryside, terrorizing Negroes, while downplaying their freedom. Mark felt that his father would be instrumental in helping to organize such a group, although he hadn't heard of anyone admitting that they belonged to the organization, and denied taking part in its activities. He remembered his friends being killed, and what Bland said just a moment ago, really bothered him, as he went on back to his plantation.

One day simply bled into another for Mark, as work in the fields, eating and sleeping became a never-ending routine. Mark smiled very little anymore, and seemed to live only to get from one day to the next. Martha worried about Mark all the time now, and hoped that her devotion to him would be enough to help him through this crisis that was causing him so much grief. Although she was the only survivor left of her family, she continued living in Mark's house and serving as maid. Since George and Ike were killed, other Negroes had been placed in charge of his plantation, for Mark wasn't able to handle everything that must be done all by himself. Although he hadn't spoken to his father, he had managed to slip back to his homeplace to visit with his mother for a few hours. She was very weak, yet his visit seemed to bring some color to her wrinkled face, and a tiny sparkle to her loving eyes again.

"Mother, when I last visited you, I told you how worried, and concerned I was about the condition the South was in right after the war, and I must admit that it hasn't changed very much," Mark told her. "I fought in the war, but my being there didn't change things one bit, except to help the South get into a worse mess, than it was in before the war started."

"I know, Son," she gently smiled, "and I'm afraid we won't ever enjoy a lifestyle quite like we had before, for it seems like we have lost all hope of ever getting ahead again. It will take a lot more than the war to destroy our Southern pride, for we're born with that, but our spirit has been broken, and our will to become successful, has crumbled right before our eyes."

"I know, Mother, for it seems like I'm living only one day at a time, and at the close of the day I lay and wonder how I made it," he sadly replied, as he felt tears coming to his eyes. "I thought that by the South losing the war it would cause folks to realize where they had been wrong, but as it seems to me, folks grew even worse than they were before. The only real friend I have left is Martha, after her family was killed, and just having Martha around, is still creating problems for me. Her family helped me during a time when I had no one else to turn to, and even though she is a Negro, she is all that I seem to live for anymore. I wish that folk understoood how a person can like other people, without being in love with them, and feel like I do toward her, without committing a sin. Do you think it's wrong, for me to feel as I do about her ?"

"Like you said, there's a great difference in loving somebody, and being in love with them, but that's hard for an evil-minded person to understand," she replied. "Ever since you were just a child, I knew that you had a special feeling for that whole family, and as time passed, you grew closer, and closer to them, and especially to the girl. They have stood by you when everyone was against you, including your father and sister, and regardless to the color of her skin, you'd be a fool, to let her down now. That's the reason I helped her to escape after she killed the buck, for she didn't deserve the kind of punishment, that your father was putting her through."

"I appreciate that, Mother, and I'll always remember your words of wisdom 'til the day I die," he said, as he stood up to leave. "I must go now before my father gets back, for we both have all the trouble resting on our shoulders that we're able to bear." He kissed her on the cheek, and then went on his way.

Days turned into weeks, weeks into months, and months into years. Plant and harvest the crop, collect from the banker, pay the workers, and start all over again. Life became a mechanical existence for Mark. His guilt over the death of many of his friends, had certainly taken its toll on him. There were Bill and Liza, their two sons, and yes, those who were killed for not telling where he was hiding, and now the new group Bland spoke about, were threatening those who had managed to survive.

As if to complicate his life even more, Martha had given birth to a child out of wedlock, and rumors began to fly. She named the child Rebecca, and of course, everyone accused Mark of being the child's father. Because of all the gossip, Mark withdrew from all social activities, and seldom ever went off the plantation for any reason. He had already been branded as a "nigger lover" in the past for freeing the slaves, and paying them for their work, and the birth of Martha's child, only added fuel to the fire. His mother told him about his sister getting pregnant before she got married, and about her giving her child to a relative to raise, and Mark wondered why folks hadn't blamed him for that as well. Other farmers had fathered children by Negro girls, and nothing was said about them, but because this happened to Martha while she lived in Mark's house, and even without any proof, everyone made it seem like he had committed an unforgivable sin, simply because they thought he was guilty.

Forced to go into town one day to pick up supplies, he was confronted by a hot-tempered man, as he approached the General Store. Although Mark had not knowingly come in contact with a member of the White Supremacy group that came into being immediately after the war ended, the man left an impression that he was possibly a member of that group.

"This is a clean and respectful town," the man taunted Mark, "and folks like you aren't welcome in our presence. You are classed like the scum of the earth for the way you treat the niggers, and now that you have a baby by that gal who lives in your house, you've become as low as a snake's belly."

"Sir, I have no quarrel with you," said Mark sternly, trying to avoid an argument. "I came to town on business, like anybody else, and my being here is no concern of yours, and if you know what's good for you, you'll keep what you think of me to yourself. Excuse me, for I have business at the store."

"You're a nigger lover, and that does concern me!" The man shouted, in an angry voice. "You were hated before the war, because you stood up for niggers, and now you have a baby by one of the black-bastards! Folks have had all they can stand out of you, and it's time for us to take action!"

"But, the child don't belong to me!" Mark snapped. "You're accusing me of something you know nothing about. And, let me warn you now, if you and the so-called Christian group don't keep your mouth shut about me, you'll be sorry that you said what you did." Mark was growing angry with the man.

"We'll see how true it is, when we come out there and burn your house down on you, and that sorry hussy!" He yelled, suddenly looking as though he might have said something that he shouldn't have said.

Then, it dawned on Mark what Bland had said about the new group, and how they planned to take control of the freed-slaves.

"So, you're a member of that so-called Christian group that's been going around over the country and harassing the Negroes!" Mark replied "Do you fellows plan to clean up the country? Is that what you mean."

"No, I don't belong to anything like that," the man replied. "All I was told, they said, oh, never mind. Forget that I ever said anything."

"You had better tell them to stay away from my house, for I'll be ready to kill anybody who messes around my place!" Mark threatened. "Just in case you think that I'm bluffing, and if you're ready to die, go ahead and set foot on my property, or try to bother any of my workers."

Mark noticed that the man's face was bright red now, and it appeared that he had said somethng that he shouldn't have.

Though it didn't show on Mark's face at all, what the man said really frightened him, and he decided to go back home without even bothering to pick up the supplies from the store. He felt an urge to warn his workers so they would be prepared, just in case something took place tonight. Hurrying to get in his buggy and go home, he stopped at the door leading to Dr. Hall's office, to allow a man on crutches to enter. As the man turned to thank him, they looked hard at each other.

"Mark Simpson!" The gray haired man gasps, as he eyed Mark intently. "You stay away from me!" The man looked horrified at the sight of Mark. His right leg had been amputated, and the foul odor attested to a massive infection that had taken over his body. He trembled, as Mark stood holding the door for him to enter the doctor's office.

"Well, if it isn't my old partner, Mr. Powell, in person!" Mark said, in a stern voice. "I heard that you were still around these parts, and I wonder if you've been shooting any Negroes here lately. I heard that you were in the group that killed some of my workers, while I was away at war."

Powell's face was ashen now, for he realized that Mark knew that he was in the group that night, when they killed several of Mark's workers.

"I don't know what you're talking about!" Powell nervously replied. "Don't be accusing me of something, that I didn't do."

"You know perfectly well what I'm talking about," said Mark, as he stood and shook his head. "I told you that I'd kill you if I ever ran upon you, but I see that the Almighty has taken care of that for me. You are a dead man already, and don't know it."

Then, Powell's wife came running up to them. She had also aged an awful lot, and looked very much like a hag.

"Simpson!" She yelled, in a cracking voice. "Leave him alone! Are you too ignorant to see that he's dying? Almost dead now, as it is."

"Yes Madam, I sure do realize that he's dying," Mark said mockingly. "He and I were just talking about his physical condition. Good-day, to both of you!" Mark gave a quick bow, and then turned to walk away.

"You'll burn in hell for this!" Mrs. Powell ranted after him. "You will reap what you sow. The Bible says so, if you'll take time to read it for yourself sometime."

Turning back, Mark looked harshly into her eyes. "Yes, that's how I feel myself," he said very seriously. "You and Mr. Powell are living proof that a person will reap what they sow. Sow to the wind, and you'll reap a whirlwind. Maybe I read that in the Bible too, I'm not really sure."

As Mark neared his buggy to go back home, a thought came to him. He had only one handgun in his house, and if the mob did happen to come to his house as he thought they might, he would be in a lot of trouble. Not knowing quite what to do, or if he should even take what the man said seriously, he decided to go to the General Store and purchase some weapons and ammunition to take to the Negroes to use for protection, just in case.

Expecting to find Mr. Wilson tending the store, and knowing that this man and his father were great friends, Mark really didn't know if Mr. Wilson would even let him buy any weapons from him. However, as he neared the counter, an unfamiliar young man greeted him.

"Excuse me, Sir," Mark spoke politely. "Is Mr. Wilson around, or did he step outside for a moment. I wanted to purchase some special items, but I can come back later on, after he gets back."

"No Sir, he's not in," replied the young man, nervously. "Mr. Wilson is dead, or haven't you heard? He, uh, well, he's dead," he added.

"I'm sorry to hear that," Mark responded, realizing that the man didn't know him. "I haven't been to town in quite some time now, and this sure is news to me. What happened to him, if I may ask?"

"Well, I uh, I guess it's all right to tell you," replied the clerk, in an edgy voice. "He, well, he got shot one night, that's what happened."

"And you, Sir, what's your name?" Mark inquired. "Did you buy the store after his death, or could it be that you're related to him?"

"I'm John Holden," he answered. "Mr. Wilson's wife is my aunt. I came up from Savannah, to mind the store for her. Aunt Daisy's in foul shape after what happened, for he was . . .." The young man hesitated.

"I hope he wasn't shot during a robbery," Mark pressed him. "There sure has been a lot of that going on since the war, and I just wondered if the same thing might have happened to him. That's all I meant."

The young man looked keenly at Mark for a moment, and not knowing him, or if he belonged to the newly organized group he'd heard about, he hesitated for a moment, before telling Mark what really happened.

"He got involved with the wrong bunch, and he wound up losing his life in the meantime," he reluctantly replied, in a low voice. "Now, Sir, I'd rather not discuss it any further, if you don't mind."

"I'm sorry, for I didn't mean to pry into your business, but I've come to this store ever since I was a child," said Mark. "What happened to his son, "Josh," as they called him? He and I were great friends, before I was called off to the war, and I haven't seen him since I came back. He didn't get killed in the war, did he?"

"No, but he deserted the war, like many other soldiers did before it ended, and he lives somewhere in Virginia," John replied. "I don't know why he didn't return like other soldiers did, and in fact, he didn't even return home to attend his father's funeral. Between me and you, I think that he was ashamed of the way his father died."

"That's a shame, for I always liked him, and he and I saw eye to eye on a lot of things," Mark told him. "I need some items for my house, but first, I need some rifles and some ammunition, if you have any in stock."

"Did you say that you need some rifles and ammunition?" Asked the young man, in surprise. "Sir, are you one of those men?"

"What men are you talking about?" Mark quickly asked. "We might not be thinking about the same thing, and I don't quite understand what you mean."

409

"Never mind, Sir,' he said nervously. "It's none of my business who you are, so forget that I asked. Now, what was that you needed?"

Mark noticed that the young man was jerking all over, and he decided to put his mind at ease.

"I'm Mark Simpson, I operate a large farm, and you don't have anything to worry about from me," Mark explained. "I'd like to buy some rifles and a few boxes of cartridges, for I've been told by those men whom you just mentioned, that trouble might be headed my way. In fact, that same mob that you just now referred to, killed several of my wokers a few years back, and I intend to be ready for them, the next time around."

The young man heaved a visible sigh of relief. "Mr. Simpson, I wasn't sure who you were, for a man has to be mighty careful these days, with the so-called White Supremacy around." John smiled. "A man might teach a Sunday school lesson in the morning, then kill a bunch of Negroes, as soon as the sun goes down. That's why I have to be very careful what I say."

"I'll gladly tell you which side I'm on," Mark replied. "I believe that we should do right toward everybody, black or white, and I don't intend to let that hooded-mob hurt any of my workers, if it can be prevented. If you have a few rifles and ammunition, I'd like to buy them."

"Sure thing," John winked. "Now, just how many rifles do you need, and how many rounds of ammunition would you like?"

"Make it twenty, or twenty-five repeating rifles, the kind the North used before the war ended, and a case of ammunication," he replied."

After checking his stock, John returned with twelve rifles and five shotguns, a case of cartridges, and two boxes of shotgun shells. "Can you get by with these, 'til I order some more?"

"That's fine, and I appreciate your help," Mark replied. "I promise not to tell where I got them, so you don't have to worry one bit about that."

John wrapped the weapons in feed sacks, so no one could see what Mark had purchased. After Mark gathered up a few other items he needed, John helped to load everything into Mark's buggy. When John glanced across the street, there stood a group of men looking that way.

"Don't let on as if you see them, but there's some of those very same men standing across the street, and they're eyeballing us right now," John softly said. "Is the man who threatened you, one of them?"

"Yes, he's the tall one, leaning up against that tree," Mark replied, as he glanced that way. "I don't recall ever seeing him before. Who is he?"

"Jim Phillips, that's his name," John whispered, as he turned to go back into the store. "He works for Ephriam Johnson, and from what I hear, he's the leader of the clan. Good-day, Sir, and I hope things work out for you."

Mark climbed into his buggy and headed back toward home, and as he drove past where the men were standing near the edge of the street, he noticed that Jim was whispering something to the other men.

"Better get back to your nigger woman and baby!" Jim yelled. "Better be enjoying them while you can, which won't be long, now!"

Mark suddenly stopped, whipped out his pistol, and fired a shot into the tree, just above the men's head.

"I can take care of my business, and I expect you to do the same thing!" Mark yelled, in reply. "If you, or any member of your clan bothers me or my workers, you'll have the devil to pay! I'll kill anybody who acts like they intend to do us harm. When you drive through the gates of my plantation, you'll be entering the gates of hell."

Mark waited a moment longer, and when neither of them replied, he headed on toward home. The shot had quieted them down for the moment, but Mark knew that he hadn't heard the last of this.

As Mark drove back home, a strange feeling came over him, and he realized that the weapons might be needed after all. He hoped and prayed that nothing would happen, yet at the same time, he couldn't stand idly by without any kind of protection, and take a chance of him, or his workers being hurt. Mark was not a real violent person at all, but past happenings had taught him a lesson he would not soon forget, and the death of so many of his friends had caused a great change in the way he looked at other persons. Even though they were Negroes, Martha and her young daughter lived in Mark's house, and because they trusted him to look after them, as did the other Negroes on his farm, he felt more obligated to care for them, than he did for himself.

411

The sun was almost down, when Mark arrived back at the mansion, and three Negroes who had been raking leaves off the yard, walked over to Mark's buggy to see if he needed help in unloading the supplies. They knew that Mark was a gentle natured person, but when they saw the weapons, their eyes blared.

"Mr. Mark, is you gon'a get the war started up again?" Asked Jimbo. "It looks like you's got 'nuf guns to whoop a big army wid. Ain't you done went and kilt 'nuf of them mens, er is you gon'a send us off to war, and let us get kilt, too? I's ain't never been kilt befo', and don't know how to act like no dead man, so you's better send somebid'ee else, 'cides me."

"I'll explain it all later," said Mark, as he handed the weapons to the three men. "Stand them in the corner of the parlor, and tell everybody to be up here at my house before dark. And, tell them to make sure that they leave a lamp burning in the house, as well. I want everybody up here!"

Mark took the items he had bought for the house and set them on the kitchen table, where Martha and her daughter Rebecca, were making decorations to hang on the Christmas tree, for soon it would be Christmas. Mark knew that Rebecca would see the guns standing in the parlor, and would become frightened at the sight of them, so he decided to explain to her why they were there.

"Rebecca," he spoke softly, kneeling down by her chair, "there might be some disturbance here tonight, and I don't want you to be afraid. If it comes to that, I want you to go with your mother to a special room I have somewhere, and be very quiet. Do you understand what I mean?"

Before the child could reply, Martha grabbed Mark by the arm, and led him out into the hallway, for she knew that something was fixing to go wrong.

"Mark, what kin'a trouble is you spect'n?" She asked. "Did you's happen to hear of sump'um while you wuz in town, to cause you to thank that we gon'a be having trouble 'round here?"

"Yes, I heard a threat made in town, and I have reasons to believe that a hooded-mob might come around here pretty soon, maybe even tonight, as far as I know," he whispered. "Nothing might happen at all, then again it might, so to be on the safe side, I wanted to be prepared."

"Oh Lord, no!" Martha wailed. "They gon'a kill me and Beckie, like they done kilt all my folks! Ain't that what they gon'a do? Mark, did you happen to axe 'em, if they wuz gon'a kill lit'l Beckie, too?"

"Not if those rifles and shotguns in there will fire," he replied, as he pointed toward the weapons that were standing in the parlor. "If they do come tonight like I think, I want you and Rebecca to hide in the secret room before the others arrive. I don't want them to know anything about the room. I'll make them lay down on the floor, in the hallway."

As darkness hovered over the plantation, all the other Negroes arrived at the mansion, and Mark told them what they must do in case there was trouble. Martha and Rebecca were already in the secret room, and their names were not mentioned at all.

"Fellows, I hope nothing happens, but just in case, I want us to be ready for whatever comes," Mark told them, as he loaded the weapons, and handed one to each of them, until the supply ran out. "As far as I know, nobody will be coming tonight, except for the mob, if they come at all, and if you happen to see anybody snooping around out there, shoot to kill."

"We know what to do, but what we's don't know, is why you axed us to make sho' that a lamp wuz burning in our house," said Jimbo. "Ain't that wasting kerosene? Ain't you told us not to waste nothing?"

"If they do come tonight, like I think they will, they'll be looking for Martha and me," Mark replied. "When they see the lamp burning in your houses they'll think you folks are at home, and that we're up here alone. They won't know that we're sitting up here armed, and ready for them. Like I said, they might not even come tonight, but if they don't, we'll repeat this every night, until we feel sure that they're not coming at all."

"If they do come adder you and Marthie, is we 'spose to start shoot'n at 'em when they fus' get here, er is we 'spose to wait 'til they kill us, fo' we shoot at 'em?" Asked another one of the men.

"No, not exactly," Mark chuckled. "I want one of you to stand near each window in the front of the house, and when I give the signal, we'll all start shooting at the same time. And like I said, shoot to kill."

Although Mark had no way of knowing, trouble had already started to brew. Down at the main road, just yards from the entrance to the plantation, was an ominous-looking group of hooded raiders. Leading this pack of hoodlums, were none other than Nate Simpson himself, flanked by John Phillips, Nate's son-in-law, and of all the other men imaginable, the County Sheriff. They had sent a rider to scout out Mark's plantation.

"Well, all the niggers are still at home, for I saw a lamp burning in all their houses, which means that they won't be up there to help Mark," reported the scout. "I watched the light go out in Mark's house, which means that they are snug in bed, and won't be expecting anything to happen. Seems to me, like this is going to be easier than we expected, and we should have done this long before now."

"Very good, indeed!" Snapped the sheriff. "Then we'll just have to wake the sleepy-heads up, and have a word of prayer with them. Speaking of prayer, Brother Nate, will you lead us in prayer, and ask the Lord to be with us, as we go about doing His great work here tonight."

They all bowed their heads, while Nate Simpson asked for God to bless the hoodlums, and help them carry out this act that was a disgrace in the sight of all humanity, and an abomination in the sight of God.

"Like I said earlier," spoke up Nate Simpson, "John and me are with you fellows, no matter what happens. I might have a nigger lover as a son, but I have a real gentleman for a son-in-law, and we're ready to get started."

"I understand that we're going to give Mark a flogging, but what will we do with that nigger woman, and her gal?" Asked one of the men.

"Let us take care of Mark first, then we'll play things by ear, as we go along," the sheriff laughed.

The others knew quite well what "playing it by ear" meant, for back last spring they played a similar game "by ear," and the farmer got off some shots before he was killed. One of the shots had killed Mr. Wilson, the manager of the General Store, and another shot had caused Powell's leg to be amputated.

"Nate, just how far do you want us to go tonight?" Asked one of the men. "Do you care if we burn that beautiful house, and kill Mark, if it happens to come down to that?"

"Whatever happens, will happen!" Nate bellowed. "If he refuses to do as we say, then the sky's the limit, I suppose. Let's get on with it."

Inside the house, Mark and the Negroes patiently waited in the darkness, while they hoped that nothing would happen here tonight. It had been dark now for at least two hours, and Mark was beginning to think that the man, who spoke with him in town, was only bluffing. All of a sudden things changed, for Mark heard the sound of horses hoofs pounding on the dirt driveway that led up to the mansion. He went to the hallway and told the women and children to lay on the floor, and be very quiet, and then he hurried back to where he had positioned himself near the front door earlier.

"All right fellows," Mark softly said to the Negro men. "I hear horses walking up the driveway. The moon is shining fairly bright tonight, and I'd like to see if I can recognize any of them, before we start shooting."

Peeking through the glass in the front door, Mark saw several hooded-men on horseback, ride up and stop near the edge of the yard. They all wore white robes, and masks over their heads, with only eye-holes cut in the mask so they could see, making it impossible for Mark to recognize them. They dismounted, and Mark could hear them talking to each other, but he couldn't hear what they were saying. They worked quickly, and quietly, as they stood up an oil-soaked cross near the edge of the yard, then set fire to it. As the cross-started to burn, two of them walked up closer to the house, with weapons pointed.

"Wake up in there, Brother Simpson," a disguised voice called out, "for we want to have a little talk with you. Do you hear me?"

Mark didn't respond, for he had a feeling that his father was among them, and he wanted to wait and see if he could recognize any of their voices. Mark had no way of knowing who was among the mob, but he did think that the man who just called out, sounded a lot like his brother-in-law.

"Get on out here!" another altered voice called out. "We have something to discuss with you!" Then, a shot was fired into the air. "Did you hear me, or can you hear the sound of a rifle, a little better?"

A moment later, someone fired a shot at the house, and broke out a window upstairs, and Mark knew now, that it was time for him to do something.

"All right, I'll be out as soon as I get dressed!" Mark called back, as he slowly raised a window, and motioned to the Negroes to do the same. "Don't hurt the Negro woman or her child, for they have nothing to do with a quarrel you have with me. Is that a deal? Do you promise not to hurt them?"

"That's where you're wrong!" Growled another voice, that sounded quite a lot like his father's voice. "Bring her and that bastard-child on out!"

"I'm coming out alone, and unarmed, for I don't intend to involve them, in whatever you came to see me about!" Mark shouted, firmly.

"We'll burn the house down with them inside, unless you bring them on out with you!" The man threatened. "Do you doubt my word?"

A few moments went by, and Mark didn't go outside, as they demanded, then another shot rang out, breaking out the window where Mark was standing.

"Get on out here, right now!" Someone shouted, as six more men walked up close to the house. "We mean business, and we don't have time to fool around any longer!" Then, several more shots were fired at the house.

The Negroes had already raised the windows like Mark ordered, and as soon as Mark gave the signal; they started in firing the shotguns and rifles at the hooded-mob. This caught them by surprise, and they ran in all directions, in an effort to get out of the line of fire. Mark heard one of the men yell, and at least three of them fell to the ground, and Mark knew that they had been at least seriously injured. Some of the others began dragging the fallen men out toward where the horses were tied, and Mark called out for the Negroes to stop firing, for he figured that the men had learned a lesson tonight. After the men left, Mark and his friends went outside to look around, and survey the damage that has been done to the house.

"Is everybody all right?" Mark asked, as he took his foot and kicked the burning cross down to the ground.

"Yass'uh, we's aw'rite," replied Jimbo, who was Mark's favorite. "Does you thank that we's kilt any of 'em? Did we's do the way you wanted us to do, er is you mad, 'cause we didn't kill all of 'em?"

"You fellows did real good, for I'm sure we wounded several of them, and we might have killed one of them at least," Mark replied. "Except for a few windows being broken, and maybe a few boards cracked, we came out just fine."

"Does you want us to clean up the mess to'nite, er wait 'til moan'n, and clean it up?" One of them asked.

"No, not tonight," Mark replied. "Round up your folks and go on back to your house, for we've done enough tonight. I'll go into town early tomorrow morning, and get what we need to make the repairs, and I might get a carpenter to come out and fix up things for us."

"That's fine wid me," said one of the men. "Will you be aw'rite all by yo'sef, er does you want us to hang 'round 'til the sun comes up?"

"I'll be just fine," Mark smiled. "Take the guns on home with you, just in case you might need them later, but leave one of the repeating rifles at my house. If I know them, they'll return to finish what they started, but I have no way of knowing when that might be. We'll just have to wait and see."

Early the following morning, Mark went into town to order the supplies he would need to make the repairs on his house, and talk with a carpenter, to see when he would be able to do the work. He was sure that he'd hear something at the General Store about what went on last night, for that was the place where folks came to hear about what went on in the community.

Entering the General Store, Mark greeted John, who was busy arranging some stock on a shelf behind the counter. "Good morning, John!" Mark said, as he walked up to the counter. "Do you remember me?"

"Back so soon!" John replied, smiling. "It really did happen last night like you suspected, didn't it?" He asked, as if talking in riddles.

"I'm afraid so," Mark answered, "But I'm all right. I just need twelve of the window panes replaced, and a few boards that were splintered, when the good Christian men shot into my house."

"Well, word has it, that some of your Negroes ambushed a group of men who were returning from a political meeting last night," John told him. "The way I hear it, the County Sheriff and two other men were killed, and at least two others were injured. Those weapons sure paid off for you, didn't they."

"And the sheriff was one of them, you say." Mark asked. "And the other two, would you happen to know who they were?"

"A deacon of my church, Brother Satterfield, and another man by the name of Baxter, I do believe," John replied. "A number of others were injured by shotgun pellets, and one was hit in the leg with a rifle bullet, but I haven't heard who they were, or how serious their injuries were."

"A real bunch of outstanding citizens, huh'?" Mark grimaced. "And several of our good Christian gentlemen, our sheriff, too. Killed, while carrying out what was called their Christian-duty. That's real bad."

"Yes, it's awful bad," John, remarked sadly. "I'm going back to Savannah in a couple of weeks, for I can't stay in such a place as this, any longer. Seems like folks won't ever learn that they can't take the law into their own hands, and that Negroes are now free citizens, whether they like it or not."

"I'm sorry that you had a bad example set before you here, and that your uncle was killed," Mark replied. "You might be wise in returning to Savannah after all, for unless the hooded-mobs are stopped, there's no telling just how far they might go, or how many more lives will be lost."

"I'm not trying to run you off," said John nervously, "but I don't want any trouble with that bunch, or have them think that I'm on your side, or find out that I sold you the weapons. I hope you understand, Sir."

"You're absolutely right, for there's no telling what that bunch might do if they caught me in here, after what happened last night," Mark agreed, then he handed him a list of supplies, he needed. "I'll tell the carpenter to come by and pick them up tomorrow, and I'll stop by and pay you soon."

All the way back home, Mark was bothered by what had happened at his place, but he'd been pushed to a point where he had to stand up against these hoodlums, otherwise, they would eventually take over everything. He was sorry that the men were killed; yet he felt justified because he had prevented them from killing Martha and her daughter, maybe him too. His father boasted about "having the law in my pocket," but now the law was dead. He feared his father now more than ever before, for if he were in the group last night and they failed, he'd return to finish what he started, and Mark knew that.

Truer still, was a statement Bill made, "This ain't no place fer no free-nigga," and Mark knew that for a fact. Oh, how he missed Bill, for he was stable and trustworthy. He would have known exactly what to say to Mark now, and he could have given him courage to go on, but Bill was not here.

Had Bill lived, he would have the right to vote now, Mark thought, as he rode along toward home, but what good would it be. The main objective of the hooded-mob, was to frighten the

Negroes so that they wouldn't seek their rights as free citizens. Abraham Lincoln officially abolished slavery before the war was over; still it was very much alive in practice in the South. Although white persons outwardly admitted that Negroes were free and equal citizens, in reality they were not, for they were too frightened to attempt to vote. White persons thought it was degrading to allow former slaves to vote, or admit that they were equal citizens, and an all-out effort was made to deprive Negroes of all rights that had been granted to them.

Nate Simpson returned home to his ailing wife, after having been away for three days. Dr. Hall had treated his leg that was injured during the raid on Mark's house, and he had been staying at a hotel in town. His wife Julie was real weak, and lay propped on a pillow in bed. She'd heard about the raid on Mark's house, and about the injuries and deaths that occured, and she felt sure that Nate was somehow involved, along with Susan's husband.

"Julie, I'm home!" Simpson snapped, as he walked down the hallway. "Are you all right," he asked, as he stood there in the hallway, near her bedroom door.

"I'm as well as can be expected," she replied. "I heard that the County Sheriff got killed the other night, along with some other men, and I wondered if you knew what caused it, or who killed them. I've heard one side of how it happened, and if you know anything about it, I'd like to hear your side."

"No matter what you might have heard, or who told you, I'll tell you what really happened," he replied. "A group of men attended a political meeting, and on their way back home, they were ambushed by some sorry niggers who live on Mark's place," he lied. "Good Christian men, slaughtered by a sorry bunch of niggers. It's not safe to be outside at night anymore, and unless we wipe the sorry bastards off the face of the earth, things like that will continue. It's nigger lovers like Mark, who are to blame for what happened to them."

"Nate, why are you walking with a limp?" Julie asked. "Did you fall and hurt your leg. Why is that hole in your britches leg, above your knee."

"Nothing's wrong with me!" He shouted, as he stormed down the hallway to go back outside. "It's none of your darned business, anyway."

She knew by the way he limped, and by the hole in his britches leg, that he was one who had been injured during the raid.

Sad to say, she thought, but it might have been a blessing to Mark, and to everyone else in the area, if he had been one of those who were killed that night.

During the rest of the week following the raid, Mark could hardly sleep a wink at night, for thinking that it might happen again. Not like in times past when he had no fear, now, he always kept a rifle near by at night, and carried it with him when he went into the fields to check on the crops. He tried very hard to make himself believe that the men wouldn't strike again, however, they were determined to keep Negroes under control, and Mark knew there were no bounds as to how far they were willing to go, to accomplish their goal. Though others in the community acted like they believed the story of how the men were killed that night, they did know the truth, but were afraid to admit it, for the fear they had for the hooded-mob.

It had been only one week since the raid on Mark's mansion, Christmas was only three days away, and Martha and her daughter had been busy all day making peanut-candy, baking cakes, and popping corn to make balls to hang on the tree as decoration. Martha had cut out strips of paper from a catalog, made some paste from flour dough, and Rebecca was making paper chains that would be hung on the tree. Martha knew that her daughter was still upset because of what happened a few nights ago, and she thought that if she could keep her busy doing something, it might take her mind off what happened.

Since the night of the raid, nothing had been said to cause Mark to fear another attack, or at least no time soon. This was the time of year for folks to enjoy peace and goodwill, and he doubted if members of the group were sorry enough to do something like that now, with it being so close to Christmas. He had gone to town to pick up a few items to put under the tree for Rebecca, and to get some cloth for Martha, so she could make her and Rebecca a dress. Mark was sitting by the fireplace in the parlor, and while Rebecca was taking a nap, Martha came in and sat down with him.

"Martha, I've been thinking about your family, ever since the men came and raided my house, and about all the hard times we had starting off with only a few acres of land, and how we all pulled together as a team," Mark told her, as he wiped a tear from his eye. "When I look at what we're going through at the moment, it causes me to wonder if it was worth all that it's cost, and if I did the right thing by crying out against slavery."

"My pappy used to say, there wuzn't no need to eat sump'um that you don't like, and have to puke it up later," she replied. "You went and stood up fer what you's thought wuz rite, and if you railly thought you wuz doing the rite thang, there ain't no use fer you to feel bad 'bout it now. We's all made big mistakes, and I's make a big'un when Beckie come 'long, but there ain't no use fer me to go through lif' and 'gret what I's done, er kill the youngun, 'cause of what folks say."

"You do have a point, and I agree that it should have never happened, but like you said, we'll just have to live with the past, for it can't be changed, and it certainly can't be erased," said Mark. "We'll have to raise the child as best we can, and hope for the best, and pray that she don't make some of the mistakes that we made in life. One day, and no matter how it might hurt, you must sit her down and tell her the truth, for I know how hard it is to live a lie, and pretend that others don't know the truth."

They sat and talked for a while longer, then Mark went to the barn to see that the Negroes did their chores before dark, and make sure they put firewood on the porch, to keep a fire burning through the night. He had told Martha as he walked out the door, that he had something else to discuss with her as soon as Rebecca went to sleep tonight.

It was now a few minutes after dark, and while Martha was cleaning up the kitchen, Mark sat by the fireplace, still thinking about his conversation with Martha earlier. Then, he heard a noise outside. When he went over and peeked out through a window, he saw a group of hooded-men standing at the edge of the yard. They had slipped quietly up to his house, and a cross was burning near the edge of the yard, and by the light of the burning-cross, he could see that there were at least fifty men out there. Then, he saw four men with torches, heading around toward the back of the house. He realized now, that there was no way of escape, for if he didn't do as they asked, and without the Negroes being there to help him, the men would burn the house down. The secret room would become a tomb, if they decided to hide in it.

"Get down on the floor, real quick!" Mark cried, as he hurried into the kitchen, and shoved Martha and Rebecca down on the floor. "Lay there, and don't move!"

"What's the matter?" Asked Martha, frightened by the awful strange expression on his face. "Is sombid'ee mess'n 'round out there? Is the mens come back?"

"There's a mob of men out there, a hundred or more, and we don't have anyone around to help us!" Mark nervously replied. "From the looks of all the torches, and the way they already surrounded the house, I think they're planning to burn the house down this time, with us inside."

Martha quickly threw her arms around Rebecca, and held her real tight, as she lay and prayed for God to help them. She could see the glow from the torches through the kitchen window, and could hear men mumbling as they waved torches in the air. Mark went back and peeked out through the glass in the front door to see if he could recognize any of them, but the mask over their faces prevented him from doing so. It was obvious, that they could see him, for one of the men pointed toward the door.

"Hey, I see you standing there at the door!" One of them yelled. "We've already checked the nigger houses, and we know that you're here alone this time, so you might as well come on out. It's you against us, this time."

"Yeah, come on out, Simpson!" Shouted another man. "Come on out, and we promise that we won't hurt you, for all we want is that sorry hussy, and that bastard-gal of her's."

"Why don't you fellows go on and leave us alone, for you know what you're doing, is wrong," Mark yelled back to them. "Think it over real good, before you fellows make a terrible mistake, that you'll regret forever."

"Think it over, the devil!" Shouted the man. "Unless you come out while you have a chance, you won't get out of there alive! Do you hear me?"

Mark knew for a fact that he was outnumbered, and the only possible means of escape, was that if he could bribe them into leaving. When he stepped out on the front porch with his hands raised in the air, he saw the angry men with rifles and shotguns pointed at him. As he stood there for a moment looking at the hoods on those who were not man enough to show their face, he wondered what kind of human beings these men were.

"I'm unarmed, I don't recognize any of you gentlemen, and I'm willing to made a deal with you," Mark proposed. "Go on and leave us alone, and I'll go to the bank tomorrow morning, and have Mr. Bland close out my account, and see that all of my money is divided between you fellows. If need be, I'm willing to mortgage my property, and give you more money. What do you fellows say?"

"We don't want your darned money!" Shouted someone, who sounded to Mark like the local banker himself. "These Christian men are thirsty for nigger's blood, as you can see, and money won't quince their thirst. Hand the niggers over like the man said, and you won't be hurt."

"But listen to me, fel..." Mark was about to offer them more, when a man rushed up and struck him on the head with the butt of his rifle. Mark let out a pitiful groan as he fell off the porch into the yard, with blood gushing from his head, and it appeared to them that the blow had killed him instantly. The men jeered, and some even tossed their mask in the air, because they had killed Mark at last.

Martha and her daughter had crawled down the hallway, and with the front door standing open, they saw what happened to Mark. Not seeming to care what happened to her now, Martha jumped up and ran into the parlor, and grabbed the rifle off the gun rack, then rushed back toward the front door. Not concerned for her own life, now that Mark was dead, she ran out on the front porch, and commenced firing widly into the crowd of men, while her young daughter stood near a window, watching.

In an instant, a volley of bullets, and shotgun pellets began raining down on her, and she fell facedown on the steps, then rolled on out into the yard. This didn't seem to satisfy these crazed-monsters, however, as they continued firing shot after shot into her lifeless body, until it became a bloody pulp. This was a pathetic scene to say the least, and her daughter stood helpless as she watched her mother being brutally murdered.

"Her daughter is standing near the window, and while we're here, we might as well get rid of the whole darned bunch!" A man yelled. "Drag her out here and tie her to a tree, and we'll get some target practice."

Two men rushed inside, dragged Rebecca out by the hair of the head, and then tied her to a tree near the edge of the yard.

"Oh Lord, don't kill me too!" Rebecca cried. "I's jus' a young'un, and ain't never done nothing to nobid'ee. Please don't kill me, like youn's done kilt my mammy, and Mark!"

Her tears seemed only to enrage the angry men more. There wasn't even a shred of remorse in any of them, for what they were doing here tonight.

Nate Simpson then spoke up. "Get out of the way, fellows," he laughed wickedly. "I want to end this worthless life, myself."

"Wy Nate, you wouldn't think of killing your own grandchild, would you," one of the men teased. "Your wife would never forgive you for that."

Nate quickly turned and fired a shot pointblank at the man, and he fell to the ground, dead. "Any more jokes," Nate growled, "any more smart asses?"

The men stood looking at each other, appalled at the lack of concern Nate had for the farmer that he'd just killed. The shot really frightened Rebecca.

"Please don't kill me, like you's done that feller!" Rebecca begged, and trembled with fright as she looked at Nate, who already had his rifle aimed at her. "Mammy's done dead, and Mark too, so please don't kill me."

The other Negroes had heard the shots that had killed Martha, and they grabbed the guns that Mark gave to them, and hurried up to the mansion to see what was going on. They slipped up behind the hooded-mob without being seen, and when they saw Martha and Mark they're on the ground, and Rebecca tied to the tree, they started firing into the group from where they stood in the shadows. The hoodlums who were still alive quickly jumped on their horses and galloped away, leaving those who had been shot by the Negroes, and the one Nate Simpson had killed, lying sprawled out there on the ground.

Eight men now lay dead on the ground, their white hoods and cloaks soaked in their own blood, as the light from the burning-cross, cast a glow on their bodies like flames from the pits of hell. The Negroes stepped over the bodies as they hurried to where Rebecca was still tied to the tree, and to where the corpse of Mark and Martha lay near the porch. They cried and chanted; as they gently lifted Martha's bullet riddled body, and placed it on the porch. Then, they picked up Mark's body, and placed it on the porch next to her.

Rebecca was devastated. She ran and threw herself across the body of her mother, and wept uncontrollably. She placed her hand on Mark's chest, as she watched blood coming from his head, then she let out a loud scream.

"Why did they do this?" She wailed. "Why did they keep on shoot'n at my mammy, adder she wuz done kilt, and dead?"

"The big Mos'a in the sky, is the on'les one that's got the an'sur to yo' kin'a ques'un," one of the women sighed, and told her. "Don't guess the mens that done this, is got no an'sur to why they went and done this."

The women took Rebecca inside to comfort her, and the men spread a quilt over Mark and Martha's bodies, then they set down on the edge of the porch and cried. To them, two members of their own family were dead.

All of a sudden, one of the men let out a loud yell, as he jumped up, and ran across the yard. "Oh my God, hold my feets on the ground, fer I jus' seed the dead man move his hand!" He screamed. "He done moved on me! Oh my Lord, that dead man is still liv'!"

"No he ain't, neither!" Another man sobbed. "He be dead, fer his head's busted wide op'um, and nobid'ee ain't gon'a live like dat'. Everbid'ee needs a head, if they gon'a liv', and it's got'a be in one piece, too."

Mark's hand moved again, and Jimbo saw it. "Hey, he still be liv', fer I seed him move that time!" Cried Jimbo. "Say sump'um to me, if you is still liv'," said Jimbo, while his whole body trembled. "If you is still dead, don't bother to say nothing, fer I's don't know how to talk to no dead man."

Mark then let out a groan, and realizing that he was still alive, the men picked him up and took him inside, and gently laid him on a bed. They quickly washed his head with cold water to help stop the blood, then they took a clean towel and wrapped it real tight around his head. The butt of the rifle had cut a deep gash in the side of his head, and knocked him unconscious, and because he had lost a lot of blood, due to the fact that they thought he was dead, he was too weak to say anything. The men sat by his side for about two hours, and he finally started talking to them.

"Jimbo," Mark whispered weakly, "where is the hooded-mob that I saw out there in the yard? Are they still around here?"

Before Jimbo had a chance to reply, Mark closed his eyes, and it appeared that he had fallen off to sleep. Jimbo didn't want to disturb him.

"Are they still out there?" Mark asked, a few minutes later, while Jimbo leaned over him, listening. "Are they going to burn the house?"

"Naw'suh, they ain't gon'a bun' the house down, fer them that ain't still laying out there in the yard dead, is done left, and gone."

"What do you mean by dead? Who did you say was dead? Did somebody get killed?" Mark asked, in a weak and confused voice.

"While we wuz at home, them hooded-mens slipped up here and kilt you and Marthie, and when we's hear'd 'em shoot'n youn's, we slipped up here and kilt some of them too," Jimbo smiled, and replied. "We's didn't want 'em to kill Beckie, fer they had her tied to a tree, and wuz ready to shoot her, too."

Mark hadn't noticed what he'd said about Martha being dead. "Do you know any of the men you folks killed," asked Mark, as he grew a bit stronger.

Jimbo hung his head, and hesitated for a moment. "Yass'uh, I's purdy sho' that I's know one of 'em," he finally replied. "Yo' pappy, and a bunch of other mens wuz kilt. They still be out there in the yard, still be dead, too."

Mark tried to sit up, but he fell back on his pillow. "I want to see who you killed," he said, dizzly. "Will you help me up."

"You's need to res' fer a spell longer," another man said, as he brought mark a dipper of water. "Drank this water, and don't worry 'bout the mens out yon'a, fer they ain't going nowhere 'cept fer to hell."

While he sipped on the water, Rebecca came into the room, and when he saw the tears in her eyes, he motioned for her to come to him. He still didn't know that Martha was dead.

"What's wrong, Rebecca," he asked softly. "Did those ugly men frighten you? Go tell your mother to give you a piece of that peanut candy, you helped her make today. What about that coconut cake. It sure smelled good, when she was cooking it this evening. Tell your mother to come in here, and I'll tell her to give you a piece of the cake. I could eat a piece, myself."

Realizing now, that Mark didn't know that her mother was dead, Rebecca ran over and threw herself across his chest, and screamed. "They went and shot my mammy, and she's dead!" She wailed. "She's on the porch, dead!"

"Oh my God, please don't tell me that!" Mark wailed. "Jimbo, is Martha really dead? Did those men kill her?"

"Yass'uh, she be dead, and Beckie seed it happen," Jimbo replied. "We's got her wrapped up rail purdy like, in that new quilt she made, and she be out there on the porch, wait'n fer somebid'ee to bur'ee her, I's reck'n."

"She loved me, she always loved me. All I ever brought her was a life of grief, and now I've caused her death," he cried. "I wish they had killed me at the same time, for there's nothing left for me to live for."

"Mark, my mammy loved you, and she died try'n to save yo' lif'," Rebecca comforted him. "She be better off now, er I's hope she be, anyhow."

"Yes, she's a lot better off," Mark forced a smile, for Rebecca's sake. "Your mother really was a wonderful person, and someday we'll both be with her again. Let me rest for a moment, then you and me will go out there and see her."

About an hour later, the Negro men went with Mark outside to look at the men who lay in the yard, to see if he recognized them. He was sad because his father had been killed; yet at the same time, he knew that he had reaped what he had sown for so many years. Looking down at his father, he couldn't bring himself to cry. He felt nothing but contempt for this man, who had dogged his tracks all these years. There, in a twisted array lay the body of the deputy sheriff, who had taken over after the sheriff was killed a few days ago, along with the body of Dr. Hall, and others whom he didn't know. Leaving the hoods and robes on these so-called men of justice, he told the Negro men to load the bodies on a wagon and take them into town, and leave them for everyone to see what had happended.

"Lay them on the courthouse lawn, with their hoods and robes on them, so everyone can see what they were doing tonight," Mark instructed. "Folks need to know the truth about these so-called Christians, crusaders of justice for the community, Negro-haters, if I might add."

"Does you want us to bur'ee yo' pappy in 'hind yo' house, whu' you's done bur'ed some of yo' folks?" Asked one of the men. "He wuz yo' pappy, and that do make him be some of yo' kinfolks, I's reck'n."

"By no means, do I want him buried anywhere close to my friends!" Replied Mark, sharply. "He died with the same kind of persons he was himself, and now let him lay in death, with the same kind of persons with whom he lived."

Something shiny on the ground caught Mark's eye, as Jimbo walked around with a lantern, for the moon wasn't shining, and it was dark outside.

"Jimbo, see what that is laying there on the ground," Mark told him, as he pointed to the object. "It must have been dropped by one of the men who were here tonight, for I've never seen it before."

"Looks like some kind'a jew'ry to me," Jimbo replied, as he picked it up, and handed it to Mark. "Sho' is a purdy thang, whatever it be."

It was a gold money clip, with the letters E.G.B. engraved on it. Right off, Mark recognized it to be the initials of the banker, Ellis G. Bland. So, he was here tonight as well. Helped to kill Martha too, Mark thought.

"Fine, upstanding citizens," Mark said, as he put the money clip in his vest pocket. "Go ahead and load the bodies on a wagon and take them into town like I said, for I want to spend some time alone with Martha, while you men are gone. Try not to let anybody see you, and hurry on back home."

Later the following afternoon Martha was eulogized, and laid to rest next to where her parents and brothers were buried, near the back of Mark's house. Mark stood for a long time at her grave, with his arm around Rebecca, while he thought about the sacrifices her family had made, because of his stand against slavery. He decided there and then, to leave the South soon. Now that Martha was dead, there was nothing left for him. His world had crumbled right before his eyes, and he'd been left standing alone, with no one who cared.

Mark left Rebecca standing alone at Martha's grave, as he walked out into a wooded area and pulled up a wild rosebush, and when he returned, he kneeled down, and transplanted it near the head of Martha's grave. They stood there a moment longer, as Mark wondered if the hatred those men had for Martha, would someday be turned toward her daughter as well. How long, and how many future generations will it take, for white people to realize that all persons must be treated equal, regardless to the color of their skin, he thought.

Rebecca then caught hold of Mark's hand. "That sho' wuz a pow'ful purdy thang you's done fer Mammy," she sobbed. "Ever' time the rose blooms, she can look up at it, and know that somebid'ee is still thank'n 'bout her."

"We're all better off because she was a part of our lives, in one way, or another,' Mark sighed, "and Heaven is going to be a much prettier place, now that she's there. Life won't be the same for me, now that she's gone."

Then, a strange expression came on Rebecca's face, as she looked up into his eyes, as tears trickled down her cheeks.

"Mark," she began, "my mammy told me that she railly loved you, and she sez that you wuz the bestest white feller she ever knowed. Did you love her, like everbid'ee sez, and like me and mammy knowed you's did?"

"Your mother has been a very dear friend of mine, ever since we were just children, and she meant more to me than my own sister," he replied. "All her folks were dear to me, and you can be proud that she was your mother."

"Mark, I's hear'd a lot'a talk from folks, and I's want'a know if you is my, uh, never mind," said Rebecca. Quickly turning, she ran as fast as she could back to the house. Mark knew what she wanted to ask him, and by no means was he going to call her back, or follow after her to give her an answer. Someday she must have the answer to her question, but not now, he reasoned. He stood there for a few minutes longer, and then slowly turning, he put on his hat, and walked back up to the house. He hoped Rebecca would not ask him any more questions.

Mark didn't even attend his father's funeral, for he didn't want to have a run-in with Susan or her husband, or with others who were sure to attend. The following Sunday afternoon, he had Jimbo to drive him to see his mother. Susan and her husband, along with their two children, were getting in their buggy to leave, when he arrived. He smiled, and politely spoke to them, but they drove off as though they hadn't even seen him. Although he didn't see eye-to-eye with his father, and felt bad at Susan for the part she and her husband had played in helping to keep a distance between he and his father, he would have enjoyed a friendly conversation with them, just the same. Maybe it will come to pass one day, he thought, as he went on into the house to see his mother. He found her in bed, with her shoulders propped upon some pillows.

"Mother, I'm glad to see you again, and I must say, that you look as good as you did the last time I was here," said Mark, as he leaned over and hugged her real tight. "I spoke to Susan and John, as they were leaving, and I would have liked to talked with them longer, but they were in a hurry to get home, I guess," he lied, sparing her feeligs.

"I'm glad that you two are finally back on speaking terms, for I'm going to die pretty soon, and I'll rest better, knowing that some love has returned to this family at last," she smiled. "I hate that you couldn't come to the funeral the other day, and I wasn't able to go to the church myself, but a lot of folks came to the house to see him. Nate did have a lot of friends of his own kind, I guess. Everybody can't have the same friends, I don't suppose."

"I hate that it happened, and even though he and I had our differences of opinion on things, he was my father," replied Mark. "Like you say, I have my friends, and he had his, and I'm glad that they showed their respect."

"Susan and John said, eight men were killed that night on the courthouse lawn, by a bunch of drunk men," she told him. "Of course, when I heard about what happened at your place, and about the Negro girl getting killed the same night, well, I formed my own opinion. Why is that bandage on your head? Did you bump into something, and hurt your head."

"Well, you might say that I wasn't watching what I was doing," he smiled, and told her. "I should have been more careful, will be, the next time."

"Let's put all of that in the past, and not discuss it anymore, and go on with what little life we have left," she smiled, and took her trembling hand, and gently patted him on the arm. "I appreciate you hiring that woman and man to stay with me, for they are real nice, and they look after me like I was one of their own children. They baby me, you might say."

"I'll never be able to repay you for what you've done for me, and even if I don't come around you every day, I'll see that you're well cared for as long as you live," he said. "It's my duty as your son, you know."

"By the way," said his mother, reluctantly, "what happened to the young girl, after Martha was killed? Is she still staying there with you?"

"As a matter of fact, she is," he replied. "I feel obligated to do what I can for her, for after all, that family of Negroes stood by me when everyone else turned against me. I don't care what folks say about me, or if they call me a "nigger lover", I'll look after the girl 'til the day I die."

They continued talking for at least an hour longer, then Mark kissed her on the cheek, and waved goodbye to her as he left. Little did he realize that this would be the last time that he would see his mother alive, for less than two weeks later, his mother died.

After the funeral of his mother, he met with Susan and her husband at the lawyer's office in town, and he signed his part of his father's estate over to Susan and her husband. Her husband didn't know how to manage his affairs, and as Mark would learn later, they eventually sold the plantation, spent the money on trips abroad, and speculating in risky business deals.

From that day on, a great change came over Mark's life. Like a child who had lost its mother, he felt alone. He soon withdrew himself from everything, and everybody, and rarely left his room except to eat, which was infrequently. When he did leave the house, he felt compelled to visit the five graves of his friends before leaving. These people were now dead, because of his firm stand against slavery, which didn't seem fair at all. They were always there when he needed them, but in their time of need, he wasn't able to save even one of them. He couldn't go on claiming that the South was his home, when in reality, the South had caused him all this sorrow and grief in the first place.

One day, Mark decided to sell all his land, except for a few acres around the plantation home, which he would leave for Rebecca, and the other survivors. This wasn't going to be easy for him, for since the death of Martha, he turned his attention and affection toward Rebecca, and it would be like seeing Martha buried all over again.

"Rebecca, it's time for me to leave the South for good," he told her one morning at the breakfast table, "for there's too many sad memories lingering around here, with the five graves out back, and the others down at you folk's church. It seems like everything I put my hands on, turns to ashes, and I hope you understand why I have to leave here."

"Yass'uh, I's thank I do," she sobbed, seeing the sober expression on his face. "What's gon'a happen to me, when you's leave? Is I gon'a be kilt jus' 'cause I love you, like my mammy wuz? Who gon'a look adder me?"

"I'll leave Jimbo in charge, for he can be trusted, and I'll leave plenty of money in the bank for you, when you grow up," he explained. "You can stay in this house as long as you wish, and you won't have to suffer like your poor mother did, either."

"You know good'n well, that I's can't stay here adder you is gone," she cried. "Everthang is gon'a get all messed up, wid you and Mammy bof' gone."

"You have your whole life ahead of you, and I'm sure your mother will be proud of whatever you decide to do in life, for she loved you," he told her. "When she was your age, she was a slave, and she couldn't make choices of her own, like you can today. I know that it's going to take a long time, and some giving and taking from both races, but eventually things will change."

"She told me to treasure my freedom, fer it wuz sump'um she never got no chance to 'joy in her lif'," she smiled. "And, she say fer me to put legs on my prayers, too, whatever that means."

"That's good advice, and you should always remember that too," he gently smiled, "and there's something I wish to ask of you as well. Will you do one thing for me, if you ever get married, and leave this place, or if you make up your mind to go and live somewhere else, for any other reason?"

"Mark, you know that I's gon'a do 'zackly what you axe me to do, fer like Mammy sez, you be the only pappy I's got," she promised. "I's like to know if you is railly my... well, what wuz it, that you's want me to do?"

Mark hesitated for a moment, not quite sure just how much her mother had really told her young daughter about their relationship.

"Well, if you ever leave, I want you to dig up the wild rose bush that we planted at your mother's grave, and take it with you," Mark told her, almost begging. "Every time it blooms, you'll know that her love is still alive for you, and hopefully, for me too. Will you promise to do that?"

"Yass'uh, I'll sot it out wherever I's move to, and when I's look at it, I gon'a know that my Mammy's love is still there wid me," she told him.

Mark went into his room and began rumbling through drawers and boxes, as he sorted through his many personal items, trying to make up his mind what he wanted to take along with him, and what he intended to leave behind. He came across a small velvet covered jewelry box, which contained the engagement ring he'd bought for Carolyn Bland many years ago. His eyes welled with tears, as he stood for a while looking at the ring, and wishing that it was on her finger now, instead of still being in the box. His mind became flooded with memories of choosing the ring for her, and most of all, the anticipation of slipping it on her finger at the party that night. Then, he closed the tiny box, and put it in his pocket. He had one more very important call to make, before he finished packing up his belongings, to leave South Carolina.

Mark went directly to the barn and saddled his mare, and then he proceeded in great haste toward the Bland's country home. When he arrived, Carolyn and her mother were sitting in the parlor having tea. Mark hitched the mare to a post at the edge of the yard, then went up on the porch, and knocked on the door.

It was Carolyn who opened the door, looking as beautiful as she ever had before. She had aged only slightly, but the sparkle was gone from her eyes.

"Carolyn," Mark said softly, "may I talk with you for a moment, if you have the time to spare, and don't mind?"

"Mark!" She squealed. "Please come in! Look who's come to visit, it's Mark! Mother, it's Mark!"

"Please come in, Mark," said Mrs. Bland, kindly. "It's been such a long time since we've seen you. Would you care for some tea?"

"Yes, thank you, Mrs. Bland," Mark replied politely, as he looked at her and smiled. "It's an honor to be in your home again, and more than you can ever imagine, and I'm sorry for having barged in like this."

"We're glad to see you, and like I've told you before, we're always happy to have you in our home," she replied. "Now, let me fix you some tea."

Mrs. Bland walked slowly to the kitchen to get Mark a teacup and saucer, and she would hesitate there on purpose, so Carolyn and Mark could spend a few minutes alone. Let them work out something, she prayed to herself.

"Let me take a good look at you, Carolyn," said Mark, holding Carolyn at arm's length. "I'll have to say, that you're just as beautiful as ever."

"Oh Mark," she sobbed, "all these years I've wanted you to come back to me, for life hasn't been worth living without you. I'm so thrilled to see you again, and I hope that we can be together from now on."

"I've been wanting to see you too, and I drove almost all the way to your house one day, then I thought it best not to come," he told her, as his eyes filled with tears. "I sold my plantation, for I don't have any reason to stay her in the South now, but I had to come to see you before I left."

"Please don't go, Mark!" She begged. "We can straighten things out, for I still love you, and I always will. Won't you reconsider this, and let us live out the rest of our life together?"

"Please don't make this any more difficult for me than it already is, for I still love you too," Mark whispered. "What happened here that night, hurt me more than the death of my mother, and more than the death of…"

"I know Mark," she whispered. "But that was my father's fault, and not yours. We can still have a wonderful life together, and I'll go with you this very minute, no matter what my father says. Will you take me with you, Mark?"

"It don't matter who's fault it was, it still happened, and it was unfortunate, to say the least," he told her. 'I'm sure you heard that I fathered a child for the Negro girl who used to work for me, and a lot of other things as well."

"Yes, but I didn't believe a word of it," she quickly replied. "My love for you is strong enough to cause me to overlook such nonsense."

"Well, thank you for that," Mark smiled. "You still remember when folks thought Martha burned up in the house-fire, don't you. And how it shattered my father's nerves, when he realized that she was still alive."

"Yes, I remember," Carolyn nodded. "I remember the trick you played on your father at the party, as if it were yesterday."

"Well, she's really dead now, shot down by my father, and a group of his so-called Christian-crusaders. It happened on the same night folks claim that my father, and some other men were killed on the courthouse lawn."

"Oh Lord no!" Carolyn gasps. "And her young daughter, did they harm her in any way? Where is the poor girl now?"

"She still lives with me, but she's heartbroken and sad over what went on that night, right before her eyes," Mark told her. "She saw the mob kill her mother, saw my father die, as well as seven other men. They intended to kill her, but a group of my workers ran up and fired into the group."

"Daddy told me about your father, and the others getting killed, but from what he said, a bunch of drunks killed them in town one night," she replied. "Said it was Negroes, no doubt."

"That makes sense," Mark told her, "for the innocent seems to always be the one who gets hurt. I've walked that road myself. Those men were killed right in my front yard, and not in town, as you might have heard."

"That's what bothered me so much that night after you left, for you were innocent," Carolyn sighed. "Then after years went by, and you didn't come to see me again, it caused me to wonder if you loved me, as much as I thought you did. I finally accepted the fact that your love ended for me that night. Is that what happened? Did it cause you to stop loving me?"

"No, I've never stopped loving you," Mark smiled softly, as he held her face in his hands, "but your father thought I loved Martha. She was the only friend I had in the world, after they killed her family, that's all. What some said about her was unfair, for she never did anything to harm anyone."

"I was aware of how you felt toward her, but she really was in love with you, wasn't she." Carolyn said, blushing at her own words. "I can tell love when I see it, know when it's gone, too."

"Yes, I truly believe that she loved me," Mark replied softly, "but the way I felt for her, was only the purest of friendship, and nothing else. There were times when I thought I might love her too, but I didn't allow myself to yield to such feelings."

"I never thought differently," she told him, "no matter what folks said about you. You can love somebody, without them loving you back, you know."

Reaching into his pocket, Mark retrieved the velvet-covered box, and then opening it, handed it to Carolyn.

"I planned to give this to you that night, but your father interfered, so I've kept it for all these years," Mark said, as tears filled his eyes. "I'd like for you to have it to remember me by, when I'm gone."

Carolyn took the ring, and began to cry. "It's so beautiful, and I wish you wouldn't leave me again!" She wailed, holding his hand tightly. "We can still be happy together, it's never too late for love."

"It's too late for me, Carolyn," he told her, tearfully. "I have to get away from the South, away from this awful guilt, and away from the hatred that surrounds it. The plantation, only reminds me of how the Negroes sacrificed, and gave their lives to help me accomplish something, and the graves out back, are positive proof of the hatred that some human beings can have for another. I've lost all that I ever hoped to accomplish, even the love that you once had for me."

"I've never stopped loving you, and I've never loved anyone else, so why don't you let me help you get over this rough spot?" She begged. "Will you let me do that?"

"This is something I'll have to do myself," he told her. "I will always love you, and treasure your memory." Then gently pulling the pink ribbon from her hair, he added, "May I have it? You wore pink that night, remember."

"Of course," she cried, "and I'll always love you."

"And, I'll go to my grave, wishing that things could have worked out like I hoped they would," he said, hugging her tightly.

Then he kissed her cheek gently, and turned to walk out the door. All of a sudden, he stopped, reached into another pocket, and pulled out her father's money clip that he found in his yard, the night Martha was killed.

"Give this to your father when he returns," Mark said, as he placed the money clip in her hands. "I found it laying in my yard, the night the mob came to my house, and killed Martha. I can't imagine how your father's money clip got there, for I'm sure he wasn't a member of the hooded-mob."

Carolyn watched from the front porch as Mark rode away. Then she slipped the diamond ring on the third finger of her left hand. We're husband and wife in spirit if not in reality, she softly said to herself. As soon as she went back inside, she tossed the money clip into the fireplace.

Early the following morning Mark loaded his belongings into a buggy, as he prepared to leave South Carolina, while Rebecca and the others cried and begged him to stay. Jimbo, planned to go into town with Mark to catch a train that was headed north, then he'd bring the mare and buggy back home.

Spring was here, flowers were blooming, and the birds were chirping; yet Mark's heart couldn't have been any sadder. "You folks will be all right, for this place belongs to you as long as you wish to stay," he told them, when he stepped out into the yard, to board the buggy.

Then, as he'd done so many times in the past, Mark walked to the back of the house, then kneeled down beside the five graves. Tears streamed down his cheeks, as he offered a silent prayer for these, his only true friends.

"I'm going away now," he then said aloud, as though they could hear him, "but Rebecca, and the others will stay here with you. Martha, I've made sure that your child will be taken care of after I'm gone, so don't worry."

"Mark, you don't have to tell her that, fer she done knows that you's the bes' friend she ever had," spoke up Rebecca, who had followed him out to the graves. "I's wush you'd change yo' mind, and stay here wid us."

"No Rebecca, I can't stay," he smiled softly, "and remember what I said about the rosebush." He reached over and plucked a pretty rose from the wild rose bush that he had planted at Martha's grave, stuck it in his pocket, then slowly turned, and headed back toward where Jimbo was already waiting for him in the buggy.

A question still bothered Rebecca, and even though she was already in her mid-teens, she must not let Mark go, without having an answer. As they walked around toward the front of the house, she caught hold of his hand, and he then looked into her tear filled eyes, and forced a soft smile.

"Is something still bothering you," he asked, kindly. "I really hate to go and leave you like this, and everything I've worked so hard to achieve, but soon you'll be grown, and you'll understand why I have to do this."

"Did the war kill my pappy, like Mammy sez, and wuz he the bestest man, that ever lived?" She humbly asked. "That's what my mammy went and told me."

"Well, the war killed a lot of things, and a lot of good men, in addition to those who actually died on the battlefields, and many things changed during the war that will never be the same," he replied. "She told you how she felt in her heart about him, but he never got around to telling her how he felt in his heart about her. Your mother really loved you, and so does your father in his own way, even though you might never hear him say that freely."

As the years passed by, the horrible death of her mother became a living-nightmare to Rebecca, and it would no doubt continue to haunt her for the rest of her life, but the true love Mark has shown for her, until he finally left South Caroilina, would always be in her memory. She eventually married a man who worked with a railroad construction crew, and they settled down near where her husband's folks lived in Toccoa, Georgia. Like Mark asked her to do, she dug up the wild rose bush that Mark had set out at Martha's grave, and she reset it in the chimney corner there at her new home.

During the summer of 1947, this author walked up to a house in Toccoa, Georgia to ask for directions to where someone lived in the Red Hill Community, and spoke with an elderly Negro woman who sat on the front porch, with an old tattered Bible on her lap. He saw a beautiful rose blooming in the chimney corner, and he asked her about it. Then she told him a story about the life of her mother, who was once a slave on a plantaion in South Carolina during the 1800's. The author was duly impressed by her story, and it inspired him to write a story someday about the way Negro slaves were treated by their masters, although this is not the actual story that she told to him. When he asked about what appeared to be a dried-rose, and a pink ribbon pressed between the pages of the old Bible, she replied:

"I's got this here old Bible from a lawyer up in Ohio, several years ago, and rite off I's knowed it wuz Mark's old Bible that his mammy gave to him," she replied. "I's ain't sho', but I thank the dried-rose wuz the one that he picked from my mammy's grave when he left South Carolina, when I wuz jus' a young girl. Don't know how to 'splain the pink ribbon, fer I ain't never seed it befo'. It mout be sump'um that his sister give to him to 'memer her by, fer he never did have no girlfriend, that I's ever knowed 'bout."

Before leaving, I asked her if I could bring my mother by to see the rose, and she smiled and said-

"Son, you sho' can, any time you's feel like it. In case you happen to ferget whu' I's stay at, er don't 'memer that my name is Rebecca, jus' axe anybid'ee whu' the ole woman stays...

...where the wild rose blooms."

THE END